LUDMILA ULITSKAYA is one of Russia's most popular and renowned literary figures. A former scientist and repertory director of the Hebrew Theater of Moscow, she is the author of fourteen works of fiction, three tales for children, and six plays that have been staged by a number of theaters in Russia and Germany. She has won Russia's Man Booker Prize and was shortlisted for the Man Booker International Prize.

Additional Praise for *The Big Green Tent*

A *Christian Science Monitor* 10 Best Fiction Books of the Year
A *Kirkus Reviews* Best Historical Fiction and Best Fiction in
Translation of the Year

"Ludmila Ulitskaya's latest translated novel, *The Big Green Tent*, is a compelling testimony to the stifling atmosphere of stagnation-era Russia—and a warning, according to the author, to those Russians who feel nostalgic about the Soviet past.... Ulitskaya avoids the kind of psychologizing that is a trademark of Russian novels, but she masterfully renders psychology through the language of the body, sensory experience, and the shifting voice of the narrator."

—*Chicago Tribune*

"The characters are drawn with humor and melancholy yet endowed with hope and a love of literature. A great introduction for readers new to Ulitskaya."

—*Library Journal* (starred review)

"With both intimacy and cosmic scope, Russian novelist Ludmila Ulitskaya weaves an engaging tale of a group of cold war–era Soviet friends.... Ulitskaya's easygoing manner and sense of humor are attractive, and it doesn't take long to trust she knows what she's doing.... The translation, by Polly Gannon, is light and lively, wonderfully devoid of accent or awkwardnesses."

—*The Christian Science Monitor*

"A very interesting read, as Ulitskaya covers with breathless gusto a period of Russian history unfamiliar to most American readers... You'll laugh, you'll cry, you'll occasionally want to throw the book across the room in frustration—but you'll keep reading."

—Daniel Kalder, *The Dallas Morning News*

"One of the year's best works of straightforward realism... An attempt to reawaken a dissident past."

—*Flavorwire*

"Often it is achievement enough for a writer to depict a vast array of characters with insight and great sensitivity for each; Ulitskaya does this and more.... It is undeniable that with this novel Ulitskaya has pulled off a multipronged feat."

—Kim Hedges, *Minneapolis Star Tribune*

"As the book leaps effortlessly from year to year, character to character, it ingeniously tells the story of a generation that is at the same time in love with and at war with its homeland.... A delight to read."

—*The Harvard Crimson*

"The huge cast allows Ulitskaya to lead the reader on delightful tours of all those late Soviet phenomena most fetishized in hindsight: samizdat, underground dissidence, and steamy kitchen conversations about jazz, politics, and forbidden literature." —*Public Books*

"[One of] Fall's most promising new books...Ludmila Ulitskaya's ambitious, newly translated Russian novel tracks the lives of three young Muscovites from the death of Stalin to the fall of the Iron Curtain."

—*Travel+Leisure*

"Ludmila Ulitskaya's evocative book *The Big Green Tent*, set in Moscow after Stalin's death, has just appeared in Polly Gannon's elegant English translation. It is Ulitskaya's sixth novel translated into English and as readable as ever." —*Russia Beyond the Headlines*

"The popular Russian novelist takes a cue from the greats here, crafting a sweeping novel that's traditional in structure and scope but modern in humor and relevance." —*Bustle*

"[Ulitskaya is a] consummate storyteller.... She can create characters with the best of them." —*The Buffalo News*

THE BIG GREEN TENT

LUDMILA ULITSKAYA

TRANSLATED FROM THE RUSSIAN BY
POLLY GANNON

PICADOR

FARRAR, STRAUS AND GIROUX

NEW YORK

This is a work of fiction. All of the characters, organizations, and events portrayed in this novel are either products of the author's imagination or are used fictitiously.

ИНСТИТУТ ПЕРЕВОДА

AD VERBUM

Published with the support of the Institute for Literary Translation, Russia.

picadorusa.com • picadorbookroom.tumblr.com
twitter.com/picadorusa • facebook.com/picadorusa

For book club information, please visit facebook.com/picadorbookclub or e-mail marketing@picadorusa.com.

An excerpt from *The Big Green Tent* originally appeared, in different form, in *The New Yorker.*

Grateful acknowledgment is made to the University of California Press Books for permission to reprint an excerpt from "To an army wife, in Sardis," by Sappho, translated by Mary Barnard, from *Sappho: A New Translation.*

Designed by Abby Kagan

The Library of Congress has cataloged the Farrar, Straus and Giroux edition as follows:

Ulitskaia, Liudmila
[Zelenyi shater. English]
The big green tent / Ludmila Ulitskaya ; translated from the Russian by Bela Shayevich. —First American edition.
    p. cm.
ISBN 978-0-374-16667-0 (hardcover)
ISBN 978-0-374-70971-6 (e-book)
1. Male friendship—Soviet Union—Fiction.   2. Soviet Union—Social Conditions—1945–1991—Fiction.   3. Soviet Union—Intellectual Life—Fiction.
I. Shayevich, Bela, translator. II. Title.
PG3489.2 .L58Z4513 2014
891.73'5—dc23   2014016972

Picador Paperback ISBN 978-1-250-09744-6

Our books may be purchased in bulk for promotional, educational, or business use. Please contact your local bookseller or the Macmillan Corporate and Premium Sales Department at 1-800-221-7945, extension 5442, or by e-mail at MacmillanSpecial Markets@macmillan.com.

Originally published in Russian under the title Зеленый шатер by Eksmo, Russia
Published by arrangement with ELKOST International Literary Agency, Barcelona, Spain

English translation first published in the United States by Farrar, Straus and Giroux

First Picador Edition: January 2017

D   10   9   8   7   6   5   4   3

Do not be consoled by the injustice of our time. Its immorality does not prove our own moral worth; its inhumanity is not sufficient to render us human merely by opposing it.

—*Boris Pasternak to Varlam Shalamov, July 9, 1952*

CONTENTS

THE BIG
GREEN TENT

PROLOGUE

Tamara sat before a runny omelet on a plate, the vestiges of sleep still clinging to her.

Trying not to yank at the living pelt, Raisa Ilinichna, her mother, nudged a wide-tooth comb through Tamara's hair as gently as she could.

The radio disgorged strains of triumphal music, but it wasn't terribly loud: Grandmother was asleep behind the partition wall. Then the music died out. The pause that followed was too long, and seemed to portend something. The familiar, solemn radio voice resounded: "Attention! This is Moscow speaking. Transmitting an official announcement to all radio stations of the Soviet Union."

The comb froze in Tamara's hair. She snapped out of her half-sleep, swallowed down the last of the omelet, and in a hoarse, morning voice said, "It's probably just some dumb cold, and they have to go broadcasting it to the entire—"

She didn't get to finish her thought. Raisa Ilinichna jerked Tamara's head back with a violent tug of the comb, so that her jaw snapped shut.

"Shush!" Raisa Ilinichna's voice was tight.

Grandmother, wearing a robe as ancient as the Great Wall of China, appeared in the doorway. She listened to the announcement, and at the end, her face and eyes shining, said, "Raisa, dear, run down to the store and get us something sweet. Today is, after all, Purim. Besides, the Big Samekh seems to have kicked the bucket."

Tamara didn't yet know what Purim was, or why it required something sweet; nor did she know who this Big Samekh was who had most likely kicked the bucket. She was still too young to know that in her family they had always referred to Stalin and Lenin in code, calling them conspiratorially by the first letters of their names, in an ancient secret language—Hebrew. The letters were samekh and lamed.

Meanwhile, the beloved official voice of the nation, familiar to every household in the land, was announcing an illness far worse than a cold.

〄

Galya had already thrown on her school dress and was now looking for the pinafore. Where could it be? She fished around under the trestle bed—maybe it had fallen behind it.

Suddenly her mother burst in, with a kitchen knife in one hand and a potato in the other. She wailed in a voice so strange that Galya thought she might have cut her hand open. But there was no blood.

Her father, grouchy in the mornings, pulled his head from the pillow. "What are you yelling about, Ninka? Isn't it too early for that?"

But her mother wailed even louder, a jumble of incoherent words streaming out.

"He's dead! Wake up, you idiot! Get out of bed! Stalin's dead!"

"Did they make an announcement, or what?" Her father raised his big head; a lock of hair stuck to his forehead.

"They say he's ill. But he's dead, I swear to God! I feel it in my bones."

Then the incoherent wailing resumed, punctuated by a plaintive, melodramatic lament: "Lord in heaven! What will become of us?"

Wincing, her father barked, "Quit moaning, woman! How much worse can things get?"

Just then Galya's fingers grasped the pinafore, which had indeed fallen behind the bed.

So what if it's wrinkled. I'm not ironing it, she decided.

卍

By morning her fever had subsided, and Olga fell into a sound sleep, undisturbed by sweating or coughing. She slept all the way through till dinnertime, when her mother came in and announced, in a stern, resonant voice, "Olga, get up! Misfortune has befallen us."

Without opening her eyes, clutching the pillow in the hope that it was all a dream, but already feeling terror pulsing in her throat, Olga thought, *War! The Fascists are attacking! War has started!*

"Olga, get up!"

What a catastrophe! The Fascist hordes are trampling our holy Motherland, and everyone will get to go to the front to fight, but me . . .

"Stalin's dead!"

Her heart was caught in her throat, but she still didn't open her eyes: thank goodness it wasn't war after all. When the war started, she would be bigger and they would take her, too. And she buried her head under the blanket, muttering, "And then they'll take me, too," and fell asleep to this comforting thought.

Her mother let her sleep.

THOSE WONDROUS SCHOOL YEARS

I t's fascinating to trace the trajectories of people destined to meet. Sometimes such encounters happen without any special help from fate, without elaborate convolutions of plot, following the natural course of events—say, people live in adjacent buildings, or go to the same school.

The three boys all went to the same school. Ilya and Sanya had known each other since the first grade. Mikha joined them later. In the hierarchy that takes shape willy-nilly in every herd, all three of them occupied the lowest rung—due to their complete disinclination to fight or be cruel. Ilya was long and lanky, his hands and feet stuck out from his short sleeves and trouser legs. Moreover, there wasn't a single nail or sharp piece of metal he hadn't snagged his clothes on. His mother, the doleful, single Maria Fedorovna, wore herself out attaching unsightly patches to his clothes with her graceless fingers. Sewing was not her forte. Ilya was always dressed more poorly than the other students, who were themselves poorly dressed. He liked to cut up and play the clown, making a spectacle of his poverty and thereby overcoming it.

Sanya had it even worse. His classmates were filled with envy and disgust at his zippered jacket, his girlish eyelashes, the irksome sweetness of his face, and the cloth napkin his homemade lunch came wrapped in every day. Added to that, he took piano lessons. Many of the kids had seen him walking down Chernyshevsky Street, the former and future Pokrovka, to the Igumnov Music School, one of his hands clutching his grandmother's hand, the other clutching a folder with sheet music. Sometimes they saw him even on days when he was sick with one of his frequent minor, but protracted, illnesses. His grandmother was all profile. She would place one slender leg in front of the other like a circus horse, her head swaying rhythmically in time. Sanya walked by her side, but slightly behind, as befits a groom.

Contrary to his regular school, at music school everyone sang the praises of Sanya. In his second year there, he played Grieg at his recital with a skill that few fifth-year students could muster. The small stature of the performer was also touching. At eight years old he was mistaken for a preschooler, and at twelve he looked like he was eight. For this reason, they dubbed him Gnome at his regular school. And the nickname was not an affectionate one; they made fun of him mercilessly. Sanya consciously avoided Ilya, not so much because of his teasing—which was not directed at Sanya, but which sometimes grazed him nonetheless—but because of their humiliating difference in size.

Mikha was the one who brought Sanya and Ilya together when he appeared in their midst in the fifth grade. His arrival was greeted with delight. A classic redhead, he was the ideal target for gibes.

His head was shaved bare, except for a crooked, reddish-gold tuft in front. He had translucent magenta-colored ears that stuck out from the sides of his head like sails; but they were in the wrong place, too close to his cheeks, somehow. He had milky white skin and freckles, and his eyes even had an orangey hue. As if all that weren't enough, he was bespectacled, and a Jew, to boot.

The first time Mikha got beaten up was on the first day of school. The beating, which took place in the bathroom during recess, was a mild one—just a formality, to give him something to think about. It wasn't even Murygin and Mutyukin who did it—they had better things to do—but their sidekicks and underlings. Mikha stoically took what was coming to him, then opened his book bag to take out a handkerchief and wipe away his snot. At that moment, a kitten squirmed out of the bag. The other boys grabbed the kitten and started tossing it back and forth. Just then, Ilya, the tallest boy in the class, walked in. He managed to intercept the kitten in midair, over the heads of the makeshift volleyball team, when the bell sounded, putting an end to the game.

When they returned to the classroom, Ilya thrust the kitten at Sanya, who had materialized right beside him, and who then stuffed the kitten into his book bag.

During the final break, those archenemies of the human race, Murygin and Mutyukin, whose names will serve as the basis for a future philological conceit and so deserve mention, looked around for the kitten, but soon forgot about it. That day, school was dismissed after only four classes, and the boys tore out of the school building, whooping and hollering. These three were left to their own devices in the empty classroom bedecked with brightly colored asters—first-day-of-school offerings for the teacher. Sanya extracted the half-smothered kitten from the satchel and handed it to Ilya. Ilya gave it to Mikha. Sanya smiled at Ilya, Ilya at Mikha, Mikha at Sanya.

"I wrote a poem. About him," Mikha said shyly. "Here it is."

> He was the handsomest of cats,
> And just about to meet his death,
> When Ilya jumped into the fray.
> And now the kitten's here today.

"Not bad. Though it's no Pushkin," Ilya said.

"'Now the kitten's here today' is too pompous," said Sanya. Mikha agreed humbly.

"How about 'And now the kitten's here to stay.' That sounds better."

Mikha then told them in great detail how in the morning, on his way to school, he had snatched the unfortunate creature out of the jaws of a canine predator. He couldn't take the kitten home, however, because he didn't know how his aunt would react. He had been living with her only since the previous Monday.

Sanya stroked the kitten's back and sighed. "I can't take him home with me. We've already got a cat. He wouldn't like it."

"Fine, I'll take him." Ilya casually scooped up the kitten.

"They won't mind, at home?" Sanya said.

Ilya grinned. "I'm in charge at home. My mom and I get along great. She listens to me."

He's so grown up, I'll never be like him. I could never say "My mom and I get along great." It's true—I'm just a mama's boy. Though Mama does listen to me. And Grandmother listens, too. Oh, does she ever! But in a different way, Sanya mused.

Sanya looked at Ilya's bony hands, covered all over in bluish-yellow bruises and scars. His fingers were so long they could reach two octaves. Mikha was trying to balance the kitten on his head, above the reddish gold tuft left there yesterday "for growing back" by the magnanimous barber at the Pokrovsky Gates. The kitten kept slithering off, and Mikha kept planting him on his head again.

Together, the three of them left the school building. They fed the kitten melted ice cream. Sanya had some money, just enough for four portions. As it turned out later, Sanya almost always had money. This was the first time Sanya had ever bought ice cream on the street and eaten it straight from the wrapper. When Grandmother bought ice cream, they took it home with them, placed the sagging mound in a special glass dish, and topped it with a dollop of cherry jam. That was the only way they ever ate it.

Ilya told them excitedly about the camera he was going to buy with the first money he earned. He also laid out his precise plan for making that money.

Out of the blue, Sanya blurted out his own secret—he had small, "unpianistic" hands, and that was a handicap for a performer like him.

Mikha, who had moved in with his third set of relatives in seven years, told these boys, nearly complete strangers, that he was running out of relatives, and that if his aunt refused to keep him he'd have to go back to the orphanage.

The new aunt, Genya, had a weak constitution and suffered from some undefined illness. "I'm sick from head to toe," she would say with mournful significance. She complained constantly of pains in her legs, in her back, her chest, and her kidneys. She also had a daughter who was disabled, which put a further strain on her health. Any kind of work was beyond her strength, so her relatives finally decided that her orphaned nephew should move in with her, and that they would all contribute money for his upkeep. Mikha was, after all, the son of their brother, who had perished in the war.

The boys wandered aimlessly, chattering nonstop, until they found themselves on the banks of the Yauza, where they fell silent. They were struck with the same feeling in unison—about how fine it all was: trust, friendship, togetherness. There was no thought of who might be the leader. Rather, they took a mutual interest in one another. They still knew nothing of Sasha and Nick* or of the oath they took on the Sparrow Hills. Even the precocious Sanya hadn't discovered Herzen yet. And the run-down districts the boys had been wending their way through—Khitrovka, Gonchary, Kotelniki—had long been considered the dregs of the city, no setting for romantic oaths. But something important had transpired, and this sudden magnetic linkage between people can happen only in youth. The hook pierces the very heart, and the lines connecting us in childhood friendship can never be severed.

Some time later, after heated debate, this triumvirate of hearts, rejecting both "Trinity" and "Trio," decided to choose the august moniker "Trianon." They knew nothing about the breakup of the Austro-Hungarian Empire; they just liked the sound of it.

Twenty years later, Trianon would crop up in a conversation between Ilya and an official from the Department of State Security, a man of high but indeterminate rank, with the not altogether plausible name of Anatoly Alexandrovich Chibikov. Even the most zealous of the dissident-hunting KGB thugs of that era would have shied away from calling Trianon an anti-Soviet youth organization.

Ilya deserves most of the credit for preserving the group's memory for posterity. As soon as he laid his hands on his first camera, he began assembling a comprehensive photo archive that has remained intact to

---

*When they were teenagers, the writers and activists Alexander Herzen (Sasha) (1812–1870) and Nikolay Ogarev (Nick) (1813–1877) famously took an oath on the Sparrow Hills, vowing to dedicate their lives to fighting tyranny.

this day. True, the first file from their school years bears the mysterious label "The LORLs," rather than Trianon.

Thus, the original catalyst for a union that would, in time, be amply documented, was not the noble ideal of freedom, worthy of the ultimate sacrifice of one's own life, or, far more tedious, the dedication of one's life, year after year, to an ungrateful public, as Sasha and Nick had done just over a century before. Instead, it was a mangy little kitten, who was not destined to survive the upheaval of September 1, 1951. The poor little thing died two days later in Ilya's arms, and was secretly but solemnly buried under a bench in the yard of 22 Pokrovka Street (called Chernyshevsky Street in those days, after someone else who squandered his life on lofty ideals). The building had once borne the nickname "The Vanity Chest," but few of its current residents would have remembered this.

The kitten rested for eternity under the very park bench on which the young Pushkin had allegedly sat with his cousins, amusing them with his mellifluous little rhymes. Sanya's grandmother never tired of reminding him that the building they lived in had once been grand.

It was astonishing how everything at school changed in a matter of weeks. Mikha, of course, didn't feel the change as keenly—how could he, he was a newcomer. But Sanya and Ilya noticed it. In their class they still occupied the lowest rung in the hierarchy, but now they did not occupy it singly. They were there together. They became a recognized minority, set apart by some indefinite sign or mark that prevented them from blending into the status quo of this small world. The two leaders, Mutyukin and Murygin, kept a tight grip on all the others; but when they argued between themselves, the whole class split into two hostile factions, which the outcasts never tried to join—and they would not have been accepted anyway. At those times, gleeful, malicious, angry skirmishes erupted—with bloody noses and without— and the outcasts were left alone. When Mutyukin and Murygin made peace, their attention again turned to these odd, unsociable misfits. They were too easy to beat up. It was more fun to keep them in suspense and fear, and to keep reminding them who was boss here: not the Jewish four-eyes, the musician, and the class clown, but the "normal kids," like Mutyukin and Murygin.

Fifth grade was the first year when there were different teachers for different subjects (math, Russian, botany, history, German, and geography), instead of just one teacher for reading, writing, and arithmetic—the sweet-tempered Natalya Ivanovna, who had even taught Mutyukin and Murygin the alphabet, and who still called them, affectionately, Tolya and Slavochka.

All the teachers were crazy about their own subjects, and assigned a lot of homework, which the "normal kids" clearly couldn't keep up with. Ilya, who had not excelled in grade school, was given a boost by his new friends, and by the end of the second quarter, just before the New Year, it became obvious that the rejects, the four-eyed weaklings and misfits, were thriving, and that Mutyukin and Murygin were lagging behind. The conflict, which grown-up people would have called a social one, grew more intense and more tangible, at least to the oppressed "minority." It was then that Ilya introduced a term that would come in handy for many years to come—*mutyuks and murygs.* The term was basically synonymous with *sovok* ("a typical Soviet"), a term of later currency. The beauty of theirs lay in its apt self-evidence. It was there for the taking.

No one got under the skin of the mutyuks and murygs like Mikha, but with all of his orphanage experience, he easily weathered the schoolyard brawls. He never complained, but shook himself off, snatched up his hat, and took to his heels while the hoots and catcalls of his enemies rained down on him. Ilya played the clown with aplomb, and was often able to confuse his enemies with wisecracks or with sudden comic moves. Sanya proved to be the most sensitive and vulnerable among them. Still, it was his excessive sensitivity that served as his defense in the end.

Once, when Sanya was washing his hands in the school bathroom—a cross between a parliament and a den of thieves—Mutyukin was overcome with loathing for Sanya's unassuming pastime and suggested that he wash his mug, while he was at it. Sanya, partly from a desire to keep the peace, but also partly out of cowardice, did as he was told. Then Mutyukin grabbed a filthy rag for cleaning the floor and wiped it across Sanya's dripping face. By this time, they were surrounded by onlookers who were in the mood for some excitement. But they were

disappointed. Sanya went pale, began to shake, then fainted, collaps-
ing onto the tiled floor. The paltry enemy was, of course, vanquished,
but the victory felt hollow. He lay on the floor in a contorted pose, his
head lolling back. Murygin jabbed his side with the toe of his boot,
just to make sure that he was really out cold. He called out to him
with no malice whatsoever,

"Hey, Sanya, what're you doing down there?"

Mutyukin stared wild-eyed at the lifeless Sanya. Sanya didn't
open his eyes, despite the insistent pokes and jabs. Just then, Mikha
came in. He glanced at the mute scene, then rushed off to fetch the
school nurse. A pinch of smelling salts revived Sanya, and the gym
teacher carried him to the infirmary. The nurse measured his
blood pressure.

"How are you feeling?" she asked.

He answered that he felt fine, though he couldn't quite recall what
had happened to him. When he did remember the dirty rag rubbing
against his face, he almost retched. He asked for some soap and
washed his face thoroughly. The nurse wanted to call his parents. It
took some effort for Sanya to persuade her not to. Mama was at work,
anyway, and he wanted to guard his grandmother from the unpleasantness. Ilya was enlisted to accompany his shell-shocked friend
home, and the nurse wrote a note for both of them, dismissing them
from class.

From that day on, counterintuitive though it might seem, Sanya
rose in stature. True, they did start calling him Epileptic Gnome, but
they stopped tormenting him: What if he had another fainting fit?

On December 31 school let out for the winter break. Eleven days
of bliss. Mikha always remembered these days, each of them a revelation, and each different from all the others. On New Year's he received
a wonderful present. After secret negotiations with her son, who solemnly promised her that his direct descendants would never claim
their rights to that particular family heirloom, and he himself didn't
mind in the least, Aunt Genya gave Mikha a pair of ice skates.

They were an American make, long outmoded, a hybrid between
the standard Snegurkas and Hagues, with double blades and serrated
front tips. The blades had been affixed to a pair of beat-up boots that

had once been red, with huge star-shaped rivets. On the metal plate connecting the blade to the shoe, the word *Einstein* could be made out, followed by a series of incomprehensible numbers and letters. The boots had been thoroughly battered and broken in by their previous owner, but the blades gleamed like new.

Aunt Genya treated the skates like the family jewels, the way other families cherish their grandmother's diamonds.

And diamonds did figure into the story of these skates in a tangential way. In the year 1919, Lenin himself had dispatched Genya's older brother Samuel to the United States on a mission to organize the American Communist Party. For the rest of his life, Samuel had prided himself on his mission and regaled his relatives and close friends, of whom there were hundreds, with the details of the journey—until he was arrested in 1937. He was sentenced to "ten years of imprisonment without the right of correspondence," and disappeared forever; but his remarkable story became the stuff of family legend.

In July 1919, Samuel traveled from Moscow through northern Europe by a roundabout route, finally arriving in New York Harbor on a Dutch trading vessel in the guise of a seaman. He clattered down the gangplank in boots that had been fashioned by the Kremlin cobbler, with an exceedingly costly diamond secreted in the heel. He carried out his mission: at the behest of the Comintern, he organized the first underground congress of the Communist Party. Upon completion of his task several months later, Samuel returned and reported directly to Comrade Lenin.

The whole of his modest travel allowance was spent on presents, minus twelve dollars spent on food. For his wife he brought home a red woolen dress with berries embroidered on the collar and shoulders, and red shoes three sizes too small. The skates were the third, and most expensive, American present in his luggage. He had bought them too big (with growing room) for his son, who died soon after.

He should have bought them for himself. As a boy, Samuel dreamed of gliding out into the middle of the skating rink with his body bent over the slick ice, racing past all those who turned up their noses at him—past the fine ladies in their muffs, the gymnasium students, the highborn young boys and girls, Marusya Galperin most likely among them. The skates had been buried in a chest for safekeeping, awaiting a new heir. But Samuel didn't have any more children, and the skates, which had lain for ten years untouched, were passed down to the son of his younger sister Genya.

Now, twenty years later, they changed hands—or rather feet—again, inherited by another relative of the heroic Samuel.

Thus, the first day of Mikha's vacation culminated in this unexpected gift, and far surpassed any happiness he could ever have imagined. And there was nothing that even hinted of the misfortune to follow.

On New Year's Eve, Aunt Genya's large family gathered around the table. The neighbors who shared their communal apartment had consented to having the festive dinner set up in the common kitchen, rather than in the 150-square-foot room that Genya occupied, together with her unmarried and endocrinologically challenged daughter, Minna, and, for some time already, Mikha. Aunt Genya prepared a sumptuous feast: both chicken and fish. That night, after the memorable repast, Mikha wrote a poem expressing his abiding impressions of the day.

> The skates are the finest thing
> That ever I have seen in life,
> Finer than sun and water,
> Finer than fire.
> Fine is the man
> who is on those skates.
> On the table, bedecked as at a ball,
> Countless were the dishes,
> And one can only wish
> One's kin great victories in years to come.

At first he had "victuals" instead of "dishes," but thought better of it—it sounded a bit crude.

All week Mikha got up when it was still dark outside and went down to the courtyard, to the improvised skating rink. He skated by himself until the first kids appeared, after sleeping their fill, since they were on school break. He still wasn't very sure on his feet when he was wearing the skates, and he was afraid he wouldn't be able to fend off the other kids if they tried to jump him.

The skates were, of course, the most important event of that vacation. The second most important was Anna Alexandrovna, Sanya's grandmother. She took the boys to museums.

Mikha had a dual nature: he had a thirst for knowledge, a natural curiosity and excitement that was both scientific and unscientific; but he was also possessed of an inchoate creative fire. He was captivated by Anna Alexandrovna. He was not the only one to fall under her spell, however. The museum outings made a strong impression even on Ilya, who seemed to have more of a technological bent than an artistic one. Sanya, the proud owner of this remarkable grandmother, sauntered casually from room to room, occasionally sharing his thoughts—not with his friends, but with his grandmother. It was clear that in museums, no less than in music school, he was in his element.

Mikha fell in love with Anna Alexandrovna. He would never stop loving her until the day she died. She saw in him a budding man of that stamp she had always preferred. The youth was a redhead, a poet, and during that particular week he even limped a bit, having overtaxed himself on his new skates—exactly like the nearly great poet whom Anna Alexandrovna had secretly loved as a thirteen-year-old girl. This paragon of a man, already full-grown in that distant era, who had the aura of a freedom fighter and would-be martyr, and enjoyed adulation at the beginning of the twentieth century, didn't deign to notice the lovestruck young lady, but left a lasting impression on some Freudian underside of her psyche. All her life she would love these intense, emotional redheads.

She smiled when she looked at Mikha—a boy of the same breed, but separated by time . . . and it was pleasant for her to catch his rapturous gaze.

Thus, without being aware of it himself, Mikha's love was requited. That winter he became a frequent guest at the Steklovs' home. Countless books, even books in foreign languages, nestled in every nook and cranny of the living room, with its three windows and another half window bisected by a partition wall, under lofty ceilings with ornate plaster moldings, also bisected. An upright piano, ever battle-ready, guarded its music in its depths. From time to time, unusual but intoxicating smells wafted through the room—real coffee, floor polish, perfume.

This must have been what it was like in my parents' home, Mikha thought. He didn't remember his parents. His mother had perished during the bombardment of the last train headed east from Kiev on September 18, 1941, when the Germans were already approaching the Podol district. His father died at the front, never knowing that his wife was dead and his son had survived.

In reality, the home of Mikha's parents hadn't been anything like Sanya Steklov's. He was already twenty years old when he saw photographs of his parents for the first time. By some miracle, the photographs had been preserved after the war. He was very disappointed to see that his parents were poor, unattractive people—his mother, with a forced smile on her small dark lips and an extravagant, brazen bust; and his father, squat and corpulent, with an air of exaggerated self-importance. The photographs afforded glimpses of dull, everyday life, a setting that was not at all like the diminutive portion of the smaller reception hall of the former Apraksin-Trubetskoy mansion occupied by Sanya's family.

On January 9, as the winter break was drawing to a close, they celebrated Sanya's birthday. Before that it was Christmas, but only grown-ups had been invited to that event. It would be several years before the younger generation would be allowed to take part in the January 7* festivities. Still, there were always sweets left over from Christmas on Sanya's birthday—candied apples, cherries, even orange rinds that Anna Alexandrovna prepared like no one else in the world. But that wasn't all: they would fold up the room divider, move the dining table closer to the door, and, between the two large windows, set up a towering

*Julian calendar (so-called Old Style date). Russia adopted the Gregorian calendar in 1918, but many religious holidays were still celebrated according to their Old Style dates.

Christmas tree decorated with ornaments from a box that had been stashed away all year in a storage loft.

Sanya's birthday party was always a thrilling event. Even girls came. This time there were two of Sanya's friends from music school, Liza and Sonya. There was also Tamara, the granddaughter of his grandmother's friend, with her friend Olga; but they were still small, little first-graders, and they didn't inspire any interest in the boys. His grandmother's friend was somewhat lackluster, too. Liza's grandfather, Vasily Innokentievich, though, was marvelous, with his military uniform and mustache. An enigmatic cloud of odors clung to him: cologne water, medicine, and war. Half-joking, he addressed his granddaughter with the formal "you," while casually calling Anna Alexandrovna "Nuta" and addressing her with "thou." Vasily Innokentievich was Anna Alexandrovna's cousin, and Liza was thus some sort of distant cousin to Sanya. They even used those pre-Revolutionary terms, the French *cousin* and *cousine*, which also seemed to have been pulled out of the box in the storage loft.

Anna Alexandrovna called the girls "young ladies" and the boys "young men," and Mikha, discomfited by all these high-society forms of address, was completely at a loss until Ilya winked at him, as if to say, Take it easy, they won't bite!

Anna Alexandrovna had planned an extraordinary evening. First there was a puppet show, on a real puppet stage, starring Petrushka, Vanka, and fat Rosa. They tussled and fought and exchanged insults, all in a foreign language.

Then they played word games. The little girls, Tamara and Olga, refusing to be outdone by the grown-ups, showed a quickness of mind beyond their years. Anna Alexandrovna invited the children to take pride of place at the large oval table, while the grown-ups retreated to a corner to drink tea. Vasily Innokentievich sat in an armchair and smoked shag tobacco cigarettes. After the puppet show, Anna Alexandrovna picked out a fat hand-rolled cigarette from the silver case on the side table in front of Vasily Innokentievich and tried to smoke it, but immediately broke into a fit of coughing.

"Vasily, these are awfully strong!"

"That's why I don't offer them to anyone, Nuta."

"Ugh!" Anna Alexandrovna expelled the reeking smoke. "Where do you get them?"

"I buy the tobacco, and Liza rolls them for me."

But that wasn't the end of the evening. After the puppet show an array of desserts was spread out for them, a presentation Mikha would remember to the end of his days—everything from the homemade punch to the pale yellow napkin rings, carved from bone, cinching the folds of starched linen.

Ilya and Mikha exchanged glances. This was a moment when Sanya appeared aloof and inaccessible to them. The two of them felt set apart, like lowly interlopers. A three-way friendship, like all triangles, is a complex matter. Obstacles and temptations arise—jealousy, envy, sometimes even treachery, albeit trivial or pardonable. Can treachery be justified by unendurable, boundless love? The three of them would be granted an epoch quintessentially suited to posing this question, and a whole lifetime—shorter for one, longer for the others—in which to find out.

That evening, not only the rather inhibited Mikha, but also the expansive Ilya, felt somewhat abashed by the grandeur of the surroundings. Sanya, preoccupied by Liza, with her long, narrow face, and her hair set free from its blue ribbon, nevertheless sensed this. He called Mikha over and the two of them whispered together for a long time, then summoned Anna Alexandrovna. A little later, it was announced that there would be a game of charades. Then Sanya turned an ungainly little chair upside down, and it suddenly became a stepladder. He climbed up to the top step so that he was even taller than Mikha, who stood one step lower, and together they raucously declaimed the following lines, all the while pushing and shoving each other, tugging at each other's ears, snorting and mooing and making a general racket.

> Two names that start the same—
> A talk between two lords of the meadow.
> The second part of one's like foul disgust: "Yuck!"
> The other's like the vulgar sound
> Released after a meal of slops: "Ugh!"

The two names end the same—
A German preposition.
Add them together, you have two creatures
Misnamed, perhaps, *Homo sapiens*.

The guests laughed heartily, but no one could guess the answer. There was only one person among them who was capable of solving this linguistic riddle: Ilya. And he didn't let them down. Waiting until the guests admitted defeat, he answered, not without pride, "I know! The beasts are called Mutyukin and Murygin!"

In all honesty they should have chosen another charade, because no one had ever heard of any Murygin or Mutyukin; but no one took them to task for it. Everyone had had a good time, and that was what mattered.

But something in the boys' relationship to one another had shifted: Mikha, who had taken part in the charade, was raised to Sanya's level, and Ilya surpassed them both—he was, after all, the one to solve the riddle, and thus support the integrity of the game. It would have fallen through if no one at all had known the answer. Good show, Ilya!

The boys slung their arms around each other's shoulders in triumph, and Vasily Innokentievich photographed the three of them together. This was their first group portrait.

Vasily Innokentievich's camera was a war trophy—a fine one, Ilya noticed. He also noticed that his epaulets were those of a colonel, and decorated with serpents. He had been an army doctor.

On January 10, Anna Alexandrovna took the boys to a piano concert at Tchaikovsky Hall, to listen to Mozart. Ilya was fairly bored, and even took a little snooze, but Mikha felt a sense of elation. The music was so thrilling, and he was so deeply moved, that he wasn't even able to write a poem about it afterward. Sanya was upset, and nearly broke down in tears. Anna Alexandrovna knew why: Sanya wanted to be able to play Mozart that way, too.

On the eleventh they went back to school. That very first day, the three of them, along with another boy, Igor Chetverikov, got into a school-yard brawl with the other boys. It all began with an innocent snowball fight, and it ended in a rout: Mikha had been punched in the face and his glasses were broken; Ilya had a busted lip. It was humiliating that the fight had been two against four. Sanya, as usual, had hung back—not so much out of cowardice as from fastidiousness and tact. Murygin and Mutyukin aroused as much disgust in him as the infamous rag they had wiped his face with. This time, the bullies ignored Sanya completely. Red-haired Mikha, who had aimed a rock-hard snowball at the bull's eye of Murygin's nose and was right on the mark, was far more interesting to them. Ilya was over by the fence, spitting blood, Chetverikov was wondering whether it was time to hightail it, and Mikha was leaning with his back against a wall, fists at the ready. Mikha's fists were massive, almost like a grown-up's.

Then Mutyukin took out a jackknife resembling a penknife, only for very large pens, by the looks of it. The long, thin blade flipped open, and Mutyukin charged, aiming for Mikha's blunt fists. Suddenly, Sanya let out a shriek, leapt up, and in two short bounds was grabbing the blade with his bare hand. Blood spurted everywhere. Sanya waved his hand around and the red stream sprayed Mutyukin's face. Mutyukin bellowed like he was the one who had been slashed, and took off running, Murygin at his heels. But no one considered this a victory. Mikha couldn't see what was happening very well without his glasses. Chetverikov ran after Murygin, but there was no point in chasing him. It was too late. Ilya wrapped a scarf around Sanya's hand, but the blood continued to gush out like water from a faucet.

"Run and get Anna Alexandrovna, quick!" Ilya screamed to Mikha. "And you, go get the school nurse!"

Sanya had passed out, either from shock or from the loss of blood. Twenty-five minutes later he was at the Sklifosovsky Emergency Clinic, where they quickly stopped the bleeding and stitched up the wound. A week later, it was clear that his fourth and fifth fingers would no longer straighten out. A professor of medicine came in, took off the bandages from Sanya's little hand, and said he was very happy with how the patient's wound was healing. Then he told them that the cut was deep, going through the transverse metacarpal ligament, and he was amazed that only two of his fingers now seemed permanently curled toward the palm, rather than all four.

"Are there any exercises he can do? Massage? Electrophoresis? Some experimental procedure?" Anna Alexandrovna implored the professor, who treated her with respect.

"Of course. After he heals completely, we can partially restore mobility. But tendons aren't muscles, you understand."

"What about playing a musical instrument?"

The professor smiled at her sympathetically. "It's unlikely, I'm afraid."

He didn't know he had just signed a death warrant. Anna Alexandrovna said nothing to Sanya, and for six months after he was released from the hospital she continued taking him to physical therapy.

Larisa Stepanovna, the school principal, rushed to the hospital to see Sanya after his operation. Rumors about the knife had reached her, and she was alarmed. Sanya was firm and tight-lipped during the interrogation with the principal. Five times he told her that he had found the knife in the school yard, pressed a button, and the blade shot out, slicing his hand. Who had the knife belonged to? No idea. The evidence was found the next day. Just like in a movie, the knife lay on a mound of bloody snow. It was handed over to the principal, who locked it in the top drawer of her desk.

Aunt Genya bemoaned Mikha's broken glasses, Ilya's mother scolded him a bit for his scrappy belligerence, and Igor Chetverikov managed to hide his involvement in the event from his parents altogether.

From that day on, although Igor was never a full-fledged member of Trianon, he was acknowledged as a sympathizer. Subsequent events, stretching over a quarter of a century, would prove that nothing in the world happened without rhyme or reason. It wasn't just by chance that the two preternaturally farsighted little hooligans locked horns with this future dissident.

When all the talk about the brawl had been quashed for good through the principal's efforts, and everyone had left Mutyukin and Murygin alone, the two started to quarrel and fight with one another. The class split into two camps, and life grew interesting again. The world was full of enemy spies, deserters, negotiations, and skirmishes. The majority was gripped by the warrior spirit, allowing the minority to relax and grow soft.

———

Sanya returned to school three weeks later with a bandaged hand, made it through several days, then came down with tonsilitis, and disappeared until the fourth quarter. Ilya and Mikha visited him almost every day to give him his homework. Anna Alexandrovna served them tea with an apple pastry she called "pie." This was the first word in English that Mikha learned. Sanya had studied English and French since he was little. In school they had to study that repulsive language, German, starting in fifth grade. But Anna Alexandrovna turned out to be a stickler when it came to studying German, and began giving Sanya extra lessons, inviting his friends to join in as well. Though Ilya begged off, Mikha attended the lessons as if they were a party.

At the same time, Anna Alexandrovna gave Mikha an old English primer as a present.

"Study it, Mikha. With your abilities you'll easily teach yourself. I'll give you a few lessons to help you with the pronunciation."

And so, the rich fare from the master's table was shared and shared alike with Mikha.

Sanya was in a curious frame of mind. His two injured fingers didn't get in the way, and weren't even noticeable to others, since we all hold our fingers slightly tucked in, only rarely stretching them out completely. But the injury meant a complete transformation of his life, a total change of plans. He would listen to music all day and enjoy it as never before. It no longer disturbed him that he couldn't play like the great musicians; he was no longer plagued with uncertainty about his talent. The only one who understood was Liza.

"You're freer now than someone who tries to become a musician. I even envy you a little."

"And I envy you," Sanya said.

They would go to the Conservatory together, Anna Alexandrovna with Sanya, and Liza with her grandfather. One of Alexandra Alexandrovna's friends would sometimes join them, someone or other's niece or relative. Occasionally, when his workload permitted, Liza's father, Alexei Vasilievich, also a surgeon, like Vasily Innokentievich, would come along. They all shared a strong family resemblance: an elongated face, a high forehead, and a delicate aquiline nose. In those days it seemed that everyone who visited the Conservatory was related; they were certainly all acquainted. They were a particular subset of the huge metropolitan populace, like a religious order or a hidden caste, perhaps even a secret society.

The beginning of the year was an eventful time. Ilya's father, Isay Semenovich, came down from Leningrad. He usually visited once or twice a year, always loaded down with presents. The year before he had also brought a valuable gift—a set of German drawing instruments—but, apart from their beauty as objects, they were of no use to Ilya. This time he came with a FED-S camera, an exact replica of the German Leica. It was a prewar model manufactured by the boys at the Dzerzhinsky labor commune. His father prized the old camera. As a war correspondent, he had carried it with him wherever he went for three years. Now he was giving it to his only son, born of a romance with the homely and no-longer-young woman by the name of Masha (as Isay Semenovich called Maria Fedorovna). Masha had no expectations, made no demands, and quietly loved her son, Ilya. She rejoiced that Isay hadn't abandoned him, and would even give them money on occasion—at times it would be a lot, and then, for long stretches, nothing at all. Masha refused her former lover's advances, which was her strategy for keeping him interested. She would smile at him, offer him cake, make up his bed with starched linen sheets, and then go to bed herself on the sofa, sleeping head-to-toe with her son. Isay's fascination with her only grew, and he thought about her more and more.

Although Isay was sorry to give his trusty, beloved camera away, the guilt he felt toward his neglected son outweighed his attachment to it. He had other, better cameras. He also had another, official, family, and two beloved daughters who had no interest whatsoever in photography. The boy trembled with excitement at the present, and his father felt annoyed with his life, which hadn't turned out as it should have. Instead of the gentle Masha, whose plainness gave way to flashes of prettiness, he ended up with the shrewish Sima. He no longer even remembered why or how he had become her henpecked husband.

He explained to his son what a *camera obscura* was, that a dark box with a small aperture and a plate covered in photosensitive chemicals was sufficient to capture an image, to stop a moment in time. Masha sat there with them, resting her cheek on her palm, smiling at her small measure of joy. She only needed a tiny crumb, like a chickadee. Isay saw this, and noticed, as well, how skilled and adept Ilya was, how nimble his hands were—like father, like son!

He went away with the firm intention of changing his life so that he could see his son more often. And Masha was more attractive to him now than she had been that summer of 1938, when he had taken her more out of a sense that he owed it to her as an able-bodied young man than out of a real affinity. It was too late to change his life completely, but he could make some minor adjustments, like finally coming clean to Sima about having a son, his prewar offspring. It might be nice to invite Ilya to stay with them and introduce him to his younger sisters. But this was to be the last time he would see his son: two months later, Isay Semenovich, having lost his job at the Leningrad Film Studios, died of a heart attack.

Ilya's father had stayed with them for two days on that final visit. After he left, Ilya's mother, as usual, wept quietly, and then stopped. His life now had been clearly divided into two parts: before the FED, and after. This clever little apparatus gradually awakened a hidden talent in him. He had always collected things right and left—almost anything that grabbed his attention or entered his field of vision. Back in second grade he'd had a feather collection; next it was matchbox labels and stamps. But those were passing phases. Now, once he'd mastered the technical process, from loading the film and choosing exposures to rolling the photo paper onto glass, he began collecting moments of existence. The true passion of a collector was ignited in him, never again to burn out.

By the time he finished school he had assembled a true photographic archive, and a rather sophisticated one at that. On the back of each photograph, in pencil, he noted the time, location, and subjects; all the negatives were arranged in envelopes. The camera changed his life in other ways as well. It turned out that besides the camera itself, he needed accessories, all of which cost a lot of money. Ilya applied himself to the problem and discovered another latent talent: he had a gift for enterprise. He never asked his mother for money; he learned to

acquire it himself. The first initiative that spring was *rasshibalochka**—
winner take all. Ilya was the best player in school, and he branched
out to other games, too. This started bringing in money.

Sanya Steklov didn't approve of Ilya's pursuit of lucre, but Ilya just
shrugged it off.

"Do you know how much large-format photo paper costs? And
developer? Where am I supposed to get it?"

And Sanya would fall silent. His money came from Mama and
Grandmother, and he suspected that this wasn't the most honorable
way to come by it.

The old camera turned Ilya into a photographer. Soon he realized
that he needed his own darkroom. Amateur photographers usually set
up their darkrooms in the bathroom, where there was running water
for rinsing film and photo paper. But their communal apartment had
no bathroom—just a sort of pantry or broom closet, where three families kept their washtubs of various sizes as well as necessities. The
closet shared a wall with the WC, which did have running water, so
Ilya started devising a plan to rig some pipes to feed water into the
closet and then drain it out again. He didn't consider the neighbors,
who had equal rights to the closet.

In their apartment, along with Ilya and his mother, lived a harmless old lady named Olga Matveevna, and a widow by the name of
Granya Loshkareva, who had three children. Ilya's mother often took
the younger two to the preschool where she worked, and she helped
Granya in other ways, too.

In short, when Maria Federovna talked the matter over with her
neighbors, they didn't object. They dragged their unwieldy washtubs
out of the closet—and the rest was up to Ilya. He was just in time to
write a letter to his father requesting his help in setting up shop. His
father was deeply touched, and wired him 150 rubles. A two-line message accompanied the telegram: "I'll come down for the May holidays,

---

*A game in which players toss a round, heavy piece of metal (called a *bita*) at a stack of
coins, in order to hit or knock it over, and then take turns using the *bita* to try to flip
the coins over. If you flip a coin, it's yours to keep. —*Trans.*

and we'll do everything together." That was his last letter—he didn't live till May.

Although he couldn't hook up the water to the closet for another year and a half, Ilya now had his own private nook where he spent a great deal of time. He salvaged a bookcase he found in the trash and used it for storing all his equipment.

Fifth grade seemed endless. It was the thirteenth year of their lives. The boys had slowly filled up with testosterone. The early bloomers had grown hair in secluded places and pimples on their faces. They itched and ached all over, more fights and arguments broke out, and they yearned to touch themselves to relieve the vague longings of the flesh.

Mikha exhausted himself skating. As a result of his secret early-morning training sessions, he became a good skater. He also became a passionate reader. Even before that he would read anything he could get his hands on, but now Anna Alexandrovna was supplying him with wonderful books: Dickens, Jack London, and many others.

At ten o'clock sharp, Aunt Genya would emit a single, high-decibel snort, after which she snored gently and steadily till morning. Minna turned in still earlier, and fell asleep quickly, after a bit of restless stirring about. Then Mikha slipped down to the kitchen to read to his heart's content by the light of the communal lamp. He never got caught. He would sit there scratching at his pimples, reading a young-adult book that had nothing whatever to do with the aggravations of his body.

Sanya lagged behind his friends, not just in height, but in other ways, too: smooth face, clean collar—he was a gentle fellow. But he was also in the process of maturing. He announced to his mother and grandmother that he no longer intended to continue his physical therapy. It was obvious that his hand wasn't going to heal and that he would never become a pianist. His mother and grandmother were both musicians of the homespun variety. In their youth they had dreamed of becoming professionals, only to be forced to abandon their musical training because of the entirely unmusical times, when blaring horns, thundering timpani, and marches and battle hymns were disguised as street songs.

The two solitary women had pinned all their hopes on Sanya. He had promise as a pianist, and everything was going beautifully—he had an excellent teacher, his future was shaping up. After the accident with the knife, however, Sanya had dropped out of music school. Anna Alexandrovna and Sanya's mother, Nadezhda Borisovna, prepared themselves for a serious talk about his future. Anna Alexandrovna said that with his musical talent, it would be a waste to cut all his ties to music completely. Of course, he would never be a professional performer, but what could prevent him from playing at home? There was a certain charm in being an amateur. Sanya stubbornly resisted at first, then gave in after two weeks. He began taking private lessons with his grandmother's friend Evgenia Danilovna.

Sanya played on their beloved Karelian-birch upright piano with his futureless, maimed hands. He would go weak at the knees for Chopin's waltzes the way his peers did when girls from the neighborhood would brush against them in the mad chaos of a street game. He read, played, and sometimes did what normal boys his age did only as a form of punishment: he took long walks with his grandmother.

Evgenia Danilovna continued to give him lessons for about two years, but then the lessons faltered. This was partly due to Liza: her progress was so great, and his so minor, that he began shirking.

Anna Alexandrovna was a teacher of Russian, but with special qualifications—she taught Russian to foreigners.

And what foreigners they were! Her students were young men from Communist China who had come to study at the military academy. This was Anna Alexandrovna's eighth or ninth job since finishing high school, and everything about it suited her. She liked how she was treated by the administrators. The short hours, her salary, and the various bonuses and benefits, including the excellent military sanatorium where she was allowed to stay for free once a year, were all very much to her liking.

Nadezhda Borisovna was an X-ray technician. It was an unusual profession, harmful to her health, but she got short hours and free milk to boost her strength.

Even though the small family was relatively well-off, their life was not without problems. There was too much secret dissatisfaction pent up in both mother and daughter. They were single, having both lost bona fide husbands, and husbands-to-be. No one raised the tactless question of where their men were. Those who needed to know, knew, and everyone else left them alone.

Mikha spent a lot of time at the Steklovs'. During his visits he watched Sanya fingering the keys, and saw how they responded to his touch. He imagined mysterious negotiations transpiring between the boy and the instrument, and tried to intuit their secret meaning, but was unable to get to the bottom of it.

He sat in the corner, leafing through the pages of his book, awaiting Anna Alexandrovna's return. She would place a plain cookie and a cup of milky tea in front of him, then sit down beside him—with a self-rolled cigarette that she didn't so much smoke as hold poised between her beautiful, arched fingers. Sometimes Sanya would get up from the piano and sit down with them on the edge of the chair, but his presence ruffled them. Mikha was fast outgrowing Dickens, and Anna Alexandrovna, without a second thought, urged Pushkin on him.

"But I've already read him," Mikha said, resisting.

"This is like the Gospels—you read it your whole life."

"Then give me the Gospels, Anna Alexandrovna, I've never read them."

Anna Alexandrovna laughed, shaking her head. "Your relatives will kill me. But, to be honest, you can't understand European literature without them. Not to mention Russian literature. Sanya, dear, bring us the Gospels. In Russian."

"Nuta," he said, baiting his grandmother, "I think you're just a corrupter of youth."

But he brought over the book in its black binding.

They decided that Mikha could read the Gospels, but he was not to remove the book from their house or breathe a word about it to anyone. Mikha had never known such abundance—he had a home with his own folding cot, Aunt Genya with her soup, the buxom, feeble-minded Minna constantly nudging him, now with her ample hips, now her ample bosom, his friends Sanya and Ilya, Anna Alexandrovna, skates, books . . .

In the middle of March the thaw set in. The ice in the skating rink melted, and Mikha coated his skates with machine oil to protect them, as his uncle Marlen had taught him to do. He did it too soon, though; another frost hit, and the little skating rink again froze over. Mikha could go skating again, even though winter was clearly on the wane. Now he even ventured down to the courtyard in broad daylight, after lunch. That was how everyone got a good look at his prized possession. No one else had skates like his; everyone else just strapped any old junk onto their felt boots. Only Mikha had the real kind, affixed to leather boots. His skates became the talk of the neighborhood. Two days or so later, Murygin showed up to check them out. He stood there awhile, took a good long look at them, then left. The next day, as Mikha was returning home from the rink, he found himself pressed up against the wall of his entryway by Murygin and Mutyukin.

It was no secret why they were there—the skates had taken their fancy.

"Come on, take them off!" Mutyukin said.

Murygin twisted Mikha's arms behind his back, Mutyukin kicked him behind his knees, and Mikha collapsed. In a flash they ripped the skates from his feet and sped off. Mikha, wearing only his woolen socks, dashed after them. He caught up with them at the entrance to the courtyard and grabbed Murygin, who tossed the skates to Mutyukin. Mutyukin hightailed it down Pokrovka with Mikha in hot pursuit, shouting, in the direction of the Pokrovsky Gates. They were obviously running toward Milyutin Park, where there was another skating rink.

A streetcar was just crawling out from around the corner of Chistoprudny Boulevard. Mikha had almost caught up with Mutyukin, who flung the skates back to Murygin, but Murygin failed to intercept them, and the skates landed somewhere between the streetcar tracks. All three threw themselves at the skates. The streetcar let out an unearthly shriek, followed by a long, loud screech. Then it swallowed up the sound and ground heavily to a halt. Mikha faltered and fell.

When he opened his eyes, the skates were lying right by his nose. He couldn't see Mutyukin. On the tracks in front of the streetcar lay a messy heap. Rags, blood, a twisted leg—this was all that remained of Murygin. A frantic crowd had rushed over and gathered around him. More streetcars rattled and clanged in the background. Mikha stood up, took the skates—no, just one skate. Shoulders hunched, he trudged home. He walked barefoot over the frozen ground—his socks had vanished, somehow—but he didn't feel the cold. Near the entrance to his building, teeth chattering, he chucked the remaining skate in the direction of the ice rink, then slipped into the entryway he had emerged from just five minutes before.

He picked up his boots, stuck his bare feet into them, and ran straight to the Steklovs'. Anna Alexandrovna listened to the whole story without saying a word, then poured him a bowl of mushroom soup.

When Mikha had finished his soup, Anna Alexandrovna took the dirty bowl to the kitchen.

"I didn't want it to happen, I swear!" Mikha said to Sanya.

"Who would want a thing like that?" Sanya said, shaking his head.

> The tram shrieked out in awful pain,
> The world is not what it was before.
> All that was, and is, remains,
> Except Murygin, who is no more.

This was the poem Mikha wrote on the day of Murygin's funeral. The whole school had come, mourning Slava Murygin as though he were a national hero. The vice-principal and two upperclassmen laid a beribboned wreath, bought with money donated by the student body, on the grave. The ribbon bore an inscription in gold letters on a red background.

Mikha, the witness, and, as he believed, guilty party in this death, kept reliving that tragic instant: the skates flashing through the air, the metallic shriek of the streetcar, and an untidy raggedy heap under the wheels instead of the pathetic, mean boy who had been grimacing and racing through the streets a moment before. Pity of enormous proportions filled Mikha's mind, his heart, his entire body. It filled him to overflowing, it overwhelmed him, and it was a pity for all people, both bad and good, simply because they were all so defenseless and fragile, so soft, and because the mere touch of senseless steel was enough to shatter their bones, to break their heads open, to make their blood flow out, so that all that was left was an unsightly heap. Poor, poor Murygin!

No one but Ilya managed to hold on to the 1952 class picture. It was one of just two photographs in his entire archive not taken by himself; the rest were all his own. One was the photograph taken by Vasily Innokentievich on Sanya's birthday. The other one, the class picture, had been taken by a studio photographer. The picture displayed a motley group of underfed, postwar kids arranged in four neat rows. The first rows are sitting, and the upper rows stand on chairs borrowed from the assembly room. The boys are surrounded by thick sheaves of wheat, draped banners, stippled emblems, the decorative frame that formed the base, while the superstructure was the bug-eyed schoolteacher amid a mass of closely shaven heads. Murygin and Mutyukin are standing side by side in the top row on the left. Murygin is looking sideways; he's a small boy, bald shaven, paltry, and harmless. Sanya isn't in the picture. He was sick the day it was taken. Mikha is in the bottom corner. In the center stands the class adviser, their Russian teacher. Everyone forgot her name, because she went on maternity leave when they were in fifth grade and never came back. Mutyukin had to repeat fifth grade, but soon went on to other things. His career continued in a vocational school and, later, a prison camp.

Murygin, of course, was no more.

THE NEW TEACHER

In the sixth grade, Victor Yulievich Shengeli, a literature teacher, replaced the Russian teacher whose name no one could remember.

From the very first day he captured the attention of the entire school: he walked briskly down the hallway, with the right sleeve of his gray-striped blazer pinned shut just below the elbow, his half-arm dangling inside. In his left hand he carried an old briefcase with two copper locks—far older than the teacher himself, from the looks of it. And, by the end of that first week, he already had a nickname: the Hand.

He was fairly young, with a handsome face, almost like a film star, but excessively animated. He was in the habit of smiling for no discernible reason, then breaking into a frown, then twitching his nose or lips. He was improbably polite, addressing everyone with the formal "you"; but he could also be very caustic.

For starters, when Ilya was wending his way through the rows of desks with his unsteady gait, the teacher said: "Why are you waddling about like a duck?" Ilya took an instant dislike to him. Then the teacher picked up the attendance book to call roll. When he got to the surname Svinin (someone did have that unfortunate name, which sounded so much like "swine"), he stopped, peered closely at Svinin's small face, then said in a strange tone that could have been either respectful or mocking: "Nice name." The class erupted in guffaws, and Senka Svinin turned red as a beet. The teacher raised his eyebrows quizzically.

"Why are you laughing? It's a very distinguished name. There was an ancient clan of boyars called the Svinins. Peter the Great himself sent a Svinin, I don't recall his first name, to Holland to study. You've never read *The Silver Knight*? The Svinins are mentioned in it. It's a fascinating book, by the way."

Within three months, all of them, including Ilya, Senka Svinin, and, in particular, Mikha, thought the teacher could do no wrong. They clung to his every word, twitching their lips and furrowing their brows in perfect imitation of him.

The Hand also read poetry to them. At the beginning of every class, while they were settling into their seats and getting their notebooks out, he recited a poem from memory, never telling them who the author was. His choices seemed very idiosyncratic. One day it would be the familiar "A lonely sail is flashing white"; and the next, the enigmatic but memorable "the air is blue, like the bundle of linen of a patient just discharged from hospital." Then, out of nowhere, he'd toss out some inspired gobbledegook, like:

> Outside it was cold, *Tristan* was on the stage.
> A wounded sea sang in the orchestra pit,
> Green realm behind the bluish steam.
> A heart that ceased to beat.
> No one saw her enter the theater,
> But there she was, seated in her box,
> Like a Briullov painting.
> Women so lovely live only in novels,
> Or come to life on-screen . . .
> Men steal for them, or worse.
> They ambush their carriages and
> Poison themselves in garrets . . .

Mikha's heart leapt to his throat when he heard poems like this, though the other students were unmoved. But Mikha was the one the teacher looked at—he was almost the only one who lapped up the verses. Sanya would smile condescendingly at the teacher's weakness: some of the poems were ones that his grandmother had read to him. The other kids forgave their teacher his curious predilection. They considered poetry an effeminate affectation for a man who had fought on the front lines during the war.

Occasionally, however, he recited something very apropos. When they began reading *Taras Bulba*, he came to class with something that was clearly about Gogol:

> Our own wayward riddle,
> You alighted on the earth,
> Our own thoughtful mockingbird
> With sorrow on your brow.
>
> Our Hamlet! Laughter mixed
> With tears, inner woe,
> Outer cheer, burdened by
> Success, as others by ill luck.
>
> Darling and martyr of
> Fame, always gentle to you,
> Drone of life, wanderer,
> Struggling with an inner storm.
>
> A ruined ascetic in spirit,
> An Aristophanes on the page,
> Physician and scourge of all
> Our ills and wounds!

It seemed there wasn't a single occasion in life for which he didn't have a poem at the ready.

"We are studying literature," he would constantly remind them, as though it were breaking news. "Literature is the finest thing humankind has created. Poetry is the beating heart of literature, the highest concentration of all that is best in the world and in people. It is the only true food for the soul. It is your own choice whether you grow up to become human beings, or remain on the intellectual level of beasts."

Later, when he had learned all the students' names and assigned them seats after his own idiosyncratic fashion (not in the same order as their class picture, and not alphabetically, either), after everyone had formed a bond through discussions about cunning Odysseus; the mysterious chronicler Pimen; the unfortunate son of Taras Bulba; Pushkin's honest but slow-witted Alexei Berestov; and swarthy, clever Akulina—all part of the school curriculum, by the way—the boys started asking questions about the war: What was it like? And it immediately became clear that Victor Yulievich loved literature, and hated war. A strange bird! In those days, the entire population of young men who hadn't had the opportunity to shoot Fascists was enamored of war.

"War is the greatest abomination ever invented by man," the teacher told them, curbing their tongues before they could even ask: Where did you fight? How did you get wounded? How many Nazis did you kill?

One day he told them.

"I had just finished my second year of college when the war broke out. All my classmates immediately reported to the recruitment office, and all of them were sent to the front. I am the only one from my group who stayed alive. Everyone else perished, including two girls. That is why I am against war with all my heart and with both my hands."

With that, he lifted up his left hand. He tried to raise his right half-arm in tandem, but was unable.

On Wednesdays, literature was the last class of the day. When it was over, Victor Yulievich would say, "So, shall we go for a walk?"

The first of these walks took place in October. About six of them went. Ilya had rushed home, as usual, and Sanya had skipped school that day, which he often did, with his grandmother's permission. The Trianon was represented solely by Mikha, who later recounted word for word the stories he had heard from the teacher on the way from school to Krivokolenny Lane. Victor Yulievich had told them about Pushkin, but the way he talked about him made them wonder whether he and Pushkin hadn't been actual classmates. It turned out that Pushkin was a card shark! And a skirt-chaser! He was a real womanizer! On top of that, he was a brawler, held grudges, was always ready to make a scene or kick up a row, to fight in duels.

"Indeed," Victor Yulievich said, "it was this kind of behavior that led people to consider him a *bretteur.*"

No one asked what this foreign word meant, because it was obvious anyway: a troublemaker.

Then he led them up to the shabby building on the first corner of Krivokolenny Lane after its intersection with Kirov Street. With a broad gesture of his left hand, he said, "Just imagine what it was like here in Pushkin's day. Of course, there wasn't any asphalt, and the roads were paved with wooden blocks. A carriage pulls up from the direction of Myasnitskaya Street. Well, most likely not a carriage, but a small cart with a coachman. Pushkin was visiting Moscow, partly on business. He had many friends and relatives here, but he never had his own home in Moscow, or his own equipage—with the exception of the apartment he rented on the Arbat; but that was only for a little while, after his wedding. Then he moved back to St. Petersburg. He did not like Moscow. He said there were 'too many old Aunties' there.

"Now imagine it's more than one hundred years after Pushkin's death, after the Revolution. A woman is walking down this lane, and, suddenly, from the direction of Myasnitskaya, she hears, clip-clop, clip-clop: a carriage rounds the corner and stops right at this spot. Pushkin alights from the carriage, his heels clicking on the wooden pavement, and disappears inside the house. The lady gasps, and then everything disappears—the wood pavement, the carriage, the coachman, and the horses. There were rumors that this building was haunted. We'll never know whether that's true or not. But what happened in this very building in October 1826—a poet named Venevitinov was living here then—many eyewitnesses confirm: in the main hall of this house, Pushkin read his tragedy *Boris Godunov* aloud for the first time. There were about forty people present, and almost half of them wrote about the reading in letters to their relatives immediately afterward, or subsequently, in their memoirs. You've all read *Boris Godunov*, haven't you? Who can summarize the plot for me?"

Mikha was always ready to be called upon, but this time he had forgotten some parts of the story and didn't want to embarrass himself.

For a while, nobody said anything. Finally, Igor Chetverikov said tentatively:

"He killed Tsarevich False Dmitry."

"Congratulations, Igor. History is a rather muddled affair. There are in fact two versions of the story. In one, Boris Godunov killed Tsarevich Dmitry. In the other, he didn't kill him, and was really quite a decent man. Your version, charging him with the murder of another person altogether—False Dmitry—flies in the face of long-held historical beliefs. Don't worry, though, history isn't algebra. It's not an exact science. In some ways, literature is a more exact science than history. What a great writer says can become a historical truth. Military historians have found many discrepancies in Tolstoy's description of the Battle of Borodino, but the whole world imagines the event just as Tolstoy described it in *War and Peace.* Neither was Pushkin standing in the rear courtyard of the palace of Maria Nagaya, mother of the young Tsarevich, where the murder of Dmitry did—or did not—take place. The same principle applies to his story about Mozart. I suppose you've all read *The Little Tragedies.*"

"Yes, of course! Evil and true genius are incompatible," Mikha said.

"I hold the same view. There is no definitive proof that Salieri poisoned Mozart. This is just historical speculation. Pushkin's work, however, is what one could call undiluted fact. A great fact of Russian literature. History may find proof that Salieri never poisoned Mozart, but there will still be no gainsaying *The Little Tragedies.* Pushkin expressed a great idea: a man cannot be both evil and a true genius."

It was getting dark. Victor Yulievich said good night to the students, and they all scattered to their homes in various parts of Kitai-Gorod.

This first literary walking tour led to the foundation of a club, which by the end of the year had settled on a name for itself: LORL, the Lovers of Russian Literature.

After finding out about the first excursion, Ilya never missed a single one of these "nature walks"—what Victor Yulievich called their Wednesday afternoon literary wanderings. Ilya would compile reports on their meetings; he was the recording secretary, and a conscientious one, at that. He stored the LORL protocols, together with his photographs, in the bookcase of his sacred space, the closet darkroom.

While they were being initiated into the mysteries of nineteenth-century Russian literature, the LORLs also learned, piece by piece, about the war experiences of their teacher.

With his nostrils and cheeks twitching (which they now knew was the result of an injury), Victor Yulievich told them about how he and his classmates had reported to the recruitment office the day after war broke out.

They sent him to a field artillery school in Tula. The boys wanted concrete details—battle, advance, retreat, wounds. What kind of weaponry? What kind of ammunition? What about the Germans, what were they armed with?

The teacher's answers were brief and to the point. Remembering was painful for him.

Training at the Tula program was accelerated, but the German advance still outpaced it. By the end of October, the Germans forces had already pushed as far as Tula. The trainees were thrown into battle to defend the city. Each of them was given a platoon of militiamen, and the gun emplacements were manned by student commanders and rank-and-file volunteers. This would have resembled "playing war" as kids, if they had not all been cut down within twelve hours by enemy fire. Victor was saved by his politeness—the first time good manners ever saved anyone's life in any circumstance. He ordered a soldier, whose name he couldn't recall, to fetch a box of shells. The fleshy older man cursed the young commander, saying, "Who do you think you are, ordering me around? I'm fifty and you're only eighteen. You lug the boxes."

Victor, who was in fact nineteen at the time, ran to fetch the shells without a word. He ran a hundred yards there, empty-handed, and a hundred back, carrying a hundred-pound crate. But when he returned, the panting and winded student commander couldn't find the gun crew anywhere—there was just a giant smoking crater in the spot where the gun had been set up. None of the crew survived.

There wasn't even anyone to bury. It had been a direct hit. The trainee sat down on the box, his mind empty, feeling like he was the scorched earth itself, a blast of searing metal, boiling blood, and burning rags. Then, abandoning his useless box, he left, amid the whistles and explosions that he no longer heard.

When the siege of Tula was lifted, they transferred the trainees to Tomsk—those who were left alive after the onslaught, at any rate. For a long time Victor had nightmares about the perished gunners, and the fleshy man cursed him darkly—not about the box of shells, but for something far more serious. A thousand times Victor returned to the scene in his thoughts. What should he have done? How should he have acted? If he had shouted down the fleshy older man, which was his duty as a commander, that guy was the one who would still be alive today, and not he himself.

He decided that he wasn't cut out to be a commander, only a private. He submitted a request to be assigned to active duty. It was refused— he had only six weeks until graduation. A slight transgression—that was what was called for. Not so great that he would be court-martialed or sent to a punitive battalion, but enough to get him sent to the front as a private instead of an officer.

He came up with a plan for a fitting offense. On the eve of his swearing in as an officer, he went AWOL, got drunk in the city, sneaked into the women's dormitory, and spent the night with a girl in the recreation room. Early the next morning, at his request, she turned him in to the military patrol. It worked like a charm. He was thrown into the guardhouse for ten days, and then sent into active duty as a private. There he remained until the end of the war, which for him was in 1944, after he was wounded. He never once had to give orders, only carry them out. The task was always the same: make it from point A to point B alive. And myriad petty concerns: eating, drinking, sleeping, not getting blisters on his feet. And it would have been nice to have a good wash once in a while . . . They gave the order—he fired. No orders—no firing. He didn't talk about that. He chose to keep silent.

"Where did you get wounded?" the boys asked.

"In Poland, during the invasion. Look, they took my hand."

What happened after that, he wouldn't tell the kids. How he learned to write left-handed—in a rounded, slanting script, not devoid of elegance. The stump of his right arm still helped him out a little, but he

never wore the pink celluloid prosthesis. He figured out an easy way
of donning his rucksack—with his left hand he arranged the first strap
over the stump of his right arm, and then reached around behind him
with his left arm, slipping it under the other strap. After he left the
hospital he went to Moscow. The institute where he had studied before the war had been reorganized, and the vestiges of it had merged
with the philological department. That was the place he returned to,
in his military overcoat that still reeked of war, and in officer's boots
that didn't match his rank.

The university on Mokhovaya Street! What a sweet luxury it was—
for three whole years he recuperated there, regaining his health
through his own efforts: he washed the blood off with Pushkin, Tolstoy, Herzen . . .

In 1948, shortly before graduation, he was encouraged to take up
graduate studies. His academic adviser would be a marvelous medie-
valist and renowned scholar in the field of European literature. The
subject of Victor's research was intriguing—it examined Pushkin's
relationship to his European counterparts in a primarily Romano-
Germanic context. But Victor Yulievich wavered: he also wanted to be
a schoolteacher, and he felt that he now knew what he wanted to teach
them. Choices, choices . . .

Where was that voice that prompts you at critical moments and
tells you what to do? Yet it turned out he didn't need that voice after
all. The would-be academic adviser was officially reprimanded for his
Western leanings and his "cosmopolitanism," and was later sent to a
prison camp.

Victor's graduate studies ended before they began. He was assigned
to teach Russian language and literature in a middle school in the village of Kalinovo, in the Vologda Oblast.

They gave him room and board at the school—one room and an
entrance hall, where there was a wood-burning stove. They supplied
him with wood. The local store sold hard candy and crabs from the
Far East, awful wine, and vodka. Bread was delivered twice a week,
and lines started forming in the early hours of the morning. The store
opened at nine, when the first lesson at school was just ending. The
mothers, observing time-honored village custom, would bring him eggs,

cottage cheese, or homemade pies that had the remarkable quality of tasting delicious when warm, but being completely inedible once they had cooled off. From time immemorial this had been the accepted form of payment for the services of doctors, priests, and teachers. He would share these offerings with the cleaning lady Marfusha, an asocial, eccentric widow, but he always drank alone. Not too much and not too little—one bottle an evening. Before going to bed he would read the only author he never got tired of.

Besides literature, he also had to teach geography and history. The school principal taught math and physics, as well as the social sciences, which were all versions of the history of the Communist Party, only with different names. The other subjects—biology and German—were taught by an exiled Petersburg Finnish woman. Besides her nationality, she had one other blemish in her biography: before the war she had worked with Academician Vavilov, an unrepentant Weismann-Morganist, who dared insist on the validity of the theory of genetics.

Everything in Kalinovo was meager. The only thing in abundance there was virginal, unsullied nature. And the people were perhaps better than city-dwellers, because they, too, were almost untouched by spiritual dissipation.

His interactions with rural children had undone all the illusions of his student years. His notions of "the good, the eternal" had not changed, of course; but the circumstances of everyday life here were so coarse, so very difficult. The young girls, wrapped in their patched and mended kerchiefs, who managed to care for the farm animals and their younger siblings before school, and the boys, who already did the work of men in the summer—what use were these cultural values to them? What was the point of studying on an empty stomach and wasting time on knowledge they would never need under any circumstances?

Their childhood was already over long ago. They were simply underdeveloped men and women. Even the ones whose mothers eagerly sent them off to school, by far the minority, seemed to feel awkward, as though they were busy with trifling pastimes rather than serious work. This caused the young teacher to feel uncertain about his role as well—and, really, wasn't he distracting them from the fundamental concerns of life by exposing them to superfluous luxuries? What did

Radishchev mean to them? Or Gogol? Or even Pushkin, for that matter? Teach them to read, and send them home to work as soon as possible. That's all the students really wanted themselves.

This was when he first started thinking about the phenomenon of childhood. When it began wasn't the issue; but when did it end? Where was the boundary beyond which a human being became an adult? It was obvious that childhood ended earlier in the country than it did in the city.

The northern countryside had always lived hand to mouth, but after the war the poverty was profound. The women and children did the lion's share of the work. Of the thirty local men who had gone to the front to fight, only two had returned: one with only one leg, the other with tuberculosis. He died a year later. The children, miniature peasants, shouldered the burden of labor early, and their childhoods were stolen from them.

And, truly, how was one to reckon it, to weigh the losses? Some had had their childhoods stolen from them, others their youths, still others their freedom. Victor Yulievich himself had lost the most insignificant thing of all: his graduate studies.

After his three-year term of quasi-exile—after all, he was living in the same part of the country to which clever young people like himself, with a sense of their own dignity and self-worth, had been sent during tsarist times—his seventh-graders graduated, and he returned to Moscow to live with his mother on Bolshevik Lane, in the building with the knight standing in a niche above the entranceway.

By some stroke of luck, the first place he was offered a teaching job in Moscow was only a ten-minute walk from his home, near the History Library. The library held a strong attraction for him. He had felt starved of literary culture and missed it more than theaters and museums when he was away.

He tried to reestablish his university connections, seeking companionship. He got together with Lena Kurzer, who had spent the war as a military interpreter, but they couldn't really communicate. He found two more of his former classmates, but again nothing clicked. The mood of the time was taciturn, disinclined to frankness. People started to open up and talk only several years later. Of the three classmates who had survived the war, one of them embarked on a career in the Party and a second taught school. His first and last meeting with them was limited to splitting a bottle of vodka. The third, Stas Komarnitsky, was out of reach: he had been sent to prison, either for telling a joke or just for talking. The only one of his friends he was always happy to see was Mishka Kolesnik, his former neighbor. They made for an amusing postwar pair: Mishka was missing a leg, and Victor an arm, so they called themselves "Three arms, three legs."

Mishka had meanwhile become a biologist and was married to a nice girl, also from their neighborhood, but younger.

She was a doctor and worked in the municipal hospital. She was desperate to marry Victor off, and kept trying to hook him up with one of her unmarried colleagues. But Victor had no intentions of marrying. After he returned from Kalinovo, he had fallen in love with two beauties at the same time. One he had met in the library, and the other had approached him in a museum, where he had taken his students on a field trip. Mishka joked, "It's your good fortune that the dames flock to you in pairs, Vic. If there were only one of them, she'd collar you for sure."

But it was, in fact, work that "collared" Victor. It turned out that teaching his thirteen-year-olds was the most fascinating experience in his life. These Moscow youths had nothing whatsoever in common with their country counterparts. They didn't plow the land, didn't sow, didn't repair the horses' harnesses, and had none of the peasant's sense of responsibility for family.

They were ordinary kids—in class, they cut up, threw paper wads and spitballs, sprayed one another with water, hid one another's book satchels and notebooks, and grabbed and pushed and shoved like puppies. Then they would suddenly freeze in wonder, and ask him real questions. Unlike the country lads, they had had a real childhood, which they were now leaving behind once and for all. Besides pimples, there were other signs, in a higher register, of their maturing: they asked the "accursed questions," agonized over the injustices in the world, and listened to poetry. A few of them even wrote something that vaguely resembled it. The first one to bring the teacher a neatly copied page of verse was Mikha Melamid.

"Yes, I see," Victor Yulievich said out loud, smiling. *Jewish boys are particularly sensitive readers and writers of Russian literature*, he mused.

Half of the class did not quite understand what the literature teacher wanted from them. The other half clung to his every word. Victor Yulievich tried to treat everyone equally, but he did have his favorites—Mikha, emotionally intense and sensitive to a fault; Ilya, energetic and capable; and Sanya, polite and self-contained. The inseparable trio.

He had belonged to just such a triumvirate at one time, and he often thought about his college chums, Zhenya and Mark, who had died in the first days of the war. They were still just boys, really, who hadn't completely outgrown childhood. Full of overblown romanticism, with their infantile verses—"Brigantine! Brigantine!"—who would they have become now, had they lived? The red-haired Mikha could have been their younger brother, and if you looked closely you could read his complicated future on his face. Not that Victor claimed any sort of clairvoyance; he was just concerned.

It was 1953, not yet March, and the anti-Semitic campaign was raging. In those rotten times, the eighth of him that was Jewish moaned in horror, and the fourth of him that was Georgian burned with shame.

Victor Yulievich was a man of mixed ancestry. He had a Georgian name, he was registered as Russian, but he in fact had very little Russian blood. His Georgian grandfather had been married to a German woman; they had studied together in Switzerland, and Victor's father, Julius, had been born there. The ancestry of Ksenia Nikolayevna, Victor's mother, was no less exotic. Her father, the product of the union of an exiled Pole and a Jewish girl, one of the first females to become a trained field doctor, had married a priest's daughter. This ecclesiastical blood was the sole source of Victor's Russianness.

From his Georgian grandfather he inherited his musical talent. From his German grandmother, who carefully concealed her origins and with prudent foresight registered herself as Swiss upon her arrival in Tiflis in 1912, he inherited his rational cast of mind and his prodigious memory. His Jewish grandmother gave him her thick hair and small bones; and from his Vologda grandmother, he got his light-gray northern eyes.

Ksenia Nikolayevna, who was early widowed, was the only surviving descendant of two family lines that had gone extinct during the Revolution. She would carefully wipe dust from bookshelves, battle clothes moths, and water the orange marigolds that bloomed nearly year-round on her windowsill.

She had two favorite things in life: taking care of her son, and painting silk handkerchiefs to sell. She was also good at frying meat patties and making French toast. After Vika (that was what she called him—almost like a girl) returned from the front, she quickly learned to do things for him he couldn't manage with just one hand: slice bread, butter it when butter was to be had. In the mornings, she would make shaving lather for him out of soap.

The one thing that was categorically absent in Victor Yulievich was a proud sense of belonging to some particular people or ethnic group. He felt like an outcast and a blue blood, in equal measure. The Jew-baiting that was endemic to the times was anathema to him primarily on aesthetic grounds: ugly people dressed in ugly clothing whose behavior was ugly, too. Life outside the bounds of literature was harsh and abusive, but the world of books offered living thought, and feeling, and learning. It was impossible to bridge these two realms, and he retreated farther and farther into literature. Only the children he taught could make the nauseating reality outside of books bearable.

And also women. He loved beautiful women. They flashed through his life like brief festivities, often in succession, sometimes even parallel to one another, and all of them were equally beautiful to him.

It must be said that women liked him, too. He was handsome, and even his physical defect (this took him some time to realize) was attractive in its own way. Beautiful women would fall for him not just for the obvious reason that there were fewer men than necessary for the purposes of reproduction, as a veterinarian might put it. What made him especially attractive to women was their mistaken assumption that he would belong to them completely, now and forever, because of his disability.

They were wrong. He had no intention of handing over exclusive rights to himself to anyone, which marriage implied.

In the early twentieth century, Bunin, Kuprin, and Chekhov, in his

"Lady with a Dog," all wrote about "profane" love, a still largely unexplored territory in Russian literature: the sudden blooming of desire, adultery, sexual relations—all that the nineteenth century had deemed "vulgar."

Not one of these writers was aware of the primary problem of our postwar era, however: the problem of territory, which preoccupied the devotees of divine love, and lovers with the most primitive longings and aspirations, alike. Where? Where could a person who lived in a single room with his mother arrange a lovers' tryst? Where, in a city without hotels, could one experience mutual "sunstroke"* with a lady friend? There wasn't even a narrow berth to be had for such purposes. Well, perhaps in summer, *en plein air*; but summers are so brief in our latitudes.

Bringing a girl home and entertaining her behind the tapestry curtain that divided the male, filial half of the room from the female half occupied by his mother was unthinkable. Renting a room just for trysts was both distasteful and expensive. Borrowing the key to the room of one of his single friends was awkward. Fastidiousness stood guard over Victor Yulievich's morality.

But he lucked out. All his girlfriends had places at their disposal. Lidochka, a divorcee he saw sometimes, with an elegant neck and beautiful breasts, had her own room. Then there was Tanya the tomboy, who was diminutive and seemed to be walking on springs. Her husband worked as an actor in Saratov, and she rented a room on Sretenka Street within walking distance of Victor's place. There was also Verochka, a well-educated translator of French, who would take him to her parents' empty dacha.

He never took a single one of these women home with him to meet his mother. Ksenia Nikolayevna couldn't abide other women. Mother and son lived peacefully together, and Victor Yulievich wasn't trying to change that arrangement.

On the morning of March 2, they were eating breakfast—French toast, soft and tender on the inside, crisp on the outside. Ksenia Nikolayevna had cut it up into small pieces for her Vika. This kind of

---

*The title of an eponymous story by Ivan Bunin.

meticulous care, sometimes quite gratuitous, took her back to the days when Vika was still a small boy, she was still young and pretty, and her husband was still alive.

She made the tea strong, just as her late husband had preferred it. Their peaceful breakfast was suddenly interrupted by an official announcement informing the nation of Stalin's illness. Ksenia Nikolayevna threw her hands up, and Victor's face jerked. He was silent for a moment, then said, "I swear he kicked the bucket. They'll try to pull the wool over our eyes for a week, then they'll admit it."

"That's impossible."

"Why impossible? It's happened before. When Alexander the First died in Taganrog, a courier was sent to Petersburg with news of his death, and even after the courier had made it as far as Moscow, Golitsyn ordered bulletins to be made up and distributed about the state of the Tsar's health. For a whole week the city police spread this disinformation."

"Oh, come now! Wherever did you hear such a thing?"

"I first came upon it in the notes of Prince Kropotkin, he wrote about these very bulletins. Later, in the History Library, I found the bulletins themselves. Compose your face, madame, and simulate grief. Change is on the way."

"I'm scared," she whispered. "Vika, I'm scared."

"Don't worry. Things can't get any worse."

And he left for school. A tense silence gripped the teachers' lounge. No one spoke louder than a whisper, if at all. He greeted the others, took up his attendance book, and went to see his boys.

As he opened the door to his classroom, the Hand began to recite, and the din died away.

> Some say a cavalry corps,
> some infantry, some again
> will maintain that the swift oars
>
> of our fleet are the finest
> sight on dark earth; but I say
> that whatever one loves, is.

> This is easily proved: did
> not Helen—she who had scanned
> the flower of the world's manhood—
>
> choose as first among men one
> who laid Troy's honor in ruin?
> warped to his will, forgetting
>
> love due her own blood, her own
> child, she wandered far with him ..."

"Now, who can tell me what a lyric is?" the teacher said, when the lids of the desks had all closed with a thump and it had gone quiet.

The class was rapt with attention. Victor Yulievich savored the moment—he had learned how to create this meditative silence.

"It's about love," a brave soul piped up.

"Correct, but that's not all. A lyric is about human experience, about the inner life of a human being. And that includes, of course, love. And sadness, and loneliness, and parting from the beloved. And the beloved doesn't necessarily have to be a person. There is a famous poem, written long before our time, about the death of a sparrow. I'm not joking.

> "All ye gentle powers above,
> Venus, and thou god of love;
> All ye gentle souls below,
> That can melt at others' woe,
> Lesbia's loss with tears deplore,
> Lesbia's sparrow is no more:
> Late she wont her bird to prize
> Dearer than her own bright eyes.
> Sweet it was, and lovely too,
> And its mistress well it knew.
> Nectar from her lips it sipt,
> Here it hopt, and there it skipt:

*Trans. Mary Barnard, 1962.

Oft it wanton'd in the air,
Chirping only to the fair:
Oft it lull'd its head to rest
On the pillow of her breast.
Now, alas! it chirps no more:
All its blandishments are o'er:
Death has summon'd it to go
Pensive to the shades below;
Dismal regions! from whose bourn
No pale travelers return . . .*

"This is also a lyric.

"We've already discussed Homer, read a bit of the *Iliad*. We know about Odysseus. We learned what an epic poem is. Scholars claim that the epic preceded the lyric. The first poem I recited to you was written in the seventh century BC and mentions Helen. Did anyone guess that this was the same Helen who, according to legend, was the cause of the Trojan War? The speaker in that poem compares the beloved to her. Even today we come across this 'beautiful Helen,' wife of King Menelaus, who was abducted by Paris. In this way she migrated from the epic to the lyric—an image of a beauty who captivates mens' hearts.

"In the depths of antiquity, when human culture was just beginning to emerge, the word was much more intimately connected to music. Verses were recited aloud, to the accompaniment of a musical instrument called the lyre. This is the origin of the term 'lyric.' Two and a half thousand years later, a great deal has changed: it is rare for poetry to be accompanied by music, although new genres have appeared in which music and words are intrinsic to each other. Any examples?"

The bell rang, but none of them stirred, as though transfixed by his words. Why didn't they slam the lids of their desks shut, tear out of their seats, and hurl themselves toward the door with leaps and wild yelps, blocking up the exit with their jostling bodies—move it! Come on, hurry up! Into the hallway, down to the coatroom, out onto the street!

*"The Sparrow. From Catullus" by Francis Fawkes (1761).

Why did they listen to him? Why did he feel it was so urgent to stuff their heads with things they didn't need to know? And he was moved by a sense of very subtle power—they were learning to think and feel. What an oasis amid the general dull and meaningless chaos!

Three days later, Stalin's death was announced, and Victor Yulievich felt a small sense of satisfaction—he had predicted it before anyone else. Moreover, he belonged to the absolute minority of people who did not intend to mourn the loss. When he was growing up, his parents had sent him to Georgia for the summers. The last time they had all been to Tbilisi as a family was shortly before his father's death, in 1933.

He knew from his father how much his Georgian relatives all despised and feared Dzhugashvili.

The tyrant was no more. The titan was no more. A loathsome creature that had crawled out of the underworld, ancient and tenacious, with a hundred arms and a hundred heads. And a mustache.

Classes were canceled, and the kids were rounded up for an assembly. Victor Yulievich led his sixth-graders, lined up in pairs, to the auditorium on the fourth floor. Mikha hovered around him, then thrust a piece of paper covered with large lilac handwriting into his hand. It was a poem.

A black frame at the top enclosed the words "Stalin's Death."

> Weep, people, living here and yon,
> Weep, doctors, typists, workers galore.
> Our Stalin is dead, and never will one
> Such as he return. Nay, nevermore.

Well, hello there, Catullus, Victor thought, stifling his amusement. Then he said quietly, "Well, 'doctors' makes sense. But why 'typists'?"

"My aunt Genya was a typist. All right, let it be 'typers' then," Mikha said on the fly. "Maybe I could recite it?"

Nothing good could come of this ready enthusiasm.

"No, Mikha, I wouldn't advise it. In fact, I categorically advise against it."

Mikha wanted to take back the paper, but the teacher folded it deftly in half, pressing it to his chest.

"May I keep it as a memento?"

"Sure!" Mikha said, beaming.

The auditorium was full. Beethoven was playing on the radio. Damp-eyed teachers arranged themselves around a plaster bust. The scarlet velvet of the school banner draped its folds onto the floor. Victor Yulievich stood at the back with a grim look on his face. Borya Rakhmanov, an eighth-grader, was pinned up against a windowsill by the crowd of students. The windowsill was digging painfully into his right side, but there was no room to wriggle free from the torment. This was a light dress rehearsal for what would happen to him only three days later.

After the solemn assembly, with copious sobbing—the teachers provided the example of sincere grief, and the children emulated them, struggling to reach the tragic note—they dispersed and returned to their classrooms. The principal tried to call the school board to find out whether school should be canceled, and for how many days, but the line was always busy. Only at one o'clock was it announced that students should be dismissed and sent home for public mourning. Later they would announce when school was to resume.

When he was sending his students home, Victor Yulievich asked the children to remain there, at home, and to stay off the streets. The best thing of all would be for them to read some good books!

Sanya Steklov was glad to follow his teacher's advice. He was, it seemed, the only one who had the collected works of Tolstoy on his bookshelf at home, and during the four days of official mourning Sanya devoured all four volumes of *War and Peace* (though, it's true, he did skip some of the passages). After he had read the first volume, he gave it to Mikha, but Mikha didn't so much as open it; he had other problems. Aunt Genya had collapsed from a minor heart attack; Minna was having stomach trouble, which happened whenever the going got rough; and Mikha was run ragged, catering to his woeful aunt's every whim for three whole days (although her mad grief was somewhat overblown).

Ilya didn't give a hoot about his teacher's advice or his mother's pleas. The alarming significance of the event lured him down into the streets. Early in the morning on March 7 he grabbed his camera and left home with the confidence of a hunter anticipating a run of luck.

For three days Victor Yulievich never left the house, and forbade his mother to go outside as well. The bread had run out, but he said, "Bread? What are you talking about? We don't even have any vodka."

Indeed, on the evening of the fifth he had drunk the bottle his mother kept on hand for special occasions. He had decided that until the moment the Leader was taken away and safely buried, he would stay right where he was.

Dressed in his striped pajamas, he lay down on the divan behind the tapestry curtain with a pile of books beside him. The ultimate happiness.

At ten o'clock on March 9, the body was ceremoniously removed from the Hall of Columns, where it had been lying in state. It was carried out by squat people in heavy overcoats with astrakhan collars.

That was when Victor finally left the house—to get bread and vodka. The streets were almost deserted. Trucks were still lined up. The scene that greeted him was reminiscent of the aftermath of St. Petersburg's infamous flood: crushed shoes and hats, briefcases forever parted from their owners, broken lampposts, smashed-in first-floor windows. By the archway to a building, there was a wall covered in blood. A trampled dog lay in front of it. Victor recalled Pushkin:

> Yevgeny—evil is his lot!—
> Runs to the old familiar spot
> Down the old street—and knows it not.
> All, to his horror, is demolished,
> Leveled or ruined or abolished.*

*Trans. Waclaw Lednicki, 1955.

He recited *The Bronze Horseman* to himself from start to finish:

> Upon the threshold, they had found
> My crazy hero. In the ground
> His poor cold body there they hurried,
> And left it to God's mercy, buried.

Just there, on a lane a good distance from his home, Victor found a little shop that was open. The stairs led down into what was nearly a cellar. Several women were talking with the proprietor in hushed voices, but fell silent when Victor entered.

It's as though they've been talking about me, Victor Yulievich said to himself, amused.

One of the women recognized him as the teacher, and peppered him with questions.

"Victor Yurievich, what happened? People are saying that the Jews were behind the stampede, that they organized it. Is this true? Maybe you've heard something yourself? Do you know anything about it?"

She was the mother of a tenth-grader, but he couldn't remember which one. Unsophisticated women often called him by the more common name Yurievich, rather than Yulievich, and this usually annoyed him. But now he was overcome with a strange feeling of humility, uncharacteristic of him.

"No, sweetheart, I haven't heard anything like that. We'll down a glass or two this evening for the repose of the soul and then get on with our lives. Why single out the Jews? They're people just like us. Two bottles of vodka, please, a loaf of white bread, and half a loaf of dark. Oh, and two packages of dumplings."

He took his groceries, paid, and went out, leaving the women behind in a state of confusion: maybe it wasn't the Jews after all, but someone else. It could have been anyone, they were surrounded by enemies. Everyone envies us, everyone is afraid of us. And their conversation shifted to another key, prouder and bolder.

———————

Victor and his mother sat at the round table dotted with burn marks, a carafe between them. Ksenia Nikolayevna brought in the dumplings, overcooked as usual. She placed the pot on an iron trivet. Victor poured them each a glass. Suddenly, the doorbell rang in the hallway. Three rings—that meant they were calling on the Shengelis, not the neighbors.

Victor went out to open the door and beheld a strange vision standing in the doorway. Wrapped up in a black lace shawl draped over a fur hat, wearing a man's coat with a raccoon-fur collar reeking of mothballs and cats, odors harking back to a distant past, was Nino, his dead father's cousin. She was an aquiline-nosed beauty, a singer, embroiderer, and nun *manquée*, who radiated warmth and laughter.

"Is it really you?"

The last time he had seen her was twenty years earlier. As a child he had stayed in her Tbilisi home, but an aura of doubt clung to this memory: Did that house really exist, or had he just dreamed it? But here she was, the same dear Nino, darling Niniko. She had hardly aged at all.

"Vika, my boy, you haven't changed a bit! I'd have recognized you anywhere."

"My goodness, Nino, how are you? How did you get here?"

"Well, invite me in, don't leave me standing here on the threshold!"

They exchanged kisses, stroked each other's hair, pushed away from each other to get a better look, and then kissed again.

Ksenia Nikolayevna stood at the door to their room wondering indignantly—who could Vika be kissing out there? Good Lord, it's Nino! The Georgian cousin, her dearly departed's favorite! It was like she had just stepped out of the distant past. How is it possible? Come in! Sit down, sit down! But wash your hands first!

"By all means! Coming back from the graveyard, the first thing you do is wash your hands," she said. Her Georgian accent was thicker than it had been before. Her voice was rich with celebratory laughter.

She washed her hands, used the facilities, and washed them again. Ksenia Nikolayevna had already set the table for three. All their plates were old, chipped and cracked all over.

Victor poured out the vodka.

"First, let's drink to our liberation! It's like the forty years in the desert. He's croaked, but we've survived!" she said, flouting the protocol at table that was strictly observed in Georgia. A woman—especially a guest—never spoke first!

They drank. Nino broke off a small piece of a single dumpling with her fork, and popped it daintily into her slightly opened mouth. Victor recalled how she had taught him to eat, to drink, to sit down properly, and to greet people. He had clean forgotten all of it. Yet he still did everything just as she had instructed him to back then, without being aware of it.

"How did you manage to end up here, Ninochka?"

She leaned against the back of the chair, clasped her hands behind her head, and broke into merry, youthful laughter. Then she stopped smiling abruptly, removed the black lace shawl from her shoulders, wrapped it around her head, and stood up. She raised her exquisite, ageless hands above her head and let out a long, ascending wail. When the sound reached its apex, it came crashing down, nearly wordless, because it was mourning the dead. It was an ancient keening beyond the need for words, a howl of despair filled with great pain, and longing, and solemnity.

Nino completed this ancient, wordless utterance and broke into wild laughter again.

She's inebriated, poor thing, Ksenia Nikolayevna thought.

When her laughing fit was over, Nino told a story that for years afterward would be a favorite among close friends and family.

On March 5, before they had formally announced the death of Stalin, two NKVD officers came to fetch her and take her away. They wanted to take her sister Manana, too, but she had gone to Kutaisi the week before and hadn't yet returned.

"Mama starts to gather my things, she's crying, and she whispers under her breath, 'He just won't leave us alone, the devil!'

"But the officer, watching Mama pack, understood her, and said, 'Your daughter will be back home in three days, five at the most. I give you my word.'

"You remember Mama, don't you, Vika? Ksenia remembers, of course! She's ninety years old. Even when she was young she was absolutely fearless; and what is there for her to be afraid of now?

"'Well, maybe your word is goldeh. But your hands are like iron!' she says.

"'There's no need to insult us, Lamara Noevna,' one of the creeps says to her. 'This is a great honor for your daughter.'

"They took me to the local Party headquarters. What an honor, indeed! The lights are always on there, people rushing to and fro like it's Rustaveli Avenue on a holiday. They take me into a large hall. The hall is full of women—every shape and size. There are village women—but also Veriko, and Tamara, and the Mehabde sisters, singers.

"Two men come out—the first one says something like: the world has lost a great leader, the people are inconsolable, grief abounds. And I'm thinking, *This is what they brought me here to tell me?* Then the second one says, we've brought you here because according to ancient Georgian custom women lament the deceased. Only women can do this. We've brought you here to carry out a proper lamentation.

"My goodness, right then and there I wanted to sing, 'Halleluja! *God shall arise, and his enemies be scattered!'*

"'We know all about you,' this dirty little spy says. 'We know you have sung at funerals and know the Georgian laments. We've gotten word from Moscow that they want you to keen for the Great Leader.'

"I don't know the first thing about it, of course. I've sung at many funerals, but Christians don't sing these pagan laments. It's just wailing, not true song. Well, never mind, I think, I'll go anyway! How could I deny myself the pleasure?

"It's impossible to say how many of us there were altogether. Enough to fill an airplane, at any rate. Some of the others were weeping, some were proud, but all of us were shaking with fear. I admit, I'd never been on a plane before, and I'd never agree to do it except in that kind of situation.

"We landed in Moscow at night, and they took us in buses to some sort of hotel outside the city. They didn't let us sleep our fill; some Georgian comes to fetch us. A musician, he tells us. He'd be directing us. His face looked familiar, I felt like I'd seen him somewhere before.

I stare and stare, and he calls me over and whispers: 'I'm Mikeladze's brother.' Oh, that Satan, how many died at his hands!

"So we wail and lament all day, wail and lament all night, wail and lament all the next day. I'm already sick of it. And we're only just rehearsing!

"On the evening of the eighth, they announce that plans had changed, there would be no keening. Why they wanted it in the first place, then stopped wanting it, God only knows! Then they loaded everyone into the buses and took us to some godforsaken place. And I lie in bed, screaming to beat the band, 'Oh, lord! The pain is unbearable! I'm having some kind of attack, oh, the pain!' I'm thinking there's no way I'm going back home until I see the two of you. Some bigwig tells me, 'You'll have to buy your own ticket, then.' 'Owwww!' I cry. 'The pain is too much for me to bear! I'll buy my own ticket.'

"Pour me another glass, Vika. This is the first time in my life I've drunk vodka, the first time in my life I've ever lied, and the first time in my life we've buried a great villain."

"Not so loud, Nino," Ksenia Nikolayevna said, touching her shoulder.

Nino nodded and placed her lovely hands over her lips. Victor took her right hand in his left one and kissed it. Something in life was changing. For the better.

CHILDREN OF THE UNDERWORLD

Ilya dashed through the city, trying all the while to figure out where this extraordinary demonstration was headed. He had established that it had many tails, and one of them began—or ended—at Belorussky Station, while another started at the point where three boulevards meet: Petrovsky, Rozhdestvensky, and Tsvetnoy. He pushed his way there, then realized he didn't have enough film, and, when it was already completely dark, he groped his way home. In one spot, next to the Central Post Office, he had to crawl over a fence. No one, not even the police in that precinct, knew the terrain like the local boys. For years they had played Cops and Robbers here, and they knew all the shortcuts, the back alleys, even the sewage drains and manholes, by heart. There were back stairs in many buildings. If you went in through the main entrance of the building, you could ring the bell at the apartment of one of your classmates, slip in and make a dash down a long corridor, and end up at a door that led to the back stairway, down through another courtyard altogether, and finally into another street.

On the morning of March 7, he loaded his camera, and as soon as his mother had left for work, he hit the streets. That morning, the crowd of people was even denser than it had been the night before.

Now Maroseyka Street, where it runs into the square, was blocked not only with trolleybuses, but also with a second line of trucks. It was possible to reach the Hall of Columns only from the direction of Pushkin Square—but you could get there only through Pushkin Street, not Gorky Street. Later they let the crowd onto Neglinnaya Street.

All three of the neighboring boulevards were jammed with people, but at midday the crowd seemed to thin out. The mass of bodies that had been pressed from all sides started to move, and then to run. Some side streets and lanes were opened up and people streamed into them. No one ever found out who laid these traps and ambushes, who contrived these dead ends that people were herded into like cattle; but they eventually squeezed into the back alleys and passageways, through connecting courtyards. They poured in and poured in like water gushing from a burst main.

Imposing Studebaker trucks blocked the streets, and there were countless soldiers and police. Ilya, pressing his camera to his stomach, slipped in and out among the cars. He crawled under one of them, and when he emerged on the other side, he ran right into Borya Rakhmanov, an eighth-grader. Borya was determined to maneuver through the pandemonium to get to the Hall of Columns. For Ilya, it was the pandemonium itself that was most interesting.

This was not unlike the annual May Day and November 7 celebrations, with their serried ranks of vehicles and uniforms, cordons, and barricades. Boys who lived in the center of the city had long been familiar with this kind of holiday turmoil and never missed a chance to mingle in the throng. But this time something truly monumental was unfolding. Ilya wanted terribly to clamber up above the level of the crowd, so he could get a shot looking down on it. He tried to get Borya to come with him to a roof he knew of, but Borya didn't want to.

Idiot, Ilya thought. *I'll get to the Hall of Columns faster by rooftop than he will on foot.*

He decided to go by way of Krapivensky Lane. Just then the crowd staggered, then surged, carrying him off toward Neglinnaya, while Borya was swept off in another direction.

Ilya caught one last glimpse of him—his face gone red, his mouth agape. He was shouting something, but Ilya couldn't make out what it

was above the din. The air was filled with a strange, haunting roar—
a composite of howls and screams, and something resembling song.
For the first time in two days, Ilya was suddenly beside himself with
alarm.

He had to make it to an archway that he knew led into a courtyard
with a toolshed. From that roof he could easily climb up to the roof of
the building next to it, a four-story structure. Ilya lurched off in the
direction of the archway, but realized that people were trying to stay
away from the buildings, keeping well within the throng so as not to
be crushed against the trolleybuses lined up bumper to bumper along
the edge of the street. People were thrashing and struggling on the
road right next to the trolleybuses. Some people, crushed and lifeless,
were slumped against the sides of the buses; others trampled them
underfoot. In order to made it to the sidewalk, Ilya had to squeeze
between these bodies—could they really be dead? No, it can't be true.
But there was no other way. He realized he would have to duck for
cover immediately under the big belly of the trolleybus or get smashed
against the side of it. All the while he looked after "Fedya," his trusty
camera—he didn't want the lens to get smashed. He stamped out a
tiny space for himself next to the wheels, then dove underneath. There,
under the bowels of the trolleybus, it was pitch-dark and stuffy, crammed
with bodies, arms and legs entangled, wearing heavy overcoats. He
crawled over them, struggling through the dank stench. Someone
moaned. He emerged on the other side, landing right in the arms of a
fat soldier with a trembling, moist face. A little boy of about five, pale
and immobile, dangled in his arms.

"Where do you think you're going?"

"This is where I live."

"Scram. Go home, and stay there."

The soldier shoved him toward the archway, and Ilya darted into
the courtyard. The toolshed was still there, where it belonged, a
wooden garbage-can shed flush with its outside wall. Ilya climbed up
on the shed, then onto the roof of the toolshed. He knew that above
it there were some convenient ledges and niches—he remembered
them from the last time he had played Cops and Robbers—that made
it easy to clamber up to the roof of the "spotted house," made of alter-

nating red and white bricks, provided that the third-floor window was still smashed and he could wriggle through.

The winds of fortune were still at his back. He had escaped the deadly throng unharmed, and now there was another stroke of luck— the window had still not been fixed.

There was one terrifying moment when he tried to pull himself up by the window frame, and it wobbled unsteadily, as if it might fall off. But he didn't plunge to his death: He made it onto the broad windowsill and scrambled inside. But another surprise lay in wait for him. The attic was locked, with a new big padlock dangling from hasps so sturdy he would never be able to break them off without special tools.

But the building was an odd design, and the windows in the main stairwell faced in two directions: on the third floor they looked onto the courtyard, and on the second and fourth, onto the street. Ilya went down to the fourth floor and peered out at the street. It looked like a black river. The heads on the surface of this river looked like curly clumps of fur, and they undulated and stirred like the pelt of some dreadful beast. Ilya got out his camera. He realized that he wouldn't be able to get a good shot from this distance, so he decided to take it from the second floor. On the second floor he was able to open the window. From below he heard a sound that was not so much screaming as a rhythmic howling, punctuated with piercing shrieks and cries. From this vantage point the crowd no longer resembled a living pelt. The heads were like dark stones pressed tightly together. They oscillated in place, moving to and fro, locked in rhythm, but unable to gain any momentum and break free. It was a road of living cobblestones dancing in place.

Ilya took a few photographs, then decided that it would be more effective after all if he took them from the fourth floor. He had already gotten over his recent scare.

Suddenly, a drunken woman in a red housecoat poked her head out of an apartment and barked, "What's going on? You got nothin' better to do?"

She reinforced her indignation with a string of curses. Ilya was at a loss for words.

He was clever, so he didn't bother to answer her back, but gestured to his mouth and waved his hands around his ears, as though he were a deaf-mute. The woman spat in disgust and turned away.

On the fourth floor, Ilya used up almost all his film, and started thinking about trying to head home. It was clear to him that his usual route up Rozhdestvensky Boulevard from Trubnaya Square, then crossing Sretenka and coming out on Chistoprudny, was impossible. But he thought that if he were able to push through the crowd on the square and make it to the other side, it might be easier. He had no way of knowing that the crowd was streaming down Rozhdestvensky to Trubnaya Square, where it collided head-on with the living human current emerging from Petrovsky Boulevard, forming a giant, deadly whirlpool.

He had no intention of holing up in this building forever, though, and his mother was already no doubt frantic with worry. He sat there on the windowsill a little while longer, wondering whether he should use up the last of his film now, since the light was fading, or save a few shots for later. Then he got sick of sitting and decided to get out of there, no matter what.

It was even harder to get out of the courtyard than it had been to get in. But he made all the right moves: he rang the doorbell of an apartment on the first floor and asked the resident, an old man, to let him exit through the other door, and thus reach the street. The old man shook his head, and struggled to explain, through inarticulate moans and gestures, that the front entrance was locked, but that he could go out through the boiler room.

This old guy isn't just pretending to be a deaf-mute. Ilya laughed to himself, always amused by coincidences of this kind. The courtyard was completely deserted, but through the walls he could hear the dull but mighty roar of the compressed horde. Ilya saw the boiler room, but discovered it was locked. He went around it to the other side and climbed onto the roof, then scrambled up to the top of the outside wall and leapt down onto a stretch of cordoned-off sidewalk. Now he had to slip through the military cordon to blend into the crowd. He ran a ways to get nearer to the intersection, and slid between two soldiers onto the pavement packed with people. He understood immediately that he had made a mistake; he should never have left the building where he had taken cover. He was dragged off by an unremitting force, like the undertow in a great ocean. The traffic light was blinking up ahead.

Now Ilya became truly paralyzed with fear: he was afraid not for his Fedya, which might be smashed to smithereens against the pole of the stoplight, but for what might happen to his own head. He wasn't even able to move his hands, which were trying to shield the camera from blows. The camera was pressing hard into his stomach. He felt no pain, but rather a terrible despair. He was carried along toward the traffic light, and just to the left of it. A man with a crushed face was pressed up against the pole. He was dead, but there was no room for him to fall down.

Suddenly, the ground under Ilya's feet shuddered and opened up. He plummeted into a sewer—the manhole cover had given way under the trampling feet of the crowd. Ilya made a soft landing on top of a roll of oakum left behind by a water department crew. To his left was a grate, one side of which was slightly ajar. Ilya pulled, and it opened completely. He stuffed himself into this little burrow, and for some reason closed the grate behind him. This instinctive motion saved his life. People kept falling into the sewer after him for several minutes, until it was crammed to the top with bodies; as the one on the very bottom of the pile, he would certainly have suffocated. The bodies of the others were compressed so tightly and compactly that the thousands of people trampling over them had no idea they were walking on human flesh. Inside his burrow, he heard their screams.

Meanwhile, aboveground, a monstrous, invisible wave suddenly swept everyone off, hurling them against walls and barriers, into the sides of trucks, and against the chain of trolleybuses. The guards had opened a passage leading into the depths of a closed-off area, and people assumed that they were finally about to escape to safety, somewhere beyond the bone-crushing pressure. Ilya saw none of this. In fact, he saw nothing at all. It was pitch-dark.

Ilya lay in his dark burrow for what seemed a long time, then began groping the walls. He discovered a large pipe leading slightly downward. He started to crawl along it. He crawled and crawled, and then the pipe made a slight turn and started leading upward. He had wrapped his camera in his woolen cap and stuffed it under his belt. After some time, he paused and slept a little while, and when the bitter cold forced him awake, he couldn't remember right away how he had come to be in this dank hole. He lifted up his head and saw a large, rectangular grate about six feet above him. It wasn't that there was light on the other side—just that the darkness there was not as thick. He was terribly thirsty. The stench was foul, but not from sewage; it smelled of rusty iron and rats. He didn't see any rats, though—they must have been running in a dense mass toward the Hall of Columns, too.

He had to get out of there. Thin, ladder-like iron brackets jutted out from the vaulted walls leading up to the grate above his head, and he began to climb. He made it to the top with ease, but the grate turned out to be welded shut. He couldn't possibly force it open to get through. He descended again, curled into a little ball, and fell asleep. When he woke up, the light from above seemed stronger. He moved farther along the pipe—it grew wider.

He came to another grate, about fifty yards from the first. He felt around for the brackets and began to clamber up them. The grate wasn't welded shut this time; it was secured fairly loosely, but there was a lock on the outside. Ilya kept going. The grates appeared at regular intervals, fifty yards or so apart. He passed eight of them, investigated each one, and found that almost all of them were welded shut, except for two, with locks on the outside. Soon he lost count. He dropped off to sleep several more times from exhaustion, woke up, then kept going.

Three or four grates in a row were directly under the feet of the surging crowds. He couldn't see them, since there was no light, but he heard the dreadful roar, and understood that he shouldn't even try to exit there. Once he came upon a broken grate—half a dead body dangled through the gaping hole.

He had no idea what direction he was headed in, but he understood clearly that the pipes were his only way out, and that he had to keep moving along them, though he didn't know where they would lead.

He lost track of time. Suddenly, he saw a grate, beyond which shone a bright yellow light. He climbed the brackets, touched the grate, and it opened. He crawled out and discovered that he was standing under the streetlamp in the courtyard of the building where Sanya Steklov lived. He had just enough strength left to make it to Sanya's door and ring the bell.

Anna Alexandrovna opened it.

Ilya collapsed. His hands were clasping his stomach, where Fedya was still safely tucked away under his belt.

It was eleven in the evening on March 7. Anna Alexandrovna did what she could for Ilya: she undressed him, carried him to the bath with the help of a neighbor, and waited for him to open his eyes. Then she washed him off with a big shaggy sponge, carefully avoiding his wounds. His whole body was black and blue; his stomach was one big bruise. She was surprised that this skinny boy, with a completely boyish face, was already so well equipped for manhood. He got out of the bath by himself, made it to the divan, and collapsed again. They put a woman's nightgown on him, covered him with a blanket, gave him sweet strong tea. Then, stuffing a big pillow behind his back, they propped him up to feed him some soup. He fell asleep.

The Steklovs sat at the table in silence.

"Nuta, I think a lot of people must have died today," Sanya said to his grandmother, his voice a whisper.

"Most likely."

Then Sanya sat down next to the sleeping Ilya, hoping he would wake up and tell him everything that had happened. His feelings for his friend were strong and complex: he was proud of him, and a bit envious that he himself wasn't like Ilya, but he didn't really want to be, either. He also understood that Ilya was a man—and it was not only the dark fuzz on his upper lip that attested to this, but the dark path of hair under his belly leading down to his large male member, which was not made just for peeing. He had never seen a naked man before today: he had never been taken to the public baths.

He had never seen a naked woman, either. Why would two proper, well-educated ladies, his mother and grandmother, take a notion to start undressing in front of him? But Sanya could guess what women were about—the breasts under the dress, the dark nest below the stomach. This naked man, his friend and classmate Ilya, surprised him much more—with a pang, Sanya sensed that he was not, and never would be, like his friend. Portraits of naked women—Sanya had seen many of them in museums and in art books—for some reason did not awaken such confusion and excitement in him as the nakedness of a man. He felt he might faint from the crudeness and power of it.

He had almost finished reading *War and Peace*, and the female shades didn't move him in the least—Natasha, with her silly enthusiasms, Princess Liza with her short upper lip, Princess Marya, whose unattractiveness was stressed throughout; but the men . . . They were magnificent—their strength, generosity, their wit and intelligence, their nobility and sense of honor. Now, looking into Ilya's face, he tried to figure out which of these magnificent men his friend resembled. No, certainly not the dry, aristocratic Bolkonsky; nor the fat, intelligent Bezukhov. And not the wonderful Petya Rostov, beloved by all. Not Nikolay, either, of course . . . Most likely it was Dolokhov.

Maria Fedorovna, Ilya's mother, had been sitting on a chair by the door to the apartment for two days running. They didn't have a telephone yet, and Anna Alexandrovna couldn't inform her that her son was alive. It was terrifying, and too dangerous, to venture out onto the streets. And, in any case, crossing the streetcar tracks at the intersection of Chistoprudny Boulevard and Maroseyka was impossible because of the military and police cordons blocking the path.

A pall of fear hung over the city—an ancient terror, familiar from Greek tragedy and myth, enveloped it, drowning it in its black waters, the kind of terror that visits one only in dreams, in childhood nightmares, a terror that rises up from the bottom of the soul. It was as though some underground deposit had ruptured, and was now threatening all human life.

Borya Rakhmanov's parents were also sitting, paralyzed with fear. It was impossible to reach the police, the hospital, or the morgue. All the lines were busy.

They would find Borya only four days later, among the bodies lying in the snow next to the overflowing Lefortovo Morgue. They would identify him by the laundry mark on the shirt—Galina Borisovna Rakhmanova never washed white shirts herself, preferring to take them to the cleaners. There was one other number on the hand of her dead son, written in violet ink: 1421.

These people, the victims of the stampede, were buried quietly, in secret. No one counted them a second time, and only the number on Borya's hand witnessed to the fact that there had been no fewer than fourteen hundred of them.

No wreath from Borya's school was laid on his grave. There were no flowers to be had in those days, anyway—all of them had been lavished on the Great Leader. During those terrible days, one other person died, a private death at home—the composer Sergei Prokofiev. This went completely unnoticed.

Of all Ilya's photographs, only two came out. As he had suspected, the light was insufficient. But apart from the official images of the coffin in the Hall of Columns, which appeared in all the papers, no other photographs of that event existed.

THE LORLs

On Wednesdays, Victor Yulievich would make the rounds of Moscow with the LORLs (as they called themselves) in tow. Like some latter-day Pied Piper blowing on his flute, he would lead them out of their poor, sick time into a world where thought labored and lived, a world of freedom, and music, and the other arts. This is where it had all happened, right here, behind these very windows!

Their peregrinations through literary Moscow had a wonderfully chaotic character. On what was once called Gendrikov Lane, they looked into the courtyard of a building where Mayakovsky was rumored (mistakenly) to have shot himself. From there they walked down Dzerzhinsky Street, formerly Lubyanka, to the Sretensky Gates. This renaming of Moscow streets disturbed Victor Yulievich, and he always called them by their original names when he was with his students.

They walked down the boulevards to Pushkin Square, where their teacher showed them the house of Famusov, and they stopped at all the addresses associated with Alexander Sergeevich Pushkin: the houses of Vyazemsky and Nashchokin, and the house where Yogel's dancing classes were held. This was where Pushkin had first seen the young Natalia, who would later become his wife.

"Tverskoy is the oldest of the boulevards. At one time it was just called the Boulevard. There was only one. They call it the Boulevard Ring, but there is no ring, and never was. It's a semicircle. It runs down to the river. All the boulevards are built on the place where the stone walls of Bely Gorod, the White City, once stood."

From Pushkin Square they would pick out some unfamiliar route to explore. They walked through Bogoslovsky Lane to Trekhprudny, to the house where the poet Marina Tsvetaeva had lived. Or they would take Tverskoy and Nikitsky Boulevards to the Arbat, and cross Malaya Molchanovka near the little house where Lermontov had lived. Passing through Sobachya Square they found themselves in front of Scriabin's last apartment. This was where he played, and people still alive today attended his private recitals at home. The students asked questions, and the names stuck in their memories. They ambled through the city without any preconceived plan, and it was impossible to imagine anything better than these aimless pilgrimages of discovery.

Victor Yulievich spent long hours in the library preparing for these outings, digging through old books and scouting for rare tidbits of information. In the History Library, he discovered rich deposits of handwritten memoirs, photographs, and letters. Some of the materials, judging by the library's records, had never before been examined. He came across a great deal of valuable and intriguing information. He was surprised to learn that many, if not all, of the notable people of the nineteenth century, while living very disparate lives, were related by blood. Certain far-flung clans were intimately intertwined by birth, like a tree with myriad branches. Letters from before the Revolution constantly witnessed to this remarkable web of kinship, and all these connections, as well as family disputes and quarrels and *mésalliances*, were transformed in Tolstoy's novels into something larger, greater, than just a family chronicle. *It's like the Russian Bible*, thought Victor Yulievich.

Like Gulliver in the land of the Lilliputians, Victor Yulievich was tied by every strand of hair to the ground of Russian culture, and these ties extended to the boys, who were acquiring the taste, growing accustomed to this dusty, papery, ephemeral nourishment.

With the group of boys he would walk down Gorky Street, past Eliseevsky's, the finest grocery store in the capital, telling his LORLs about Zinaida Alexandrovna Volkonskaya, who had owned this palatial house before its reconstruction.

"She held a literary salon, famous all over Moscow, and all of Moscow's high society would gather here. Writers, artists, musicians, and professors would all attend, among them Pushkin. Not long ago I came upon an interesting document in the library—a report from Colonel Bibikov dated 1826, in which it was spelled out in black and white: 'I keep a close eye on the writer Pushkin, insofar as possible. The homes he visits most frequently are the homes of Princess Zinaida Volkonskaya, Prince Vyazemsky, former minister Dmitriev, and Prosecutor Zhikharev. Conversations there revolve primarily around literature.' You understand what this means, don't you?"

Ilya was the first to respond. "What's there to understand? They were spying on him."

"Precisely. Because all through the ages there have been people who want to 'revolve primarily around literature.' Like all of us here!" The teacher laughed. "And then there are the Colonel Bibikovs, who are charged with keeping a close eye on them. Yes, such are the times."

He hadn't said anything in particular, but hovered just on the brink of it. He had understood long ago that the past was no better than the present. That was as plain as day. One had to try to escape, to wrestle free from every era, so as not to be devoured by it.

"Literature is the only thing that allows us to survive, the only thing that helps us to reconcile ourselves to the time we live in," Victor Yulievich told his charges.

Everyone agreed eagerly. Only Sanya had his doubts—what about music?

From listening closely to Mozart and Chopin, he had grasped that there was another dimension quite distinct from literature, a dimension into which his grandmother, then Liza and his music teacher, Evgenia Danilovna, had initiated him. This was the place he had escaped to every day after school, when his hand was still whole and intact. But even now, with his mangled fingers, he had not parted ways with music—he listened to it constantly, picked out melodies on occa-

sion. How could he play, without the use of two fingers? He wasn't
going to fool himself.

For Mikha, these literary journeys were also a form of escape—
from his dreary aunt Genya, with her trivial concerns—and a flight
into a rarified atmosphere inhabited by noble men and beautiful women.

Ilya didn't miss a single one of these walks through the city, either.
He had set his own task—to document all the events and compile reports accompanied by photographs. Some of these reports were stored
at Victor Yulievich's home, and the others in Ilya's closet.

More than a decade would pass before the degenerate heir of Colonel
Bibikov, Colonel Chibikov (the immortal Gogol grins each time such
echoes in nomenclature spring up), would get his hands on the childhood archive, and fifty more years would pass until an Institute for
Central and East European Studies, in a small German town with a
fairytale name, would register this archive under a seven-digit number with a forward slash, and the archive would pass into the hands of
another one of the LORLs, also a student of Victor Yulievich's, but a
year younger, for safekeeping.

Getting to know these Moscow boys after his experience at the
village school, Victor Yulievich again returned to his musings about
childhood. He lacked knowledge of the subject, so he began reading
scholarly works on the matter.

He managed to get access to semiforbidden books on child psychology, from Freud, whose books stood gathering dust on the bookshelves of the major libraries, to Vygotsky, whose books had been
withdrawn from circulation and placed in restricted-access collections. Victor found almost all Vygotsky's published works in the home
of one of his friends, whose grandmother had been fired when the subject of "pedology" had come under fire from above. She had learned to
knit sweaters to get by, but she guarded all of Vygotsky's books like
rare treasures, only allowing a select few to read them—and that
without "borrowing rights." Victor Yulievich came on Sunday morning and sat until evening, with a few leisurely breaks for traditional
Moscow-style tea-drinking.

Everything he read was very intriguing, but put too great an emphasis on "scholarliness." Matters that were self-evident, like the well-known fact that adolescent boys stop respecting their parents, become irritable and argumentative, experience heightened sexual curiosity, and that all of this is the result of the hormonal storm assaulting the body, were presented as discoveries. The author's explanations and interpretations sometimes seemed to Victor Yulievich to be purely speculative and unfounded.

He didn't find what he was seeking. He had come across a very important notion in his reading of Tolstoy, who called this tormented period "the wilderness of adolescence." Tolstoy came closest of all to describing what he saw in his agitated, disheveled students. There came a moment when they seemed to lose everything that had accumulated in them until that time, and life seemed to start anew. But not all of them were able to find a way out of the wilderness; a significant number of them remained lost in it forever.

Victor Yulievich's sole interlocutor on this subject was Mishka Kolesnik, his neighborhood friend from childhood. Mishka was a war invalid, a biologist and an intrepid homespun philosopher. He listened attentively, but couldn't abide long-winded deliberation. He interrupted Victor Yulievich, grumbling, "Yes, go on, go on. I get the point." He tried to hasten his friend's train of thought, interjecting strange, at first incomprehensible observations and comments—which were in fact the articulation of a biological perspective.

Victor Yulievich gradually grew accustomed to his interlocutor's unusual thought processes, and was gripped by the idea of the universalism of knowledge toward which the lame Kolesnik was pushing him. He was the one who introduced Victor, an inveterate man of letters, to the principles of evolution, the one who enlightened him on the conflict between the theories of Lamarck and Darwin, and even elaborated on such technical particulars as metamorphosis, neoteny, and chromosomal heredity.

Now, when he reflected on his growing boys, he observed how close their maturation processes were to the metamorphosis that insects undergo.

Small babies with unformed minds, human larvae, devour whatever food comes their way—they suck, munch, and swallow ideas and impressions at random, and then pupate; and within their cocoons everything falls into place in the required order—reflexes are developed and refined, skills are learned, initial impressions of the world are mastered. But how many cocoons perish without reaching the final phase of growth, never bursting the seams and releasing the butterfly within? Anima, anima, little soul . . . colorful and airborne, a short-lived marvel. And how many of them remain larvae until their very death, never realizing that their maturity has eluded them.

Vygotsky discussed the differences between the process of habit-formation and the unfolding of interests. But Victor Yulievich saw the picture otherwise—he observed in his pupils the unfolding of wings, and the meanings and designs imprinted on them. But why did some, like insects with a full cycle of development, undergo metamorphosis, while others did not?

Victor Yulievich sensed almost physically these moments when the horny covering of the chrysalis bursts apart. He heard the flutter and rustle of wings, and was filled with happiness, like a midwife attending a birth.

But for some reason this metamorphosis didn't occur in all of his pupils, or even most of them, but rather in the minority. What was the essence of this process? The awakening of a moral sensibility? Yes, of course. But why did it happen in some, and not in others? Is there some kind of mysterious module of transition: a ritual, or rite? Or perhaps *Homo sapiens*, rational man, also undergoes a phenomenon similar to neoteny, which is observed in worms, insects, and amphibians—when the ability to reproduce appears not in mature specimens, but already in the larval stages? And then the immature organism spawns analogous larvae, which will in their turn never mature.

"Naturally, this is only a metaphor. I understand that my adolescents are, physiologically, full-grown beings. Imagos, so to speak," he said for Kolesnik's benefit. But Kolesnik grasped the idea at once and needed no interpretations.

Kolesnik raised his thick, arched eyebrows, and drawing out his *R*s, spoke with feigned amazement.

"Well, Mr. *Littérateur*, you've certainly grown wiser during the last five-year plan. But can you provide a definition of the imago, the 'mature' person? What are the criteria for 'maturity'?"

Victor Yulievich thought about it. "Not simply the ability to reproduce. Responsibility for one's actions, perhaps? Independence? A degree of self-awareness?"

"Those are qualitative criteria, not quantitative," Kolesnik said, jabbing him with his finger. "Look what you end up with: initiation—some indeterminate thing—and responsibility—how do you measure it? So, according to you, the human larva becomes an imago as the result of some process of initiation?"

Victor Yulievich pressed on. "You admit, Mishka, that we live in a society of larvae—immature human beings, adolescents disguised as adults?"

"There is something to that. I'll think about it," Kolesnik said. "The question you pose is purely anthropological, and modern anthropology is in a period of stagnation, which is a problem. But, indeed, some element of neoteny can be observed."

Victor Yulievich combed through the pages of a stack of books. He was searching for the coming-of-age ritual he had in mind.

He found descriptions of all manner of rituals—those connected with sexual maturity, with a change in social status, with entering a select community of warriors, shamans, or wizards. He kept looking for something that touched upon the moment when the wildness and rudeness of youth underwent an instantaneous transformation into a cultured state, into mature adult existence. Of course, one could consider the graduation ceremony of European universities, when the newly educated youth are swathed in robes and silly hats, to be this kind of rite of passage. But weren't they the very people—doctors, psychologists, and engineers—who devised that most rational system of enslavement and extermination of human beings, the Third Reich? The volume of knowledge digested did not guarantee moral maturity. No, that wasn't the answer, either.

Although his reading failed to provide direct answers, it was fruitful nonetheless. He learned to discern the outlines of ancient rites and rituals distorted beyond recognition, watered down or taken to extremes, in the rules and customs of contemporary Soviet life. Even the induction of Pioneers into the fold, accompanied by oaths and a change of attire, was a parody of some sort of ancient initiation rite. True, these were not the new white robes of the ancient Christians, not the aprons of the Masonic order, but a simple red kerchief tied around the neck. Still, the connection was not far to seek.

When he had come to the bottom of his small mountain of books, he turned again to the Russian classics—the source of authority he trusted implicitly. He reread Tolstoy's *Childhood. Boyhood. Youth*, Herzen's *My Life and Thoughts*, and Aksakov's *The Childhood Years of Grandson Bagrov*. To these he added Kropotkin's *Notes of a Revolutionary* and Maxim Gorky's trilogy, which already fell outside the bounds of Russian literature's Golden Age, and describe the sense of injury in the childish psyche at the absolute injustice and cruelty of the world, and how this can awaken compassion and empathy.

He led his boys down the paths of little Nikolay Irteniev, Peter Kropotkin, Sasha Herzen, even Alesha Peshkov—through orphanhood, humiliation, cruelty, and loneliness, to their acceptance of things that he himself considered absolutely basic: the sense of good and evil, and the understanding that love is the supreme value.

His boys responded to his call, and learned to identify important episodes in the books on their own—Garin's descriptions of Tema descending into the darkness of a slimy well, as though into the underworld, to rescue the dog that had fallen down it; the triumph over fear; the cat, killed by the house caretaker before the very eyes of Alesha Peshkov; and on, and on ... The execution of the Decembrists, which so deeply affected Sasha Herzen. Some kind of change was under way. They were becoming more conscious and conscientious—or did it just seem so?

Victor Yulievich himself, who had to remain within the confines of the school curriculum, continually sought what he termed a "strategy of awakening."

To this end, he gave everything he had. Those were, in essence, simple things—honor, fairness and justice, contempt for baseness and greed. He grounded them in what he considered the absolute pinnacle of classical Russian literature—he opened the door to the room, in Pushkin's *The Captain's Daughter*, where the fifteen-year-old adolescent, seduced by the breadth and quality of paper that had been used for a geography map, affixed a bast tail to the Cape of Good Hope while Monsieur Beaupré slept his drunken slumber, and his aristocratic father sent the worthless teacher packing, to the delight of the boy's servant, the peasant Savelich.

And Petrusha Grinev, enduring the cruelest forms of torture, preserved his honor and dignity, which became more valuable to him than life.

Still, there was one strange feature in this whole magnificent body of literature: it was all written by men, about boys. For boys. It was all about honor, about bravery, about duty. As though Russian childhood were solely a male affair. And what about the childhood of girls? What a paltry role they played! Natasha Rostova dances and sings exquisitely, Kitty can skate, Masha Mironova fends off the unwanted advances of a scoundrel. All the young cousins and their girlfriends, with whom the boys are so smitten, are admired for their curls and frills. All the rest are hapless victims: from Anna Karenina and Katyusha Maslova to Sonya Marmeladova. Very curious. What is their story? Are they only the objects of male interest? Where is their childhood? Do they undergo the same inner transformation that boys experience? Can it be just a mere function of physiology? Of biology?

In September 1954, a monumental event took place: separate education was abolished. Girls were admitted to their school, and thereafter began to appear in Ilya's photographic archive.

Everyone lost their senses, most notably the teachers of long standing, who were accustomed to their boys and believed that girls put them in grave moral danger.

The girls troubled everyone. And it wasn't these girls in particular, so much as what they represented—an attractive and rather frightening elemental force. The Trianon boys didn't deign to broach the subject, most likely because of Sanya, who couldn't bear "impropriety." This included a variety of things: physical uncleanliness, dirty words, lies, and disproportionate curiosity. Ilya, who allowed himself to indulge in bad language and crude jokes around others, kept himself in check in Sanya's presence. They did not permit themselves to talk about the girls precisely because their classmates did—and their conversation was always tinged with unseemliness. But a cloud of silence hung above the heads of these three, prefiguring a still unknown rule of thumb: self-respecting men do not discuss women.

The small fry—first- and second-graders—were not fazed in the least by the girls, but the eighth-graders went nuts. The very idea of a girl was enough to unhinge them. Girls were indecent by definition. They wore stockings, held up by elastic bands; the hems of their uniforms would sometimes ride up and reveal glimpses of bare flesh, and something pinkish or blue. Even the least attractive girl had noticeable breasts hidden under her black pinafore, though it wasn't as if the boys hadn't known this all before. They knew, of course, but now it was all unbearably close to them. And gym class! They had a girls' changing room where they undressed. Maybe even completely.

Excitement hung in the air like dust on a playground. All of them, boys and girls, gave off an electrical current, and all of them were love-struck.

The boys were transformed externally as well. Now they wore uniforms that resembled those of pre-Revolutionary preparatory school students: dove-gray coats and dress shirts. All wore uniforms that were too big, so they could grow into them, except Sanya Steklov, whose grandmother bought him just the right size. Although he had grown a little over the summer, he was not destined to catch up to Ilya or Mikha. Strange as it may seem, however, little Sanya enjoyed the most attention from the girls. Notes flew thick and fast through the classroom, like dangerous, honey-laden bees. The only thing missing was the buzz.

By the New Year, sympathies and antipathies had formed, and the first pairs of lovebirds had emerged. Those who had so far been unsuccessful at attracting someone of the opposite sex had high hopes for New Year's Eve.

All these hopes collapsed in the middle of December, when the whole school came down with measles. It started with the youngest pupils, then broke out among the older students, until a strict quarantine was imposed at the end of the month. Students were even forbidden to move between floors and to use the cafeteria. More than a third of the eighth-grade students came down with measles. Sanya kept waiting to get sick, checking his face every morning for signs, but the reddish rash didn't appear.

Students were allowed out of the classroom only to go to the bathroom. During the lunch break, the nurse and the lunch lady would bring pies, beet salad, and pots of sweetened tea to their rooms. At first it was exciting, but very soon it palled. The most unpleasant consequence of the whole epidemic was the cancellation of the New Year's party. The second quarter ended on an anticlimactic note, and they all dispersed for the winter vacation. On December 31, Sanya did come down with the measles after all, which deprived his friends of yet another celebration, their favorite one—Sanya's birthday.

Victor Yulievich brightened the dull winter break. Usually, the LORLs' meetings were suspended during the break, but that year they met nearly every other day. In any event, Ilya had taken many photographs during this period. Many others joined them on their walks— everyone who hadn't gotten sick. They would walk for about three hours, and then drop in at Victor Yulievich's home to drink tea. Those were the first of the pictures in which the two friends, Katya Zueva and Anya Filimonova, appear. They were the first girls to join their previously all-male club.

Katya had still not cut off her long braids bound with black hair ribbons, which hung over the collar of her coat. Anya Filimonova, in a ski cap with the brim overhanging her face, looked like a boy, with pimples on her forehead. She was trying to conceal them with the hat, Ilya surmised. He was also the first to notice that Katya was in love with their teacher.

When she went to school, she gathered her braids into an unattractive bun; but at the LORL sessions at Victor Yulievich's, she unbound her mane and suddenly looked very pretty. She sat at the round table, always in the same spot, resting her chin in her palm. Her hair almost completely covered her face, and Mikha had to bend lower to catch a glimpse of it. He liked her immensely, especially outside of school. He also liked little Roza Galeeva, from the seventh grade, and Zoya Krym, who was in the other eighth-grade class.

Every time Victor Yulievich addressed Katya, she blushed so violently that only the tip of her nose remained white. Katya was shy and quiet, and even with Anya, her best friend, she didn't share her greatest secret—that she had been head-over-heels in love with the teacher at first glance, on September 1, when she saw him standing in the school yard before the opening ceremony, surrounded by his boys, animated and laughing.

She would use any opportunity to see him, and would even follow him home (keeping her distance, of course). Sometimes she would stand by the entrance to his building in the evening, but she never ran into him. She decided to join his club, but only after she had persuaded Anya, who much preferred volleyball, to attend with her.

Closer to spring, something happened that Katya would tell her husband about, not omitting any details, only two years later. Katya managed to get hold of a ticket to Prokofiev's ballet *War and Peace*. The whole of Moscow wanted desperately to see the performance, and Katya's grandmother gave her a single ticket that she had acquired through her vast circle of connections. After the first act, Katya peeked into the theater buffet, just out of curiosity. There was a terrible crush, a noisy throng, and a long line had formed to the buffet. At the table nearest the door, Victor Yulievich was sitting. He was with a beautiful woman with slightly Asian features. A bouquet of flowers was lying on the table. They talked, and then he placed his left hand on her shoulder. Katya was overcome with nausea. She went home without staying to see the rest of the performance. She told her grandmother that she had a splitting headache.

A week later, she waylaid him in the entrance hall of his building and told him she loved him. She was terrified that he would laugh at her. He didn't. He put his hand on her shoulder, as he had done with the beautiful woman in the buffet, and said, in all seriousness, that he had already guessed her feelings, and that he hadn't known what to do about it.

"Never mind. It's just that I die inside whenever I think about that woman you were with in the theater. Are you going to marry her?"

"No, Katya. I'm not going to marry her. She's already married," he said somberly.

"Then you're going to marry me!" And she left.

"When you finish school!" he shouted after her.

The front door slammed behind her. He smiled, shook his head, and, pulling out his metal cigarette case, extracted one from it nimbly. He could do many things with the use of just one hand—he flicked the lighter and started to smoke. He stood for a while, smoking and smiling to himself. When he had lost his hand, he immediately vowed never to marry, never to put himself in a position of humiliating dependence on a woman. For more than ten years already he had managed to evade marriage and turn his back—timidly, decisively, sometimes cruelly, sometimes kindly—as soon as the idea of a permanent family bond cropped up.

But now he smiled: the girl was enchanting, in love with him in a way at once passionate and childlike. She seemed to pose no danger to him. He could never have imagined that he would indeed marry her as soon as she finished school.

All the next year the ninth-graders were steeped in the nineteenth century. From afar, it appeared very attractive. Ordinary conversations, just as in Zinaida Volkonskaya's salon, "revolved around literature." And "history." As Colonel Bibikov's report had revealed.

The Decembrists—the beating heart of Russian history, its finest legend—appealed strongly to everyone. Ilya even collected his own portrait gallery of the Decembrists (yet another collection he began, then abandoned to the whims of fate), and rephotographed their portraits from books, thus becoming very handy in the art of reproduction. Once Sanya, while he was examining Ilya's amateur reproductions, pointed at a certain mustached and rather shaggy-haired fellow, and, as if it were the most ordinary piece of information in the world, said, "This Lunin was a brother of one of my great-great-grandmothers. Grandmother says he was without fear and reproach. We're related to two Decembrists, in fact. The other one was my grandfather Steklov's great-great-something. You should ask Nuta about it. She'll tell you. She even has some of his letters."

Mikha and Ilya were astounded: Could this be true? And they rushed off to ask Anna Alexandrovna.

Anna Alexandrovna gestured vaguely with her hand, a cigarette between her fingers, and frowned. "Yes, we're related to them."

Like all people of that generation, she avoided talking about the past, even a past as distant as this one. Nevertheless, the boys peppered her with questions. She answered tersely. Yes, Mikhail Sergeevich Lunin was her great-grandmother's brother. And Sanya's late father, Stepan Yurievich Steklov, was a descendant of Sergei Petrovich Trubetskoy. Sergei Petrovich's son lived on Bolshaya Nikitinskaya Street. There had been many Trubetskoys; it was a real clan. This very house belonged to one of them about a hundred years ago. The first owner was Dmitry Yurievich, but that was a different line—not the line related to the Decembrist. She herself was not directly related to Trubetskoy, but Sanya was a descendant through the matrilineal line.

Here Mikha grew indignant. "And you never told us, Sanya?"

"Why should I go spreading it around?" Sanya said uncomfortably.

"Oh, come on! Most people would be proud." Mikha seemed to see Sanya in a different light now. "That poem, you know the one—'In the depths of the Siberian mines . . .' and all that. That's about them!"

Such rapturous admiration was written all over Mikha's reddish face that Sanya had to pull the rug out from under him. He bent down close to his ear, and, quietly, so that Anna Alexandrovna couldn't hear, said, "Yep! In the depths of the Siberian mines, two men sit to take a shit. Their sad labors won't be lost—their shit makes the best compost!"

Anna Alexandrovna had raised him on these stories of his ancestry, but he was indifferent to the birthright of his ancestral roots.

Ilya either overheard or guessed what Sanya had said, and he let out a long peal of laughter. Mikha's expression of shocked dismay thoroughly amused him. Batting his long, childish eyelashes, Mikha said, his voice trembling, "How dare you? How do you dare? I should challenge you to a duel for such words."

Anna Alexandrovna savored this little scene. Her red-haired favorite, whose ancestors would never have been allowed to set foot in an aristocrat's home, was prepared to challenge her grandson to a duel.

"You're still just silly boys, your sprouting mustaches notwithstanding. Go put the kettle on for tea, Sanya."

Sanya went out to the kitchen obediently. Anna Alexandrovna

rummaged around in the sideboard. There was nothing special for tea today—just rusks and dried bread rings. But the scent of vanilla, and something else, something pre-Revolutionary, always wafted out when the upper door of the cabinet was opened. Mikha loved it.

They drank their tea in silence. Mikha and Ilya were mulling over what they had learned, amazed that people they had known so well, and for such a long time, were so highborn. They even sensed their proximity to the grand sweep of history in the present moment.

I've got to take pictures of them all, Ilya thought. *Anna Alexandrovna, and Nadezhda Borisovna, and Sanya. So that the collection will be complete. Anna Alexandrovna, especially, since she'll probably die soon.*

And he already started to envision how he would make a real portrait, so that the nose with the little hump, and the bun fastened with a large brown hairpin, and the short wisps of gray curls falling behind her long ears onto her wrinkled neck would all be visible. And he imagined taking it at such an angle that her sunken cheek, and her long ear with the diamond in the lobe, would all be in the picture.

Mikha munched on rusks and wondered whether it would be proper to ask Anna Alexandrovna why Colonel Trubetskoy had not gone out onto Senate Square, and why he betrayed his comrades. But he was too shy.

Anna Alexandrovna, meanwhile, had gotten up and disappeared behind the room divider. The wardrobe door creaked, and she reemerged with a sizable box, covered with golden tapestry fabric. It contained a valuable book, published in London at Herzen's Free Russian Press in 1862: *The Notes of the Decembrists.*

"Here. Wash your hands, wipe your noses, and be careful when you turn the pages. And don't believe everything you hear or read about the Decembrists." She seemed to have intuited Mikha's silent question. "No matter how you look at it, the history of Russia has been rotten, but those times were not the worst imaginable. There was a place for nobility, and dignity, and a sense of honor. Now let me see your hands."

Mikha gently removed the cat that had settled on his lap and placed it on a pillow. Then he rushed to the bathroom to wash his hands, to show the proper respect for the rare edition he was so eager to touch. When he came back, he opened the book to a random page and started reading:

"'It was difficult to owe a debt of gratitude to a person whom one held in such low esteem.'"

"Wait a moment, give it here," Anna Alexandrovna said. She threw a cursory glance at the open page and smiled triumphantly. "You see, this is just what I was talking about. Sergei Trubetskoy wrote this after his interrogation. On the night of the fourteenth of December, he was arrested, and His Imperial Majesty Nikolay Pavlovich himself interrogated him. The Tsar was horrified that a prince descended from the Gediminids, a more aristocratic family than the Romanovs, could have 'gotten mixed up with this filth.' At the end of the conversation, the Tsar said, 'Write to your wife to tell her that your life is not in danger.' In other words, the Tsar made the decision even before the investigation. But Trubetskoy knew he was guilty of wrongdoing, and accepted all the charges, even that of plotting to kill the Tsar, though in reality he had been vigorously opposed to it."

"Victor Yulievich said that all the Decembrists gave testimony, admitted everything honestly, because they thought the Tsar would understand them and change his policies," Mikha said. He was eager to be seen in a positive light in this aristocratic company.

"Yes, they told the truth. Trubetskoy repented his actions bitterly during the interrogations, but never betrayed others. They never stooped to lying. As for Sergei Petrovich, many memoirs testify to the fact that he was loved and respected in exile. As far as I know, there was only one traitor among the Decembrists: Captain Maiboroda. He informed the authorities about the planned uprising three weeks in advance. I don't know for certain—there may have been one or two others. But there were more than three hundred involved in the plot! Read about it, the interrogation protocols have been published. Informing on others was not in fashion back then, that's the point I want to make," Anna Alexandrovna said with peculiar emphasis, which only Ilya picked up on.

"Truth be told, it's a story that recalls the Gospels. Maiboroda hanged himself—albeit many years later."

"Like Judas!" Mikha said, revealing his knowledge of biblical history.

Anna Alexandrovna laughed. "Good going, Mikha! You're a man of culture."

Mikha grew bolder with the encouragement.

"Anna Alexandrovna, which Decembrist was the . . ." he began, then faltered. He wanted to say "best," but decided it would sound too childish. So he said, "Your favorite?"

Anna Alexandrovna leafed through the book. It contained several reproductions. She removed a portrait on yellowing paper that had been cut out from somewhere.

"This one. Mikhail Sergeevich Lunin."

The boys leaned in over the picture. They had already seen the face, it was part of Ilya's collection. But in that picture he was young, full-lipped, and mustached, and in this one he was twenty years older.

"Look, he was decorated. See? There's the cross, and there's something else I can't make out," Ilya said.

"He took part in the 1812 campaign. The only thing I know about his decorations is that they were publicly cast into a fire when he was sentenced," Anna Alexandrovna said, smiling. "But it didn't prevent him from remaining a hero."

"The bastards!" Mikha exclaimed. "War decorations—throwing them into the fire!"

"Indeed. He wasn't even in St. Petersburg during the uprising. They caught up with him in Warsaw and shipped him back home. He was one of the organizers of the Northern Society, but by that time he had already ceased to play an active role in the conspiracy. He believed that they were not acting decisively enough. Lunin was among those who believed they should kill the Tsar, but others didn't support him in this. And Trubetskoy, chosen subsequently as their 'dictator,' was opposed to the murder."

"But if Lunin had been able to win them over to his idea the October Revolution would have happened a century earlier!" Mikha said, his eyes wide with excitement. Everyone laughed.

"It wouldn't have been called 'October' then, Mikha," Anna Alexandrovna said, curbing Mikha's enthusiasm.

"Oh, that's true. I didn't think about that. And what happened to Lunin afterward?"

"Mikhail Sergeevich was arrested again, after serving his sentence to hard labor, this time for his letters. He had also analyzed the reports presented to the Tsar by the Secret Commission. These were published. That was why they arrested him a second time, and why he was sent to prison again. And there he died. Rumor has it that he didn't die of natural causes, that he was killed on orders from the Tsar."

"How despicable!" Mikha said. It took him several days to get over Lunin's death. He wrote a poem called "On the Death of a Hero."

This was the most beautiful, the most heroic page of Russian history. Under the guidance of Victor Yulievich, it became the cornerstone of what inspired them, the event that honed their young minds and hearts.

Mikha Melamid wrote an essay, quoting lines from Herzen:

I was present at the mass, and there, before the altar defiled by a murderous prayer, I swore to avenge the executed, and vowed to struggle against the throne, against this altar, against these guns. I did not avenge them; the guardsmen and the throne, the altar and the guns—all remain; but now, thirty years later, I am still standing under the same banner, which I have never once forsaken.

Later in the essay, the boy wrote, now in his own words: "And they remain unavenged till this very day."

The teacher was moved by Mikha's essay. Here was one of his boys grasping that moment of transition, the moral crisis of another adolescent, who had lived one hundred years before.

But life, of course, is more than just heady knowledge about the Decembrists. For instance, the New Year was coming up. It was the most important holiday, the only one that wasn't for the greater glory of the state, the only one without red flags. It was the only completely human holiday, with the rehabilitated Christmas tree, sanctioned drinking (for adults), presents, and surprises.

This year there were no epidemics, and everyone was eagerly anticipating the New Year's Eve party. For two weeks before the school celebration, planned for December 30, everyone was mad with excitement: all their dreams of love were about to come true.

This was the first party with girls. They weren't wearing their uniforms. Instead, they came all dressed up, as colorful as butterflies, and some of them even wore their hair loose. The teachers were also dressed up. Victor Yulievich found it touching that the holiday excitement had affected everyone without exception. Even the principal, Larisa Stepanovna, was wearing high heels and had pinned a brooch to her collar. It was a butterfly with outspread wings—a creature she in no way resembled.

The older students had begun to make preparations for the party so long before, and so carefully, determined as they were not to overlook a single detail in their arsenal of sanctioned pleasures, that plans kept changing throughout December. At first they considered a costume ball. Then they changed their minds—instead of spending time on elaborate costumes, they would have a talent show. They even thought of inviting a real band, but their money didn't stretch that far. Maybe skits would be a good idea—or a cultural program with poetry, and Natasha Mirzoyan performing Schubert? Or even a real play?

As often happens when there is an overabundance of ideas, it ended up being an incoherent jumble of everything, with no particular rhyme or reason. Those who were in favor of a costume ball or carnival threw on something funny or ridiculous. Katya Zueva, bringing to fruition a long-held plan, appeared in the guise of a postal worker, with a ticket-taker's bag instead of a mailbag. On her chest she wore a piece of cardboard painted with the number 5, supposed to resemble a badge; instead of the official blue cap of the uniform, she wore a tricorne hat made of folded newspaper. On her back, for those who were completely slow-witted, she had stuck a piece of blue cardboard with a white inscription reading POST. Her friend Anya Filimonova dressed up like a gypsy in a colorful skirt, with hoop earrings, a necklace she had made herself, and a large shawl that her mother had dragged out of a trunk and warned her to treat with the utmost care, since it was very old. In her hand she held a deck of cards for fortune-telling—but she was too shy to use them. She hadn't even wanted to dress up at first, but Katya had persuaded her to—she needed the moral support.

The evening also featured a poetry montage and a human pyramid, which the whole gymnastics team had practiced to perfection. Twelve people, balancing one on top of the others, representing a Christmas tree hung with ornaments.

The shop teacher, crippled Itkin, was wearing his war decorations, and the gym teacher, Andrei Ivanovich, for once appeared not in his everyday blue zippered working vest, but in a white sweater. Both of them smelled strongly of eau de cologne—Itkin of Troynoy, and Andrei Ivanovich of Chypre. They played records with old songs that only a trained circus bear could have danced to. When "Rio Rita" came on, the girls started to shuffle their feet, but no one dared to venture out into the middle of the room until the gym teacher invited the senior Pioneer instructor to dance. They danced "Rio Rita" together, the only couple, under the stern gaze of their older colleagues. Tasya Smolkina, an enthusiastic tenth-grader who was a member of the Komsomol committee, saved the day by initiating several games: Freeze Dance and Duck Duck Goose for the younger ones, and Love Mail for those who had romantic hopes for the evening.

Katya Zueva, the mail girl, passed out numbers, and everyone began writing love letters. Katya darted around the room delivering them. Victor Yulievich stood over by the window, waiting for the moment when he could slip away to the teachers' lounge for a smoke. Just as he got to the door, the mail girl intercepted him and thrust two letters into his hand at the same time. He tucked them away in his pocket. "I love you" was scrawled on one of them; it had no return address. The other one read: "Do you like Pasternak's prose?" That one was from number 56.

Victor Yulievich went downstairs to the teachers' room, where two young elementary-school teachers—one pretty, the other rather plain—were whispering and giggling together like eighth-graders. They were also obviously hoping to get some romantic pleasure, their small share of happiness, from the evening.

Victor Yulievich tore up the love note and threw the pieces in the ashtray. The older girls at school fell into two groups: those who adored Victor Yulievich, and, a smaller group, those who preferred the gym teacher. The literature teacher opened the other letter—it had been written with a hard pencil in a round, girlish script, very faint. Rising to the challenge, he wrote his answer: "Except for *The Childhood of Zhenya Lyuvers*." He folded it up and wrote "56" on the back, and then began to muse. He had been thinking that nothing had ever been written about the childhood of girls in Russian literature. How could he have forgotten Pasternak's early novella? He had read it before the war, when he was just a boy, and its intricacy, its contrived unevenness, its elusive structure, and its superfluity of words had not appealed to him. But this was, it seemed, the only work about a girl's childhood in all of Russian literature. How could he have overlooked it? It contained everything that preoccupied him now: the awakening of consciousness, a psychological catastrophe that prefigured the enormous physiological changes the girl would soon, without warning, undergo. Even her first experience of death! He wanted to reread it immediately, without delay. But his home library contained no Pasternak. He'd have to look for it at the Lenin Library.

He went back to the auditorium, and passed the note back to the mail girl, Katya. He had missed the human pyramid and Schubert. The music had died down altogether now—a waltz had just ended. People shuffled back to their places by the wall. Suddenly, a ringing slap, uncannily loud, resounded through the dusty stillness. Everyone turned to look. In the middle of the room stood a lanky couple—Anya Filimonova in her absurd gypsy attire and Yura Burkin. Anya was clutching her shawl, which she had removed, to her chest. Yura was pressing his hand to his cheek, where the trace of the sturdy volleyball-playing hand was blooming, compliments of his resolute partner.

It was a scene worthy of Gogol. But the curtain did not fall. Everyone continued to stand rooted to the spot, expecting the plot to unfold. And unfold it did: Yura removed his hand from his cheek, raised it slightly, and brushed it across his partner's face. It made the sound of a smacking kiss.

The crowd let out a quiet gasp—*Oooooooh!* Katya threw herself at her friend, everything came to life, everyone was overwrought. Anya, who had turned scarlet, wept on Katya's shoulder. Through sobs, one could make out:

"He . . . He . . . blew his nose on my shawl!"

Yura rushed out of the auditorium. Katya looked around. "Is there no one here willing to stand up for her honor?"

She was pale, trembling, filled with fury, and it was clear that she would lose no time in trying to destroy the offender herself. All year she had talked about nothing but noble men and beautiful ladies!

Mikha flew out the door, as though he had wings on his feet. He caught up to Yura in the boys' bathroom. His hands shaking, Yura was smoking one of his father's cigarettes, which he had pinched the night before. He didn't even smoke, it made him queasy. He had been trying to get used to it since sixth grade, but couldn't. But he liked the act of smoking, just to hold the cigarette in his hand, and this time, he suspected that it wasn't even going to make him feel queasy.

Mikha grabbed the cigarette out of his hand, broke it in two, tossed it aside, and then said in a slow, calm, contemptuous voice, "A duel! I challenge you to a duel!"

"Mikha, are you nuts? A duel? What duel? She just can't take a joke, the idiot."

"We won't shoot, we have no pistols. We have no weapons whatsoever. Hand-to-hand combat will have to do, but we'll stick to all the rules."

"Are you out of your mind?"

"So you're a coward. On top of being an insolent boor," Mikha said.

"Okay, okay, if that's what you want," Yura said, reluctant but also conciliatory. "When?"

"Today."

"But it's already nine thirty!"

Mikha summoned up all his organizational skills and the duel took place an hour later at Milyutin Park.

The tenth-graders tried to talk Yura out of it, and the ninth-graders worked on Mikha. The rules of the duel were invented on the fly.

Yura whined the whole way, "Mikha, why are you itching to have your face punched in? I need to get home. My father is going to yell at me, my mother has probably gone to school to find out what happened to me."

But Mikha was adamant.

"A duel! Till the first drop of blood."

Ilya and Sanya exchanged glances, winked at each other, and even snickered a bit between themselves. Sanya said, "Our little bleeding Jesus!"

Mikha's second was Ilya, and Yura's was Vasya Egorochkin. The snow in the park had settled in big drifts, and the seconds had to stamp out a small area for the fight. Sanya suggested that they use leather gloves for the fight, but none of them owned such a luxury. For some reason, Sanya felt sure that fighting with bare fists was against the rules.

"The ancient Greeks wrapped leather belts around their fists."

Where had he picked that up? But he spoke with confidence. He just knew, that's all. And they had belts galore. The seconds took off their own belts, hooked them together to make one long one, and laid it in the snow between the duelers, as a barrier. The duelers were supposed to approach it and start to fight on the count of three.

The duelers wrapped their school-uniform belts around their fists, but with the clasps inside their palms. It was very uncomfortable.

"Maybe we can manage without the belts?" Yura suggested. Mikha didn't even deign to answer him. Ilya suggested that Burkin convey his formal apologies. Mikha rejected this on reasonable grounds.

"The apologies are due to the lady herself."

Yura's spirits lifted. "By all means! I'll apologize right away!"

In view of the absence of the lady in question, the truce was declined. Mikha took off his glasses and handed them to Sanya. They threw off their coats.

"Maybe that's enough already?" Sanya whispered.

"Just hold it!" Mikha burst out, infuriated. Ilya started counting. On the count of three, they went at each other.

They stood face-to-face: heavyset Yura, Mikha, thinner, but also madder. Mikha jumped up and down in place, and with both fists at once, somehow, popped Yura in the face, awkwardly and painlessly.

Yura's anger finally kicked in. He launched a single punch at Mikha's nose. Blood gushed out instantly. Sanya groaned, as though he had taken the blow himself, and pulled out a clean hanky. The punch wasn't exceedingly strong, but it was perfectly on the mark. From that moment on, Mikha's nose would be a little crooked. It was sore for a long time. Most likely it had been broken.

The duel was, for all intents and purposes, over.

Meanwhile, when the students had already left for home, the two young elementary-school teachers were sitting with Andrei Ivanovich and drinking a modest nightcap. Only the cloakroom attendant and the cleaning lady, who sometimes stayed overnight in the utility room when her husband drank too much, were left behind. Katya Zueva, now without her tricorne newspaper hat, wearing her brown coat, its cuffs and hem lengthened with black wool, sat on a chair in the cloakroom waiting for Victor Yulievich.

When he came downstairs, she handed him a note.

"A letter for you."

He looked puzzled—he had already forgotten about the game. "Oh? Thank you," he said, stuffing it absentmindedly into his coat pocket.

He found the scrap of paper in his pocket the next morning. It said:

I can lend you his new novel. Do you want it?
                                    —Katya

He didn't immediately understand what she was talking about.

On January 3, Katya called for him, and, still in postal-worker mode, delivered him a typewritten manuscript.

Pasternak's new novel was called *Doctor Zhivago*. The first pages— even those before the death of Maria Nikolaevna Zhivago—affected Victor Yulievich deeply. This was the continuation of that legacy of

Russian literature he had thought was over and done with, lost forever. It seemed that this tradition had sprouted anew, in the present. Every line of the new novel echoed that tradition and spoke of the same thing—of the ordeals of the human heart in this world, of the growth of the human being, of physical death and moral triumph; in short, of the "creation and wonder" of life.

For the entire school break, Victor Yulievich was completely absorbed in Pasternak's novel. He was enchanted by the poems, though they seemed to be tacked on at the end in a clumsy and gratuitous way—they were recognizably Pasternak, but with a newly minted directness and simplicity. This was, evidently, the "unprecedented simplicity" the poet had long dreamed of.

As soon as he had finished the book, he began reading it again from the beginning. He discovered in it more and more gems of thought, feeling, and word. At the same time, he discerned its weaknesses, and the weaknesses appealed to him as well. They forced one to think, to ponder. Victor Yulievich felt no fondness for Lara, a rather thinly drawn character who kept doing things that attested to her foolishness and narcissism. But boy, how the author loved her!

Victor Yulievich was dismayed by the insistent coincidences, chance meetings, and convergences, until he realized that they were all connected, the loose ends all tied up, during the scene describing Yury Andreevich's death, the parallel movement of a streetcar carrying the dying Zhivago, and Mademoiselle Fleury, proceeding on foot, without haste, in the same direction, to freedom—one departing from the land of the living, the other leaving the land of her captivity.

A magnificent postscript to the classical tradition of Russian literature, Victor Yulievich thought, pronouncing his verdict.

On January 10, the last day of school break, Victor Yulievich phoned Katya. They met in front of the fabric store on Solyanka Street. He thanked her for the enormous happiness she had afforded him.

"As soon as I read the book, I realized there was someone I had to give it to," she said.

Then she revealed something to him that he would on no account have asked her: how she had acquired the book. "My grandmother has known Boris Pasternak nearly her whole life. She typed out the novel for him. This is Grandmother's copy."

Victor Yulievich placed a warm hand over the babbling mouth. "Never tell that to anyone. And you didn't tell me, either."

He kept his hand over her lips, and they moved ever so slightly, as though she were whispering to him silently.

She had just turned seventeen. She was barely out of childhood, and she still displayed some of the ways and manners of a child. Her long, bare neck stuck out of her coat. She had no scarf. Her hat was a child's bonnet that tied under her chin. Her light brown eyes showed hurt, and a film of tears.

"No, no one—just you. I knew you would like it. I was right, wasn't I? You did like it?"

"More than you can know, Katya. More than you can ever know. A book like that changes one's life. I will be grateful to you until the day I die."

"Really?" Her eyelashes opened wide, and her eyes lit up.

My God, it's Natasha Rostova! Natasha Rostova in the flesh!

It took his breath away.

After Katya finished school, they got married. The first to know about it were, of course, the LORLs. They were thrilled. By September, Katya's belly was noticeable to anyone who was paying attention, and the LORLs were doubly happy.

These circumstances drew them still closer to their teacher. Now, after their sessions, they would occasionally share a good bottle of Georgian wine, which flowed freely at Victor Yulievich's home. They even started calling him Vika—to his face. And he didn't object, though he preserved the custom of using the old-fashioned and respectful form of "you" when addressing them.

The sessions of the Lovers of Russian Literature continued to be held in Ksenia Nikolayevna's room, but Victor Yulievich and Katya now lived in an apartment that belonged to one of Katya's relatives.

He had moved to the Russian north, having gotten a better job, and offered them the use of the apartment, in a residence for railroad workers, with windows facing onto the rail yards. They began their new life together against the background of an unceasing twenty-four-hour refrain: train departing, train arriving . . .

THE LAST BALL

These were Victor Yulievich's best years: a meaningful job, the adoration of his students, and a happy marriage—at least for now. He even earned a little extra on the side—two evenings a week, he gave private lessons.

He worked very hard, but the LORLs still gathered at his home on Wednesdays. The graduating class of '57 was his favorite—he had been their class adviser since the sixth grade, knew all their mamas and papas, grannies and grandpas, and siblings. The fifteen-year age gap became less and less palpable. The boys were growing into young men, and the marriage of their teacher to one of their classmates made the gap in their ages still less significant.

At the end of 1956 they announced the birth of a daughter. On December 1, in her eighth month of pregnancy, Katya had given birth to a fine four-and-a-half-pound girl. They named her Ksenia, after her grandmother. But even this diplomatic gesture could not soothe the hurt Ksenia Nikolayevna had suffered after her son's marriage. She couldn't bear the thought that another woman would make Vika his breakfast, talk with him in the evenings, wait for him after school, and wake him up in the morning. Moreover, she felt a particular antagonism toward Katya—relations between a mother-in-law and her son's wife are a chemical reaction in the blood. She believed that the underage girl had seduced him, perverted him, lured him with her wiles. In short, she had roped him into marriage.

Victor Yulievich's colleagues at school took a different view of the matter. The teachers' lounge was rife with backbiting rumors and gossip, which were especially ruthless and damning among the female teachers. When the little girl was born, the entire teaching staff experienced a thrill of malicious pleasure. Vera Lvovna, the mathematics teacher, counted off the months on her fingers, incontestably demonstrating that Zueva would have had to conceive in the third quarter of the school year to give birth in December.

Rybkina, the local Party organizer, who was also the head teacher, consulted with the higher-ups on the school board, as well as the regional committee of the Party, about how to deal with a criminal in their midst. The case was clear: the teacher was guilty of the corruption of a minor. On the other hand, the underage girl had come of age in the months that followed, and at the same time the transgressor of the law had made her his legal wife. But could he go unpunished?

The teachers maintained a unanimous tense silence whenever Victor Yulievich entered the room. The school administrators—the holy trinity of principal, Party organizer, and labor union organizer—had initially wanted to convene a faculty meeting to discuss the issue. But Larisa Stepanovna preferred to launch a probe with the authorities first. Reports were sent to the school board and the regional committee of the Party.

It was during this last winter of school that Victor Yulievich began writing the book he had been mulling over for several years. The title had already suggested itself: *Russian Childhood*. He wasn't sure about the genre—whether it would become a collection of essays or a monograph.

He laid no claim to any discoveries. He was distinctly aware that his interests partook of a variety of disciplines: developmental psychology, pedagogy, and anthropology in the broadest sense of the word. At the same time, the logic of his thoughts developed according to the

terms deployed by medical doctors and biologists. The influence of
his friend Kolesnik was undeniable.

He was at pains to describe the moral awakening of the adolescent,
which is as fundamental and necessary as cutting teeth, babbling, and
the first steps the baby attempts during the early months of development. In other words, it was the whole thrilling yet routine growth
pattern that he was observing in his own child:

> Thus it begins. At two or so they rush
> From breasts into the dark of melody,
> They chirp, they crow, they warble—then words
> Appear already by the age of three . . .

The lyrical model that Pasternak outlined was far more obvious to
him than all the tenets and premises of developmental psychology.
Moral maturation seemed to be as valid a dimension of human devel
opment as the biological processes that unfolded in tandem with it. But
moral awakening occurs in different ways, and the framework within
which it takes place varies according to the individual cast of mind,
and other contingencies. Moral awakening, or "moral initiation," as he
called it, occurs in boys between eleven and fourteen years of age, most
often spurred by unfavorable circumstances—an unhappy or difficult
family situation, an assault on one's sense of self-worth and dignity (or
the dignity of those one holds dear), or the loss of a loved one. In short,
an internal upheaval that calls the soul to life.

Every person has his "sore spots," and this is where the inner revolution of the personality begins. According to Victor Yulievich's notions,
the presence of a catalyst or "initiator" is almost a sine qua non of this
process, whether it be a teacher, a guardian, an older friend, or even a
relative (usually a fairly distant one). As in baptism, a child's parents
rarely assume the role of godparents (unless, for example, the child's life
is in some sort of danger). In exceptional circumstances, even a book
that falls into a child's hands at the right moment can serve as an
"initiator."

Following a comprehensive analysis of this phenomenon, the author
went on to describe several cases of initiation derived from classical

Russian literature, examining the maturation of contemporary adolescents and analyzing the reasons for their tardy development. He also discussed the most alarming phenomenon of all: "initiation avoidance."

It also occurred to Victor Yulievich that at just this age, Lutherans and Anglicans undergo the process of Confirmation, conscious acceptance of the faith; Jewish boys celebrate their bar mitzvahs, in which they are inducted into the adult community; and Muslims are circumcised. Thus, it seems that communities of believers attach particular significance to this transition from childhood to adulthood, whereas the atheist world has completely foregone this crucial mechanism. Becoming a Pioneer or a Komsomol member could hardly be considered a serious replacement for this practice.

The community sinks below the level of a moral minimum when the number of people who have not undergone this process of initiation in early youth exceeds half the population—this was the view that Victor Yulievich held at that time.

He and the late Vygotsky had serious differences of opinion about the formation and displacement of cultural interests, but that hardly mattered, since developmental psychology was a "closed" subject, forbidden, along with genetics and cybernetics. In truth, Victor Yulievich did not hold out any hopes that his future book might be published. But these kinds of pragmatic considerations could gain no toehold amid the heady pace of his life, which gave him every happiness he could ever have wished for—creative work, a marvelous young wife holding up that very diaper with the yellowish stain, a diminutive miracle with wonderful tiny fingers and lips and eyes, a little creature that grew more human by the day, and students whose enthusiasm raised him to heights hitherto unknown. He smiled in his sleep, and he smiled upon waking.

The country was, meanwhile, in the throes of its own mad existence. After the unseen wrangling at Dzhugashvili's coffin, the hidden struggle for power, after the return of the first thousands of people from the prison camps and from exile, after the inexplicable, unanticipated Twentieth Party Congress, the uprising in Hungary began and ended.

Victor Yulievich, steeped in the affairs of his own life, was only half-aware of these events. His "inner" life during this period seemed more important than the "outer."

In September, during the first days of school, Tasya Vorobieva, a pretty student who took night classes at the pedagogical institute and with whom Victor Yulievich was on good terms, slipped him a packet of faded pages with Khrushchev's address to the Twentieth Party Congress typed on them. Although half a year had already passed since that event, it had still not been published anywhere. This address, full of cautious half-truths, was distributed only among the highest echelons of the Party. Rank and file Party members were informed about it during closed meetings, and only orally. The top of the document was marked "For Official Use Only"—thus, not for ordinary people. This was the run-of-the-mill Soviet phantasmagoria: a secret report for one sector of the populace, which it was required to keep secret from the other. A government with an impaired faculty of reason.

Victor Yulievich also read Khrushchev's address, which so many people were talking about. It was, indeed, very interesting. History was unfolding before their very eyes. The tyrant had fallen, and three years later the whole pack dared raise its voice against him. Where were you before, all you clever ones? The document, which had momentous consequences, was in equal measure terrifying and revelatory for the Party bosses. This typewritten report, which was continually reproduced and passed from hand to hand, was the first underground samizdat, which in those years had not yet received its name.

While this domestic typing and dissemination of Khrushchev's report was already under way in Moscow, *Doctor Zhivago*'s hour had not yet arrived. The poems from the novel, however, had already begun to circulate through these clandestine channels.

A curious state of affairs, mused Victor Yulievich. *Just as in Pushkin's time, notes in verse are passing from hand to hand. What next? Will they stop sending people to labor camps?*

The nation, once paralyzed with fear, began to revive. It whispered more boldly, tuned into "enemy" broadcasts, typed, retyped, photographed, and rephotographed. Samizdat spread around the whole country. Although this underground form of reading was still not established as the new social phenomenon it would become in the next decade, the rustling of typewritten pages at night in the hands of bold and eager readers was already audible.

Khrushchev had so effectively unmasked Stalin's cult of personality that something inchoate and uncertain had overtaken the previous state of clarity. Everyone was frozen in expectation. And the fate of the literature teacher, who had married his student and produced a child not quite according to schedule, was still hanging in the balance, despite the efforts of the school officials to resolve it as they saw fit.

At long last Victor Yulievich's case was reviewed. The school board judged him more severely than the district Party committee. It was agreed that he should be fired, but with the proviso that he should first see his students through to graduation. So as not to alarm the teacher about the planned dismissal, they decided not to inform him about the decision at all. If he were to leave in the middle of the year, who would replace him? Victor Yulievich got wind of all sorts of unpleasant rumors, but he had already made up his mind to resign at the end of the school year, anyway.

In the spring of 1957, the LORL meetings were transformed into review sessions in preparation for the matriculation examination—a good three-fourths of the class planned to enter the philology department. Mikha attended these sessions regularly, though he was already first in his class in literature. He knew that the philology department at Moscow State University didn't accept Jews. He also knew that it was the only place he wanted to study.

His older cousin Marlen teased him, offering to help him get admitted to the Fishery Institute, insisting that fish were a far more solid profession for a Jew than Russian literature. This incensed Mikha, naturally.

By spring, the rumor that Victor Yulievich was going to be fired reached the ears of the tenth-graders. It was said that the teachers had incriminated him on the basis of a clause regarding marriage with a former student. The young people were prepared to go to any lengths, to appeal to any authority, to defend their favorite teacher. He finally managed to convince them that he himself wished to leave the school, that he had long wished to engage in his own scholarly activity, to write books. He said that they should be able to understand how sick he was of school notebooks, meddling old biddies, political informa- tion meetings and other such nonsense, and that it was only because of them, his beloved LORLs, that he hadn't left immediately after his marriage.

"Moreover," he said, "I've already ensured that I'll have replace- ments. You know yourselves how many literature teachers our school will have turned out a few years hence."

This was true. Since he had begun teaching at the school, half of every graduating class had entered a philology department—some at Moscow State University, others at the pedagogical university. Girls who were not quite up to the mark went on to library school, to the Archival Institute, or the Institute of Arts and Culture. A small but mighty army of young people had learned the art of reading Pushkin and Tolstoy. Victor Yulievich was certain that his students were thus inoculated against the ills and evils of existence, both petty and grand. In this he was, perhaps, mistaken.

The LORLs were far more preoccupied with getting ready for their graduation party than for their matriculation exam. They were plan- ning a spectacular event. It had been announced beforehand that alcohol would be forbidden. On the one hand, there were ways to get around this ban quite easily; on the other hand, no one was particu- larly upset by the ban on alcohol, anyway. The main thing, which everyone understood very well, was that they would be saying good- bye to Victor Yulievich. It would be a double good-bye, since Victor Yulievich would be taking leave of the school, along with his gradu- ating class.

The students kept their preparations under wraps, but Victor Yulievich guessed at the scale of the event. News had reached him that several of the boys were spending day and night in the art studio of the sculptor Lozovsky, who happened to be Volodya Lozovsky's father, instead of studying for their examination. They were said to be building something truly magnificent.

Ilya was blowing up photographs and making shadow pictures that he projected onto a wall. This was an unprecedented kind of set design, which he had conceived all on his own.

Mikha, laying his textbooks aside, had begun working on a play in verse. The characters numbered in the millions—from Aristophanes to Ivan the Fool, from Homer to Ehrenburg.

When the matriculation exams were at last over and had all been passed, it was time for the graduation ball. This annual celebration had its own long-standing traditions. The girls had fancy new dresses made, even white ones. Elaborate hairdos were whipped up for them at the hairdresser's. The girls wore mascara, and were even allowed to put on nylon stockings.

This was the dress rehearsal for the first ball of the future, which for most of them would never take place. It was the false promise of a 24/7 holiday that never arrived. And it was a parting of the ways with school, which was for each of them without exception a happy event, but which was bemoaned with maudlin insincerity.

Row upon row of chairs had been set up in the auditorium to accommodate the parents, primarily mothers, who were also dressed up, and no less excited than their children.

After the complex choreography of seating arrangements was over, an unpleasant incident occurred. Two ninth-graders, Maximov and Tarasov, smuggled themselves into the crowd of graduates, intending to steal a piece of a celebration they were not allowed to share. They were publicly humiliated and banished. Everyone assumed they had left the school premises.

The ceremony began. Diplomas were distributed, and speeches made. The ritual began with the announcement of medalists, recognized for exceptional academic achievement. There were four that year: three silver medalists, and one gold. Natasha Mirzoyan, an eastern beauty and champion brownnose, won the gold medal. The silver medalists were Poluyanova, Gorshkova, and Steinfeld—nicknamed "Muchable." He had received the nickname in elementary school for his habit of saying "much obliged" instead of just "thank you."

The Trianon never rose to scholastic heights worthy of medals. They were all serious about their studies but had never been straight-A students.

After the ceremonial portion of the event, the proceedings stalled. According to the program, a play was supposed to get under way, but for dozens of reasons, it did not. They needed at least forty minutes to tack together all the disparate scenes and acts. They turned on some music instead, but no one felt inspired to dance yet, so they all just shuffled around aimlessly. In the neighboring classroom the actors and stagehands were just stitching the last flowers to the wreaths, making up their faces, and memorizing their lines.

Victor Yulievich was standing by a window, conversing with one of the parents. He looked up to see Andrei Ivanovich gesturing to him from the doorway—Come here, quick!

It turned out that the exiled Maximov and Tarasov had not left the school premises at all, but had instead taken refuge in the attic, and had downed a bottle of port wine between the two of them. They were caught red-handed with the evidence just outside the attic, and were led down to the principal's office. Both of them were drunk, a fact no one with eyes would have disputed.

Victor Yulievich walked into the office, and the principal turned to him theatrically, saying, "Just look at our fine students!"

They had such a pathetic, hangdog look about them that it was clear they needed to be comforted, rather than punished. Victor Yulievich reached for the empty bottle on the principal's desk, turned it around to look at the label, and said, "This is certainly worth a reprimand. Godawful stuff."

The principal launched into her spiel.

"Now then. Your parents have been informed, and we will discuss the matter further when they arrive. In the meantime, I want to know who else was in on this. If you don't tell me their names, you will be expelled from school."

They had acted alone, but Larisa Stepanovna was certain there had been a whole gang of them up there.

"Tarasov, why are you looking at me with such an insolent expression on your face? That goes for you, too, Maximov. Tell me the names of your accomplices. I want their names! And don't think you can cover for them, and they'll be off the hook. We'll find them out anyway. Only it will be all the worse for you."

"Hmm, this stuff is truly vile," Victor Yulievich said with emphasis. "Where did you get it?"

"Bought it," Maximov answered readily.

"Do your parents drink this at home, too?"

"No, my mother doesn't drink at all," Maximov lied.

This shady investigation continued until Tarasov's father, a lieutenant colonel in the Ministry of Internal Affairs, arrived in his official car. Larisa Stepanovna told him the whole story. He stood there, shaking with fury. "We'll sort it out," the lieutenant colonel said darkly. It was clear that his son would pay dearly for this.

"When is your mother going to get here?" Larisa Stepanovna said. Obviously, she was getting bored with the drawn-out, fruitless interrogation. Moreover, her presence was required in the auditorium.

"My mother went to Kaluga to visit my aunt."

Larisa Stepanovna paused. Her train of thought was etched on her face.

"I'll take responsibility for him. When the party has ended, I'll make sure he gets home. So that he isn't picked up by the police, by mistake," Victor Yulievich said, placing his left hand on Maximov's shoulder.

"Leave," she said, waving her hand dismissively. "And don't come back to school without your mother, Maximov."

This warning meant absolutely nothing, since school had already let out for the summer. It would be three months before it started again.

Victor Yulievich led poor Maximov to the auditorium, and pointed at a chair.

"Sit down, Maximov. Be quiet, and try not to attract attention."

Maximov nodded gratefully. His mother wasn't in Kaluga at all. Her boyfriend from Alexandrov had arrived, and the two were at home getting drunk.

When he was writing his play, Mikha tried to capture in rhyme the whole of his vast knowledge of literature. The actors also took a creative view of Mikha's masterpiece and made their own contributions to it. In the end, the script had ballooned to two hundred pages.

Two weeks before the graduation party, when exams were already in progress and everyone was cramming for algebra and chemistry, Ilya took Mikha's script, cut it up into chunks and bits, then reshuffled them until a plot—at first impossible to discern—emerged. The story described the journey of a group of dimwits, all recognizable by their real names, who would just be on the verge of misfortune or catastrophe, when the higher powers—an incarnation of Victor Yulievich, from Zeus to the policeman—would intervene to save the day.

Victor Yulievich was played by Senya Svinin, the best actor in the class—he was going to enroll in the theater academy. He wore a papier-mâché mask that bore a passing resemblance to Victor Yulievich. His right arm was not in the sleeve of his jacket. Instead, they had folded up the sleeve halfway and pinned it.

It was all terribly silly and terribly funny. A statue of Zeus toppled over and smashed into bits, and Svinin-Shengeli, shaking the dust off, crawled out. Alexander Sergeevich Pushkin searched high and low for some lost object. In the end it turned out that he had been looking for a dainty little foot. About fifty mannequin legs, their stocking feet aloft, floated out onto the stage. Chekhov's gun, in the guise of a child's toy wooden rifle, ended up in the hands of one of Turgenev's hunters, and fired a shot—after which a seagull made out of an old rag plummeted down with a hideous screech.

The whole phantasmagorical drama centered on dear Victor Yulievich, of course.

Sanya Steklov, in a curly wig and a velvet robe, sat at the piano and played to perfection in the spots where the text faltered a bit.

Then, raising their voices in unison, they sang an anthem, also written by Mikha, which it would be a crime to omit.

> Both many-armed and many-eyed,
> He faced our death, and death defied
> (For each of us one time he tried)
> And that is why our time we bide
> To tell his story far and wide.
> Yes, Yulievich, we're on your side!
> You showed the truth, you never lied—
> That we have noble blood inside.

At your command, it is our pride
To rally to your call, not hide,
And follow in your footsteps, ride
The waves, or fly, to keep in stride
With Victor Yulievich, our sun,
Who'll light our way for years to come.

When the song was over, there was not a single teacher left in the auditorium. All of them had escaped to the teachers' lounge, fuming in indignation. They had been scorned! For this reason they hadn't even seen the end of the play, when the actors gathered in a circle on the stage to discuss what to give their beloved teacher as parting gift. They entertained, and dismissed, several highly comical suggestions before deciding that the gift had to be something unparalleled, something invaluable, something that "wouldn't run out" (that is, it couldn't be eaten or drunk). And it had to be useful! And bring joy! At last, they dragged onto the stage an enormous box, the size of a person. They removed the top lid and revealed a plaster statue inside: a slender young girl in a tunic. She stood there quite naturally in a Classical pose, until they commanded: "Forward!"

The statue came to life. It was Katya Zueva, covered in whitewash. It must be said that it hadn't been easy to talk her into playing the role.

Then she walked through the auditorium amid rousing applause, and kneeled down at Victor Shengeli's feet.

After it was all over, they removed the extra chairs from the auditorium and set up tables. The teachers were nowhere to be seen. Victor Yulievich went to the teachers' lounge to negotiate for the strikers to pick up their tools again.

They were waiting for him. Larisa Stepanovna was the first to speak.

"On behalf of the teachers' collective, Victor Yulievich, I am obliged to inform you . . ." the principal began with a triumphal air.

But Victor Yulievich quickly realized what she was going to say. He did the first thing that came to mind—he took a glasses case out of his jacket pocket, removed a pair of old-fashioned steel-rimmed glasses, perched them on his long, regularly formed nose. Then he went up to Larisa Stepanovna. He leaned down to peer at her infamous butterfly brooch pinned to the collar of her blouse, and said in a saccharine tone, "Oh my, how charming! What a dear little piglet it is!"

"Get out!" Larisa Stepanovna shouted. *In a voice scarlet with fury*, the literature teacher thought.

Strains of music sounded from the auditorium.

"Why are you all so on edge? Let's go drink some lemonade and dance. The kids are waiting for you!"

He smiled his disarming smile, while thinking to himself: *What a pompous son of a gun I was. I shouldn't have behaved like that. Why did I have to humiliate them? And poor Larisa Stepanovna, the corners of her mouth turned down, like a hurt little girl. She looked like she might start sobbing. What bad kids they were . . . But what can I do about it now? Surely not ask their forgiveness.*

The notice of termination was lying on Larisa Stepanovna's desk. She had intended to hand it to him at the end of the evening, but now was the perfect time. Her hand trembling, she shoved the fateful document across the table.

"You're fired!"

There was a knock at the door. The LORLs were looking for their teacher. They had something to give him. And it wasn't bad port, but very good Georgian wine.

FRIENDSHIP OF THE PEOPLES

It was 1957. Moscow was aflutter with anticipation: The International Youth and Student Festival was about to open. The recent high-school graduates were preparing for entrance exams to the university. In passing from the category of ordinary young person to the category of student, they also got a dispensation from compulsory military service, along with the advantages of an education. They all sweated it out from morning till night, and Victor Yulievich coached the aspiring college students. In addition to his regular private students, he tutored several of his "own" without charge.

Conscription posed no threat to the Trianon. Ilya possessed the unique gift of having flat feet, Mikha was nearsighted, and Sanya, with his crooked fingers, was unfit for handling a weapon. In short, they all had minor defects or shortcomings that disqualified them from their military obligations. Ilya studied perfunctorily. Sanya, who had applied to the Institute of Foreign Languages on the advice of his grandmother, didn't study at all, but lolled on the divan listening to music and reading books (even foreign ones). Mikha's position was the most vexed. Jews were barred from entering the philology department, and he had decided once and for all that it was the only place he wanted to study. As if that weren't problem enough, he was also the only one of them who needed a scholarship to be able to study. His relatives had pledged to help him only until he finished high school. Of course, as a last resort he could go to night school, but he so desperately wanted to experience the authentic life of a student.

"I can't understand your passion for the humanities. It's one thing to read books, to try to figure out what they mean, to enjoy them—but why do you want to make a profession out of it?" Ilya would say. He spurned philology, and made the independent decision to enroll in LIKI, the Leningrad Institute of Cinema Engineering.

Ilya had an uncle in Leningrad who had sought him out soon after his father's death. He invited Ilya to come to Leningrad to live with him until he started college. After Ilya received his high school diploma, he immediately took off for Leningrad. He had saved a considerable sum of money, earned through illicit means—fifteen hundred rubles. This was three times his mother's salary. He also intended to live it up before the semester began.

That year in Moscow, the dates of the entrance exams were shuffled around so the aspiring students wouldn't arrive all at the same time and thus inconvenience the guests in the city for the festival.

Ilya liked the Institute of Cinema Engineering immensely. His uncle Efim Semenovich said that Ilya's father had worked there before the war, and that some people might still remember him. He began to call around to various numbers; but, unfortunately, those who remembered Isay Semenovich weren't there anymore, and those who were there didn't remember him after all.

Ilya left Leningrad abruptly on the day he found out that the entrance exams would coincide with the first day of the festival. He wouldn't miss that great event for the world. He grabbed his camera and returned to Moscow, clutching his passport. He was required to show it five times, from the time he bought the one-way ticket at Moskovsky train station in Leningrad until the moment he made it home: to policemen, conductors, volunteer patrolmen, and to other random officials who demanded to see his documents. Only Muscovites were permitted entry into Moscow.

Ilya stopped over to see Mikha. Mikha had already been accepted as a student, it turned out. He hadn't been accepted to Moscow University, as he had hoped, but to the less prestigious Pedagogical Institute, where (as the story went) there were eight females for every two males—one of them lame, another one cross-eyed. Self-respecting young men without such shortcomings were not eager to enroll there.

Mikha had had no trouble getting in. His gender and his thorough academic training outweighed his unfortunate ethnicity. But his triumph was made bitter by loss: on the day he found his name on the list of successful candidates for admission, poor Minna died of pneumonia. He had never even visited her in the hospital. She suffered from pneumonia at least three times a year, and he couldn't have imagined that this bout of illness would be her last.

Now he was left alone with a dreadful secret and with the sinking feeling that this burden of guilt would stay with him until the end of his days. Slow-witted Minna was in love with him, and he had somehow become entangled in a strange sexual relationship with her. There was no other name for it, although sex in the absolute sense of the term was not what went on between them. Minna would lie in wait for him at the secluded end of the corridor, next to the WC, lure him into the corner, and press herself against him with all the warm and soft parts of her body, until he slipped away, flushed, shaking, and quite satisfied. He wanted to kill himself after every episode of fondling, and swore that next time he would push her away and flee; but he could never bring himself to refuse her. She was affectionate, soft, thrillingly hairy in places, and had a strong speech defect, a quality that protected their anonymity and guaranteed they wouldn't be found out. He was being slowly strangled with a sense of guilt and disgust, and the thought of suicide always hovered in the back of his mind. No one dared mention the unconscious in those days.

This was the state Ilya found him in. Ilya decided not to pry, but dragged him outside to get him to relax.

Moscow was uncharacteristically clean, and fairly empty. The festival was opening the next day. Through the deserted city streets, in various directions, passed motorcades of passenger automobiles, pickup trucks, some with their sides lowered, some with their sides up, old-fashioned buses—even Hungarian-made Icarus buses.

Everywhere you looked there were flags and giant paper flowers. That summer the girls were wearing full, brightly colored skirts on top of thick umbrella-like petticoats. Their waists were cinched with wide belts, and they wore their hair in "beehives."

After they managed to get through two light cordons, the boys came out into the small park in front of the Bolshoi Theater. Quite a few people were milling around. Ilya pointed out two confused-looking and not especially pretty girls to Mikha, saying: "Come on, let's pick them up!"

"No way," Mikha said, offended by the suggestion, and turned to go.

"Aw, I'm sorry, Mikha. I'm a boor! Shall we go and get drunk somewhere? Come on, let's go to the National."

Somehow they were able to get into the National. Possibly, the doorman had gone to relieve himself and had forgotten to close the latch; or maybe he was relying on the effectiveness of his sign, which read "Closed for a Special Event."

"We're drinking cognac," Ilya said confidently, and ordered doubles from the discombobulated waiter.

They drank their double cognacs with two pastries, then repeated their order. Between the first and second rounds, Mikha's spirits visibly lifted. Just then, a young man with a Hasselblad camera on a strap came up to them. He looked Russian. He asked them whether he could join them.

"Sure, go ahead," Mikha said, offering him a chair.

They immediately hit it off. He said his name was Petya. It turned out, though, that he wasn't just an ordinary Russian "Petya," but a Belgian whose real name was Pierre Zand. He was of Russian descent, a student at the University of Brussels. They split the second round three ways, then went to wander through town. On Ilya's advice, Pierre left the camera behind in the hotel room.

They strolled through the center of Moscow, and it would have been hard to imagine a better tourist than Pierre was. He recognized all the places where he had never once set foot—the reminiscences of his mother and grandmother, and a deep familiarity with Russian literature, were coming to life for him.

And the veteran LORLs were the best possible guides for Petya, with his nostalgia for a place he had never seen before.

At Trekhprudny Lane, by a small wooden house, Ilya stopped and said:

"Marina Tsvetaeva lived somewhere around here."

Pierre seemed to melt and go soft, and all but wept, saying:

"My mother knew Marina Tsvetaeva well, in Paris. They won't publish her here . . ."

"Tsvetaeva may not be published here, but we all know her," Mikha said:

> "Some are of stone, some are of clay,
> But I am silver and sparkle!
> My crime is betrayal, my name is Marina.
> I am the ephemeral foam of the sea."

"Actually, I like Akhmatova more. As for Ilya, he's obsessed with the Futurists."

But never mind their preferences. What was astounding was the fact that they were standing there with a real person, their own age, whose mother had known Marina Tsvetaeva in real life. For them, Pierre himself represented a vast, already nonexistent country that had gone into exile. While they were walking, he told them about his family, about that former Russia, which to his interlocutors seemed as insubstantial and distant as Brussels or Paris. And how bitterly Pierre hated the Bolsheviks!

Mikha and Ilya, who had often discussed the shortcomings of socialism, had for the first time met a person who didn't talk about the shortcomings of the Communist regime—rather, he raked it over the coals, condemning it as satanic, dark, and bloody. He saw no fundamental difference between communism and fascism. In some unaccountable way, Pierre was able to unite a love for Russia with a hatred of its system. For the next two weeks, they were almost inseparable. Thanks to Pierre, they all managed to cram themselves into a Belgian bus and get into the opening of the festival at Luzhniki Stadium. More than three thousand of the finest athletes bloomed in formation as a single flower, or spread themselves out in geometric patterns, hands, feet, and heads rising up or descending in perfect unison. It was a thrilling spectacle.

"They did this sort of thing at Hitler's rallies, too," whispered Pierre. "Leni Riefenstahl's films were shown all over the world. The great power of mass hypnosis. But it really is powerful to witness it! And amazing!" Pierre sighed and pressed the button on his camera. Ilya did the same.

Then there was a jazz concert, a mass relay race with torches, some water ballet, along with countless song-and-dance ensembles of the Soviet Army and Navy, industry and trade groups, and cooks' and hairdressers' labor unions.

Pierre had absolutely no interest in the Egyptians chanting "Nasser! Nasser!," the black citizens of newly independent Ghana, or the Israelis, who were also very popular among Soviet citizens branded with the same ethnicity in the "fifth line" of their passports.

On the third day of the festival, after he had recovered from another case of tonsillitis, Sanya joined them. For two more weeks they reveled, rushing around from one place to another and having fun. Mikha didn't have time to dwell on Minna.

Nor did Ilya think about his unrealized attempt to enroll in the cinema engineering program, or Sanya his thwarted career as a professional musician. All of them were enamored with Pierre, whom they nicknamed "Pierrechik," and not one of them contemplated how the foreign friend might influence their fates.

They learned that Pierre had been sent to the festival as a representative of a young people's newspaper on an assignment to photograph life in Moscow. His photographs of Moscow were superb, in large part thanks to his new friends. He photographed the bread store when fresh bread was being delivered; the river port, with its tall cranes and stevedores; kindergartens; inner courtyards, with clotheslines and sheds; girls reading in the metro; old folks standing in lines; grown men kissing and hugging; and myriad other joys and pleasures.

Fast-forward, and the photographs were rejected by the editor of the newspaper. They were deemed to be inauthentic—mere Soviet propaganda. Pierre, who could never have been accused of sympathy for the Communist regime, accused the editor of bias, and they quarreled.

On the day before Pierre's departure, they all went to Gorky Park together to drink beer. There was a wonderful Czech beer garden, masquerading as a restaurant. The line stretched all the way around the place, like foam around the rim of a beer mug, but they obediently went to stand at the tail end of it—they were in no hurry.

They had planned a rendezvous there with someone—a distant relative of Pierre's, the second or third cousin of his mother, who was working in Moscow in the French embassy. Standing in line was not in the least dull; exciting things kept happening all around them. First a group of people on stilts galloped past, followed by a procession of Scottish bagpipers, Mexicans with maracas in their hands, and costumed Ukrainians.

Sanya and Mikha saved their place in line, while Ilya and Pierre kept darting off to get a good shot of something or other. They managed to capture a fight that broke out between a powerful, stocky black man and a Scot wearing a green-and-white kilt from some obscure clan. The fighters were surrounded by a crowd of boisterous people egging them on:

"Kill the blackie!"

"Nail the faggot!"

In short, the people amused themselves in the ancient and time-honored tradition of gladiatorial fights. Strains of Soloviev-Sedoy's ubiquitous "Moscow Nights" were heard in the background as they battled—it was a song you heard everywhere you went that summer.

The black man threw the deciding blow, and the Scotsman crumpled into his skirt.

The music changed. "The youth will strike up a song of friendship, you cannot strangle it, you cannot kill it . . ."

The Scot stirred. "You cannot kill it, you cannot kill it," the loudspeaker blared.

Two hours later, when the boys had already entered the pub, Pierre's uncle found them. He was a Frenchman by the name of Nikolay Ivanovich, with the Russian surname Orlov. He was aging, pink, and rotund, reminiscent of the merry little pig Nif-Nif. He spoke in the Petersburg slang of another age. His clothes were funny—a straw hat and a Ukrainian peasant blouse with an embroidered collar—like Khrushchev's. No one would ever have suspected that he was a foreigner. He resembled a provincial accountant with a small, tattered briefcase.

As soon as Pierre set eyes on him, he roared with laughter.

"What a getup!"

Pierre introduced the boys to his uncle so that they could keep in touch through him.

They didn't trust the postal system. They exchanged phone numbers. It went without saying that they could make calls to him only from public pay phones. They agreed that they would continue to rendezvous at this same place by the Czech restaurant so that they wouldn't have to risk saying anything over the phone.

So began their illicit dealings with a foreigner.

The famous Czech beer was a pilsener served in sweaty mugs, evidence that it was the ideal temperature. Of course, those mugs were on the neighboring tables. By the time their little group had entered the pub, the Czech beer had run out. The sausages were also gone. The waiters were serving Zhigulevskoe beer, a local brand, with salted pretzels, a hitherto unknown treat. At the adjacent table, they had smuggled in dried fish, which they were picking at like lint, and pouring vodka into their beer—under the table.

The friends wanted to take photographs, but it was, first, too risky, and, second, too dark.

Mysteriously, the Czech beer suddenly reappeared, and they had to drink another two mugs each. They left sated and happy. As a parting gift Pierre gave Ilya his Hasselblad. Actually, he had first offered to exchange it for Ilya's Fedya, but Ilya wouldn't think of it.

"It was a gift from my father; it's not a thing, but a part of my life."

Then Pierre removed the strap from around his neck, and said: "I understand. Here. It's yours."

Uncle Orlov gave them his accountant's briefcase. It was laden with books. By the metro they parted ways, in different directions. Ilya and Pierre had decided to go on foot to the center of town. Orlov also went on foot, but in the opposite direction. He lived on Oktyabrskaya Square.

Mikha was carrying Orlov's briefcase full of books. He and Sanya went down into the metro. The revels were still in full swing, though the festival had formally ended.

Happy, drunken crowds, somewhat the worse for wear after two weeks of festivities, were spending their last evening together.

The foreigners, who had temporarily brightened up the Moscow cityscape, were few. They had most likely gone to pack their suitcases, sleep, exchange their last gifts, sell the remainder of their hard currency, and give and receive their final kisses from the Soviet girls who had discovered the wonders of an affair with an Austrian, a Swede, or a citizen of independent Ghana.

The friendship of the peoples had triumphed. In spite of years of inculcation of the opposite view, it turned out that foreigners were decent people—they weren't capitalists at all, but Communists and their sympathizers. Like Picasso the dove painter, and the progressive Federico Fellini.

Sanya and Mikha sat till deep in the night on a bench in the yard of the Vanity Chest house on Chernyshevsky Street, talking about the improving social mores and habits of Russia, praising Khrushchev, who had "opened" the iron curtain. Then they began talking about more personal matters: Mikha informed Sanya about what he had explained in so many words to the mocking Ilya—about poor Minna, about their impure relations, about the bitter aftertaste he would now have to suffer his entire life.

Sanya nodded in silence. He had always imagined this secret between men and women to be dirty and at the same time vulgarly attractive. He couldn't fathom it—there were no words for it.

The two friends grieved, grumbled, and moaned, and then parted ways.

Outside, echoes of "Moscow Nights" still hovered in the air: "Not a whisper is heard in the garden, all grows still till morn, if you only knew how dear they are to me, these Moscow nights . . ."

Mikha forgot about the brown briefcase with the books under the bench. Sanya didn't remember it, either.

Uncle Fedor, the street sweeper, immortalized subsequently by Yuly Kim, sobered up suddenly and went out to sweep the yard. He found the briefcase—there was nothing interesting in it. Just some books. He turned them in to the local police.

The parents of the stout Orlov's former wife considered him to be a complete dolt, and they were very disturbed by his appointment to the diplomatic mission in Moscow. He was the first one in their family to cross the border of the Motherland in the wrong direction after 1918.

The briefcase contained a priceless gift—six volumes of *The Journal of the Russian Christian Student Movement*, and Orwell's *Nineteen Eighty-four*, which had just been translated into Russian and published by Posev. It was unfortunate that the boys would read the book with a five-year delay, and only in a poor copy. The real misfortune, however, was that in a side compartment of the briefcase there was a letter from Masha, the wife who had left him. It had been sent in the diplomatic mail pouch. Orlov's name was on the envelope, and it proved to be no problem to hunt him down.

The festival was over. The girls who were pregnant with brown-skinned babies had not had time to realize it, but Orlov was already in trouble. Luckily, they didn't throw him in prison; but he was expelled from the country forthwith. His diplomatic career was over. His ex-wife and her parents now had indisputable proof that Nikolay Ivanovich was an absolute dolt, and that so he would remain.

But the boys came off unscathed.

THE BIG GREEN TENT

Dear little Olga, like a lovely pinkish-yellow onion bulb, slightly plump in her silky transparent skin, unmarked and smooth, was pleasing to men and women, cats and dogs alike. How was it that she, so healthy and cheerful, with her dimpled smile, had been born to such dour, aging parents, career Party officials whose services to the state were both significant and highly confidential, and who enjoyed all the outward signs of official favor: medals and decorations, private automobiles, a dacha in the Generals' Compound, and groceries delivered to their door in brown paper bags and cardboard boxes through a closed distribution network?

Even more remarkable was how credulously, in what good faith, she absorbed all the good things they told her, and failed to notice the bad things they did. She grew up honest and principled, always putting collective concerns first, and personal concerns second. From her parents she inherited a hatred for the rich (where were they, anyway?), as well as respect for the working man (or woman)—Faina Ivanovna, their housekeeper, for example, or Nikolai Ignatievich, who chauffeured her father's official Volga automobile, not to mention Evgeny Borisovich, the chauffeur of her mother's gray one.

How joyfully easy it was to be a good Soviet girl! The Artek Pioneer

Camp, with its blue nights and red bandanas, was perfectly in keeping with the closed grocery distributor; and her parents' private cars, which dropped her off at the dacha on Saturdays, were not in the least incompatible with equality and brotherhood. She was guilty of nothing, before no one, and she loved Lenin-Stalin-Khrushchev-Brezhnev, the Motherland, and the Party, with a love both joyous and serene. She was morally stable and highly politically aware, as was noted in her letter of recommendation upon entering the Komsomol in seventh grade.

Afanasy Mikhailovich, Olga's father, worked in the Army Construction Corps, and her mother was the editor of a magazine that had more to do with upbringing than with literature.

Antonina Naumovna, her mother (the descendant of Orthodox believers who named their children after the calendar of saints, and not in the least Jewish), had graduated from the Institute of Philosophy and Literature, and was thus practically a writer. Olga was being equipped, according to her parents' wishes, to study in the philology department at Moscow State University.

The first year of university did not portend any ill. The girl eagerly carried out her mandatory stint of social volunteer work, was elected to the Komsomol committee board, studied zealously and with fine results, and acquired a fiancé—an upstanding young man. He was from a military family—a smart fellow, not a philologist, but a student at the Aviation Institute. Senior year. Antonina Naumovna liked Vova, as he was called—he was broad-shouldered, tallish, with fair hair that fell in a wave on his forehead. He was always immaculately clean and wore a hand-knitted reindeer sweater; but in winter he wore a leather bomber jacket, the epitome of chic in the 1930s, which made a strong impression on Antonina Naumovna.

The wedding took place after Olga had completed her first year of study, at the beginning of June so that Olga wouldn't eventually "rue the day" by marrying in May, as Faina Ivanovna, the housekeeper—a true fountain of folk wisdom—warned.

Vova moved into the general's apartment, into Olga's room. The apartment easily accommodated one more person, though they did invest in another, wider bed. Strange as it might seem, it was the general who bought it. Olga refused point-blank to take part in such an ambiguous shopping expedition, and Antonina Naumovna was up to her ears in preparations for yet another congress of Soviet teachers; or was it Soviet doctors? Afanasy Mikhailovich recalled that he had seen a furniture store on Smolenskaya Embankment, and told his wife that he would buy the bed. He went there after work. The store turned out to specialize in antiques. The general wandered among the pieces of furniture of all times and nations, and thought about his grandfather, a mahogany carver. He hadn't thought about him for some fifty years, and, suddenly, amid the flimsy bamboo whatnots, the monumental writing desks with their secret drawers, the new forest growth of white-and-gold empire chairs and love seats, a scraggly old man, small of stature, with massive blackish brown hands, and sharp eyes with delicate, watery pouches underneath, came back to life. And the smell of his grandfather's workshop struck his nostrils—turpentine, spirits, lacquer—so thick and palpable he could almost taste it. He remembered how his grandfather had taught him, still a little tyke, to sand, to strip, and polish . . .

Afanasy Mikhailovich walked and walked, forgetting why he had come. Then he remembered, and bought a Karelian birch double bed, the work of a peasant craftsman with an imaginative bent, not thinking for a minute about the two young Komsomol members, who loved sleeping under the stars in tents and would now have to labor for the future between ornate little scrolls and columns, watched over by four cherubs.

The bed, with all its whimsical splendor, made a strong impression; but it didn't get in the way of business—his grandson Konstantin was born exactly ten lunar months after the wedding day.

But the general, after that first visit to the antiques store, had begun frequenting it. To the surprise of Antonina Naumovna, he gradually started exchanging their sturdy, Stalin-era furniture for intricate, inspired pieces of ancient vintage that he would refurbish himself.

Afanasy Mikhailovich was older than his wife by ten years. She had long begun to sense the approach of old age in him, and she viewed this new passion of his as an old man's eccentricity—albeit a fairly harmless one. He fitted out a workshop for himself at the dacha, and puttered around in it happily; meanwhile, his military bravura and political acumen, which his wife had always admired, diminished by the day.

Antonina Naumovna was not particularly thrilled about the birth of a child so early in the marriage. Olga was not yet nineteen when they brought the bundle, wrapped up in a blue silk receiving blanket tied with a blue ribbon, home with them from the maternity hospital. The little bundle turned out to be exemplary, just like its parents: it ate, slept, and pooped like clockwork, made everyone smile, and permitted Olga to continue her literary studies without even taking maternity leave until the child learned to walk.

Faina Ivanovna, who had worked in the family since the war ended and had raised Olga from infancy, had planned to leave after the birth of the child—to work for another family of only two people, who had long been courting her, and where there would be less work—but the baby, Kostya, so captured her heart that she stayed with him until her own death.

Toward the end of her university studies, in which Olga excelled, something happened that would shatter the family's world. Olga, herself so pure and good, had succumbed to a degenerate influence at the university. One of her teachers, secretly anti-Soviet and an enemy, it went without saying, of the people, was arrested for libel published abroad. Olga and some fellow students, misguided fools, signed a letter in his defense.

As a consequence, she and the other signees were kicked out of the university. Antonina Naumovna repented of ever having sent her daughter to the university, but it was already too late. If he had known that her venerable education would turn out this way, Olga's courageous and manly father would doubtless have quoted, if only loosely: "Who increases his knowledge, increases his sorrows." He didn't know Ecclesiastes, however, and for that reason, when the pernicious influence of a university education affected his daughter so dramatically, he told his wife with bitterness:

"This is what all your university nonsense leads to. I told you that we should live more simply, closer to the people. The girl's brains have been warped . . . if we had enrolled her in an engineering school, she wouldn't have picked up any of that rot . . . they would have left the girl alone."

And Afanasy Mikhailovich was most likely right about this. From time immemorial, the university had been a source of intellectual ferment, and the general condemned this not out of his sense of duty to the Party, but from personal conviction.

"Everyone is such a know-it-all," he said angrily, each time he was faced with something he didn't understand. And he was more and more baffled by his own daughter. She spoke about even the simplest of matters in such a way that it sounded like nonsense, just to confuse him, it seemed. His son-in-law, to give him credit, did not share Olga's views. They quarreled now and then—about politics, since there was nothing else to complain about. They had everything they could possibly need: a nanny, a country house, grocery delivery service . . . and yet the situation got so bad that Vova slammed the door behind him one day, and left to go live with his parents.

If Olga had listened to her parents, if she had repented at the university meeting, cried, and signed a recantation, which is what they had demanded, her expulsion could have been avoided. However, as we know, she had been raised to be honest and principled—her parents had instilled this in her since childhood—and for this reason she refused outright to repent, to admit her mistakes, and to denounce that scum of a teacher, who was also her thesis adviser.

The teacher was arrested at the beginning of September, and Olga was summoned for the first interrogation at the end of the month. The honest girl told the whole truth, and nothing but the truth. What else could she have done? Her truth consisted in the fact that the teacher was, indeed, an outstanding scholar; that he was critical of many aspects of Soviet life, and his criticism was warranted; and that she, as his student, fully shared his views on literature and life.

Her testimony did no great harm to the arrested man, but her parents paid dearly for their daughter's mistakes. Afanasy Mikhailovich was summoned to a secret place for a very serious conversation, where they put the screws on him (figuratively speaking). Soon afterward, he submitted his resignation and moved to the dacha. In his heart of hearts, he even felt glad about the changes. He liked living outside of town, where he could carry on the tradition of his family craft. While he nursed a quiet hurt and resentment toward his daughter, he didn't allow his domestic troubles to poison his mood or elevate his blood pressure. What's more, he had another diversion.

Antonina Naumovna, on the other hand, struck a preemptive blow. Even before the higher-ups could get together to shake their collective fingers at her for the way she had raised her child, she managed to publish a vicious article about the former teacher's libelous book, and offered to testify as a citizen prosecutor at the trial of the miscreant. After this, her relationship with her daughter foundered once and for all.

Olga felt like a stranger in her own home. She never told anyone anything about herself; she came and went, sometimes taking Kostya out for a walk, sometimes disappearing altogether for a day or two. In February the trial of the teacher and his friend, also a frustrated writer, who had sent their manuscripts to the West for publication, got under way.

Olga would go to the Krasnopresnensky District Courthouse to assume her place in the crowd of young men and women, whose faces all bore intelligent and daring expressions. They all seemed to know one another. Sometimes someone would take a bottle out of his briefcase, or a flask out of his pocket, and pass it around. At these moments Olga felt lonely and unhappy: they never offered it to her. One day, when she stepped into an eatery next to the courthouse, more for the warmth than from hunger, she found herself at a table with this group of people. They accepted her as one of their own when she told them that the accused was her teacher and adviser, and that she had been kicked out of the university because of it.

A tall young man whom she had noticed before in the crowd—because, despite the bitter frost, his head was bare and his curls were dusted with snow, and he pulled out a camera now and then, and thrust pieces of paper at someone occasionally, and had once been packed into a paddy wagon and taken away right in front of their eyes—this very same young man handed her a glass of vodka directly underneath a warning sign that said bringing in and drinking alcoholic beverages on the premises was strictly forbidden. She drank almost half the glass.

And happiness arrived at that very moment. Happiness smelled like overcooked dumplings and damp fur coats and hats, with a slight tinge of chlorine and a whiff of stale alcohol. It smelled of danger and daring; and Olga felt that the group of sympathizers with the accused had finally accepted her. The feeling reminded her of the collective childhood joy of Young Pioneer gatherings, sparks floating above a campfire under electric blue skies, Komsomol trips to harvest potatoes, and singing songs there and back on the commuter train. Only it was clear that all she had experienced in her childhood had just been a substitute, a prelude, to this genuine unity of intelligent, serious, and courageous people. They looked like true comrades, and they clapped one another on the shoulders, sometimes exploding with laughter, but more often whispering something in secret. The most attractive person at the table was the tall, curly-haired one. They called him Ilya. He was also the one in charge of the vodka.

And so it happened that Olga's family continued to live its former life, and Olga found herself in a completely new one. The trial ended, the anti-Soviets received the prison sentences they had earned and were sent off to serve their terms. And the group of people that had gathered in the courtyard of the Krasnopresnensky District Courthouse grew even closer.

The word *dissident* had still not entered the Russian language, and the term "men of the sixties" was still associated only with the followers of Chernyshevsky in the previous century; but inside astute and reflective minds, thoughts—quiet as worms and dangerous as spirochetes—were taking shape. Ilya expounded on them to Olga in a form she could grasp during the intervals between their embraces, which took place in the room on Arkhipov Street. This was where Ilya had lived with his mother before he had gotten married; and even afterward, he never completely moved out. He took Olga there from time to time, only during the early hours of the day, as his mother worked as a kindergarten nurse from eight to three.

Ilya had known the imprisoned teacher well. He knew almost all the people who had gathered in front of the court. Moreover, he knew everything there was to know, period; and especially what was written in the fine print. He even created the impression that the smaller the print, the more interesting it was for him. He was especially knowledgeable about what was left out of college textbooks. He gleaned his information from the libraries where he buried himself during his school years and after. To Olga's great surprise, the erudite Ilya did not even have a college degree. He had graduated from high school, but hadn't wanted to work for the government; and to avoid being persecuted by the state for "parasitism," he began to work as a secretary for some professor (a job that existed only on paper).

Olga and Ilya's romance unfolded for the most on foot, during strolls through the sacred sites of Moscow's literary past, which Ilya knew well. He would stop in front of a crooked little house with a lopsided porch and tell her: "This house survived the great fire of 1812. Vyazemsky used to frequent it . . . And here, Mandelstam stayed, with his brother . . . Bulgakov's wife, Elena Sergeevna, use to stop by this pharmacy to get medicines for her husband . . ."

But the subject he knew most about was the Futurists, and the whole Russian avant garde. He used to spend hours at the counters of antiquarian booksellers, where he also knew everyone, and they knew him, paging through thin volumes printed on damp gray paper. Sometimes he bought them, sometimes he would only smack his lips in delight. Once he made Olga run home to borrow a hundred rubles from her parents so he could buy a rare edition of Khlebnikov.

Thus the year passed, and they continued to stroll through the streets and lanes, drinking with friends of Ilya's, all of whom were special, like a select group: one a music historian, another a jockey, a third a park ranger whom they went to visit on the Oka River, and yet another, a real Orthodox priest. The sweetest one was a redheaded teacher of deaf-and-dumb children. Olga had never realized how many interesting people there were in the world, and how different they were from one another, all of them with their distinctive philosophies and religions. There was even a Buddhist! Olga read books, and it was like getting a second university education, but much more interesting; and the books Ilya gave her to read were either antique or had been smuggled in from abroad. Once he even asked Olga to translate a book from French—a Catholic book, about miracles at Lourdes.

They were so happy together that Olga found it hard to believe he had a wife somewhere, to whom he would return late in the evening.

Then something changed in his family life. He went to see his wife in Timiryazevka less and less often, until he finally moved back into his mother's communal apartment for good. He introduced Olga to the quiet Maria Fedorovna.

The more distant Olga grew from her parents, the closer Vova grew to them. He would visit on Sundays, and Faina Ivanovna, the nanny, would deliver his son, all dressed to go out and play, into his safekeeping. They would spend the afternoon together, then return in time for dinner. Vova fed his son himself, put him to bed, and then had a meal with his parents-in-law. They pressed him to stay for the meal each time, and each time he made as if to refuse, wanting them to know that he didn't visit because of the special (though not extravagant) Sunday meal; and it wasn't Faina Ivanovna's plump, undersalted pies that kept him coming week after week, but family.

Olga was absent on Sundays, and they usually didn't mention her. She was a sore spot for all of them, and they shared the same sense of injury, bewilderment, and inexplicable betrayal. The abandoned husband also suffered from a young man's wounded pride. To his honor, it must be said that he only took his first lover two years after their separation, when Olga demanded a divorce. Until that moment he had felt himself to be a married man, away on an exceedingly long business trip. He maintained a senseless fidelity and paid forty rubles in alimony each month, which no one had asked him for. He kept thinking that Olga would come to her senses and they would pick up their married life where they had left off, when their conjugal life had faltered . . .

When she found out that Olga had filed for divorce, Antonina Naumovna fell into a quiet rage. But she knew how to restrain herself; her passion seethed in the deepest part of her. The more she restrained herself, the tighter her jaw clamped shut, and the more her pale eyes seemed to bulge in their sockets. She didn't say a word to Olga, and she didn't let off steam at home; she knew how to unleash her fury at the editorial office. Her subordinates quaked: one of them resigned from fright, and the secretary, who was devoted to Antonina Naumovna heart and soul, suffered a ministroke.

Since his retirement, Afanasy Mikhailovich had quietly reveled in his uncomplicated existence. He was not as emotionally high-strung

as his wife, and he was somewhat reluctant to expurgate his daughter
from his life; he simply set her aside. Unlike Antonina Naumovna, he
refused to let his suffering get the better of him.

Evidently, Olga herself sensed her father's weakness. He was the
first one in whom she confided about her changing circumstances, not
her mother. But this was a calculated move.

In the middle of February, Olga moved to the dacha. She arrived
on the bus like an ordinary person. On a weekday; not in the morning,
nor in the evening—but after midday. They had just delivered her
father a meal from a nearby military sanatorium where he had a voucher:
a three-course meal and a delicious sweet roll from their own bakery.
Afanasy Mikhailovich was just busying himself with the lunch pails
when Olga showed up. He was glad to see her—it had been a long time,
and the memory of the family quarrel was fading. She was cheerful,
just like her old self. She shared her father's meal without balking, and
even joined him in a preprandial drink. After their lunch she put her
feet up on the leather armchair with the aluminum tag on the neck
rest. There were still vestiges of the government-issue furniture that
the general had purchased for mere kopecks when he bought the dacha, and Olga chose this monstrosity, so familiar to her from childhood, over her father's refurbished antiques, made entirely of wood,
and devoid of softness and coziness, all of them from the same antiques
store where he had found her bed.

"Daddy," Olga said, calling him by her childhood name for him,
"I want to live at the dacha with you. I could bring Kostya, too. What
do you think?"

Afansy Mikhailovich felt a surge of happiness. He didn't even suspect that there might be a catch.

"Sure, live here as long as you like, why bother to ask? But what
about work? It will be hard to get around without a car . . ."

Traveling back and forth to the city was complicated: to Nakhabino by bus, which didn't run on schedule, but according to whim, and
from Nakhabino by commuter train to Rizhskaya Station.

"It's no problem for me," Olga said, laughing. "I don't work, I study."

Afanasy brightened: his wife hadn't told him that Olga had gone
back to school. But his joy was short-lived. Olga was not studying in

the university, she was taking evening courses in Spanish, for some reason. She didn't have classes every day. And she didn't intend to re-enroll at the university.

Afanasy Mikhailovich was weighing all of this in his mind, trying to understand why his daughter had suddenly taken a notion to make this change, and wondering how his wife would react to it, and whether he should have discussed the matter with her first, before agreeing to it. But Olga cut through the confusion abruptly.

"My friend might come here to live, too."

The old general choked with indignation: she had divorced without asking them, and now she had taken a lover, whom she wanted to bring home with her, and she was asking for her father's blessing! But, after a moment of silence, he relented.

"Go ahead, live with whoever you want. Why should I care?"

He frowned, consumed the last of his government-issue meat patty, and went to carry out his postprandial ritual—a nap.

Several days later, an old Pobeda drove into the general's huge property. Out of it tumbled Kostya in a sheepskin coat, a puppy that seemed to be dressed in an identical fur coat, Olga, with a pile of books in her arms, and a tall, shaggy-looking man with a pair of skis.

The windows of Afanasy Mikhailovich's workshop, where he was engrossed in his wood, were on another side of the house, and he didn't see them arrive on the porch, jostling one another, falling down in the snow, and dropping mittens and books along the way.

When he went to answer the doorbell, he saw what appeared to him to be a whole crowd, after the seclusion of his dacha life. Kostya was shrieking, the dog was barking, Olga was laughing artificially, and over all of this mayhem loomed a tall, gangly man—whom the general instantly recognized to be the root of all the evil.

This evil root was Ilya Bryansky. He extended a bony, lean hand. He smelled of cheap tobacco, some familiar chemical reagent, and veiled hostility. Olga also smelled different—audacious and alien. Only his grandson, Kostya, and the mutt of a puppy seemed like his own. But Afanasy Mikhailovich didn't indulge in analyzing his feelings. He kissed his daughter and grandson and went back upstairs to the second floor, to take up his handiwork again. The smell of varnish, carpenter's glue, and sawdust soothed him more effectively than valerian. He took the finest grade of sandpaper and began to rub the side of a chair, removing the offensive layer of varnish, and his hand delighted in the curvy smoothness of the scroll that supported the armrest.

From downstairs he heard explosive laughter, snorting and guffaws, trailing off into groans and squealing—sounds not at all befitting a quiet, well-mannered household.

How brazen she is—showing up here with her lover and her son in tow, acting like it's nothing, thought the general.

They began to live in two households, under one roof. Afanasy Mikhailovich, on his military sanatorium provisions, carried on according to his habitual schedule: rising at seven, dinner at eight, bed at eleven. Olga's family lived any which way. They would sometimes throw together some insubstantial meal, but mostly just eat sandwiches. All day long they opened and closed the refrigerator. They got up and went to bed when it pleased them, and not by the clock. They would take walks, drink tea in the middle of the night, sleep till all hours, laugh and bang on the typewriter till dawn. And they worked erratically, too. Sometimes they left for work in the morning, sometimes in the middle of the day. Olga left for her evening courses at four and returned on the last bus. Ilya would pick her up at the bus stop. Sometimes with Kostya. But why take the child out at night, in the bitter cold?

Although, it was true, they never left Kostya alone—they took turns going out. And if they would be gone overnight, they called on Faina Ivanovna. During the past two months, they had asked Afanasy Mikhailovich to look after Kostya only once. He had taken him up to his workshop, and the child had lent him a hand. He was a smart boy.

On Saturdays, Antonina Naumovna arrived in the gray Volga, laden with cake and groceries. She organized the Sunday family dinner. The new fiancé avoided running into her for a long time; when the weekend rolled around, he would make himself scarce. Only at the beginning of April did they finally meet. Antonina's anticipatory hostility was not misplaced: she didn't like him. How could she? Except for his curly head of hair. But otherwise—his face was gaunt, his nose was like a crow's beak, his lips were thick and red, like he was feverish.

He cut an absurd figure: narrow shoulders, spindly legs; he looked like he might snap in two at the waist. His trousers were tight, and they bulged out in front, as if they were well-packed. But he was a scrawny little runt! Ugh.

Antonina nodded, pursing her lips.

"Pleased to meet you. I'm Antonina Naumovna."

"Ilya."

"And your last name?

"Ilya Isayevich Bryansky," he said.

Bryansky is just Bryansky, Antonina Naumovna reasoned, bringing her accumulated expertise in categorizing personnel to bear. But Isayevich! Only priests and Jews were named after prophets . . . and Old Believers. She knew this issue inside and out, having had to defend herself on this count her whole life.

But what did the girl see in him? She had traded Vova, such a decent sort, and a good husband, for this scraggly beanpole. And, what was worse, Kostya couldn't take his eyes off him, and crawled up and down him like he was some sort of human tree.

When they were at the table, the young family started giggling. Antonina Naumovna noticed that Ilya had tossed a little ball of bread onto Kostya's plate, and Kostya sprinkled salt on his, as if by chance. Olga sat there with a dumb grin on her face, screwing up her eyes . . . Ilya ate two pieces of the cake. He licked the cream off the top, like a cat. And he ate up the rest of Kostya's. And he sucked on his spoon. Disgusting! Afanasy shouldn't have allowed them to move in. Let them fend for themselves; they've had it far too easy in life. And a spiteful dry tear clouded her eye . . .

Olga's poor parents couldn't imagine what on earth this unprepossessing suitor was up to, why the typewriter keys clattered ceaselessly into the night, and why he always had to rush off, abandoning the peaceful luxuries of the dacha. But Olga knew: she was the one who typed all the anti-Sovietism from the onionskin paper. Granted, Olga was not entrusted with any sizable texts. She had neither the speed nor the skill for that. She opted for the poetry, most often Osip Mandelstam and Joseph Brodsky. She considered this to be a kind of community service. The thick books were passed on to more dexterous typists, who were paid for the work—either Galya Polukhina, a girl-hood friend, or Vera Leonidovna, a professional typist.

Sometimes Ilya delivered the pages to his friend Artur, to be bound, and sometimes he distributed them just as they were. Artur made lovely volumes of poetry covered in chintz. Books of a religious nature were bound appropriately—in leatherette or plain calico. It wasn't easy to pin him down, though. He forgot about what he had agreed to do, and when it was expected to be finished. Ilya made a living from samizdat. Contrary to most of these other heirs of Gutenberg, his intellectual contemporaries, he felt no moral qualms about material compensation. He expected to be well paid for his time and effort, and he invested his earnings in his photography and his expanding archive.

What an abundance of poems there was! What lyrical abundance! Never before nor after had there been such a time in Russia. Verses filled the airless space, and themselves became the air people breathed—albeit "stolen air," in the words of Mandelstam. The Nobel Prize, it seemed, was not the supreme literary honor. Rather, it was the honor of being printed and read on these dry, rustling pages, crudely typed or handwritten, full of misprints and errors, sometimes barely legible—conferred on Tsvetaeva, Akhmatova, Mandelstam, Pasternak, Solzhenitsyn, and, finally, Brodsky.

"Our high-school literature teacher, Victor Yulievich Shengeli, is someone you ought to meet. You'd really like him. He hasn't taught for a long time, though. He works in some museum—trying to escape notice."

The Soviet authorities persecuted the unemployed, including those whom they themselves banned from official employment. The "parasite" Joseph Brodsky had already been released from exile in the village of Norenskaya, but no one could have anticipated that fifty years hence, a memorial room would be established in the local library in his name, and that a down-at-the-heels woman in her waning years would show people around, calling the tour "Brodsky in Norenskaya."

Olga became more and more adept at translation. She had studied French at university, and Spanish at night school. She picked up Italian as well, studying it on her own in the commuter train on the way to and from the dacha. She made connections, and was sometimes asked to translate film scripts, a task she was very good at. She did other forms of moonlighting—writing research papers, patents. Her earnings were meager at first, but they grew steadily. These jobs were all "unofficial," of course—officially she was registered as a research assistant, like Ilya. This was a front used by many people at the time.

After the death of his former father-in-law, Ilya found someone else who would register him as an assistant. For Olga, he found an old professor willing to take her on as a secretary. They both joined some sketchy labor union that seemed tailor-made for people trying to evade the Soviet authorities.

At the dacha, Ilya rigged up a darkroom in the broom closet next to the bathroom. He ran a pipe from the WC into the broom closet, just as he had done back in his school days, and performed his magic there during the nights. Afanasy Mikhailovich didn't notice a thing, since he bathed only on Saturdays. The rest of the week he never so much as glanced at the bathroom or the broom closet.

What happy years they had together! Ilya divorced his first wife. Eventually, without much fuss or bother, he and Olga got married. Olga devoted herself to him heart and soul. Everything he said or did was fascinating and unprecedented: samizdat, photography, travel—he adored the Russian Far North, the Central Asian south, and often set out for the back of beyond. Sometimes he took Olga and Kostya along with him.

Once they took a trip to the region around Vologda—to Belozersk and Ferapontovo. Kostya remembered this long afterward as a magical journey. Everything that happened, every hour of every day, stayed in his memory like a movie he could watch at will—how they went fishing in a rowboat, and slept in a hayloft; and how they climbed the scaffolding surrounding the monastery and he nearly plunged to his death, only Ilya grabbed hold of his jacket just in the nick of time and saved him. And the horribly amusing story of the bee that he ate along with a piece of homemade jam pie, and how Ilya fished the pie right out of his mouth, and then plucked the stinger deftly from his lip.

Olga had other memories: of the vanishing frescoes of the icon painter Dionysius, the crumbling monastery, and the slow, somnolent beauty of the north, which, from that very first sunset, shimmering and pellucid, she recognized as her true home.

It was here, near Vologda, that she finally came to terms with her keen disappointment in her parents' ideals, in the whole edifice of power and authority of the country she was born in, in the country itself, with its cruel and inhuman regulations and customs. Now she was overcome by a new and heart-wrenching love for this austere, impoverished north, where her father had been born. Her heart leapt to her throat when she watched the late-evening sun sink into the big lake, and saw how the crimson sky gradually gave way to silver, and how this silver spread over everything else, in turn—the fields, the water, the air. This greenish-silver hue was also a revelation of this journey, and it was Ilya who first noticed it, and spoke of it.

During these years the general ensconced himself in his workshop for good, leaving it only rarely. Olga's mother was afraid of losing her position at the magazine, but no one tried to remove her: she was a Party-hack writer, a real bigwig.

When Kostya started school, they moved to the Moscow apartment and Antonina Naumovna began staying overnight at the dacha more and more often. The official automobile went back and forth twice a day, nearly every day—dropping her off and picking her up again.

When they had been together ten years, their marriage started to falter.

Ilya became nervous and importunate: his playful effervescence changed to gloominess. At the beginning of 1980 he announced to Olga that they would have to leave the country. They had been talking about it for a long time, but only in a perfunctory way. Suddenly, out of the blue, Ilya started treating it as a matter of grave urgency.

"I'll request an invitation for the whole family. If you don't want to come with me, we'll have to get a divorce."

"Of course I want to go with you. But think about it—Vova will never let Kostya leave, if only to spite me. When he turns eighteen it won't be an issue any longer; we won't need Vova's permission." Olga thought Ilya was being unreasonable and demanding. They hadn't left ten years ago—what was the big hurry now?

Ilya insisted and kept trying to rush things along. Olga met with her ex-husband to discuss it. It was no go. Vova proved to be as intransigent as she had anticipated. It even surprised her how mule-headed he was. He flatly refused to let her have her way, and even gave her a piece of his mind.

Olga begged Ilya to wait another year. He was in a feverish haste: they had to leave; it was now or never. And he had reason to be nervous about his situation. Unpleasant rumors about him were making the rounds, and he was afraid Olga would get wind of them. One day, almost on the spur of the moment, he announced, without going into much detail, that if Olga couldn't go with him because of Kostya, they would have to divorce immediately.

For Olga this was akin to a disaster—but a strange one, somehow unnecessary, or avoidable. It wasn't at all clear why Ilya was so adamant about leaving all of a sudden. If they waited a year, Kostya could go with them. Many of their friends had already emigrated to all corners of the earth. There really wasn't any hurry.

Finally, things broke down, and they filed for a divorce. Now a honeymoon began, only in reverse. The expectation of having to part ways—for one year? maybe two?—lent a bittersweet poignancy to their relations. Even Kostya was overcome by these tangled emotions. He had reached the age when he should have felt most alienated from his parents, but he clung to Ilya so stubbornly that he proved a constant threat to their solitude and emotional intimacy.

In these trying circumstances, their love reached such a fever pitch that their nocturnal passion destroyed the last boundaries between them—they made crazy vows to each other, oaths and promises so outlandish and unrealizable that they seemed to be fifteen years old rather than forty. They swore that no matter what obstacles arose, they would devote the rest of their lives to reuniting with each other.

The mechanism of departure was set in motion. The process was an unusually speedy one. Two weeks after submitting his documents, Ilya received permission to leave. He flew by the conventional route:

through Vienna, then on to anywhere in the world. He had his sights set on America. A place far away.

His going-away party was held at the apartment of some friends. The general's apartment in Moscow wasn't suitable for any number of reasons.

The send-off was noisy, with peaks and valleys of emotion— sometimes it felt like a funeral, sometimes like a birthday party. In a way it was both.

At Sheremetyevo Airport, Ilya stood out in the crowd of people who were abandoning the country forever. They were nervous, sweaty, and burdened with children, the elderly, and piles of luggage. He wore a serene expression and carried no luggage. He had sent his collection of books ahead of him in a diplomatic mail pouch, arranged through a friend who worked at an embassy. The same friend had also sent the negatives from Ilya's photo archive. Colonel Chibikov was unlikely to have been privy to this information.

Many facts remained obscure. Why, for example, had Chibikov, who was by then already a general, helped him to emigrate? What did he stand to gain by it? Was Ilya's job at Radio Liberty a happy escape into freedom or a continuation of the ambiguous game he was mixed up in until the moment of his death?

It was unlikely that anyone would ever know.

Ilya receded into the black hole that yawned beyond the border guards. A camera with no film dangled from his neck—the film had been confiscated by the officials. A half-empty backpack was slung over his shoulder. In it was a change of underwear and an English grammar book, which he had been carrying around with him for two years.

During the night, after Ilya's departure, Olga started bleeding profusely. She was taken to the hospital in an ambulance. The illness, which had in fact begun long before, had chosen this day to manifest itself.

The first year of Ilya's absence was marked by feverish correspondence as well as bouts of fever. Olga lost her appetite, grew alarmingly thin, and had to force herself just to eat three spoonfuls of oatmeal a day. Her old friends rallied around her in sympathy. Antonina Naumovna also felt sorry for Olga, and the more she pitied her, the more she hated her former son-in-law.

Ilya had already made it to America by this time. Things were far worse there than he had imagined they would be. Moreover, the German to whom he had entrusted his collection of avant-garde literature, which he had begun amassing in his school years, was dragging his feet about sending it on to him. The value of the books, according to the auction catalogs, was far greater than Ilya had supposed.

Ilya wrote infrequently, but the letters were fascinating. Olga lived from one letter to the next. She inundated him with her missives, paying no heed to the vagaries of postal delivery: for every one he sent, she replied with ten.

A year later, Olga received a terrible blow. Some mutual friends of theirs informed her that Ilya had gotten married. She wrote him a wrathful letter. She got a tender and repentant letter in reply: yes, he had gotten married, the flesh is weak, his marriage was virtually fictitious, he wasn't actually living with his wife, since she lived in Paris. And she, Olga, must understand—here in America things were just not working out. He had to try to relocate to Europe. Marrying a Russian-French woman would give him that opportunity. It was the only way out.

Then there was a little throwback to the past/glimpse of the future: it was a temporary detour, unavoidable, their happiness still lay ahead of them . . . and a gentle reproach: you could have left Kostya there for a year, and we would have come back for him . . .

Olga was consumed with jealousy: Who was this woman, what kind of woman was she, where had she come from? She found out her name from her friends. She had been born in Kiev, had married a Frenchman, lived many years in France, and was then widowed. She was obviously no longer young. That was the only information she could dig up. Olga decided to go to Kiev, where they had mutual acquaintances galore. Truthful by nature, she nevertheless started lying to her Kiev friends right and left, and they told her everything she wanted to know. She even managed to wheedle a photograph of the newlyweds out of one of the bride's more gullible friends. The photograph showed a plump, middle-aged woman, her fleshy hand resting brazenly on the shoulder of a smiling Ilya. It had been taken at the Paris City Hall. This hand became the primary piece of documentary evidence in the case against him.

Olga carried out a full investigation and uncovered a plethora of details and facts. She returned home, reeling from the heaps of contradictory information, but certain that Ilya had deceived her and that the marriage was in no way fictitious.

When she got back to Moscow, she ended up in the hospital again. More hemorrhaging. The doctors removed a large part of her stomach, a measure that was necessary to save her life. But the main culprit, the biggest ulcer, was the colored photograph of the newlyweds, wrapped up in a plastic bag and tucked away in her cosmetic case. The misdeeds of her ex-husband were all she could talk about. When she came out of the anesthesia, the first thing she said to her friend Tamara, who was sitting next to her and taking care of her, was:

"Did you see the flowers in the picture? That bouquet was huge, wasn't it?"

The doctors had taken out a part of her stomach, but they couldn't remove the bleeding wound of her heart.

Olga expected the whole world to take her side in the conflict. Really there was only one side to take: a divorced man had gone away and married someone else at the other end of the earth. The promises, oaths, and vows of eternal love didn't add up to a side in the conflict at all; they were just words . . .

In the meantime, Olga's son, Kostya, was preparing to deal her another blow. He had fallen in love with a girl he had met in college, and they were going to live together for all eternity. The most improbable, and perhaps banal, part of this whole story is that Kostya and Lena, his first and only love, are still living in the general's Moscow apartment today, with their already grown children.

Olga demanded sympathy and loyalty from Kostya, the person she felt closest to; he, in turn, stubbornly resisted. He didn't want to sympathize with her, nor did he wish to take anyone's side in the matter. He loved his mother, but he loved Ilya, too. He didn't want to hear his mother's constant reproaches of his stepfather. Olga was deeply offended by this. She grabbed a handful of fabric on the shoulder of his new black sweater, and hissed:

"From Ilya? It didn't take much to buy you off."

Ilya did send parcels addressed to Kostya from time to time. Besides the clothes for him, there were also things "for the house," which were in fact meant for Olga. Olga fastidiously passed these things on to her mother—newfangled can openers, oilcloth for the table in highland plaids, and other cheap rubbish.

Antonina Naumovna was delighted with any sort of foreign household appliance or trinket, but she attempted to put the infidels in their place:

"In Russia, all our might, all the intellect and know-how of our scientists, is for exploring the cosmos and making atomic power stations. They just invent can openers. Well, I have to admit, they do know how to make those."

Of all the people involved in the situation, Antonina Naumovna was the only happy one. She basked in her triumph. Olga couldn't bear to look at her; it filled her with rage.

Kostya kept silent. He didn't want to hear anyone speak ill of Ilya, never mind foreign can openers. Just then he was completely absorbed in his own feelings—his beloved Lena was in her third month of pregnancy and he couldn't take his eyes off her. He was endowed with the same gift for loving as Olga was.

Olga built up a dossier on Ilya. For some reason, she now felt compelled to prove that her ex-husband was an evil man in every respect, in every sense of the word. She began communicating with her humble and unassuming mother-in-law, who had never inspired any interest in her before now, with Ilya's female cousins, with his childhood friends, and with anyone whose name appeared in his old address book. It transpired that in the seventh grade Ilya had been kicked out of school for stealing some sort of camera lens from the photography club at the House of Pioneers, and even had a police record for this minor infraction.

He had also been caught forging some documents—not very important ones, just a library card from the History Library. But it was still wrong, wasn't it? Some things about his first family came to light as well—that the child he had abandoned was sick, and he had never provided the family with any financial support. That his first wife, who was a quiet sort, and none too bright, had nevertheless supported Ilya all the years they were together.

"Yes, it figures!" Olga was almost glad to get the lowdown on Ilya's shady past from completely random people or those with only the most tenuous connection to him. He had been the same kind of cad and opportunist with her as well! She had worked her fingers to the bone to make a decent living, while he had been sitting in the library, or taking photographs, or riding a bicycle, or traveling; and all on her income! Well, he earned something from his books and photography, it was true; but she never saw a kopeck of it. He spent it all on his own pastimes and pleasures. He was just a plain, old-fashioned parasite—and the Soviet authorities had nothing to do with it!

Her friend Tamara was the first to realize that Olga was losing her mind. It was as though a demon had taken over this once kind and magnanimous person. When Olga talked about Ilya, the tone of her voice changed; her manner of speaking, even her choice of words, was different. The former Olga had not even known such words. Tamara equivocated for a long time, but finally told her friend that she needed to face her obsession head-on and that if she couldn't rein in her runaway jealousy, she would end up in a psychiatric ward.

Olga was eloquent and articulate, however, and knew how to convince everyone that it wasn't about obsession or jealousy, but about truth and justice. While she was talking, it all sounded very logical and self-evident, but no sooner had you walked out the door than you sensed that all her arguments were the product of this very madness she tried so hard to deny. Such was the power of Olga's persuasion that only Kostya was unmoved by it. His love for Ilya remained steadfast, and he had no intention of judging him for any sort of baseness of character or cruelty.

Besides, Kostya was oblivious. These days he belonged heart and soul to his fragile, vulnerable young girl with the hangnails. He had no thought of leaving for anywhere: his whole life was bound up with this place, this person.

"Mama, dear, you can leave if you want to. Without me."

Olga was also provoked by another incident concerning Kostya. She discovered that he had a whole packet of letters from Ilya that had been sent poste restante to the local post office, which happened to be on the first floor of their building. The first thing she did when her hands and legs stopped trembling was to read the letters. They were long letters, wonderfully expressive—the thoughts and impressions of someone who has left the Soviet Union for the first time. The first letter he wrote Kostya, from Vienna, was very similar to the letter he had written Olga. He wrote about feeling that it was all a mirage, about his sense of disorientation about what was real and what was not, in a place where everything was so different from what his eyes, his nose, his mouth had been accustomed to till now. In another letter, written to Kostya on the eve of his departure from Vienna to America, she read something that cut her to the quick—that "the ability to survive here, in the West, is a function of one's willingness to reject everything one experienced before, in Russia." Now she herself was a part of what had to be rejected in order for him to survive.

The next letters were from New York, and much of what he wrote coincided with what he had written to her—about the tragic incommensurability of the two cultures, Russian and American; about the "superficiality" of American culture, not in the banal, generally accepted sense of that term, but from the perspective of superficiality as such: the scrubbed and deodorized surface of the American body, which smelled like chemicals and laundry detergent; the blinding cleanliness of the asphalt; and the fact that every cover, wrapper, or envelope was just as important as what it contained. About how he had once searched all day for a subject to photograph, and finally found one: an enormous heap of garbage, both cast-off building materials and ordinary household refuse, right in the middle of Harlem, with a smiling, toothless black man in a snowy white tank top, his hands gripping a banjo, in the foreground.

The last letter from America was sad and strange. Ilya wrote to the still very young Kostya: "Only shedding your skin completely, acquiring a new surface with new feelers, can ensure your survival here. However strange it might seem, the same does not hold true for one's inmost self. You can keep your thoughts, however original, however jarring to their sensibilities and at odds with their incomprehensible (to me) way of life, to yourself. No one is interested in them in the least. In order to become part of this society, you just have to carry out their elementary rituals of communication. The idiotic ballet of Western life. I am prepared to do this, though it forces me into a number of painful decisions."

After reading these letters, Olga felt as though the scales had fallen from her eyes. She even found herself thinking that it might have been easier for her to endure this rupture with Ilya if he had really fallen in love with some brilliant, youthful beauty. But she nipped this feeling in the bud—no, it would have been just as painful. In the long run, wasn't it all the same, whether he had turned away from her because of a new love or only out of self-interest? Either way she was bereft. The real reason for his departure always eluded her. Her love, trust, naïveté, and spiritual innocence prevented her from seeing it.

Olga reproached Kostya for betraying her, though she was aware of the unfairness of her judgment. Nevertheless, she confiscated the letters from him. Kostya held his tongue.

He also felt sorry for his mother, still, he couldn't agree with her. He felt especially violated by the fact that not only had she broken into the desk drawer where he kept the letters, but that he had a stash of condoms in the far corner of the same drawer. This both embarrassed and infuriated him. He didn't realize that, blinded by her jealousy, she hadn't paid the slightest bit of attention to the paper package or its contents.

Meanwhile, it emerged that the cousin of one of her university friends was living in Paris, and knew Oksana from Kiev very well. She shared new information that confirmed Olga's worst suspicions. It was not a fictitious marriage at all! Oksana, the old vixen, was very much in love with Ilya, and had even given up her two-room apartment for a larger, three-room flat, anticipating the arrival of her young husband.

Tamara begged her: "Olga, enough is enough! Stop dwelling on it. He's gone—consider him dead. Live your own life!" Olga brushed off her pleas.

Not a year had passed since Ilya's departure, when Afanasy Mikhailovich died. He was buried at the Vagankovo Cemetery, in a good spot, with other soldiers of the highest rank, but without a salute. No one recalled how, exactly, he had been made a general. During the war he had traversed all of Europe on foot, ending up in Vienna as a lieutenant colonel. He was certainly no armchair officer. He had constructed bridges and built ferries.

Olga hardly noticed her father's death.

She was furious that now she would be stuck in this Party-owned apartment with her mother, who was on the verge of retirement, and with Kostya and his sweetheart Lena. What would become of her?

What a fool she was not to have left with Ilya when she had a chance! Now everything had been shot to hell, it was all a shambles. This was the hardest thing of all to reconcile herself to. If she had left when the time was ripe, her life would have taken another course.

As the tempestuous hurts and grievances occasioned by her exhusband turned into rigid, formulaic mantras, her livid anger turned into a hatred every bit as livid. She continued to lose weight and started turning yellow, like a withered onion; her stomach hurt, and she suffered other unpleasant symptoms, besides.

By this time, Ilya had learned to make his way in the West, but success still evaded him. Olga's correspondence with Ilya was cut short after Olga sent his wife Oksana the letter he had sent her about the necessity of entering into a fictitious marriage to further his plans in life, and about their love, eternal and immortal.

During the second year of their separation, Olga was diagnosed with cancer. She began to undergo treatment at the Oncological Institute, but her condition steadily worsened. The doctors told her friend Tamara, in so many words, that the process was irreversible and that they should prepare for the worst. Antonina Naumovna stopped going to the hospital. She feared more than anything that Olga would die in her presence.

Tamara, a recent convert to Christianity, was tireless in her efforts to guide Olga onto the righteous path of reconciliation and love. To no avail: Olga was completely indifferent to the Church, she refused to see a priest, and was even alarmed when Tamara mentioned one. She blamed all her suffering and misfortune, including her fatal illness, on Ilya. By this time, Ilya had managed to rise out of poverty and obscurity and had moved to Munich, where he worked at Radio Liberty. He broadcast to Russia. Olga never missed a program. At night she would

turn on the transistor radio and listen in rapt attention to the penetrating voice out of Munich that defied the censor's scrambling. What
must she have felt during those nights?

Tamara, seeing the bitterness etched on Olga's face, decided to
write to Ilya, informing him that Olga was dying, that God expects
forgiveness and love from all of us, and that Ilya would have to make
the first move . . .

The letter contained nothing that Ilya didn't know already, since
he had been corresponding with Kostya and was aware of the sad situation. He was not callous. He spent a long time composing a letter to
her, weighing every word, contriving every phrase, and tailoring it to
Olga's needs and expectations.

It was the end of December, and many patients checked out of the
hospital for the New Year; some were even allowed to spend several
days at home.

Tamara went to Olga's doctor to ask whether Olga could celebrate the New Year at home too. "I assume all responsibility," Tamara said.

The doctor looked at her searchingly and said:

"All right, Tamara Grigorievna, we'll discharge her. If she makes it
till then . . ."

That was when the letter from Ilya arrived. Letter? No, it was a
masterpiece. He glorified their past, describing their time together as
the best days of his life. He repented of his sins, asked for forgiveness,
and hinted (laying it on a bit thick, but still not missing a beat) at their
imminent reunion, which grew nearer with each passing day.

And the letter caused a turnaround in Olga's life and in her illness.
She read the letter, put it aside, and asked Tamara for her cosmetics.
Looking at her reflection in a small mirror, she sighed and powdered
her nose—the powder showed up as a pink blotch on her waxen yellow skin, which didn't escape Olga's notice. She asked Tamara to buy
her some more powder in a lighter tone.

"This light pink will look like rouge on my complexion!" And she
smiled her former smile, which featured four dimples at once—two
round ones at the corners of her mouth and two longer ones in the
middle of her cheeks.

She reread the letter, reached for her cosmetics, and corrected her face again. Before Tamara left she asked her to bring a good large envelope the next day.

She wants to reply to the letter, thought Tamara. But she was wrong. The next morning Olga placed the envelope with the foreign stamps into the larger one, and stashed it away on the bottom shelf of the bedside table. Tamara had expected that Olga would read her the letter from Ilya; this took her by surprise. At last, Tamara couldn't contain herself any longer and asked what Ilya had written. Olga smiled a ghostly smile and replied enigmatically.

"You know, Brinchik," she said, calling Tamara by her nickname. "He didn't write anything in particular. It's just that everything seems to have fallen into place. He's an intelligent man, and now he understands. We just can't live apart."

On that very day, Olga got up and made her way down to the dining room.

They say that this is not unheard of; it does happen sometimes. Some backup program in the body kicks in, a blocked switch turns on, something rejuvenates itself or springs to life, who the hell knows . . . God only knows . . . the very same thing that happens in miracle healing. Saints who perform wonders in the name of the Lord Jesus Christ know nothing about biochemistry, and biochemists, who are well aware of the destructive processes associated with oncological diseases, are at a loss to explain the workings of the magic button setting in motion this backup program that Father John of Kronstadt or the Blessed Matrona of Moscow knew to press.

After the New Year, Olga didn't return to the hospital. She began to heal herself, like a sick cat who steals into the woods to eat healing grasses and herbs. Now Olga surrounded herself with herbalists and wisewomen. The well-known herbal healer from Pamir was summoned, and he prescribed infusions and potions. She ate the earth from sacred spots, drank urine. And sages and soothsayers came to see her as well. Where on earth did she dig them up?

Antonina Naumovna, already reconciled to her daughter's death, was disconcerted by all of this. Death from cancer was more comprehensible than all this healing by methods bordering on the indecent.

The doctor who had foreseen Olga's imminent demise made a house call, examined her, probed and pressed her, and asked her to undergo further tests and analyses. But the patient merely smiled her enigmatic smile and shook her head: no, no, what need is there for that?

The doctor was deeply perplexed. Such tumors can't dissolve just like that. He probed her underarms, pressed her groin. The lymph nodes had shrunk. But if the tumor had disintegrated, traces of toxicity should be manifesting themselves. And Olga's jaundice had disappeared; she was even gaining weight. Remission? How? Why?

Half a year later, Olga began going outside, and her friend Tamara stopped visiting so frequently. Tamara was somewhat hurt that Olga didn't appreciate this miracle of God that had been worked before their very eyes. Tamara kept bringing up the subject of baptism, which she suggested Olga should consider if only out of gratitude to God for what had transpired. Olga laughed, and it was almost her old, childlike laugh, interspersed with little breathless gasps:

"Brinchik, you're an intelligent, well-educated woman, a scientist—how could you endorse such an absurd faith, a God who expects gratitude, and punishes us like little puppies, or rewards us with treats? You could have at least become a Buddhist . . ."

Tamara took offense and fell silent; still, she lit candles in church for restoring Olga's health and offered prayers of petition for her during church services. Despite her preoccupation with her own hurt feelings, Tamara couldn't help but notice another significant change in Olga. She no longer talked about Ilya. Ever. She spoke no ill of him, nor any praise. And when Tamara herself brought this up, Olga shrugged off the subject:

"Everything's fine. He's already made his decision; now it's just a matter of time. There's nothing to say."

And this was a miracle in its own right. After months of talking only about him, and about him only . . .

Olga, absorbed in her own rejuvenated life, didn't pay much attention to Kostya's marriage. Kostya moved away from home, and the newlyweds settled in with his mother-in-law outside of town, in Opalikha. Very soon he became the father of two children—twins, a girl and a boy. Olga was touched by this, but only momentarily. She didn't

have the energy for anything other than healing. All her spiritual re-
sources were devoted to this end.

Although her illness was clearly on the retreat, Olga was tireless in
her efforts to chase it away. On the dining room windowsill she grew
wheat from seedlings. She scorned the ubiquitous sourdough bread
and baked herself flatbreads from bran and straw. She boiled herbs
in "silver" water. On the same windowsill stood two pitchers of water
containing silver spoons, which was what lent the ordinary tap water
its healing properties . . .

Fate took a deep breath; shaking off the dust here, reevaluting this
and readjusting that, a year later Olga's health had been almost completely restored. She set to work again, hammering on the typewriter
six hours a day or more. She now lived alone in the large apartment
with her mother.

Olga was so preoccupied with herself, or, to be more precise, with
the promise of her impending conjugal happiness with Ilya, that she
didn't notice how thin and wan Antonina Naumovna had grown. Most
likely she was suffering from the same illness that had abandoned her
daughter. It also began in the stomach, then spread to the intestines.

Olga began looking after her mother with great skill and devotion.
It was a strange sensation—almost as though she were taking care of
herself, since the same thing had so recently happened to her.

They had never been so close or so tender in their emotions with
each other. Now Olga was glad she hadn't left with Ilya, so that she could
stroke her mother's hand, boil bouillon for her, which she would most
likely not be able to get down, smooth out her sheets, and wipe the
corners of her mouth. Antonina Naumovna kept asking Olga to have
her admitted to the hospital, but Olga just smiled and said:

"Mother, dear, only a healthy person can survive the hospital. Are
you uncomfortable here at home? No? Then forget about the hospital."

Antonina Naumovna's mind was failing. She forgot huge swathes
of her life. Other, more trivial details floated up out of nowhere. During
her final days she remembered only the distant past: how all her grandmother's chickens had died on the same day, one after the other; how
a horse had bolted, throwing her mother and herself out of a sleigh; and,

at last, how she and Afanasy had met at a Party-education meeting. All of her former life—meetings of the editorial board at the magazine, briefings at the regional Party committee meetings, presidiums, reports, conferences—was consigned to oblivion. Only random vestiges of her childhood remained.

"My goodness, something's not right with my head, it's all turned around," she whispered, and struggled to recall something from the recent past. "It's like everything fell right through a hole in the ground."

In the room illuminated only by a green desk lamp, she died alone, easily and unaware, saying, quite audibly, "Mama, Mama, Papa . . ."

But no one was there to hear the words. In the morning, Olga discovered her mother, already cold. She immediately called the Union of Writers, where there was a special department of funeral services . . .

Everything was carried out in the most proper and dignified manner. She already had a gravesite marked out for her, next to the general in Vagankovo Cemetery.

The funeral was a sad and bitter affair. Not, however, due to tears and sobbing, loss and grief, or even, perhaps, regret accompanied by a sense of guilt. Rather the contrary. Not one of the mourners shed so much as a tear; there was no sadness, nor even sympathy. Their slightly benumbed faces expressed the decorum appropriate to the occasion. The absolute indifference to the death of the literary worker among those who attended the funeral did not go unnoticed by Ari Lvovich Bas, who officiated at these events of the Union of Writers.

Without much enthusiasm, Kostya returned to Moscow after his grandmother's death, according to Olga's wishes. Kostya was in his fourth year of university, and Lena in her third—she had taken a year of academic leave when the children were born.

They changed around the whole apartment, remapping the floor plan. On Olga's insistence, Kostya took over his grandfather's former room. It had a large, comfortable desk, and another smaller working space—a fold-down desk. This was the study. His grandmother's old room became the bedroom. Kostya dubbed it the "Communist nook" because of its spartan government-issue furnishings, the green lampshade on the oaken table, and the picture of Lenin, with a log resting on his shoulder, looking down from the wall. Lena bought a foldout bed to replace the leather divan, and brought in pillows with flounces and frills. She replaced Lenin with some Van Gogh sunflowers.

Olga gave up her room to her grandchildren, and moved into the former dining room. The infamous bed with its fluted columns and cherubim migrated back to the antiques consignment store on Smolenskaya Embankment. They ate in the kitchen now, like ordinary Soviet citizens who by this time had managed to move from their communal apartments into private family apartments, but for whom bourgeois "studies" and "dining rooms" were still out of the question.

The quiet, competent Lena took the household into her own two hands, organized and took care of everything, cleaned and scrubbed, and prepared delicious meals. Every morning, Anna Antonovna, Lena's mother, would arrive to feed the children, take them for walks, and put them down for their naps.

Her daughter Lena was a paragon. She rushed home from classes, saw her mother out, and took over the next shift. Olga wasn't involved in taking care of the children, but Lena felt no resentment toward her mother-in-law for this failing. On the contrary, she was grateful. They had spent the first years of their family life in Opalikha, outside Moscow, where they had a small room with two windows and slanting floors; they had to prop up the children's beds with wooden boards to keep them from sliding away. The four of them all shared a single room. There was no hot water in the dilapidated cottage, though running water and indoor plumbing had been installed two years before the children were born.

The general's apartment was always full of commotion. The furniture that had been acquired and lovingly refurbished by Kostya's grandfather was not spared, and was constantly being pushed around from place to place. The two-year-old Mishka and Verochka clutched and poked at the Karelian birch with their little paws, and Mishka developed a passion for trying to pry off the birds' heads adorning the living room furniture. Finally, Kostya decided to take the entire set back to the antiques dealer's. The manager, who was by now an old acquaintance, offered an unusually large sum of money in exchange.

The loyal Tamara stopped in fairly regularly. But the stronger Olga's health became, the more things fell into their old pattern: Olga gave orders, Tamara carried them out. Their friend Galya was preparing for a transition in life. She studied a foreign language at night school and rarely had time to socialize. Besides, Galya's husband, Gennady, was opposed to their friendship—Olga was bad news!

It was almost as though Olga had forgotten about Ilya. Tamara was glad that the delusion had fled, and was surprised at how closely bound up with the illness it had been . . .

But there were things Tamara didn't know. Olga was keeping an eye on Ilya from a distance. Although their communications had seemed to break off again after his farewell letter, she now knew that Ilya had made a life-changing decision and it was just a matter of time before the final victory. Olga knew that Kostya continued to correspond with his stepfather. She saw the signs of their interaction—unusual children's toys and foreign-made clothes kept appearing out of nowhere. Now, however, this didn't exasperate her. Rather, it offered proof that change was in the offing.

In addition, Olga had a secret informer who told her that Ilya's wife had taken to drink, and that she embarrassed him. He never wanted to be seen with her in public, and from time to time he sent her away from Munich, back to Paris. She was an albatross around his neck.

This information was a great comfort to Olga. She kept to herself and waited; soon, very soon, Ilya would show up. That was enough.

Olga's health had stabilized completely, and she was again inundated with work. She spent long hours with her dictionaries and papers, and worked with even more enthusiasm and enjoyment than before. At night she listened to Radio Liberty, eager to catch Ilya's voice over the sound waves. She was sure that now everything would end well . . . She was still receptive to "opposition to the Soviet regime," but her former indignation and outrage had cooled significantly since Ilya's departure.

Olga was now translating technology patents, and the pay was excellent. Before her illness, she had attended courses to receive the proper qualifications. From time to time she mustered up the energy to go to the Central Telegraph Office and book a prepaid call to Paris. Sometimes there was no answer, but often she heard a woman's voice on the other end. The later the hour, the more slurred her speech was: *"J'écoute! Allô! J'écoute!"* Olga would hang up immediately. Ilya never once came to the telephone. It was obvious they had divorced or, at the very least, separated.

Thus, working hard and anticipating the imminent fulfillment of her fate, Olga remained absolutely certain that everything would resolve itself soon, and that she and Ilya would again be together.

The day came when Ilya himself called from Munich. The voice was recognizable, but sounded weak with exhaustion.

"Olga! I think about you all the time! I love you. You are my whole life! I've caught up, and even overtaken you. I have kidney cancer, they're operating next week."

"How do you know it's cancer? Nothing is certain until they do a biopsy! I know everything about it. You know that I recovered! On my own!" She screamed into the phone, but he remained silent and didn't even try to interrupt her. "The main thing is not to let them operate!"

But the main thing was something else entirely: he loved her, only her, and would love her forever.

The second time he called was from the clinic after the operation. Now they spoke nearly every day. He read her the results of the tests, and she replied with a long list of the medicinal herbs he should be taking. She bought them in Moscow from her herbalists and apothecaries, and sent them through friends traveling to Munich. She sent him ointments and creams, with detailed explanations about when and where to apply them. When they began giving him chemotherapy, she flew into a rage and screamed into the receiver that he was destroying himself, that the drugs were always far more damaging than the cancer itself.

"Check out of the hospital immediately and come back! I know all about this! I'll pull you out of it, I pulled myself through all on my own!"

There was something in the air, and Olga, although she had completely distanced herself from her former dissident friends, could feel it. The eighties, heavy and moribund, were in decline, staggering to a halt, and her urgent cry for Ilya to return no longer seemed like complete madness. He gave her the answer she most wanted to hear:

"No, Olga, it's not possible just now. If I get out of this alive, we'll arrange for you to come here to me."

He continued to call her, but his voice became ever weaker, and the calls more and more infrequent. Then came the last call, sounding as though it came from the bowels of the earth:

"Olga, I'm calling you on a mobile phone! My friend brought it right to my bedside. Imagine, things have come that far! That's what you call progress. And I'm covered in tubes and wires, like a cosmonaut. The countdown has started, and I'm ready for takeoff . . ."

And he laughed quietly, the same choking, slightly shrill laugh.

Two days later, Olga received a call from Munich informing her that Ilya had died.

"Oh, so that's how it is," Olga said enigmatically, and fell silent.

In the evening, Tamara came over. In silence, they each drank a glass of vodka to his memory. Kostya officiated, pouring the vodka and serving them a plate of cheese and sausage.

Several days afterward, Olga discovered some strange growths on her head, like little balls of fat. They rolled around painlessly under her skin. Under her armpits, too, she found these little balls, attached somewhere like a cluster of grapes.

The news of Ilya's death sapped Olga of all her strength. She lay down and didn't get up again. Tamara stopped in every evening and sat with her until late at night, trying all the while to persuade her to see a doctor. But Olga just smiled vaguely and shrugged. Although she had studied endocrinology her whole life, and had a Ph.D., Tamara had never practiced medicine, never treated the sick or examined patients. Still, she understood that a violent metastasis was under way, and that Olga urgently needed chemotherapy. But Olga merely smiled her beatific smile, stroking Tamara's hand and whispering brightly, "Brinchik, you still don't understand."

One evening, Olga told Tamara about a dream she had had the night before. In the middle of an enormous carpet of meadow, a large green marquee rose up into the air. It was like a huge tent, and there was a long line of people waiting to get in, ever so many people. Olga went to stand at the back of the line, because she just had to get into the tent.

Tamara, her burgeoning mystical sensibilities on the alert, froze: "A marquee?"

"Well, sort of—like a circus tent, a big-top canopy, but much larger. I look around and see that all the people in the line are people I know—girls from Pioneer camp that I haven't seen since we were kids, teachers from school, friends from college, our professor . . . it was like a demonstration!"

"Was Antonina Naumovna there?"

"Yes, Mama was there, of course, and my grandmother, whom I never once laid eyes on, and all the other familiar faces—Mikha, with some little kids, and Sanya was there, too, and Galya, with that creep of hers."

"You mean the dead and the living were there together?"

"Well, yes, of course. And some little dog kept getting underfoot, and seemed to be smiling. And there was a sweet young girl named Marina. I've forgotten the name of the dog . . . Hera! Yes, the dog's name was Hera! And there were many, many other people . . . And suddenly, just imagine, in the distance, right by the entrance, I see Ilya, and he waves to me from the very front of the line and calls out: 'Olga! Olga! Come here! I've saved you a place!'

"And then I start to push my way toward him, and everyone gets upset because I'm going out of turn, and Mama asks me why I'm budging in line ahead of everyone else. Then a big old man with a beard appeared, he had a wonderful face, and I understood that this was my own grandfather, Naum. He waved his hand over the crowd to disperse them, and I ran up to the marquee. But it wasn't a green marquee at all, it was a pavilion, all shining and golden. I look—and there's Ilya, smiling, and waiting for me. He looks fine, very healthy and still young. He pulls me into the line next to him, placing his hand on my shoulder. And then Oksana appears, and she keeps trying to wriggle her way up to him, but he seems not to see her. And there was not really a door at all, but a thick piece of cloth, like a curtain, and then this curtain folds back, and there's music coming from inside—I can't describe it, and there's a particular scent, something you can't even imagine, and everything is shining."

"A palace," Tamara said breathlessly.

"Oh, Brinchik! What the hell kind of palace could it be?"

"Olga, don't say hell!" Tamara said, horrified.

"Oh, all right, calm down. Have it your way—a palace, then. Words can't describe it, in any case. So we went inside together."

"And what did you see there, inside?" Tamara could hardly get the words out.

"Nothing. That's when I woke up. A good dream, don't you think?"

Olga died on the fortieth day after Ilya's death.

LOVE IN RETIREMENT

Once a month, Afanasy Mikhailovich rose at five in the morning instead of the usual seven, shaved with special care, and changed his underclothes. He ate his bread with tea, pulled a woolen overcoat over the old army uniform jacket, and donned a hat with earflaps. In civilian attire he felt like someone wearing a crown at a masquerade. And, it was true, no one recognized him; even the guard who stood sentry at the entrance to the dacha settlement failed to greet him.

After yesterday's snowfall, everything was as clean and fresh as it was after a spring cleaning. Afanasy Mikhailovich walked to the bus stop. The schedule was illegible, encrusted with a thick layer of snow, so he couldn't tell when the next bus would come. He waited under the overhang at the stop. Two women were waiting for the bus, too—one a nurse, who didn't recognize him, and the other a stranger. She also seemed to be a local, though. He turned away and began looking in the other direction.

He was on his way to a secret rendezvous with his sweetheart, Sophia, to grumble about things and mull over them, pouring out his heart—or whatever a general had in its stead, for there was certainly something—and listen to what she had to say about why he was suffering so.

She had a gift for getting to the heart of his troubles, and putting it into words. From that first day in 1936, when he was working in the department of construction at the People's Commissariat of Defense and she showed up to work as his secretary, she had known how to find just the right words for all those things he couldn't express himself.

She had never been wrong. Not once. She said just what needed to be said. Nothing more, nothing less. What was better left unsaid stayed that way. That's how it was right up to 1949, with a break during the war. After the war, when Afanasy Mikhailovich was appointed head of the Military Construction School, he sought out his former secretary, and she rushed to his side again. They were like Aaron and Moses. He would mutter some incoherent, garbled words, and his subordinates would rush off to find Sophia for an explanation.

She was tactful, and had had a good upbringing. She received her upbringing in the girls' gymnasium, which she attended until she was fifteen, at which time the gymnasium was shut down because of the Revolution. Her tact was a natural gift. Nature had also endowed her with copious beauty. She had thick brows and large eyes. Her regal head tilted back slightly from the weight of her luxuriant braid, twisted into a simple knot until 1949. After that she cut it off. Although Sophia was small in stature, her ample bosom inside her sizable blue and green dresses, her plump hands with their long red fingernails, and her broadly curving gestures gave the impression of a large woman. Oh, what largesse she had—not only in the salient points of her figure, but in her whole character. Her nickname was the Cow. And she really did resemble one—Europa the cow. But the general didn't know this. He only knew she was a goddess. And he worshipped her. He was never plagued by the trifling thought that he might be betraying his wife. His wife was one thing; Sophia was another. Completely other. And if she hadn't turned up in Afanasy Mikhailovich's life, he would never have known that love was sweet, or what a woman was, and what profound solace she could bring to the troubled life of a builder.

In all those years she worked for him, right up till 1949, there was only one time, just at the end, that she put him in an awkward position. She knelt before him and buried her head in his gabardine jodhpurs, leaving a trace of red lipstick in an immodest spot. But what could he have done? No, don't talk to me about your brother, he had said.

Why go to such lengths for your brother? he remembered thinking. *You're the one who needs saving.* But she wasn't.

The general was called before the administration and ordered to fire his secretary.

Although tongue-tied and inarticulate, he was still indispensable, a valuable asset. But his interlocutor—a young captain, blond, with stubbly remains of hempen locks, close-set eyes like a pale, washed-out figure eight, blue shoulder straps—didn't care that he had fought at the front, that he was a distinguished general; they could at least have sent a colonel to question him.

"You're trying to protect your mistress!" he said. "You know that I know that you know . . ."

"Well, do what you know, then," Afanasy Mikhailovich said, re-treating after the second hour of interrogation. "You have your area of competence, I have mine—bridges, roads, and access routes."

The pale wisp smiled a cold smile, and nodded. But agreeing to fire her wasn't enough for him. The haggling continued, step by step. It was like bargaining in business, but the captain kept turning the screws tighter and tighter. He knew everything—about what went on in the office, and about their secret rendezvous. He would drop oblique hints, avoid saying anything outright, and then—bam!—and didn't you visit her on Dayev Lane? And didn't you ever meet Sophia's sister, Anna Markovna? A professor, isn't she? And Iosif Markovich, her brother, an actor in the Moscow State Jewish Theater? You're not acquainted with him?

Is Sophia the only one they're after? he asked himself suddenly. He was drenched in sweat.

Are we quits, then? They were—and all it took was one signature. The next day a new secretary was sent to him, and Sophia was gone. For just over four years. At the beginning of 1954 she returned from the labor camp at Karaganda. Another year passed before they met again. And what a place to run into each other! It was at the market at Nakhabino, early one morning in June. Afanasy was buying radishes and carrots. It was Sunday, and guests were expected. Antonina Naumovna was bustling about, she had forgotten to send the housekeeper to the market. Afanasy Mikhailovich volunteered—glad to get out of the house to avoid the kitchen confusion. He went by himself in his private Pobeda, without the chauffeur.

She recognized him first—and she stepped aside to avoid him. Her braid was gone, her plumpness had sagged, her hand flew up to her face and covered it: the same large hand with dimples at the base of every finger. Only now she didn't wear red fingernail polish—it was a faint pink. He recognized that hand. It had stroked his bald head for many years, and with that one deft motion had vanquished his troubles and woes. He rushed to catch up with her.

"Sophia Markovna!"

"Afanasy!" she said, covering her mouth. "My God!"

Every other one of her sugary white teeth was missing.

"They released you?"

"Eleven months ago, July last year."

"Why didn't you let me know?" When they were face-to-face he was unable to call her by name. Addressing her formally was impossible, too.

She waved her beautiful hand dismissively and turned down the road, as if to walk away from him.

He chased after her and touched her on the shoulder. She stopped and began to cry. He removed his civilian straw hat and started crying, too. She wasn't the same as she had been, she was someone else altogether; but in a single moment the two merged and became one—that former regal beauty, and the haggard, homely woman standing before him now, who was still the most wonderful in all the world.

She lived with her sister, Anna Markovna, at her sister's dacha, not far away. He left his car by the market so he could walk her home. They didn't say a word along the way, as if the breath had been knocked out of them. His mind kept returning to the same question: Did she know that he'd signed the document? Before they reached the dacha, she turned to him and said:

"We have to say good-bye here. My family can't see you. And you don't need to see them, either. You know they shot my brother."

She knows, he thought. His heart seemed to drop to his stomach. *But what does she know? Maybe she thinks I betrayed her brother.*

Sophia had introduced him to her brother, Iosif. He was a good-natured fellow, and worked at Mikhoels's Moscow State Jewish Theater. He had even written a few tales in Yiddish. They had met two or three times. But Afanasy Mikhailovich had put his name to paper only once—and that one signature had nothing to do with Sophia's brother.

"Do you still live on Dayev?"

"I live at my sister's. They took the room away from me. A yard-keeper lives there now," she said indifferently, and he recalled the room that smelled like Red Moscow perfume, the flock of pillows, her collections of flacons and cats—of porcelain, glass, stone. "They tell me they'll get the room back for me, and kick the yardkeeper out."

Indeed, it was not long before they did return the room to her. Afanasy Mikhailovich began to call her from public phone booths now and then at the old, prewar number. He wanted to see her. For a long time Sophia refused him.

"No, please, I don't want to, I can't."

But one day she said: "Yes, come."

And once again he went through the courtyard and up the back stairs, which were adjacent to one wall of her room. As before, he avoided going through the main entrance, where the door to the communal flat was covered with doorbells for all the families living there. Instead, he knocked on the wall to her room, and she undid the huge iron latch to the back door, filling the darkness of the corridor with her body and her sweet scent. Then she led him into her little nest of pillows and blankets, where he basked in the warmth of her luxuriant body, which sank underneath him.

And all their former closeness returned, even more intense than before—for they had lost each other forever, and found each other again by chance.

And the second part of their double-feature true-love movie began. One thing, it goes without saying, had changed. They never talked about work. Sophia Markovna was as tactful and circumspect as ever.

She never asked him anything. She never talked about her own trials and misfortunes. They talked about the subjects he brought up. The conversation usually concerned domestic matters, his family affairs. And he always talked about his daughter, Olga. Sophia Markovna had known her since she was born, of course—from a distance. Only from photographs. Once, not long before all the trouble, in 1949, he decided that Sophia Markovna should see Olga in person. He bought three tickets to a children's theater, a ballet performance of *Doctor Ouchithurts*. He gave two of the front-row tickets to Olga and her girlfriend, and the third ticket he gave to Sophia Markovna. The girls sat next to Sophia Markovna; she watched them, and they watched the performance.

Framed photographs of the little girl adorned her walls. And that's how things continued. Sophia took a great interest in Olga. It is likely that Afanasy Mikhailovich would not have known as much about his daughter as he did if he hadn't been assembling this domestic dossier on her for Sophia Markovna. He reported what grade she had gotten on dictation, what museum she had visited the previous Sunday, and so forth . . .

The years passed, and Sophia heard all about Olga starting college, and about her early marriage. She'd had her doubts about the marriage from the very beginning. No, she said, our Olga is head and shoulders above Vova as far as intellect is concerned; mark my words, she'll find someone far more interesting. And she was right. She was always right about everything. When Olga's travails began, Sophia Markovna again gave Afanasy the right advice: she told him to retire.

He wouldn't have been able to make the decision himself—but, at her urging, he submitted the necessary papers. This decision bolstered his health. After he retired, his life changed, and the changes were much for the better.

Afanasy Mikhailovich never notified Sophia of his impending monthly visit. He didn't announce himself beforehand. She never left the house before noon, in case he decided to drop by. She always kept frozen minced meat on hand, ready for preparing pancakes at a moment's notice. She would make the dough, then fry up the paper-thin crepes, two for wrapping around the meat filling and one for the sugar-sweetened cottage cheese. He washed down the meat-filled pancakes with thyme-infused vodka, and the sweet one with tea. All the food Sophia made was slightly sweet—even meat and fish. And the sweetness seemed not to come from the sugar, but from Sophia herself, from the smell of her body, her clothes, her bed.

On March 12, he went to see his girlfriend for the last time, though he didn't know this yet. He only knew that it hadn't even been a full month since he had last visited her, but just over two weeks. And already he was filled with longing; he couldn't contain himself. The bus was running on schedule, and the electric commuter train didn't let him down, either. He arrived at Rizhskaya Station promptly at 9:50. It had been quiet and still outside of town, but here snow was blowing through the squares. While he was buying flowers—mimosa—the squall died down and the sun peeped out. He boarded the trolleybus. Everything was happening right on time, but for some reason Afanasy felt uneasy. What if she wasn't home? Something could have come up—maybe she had gone to see the doctor, or gone out shopping. He felt around for the key in his pocket. Sophia had given him the key to her room long ago, just in case. Which was quite pointless, since he didn't have a key to the main entrance. And he couldn't have gotten into her room through the rear, because the back door was always latched.

When he was nearing the building, the snow squall started up again. Afanasy Mikhailovich noticed that there was a crowd standing in front of the house. There was a bus, and several smaller vans. But this was not his affair; he had nothing to do with them, or they with him.

He went up the back stairs, knocked on the wall and waited at the door, expecting her to come to undo the latch. He waited for what seemed a long time, but she didn't open the door. He knocked again—he ought to have telephoned, at least. But they weren't in the habit of calling each other. Sophia Markovna still didn't trust the telephone, though times had changed.

I'll try the front entrance, Afanasy decided, and he went back out into the courtyard.

The bus, its windows draped in black, was performing a difficult maneuver, trying to pull right up to the front entrance of the building. People holding flowers leapt aside to make way.

A hearse, Afanasy noted impassively.

And, at almost the same moment, he was struck with alarm: Who had died?

And, right away, he knew it was Sophia Markovna.

He looked at the window farthest from the entrance—at that very moment it flew open, as though confirming what he had already guessed. The two halves of the large entrance door were propped open, and an enormous, plain coffin was carried out, not in the proper way, feet first, but head first. And the head, propped up high on a pillow, was that very same beautiful head, with a pale yellow face and red-painted lips. And the sweet smell assaulted his nostrils.

The general started to reel, and his legs began crumpling underneath him. Someone grabbed him, breaking his fall. They put smelling salts under his nose, and he came to. The face of the woman he saw standing before him looked familiar, for some reason. She was of the same stamp as Sophia Markovna—a noble head, large, dark-brown eyes, shoulders almost as broad as a man's. But, of course, it was her sister, Anna Markovna—Annie.

"You! You!" She spat the words out with quiet rage. "What are you doing here? How dare you? Get out of here! Get out!"

And he did. He didn't witness the custom-made coffin—ready-made coffins for people of her girth were not available—being stuffed, with great effort, into the back of the bus, or her many Jewish relatives piling in behind it. Nor did he see his two former colleagues, with whom Sophia Markovna had kept up relations after her return from Karaganda.

They saw him, however, and exchanged glances with each other. For a long time afterward they would prattle about him, and about Sophia; they would surmise all kinds of things. They would finally conclude that Sophia Markovna had tried to pull the wool over their eyes with stories about her high blood pressure, about her advancing years and her loneliness, when all the time she had been secretly carrying on with her retired lover. They thought hard about it, and did the calculations. Since 1935—that meant they had been together for thirty-two years, not counting the years of forced separation.

The general, crushing a whisk of mimosa in his bluish fist, walked to the trolleybus. It turned out that Sophia had known everything. And had forgiven him.

ORPHANS ALL

The funeral was a sad and bitter affair. Not, however, due to tears and sobbing, loss and grief, or even, perhaps, regret accompanied by a sense of guilt. Rather the contrary. Not one of the mourners shed so much as a tear; there was no sadness, nor even sympathy. Their slightly benumbed faces expressed the decorum appropriate to the occasion. The absolute indifference to the death of the literary worker among those who attended the funeral did not go unnoticed by Ari Lvovich Bas, who officiated at these events of the Union of Writers. He had been organizing funerals for sixty of his seventy-four years. It was the family business. His grandfather had been the head of the funeral guild in Grodno. Ari Lvovich knew his craft down to the smallest detail. Not only was he one of the foremost experts in the dying profession of burial, he was also a poet of this ancient trade.

He was a consummate master of ceremonies, and he had laid to rest all the great writers: Alexei Tolstoy, Alexander Fadeev, even Gorky himself (though his contribution was minor) . . . The first big funerals he had a hand in, still not as the main organizer, but as the first assistant, were in the 1930s. That was when he first met Antonina Naumovna. He remembered her. Oh, how well he remembered!

On that day in April, he was called to take the measurements of someone recently deceased, a suicide. Ari went to Gendrikov Lane, but it turned out to be the wrong address. The well-known poet had shot himself somewhere else, on the Lubyanka, where his office was. On Gendrikov Lane, instead of the deceased poet, Ari found two men from the Political Directorate, and this very Antonina, also some sort of writer.

The men were seizing papers and wrenching them out of a desk, and she was writing something down. A man with a thick head of hair looked up at Ari, his insolent gypsy eyes flashing fire—beat it! Ari, scared half to death, turned on his heels and rushed downstairs, re-covering his composure only when he was outside again. Seasoned by his profession, he did not fear the dead. It was the living he feared. Two hours later they brought the body, carried it on a stretcher up to the fourth floor, and only when the three men, armed with two brief-cases, had left the building did Ari go upstairs to the apartment again.

Several people, among them two women, stood in the corridor. One of the women was weeping desperately. The door to the room had been flung wide open, and two people were standing next to it. They were bickering about the seal, which one of them had just re-moved from the door. The other one said:

"You'll pay for this. You're not supposed to go inside—that's why it was sealed."

The other one snarled back crudely:

"Well, where in the hell should we put the deceased? In the hall-way? Why are you such a chickenshit about every little seal? I've got my orders—put the body where it belongs!"

Ari measured the body—six feet, three inches. The coffin would have to be custom-built.

The funeral was unprecedented. Thousands of people packed into Vorovsky Street, and then the whole crowd followed on foot to Donskoi Monastery behind the truck carrying the coffin and a single wreath, a bizarre iron monstrosity of a thing fashioned from random parts, hammers and sickles. And not a single flower. The funeral was strange and magnificent, truly magnificent. Never before had he witnessed such an outpouring of public grief. Never before nor after. Except perhaps thirty years later when Pasternak died.

Ari became firmly established in his profession. Now not a single person from the ranks of writers was buried without him. Provided the death occurred in the environs of Moscow. After the war he constantly ran into Antonina, either in the honor guard next to writers' coffins, or among the eulogists.

As a young man, he could never have imagined how many people he would end up burying. Ari loved all his deceased. The deceased were the only ones he read. He never got around to reading them, not to mention loving them, while they were still alive. But again, their true stature would only be determined at their funerals.

Antonina, now—it turned out she was a nobody. Zilch. And hardly anyone attended the funeral: six people in all. Her daughter, Olga; her grandson, Kostya, with his wife; a friend of her daughter's; her neighbor from across the hall; and the sister of the deceased, Valentina, whom the family hadn't seen in about ten years. The daughter seemed very pleased with herself. She had made amends with her mother toward the end, she fulfilled her obligations down to the last detail— moreover, Antonina had died quietly, without excessive suffering, under the effects of morphine. And there had been no love lost between them for quite some time, it must be said.

On this day, Ari Lvovich, it seemed, was suffering more than anyone else. He hadn't seen such a paltry funeral in a long time. Antonina Naumovna was buried according to the official Writers' Union rituals. The coffin lay in state in the Central House of Writers, where actual public wakes took place, sometimes up to a thousand people. She was placed in the Minor Hall, which was all but empty. There were neither friends, nor officials. The new editor of the magazine couldn't stand her predecessor and called a meeting so that her editorial board would be prevented from attending the funeral. She did send a wreath through her elderly secretary, however. It was made of funerary fir branches and decorated with white ribbons, reading "From the Collective." Ari Lvovich delivered the official eulogy, a skill he had long since acquired, saying that the departed had been a true Communist and loyal Leninist. He also gave the family a chance to bid their farewells.

Then the coffin was removed to Donskoi Crematorium. The secretary didn't accompany it, prevented by the infirmities of age. The coffin was placed on a special pedestal, and at this height Antonina Naumovna's gray face, with its sunken mouth and prominent nose, looked like it was made of cardboard. Music played until she had sunk through an opening in the floor, and the doors to the subterranean realm folded shut.

Kostya held his arm around his mother and could feel through her coat how narrow her shoulders were, how small she was, and how infinitesimal the span of a human life was—even a life as long as his grandmother's. And how sad was the funeral of a person whom no one loved, or pitied . . .

They threw her away like an old felt boot on a garbage heap, Kostya thought bitterly. He acknowledged that he hadn't loved his grandmother, either.

After the coffin was consigned to the artificial underworld, Ari Lvovich pressed Olga's and Kostya's hands and said that if they wished to submit a request for material assistance, he would see to it that it landed on the right desk.

After the cremation, it would be two weeks before they could pick up the urn.

Why can't she go into the ground right away? Kostya wondered. *Who knows where she'll be for the next two weeks? It's like they'll be taking her to a left-luggage room.*

Olga invited everyone home to a wake for the deceased. Her daughter-in-law, Lena, had rushed off early to tend to the small children. Ari Lvovich considered it his duty to be in attendance until the late evening, and he opened the door of the bus, admitting the dreary women. Kostya got in last. He had wanted to sit with his mother, but she was already seated next to the newly arrived aunt. The aunt was younger than Antonina Naumovna, but she had similar features and a sharp nose. Ari Lvovich looked out the window. He had a lot to think about.

Olga had set the table before leaving home. Her mother's body had been taken directly to the morgue after she died, and Olga had had plenty of time to put the house in order, airing out all the rooms. Even after three days had passed, however, the smell of medicine still overpowered the smell of resin and floor polish.

They all sat down at the long, oval table, which had been restored by Afanasy Mikhailovich, and Olga, placing her clean hands on the rough linen tablecloth, suddenly felt a pang of longing for her father. She remembered his fleshy nose, his slightly protruding upper lip, his boyish seriousness when he was busy with his woodworking at the dacha, and the smell of furniture polish and wood shavings that always clung to him. This was toward the end of his life, when he was already retired. Because of her own foolishness, that whole mess at the university . . . Her mother had been beside herself with fury, and had screamed in rage; her father, impassive, his eyes closed, had observed a strict silence. He had remained silent—and just as silently had gone into retirement.

"Father, Father," Olga whispered.

Tamara, who was sitting next to her, heard. A perceptive soul, she understood the words in her own way. She whispered:

"Yes, Olga. I also think that your parents have found each other there and are reunited."

Ari Lvovich, examining the valuable furnishings restored by Afanasy Mikhailovich with a trained eye, revised his estimation of the family's status. Empire furniture was fashionable in prosperous households, and he hadn't expected to see such rarities in the home of the deceased, a simple Party functionary. Very, very interesting. Holding back just to be sure that no one more significant would take the initiative, he stood up:

"Let us drink, according to old custom, to dear Antonina Naumovna. Don't clink glasses, don't clink glasses!"

Everyone drank. Kostya took a sip, then put down his glass. He didn't like vodka. He would have preferred wine, but no one offered him any.

Olga drank her glass and grew tipsy almost immediately. The warmth from the alcohol rose to her head, then dropped to her feet, and she seemed to go soft and limp. She sat, resting her haggard cheek on her palm. Her freckles grew more vivid, and her face grew rosy and more youthful. Her hair, which had fallen out completely after her long course of chemotherapy, was growing back again. It was new, fresh growth that even curled above her forehead a bit, and the color—the dark, lustrous amber of Easter eggs dyed with onion skins—was the same as it had been before the terrible treatment.

Her friend Tamara, surprised by her new loveliness, rejoiced: Olga had risen up again, she had revived after her grave illness. And she also thought: *Antonina Naumovna took Olga's illness into herself.* These were Tamara's new thoughts, flowing seamlessly from her Orthodox mindset. Now she no longer viewed all the movements of life, the turns and twists of fate, as random or fortuitous, but as though they were filled with meaning, unequivocally purposeful and wise.

Olga's thoughts moved in another direction altogether: If she had left with Ilya, who would have been there to bury her mother? But now, after her parents had both died and Kostya had married, it was just the time to leave. How much longer would she have to wait until she and Ilya were together again?

Valentina, Antonina Naumovna's sister, sat timidly off to the side. Her appearance was not exactly provincial and backward—just somewhat homely and simple. She lived in Protvino, sixty miles from Moscow, a scientific research town. And she was not at all the cleaning lady or housekeeper she resembled, but a respected biologist with a Ph.D. Olga did not know this, however. She only recalled that her mother had not had a very high regard for her, and had spoken, not without mockery, about the sheep to which her sister had devoted her whole life. And this was true. Valentina had graduated from a veterinary college. But her older sister, a big Party boss, clearly viewed this with contempt.

Valentina was seated next to Olga. She looked neither to the left nor to the right; her eyes remained fixed on her plate. Suddenly, she turned to her niece and said, "I'm going to leave soon, Olga. I'm spending the night here in town, with a girlfriend of mine. But I've brought something to give you. It's our family . . ."

This took Olga by surprise, but she stood up from the table and led her aunt into her mother's study. Her mother had spent the better part of her life here, sleeping seldom and working long hours, writing about weavers, carders, and milkmaids, drafting reports and speeches, composing official orders and reprimands. She once wrote a novel for which she almost received the Stalin Prize. The ancient typewriter with its faux leather cover, which the writer lovingly called "the martyr," stood in the middle of the table like a tiny coffin. It was an Underwood. Next to it stood an iron receptacle for writing utensils depicting a muscular laborer, a bust of Tolstoy, and a photograph of herself—the most flattering picture ever taken of her: a girl in a leather jacket, her lips firmly compressed.

Antonina had not permitted any of her husband's antique furniture in her study. Everything was from the Stalin era. The massive objects even bore small metal tags in their intimate folds, attesting to their origins at the state distribution center. The writer had also died on the leather government-issue divan.

After her mother died, Olga promptly removed the mattress from the divan, and Kostya took it to the dump. She threw away the medicine bottles and paraphernalia. All that was left was the smell.

Valentina Naumovna entered her sister's room and was surprised at how uninhabited it looked, though she kept her surprise to herself. There were three official portraits on the wall: a large one of Lenin with a log, and two smaller ones, of Stalin and Dzerzhinsky. She sat on the edge of the leather divan and placed her briefcase neatly across her lap.

Mama had the very same briefcase, Olga noted. Her aunt was shorter than her mother, but she had the same long nose and desiccated appearance. She was dressed in a similar fashion—a worn-out sweater over a gray blouse, and a skirt covered in cat hair.

I should give her Mama's clothes—her fur, her raincoat, Olga thought.

"Olga, I really don't know whether your mother would approve of this . . . most likely she wouldn't. But I've decided to give you the family photographs I've managed to save."

Well, that's a solemn beginning . . . oh, and shoes, too. The fur-lined boots Mama brought back from Yugoslavia fifteen years ago—I can't forget to give her those.

Meanwhile, Valentina fiddled with the lock on the briefcase, and then extracted from an envelope a diminutive packet wrapped in newsprint.

"This is, so to speak, our family archive—everything that has survived." She carefully unfolded each layer of the newsprint, one after the other, until the photographs were visible. Then she stood up and laid out one cardboard-framed picture from a pre-Revolutionary photography studio and two faded amateur photos.

"I've written on the back, very lightly in pencil, who they are, and when . . ." She gently smoothed over the photograph glued to the cardboard. The other photos had rolled up into a tube, and she pressed them flat. "If I don't give them to you and Kostya now, there will be no successors to remember our forebears."

Forebears? Successors? What is she talking about? Mama told me that she had been orphaned when she was little. She didn't know her relatives; the ones she could remember had all either perished or simply died off.

"This was our father, Naum Ignatievich, with our mother. Your grandfather and grandmother, that is." Her gnarled old woman's finger tapped the edge of the photograph. In an armchair sat a priest with a mane of hair down to his shoulders and beard almost to his waist. He had black eyebrows that looked almost as though they had been pasted on. Behind his chair stood a pretty woman in a dark headscarf, tied simply, in the style of the common folk, and wearing a fine silk frock, decorated around the collar with what looked like beadwork. Next to the father were three boys, and with the mother, two little tykes. She held one toddler in her arms. The second was holding the hand of a dark-eyed young girl with a stern, matronly expression on her face.

"Our mother, Tatiana Anisimovna—her maiden name was Kamyshina—was also from a clerical family. Her father was the inspector of the Nizhegorodsky Seminary. All of us, from the very beginning, were in the Church—grandfathers, great-grandfathers, uncles."

"Mama never told me . . ." Olga whispered, her voice faltering.

"That's why. They were all priests," her aunt said, nodding, still pointing at the sepia cardboard picture. "My father, Naum Ignatievich, looked like his mother, Praskovya. She had dark eyes and black hair.

She was of Greek origin, also from a line of priests. After Praskovya, the line was ruined and the Greek strain of black hair and eyes appeared."

"Mama told me nothing about this."

"Of course she didn't. She couldn't. She was afraid. I'll tell you everything I know. When Antonina was little, she always helped around the house. She was a good girl. At first she was the only girl among five brothers. There were three older boys and two younger ones. She took care of the younger ones. Andrei and Panteleimon both took after our mother, with their light hair. And they both died in the same year, in exile. She was ten years older than me—I was born in 1915. I wasn't born yet when this picture was taken. But I remember how your mother would feed me and dress me when I was little. She was very good, very kind," her aunt repeated several times.

Valentina smoothed over the formal portrait. The amateur photographs had rolled up into a tube again.

"In 1920, our father, Naum Ignatievich, who was a priest at the church in Kosmodemyansk, was sent into exile." She let her finger rest on the girl with the stern face, whose hand was placed on the shoulder of the small child. "I don't really remember my parents. Most of what I know, Aunt Katya has told me. I saw my father for the last time in 1925, when he returned from exile. By that time Mama had already died. Aunt Katya took me to see him."

"Who is Aunt Katya?" Olga looked at her mother's sister and realized suddenly that she was not at all dowdy and shabby. She was quiet and calm, and her diction was very correct, even impeccable.

"Aunt Katya, Mama's sister, Ekaterina Anisimovna Kamyshina, took me in as a small child, after our parents were sent into exile. Pyotr and Seraphim were already big lads; they renounced the old ways immediately, and weren't exiled. Nikolai went with Father. By that time he had already finished seminary and was serving as deacon in a small settlement on the Volga. He's wearing a cassock in the photograph; he was still studying. He was ordained, became a priest, then disappeared in the labor camps. I don't know what year it was, I don't know anything more about him. Katya had lost touch with him. The two younger boys, Andrei and Panteleimon, went into exile with our parents. Both of them died."

"And Mama?" Olga had already guessed what she was about to hear.

"Antonina followed her brothers' example. She left home at fifteen. Pyotr and Seraphim had already left for Astrakhan before her. They all renounced their father the priest when they were there. They put a notice in the newspaper saying that now Lenin was their father, and the Party was their mother."

The girl in the leather jacket looked out on them from her frame, confirming that this was true.

"What became of Grandfather?"

"Five years in exile in the Arkhangelsk region; after that he returned to Kosmodemyansk. In 1928 they sent him to prison, and then released him one more time. In 1934, he disappeared for good. Katya was never able to trace his whereabouts. Katya and I went to see your mother in 1937. We begged her on bended knee to intervene, to help find out where he was. But Antonina said that there was nothing to find out."

There was a polite knock at the door, which stood ajar, and Ari Lvovich poked his head in to say good-bye. In the living room, everyone was talking quietly at the table. With Zoya, the neighbor, Tamara discussed the mysterious illness that had abandoned Olga and had migrated to Antonina Naumovna. Zoya asked Kostya about Ilya. Despite being on very friendly terms with the neighbor, whenever the subject of her ex-husband was broached, Olga pretended that she hadn't heard the question.

Olga thanked the funeral director. He nodded deferentially. When he was already by the door, tipping his lush fur hat, he bowed with aristocratic aplomb and said in a dignified manner:

"At your service, Olga Afanasievna. Always at your service."

Brainless idiot. As though his services are in such high demand, she thought. While she was walking down the hall, she was bracing herself to hear more of what she could already anticipate: exile, arrest, persecution, execution.

But Aunt Valentina said nothing of the kind. She unrolled the two faded photographs: one showed an old man with an oversize jacket hanging off him. He was standing by a wicker fence with two earthenware pots affixed to its posts, and his face was such that it took Olga's breath away. On the other one, he appeared again, this time in a black cassock. He was sitting at a table covered with a tablecloth. In the middle of the table was a small white mound of Easter curd cheese, and a plate with three dark eggs.

"This was from Easter of 1934. Evidently he had served at Easter matins."

They sat and mused silently. Then Valentina wrapped everything up in the newsprint and put it back in the envelope.

"Olga, I have no one else to leave these to. You and your Kostya are the only ones left from our family. I really don't know you at all. Perhaps you don't want these photographs at all. I've saved them my whole life. First Aunt Katya had them, then me."

"I'll take them, of course, Aunt Valentina. Thank you. How terrible it all was, though!" Olga took the envelope from her knotted old hands and her aunt immediately began getting ready to leave.

"Well, I must be going. I've stayed longer than I had planned already. I have to make it to Teply Stan."

"Aunt Valentina, what about your older brothers? How did they fare?"

"Pyotr took to drink. Seraphim disappeared without a trace in the war. Pyotr, it seems, had a family, but his wife left him, taking the daughter with her. I don't know whether Seraphim left anyone behind when he went to war or not."

"What a story. But come back to visit us. I'd like to give you some of Mama's things . . ." And she faltered, because the expression on Aunt Valentina's face was such that it was impossible to bring up the Yugoslavian boots. "I'll call you, I'll be in touch," Olga murmured, trying to kiss her aunt's cheek, and kissing her gray knitted cap instead, as she led her to the front door. "We'll certainly see each other again, and you will tell me everything you can remember."

"Yes, yes, child, of course. Only don't be angry with your mother. Those were terrifying times. Terrifying. Indeed, all of us were orphans. Now we all live so well . . ."

Kostya stood behind his mother, unable to understand why she had suddenly lost her nerve and broken down in tears; the whole day she had shown such admirable self-control. Olga went back into her mother's study. Again she laid out the photographs, which seemed to have floated up out of the abyss of oblivion.

Her mother was no more—her mother, who had long ago turned into a brittle shell of a human being, into a pile of sterile habits and mechanical phrases. And in her place there was now a stranger with a beautiful, expressive face, who had survived betrayal by his adolescent offspring, the death of his wife and his little children, prison, and who knows what else. The dim photograph with the Easter feast opened her eyes. Olga, tears streaming down her face, sat in her mother's study, undergoing a sea change the likes of which she had never known before. She felt like a shoot, slashed off with a knife, then grafted to the parent tree, which was her grandfather Naum, and all those myriad bearded men, with their long locks of hair, both village and townsmen, scholarly and not especially scholarly priests, their women and children, both good and not especially good. She couldn't find words to explain the upheaval that was taking place inside her. And Ilya, who would have been able to find the precise words, who would have known how to put everything in its proper perspective, wasn't there.

The B trolleybus, its rods hooked up to the wires above, rattling, pulled out from around the corner. Ari Lvovich quickened his pace: the trolleybuses ran infrequently during the late-evening hours. He had already forgotten about today's deceased. One of the secretaries of the Writers' Union was now at death's door. Ari was already planning the pompous funeral solemnities. He hoped it would happen during the week so he could go to the dacha on Friday. He was hurrying home to his young wife. Ten years earlier, a newly minted widower, he had met the wonderful, tender Klara at one of his funerals and had fallen in love. He had married her, and a new daughter, Emma, was born. He felt he had been granted a fresh life, a happier life—so that it was almost impossible to imagine he would ever have to die. And he had been on such close terms with death for such a long time that he served her not out of fear, but out of duty and compunction. Hadn't he earned a rebate?

Maybe I'll live until ninety-five, like my grandfather. And why not? I have adult grandchildren, thanks to my eldest daughter, Vera, from my first marriage. Great-grandchildren will be here before you know it. And if I make it to ninety-

five, I'll live to see Emma's children, too. And why not? My health is good, knock on wood, I have an excellent job—a good income, as well as respect. And the work is interesting; it feeds the soul. Yes, it would be a good thing if the secretary—a rogue if there ever was one, by the way—died not today, and not tomorrow, and not even on Monday, but would hold out until Tuesday. Then everything could be organized without any rush, and it would all be over and done with before Friday. And the wake could be held in the Oak Hall, with a table set for one hundred guests.

KING ARTHUR'S WEDDING

Even as a child, Olga had known that people were reassuringly predictable. She already knew beforehand what her girlfriend, her teacher, or her mother would say. Her mother in particular. Very early on, Antonina Naumovna began schooling her daughter in the rare virtue of sacrificing one's own interests for those of society. The girl seemed to have had an innate sense of justice. When one of the children came out to play bearing a precious piece of bread and butter sprinkled with sugar, Olga was the one (and the only one) entrusted with the task of doling it out among all the mouths present in the courtyard. If the piece of bread was misshapen and hard to divide into even pieces, only Olga knew how to add a piece here, and take away a piece there, so that everyone got the same amount. She didn't know what bread rations were—she had been born at the end of the war—much less labor camp rations. But the instinct for them was bred in the bone.

Antonina Naumovna admired her belated offspring—she was made of the right stuff! She had inherited all her parents' good qualities. From her mother: integrity and firmness of character. From her father: kindheartedness and good looks, with fair skin and hair. The Greek strain, the black hair and prominent nose from her mother's side of the family, was nowhere in evidence. Nor did she exhibit any of Afanasy

Mikhailovich's fleshiness, a trait that had been noticeable in him since childhood.

During Olga's childhood, Antonina Naumovna was the editor in chief of a magazine for youth, and she put her pedagogical and child-rearing theories into practice in her own life, with her own daughter. Her observations and experiences, in turn, became fodder for her articles. After watching her little one at play in the sandbox—pouring water on the sand and building a clumsy sandcastle—she even resorted to artistic imagery: the sand represented disparate individual personalities, and water was the ideology that served to mix and knead the dough. Out of this substance a great building was created. She used this metaphor in both her editorials and her reports. Her speeches were always distinguished by their imagery, especially when she had occasion to speak at official Party events. She had studied at the Literary Institute, which was a rarity in such circles. The writers were unimpressed; they all had a way with words. She had other means at her disposal for them. But in Party circles she was regarded as having a golden tongue.

Still, Antonina Naumovna had never felt as comfortable in the collective as her daughter. With her hand on her heart, Antonina Naumovna had to admit: they envied her! However sad she was to have to acknowledge it, there were still petty people who were jealous of her position, her authority, and the respect she commanded among the higher-ups.

But Olga, as a small child, had always enjoyed the collective experience. The collective of children was healthier, Antonina Naumovna mistakenly concluded. But that had nothing to do with it. In fact, Olga was a born leader, and knew how to use her gifts without being aware of it herself. She employed them without any coercion on her part, and both girls and boys were prepared to go to the ends of the earth for her. Pretty, good-natured, and endowed with cheerful vivacity, she always had a string of girlfriends trailing in her wake. She liked joining in the main current of activity, sometimes heading it up; she liked the feeling of togetherness and unity, which reached its apotheosis during the annual May Day celebrations.

One day her mother had taken her daughter to witness the parade from the guest viewing balcony of Lenin's Mausoleum. Olga was entranced by the spectacle from the very first moment, but she later remarked:

"Yes, it was really great! But when you're walking together with everyone else, it's better still."

Oh, the sweet sense of togetherness and unity! The equality and interchangeability of grains of sand, their ability to blend into a single, powerful current that sweeps away everything in its path! And the joy of being a tiny particle in it. Beloved Mayakovsky! Beloved Vladimir Vladimirovich!

But Ilya had opened her eyes. Everything that Olga knew, he knew otherwise. The early Mayakovsky was the most valuable part of Ilya's collection. On fragile yellow newsprint, crumbling, ancient, fiery Mayakovsky . . . And Ilya had told her so much that she never learned from her textbooks! The Mouthpiece of the Revolution—with his fear of infection, his childish braggadocio, his lifelong love of a woman involved with the secret police—he was far more intriguing and complex than Olga, or millions of her compatriots and peers, had ever imagined. But Ilya himself was most interesting of all. When she was with him, everything seemed different, extraordinary—even the weather seemed unprecedented. And his photographs! Rain, for instance: trees viewed through a window, distorted through the traces of drops along the glass, a fur collar with beads of water stranded in it . . . a puddle, in the middle of which is a newspaper, with the word *Communist* sinking under the watery surface.

Before Ilya, Olga was completely unaware of how many interesting people there were living on the earth, how different they all were, with their various philosophies and religions. During her entire life, Olga had met only one absolutely remarkable person, perhaps even a genius. This was the university teacher, her academic adviser, an underground writer who published his books abroad, on whose account she was expelled from the university. Everyone who surrounded Ilya was remarkable, however. Not every person was a writer, of course; but each of them was an outstanding personality with eccentric interests, rare knowledge, or expertise in every imaginable and unimaginable field, and all of it absolutely superfluous to ordinary life.

There was an older woman with kimberlite pipe diamonds, a lame expert in nonexistent (banned) forms of theater, an artist from the outskirts of town who painted garbage dumps and fences, a scholar on UFOs, an astrologer, and a Tibetan translator . . . and all of them, except the woman with the diamonds, worked as security guards, elevator operators, truckers, fictitious research assistants, were spongers living off their wives or mothers, creative layabouts who never lifted a finger, parasites, pariahs, and outcasts, all of them equally dangerous and fascinating. It was never completely clear whether they refused to work for the state, or the state refused to have anything to do with them.

The first of these people Ilya took Olga to meet was Artur Korolev (Arthur Kingsley, in English—hence his nickname: King Arthur). He was a retired sailor. He lived in Tarasovka in a large, dilapidated old house with a wood-burning stove, a well by the gate, and an old wooden outhouse in the far corner of the property. The gate was affixed with a rusty lock, and Ilya had to knock for a long time on the metal sheeting that backed the gate and propped it up. At last Artur appeared on the porch—an enormous bald man in an officer's black uniform jacket. He sauntered leisurely up to the gate with a sailor's rolling gait and flipped a latch with one of his fingers. It swung open easily. He thrust his giant hand, which resembled a shovel, at Ilya. His fingers were like large carrots, and they were rosy yellow, as though they had just been hard at work in a laundry tub. Olga had never in her life seen such a person. She peered at him closely—and saw something that took her aback: he had no eyebrows. He was florid, like a peasant; even his bald head was sunburned. His voice was a booming bass, stentorian—but he laughed softly, as though the sound came from another body. He didn't give Olga a second glance after they were introduced. He hadn't even told her his name. Olga was flustered: what a boor! And he was a former naval officer, too!

The host led the way up to the house. She noticed he was wearing flip-flops—in the snow! What an oddball. And the house was par for the course: dusty, full of clutter. They stood by the door and heard rustling all around them: the fire in the big peasant stove, mice between the walls, old books piled up everywhere in small hillocks, bales, and

bundles. There were books on the floor, on the table, and on the workbench, which stood right inside the room.

Ilya shrugged off his big camping backpack and took out a bottle
of vodka. The host sat down in an armchair with patched armrests,
and looked at the bottle disapprovingly. Ilya caught his glance.

"Your highness, you don't have to drink it if you don't want to."

The King snorted:

"Well, what are we going to do with it, then? Go set the table, beautiful. The silverware is out there. Everything you need. I'm the first to
admit that I don't like domestic chores."

Olga gasped with indignation. Of all the nerve! What impudence!
"Beautiful"! What next, "sweetheart"?

She shot Ilya a look of fury, but he seemed to be either laughing or
just winking at her.

Unable to elicit the sympathy she was seeking, Olga smiled, flashing
her famous dimples. Looking directly at the King, she said simply:

"I'm the first to admit I don't like domestic chores, either. Especially
in someone else's house."

"Got it," the host said with a nod, and walked out to get the table-
ware. It was all very natural.

"Touché, Olga!" Ilya whispered. And Olga felt a rush of happiness,
pride, and vindication.

King Arthur brought back a black pot, three stacked bowls that
served as a cover, and on top of them, in a mound like a pyramid, a
large pickle, a loaf of roughly sliced bread, and three shot glasses. The
forks jangled in the pocket of his jacket. He moved with the slow grace
and precision of an athlete or a dancer—small objects stuck to his hands
like magnets. Nothing lost its balance and fell; everything stood upright, as though anchored to the spot on which he had placed it. He
fished around in his pocket and pulled out an onion and a large clasp
knife. He cut off the end, then sliced it into quarters, not bothering to
peel off the skin. The onion lay in the middle of a wooden cutting
board, its insides exposed, arranged like the petals of a white water
lily. He put a plate in front of each of them—the pot contained potatoes, still in their jackets and steaming hot. He reached behind him
without looking, then swung his long arm back around and placed a

silver salt bowl in the shape of a swan on the table. Everything was just as it should be. Happiness was spreading inside Olga like yeast; she felt she was rising like leavened dough.

"Well, open it," Artur said gently to Ilya, who tore off the tin cap from the greenish bottle.

Ah, that's why they call vodka the "green wine"—the flasks are green, Olga mused.

Olga covered her glass with her palm.

"No thank you. I don't want vodka."

"Cognac?" the host asked.

"No thank you. Not in the middle of the day."

He nodded.

He cut the pickle into thin slices, took a potato and stripped its jacket off, and then cut it into pieces, too. He and Ilya drank. Pinching the salt from the small bowl with his fingertips, he salted the pieces and ate them with his hands; but his mannerisms seemed elegant, even aristocratic.

"How's Lisa?" Ilya asked. He had already told Olga on the way there that Artur's lovely wife had recently left him.

"She's still around. She came by a few days ago."

"Is she begging you to take her back?"

"No, Ilya, she's not coming back. But she can't stay away, either. She filed for a divorce, she's planning to marry someone else—but she doesn't have the guts to leave. We'll see what happens. We've been together for fifteen years. She wants to get out of the country, to go abroad. She found herself a Finn."

"Really? I thought there was some guy from Iraq."

"There was. He was loaded. But she got rid of him. Said that a European woman like herself couldn't survive in the Middle East. The Finn is from Lapland. Lisa's used to the cold—she grew up in the Far East. She actually had her heart set on Italy, but no Italians have turned up."

Olga sat wide-eyed listening to their conversation. What kind of girl was this, who had her pick of foreigners? Was she some sort of prostitute? She would have to ask Ilya about it later.

Afterward they drank tea. Artur brewed it slowly, enacting a ceremonial ritual around the teapot. The teapot was, it must be said, unlike anything she had ever seen. It was made of enameled metal and adorned with dragons and tongues of blue flame.

"Chinese," King Arthur said tenderly, stroking its convex flank. He caressed it with his eyes just as tenderly, like a man caressing a woman. "I bought it in Singapore. A real beauty!"

That's what Ilya had told her—that Artur had worked on a merchant marine vessel and had sailed all the oceans and seas. Olga's eyes were already growing used to this unusual fellow. She liked him more and more. Although, upon closer inspection, his hairlessness had something strange about it—as though no hair had ever grown upon his head, or on his childishly soft face. And something else—his hands trembled ever so slightly, almost imperceptibly.

The King removed the plates in the same manner he had brought them in, piling them on top of the black pot. He wiped off the table, and Ilya put down a large bundle of typed pages. The thin paper rustled.

"I don't have any fitting material, only chintz," Artur said.

"Just so long as it's not floral."

"It will be a dark blue binding," the King said, nodding.

Then, with an even more solemn expression, he went into the other room. When he came back, he was carrying an ancient book in a dark leather binding. He passed it fastidiously to Ilya.

"Unbelievable! Eighteenth century—1799! *The Compleat Distiller*. Everything you ever wanted to know about moonshine? I'm floored!" Ilya sighed, then laughed out loud.

"That's not the point. Look at the title page. Then you can ooh and aah!" And King Arthur opened the cover of the book.

Ilya whistled under his breath.

"This beats all . . . From the paper collection center? It was trashed?"

"Yep. It bears the inscription of the owner—none other than Berdyaev. Of course, it needs to be verified."

"You need an expert—I can show it to Sasha Gorelik," Ilya said.

"No, I'm not letting it out of my sight. You can bring him here. I'll stand him a bottle."

"He'll stand you one. He might even buy the book."

"There's no way I'm selling this."

Olga took a peek over Ilya's shoulder. She saw the name Nikolai Berdyaev, written in lilac ink.

The name seemed familiar; she had heard the name mentioned among Ilya's friends. She didn't dare ask, though, so as not to compromise the aura of sophistication she was cultivating. Besides, it was already obvious that Ilya, who had no formal university training whatsoever, knew much more about literature than she did. And she would soon be graduating. Judging by the books that packed the room, this retired sailor was a well-educated man. Her surmise was confirmed when he pulled out a palm-sized volume of Dickens from behind the divan.

"Here is a truly remarkable writer, Ilya. Oh, the rubbish they made us read as children!" He laughed, waving his hand dismissively. "Actually, I read almost nothing as a child. In the entire city of Izyum, I don't think there was a single English book. It's a Cossack settlement. They put boys on horses before they can walk. They can wave their sabers around, but they don't even know the alphabet."

Although she had promised herself to keep quiet, Olga couldn't resist asking: "So you know how to use a saber?"

"No, my child, I've hated all that Cossack derring-do since I was small. I ran away from home when I was thirteen. I entered the Nakhimov Naval Academy. I was a romantic. An idiot, in other words. I had no idea what the military was all about."

"My child"—that was patronizing, of course; but Artur's tone was completely friendly and open. He looked directly into her eyes, not past her.

Soon they got ready to leave. Ilya put a packet of books, neatly wrapped in newspapers and tied with twine, in his nearly empty backpack. He gave King Arthur a small pile of bills in return. Then they hurried to the station. It was nearly ten o'clock, and the electric commuter trains came less frequently. Along the way, Olga asked Ilya about Artur, and he replied briefly. "Yes, he's a former naval officer who survived some sort of blast. He was discharged, with a detour through a psych ward, receives a small pension, works as an assistant at the paper collection center.

"At first he didn't know a lot about book collecting, but over the years he learned the tricks of the trade. He developed a feel for it. And it would have been hard not to—people bring in books by the bagful. It's amazing what turns up among the old newspapers and the scribbled-over textbooks—an original edition of Karamzin, or Khlebnikov. A Rudolf Steiner. You can't find those at the antiquarian booksellers—turn-of-the-century editions.

"You don't know him? It's not my kind of thing, but you need to know who he is. Artur has taken up yoga recently. He found a volume of Vivekananda at the collection center. He practices meditation."

"I also want . . . Vivekananda." Olga wanted everything: all the books, all the conversation, and music, and theater and film, and Berdyaev, and the Indian Vivekananda, and she wanted to read Dickens in English right away. And, as in childhood, when she wanted to hurry to join the Young Pioneers and the Komsomol Youth Group so she could be in the vanguard, she now wanted to be accepted by Ilya's amorphous group of acquaintances—King Arthur, and the others whom she didn't know yet, but about whom she had heard. They were the ones who had been standing outside the courthouse when her professor was on trial, and being part of their company was far more appealing to her than serving on the Komsomol committee of the philology department.

Ilya gave Olga both Berdyaev and Vivekananda, as well as Orwell, who truly astonished her. After her expulsion from the university, Olga now had plenty of free time. She lolled around in her room for days at a time while Faina took care of Kostya, feeding him, taking him out for walks, and putting him down for naps. Toward evening, when her mother came home from work, Olga would go out to meet Ilya. They had several favorite meeting places: by the monument to Ivan Fedorov, the printing pioneer; by the Kitai-Gorod wall; at an antiquarian bookseller's; in the old apothecary's on Pushkin Square. When the weather got warmer, they started meeting at the Aptekarsky Garden, a small botanical garden founded by Peter the Great.

Half a year passed before Ilya invited Olga to Tarasovka again, this time for a wedding. Olga was surprised. Who would want to marry such an eccentric man?

"Olga, you don't know what you're saying! Before he married Lisa, women were lining up for the privilege to become his wife. They dreamed of the honor of laundering his trousers! A famous actress flew all the way from Vladivostok to Moscow twice a month, just to get screwed by him. She arrives, and he says: 'Sorry, I'm not on furlough today.' And he goes off with the barmaid. When Lisa appeared on the scene, all that ended. He became a faithful husband. He never so much as glanced at another woman. Then Lisa began whoring around, too," Ilya said, and laughed.

Olga always admired how freely and simply he spoke about things that she couldn't even have named before she met him. Olga couldn't say the word *shit* out loud—it stuck in her throat; but coming from him, even the most unmentionable vulgarities sounded natural and amusing.

"Who's he marrying?" Olga said.

"It's a curious story, as you might imagine. He's marrying Lisa's elder sister. It's something Lisa cooked up herself. You'll see."

King Arthur's wedding took place in mid-July. The summer was still fresh. It was the first sunny day after a month of steady rain. On the eve of the wedding, Maria Fedorovna, Ilya's mother, went to visit her sister in Kirzhach. That evening, Olga went to see Ilya at home. For the first time they were able to spend a night together alone, without hurry, interruption, or the furtive awkwardness Olga always felt in the strangers' beds that Ilya took her to from time to time.

In the morning they felt calm and spent, emptied out, and this rapturous vacancy lent them a sense of weightlessness, both physical and emotional. They were both aware of the unprecedented nature of what had happened to them: through bodily self-expression, extreme and urgent, bordering on the edge of possibility, through the feat of the sexual act, they had traversed a generally prescribed boundary—as though making a discovery where they had least expected to find it. Beyond the supreme pleasure of sex, another, inexpressible kind of bliss opened up to them—the dissolution of the individual self, of the "I," into an ineffable, hitherto unknown freedom of soaring flight.

"It's so wonderful, it's even frightening," Olga whispered when they were already sitting in the commuter train.

"No, it's not frightening. We were shown what they call seventh heaven. I feel I need to perform an act of gratitude."

"What kind?" Olga said. "What kind of act could it be?"

"Well, I don't know. Maybe we should get married? Then I can fuck you like an honest man." And he laughed out loud, as though he had said something quite witty.

Olga felt seared by the expletive, but for some reason her body responded with immediate assent. She blushed—*I've completely lost my mind*—and said awkwardly:

"No. I think we need to have a baby after all of this."

Ilya stopped laughing abruptly. His experience with fatherhood was terrible, and he had no wish to repeat it.

"No, that's going too far. No way, never. Remember that."

Something collapsed inside her: what a roller coaster ride! What was this? Cruelty? Stupidity? How could he say such a thing? But he was neither cruel, nor stupid: he realized immediately that he had offended her. He took her arm above the elbow and squeezed it.

"You don't understand. Only freaks of nature are born to me. I'm a freak myself. You can't bear any child of mine."

Olga grabbed hold of his hand. Her hurt was transformed into poignant sympathy; he had hinted to her before that his child was not entirely healthy. Now she understood that he had not been talking about an ordinary childhood illness; he was talking about an unmitigated catastrophe. They both fell silent, and stared out the window. The leafy green verdure beyond the window, so fresh, and washed clean by the long rains, seemed to call for silence. After this confession, their intimacy grew even more profound than they could have imagined possible.

Tables had been shoved together and placed along the path leading up to the house. The grounds around the house were so overgrown with burdock, raspberry, and nettles that there was no other place to set them up. There were about forty guests, and not everyone had arrived yet. At the back of the property wood was burning in a makeshift outdoor grill. Smoke was rising into the air, and it smelled of wet grass and jasmine. Two young men were fussing happily around the grill.

No one was sitting down yet, although bowls of various kinds of salads crowded the middle of the long table. Some of the guests had already started drinking, having sought out comfortable, conducive spots—in the ramshackle gazebo, long on the verge of collapse, next to the rain barrels, or on a stump near the outhouse. Loud peremptory cries could be heard coming from the house—Lisa was taking charge of everything. Then she emerged onto the porch: a real beauty, a sex bomb, a starlet—from her slender, shapely legs in spiked heels to the fountain of hair on her head and the oversize, slightly tinted glasses. She smiled, revealing a pair of sharp, fanglike teeth on either side of her mouth. What was she, a vampire? A witch?

"Pannochka!" Olga whispered to Ilya. "It's like she just stepped off the movie screen. She should be playing Pannochka!"

"Maybe," Ilya said.

Then Olga saw the King. He was sprawled on a chaise longue, either meditating or just sleeping. His eyes were closed, his large, smooth chin pointed up to the sky.

"Your Highness! Come to the table!" Lisa shouted, and the King opened one eye. "Why are you being such a layabout? We can't start without you!"

There was a stirring in the thickets and the undergrowth—the guests, some of them already in their cups, made their way to the table and settled onto the benches. Ilya was one of the first to throw a leg over a bench and sit down. Olga sat beside him. She knew some of the people there, though not all.

But what people they were! All ages—young and middle-aged, two octogenarians, and one very amusing elderly lady. And all of them less than Soviet in their persuasions—to be more precise, they were downright anti-Soviet! Marvelously anti-Soviet! And, of course, her imprisoned professor had been part of this circle.

"Tell me who's who," Olga whispered.

"Which one in particular do you find interesting?"

"Well, the red-haired one, for example."

"Ah, that's Vasya Rukhin, a philosopher and theologian. He's extremely erudite. Fascinating conversationalist. He gets drunk quickly, though, and all he can talk about then is the Jewish-Masonic conspiracy."

The philosopher-theologian was completely sober, and maybe for that reason he seemed rather downcast. He poured some generic alcoholic liquid into a glass, and the woman sitting next to him, whose hand kept straying to the tightly braided bun at the back of her neck, quietly protested. A stooping, almost hunchbacked man with the chiseled features and decorative mustache common among people from the Caucasus Mountains, raising his right arm and gesturing broadly with his left, began slowly declaiming what sounded like verse:

"Alas, the printed word has scruples, but the lyre favors nonsense . . ."

"That's Damiani. He's a genius. A modern Khlebnikov. He writes palindromes, acrostics, all kinds of formal wordplay. And his poems are brilliant. He's a true genius. He was born too late. If he had lived at the turn of the century, Khlebnikov wouldn't have been able to hold a candle to him. I haven't seen Sasha Kuman yet. They're like bosom enemies. They always go everywhere together. Sasha is also a poet, but of a different stripe. They're always at each other's throat, and poetry is the bone of contention."

Ilya was no longer waiting for Olga to prompt him with her questions. He waxed loquacious.

"And those two are human rights activists. The fat one is a mathematician, his name is Alik. Theoretical mathematics. His logic is ironclad. I guess he's the only one the KGB is afraid to tussle with. You can't have a conversation with him—he proves every point. No one can keep up with him; his mind is like an automatic weapon. And the one sitting next to him, in the cowboy hat, a born-again Jew—his name is Lazar—is the inventor of machine translation. He's a linguist and a cyberneticist. And next to him, in the blue dress, is his wife, Anna Reps. Also a poet. A fair-to-middling one, I'd say."

"How did the King come to know all of them?" Olga asked.

"It's a circle of like-minded people. They all live and breathe books. The King is a fine bookbinder. Everyone knows him, and has good relations with him. There are several different groups of people who are connected only through the King. It's a circle," Ilya said, stressing the word again, as though it summed everything up.

At that moment, Lisa's cry—"Shura! Shura! Where's the pie?"—carried up to the porch. The door opened, and a large, red-faced woman stuffed into a white dress two sizes too small for her appeared in the doorway. In her outstretched hands, she held a baking sheet with a voluminous home-style pie. She had a fresh red burn mark on her forearm. A young girl, with an equally red face, also wearing a white dress, peeked out from behind her shoulder. She was carrying two large buckets. Olga craned her neck to get a better look—the buckets were full of sliced meat. The shish-kebab experts jumped up, grabbed the buckets, and disappeared.

"Olga, that one there, the thin one with the dark eyes, is the famous Sinko. We listened to recordings of his songs at Bozhenov's, remember?"

"Yes, of course I do. Wonderful songs."

"He has a guitar with him, so he's going to sing."

"Shura, put down the pie and go get the herring. Did you forget it?" Lisa admonished the plump one, her voice raised again. The sharp end of Lisa's nose wriggled like that of a small creature, and Olga realized that her name was a reference to *lisá*, meaning "fox" in Russian, rather than a nickname for Elizabeth. Her pointy little nose was so mobile and alert, it seemed to have a life of its own. The plump one ran into the house, her behind jiggling. Lisa shook her head and smiled a condescending smile, as if berating a dull and inept assistant. The young girl in white went up to Lisa and told her something, but Lisa dismissed it with a wave of her hand:

"Your job is to help. You didn't bring the aspic!"

And the younger one also trotted back to the house at a rapid clip.

At last, King Arthur peeled himself from the chaise longue and went to sit at the head of the table. He sat in his armchair with the patched armrests. A girl with an expressive eastern countenance, large eyes, lips, and nostrils, her hair cut short, and wearing white jeans and a white T-shirt, sat down next to Artur on a bentwood chair. He put his arm around her.

"What a stylish bride!" Olga whispered to Ilya.

"No, that's Lenka Vavilon. She has nothing to do with Artur at all. She's Ossetian; she graduated from the Institute of Foreign Languages. She knows all the languages of the Caucasus. And Persian, too. I've never laid eyes on the King's bride myself."

At that very moment, Lisa went up to the stylish young woman and yanked the chair out from under her.

"Lenka, that chair's not for you."

Lenka remained unruffled.

"Lisa, don't order me around."

"Well, you get out of that chair, it's for the bride!" Lisa shouted at her raucously. Lenka turned the chair with its back to the table, and then got up to sit in Artur's lap.

He didn't seem to mind.

"Shura, let's get started! Come to the table!" Lisa screeched. The door flew open, and Shura appeared with a dish towel in her hands.

"I'm coming, I'm coming!" On the way, she wiped her hands off with the dish towel, then fanned herself with it, saying quietly to Lisa (though Olga managed to catch what she said): "Lisa, tell Masha to sit down. You know she won't, unless you tell her to."

Masha came out balancing a large oval platter of herring on the outspread fingers of each hand.

Shura, going up to the bentwood chair, turned it around toward the table again, hung the dish towel over the back, and sat down heavily. This was the bride. In the meantime, Lenka Vavilon had vanished from Artur's lap as though she had never been there at all. Shura's hair was a hopeless mess. Early in the morning she had rushed out to the hairdresser's, where they had whipped her hair into a tower of curls. This made Lisa furious. She harangued her sister, then ordered her to wash her hair at once, getting rid of both curls and hairspray. Shura used an entire bottle of her sister's foreign-made shampoo. Now her hair was cleaner than it had ever been before; but it was so limp and flyaway that no amount of pinning and clipping could contain it. Shura kept reaching up to fiddle with her plain reddish locks, revealing dark stains under the armpits of her white dress. Her face was as flushed as if she had just emerged from a steam bath. It was clear she had been laboring in front of the stove all day.

Now Lisa's voice, with a metallic edge, rang through the air again:

"Well, come on, pour us a glass! Fill up the glasses, Artur! Why are you such a deadbeat? Get up, bridegroom! Who's going to make a toast? Sergei Borisovich, you're the head honcho here!"

A short, small-boned man in glasses, who looked about fifty, with an unhappy, self-contained air, refused outright.

"Lisa, you dragged us all into this farce; you see it through to the end."

"Who is that?" Olga said, startled by the exchange.

"Chernopyatov. A lot depends on him. He's a strong, uncompromising man. He was sent to the labor camps when he was only fourteen. He was still in school. I'll tell you more about him later."

Lisa waved her hand indignantly.

"Fine! It's my wedding, after all. My own husband is marrying my own sister."

She gestured toward her sister dismissively, as if brushing her aside. Shura stood up, and Lisa jumped up onto her chair. Her getup was like something from another world. She had on a white silk blouse, on top of which was a black lace bra; short shorts peeked out from under her shirttails. She stood on the chair unsteadily; the chair legs wobbled, sinking into the soft, uneven ground. Her spiked heels only made matters worse. Strands of unruly hair blew around in the breeze. Artur, watching the orator attentively, prepared to catch her if she lost her balance. On the other side of her, Shura shuffled around in place, arms outspread, watching the precariousness of the situation in alarm. Still, Shura hadn't foreseen just how precarious the situation was—suddenly it dawned on her that Lisa was totally smashed.

"Hey, where's the champagne? Pass me a glass!"

Someone gallantly thrust a glass into her hand. She raised it into the air and shouted:

"It's bitter!"*

Artur grabbed her. She clung to his neck and began kissing him: on his bald head, on his cheek, on his nose—until she came to his mouth, when she fastened her lips to those of the imperturbable King.

"I am giving my beloved husband away in marriage! To my dear sister! Hey, Masha! Hey, where's my niece? Come over here, Masha! I've found a daddy for you!"

---

*At Russian wedding parties, it is customary for guests to cry out "It's bitter!" when they drink. This is a cue for the bride and groom to kiss and make the wine sweet, a call-and-response ritual repeated throughout the wedding party. —*Trans.*

Masha was standing next to her mother; the expression on her face was no laughing matter.

No one knew what would happen next, but it was clear there was trouble afoot.

Olga was riveted by the scene and didn't notice that Ilya was gone. He reappeared a few minutes later laden with shish kebab skewers. He was accompanied by one of the grill tenders.

Lisa grabbed a skewer and thrust it at the King.

"Shura! Look at me, goddammit! The first piece always goes to him! Masha, you too! I'll tear your eyes out if I have to!"

But there was no need to tear out Shura's eyes—they were already filled with tears, and she wanted to die of shame. She stood rooted to the spot. Ilya passed out skewers, and the shish kebab distracted the attention of the guests from the main wedding ritual—the bitter-sweet kissing.

"Ilya, she's just a rogue, she thrives on chaos!" Olga fumed, when Ilya brought her the shish kebab.

"Of course she's a rogue! A brilliant rogue. She's the one who got the King out of prison and into the loony bin, then got him discharged. She paid some, turned tricks for others. She became a lawyer. No, it's true! She graduated from law school, taking evening courses. You can't imagine what all she's done. I knew her first, before I met the King. She was a girl from the Far East, her father was a hunter. She went out hunting in the taiga with him when she was just a little tyke. And she can hold her liquor; she keeps up with the best of them. She's an iron lady, except when she's got the hots for someone. That's her only weakness. And the King is impotent, which she herself will announce shortly."

And that was just what happened. There was a lull in the drama while the guests were amicably partaking of the grilled meat. It ended when Lisa, having polished off her shish kebab, started brandishing her skewer.

"Friends, I take my leave of you! That's it—I'm going to the land of the Finns. I've fucking had it with all of you!" She wriggled her nose and tittered. "But I adore you. Remember that I'm coming back to check up on you! You can't hide from me! The KGB is amateur hour next to me! I'm a one-woman secret agent bureau! Don't you dare insult the King! Or Shura, either. She may be just a dairy cow, but she's a good person. Good Doctor Ouchithurts will heal the masses; she'll feed one and all. She's a nurse. If you need a shot, whether it's in the ass or in your arm, you can count on her. But don't put the moves on her, she hates that. Her hormones are on strike. Whereas mine are raging! They make the perfect pair: one more impotent than the other!"

Going limp, she clung to the King's neck again, then set up an urgent, primal peasant's wail, singing:

"Oy, sweet lord of my soul, you poor little thing! Poor impotent King! Well, why are you all smirking and grinning? He's better than any one of you! If he could get it up, his worth would be beyond compare!"

The King patiently indulged his ex-wife in her wailing. He was completely impassive in the face of her public indictment, which would so devastate any ordinary man. He towered over the rest of them in height, and nobility, and dignity—even in the privilege of impotence among all the sexually obsessed and tormented lovers, the beloved, and the forlorn and unloved, men and women.

He's a king among men, thought Olga.

Shura and Masha hid away in shame in the house, in the kitchen. Shura howled, and her daughter comforted her:

"Mom, stop—you know what Auntie's like! She'll go away, and everything will go back to normal again."

Masha was indifferent to all this sophisticated riffraff. She had her own plans: to settle down in Moscow, to marry a man with an apartment, and to graduate from college. She was just as ambitious as her aunt, but she had been hewn with an axe, rather than a fine chisel.

The wedding party was gaining momentum. An enormous bottle of Absolut that had been bought in a Beryozka store was put away in minutes. The supply of home brew bought from the neighbors in three-liter jars, however, never ran out. The bitter Bulgarian Gamza, in pretty bottles covered with woven straw, was nearly untouched, though an entire case of cheap port had already been consumed. An Ampex tape recorder, one of the King's trophies from his final voyage, had been set up on a table pushed against the window. Bebop music, powerful and exuberant, poured into the yard. Everything seemed jarring and incongruous, almost a travesty—the American tape recorder, a true rarity, the epitome of a boyhood dream come true; the refined, inspired music of another culture; the awkward, reeling drunken wedding against the background of lush July greenery, in which the single indispensable thing was lacking: mutual love between the man and the woman. Soon the tape recorder, exhausted, emitted a little hiss and then fell silent.

Sinko picked up his guitar then, and everyone gathered around him. He brushed his elongated fingers, with their long, chipped fingernails, over the strings of the guitar, and they seemed to coo like a woman. He touched his fingers to the strings again, and they answered him in kind.

"It's almost like his fingers are talking to the guitar," Olga marveled.

Ilya put his hand on her shoulder, and she felt happy. They had been sitting at the table for several hours already, and she longed to touch Ilya, to experience the "awareness of the body" that had begun to melt away. She was too shy to be the first to touch his hand or his shoulder. But he touched her, and this was proof that the feeling was still present.

"Have you never heard him live?"

"No, only on recordings."

"That's completely different. He's a true artist. He sings Galich's songs better than Galich himself."

Lisa left for Helsinki the same evening. By train. At half past nine Sergei Borisovich Chernopyatov, who had been keeping a close eye on Lisa the whole time, went up to her, put his hand on her shoulder, and said:

"It's time to go, Lisa."

Lisa seemed to shrink back, but she went into the house with Chernopyatov. Soon they emerged with a suitcase. Sergei Borisovich was taking Lisa to Leningradskaya Station; they had agreed on this beforehand. Everyone streamed out into the road to gather around the car. Sergei Borisovich wore an air of practical efficiency, and looked irritated. He opened the trunk of his old blue Moskvich. At that moment, Lisa began to hum and spin like a top. She clung to the King's neck again, scolding him rather incoherently for past sins, and again reminding him of his impotence. Artur stroked her head with his hairless pink hand, and suddenly began trying to persuade her to stay:

"Forget about that Finn, Lisa. Stay with us, no one is driving you away!"

Lisa suddenly howled in rage and let her ex-husband have it.

"Not driving me away! What about Shura? I've arranged for Shura to live here with you! Where would she go now? She sold her house! She came here with her child in tow! No way, I'm no longer your wife! Enough! Shura's your wife!"

Then she turned to Shura.

"Well, why are you standing there with your eyes bugging out? Get ready! You're coming with me, to see me off! Artur doesn't need you here to scratch his back—there's always Lenka Vavilon. You'll scratch his back, won't you, Lenka? Shura, get a move on! Let's go!"

Chernopyatov stopped Lisa.

"Listen, I'm not driving all the way back here again. How is she going to get to Tarasovka from the station in the middle of the night?"

Lisa took a sizable packet of money out of her purse and waved it around.

"My sister's coming with me to Leningrad. Aren't you, Shura?"

Shura looked haggard and drawn. She hadn't eaten a thing all day— she had only drunk one glass of champagne. Her head ached and her stomach was cramping from hunger.

"Wait a minute, I'll just get my jacket."

Sergei Borisovich's face darkened. He stood next to the car, its doors agape, then got behind the wheel impatiently. Lisa had sobered up a bit. She shoved Shura, clutching her jacket, into the car. Lisa got in behind her. She rolled down the window, and shouted:

"Hey, people, keep it up! Keep it up! In our village, weddings last at least three days!"

The car started moving, carrying off the King's wives. The King waved magnanimously.

Olga touched Ilya's shoulder.

"Let's go home. I think I've had about enough of this."

Ilya finally managed to find his backpack in the house, and they left the celebration without any ado—they didn't even bother to say good-bye. They were just in time for the commuter train; they didn't even have to wait. They boarded, put their arms around each other, and fell asleep. They slept all the way to Moscow.

Early the next morning, the King in his lair set about repairing the tape recorder.

Guests lay scattered about in unlikely places, having dropped off to sleep from an excess of celebratory cheer. Lenka Vavilon woke up and went into the yard, where she saw an unfamiliar man peeing next to the outhouse. She was surprised—he had made it all the way to the outhouse, why hadn't he done his business inside? She understood the reason when she tried to go into the outhouse herself. She found a comfortable spot in the raspberry bushes, where she discovered that she was not the only one who had come there in search of cozy intimacy.

A flock of sparrows was feasting on the leftovers strewn about the table. Meanwhile, two chickadees were sitting in the branches of an aspen tree, speculating about whether there was room for them among the rabble. Lenka Vavilon gathered up the dirty dishes, poured the rest of the water from the bucket into a large pot, and turned on the gas, preparing to boil water for washing up. She began scraping the left-over scraps of food into the slops pail, fishing out stray cigarette butts that might harm the neighbor's piglet.

Shura accompanied Lisa all the way to Leningrad. Lisa bought her a ticket—albeit in a crowded sleeping car, rather than a separate compartment. Shura was offended, but said nothing. She put her sister to bed, then returned to her own car.

"I'm just a spineless idiot. My whole life I've let Lisa push me around, even though I'm six years older," Shura berated herself.

Shura slept the sleep of the dead, but she was the first to rise in the morning and emerge onto the station platform. Lisa was the last. Still not completely sober, she begged forgiveness and kissed Shura's chapped hands, lingering especially on yesterday's burn mark. Shura was always flustered and clumsy. She always burned herself on this spot when she took her pies out of the oven.

Although she was not very fresh herself, Lisa was wearing a freshly laundered blouse—Shura had not forgotten to wash and iron one for her. Now her bra was underneath the blouse, where it belonged, and she wore a string of beads she had made herself out of tightly rolled strips of paper from shredded pages of the magazine *America*. Her fingers, with their stubby fingernails, were loaded down with cheap silver jewelry and stones. She wore a short, light blue skirt. The new stockings that Ville had brought her for the wedding—he had given her a whole pile of them, twelve in all!—already had a very visible run along the calf.

The sisters kissed and embraced one last time, and Lisa barked out her final instructions as Shura retreated.

An hour and a half later, at the Soviet-Finnish border, Lisa was already going through customs control. The Russian customs officers were the first to search her suitcase and her purse. Lisa, still a bit tipsy, pulled out a packet of photographs and showed the officials her father, and her mother, and her older sister, and her hunting trophies, and some pictures of the natural scenery of the Far East. She had no foreign currency; all her Russian money—every last kopeck of it!—she had given to her sister. Her documents were all in order: a new passport, a visa, a marriage certificate. The border guards laughed at her good-naturedly—she was a strange bird! A little prostitute who had found a scrap of Finnish happiness for herself.

One of them with fewer moral scruples had managed to put his hand on her skinny behind, and she giggled. The other one, an older man, had given her some fatherly advice:

"Go easy on the alcohol over there, sweetie. All Finns are drunks, never mind the dry laws!"

The train rolled over the border—an invisible line running through identical unprepossessing forest tracts, bald patches, and boulders.

Then the train halted. The Finnish customs officers and border guards came aboard, and the whole process was repeated—only they didn't rummage through her suitcase and purse. And it all happened much more quickly and efficiently.

The Finns left, and the train pulled away from the station. Lisa got up, swaying, her little purse swinging on its thin strap, and walked down the aisle to the bathroom. She hung the purse on a hook. She looked at herself in the mirror, and didn't like what she saw, so she stuck her tongue out. Then she sat on the toilet. From her secret place she pulled out a tube of much smaller dimensions than what it normally accommodated, and peeled the condom off it. She threw the condom in the toilet, and without opening the tube, she put it in her purse. Then she stuck out her tongue at her reflection again. Three microfiches—an entire book—were on a treacherous journey. But the main leg of the journey, the most dangerous of all, had already been traversed.

Ville adored his Russian wife. From the very beginning, he had said: "I know you'll ditch me. But I never loved anyone until you, and after you I'll never love again."

At one time he had worked in Russia as a journalist; now he had lost his job. It didn't matter. Tomorrow they would fly to Stockholm, and from there on to Paris. And the banned manuscript, the author of which was doing time in the camps, would be lying on the desk of the publisher, who had been eagerly awaiting it for a long time.

Ville hated communism, loved Russia, and adored his wife, Elizabeth. Ilya loved his work. The microfiche of the manuscript, which had been smuggled out of the prison camp by the author's wife in another of the most secret places, had been expertly photographed. Sergei Borisovich Chernopyatov, who was directing the entire three-stage (at least) anal-gynecological operation, had always known that everything would work out just fine. Lisa never let anyone down.

A TAD TOO TIGHT

After she had seen her sister off, Shura returned to her new husband and the remains of their wedding. Most of the guests had departed, of course, but the truly inveterate revelers were still celebrating on the third day. By this time, they had forgotten all about the host, not to mention the hostess. Shura threw herself into the cleanup. After fashioning new rags out of two old shirts of Artur's, she began from the kitchen and moved backward through the house like a quiet but powerful tractor, scraping off successive archaeological layers of dirt. Masha assisted her silently: she drew water from the well, washed the windows, and laundered the ancient curtains. Artur didn't allow them into his room, but Shura knew that sooner or later she would gain admittance to it. Although Artur had ascended to the rank of husband, she continued to regard him as a beloved brother-in-law.

On the fourth day, when all the guests were gone except for a certain Tolik, who still couldn't manage to sober up, Artur summoned her to his den, opened his desk drawer, and, pointing a huge finger into its depths, said:

"Shura, take money from here when you need it."

There was a lot of money. Shura felt abashed, and waved her hand dismissively:

"You give it to me yourself."

Without even looking, he grabbed as much as his hand would hold and thrust it at her. She was surprised: it turned out he was a rich man. Lisa had always claimed that his pockets were empty, that she had to try to make do as best she could. It didn't tally.

It was awkward enough taking it directly from the drawer, but accepting it right out of his hand like this made her even more uneasy.

She had lived on her own for many years. Her husband had died on the job, log rafting, when Masha was only two.

"I'd like to send Father some," Shura said on the fly, though the thought had only just occurred to her.

"Go ahead, send something to Ivan Lukyanovich. Here, take some more." Again he put his hand in the drawer and drew out a wad of bills. He was amused that he had switched wives, but that he still had the same father-in-law.

"Thank you, Art. Father hasn't been doing too well recently."

The next day Shura sent Masha to the Central Telegraph Office to dispatch the money to her father in Ugolnoe. Even though Masha was not even eighteen, she knew her way around the city far better than Shura did. Lisa had twice taken Masha with her to Moscow. The last time Masha had stayed with Lisa in a rented apartment for a month and a half, and she had wandered the streets alone from morning till evening. She liked walking around alone and getting to know the city.

Now Masha was hurrying to the telegraph office to send the money. After that she planned to go to Red Square to visit Lenin's Mausoleum, if she was lucky enough to get in. But the window she needed at the telegraph was closed. A spurious, hand-lettered sign dangled in front of the window, reading: "Maintenance break. Back in fifteen minutes." Masha stood in line for fifteen minutes, then left, walking toward Red Square. Nothing had changed in the past three years; only, it seemed to Masha, there were now more people. Suddenly, Red Square opened out in front of her. Her thoughts leapt back to Ugolnoe, to her friends Kate and Lena. If only they could see all this beauty with their own eyes.

When I settle down here, I'll invite them. First Lena, then Kate, Masha decided.

The line at the Mausoleum seemed to go on forever, so Masha headed in the direction of GUM, the state department store. There she found another line, spilling out the side doors. A girl of about Masha's age took a pair of boots out of a long white box and showed them to another girl. The other girl went pale with envy. The sight took Masha's breath away, too; she had never seen such boots! Tall, reaching almost to the knee, they had a small heel. They were made from beautiful brown suede. Her grandfather, who was good at leatherwork, would never have been able to make anything like this.

Masha had never been subject to secret passions or mad longings, but now she was burning inside. She would have given anything for those boots. Unfortunately, she had nothing to give. At that moment, she had even forgotten about the money wrapped up in a handkerchief in her pocket, secured with a safety pin.

"Are you last in line? I'm after you!" a girl with a big hairdo said, nudging her.

That was when Masha remembered about the money—she had a hundred rubles with her! And it seemed she was already standing in line; there was even someone behind her.

She stood there for four hours. Twice a rumor spread down the line that they had run out of boots. It turned out that there were no more size 37s, but other sizes were still available. By the time Masha got to the front of the line, all the boots were gone, both large and small. But mounds of boxes were stacked on the counter. Women who didn't have any ready cash were writing layaway checks, valid for two hours, and rushing off to fetch the money. Whoever didn't manage to redeem the boots within the allotted time would lose them forever— other anxious women, their happiness almost within reach, were clamoring to buy them, bills clutched in their sweaty fists. Masha was one of them. And she was in luck. The long cardboard box with the soft, brown creatures inside was hers. The whole way home her hand kept straying into the depths of the box, to touch the tender flanks enveloped in darkness . . .

You have absolutely lost your mind, Masha told herself; but she couldn't do anything about it. Riding on the commuter train back to the dacha in Tarasovka, her new home, she started crying. What would she say now to Mama, to Artur? She had spent her grandfather's money on boots, it was shameful! What in the world was she going to tell them?

Before she got to the house, she stopped. The solution was a simple, though provisional one. She darted through the gate and crept over to the corner of the yard, near the outhouse, where she buried the box in a large pile of last year's leaves.

Shura was so worried that her daughter might have gotten lost in the city that she didn't chide her for being late. She merely asked whether the money had been sent, and Masha nodded her head.

"I got mixed up, Mama. I got out at the wrong station. And then I went to look at the university."

Masha lied so convincingly that she even surprised herself. The following morning, Shura and Artur went to the hardware store. Shura wanted to fix up the house. Artur didn't welcome the idea, but he was so mild-mannered that he had agreed, especially since Shura was doing all the work herself—from hanging the wallpaper to whitewashing the ceilings. Lisa had always laughed at her, saying that Shura could satisfy her sexual needs with a good floor mop, while Lisa herself needed a good . . . and Lisa didn't hesitate to say it.

When they had left and Masha was alone, she dragged the box out of the pile of leaves and carried it into the house, clutching it to her chest. She drew the boots out of the box, wiped off the soles of her feet with her palms, and tried stuffing her bare feet into the boots; but they wouldn't fit. She found her mother's socks in a suitcase, put them on, and tried pushing her feet in again. They were a tad too tight; they pinched. But since the leather was as soft as a baby's skin, she was able to get her feet inside them.

Feet swell up in summer, when it's humid; winter is drier. Masha consoled herself with this thought. Still, she decided to stuff them with a wad of paper, to stretch them out a bit.

She looked everywhere, but all she could find were dirty newspapers. How could she put those inside her heavenly boots? Then she looked under the table, and saw there was a thick packet of just the right kind of paper—the sheerest onionskin. Masha crumpled up one page at a time, rolled them all into tiny balls, and stuffed the boots up to the very top. She used up the whole packet of paper. They stood up straight and tall, as if there were living legs in them. Masha rubbed a boot against her cheek—just like a baby's skin. "Dorndorf" was written on the box. Where was this Dorndorf? In Germany? In Austria? And where would she hide them now? Certainly not outside, in the pile of leaves by the outhouse . . .

She thought and thought. She decided she couldn't keep them inside the house, either; instead, she took them to the outhouse. There was a high shelf, right up by the ceiling, draped with cobwebs. No one ever looked up there. Two empty paint cans had been left on the shelf and forgotten. Masha checked the surface to make sure it was dry. It was: a sturdy sheet of tar paper covered the roof of the outhouse, and even hung over the side.

I'll get a job, Masha thought. *I'll earn some money and send it to Grandpa, and no one will ever know. Winter will come, and I'll be wearing my boots! And college? Well, I'll just apply to get in the following year.*

This was the revolution that happened in Masha's head in the space of one day. And even her heart felt lighter. She had graduated from high school, almost with honors. She had planned to enroll in college right away, and get married, and eventually get an apartment in Moscow so as not to be a burden to her mother and her uncle. But the boots pushed back all her plans by a year. She shoved the box back into the very corner of the shelf, and put the empty paint cans back in front of it. No one would ever find it there.

Artur and her mother didn't get home until much later. They had gone all the way to Pushkino, to a big store where they'd bought the wallpaper and paste, and whitewash for the ceiling and windows. They returned toward evening. Shura was happy, beaming like a copper kettle. She bustled in, carrying the big rolls of wallpaper by herself. Artur followed leisurely behind, with a weary and perpetually good-natured air.

A lord, Masha thought disapprovingly.

Before they had even managed to bring all their purchases into the house, some uninvited visitors barged in: three in uniform, two in plainclothes. They asked for Korolev, Artur Ivanovich. The senior officer, with a bleached-out face, showed his ID, then pulled out a piece of paper and shoved it under Artur's nose.

Artur sat down in his armchair, smiling a bland smile.

"Get on with it! Go ahead, get to work, fellows. Shura, you prepare some food for us. While these people work, we'll have something to eat."

The search lasted almost twelve hours, from half past four until three in the morning. They climbed into the attic, they crawled under the floorboards, they tapped on all the walls. They went out to the gazebo and broke down the wall. They threw all the lumber out of the woodshed, and turned everything upside down. They peered into the outhouse and shone a flashlight inside. Artur showed them both his discharge papers and his award certificates.

"You must answer to the law," the captain mumbled sullenly. "You have no license, you don't pay taxes. You bind all this stuff, all this anti-Soviet junk . . ."

Piles of secondhand books, in both new bindings and old, fraying ones, crowded the workbench.

"What do you mean, anti-Soviet?" Artur said, spreading out his enormous hands. "Hamsun, Leskov; and this is a cookbook. What kind of anti-Soviet stuff are you referring to, fellows?"

Masha was also a bit anxious. What if they found the boots on the shelf in the outhouse and decided to open a case against her?

The good fellows finished their work when it was already growing light in the east. They left with both books and bookbinding tools.

"Put on the tea, please, Shura," Artur said.

Masha sat fretting: What if Artur was thrown in prison and she and her mother would have to go back to Ugolnoe? And would there be enough money for a plane? By train it would take four whole days and nights.

Artur crawled under the table—there had been a whole pile of books there, and now there was nothing. The searchers had turned everything inside out and upside down. Artur sat in his chair with the patched armrests and scratched his hairless pink chin in perplexity.

"I don't understand it. It must be some sort of magic, a spell! Shura, there was a copy of *The Gulag Archipelago* lying there, under the table.

That's what they were after, I'm sure of it. Some bastard ratted on us. But where did it go? It was a huge packet of paper! How could it just disappear? Am I crazy?"

Well, let's say that Shura, for one, knew he was crazy. They don't just throw you in the loony bin for nothing. But Masha was already asleep, exhausted by the drama of the boots, unfortunately a tad too tight, the nocturnal search, and the happy knowledge of her secret possession.

THE UPPER REGISTER

The house on Potapovsky Lane had known hundreds of residents. Its walls had been covered in silk, then in empire wallpaper, striped, or scattered with roses, later in crude oil paint, green and blue, then layers of newsprint, and cheap, porous wallpaper again, repeatedly torn. Having gone through its century and a half of wealth and poverty, birth and death, murder and marriage, densification and communalization, remodeling that only made things worse, trifling fires and petty floods, the house had begun to adorn itself in the 1960s with Czech furniture and three-cornered tables. The house existed in its own slow, incremental, virtually geological time; and only one room—the yardkeeper's storeroom under the stairwell on the first floor—had preserved its primordial aspect and purpose: the walls were bare exposed brick, never even plastered, just as they had been right after the house was built; and, as of old, it was full of brooms, crowbars, and pails of sand. It also had a hose, lying in coils—its prize possession. The storeroom was locked with a padlock. The mammoth iron padlock could have defended much more valuable goods than these, but Ryzhkov, the yardkeeper, well known in the neighborhood for his fierce expression and his exceptional bowleggedness, loved sturdy, enduring things, and among them, he particularly loved his sixteen-pound padlock. His granddaughter Nadia had to struggle with the lock, poking and prodding it, every time she took a young man there. Nadia loved this—that is, she loved any kind of mild struggle, the poking and prodding. She had been ignited prematurely and was given to disgraceful behavior; she couldn't even remember when she had first engaged in this fascinating activity. But by the ninth grade she was a master of the trade; and, like any master, she had her own signature and small predilections. She didn't like the grown men, who stuck to her like flies. She preferred boys. Her classmates and the neighborhood kids, often a year or two younger, were aware of her worth, always stuck up for her, and never said an unkind word about her; she was a highly prized public asset.

Nadia's grandfather rose early and went to bed with the chickens. There hadn't been any chickens for a long time, of course—but his body clock still remembered when there had been a stable in the yard of the two story house, with two lean to sheds, and the chickens had lived in one of them. It was at that early evening hour, when her grandfather was snoring with the long-gone chickens, that Nadia would take the key from the nail and disappear into her boudoir under the stairs for an hour or two.

There, on the armchair of Karelian birch with the broken back, in the coils of the hose, and among the brooms, many interesting things transpired. Skinny boys, sometimes too young to have broken out in pimples, tested their powers and honed their weapons for the future. Half the boys in the nearby buildings had undergone their sexual initiation here, in the yardkeeper's storeroom. It must be said that only once or twice had Nadia turned someone down, refusing them the pleasure of this simple, healthful activity.

Ilya came to her, too, taking advantage of her favors on a first-come, first-served basis.

Nadia had a weakness for virginal boys, and, with her characteristic directness, she asked Ilya now and then: "Why doesn't Steklov ever come to me? Bring him here."

Sanya was exactly to her taste—pale, slender, with clean hands, and excessively polite.

Ilya invited Sanya to visit Nadia. Blushing as deeply as the red-haired

Mikha, he refused point-blank. Afterward, he began having second thoughts; it tormented him. Until then, he had never felt any interest in Nadia. She was a big, vulgar girl in the same grade, but in the parallel class. She had dark eyes that looked out from under her bangs. He had never exchanged more than two words with her. But after Ilya's suggestion, he was agitated for a whole week and couldn't get her off his mind. He decided that if Ilya approached him about it again, he would agree to go—it was obvious where, and why.

Ilya did, and this time Sanya was easily persuaded. They arrived at half past nine. Nadia was waiting for them, and reading a book— *Virgin Soil Upturned*, which was on their required reading list.

Ilya left immediately, and Nadia fastened the large iron latch across the door from the inside.

"Should I show you, or what?" the experienced Nadia asked. She could demonstrate if need be; but she could just jump right in, too.

Sanya didn't say anything. He wanted very much to see in person what he had until then seen only in the Urban and Shwarzenberg *Atlas of Human Anatomy* on his mother's bookshelf. But he kept silent.

"Don't be afraid, it's really nice."

She unbuttoned her blue wool sweater, and he caught a whiff of warm sweat. Under her sweater he saw the top of her breasts rising up out of her tight bra, behind a pink slip with white lace.

Sanya shrank back. Nadia showed her white teeth and the pearly strip of her gums.

"Don't be scared, give me your hand."

Sanya extended his hand, like he expected her to shake it. She turned over his palm and placed it on her breast—it felt like fresh bread, warm and firm.

"You act like a complete stranger," Nadia said with a slight note of disapproval, and turned out the light to encourage the stranger to get to know her.

She was an experienced seductress, but her animal innocence prevented her from being aware of this herself. There were no windows in the storeroom; it was as dark as a dungeon.

"Come on, Sanya! You're stiff as a board, loosen up."

He *was* stiff as a board. She took his cold hands in her own large warm ones, and started guiding them around her torso as if she were a tree. He wanted to run away and hide, but where? Where was it darker than this pitch-black darkness?

There was a rustling over in the corner, then squeaking. He gripped Nadia's shoulder in alarm. It turned out that she was already completely undressed. Her whole body was like a loaf of fresh bread, not just her breasts.

"Don't be scared, it's just a rat with her babies, they have a nest. I'll show it to you later."

The rat calmed Sanya down, for some reason. He was afraid that Nadia would stop moving his hands around over her own body and would set her sights on him. And that's what she did. Oh, how he wanted to run away, but now it was too late, far too late . . . She was already holding him in her soft palms and whispering: "My sweet boy, my sweet little one . . ."

Her words were, on the face of it, quite tactless, but they were in effect encouraging, and expressed an overwhelming sympathy. The seductress was full of compassion. She held his timid manhood with gentle firmness.

"See how good it is?" said the invisible Nadia with a deep sigh. She had won; that's what she felt. Again she had won. She pressed Sanya's head against her chest—what power she felt! This was how she conquered all of them.

No, I don't want to, I don't want to, Sanya told himself; to no avail. He was already inside, and there was no place else to go.

Then came a quiet, satisfied chuckle.

"See? The little animal finds its nest."

What could have been the beginning was at the same time the end.

He seized up, then let go. Sticky and hot. And ashamed. So that was it?

Nadia sought out his lips with her mouth. He offered them politely. She licked his mouth with her large tongue, then put it under his top lip. She sucked in air, making a smacking sound.

"'Die if you will, but never give a kiss without love,'" she whispered.

Never a truer word. Even dying would be better than this.

It was still drizzling outside, just as it had been when he went in. Ilya was waiting for him across the lane.

"Everything go okay?" he asked drily, without so much as a smile.

"I guess so. It was pretty disgusting," Sanya said faintly, so faintly that Ilya couldn't even guess just how disgusted he was.

They walked to Sanya's house without speaking and parted at the entrance.

The next day, Sanya wasn't in school. He had fallen ill. The usual thing—a high temperature, and no other symptoms. In his sleepy delirium he imagined he was dying, that he had syphilis or something even worse. But he had nothing of the sort. Three days later, his temperature fell. He lay around in bed for a few more days, while his grandmother boiled fruit compote for him, and made him cookies with cream filling and applesauce. He struggled with an unrelenting sense of self-loathing for himself, for his own body, which had betrayed him and responded to the summons of a complete stranger, against his own wishes . . . or not?

He lay in bed reading *The Odyssey*. He read to the part where Odysseus's companions row past the island of the Sirens and pour wax into their ears, so they won't hear the Sirens' voices and jump into the water. And Odysseus, tethered to the mast, writhes and struggles to escape so he can throw himself into the sea and swim toward the irresistible song. He was the only one who heard their song and survived it. The stony shores were strewn with the dried-up corpses and bones of the hapless travelers who had reached the island—lured there by the bewitching, double-voiced song—and who were then sucked dry by the bloodthirsty Sirens.

"Nuta, what do you think—is the part about the Sirens about the power of sex over men?"

Anna Alexandrovna froze with a saucer in her hand.

"Sanya, I've never thought about it before; but I think you must be right. It doesn't just have power over men, though—women are under its power, too. Let's just say it has power over human beings. Love and hunger rule the world. It's terribly banal, but that's the way it is."

"And there's no way to escape it?"

Anna Alexandrovna laughed.

"Maybe there is, but I never discovered it. And I wouldn't have wanted to. Everyone is sucked into that vortex sooner or later."

She placed her cool, cruel hand on his forehead, and the touch was clinical and sterile.

"No temperature."

Sanya took her bony hand, covered in rings, and kissed it.

He's a grown-up boy. And he's so good. But he's too gentle, too sensitive . . . Anna Alexandrovna thought sadly. *He's going to have a hard time of it.*

But Sanya's difficulties had begun much earlier than Anna Alexandrovna guessed. From the earliest years, even before he started school, he had been tormented by the suspicion that he was different from the other children his age, and, indeed, from everyone else, too—and that this was due to some flaw or defect in him. Or, a less dire option, to some peculiarity. He did not doubt that it was, in some inchoate way, connected to music. Like archangels with swords, his mother and grandmother stood watch over him, protecting him from the ordinary world, which was alien to him.

In their enormous, enchanted room, all 350 square feet of it, they created a beautiful sanctuary for him, and were themselves filled with anxiety and fear: How would he cope without them, beyond the threshold of the room, and even farther afield, when they died? At first they had thought of educating him at home rather than sending him to school in the outside world; but they finally decided against such a radical measure.

Vasily Innokentievich, called in for advice, mostly so that they would have someone to argue with, rose to the occasion. He voiced crushing arguments, the most persuasive of which was that if the boy didn't learn to adapt in childhood, if he weren't run through the ringer at school, he would stand out like a sore thumb later in life, and was sure to end up in prison.

His mother and grandmother exchanged glances, then sent him off to be run through the ringer. The first five years of school were almost like being in solitary confinement. For some reason no one took any notice of him, as though he were invisible. And he cultivated his invisibility, insulating himself from boyish roughhousing and teasing

with a polite smile. His relationship with his classmates was one of
estrangement, nothing more.

A miracle occurred at the beginning of the sixth grade, however—a
kitten, tormented by a dog and his classmates, laid down his life, thus
laying the cornerstone of the friendship of Sanya and Ilya and Mikha.
And this friendship was cemented when they revealed to one another
the deepest secrets of their souls at the time.

But toward the end of their school years, new secrets grew up in
them that they chose not to confess. The friends were almost grown,
and reconciled to the notion that every person has the right to a private life. Sanya's secret had no name, but he was afraid of being found
out: What if Ilya and Mikha discovered in him what he himself
could not even name? His future had still not managed to take root
and ripen; it had not yet given way to anguished experiences, only a
dull longing. They were aware of silences cropping up everywhere,
yet these silences did not hamper their friendship.

They never quarreled. They managed to transform any differences of opinion into playful banter, ephemeral, spur-of-the-moment
theater, the rules of which were known only to the three of them—
the Trianon.

But even if Sanya had wanted to, he could not have revealed to his
friends the secret he had discovered—the words were lacking. And telling them in approximate terms, using whatever words came to mind,
would not have been possible, because of his inner need for accuracy
and precision.

Only Liza was able to understand. Vasily Innokentievich's grand-
daughter was a kindred spirit, as well as kin, to him. She was a pianist.
Almost a professional one, although she had not yet entered the
Conservatory. But she would. And Sanya would not.

Only with her was Sanya able to share his suspicion that the world
in which people brushed their teeth with mint powder in the morning, cooked food, ate it, then unburdened themselves of this food in the
WC, read newspapers, and went to bed at night, placing their heads
on a pillow—that this world was unreal. Music was the incontrovert-
ible proof of the existence of another world. Music was born in that
world, then found its way into this one in some mysterious way. And it

wasn't just the music that filled the rooms of the Conservatory, or the disorganized cacophony that roamed the corridors of the music school, or the music that lurked in the dark grooves of a record. Even the music that poured out of a radio receiver, with its gaps, its rising and sinking notes, even that squeezed through the crack between worlds.

Sanya was paralyzed with fear at the horrible suspicion that this world, the one in which his grandmother, the tooth powder, and the WC at the end of the corridor seemed to exist was a fraud, an illusion, and if the crack were to open just a bit wider, everything in this world would burst like a soap bubble in a washtub.

"Do you know what I mean? It's suffocating here, nauseating. It's impossible. But we can't get into that other world, they won't let us in. Am I some sort of freak, do you think?"

Liza shrugged and said:

"Well, of course! As for being a freak—that's nonsense! But of course there's a boundary between these worlds . . . and when you play, that's where you are, over there."

She was certain that many people knew this. Most likely because she had studied at the music school, and her classmates all played eight hours a day on the piano, or the violin, or the cello, and were chained to a musical staff by invisible shackles.

In his final year of high school, Sanya hardly touched the instrument. For him, everything was over. He refused to take any more private lessons, and Anna Alexandrovna could only sigh.

They went to concerts.

Going to a concert with Liza was even better than going with his grandmother. They listened and compared, communicating with the subtlest signs of comprehension—a half nod, a half sigh, a suspended breath, and, the most expressive sign, a touch of the hand. They were perfectly in tune with each other. Then Sanya would walk Liza to the trolleybus stop, and sometimes accompany her home, all the way to Novoslobodskaya. They talked about Chopin and Schubert, and when they were a bit older about Prokofiev and Stravinsky, about Shostakovich. And it was impossible to imagine then that they would have these musical conversations their whole lives, until one of them died—about Bach, Beethoven, Alban Berg. And they would fly across the world to hear a one-off performance by some great musician in Paris, in Madrid, or in London, so together they could savor first the music, then the conversation that went on till morning, until they flew back home to the opposite ends of the earth.

And anyway, could he have admitted to Liza about the storeroom, about the darkness, about the coitus with this pitch-darkness, about the anguish that gripped him after this celebrated manly act? About Nadia and her glistening gums?

Shortly after the New Year, Nadia was expelled from school, which was unjust: she was quite a good student. Nature had endowed her not only with a healthy physique, but with a good head to go with it. And you couldn't have faulted her for bad behavior in school—she sat drowsily through the lessons, never talking back to the teachers, and earning her Bs honestly. The school principal called her in, laid out all the facts that had been leaked to her about the storeroom, and ordered her to take her school records and leave. Nadia cried and took her records. She transferred to a trade school for working-class youth, which was only fitting.

Her former friends came by to see her, though she never had much time—from early morning she worked in a bakery on Pokrovka, and in the evening she attended classes.

Although Sanya and Nadia still lived in the same neighborhood for a few more years, they ran into each other only once, near the Uranus movie theater on Sretenka, completely by chance. Sanya was with Anna Alexandrovna, and Nadia was with her girlfriend Lilka. Sanya bowed to her in greeting from afar; she started giggling and whispered something into her girlfriend's ear.

Sanya turned away: forget it ever happened . . . forget all about it . . . never breathe a word to anyone . . . never. And it went away, as though it had sunk to the bottom of his memory.

Oh, Liza, Liza! You are . . . beyond words!

She was crystalline, fragile; it was impossible to imagine that she was made of the same stuff as the fleshy Nadia, and that she wore the same elastic harnesses—a bra, an elastic belt holding up her stockings.

It was sacrilege even to think about it. Sanya dismissed these unworthy suspicions: angels, naturally, don't wear elastic.

But Sanya was cruelly mistaken. The angel wore all those accoutrements and was not at all unfamiliar with those elemental forces Sanya had discovered in the storeroom. Slowly, but very surely, Liza had begun a romance with a young violinist, a student from the Conservatory who hailed from a well-known musical family. A bearlike fellow with a florid, porous complexion and a shaggy dark head of hair, this corpulent Boris—it was unfathomable!—had captured Liza's heart. Perhaps the name of his grandfather on a commemorative marble plaque in the lobby of the Minor Hall of the Conservatory added to his appeal. Sanya learned about their relations only four years later, not long before they got married, and was deeply shaken. All male-female corporeality was distasteful to him, tainted by the storeroom goings-on, and completely antithetical to the pure world of sound. How could Liza have succumbed to that? She played better and better. She had long ago left her apprenticeship behind and acquired her own sound, her own tone. Liza, with that fat Boris? No, it wasn't jealousy he felt; more like bewilderment.

Two weeks before Liza and Boris's wedding they played a duet—Mozart sonatas for piano and violin. Sanya sat in the half-empty hall and suffered: he knew these sonatas well and was agonized by the incompatibility of the two parts—there was no mutual support, no union of voices, but rather an alarming mutual inaudibility. There was no spiritual commingling between the piano and the violin, and he hated Boris for being so dull, egotistical, and so very conceited. Liza simply couldn't marry him, she couldn't!

He left without giving them the flowers he had brought. The three red carnations, wrapped in white paper and stuffed into the sleeve of his coat, he threw into a trash can next to the Tchaikovsky monument.

The wedding reception was held at home. It was simultaneously modest and sumptuous. There were not many guests, only parents and close friends and relatives. There were twenty-four people altogether, corresponding to the number of place settings of good china that had remained intact, given to Boris's grandmother and grandfather at their own wedding.

A portrait of his grandfather Grigory Lvovich, a well-known violinist and teacher, looked out from a frame hanging next to a portrait
of his young grandmother Eleonora, which was the work of Leonid
Pasternak, father of the famous writer. His grandfather had died, a
victim of the campaign against "rootless cosmopolitanism"; but his
grandmother, who had once upon a time been a singer, had survived
cosmopolitanism, and her husband, and her son. Now, with an iron fist,
she ruled her highly organized home according to the highest social
standards, as only she knew how.

The table gleamed like an iceberg under the sun. The silver had
been polished to a bright sheen, the crystal goblets sparkled. On the
oval and round serving dishes lay translucent slivers of fish and cheese.
Like the illustrious Teacher, she, too, would have been able to feed a
multitude with five loaves of bread, because she knew the art of fine
slicing. In truth, there were never any leftovers. The food on offer was
always meager, though the dishes were many. The newlyweds wore
their concert garb—Boris was in a tuxedo, and Liza in a lacy, pale-
yellow gown that was not at all flattering.

Among the guests were four of the most celebrated musicians in
this part of the world, with their wives. The bald pate of a great pianist shone; the soft body of a great violinist seemed to be melting into
the chair. A fifth performer, also considered a musical genius, was the
only unaccompanied woman. She had never married. She placed her
shabby handbag, a green bottle of kefir sticking out of it, on the table
next to the gleaming silverware. A great cellist, a close friend of Boris's
late father, picked at his teeth with a sharpened matchstick. A famous,
though not yet great, conductor masticated with his diminutive teeth,
looking around to see what was on each plate and pretending not to
notice his wife's angry glances. Not counting the new relatives, non-
musical society was represented by a couple who were neighbors from
the dacha—a professor of chemistry and his wife. Eleonora Zorakhovna,
a consummate socialite with a genius for prestigious social gatherings,
was disappointed, however. The wife of a great composer had just called
to say that they wouldn't be able to make it after all.

The gathering of the century, as she had conceived it, was falling apart.

"Déjà vu," whispered Anna Alexandrovna to her grandson. "I was here for Eleonora's wedding fifty years ago. In this very apartment. It was 1911 . . ."

"With the same guests?" Sanya said, laughing.

"Just about. Alexander Nikolaevich Scriabin was here. He had just come from abroad."

"Scriabin? Here?"

"Yes. He did show up, unlike Shostakovich, who wouldn't condescend to it. Everyone loved Grigory Lvovich; and no one loved Eleonora."

"Who else was there?"

"Leonid Osipovich Pasternak and Rosalia Isidorovna Pasternak. She was a marvelous pianist. Anton Rubinstein remarked on it when she was just a little girl. It was a select circle. Birth, affinity, profession . . . I was here in this house at your age—no, I was younger, of course. That wedding has stayed in my memory my whole life. As you will remember this one," she added, and sighed.

"How did you come to be at that wedding?"

"My first husband was a musician. He was a friend of the groom's. I'll tell you about it another time."

"Strange that you've never mentioned it before."

Anna Alexandrovna grew angry with herself: she had long ago decided not to burden this gentle soul, her grandson, with her entire past. The friend of the groom was sitting opposite her at the moment, picking his teeth. That was enough—just like that she had been moved, and said too much.

"Liza won't have an easy time of it here," she said, changing the subject abruptly.

Liza was comporting herself beautifully. Vasily Innokentievich and his son Alexei, Liza's father, were strangers in this company; but both of them were well-known doctors, and this put them on an equal footing with the musicians, in some sense. Liza's mother, on the other hand, was completely out of place. She was overweight, with clearly bottle-blond hair, and very much aware of not fitting in among these guests.

At one time she had been a nurse in a field hospital during the war. It was a "frontline" marriage, unequal and accidental, but solid: their daughter held it together. On the face of the new mother-in-law one could read pride, boorishness, confusion, and awkwardness. Liza sat next to her mother and stroked her hand from time to time, making sure she didn't drink too much.

Anna Alexandrovna sat on Sanya's right. To the left of him was a bohemian-looking man with a mane of hair parted down the middle, wearing a black-and-yellow leopard-print ascot. Was he a singer? An actor? They called him Yury Andreevich.

When dinner was halfway over, and they had already cleared away the bouillon cups and the empty serving dish of tiny savory pies (exactly twenty-four of them, according to the precise number of guests), but before the main dish had been served, he stood up to make a toast.

"Dear Liza and Boba!"

Ah, so he's a close friend, since he calls Boris "Boba," Sanya noted.

His mouth was unusually mobile. The upper lip was etched with a deep furrow; the lower one protruded slightly.

"You have embarked on the dangerous path of matrimony! Perhaps it is not so much dangerous as it is unpredictable. I wish for you what I consider to be the most important thing in marriage: that it not prevent you from hearing music. This is the greatest possible happiness—to hear with four ears, to play with four hands, to take part in the birth of new sounds that were never heard in the world before you. Music, once it is released by your hands, lives only for a moment before dying away, dispersing into waves moving through space. But the ephemerality of music is just the other face of its immortality. Forgive me, Maria Veniaminovna, for saying such trivial things in your presence. Boba, Liza, my dear friends! From the bottom of my soul I hope that music never deserts you, that it grows ever deeper and fuller in you."

"Nora!" a low, somewhat rasping voice called out. "Wonderful pies! Give me a few to take home with me, please!"

Eleonora answered with a spiteful glare.

"I'll have them wrapped up for you, Maria Veniaminovna. They'll be wrapped up."

"This is for your memoirs, Sanya. Don't forget it," Anna Alexandrovna whispered.

Sanya was already spellbound, as though he had a front-row seat in the theater, in the midst of all these great ones. And the man next to him in the leopard-print ascot was not merely a chance person at table; he knew something important, you could see that at a glance. But who could he be? The old lady who had asked to take home the pies, Maria Veniaminovna, had been Sanya's idol since the first concert at which he had heard her perform during his childhood.

After dinner, which passed without any ancient Russian exhortations of "It's bitter!," they all moved into the study. This was one of the last remaining aristocratic apartments on Marx and Engels Street, formerly Maly Znamensky Lane, behind the Pushkin Museum. In addition, this may have been the only family in the entire country that had lived in the building since its construction, in 1906. The great-grandfather, grandfather, father, and now Boris—none of them had been forcibly removed or had their property confiscated. None of them had been forced to communalize and partition the apartment into smaller units, admitting strangers into their midst. None of them had been arrested. Family legend had it that it was in this very apartment, and not Peshkov's, that Lenin heard Issay Dobrowen, Eleonora Zorakhovna's younger brother, perform Beethoven's Sonata no. 23. Here, in the room next door, he spoke the words (unless Gorky had made them up, for some reason of his own): "Sublime, superhuman music... But I can't listen to music too often. It works on my nerves and makes me want to say sweet nothings, to pat on the head those people who can create such beauty, despite living in a dirty hellhole..."

And the nothings turned out to be not so sweet after all, and the heads that he patted rolled by the thousands...

All these family legends, which had now become her own, Liza told Sanya when they went out on the balcony to talk. And something else: Dobrowen had not played the "Appassionata" that evening at all, but Sonata no. 14, the "Moonlight" sonata. The experts had mixed things up.

In the study, they had started smoking. A servant served coffee on a tray.

"Everything's so British," Sanya whispered to his grandmother.

"No, Jewish," Anna Alexandrovna said.

"Nuta, that sounds quite anti-Semitic. I'm surprised at you."

Anna Alexandrovna took a deep draw of her cigarette, flaring her delicate nostrils. She let out the smoke, shaking her head.

"Sanya, in our country, anti-Semitism has always been the exclusive privilege of shopkeepers and the nobility. By all accounts, our family is part of the intelligentsia, though rooted in the aristocracy. I love Jews, you know that yourself."

"I know. You love Mikha. It's a matter of indifference to me whether someone is a Jew, a non-Jew, or otherwise. But for some reason, of my two closest friends, one and a half are Jewish."

"That's what I'm talking about. Maybe there's a heightened sensibility?"

Anna Alexandrovna truly did have an aversion to anti-Semitism; she had meant something else by her comment. In her youth, she had refused to marry Vasily Innokentievich, who continued to love her his whole life. Now fate was taking revenge: Liza, his granddaughter, had rejected her refined, sensitive Sanya in favor of this flabby young Jewish man.

Anna Alexandrovna's version of things was somewhat off the mark, since Sanya had never proposed to Liza, and had wanted from her only amicable loyalty and heartfelt intimacy. Liza had had no grounds on which to reject him. But from their early childhood years, Anna Alexandrovna had been certain that these children were made for each other. In her heart she reproached Liza, believing her choice to be self-serving careerism. And, somehow, in her mind, his Jewishness figured as one of the unpleasant characteristics of Liza's new husband.

Liza came up to Sanya, a goblet in hand. Her new wedding ring shone on her finger. She was leading the man in the leopard-print ascot with the other.

"Have you met Yury Andreevich? He's a professor of music theory, Sanya. Here's a person who might be able to resolve all your musical problems."

"It's rare that one meets someone with musical problems," Yury Andreevich said, looking at Sanya with lively interest.

"Oh, what nonsense, Liza." Sanya was both embarrassed and affronted. How could she have been so tactless?

Before Sanya could say anything else, he saw the cumbersome old lady, her handbag under her arm, trundling up to the piano.

Eleonora Zorakhovna had not foreseen this impromptu performance. According to her plan, dessert was the next point on the agenda: coffee, ice cream, and small pastries that the servant was already bringing out from the kitchen. But the performer, paying no attention to the tray with pastries, was drawn to the piano like a boxer to the ring, her massive head lowered, her hands still hanging loose at her sides. She dumped her heavily laden handbag on the floor to the right of the pedals, rummaged around in it, and extracted, from under the kefir bottle, her sheet music, which she placed on the music stand. Then she sat on the swiveling piano stool, her large body swaying slightly, and looked up, as though trying to decipher some message written on the ceiling. Covering her eyes, having apparently received her message, she struck a chord heavy as a watermelon. Then there was a second, and a third. They were strange chords in and of themselves, and augured something unprecedented.

"Sit down," Yury Andreevich whispered. "This will last eighteen minutes, if she keeps up the tempo."

Sanya had never heard music like this before. He knew that it existed, agitating music, hostile to the romantic tradition, which trampled on the old norms and canons. He had picked up on the waves of disapproval and mistrust it awakened, but he was hearing it now for the first time with his own ears.

He was listening to something absolutely new, and he didn't understand how it was constructed. He was adept at listening to another kind of music, "normal" music—far more intelligible and predictable. He loved the internal movement of the music familiar to him, the almost importunate touch of the sounds; he anticipated its resolutions, foresaw the ends of the musical phrases.

He knew how absurd and empty the attempts to paraphrase the content of music through a specially evolved pseudo-poetic language were, how contrived and pompous they always sounded. The content of music was not amenable to translation into literary or visual imagery. He hated all those dreary concert-program notes—how one should perceive Chopin, or what Tchaikovsky had intended.

He viewed it the way a small child views the activities of adults, with perplexed indignation—how stupid they are!

What he was listening to now demanded intense concentration, all his attention. *It's like something written in a foreign language*, Sanya thought.

The music summoned by the old lady's hands rose in a stupefying crescendo of sound. Even in the past, Sanya had rarely experienced music so viscerally. He felt the music filling his skull and expanding it. It was as though some unknown biological process had been unleashed in his body, as though he could feel it producing hemoglobin or releasing powerful hormones in the blood. Something as profoundly inherent and natural as breathing, or photosynthesis . . .

"What is this?" he whispered, thrown off guard, to his neighbor.

The man smiled with his sculpted upper lip.

"Stockhausen. No one performs him here."

"It's like the end of the world . . ."

Sanya didn't mean the end of the world in a religious or scientific sense. It was simply a notion current among the youth, the jargon of the decade. But Kolosov regarded the young man with interest. As a theoretician, he assumed that this new music signalled the end of one era and the beginning of an unknown new one, and he ascribed great significance to this transfiguration, which was invisible and hidden from most people. He valued very highly those like himself, who were aware of the shift—possibly a shift in the evolution of the world, in human consciousness. They were few and far between, the temporal forerunners of humanity, people who not only presaged the new world, but were also able to analyze and research it.

"I don't understand how it works, how it's constructed," Sanya told Kolosov, falling at once into his mode of thought. "Perhaps it's not even a new style, but another way of thinking altogether. It's stunning, disorienting . . ."

Kolosov felt happy.

"You're a musician, of course?"

"No, not at all. I would have been . . . but I was injured. A childhood accident. I only listen to music now." He showed him his right hand, with its two bent fingers. "I'll be graduating from the Institute of Foreign Languages next year."

"Come to see me. I think we've got a lot to talk about."

Everything that happened that evening after Stockhausen was a blur in Sanya's memory. Even the image of Maria Veniaminovna herself faded a bit. He only remembered accompanying the young couple to the train station to see them off. They were going to the Baltics for their honeymoon.

What stayed with him was the sense of some portentous event. The next day Sanya went to see Yury Andreevich at the Conservatory, after the class he taught was over. They picked up the conversation where they had left off the evening before.

Later, they went together to a remote district on the outskirts of the city, first by subway and then by trolleybus. This was where Yury Andreevich lived, in an unsightly high-rise in the dreary middle ground between a village that was not quite extinct and the encroaching urban sprawl. They had agreed that Yury Andreevich would give him private lessons.

Within the demeaning confines of an almost Zamyatinesque cell, a one-room apartment with a metal number on the door (Sanya had just read the novel *We*), there was nothing but a piano and bookshelves, cabinets, and racks full of books and sheet music. There was no table to eat on, no bed to sleep on, no armoire where one could hang a coat. In his own home, Yury Andreevich looked as though he were just a guest—wearing a freshly pressed suit and a yellow ascot, in shoes polished to a high gleam and fit for the stage. For some time Sanya thought that this apartment was only the teacher's study, and that he lived in another one, more fit for human habitation. Then he spied a terra-cotta teapot and a wooden box containing Chinese tea in the kitchen. And, sometime later, Sanya realized that Yury Andreevich, in his freshly pressed suit, his ascots tied with almost military precision, was in fact a recluse, and that this masquerade costume concealed a true ascetic.

How did he manage to observe the demands of his musical monkhood in this vulgar and dirty world, amid the crushing reality of Soviet existence, nauseating and dangerous? It was completely improbable.

On that very first evening, Sanya started preparing for the Conservatory entrance exam. He wished to enter the department of music theory. Yury Andreevich taught his student in the way a carpenter teaches an apprentice to drive in a nail with a single blow, a chef to slice onions and carrots with a precision measured in millimeters, or a surgeon to wield a scalpel lightly and with the utmost skill. He taught him the craft.

And it wasn't just the explanations themselves—what tone must be doubled when resolving a dominant seventh chord into the tonic chord, how to harmonize a tritone modulation, the interplay of corresponding registers of the extreme voicings at the golden-section point, and so on. The fact was that Kolosov taught with the same enjoyment as Sanya learned.

"You don't understand how lucky you were with your hand. A true musician is not a performer, but a composer, a theoretician. Above all a theoretician. Music is the quintessence, an infinitely compressed message; it's what exists outside the range of our hearing, our perception, our consciousness. It is the highest form of Platonism, *eidos* descended from the heavens in its purest form. Can you grasp that?"

Sanya didn't understand it; rather, he felt it. But he suspected that his teacher was getting a bit carried away. He remembered too well his childhood joy when music was born under his very fingers.

Nevertheless, this was the happiest year in Sanya's life. The shell of the coarse and dirty world split open, and fresh new air gushed in through the gap. It was the only kind of air his soul needed to breathe. It was the same kind of upheaval that the sixth-graders had undergone ten years earlier, when Victor Yulievich arrived at their school and began showering the class with verse. The difference was that Sanya was now an adult, and, having overcome the devastating experience of parting with music forever, had discovered that his love had become even more profound. His gift, slumbering in the deepest part of him, had awakened and surfaced after a ten-year hibernation. The tedium of the solfeggio he had learned as a child was transformed into fascination with the science of musical structure. Several years later Sanya would become certain that solfeggio explained, in the simplest terms, as a rough approximation, the structure of the world itself.

Twice a week Sanya spent an hour and a half at Yury Andreevich's. He did complex dictations and countless ear-training exercises. Yury Andreevich played the piano, and Sanya tried to identify the various intervals and chords, progressions, and modulations.

Sanya's former piano teacher, Evgenia Danilovna, was summoned again. She was able to squeeze out two hours a week for Sanya from her tightly packed schedule (at that time she was training *Wunderkinder*, no fewer than ten of whom brought subsequent fame to the Central Music School). The well-known teacher, bent on producing superperformers, was only wasting her time with Sanya and his crippled hand; but she was a close friend of Anna Alexandrovna's, and for someone of her generation it was unthinkable to refuse a friend such a request, although the child had no prospects whatsoever. Finally, with a new fingering that took into consideration his two crippled fingers, Sanya managed to master a very cleverly selected program, crowned by a performance of the Bach Chaconne in a transposition for the left hand only by Brahms. Anna Alexandrovna sold the remains of her jewelry that year—diamond earrings and a pendant—to pay for the lessons.

Sanya flew to his lessons with Yury Andreevich as though to a lovers' rendezvous. Yury Andreevich was no less taken with his new student, who could grasp everything on the fly, sometimes posing questions that far outstripped the material they were covering. Yury Andreevich would then bloom, and break into a smile, before immediately recovering his usual composure and severity of expression. He didn't believe in indulging his students. The lessons ended precisely when they were scheduled to end. Once, when Sanya was fifteen minutes late because a bus had broken down, his teacher refused to extend the lesson to make up for the time lost.

In addition to solfeggio, harmony, and the history of music, Sanya had to take exams in other subjects: writing, a foreign language, and the history of the USSR. He wasn't in the least worried about these exams. The most challenging one for him was "general piano." He would have to play a prepared program, as well as sight-read another piece.

Naturally, students of music theory were not expected to master an instrument on a professional level, but Sanya was nervous nevertheless. From the time his tendon had been ruined by Murygin's knife, he had lost the boldness of spirit necessary for performing.

Sanya passed the theoretical subjects easily. Even "general piano" was quite satisfactory; Evgenia Danilovna had not spent her precious time in vain. But the most remarkable thing was that no one on the admissions committee had even noticed that two fingers of his right hand were crippled. This was his chief victory.

In the autumn, when his fellow students at the Institute of Foreign Languages were beginning their fifth and final year of studies, Sanya began his first year in the theory department of the Conservatory. Anna Alexandrovna was happy, Evgenia Danilovna even more so. To mark the occasion, she gave Sanya some sheet music autographed by Scriabin himself. But by this time Sanya already had his doubts about Scriabin.

Victor Yulievich had been right a thousand times over—and Sanya agreed—when he said that finding the right teacher is like being reborn. Only now it was not Victor Yulievich, but another teacher, who introduced him to a new system of coordinates, who showed him new meanings and expanded his conceptions of the world. His brightest students discovered, with shivers that traveled up and down their spines, that they were dealing not only with music, but with the structure of the entire universe, with the laws of atomic physics, molecular biology, falling stars, and the rustling of leaves. It was a commingling of science, all of poetry, and every kind of art.

"Form is what transforms the content of a work into its essence. Do you understand? The character of music arises out of its form like steam from hot water," Yury Andreevich said. "With a solid understanding of the general laws of form, which encompass all that is amenable to formulation, one can, by groping further, perceive the individual, the particular. Then, subtracting the general, one can sense a residue where wonder lurks in its purest, most undiluted form. Herein lies the goal of theory: the more fully one grasps what is available for comprehension, the more intensely the ineffable shines. Listen, and try to grasp it!" He put a black disk on the record player. The needle drew out sounds that were not perfect in themselves; but by looking at the notes while he listened, absorbing them with his eyes, and through his eyes with his ears and brain, Sanya discovered a new conception of the world, and his thoughts were drawn into unknown spaces and dimensions.

At the same time, his teacher scorned pathos, elevated words and expressions, and verbiage. He cut short any attempt to discuss music by resorting to literary devices and conceits.

"We're not applying algebra to harmony. We're studying harmony! It's an exact science, just as algebra is. And for the time being, we're putting poetry aside!" He spoke passionately, as though he were disputing with an invisible opponent.

His students adored him; the administration, always wary, regarded him with suspicion. There was something potentially anti-Soviet about him.

Yury Andreevich Kolosov was a structuralist at a time when the term had not yet been established. And the powers that be, in all eras, are particularly wary about what they don't understand.

Kolosov expanded the horizons of the courses in harmony, the history of music and musical theory systems. He immersed the students in ancient history, and also exposed them to the newest, most innovative music, the second avant-garde, which had just begun to take hold in the USSR—spiritual heirs of Webern: Boulez, Stockhausen, Nono. And side by side with them, through the corridors of the Conservatory, walked their local avant-garde counterparts: Edison Denisov, Sofia Gubaidulina, Alfred Schnittke . . .

All of this was still in its infancy, tentative and tremulous. Even the music of Schoenberg was still novel.

Sanya's head was awhirl with a powerful wave of myriad sounds: Baroque, early classical, the ubiquitous Bach, romantic music, overthrown, and then welcomed again with the passage of years, the later music of Beethoven, which approached the final threshold, it would seem, of classical music—and now all these new composers, with their new sounds and new ideas . . .

In the world outside the rains came down, snows fell, the poplar trees released their summer fluff, and the unbearable political blather about achievements and victories—that soon we would catch up with America—continued unabated. People drank tea and vodka in their kitchens, illegal pages of paper rustled, and tape recordings of Galich and the young Vysotsky, who gave birth to more new sounds and ideas, whirred. But Sanya hardly noticed any of this. This all happened in the world of Ilya and Mikha, his friends from his school days, who were drifting further and further away from him.

Khrushchev's thaw was still under way, but Khrushchev himself had exited out the back door. At some Party powwow, he was heard to say: "The notion of some sort of thaw was just an invention of that shifty rascal Ehrenburg!"

Thus, a signal was given, and received. The cold had set in again.

At this historical juncture, the government music experts traded places with the government visual arts experts. Sanya only caught the tail end of rumors about a battle in the halls of the Manezh exhibition center, primarily through Ilya.

Mikha seemed to have disappeared for good after he went to live and work in a school for children with special needs, outside of town. Anna Alexandrovna saw him more often than anyone else did. She was the one he confided in about his experiences working with the deaf-mute children, who had won his incautiously open heart. But his heart did not belong in its entirety to this younger tribe; the other half beat for Alyona, who had a habit of returning his affections, then vanishing like the Snow Queen in the rain. She was the living embodiment of this fairy-tale creature: icy, fluid, and volatile, she seemed to crystallize, flare, and fade at will.

Mikha introduced Sanya to Alyona. Sanya, conscious of her charm, felt a sense of alarm: a dangerous girl. Mikha's anxious, nervous loving was not something he had any desire to try on for size. But Ilya's easy confidence and success with women, which smacked of the dreadful storeroom, failed to inspire envy in him either. He was afraid of the female sex. At the Conservatory he socialized more often with the male students, although he never grew really close to anyone. Sanya was no less wary of the boys who looked meaningfully at him than of the women who threw themselves at him and reeked of the yardkeeper's storeroom on Potapovsky Lane. The musical milieu that seethed behind the bronze back of Peter Ilyich Tchaikovsky was predisposed to the sin eschewed in the Bible. For that matter, it was even more inclined to the sins of envy and vanity. But they didn't throw you in prison for those.

Sanya was not affected by Conservatory passions. He was even more oblivious to what was going on outside it, in the larger world. Neither the Thaw, nor the new cold snap, had anything to do with him.

Somewhere at the top, the powers-that-be had the jitters; but, luckily, Khrushchev had no interest in music, whether "sublime and superhuman" or "muddled and confused." He was completely happy with the straightforward tune of "In the park, or in the garden." Primitive, poorly educated, and drunk on power, he ruled the huge country as he saw fit. He raised his fist at Stalin, kicked his corpse out of the Mausoleum, released prisoners, cultivated virgin soil, sowed the Vologda region with corn, threw underground knitwear manufacturers, satirists, and parasites into prison, one after another, strangled Hungary, launched a satellite, and brought glory to the USSR through Gagarin. He destroyed churches and built Machine-Tractor Stations, merged some things, dismantled others, augmented this, downsized that. He inadvertently gave Crimea to Ukraine.

He set the creative intelligentsia straight with language of the gutter, and almost barely learned to pronounce that strange foreign word *intelligentsia*, which twisted the tongue without mercy. At the same time, radio announcers changed their pronunciation to reflect Khrushchev's—"communism" and "Communists" becoming "commonism" and "Commonists," for example. Sensing degeneration, deception, and bourgeois influences everywhere, Khrushchev promoted Lysenko, with his easily accessible theories, and shunted aside geneticists, cyberneticists, and all those who fell outside the scope of his limited intelligence. An enemy of culture and freedom, religion and talent, he suppressed all those his ignorant, myopic vision could discern. He couldn't discern his primary enemies, however: neither great literature, nor philosophy, nor art. He couldn't touch Beethoven, Bach was beyond his reach, even Mozart slipped out of his grasp—his simplicity of soul prevented him from understanding that they were the ones who should have been banned!

In 1964, Brezhnev came to power. The upper echelons of government were rearranged; one group of vampires changed places with another. Their mediocrity in matters of culture set a precedent for the entire country; it was dangerous to try to rise above the lowest common denominator. This diet of literary and artistic pablum was profoundly depressing. A handful of people, insignificant in all respects—surviving eggheads holed up in math and biology departments, some of them true scholars and respected academics, but far more of them marginals and eccentrics vegetating in low-level positions or languishing in third-rate research institutes, and one or two truly brilliant students of chemistry or physics or musical theory—these invisible, impractical people with spiritual needs existed illegally, outside the system.

And how numerous could they have been, these strangers who crossed paths in the cloakroom of the library, or the coat check at the Philharmonic, or in the quiet recesses of museums? They did not constitute a party, a social circle, a secret society; they were not even a cohort of like-minded people. Perhaps the only thing that united all of them was a mutual hatred of Stalinism. And, of course, reading. Hungry, unrestrained, obsessive reading. Reading was a passion, a neurosis, a narcotic. For many, books became surrogates for life rather than mere teachers of life.

In those years, the mania for reading—of a very particular kind—infected Sanya, too. He threw himself into reading musical scores, and spent all his free time in the music library. Unfortunately, borrowing privileges did not extend to many of the scores. His crippled hand limited him so drastically that now and then he was visited by compensatory dreams, one of which had recurred no fewer than five times in the past decade. In the dream, he was playing, and he experienced intense physiological gratification from this activity. His very body was transformed into a musical instrument, like some sort of multistemmed flute. From the tips of his fingers he filled up with music; it traveled through the marrow of his bones and collected in the resonator of his skull. His powers grew limitless. The instrument on which he played resembled a special, very complex kind of piano that produced unearthly sounds. He was aware of hearing music that was at the same time very familiar and completely unprecedented. The music was original, of the moment, freshly minted—but it was simultaneously also his, Sanya's, own.

Sight-reading allowed him to grasp a musical text, and even came with some advantages. "Reading" with his eyes turned out to be a more ideally refined activity, and technical difficulties ceased to exist. The music poured directly from the page into his consciousness.

Sanya derived enormous pleasure from analyzing the scores. He delighted in the art of instrumentation, the vast opportunities for interpretation. The visual—and, through it, cognitive—perception of music offered him an added dimension of pleasure: sound and sign merged into one, and an exciting picture emerged, an amalgam that contained, possibly, its own indecipherable, illegible content. Even before he had read the notes he vaguely discerned some sort of textual semantic formula, an interweaving of textual levels or planes, and it seemed to him that the key to the very secret of music was just within reach.

It seemed to him that music, too, was subject to the laws of evolution, the same ones that governed the self-organization of the world, arising from the simplest forms and becoming ever more complex. This evolution could be traced not only in sound, but even in musical notation, the semiotic reflection of the musical thought of an era. He discovered—though this was not a great discovery, since it had been made long before, by others—that musical notation, albeit belatedly, followed the changes that occurred in musical cognition through the ages. This insight led him logically to the attempt to find the laws of development of this cognition—in other words, the evolutionary law of systems of pitch.

When Sanya began, very cautiously, to set forth to Kolosov his ideas about the evolution of music, he stopped him in the middle of his halting explanation, and, with a brusque movement, pulled an American music journal out of a pile of sheet music lying under the table. He turned right to the page he was looking for. This was an article about the composer Earle Brown. The journal had reproduced the score of a piece called "December 1952." It was a page of white paper covered with a multitude of black rectangles. While Sanya was examining this page in astonishment, Kolosov, chuckling, told him that this wasn't the end of the story. Subsequently, Earle Brown had written a composition titled "Twenty-five Pages," and this was, literally, twenty-five pages covered in drawings that could be performed in any order, by any number of musicians. In light of this article, the picture that Sanya was trying to develop acquired staggering potential, according to Kolosov.

If only Yury Andreevich hadn't been emitting caustic little snorts and coughs under his breath. When Sanya realized that his teacher was mocking him and not taking him seriously, he grew upset and stopped talking altogether.

But the murky evolutionary ideas didn't abandon him. He experienced a surge of unprecedented boldness and began pursuing in secret the creation of a single law, a kind of general theory of musical systems. The only thing comparable in scope and ambition would have been the Grand Unified Theory. Like a silkworm tirelessly drawing a precious thread from its own being, he fashioned a shining cocoon around himself, and was on the verge of withdrawing into it completely, passing over into a purely speculative, but more authentic, world. This was dangerous; if he had let himself go, it would have been easy to descend into a world of pure madness.

When Sanya graduated from the Conservatory, Kolosov, with whom he still spent a great deal of time, managed to land him a position as an assistant professor in the department of the history of foreign music. (There were no openings in the department of music theory.) In the fall, Sanya began teaching, but he was still preoccupied with his theoretical constructs. Relations between Kolosov and Sanya began to unravel. Sanya wanted Kolosov's support and approval, but he was met with a skeptical grin. This hurt him.

From time to time, a sense of alarm stole over Anna Alexandrovna's heart: had her boy, perhaps, chosen too high a register in life?

GIRLFRIENDS

Galya Polukhina, nicknamed Polushka, and Tamara Brin, whom Olga affectionately called Brinchik, had always felt a bit constrained in Olga's presence. She was the only friend either one of them had. They felt they should avoid saying too much. But not for any other reason than that they loved her, and didn't want to disappoint their girlfriend with insufficiently high-minded, or even downright vulgar, thoughts and opinions.

Both girlfriends were devoted to Olga, and apart from the irrational aspect of their love, which it was senseless to question, each of them had her own reasons, and very clear-cut ones, for admiring her.

Galina Polukhina came from a poor family. She lived in a semi-basement apartment in Olga's venerable building. She wasn't particularly pretty, and was an average student—and even that took some effort. In the third grade, Olga was appointed to the task of "pulling up" Galya to improve her grades, and Olga was full of sympathy for her. Olga's magnanimity was selfless. There was no condescension of the rich and beautiful to the poor and mediocre; this poor and mediocre creature wound around the thick stem like a vine, clinging with its aerial rootlets and sucking gently. Olga, with her superabundant gifts and talents, didn't notice this.

Polushka was a placid soul. She didn't know the meaning of envy, she had no insight into the dynamics of human interrelationship, and she was filled with grateful adoration.

Things were different with Tamara Brin. In contrast to Olga, who was diligent and disciplined, Tamara was an "effortless" A student. She appraised the scholastic wisdom on offer with a single glance of her dark eyes, and imbibed it, with a flutter of the sad wings of her eyelashes. Her appearance was striking and strange. She looked like an Assyrian king from the textbook of ancient history; except that the crimped beard of the king, which descended below his lower lip, changed places on Tamara. She had a bush of hair that rose straight up from the top of her forehead. She was, in her own way, a beauty. A beauty for the connoisseur. As a Jew she inhabited a cocoon of untouchability and bore the universal repudiation bitterly but with dignity. Toward Olga she felt a certain kind of rapturous gratitude. In the winter of 1953, when the terrible word was constantly whispered behind the back of the nine-year-old Tamara, Olga was the only one in the class who rushed to the defense of the ideal of internationalism and multiculturalism, and in particular, to the defense of Tamara. When she heard the word *kike* thrown at Tamara, she cried out through hot tears:

"You're Fascists! Monsters! Soviet people don't act that way! You should be ashamed of yourselves. In our country, all cultures and nations are equal!"

Tamara never forgot Olga's characteristic unadulterated fury, and only due to the righteous wrath of the best girl in the class was she able to come to terms with the horrible school, with the world of enmity and humiliation.

As the years passed, Tamara valued Olga's independence of spirit and her courage more and more. Olga never lied, and she said what she thought. What she thought was almost always right, and it was what she had been taught at home. Tamara, because of her origins, her family history, and her not entirely Soviet upbringing, couldn't share Olga's convictions, or her enthusiasm and emotion. But Tamara would never have dared contradict her by even a single word, for fear of losing her friend, and because she didn't want anyone—Olga above all—to be moved by her tragic alienness.

The friendship among the three of them continued all through their years at school. It was strong, but very lopsided: Olga talked, and her girlfriends listened and kept silent; one in rapture but without understanding, the other restrained and skeptical.

Tamara allowed herself to voice her thoughts—independently and compellingly—only in discussions about theater and literature, and about the trivial but fascinating goings-on at school: the history teacher's new shoes, or the insidious behavior of Zinka Shchipakhina, a traitor and a cheat. Galya and Tamara tolerated each other for Olga's sake.

In the fifth grade, Galya entered a class where her own true talent emerged: She was an athlete. She trained as a gymnast, and after the sixth grade she joined a team, first in the second-class division, and soon in the first. In the eighth grade she began training to receive the title of Master of Athletics. She had fulfilled all the requirements by the time she was fifteen, but she had to wait six months to receive the title officially, as it was only awarded to sixteen-year-olds. She became a school celebrity, though her grades were too poor for her to enjoy real renown. She was still a mediocre student, always looking over Olga's shoulder.

Upon graduating from school, the unexpected happened: all three girlfriends got into college. Olga was accepted at the university (which in itself was completely predictable). Tamara, with her silver honors medal, was accepted at the Institute of Medicine. This was an exceptional achievement in the prevailing circumstances of the time. Galya, who had joined the Moscow youth team in artistic gymnastics, but still had a strained relationship with grammar, had been accepted at the Institute of Physical Education and Sports.

To celebrate this triple victory, a party was organized for their classmates at Olga's home. Antonina Naumovna ordered all kinds of delicacies from the buffet of the House of Writers—pies, tarts, and canapés (only they would have known what these were!)—and nobly retreated to the dacha. Olga's faithful knight Rifat, who had graduated two years before, volunteered to supply real pilaf. At exactly eight in the evening, he delivered it to the apartment in an enormous cauldron, hired from a restaurant at the Exposition of National Economic Achievements. His father was an Azerbaijani government official, with connections from the very highest to the very lowest levels.

The party was a complete success. Two boys and one girl got completely smashed. Vika Travina and Boris Ivanov finally went all the way, an achievement that had eluded them for a year and a half, despite wholehearted attempts. Another couple quarreled and broke up, which both of them regretted for the rest of their lives. And Raya Kozina broke out in hives for the first time—a malady that would beset her until her death.

Many, many things of great significance took place that night, but only one person, the hostess herself, failed to notice them. That night, she realized for the first time that she had been lucky from birth—whether endowed by nature, by the stars in the heavens, or by her genes. Until this day she had never been aware of her enviable lot. Now she was absolutely certain that there were many achievements in store for her, many victories, even triumphs. And the three handsomest boys—Rifat, the Persian prince, his mustache bracketing his mouth; his friend Vova, a student at the Moscow Aviation Institute, broad-shouldered and tallish, with a blond wave of hair above his eyes, like the popular poet Sergei Esenin in the early photographs where he is wearing a peasant blouse, but no jacket and tie; and Vitya Bodyagin, who had been stationed on a submarine for four years, newly discharged, with a striped sailor's jersey under his dress shirt, in funny trousers with children's clasps at the sides, and who would soon be starting at the faculty of philology with Olga—all of them looked at Olga with the hungry eyes of men, and with various shades of meaning: demanding, beseeching, searching, bold. With love, with propositions, with promises.

That would be something else! To think that I could just up and marry any one of them. Anyone I want! Olga was intoxicated with success and made a bet with herself that she would marry the one who would ask her for the next dance. She danced better than anyone else—both rock and roll and tango. And her waist was the slenderest, and her hair was the longest—though she had cut off the long braid she had grown tired of.

But her hair, which still reached nearly to her waist, was reddish, with sparkling highlights. She looked at herself from the side and very much liked what she saw. Everyone liked her, the boys, and the girls, and the neighbors, and even the mothers on the parents' committee.

They put on "Rock Around the Clock" by Bill Haley and the Comets—Rifat had brought the record. And everyone went wild. They soared to the music as if they were being carried off by the wind. The driving sounds and rhythms seeped into them. It wasn't about gentle touching, but about collisions, outbursts, and yet more collisions, and the broad-shouldered Vova seemed to be throwing her from arm to arm. But had he asked her to dance? Four months later she would marry him.

They danced and drank, smoked on the balcony and in the kitchen. Then everyone got tired. Some people left late at night, others stayed till morning. Vika and Boris fell asleep in the parents' bedroom, stunned by the earth-shattering event—their coitus, in other words. A long and happy marriage lay ahead of them, though they didn't know this, not yet. On the rug in the living room there was a pile of people, about five of them, who hadn't been as lucky. It reeked slightly of vomit.

Finally, everyone cleared out except the reliable Tamara and Galya. The girlfriends helped clean up all the traces of youthful reveling. They made coffee. They drank it like grown-ups out of the best tiny cups, but they still felt like they were just playing house, especially Galya. Toward evening, the two girlfriends left to go home, planning to get together again the following week. But the next time they saw each other was at the beginning of the following year. After graduation, life began spinning by at a breathless pace.

Tamara's house on Sobachya Square was slated to reach the end of its life span, and the residents were removed. Tamara's family was resettled in the distant outskirts of the city, in Workers' Village, past Kuntsevo. The Molodezhnaya metro station was at that time still just a point on the blueprints of city planners.

Tamara energetically shuttled back and forth between her new home, her new job, and the medical institute. The year that they moved, Tamara's beloved grandmother Maria Semenovna died. She had been a lifelong friend of the pianist Elena Gnesina; she had spent her whole life around this renowned family, working as a secretary in their musical sanctuary, the Gnesin Institute of Music. But the old lady from the Arbat was carried off by the catastrophe of resettlement.

The civil memorial service was held at the Gnesin Institute. Tamara, who had known this remarkable family since childhood, now saw what remained of them—there, in a wheelchair, sat the great Elena Fabianovna, founder of the only empire, a musical one, that had withstood the rise of Soviet power, and what's more—something absolutely unthinkable at the time—survived it.

It was a gathering of musicians, but among the mourners were also people from "the audience," participants in the world of music, which seemed to exist above the Soviet world of collectivization and industrialization, all the official state upheaval and frenzy, which appeared so paltry against the background of Beethoven, Schubert, Shostakovich, and even Misha Gnesin, an utterly forgotten composer, younger brother of the celebrated Gnesin sisters.

Tamara was astonished. She had known many of her grandmother's "old-lady friends," but here, at the graveside, she finally understood what kind of world her grandmother, who went around in a stretched-out sweater with pieces of dried egg stuck to the collar and a skirt that sported all manner of stains in varying hues, had inhabited.

Almost all the "old-lady friends," except perhaps for Anna Alexandrovna, who lived on Pokrovka, were local, from the Arbat neighborhood. They came on foot and stood in a small group nearby. They were not exactly members of the family's inner circle, not teachers or performers, but "initiates" . . .

They mourned in a musical key, performing the music of Mikhail Gnesin, written for Meyerhold's staging of Gogol's play *The Inspector General*. This was a gift of love to the departed Maria Semenovna from the Gnesin family, who were also dying out.

Then the elderly musicians all came up to Tamara and Raisa Ilinichna, her mother, to say a few words about Maria Semenovna, about music and about friendship. And it seemed that they invested these ordinary words with completely new meaning. Anna Alexandrovna also came up to them, asking them not to forget Maria Semenovna's friends, and to come to visit her. And she stroked Tamara's head, running her hand over Tamara's rough hair.

The old apartment was reproduced inside the new one. In the large walk-through room stood the piano, with the dusty divan, covered with a worn red rug, next to it. Above it hung all the same pictures from the house on the Arbat, in the same arrangement as before. Only her grandmother, who had played on the piano, was missing. Tamara soon moved from the divan in the walk-through room into her grandmother's room, the best one in the apartment. And she inadvertently became the head of this new household, which tried so hard to be indistinguishable from the old one.

Raisa Ilinichna, who had spent her whole life taking up as little space as possible, moved into the smaller room by the entrance door. Timid and unlucky, during the span of her life she had accomplished one major deed: having a child, which was Tamara, out of wedlock. The move and the death of her mother broke Raisa Ilinichna's heart. Always defenseless against the blows that life dealt, she now became nearly immobilized by grief. She was not yet fifty, but to her daughter she seemed old and completely washed out. Raisa Ilinichna had the same opinion of herself.

In the new place, without the guiding hand of her mother, she felt unmoored. She couldn't get used to the new neighborhood, and for a long time she traveled all the way back to the Arbat to buy bread. When she got home, she would sit in her narrow little room all by herself and weep, trying to hide the tears from her daughter.

But Tamara wasn't aware of this, and even if she had noticed, she would not have attached any significance to the weak-willed and pointless tears. Tamara's new life was a rich whirlwind of activity. The drowsy languor of the last years in high school vanished, and all the gears went into overdrive. Days passed in a flash, and she could hardly catch her breath. She was unaccountably, improbably lucky. Her studies were interesting, her job even more so. The academic adviser that had been assigned to her, Vera Samuilovna Vinberg, was heaven-sent. An extremely bright older woman, who had survived the labor camps, she became a mainstay in the complex picture of Tamara's life. The void was filled, all her questions answered and her fears dissipated.

As tiny and dry as a flea, Vera Samuilovna, shaking the tight stainless-steel curls that escaped onto her forehead and neck from the large cluster atop her head, would instruct the new lab assistant in a manner that implied that she knew beforehand what a remarkable scientist and researcher she would become. Vera Samuilovna looked at Tamara's luxuriant hair, at her small, agile fingers, and noted her keen intelligence—and thought that the girl could have been her own daughter; or, more likely, her granddaughter.

Vera Samuilovna even planned to invite Tamara to her home, to introduce her to her husband, to bring her into the family. But for the time being, it was merely a vague intention. Her husband, Edwin, for all his outward amiability, didn't take easily to new people.

Meanwhile, fate was busy laying down byroads upon which Tamara might meet the love of her life. The Vinbergs' home was one of the places that Tamara's lover-to-be regularly frequented.

But for now, the things that interested her most were concentrated in the old textbook of endocrinology that Vera Samuilovna presented to her lab assistant, saying:

"Tamara, dear—learn this by heart. For a start. We'll take on chemistry later. First you have to understand the connections that exist in this wisest of all systems."

Vera Samuilovna was crazy about endocrinology. In her laboratory, she synthesized artificial hormones, which she viewed almost as the key to immortality of the human species. Vera Samuilovna believed in hormones as though they were the Lord Above. She would solve all earthly problems with the help of adrenaline, testosterone, and estrogen.

A new picture of the world opened before Tamara. The human being appeared to her now like a marionette governed by hormone molecules, on which depended not only size, appetite, and mood, but also mental activity, habits, and fixations. Vera Samuilovna considered the director of this whole theater of life to be the pineal, a tiny gland hidden in the depths of the brain. A wonderful, mysterious insight afforded only to initiates! Other scientists gave priority to the pituitary gland; but in this sphere of activity, they didn't send you to prison for the error of your ways.

Tamara's personal endocrine system worked like clockwork: her pineal gland (what else?) sent out exciting signals; her adrenal gland pumped out adrenaline; her thyroid sent out serotonin for the urgent replenishment of supplies. How could her boundless energy have been explained any other way? A surplus of estrogen made little pimples bloom on her forehead. There weren't many of them—they could have been covered up with her bangs—but the hair insisted on sticking straight out and up, so she had to wrestle it down with hairpins. Everything was perfect. Only there was never enough time . . .

Galya never had enough time, either. Nor did she have any extra energy—it all went into her training. They didn't teach the athletes too much at the institute. They weren't in the business of training teachers, but of producing champions. At first everything went very well. She went from small triumphs to greater ones; she dreamed of Olympic gold, or silver at the very least. What followed, however, was a serious injury.

In her fourth year, Galya took part in the Moscow championship. When she dismounted from the parallel bars, having completed the routine without a hitch, she landed so awkwardly that she fractured her knee, severely damaging the joint. After that her career prospects as a champion evaporated, though she had almost made the national team. She spent three months in the Institute of Traumatology, where Dr. Mironova, their best surgeon, operated on her twice. Her knee became functional again, but the articulation of the joint was inadequate for an athletic career.

The heady life of training sessions, competitions, and promise had ended. They didn't expel her from the institute, however. Galya dove into her textbooks, but floundered. She still lived in her semibasement, but no one took any interest in her now. Her glory had been short-lived, and she again felt insignificant, unattractive, and worthless. Plain old Polushka she had been, and Polushka she was destined to remain.

With her unflagging energy and concern, Olga decided to take her friend under her wing. She even asked her mother's advice. Antonina Naumovna, sympathetic within reason, solved the problem: she arranged for Galya to take an evening course in typing.

"If she learns to type well enough, I'll hire her at the magazine." She immediately had second thoughts. "Though Galya's grammar isn't very good, is it?"

When she had graduated from the institute, Galya stayed on in the dean's office. Her position was not a very rewarding one—she was a secretary. Her achievements were paltry, and she had a salary to match. Still, thanks to the evening typing course, she could supplement her earnings. She was a fast typist, and she moonlighted. True, she didn't own a typewriter, so she had to use the one at work and put in long, very late hours.

When Galya's affairs had fallen into place, Olga distanced herself again. Her own life was elevated and meaningful. Even the unpleasantness that came her way was exceptional, not like what others had to contend with—she was expelled from the university under scandalous circumstances, then she broke off relations with Vova (Galya saw right away that it was a very stupid mistake, of course); but no sooner had Vova been forced to bow out than a new man appeared. Olga told Galya this and that about herself, cursorily, without going into detail; and what was surprising was that despite all the unpleasantness, her eyes still shone as before, and her hair, her smile, even her dimples were all aglow.

This was when Galya envied her for the first time. She herself had become the poorer for her misfortunes; she shed and wilted, and even started aging prematurely. Poor Galya.

Galya, naturally, knew nothing of the terrible secrets and dangers that filled Olga's life. In Galya's view, Olga's new pseudo-husband couldn't hold a candle to Vova. This Ilya fellow was also tall, and he had curly hair; but he wasn't dashing in the way Vova had been. However, Olga's son, Kostya, was all over him. As a father, Vova was a disciplinarian and treated his son with military severity; but Ilya and Kostya played noisy games together, romped around and turned somersaults, and were always exploring some new interest. Ilya was more like an older best friend. And with Kostya, Ilya was able to experience vicariously all the childhood joys that he couldn't experience with his own unhappy and constrained son. Kostya simply adored him. His own father, who saw him once a week, understood that Kostya was being "led astray," resented it, and was more and more reluctant to spend time with him. And the feelings were mutual.

Galya didn't know any of these details. Nor did she know that Olga and Ilya had quietly gotten married, without going public about it. She was hurt when she found out by chance, six months later. The event of marriage had nearly cosmic significance for her. But they hadn't even organized the most modest wedding party. She didn't even dream of ever finding a marriage partner for herself. She was twenty-nine years old, and since her career had collapsed, not a single colleague, or student, or even passerby had given her so much as a glance . . . meanwhile, in a roundabout way, through Olga, fate was preparing a valuable gift for her that would last her whole life.

It's fascinating to trace the trajectories of people destined to meet. Sometimes such encounters happen without any special effort of fate, without elaborate convolutions of plot, following the natural course of events—say, people live in adjacent buildings, or go to the same school; they get to know each other at college or at work. In other cases, something unexpected is called for: train schedules out of whack, a minor misfortune orchestrated on high, like a small fire or a leaky pipe on an upper floor, or a ticket bought from someone else for the last movie show. Or else a chance meeting, when a watcher is standing in one spot, on the lookout for a target, and suddenly a girl glides by out of nowhere, once, twice, a third time. And there's a weak smile, and then, suddenly, like dawn breaking—she's your own dear wife . . .

Isn't every person deserving of these special efforts of fate? Olga, yes, certainly . . . But Galya?

Should fate squander its efforts on an insignificant and unprepossessing couple, the daughter of the local plumber, a drunk, and the son of another such plumber from Tver, but already deceased? In fact, Galya's father, nicknamed Sir Yury Dripsandleaks, would meet a premature end. No sooner were they assigned to a new apartment than he died, to the annoyance and disappointment of the residents of the high-rise on Vosstanie Square, who would never again have such a skilled expert in all things pipes-and-leaks related, someone who knew every valve and plug by sight and by touch. In his presence, pipes seemed to join, and blockages, with a grunt, cleared up of their own volition.

And was a towheaded, suspicious, vengeful boy, the courtyard champion in long-distance pissing—no one else's stream even came close to his in the length of the arc, either in the courtyard or at school—beneath the notice of fate?

Was it possible that he, like Olga, was a darling of fate, and that it took direct aim at him, weaving its web around him, making sure he was on duty on just those days when a girl, towheaded like himself, would dart into the entrance where he was on the lookout for his target?

It's incomprehensible, improbable—but the generosity of fate also extends to the likes of these C-list extras.

Ilya never managed to find out which of his sins—the distribution of books, petty communications between hostile factions, his close connections to Mikha and Edik, by that time both in prison—had attracted the direct attention of the authorities. In the spring of 1971, he realized he was being watched.

For Galya, this was a fateful event.

The first time Galya saw him, they met at the entrance to the building. Small in stature, but handsome and appealing, wearing a gray cap and a long coat, he held the door open for her, and she smiled at him.

The very next day, she ran into him again in the courtyard. This time he was sitting on a bench with a newspaper in his hands, obviously waiting for someone. And Galya smiled at him again. Then, the third time, he was standing in the entrance hall, and they greeted each other. He asked her her name. At that point, Galya realized that he wasn't standing there just by chance, but was waiting for her, and she was happy. Now she liked him even more. His name was Gennady. A nice name. His appearance wasn't striking—but neither was it lacking in anything. He and Galya were similar, as they would discover, if you looked closely: their eyes were narrow-set, close to the bridge of their rather long noses, and they had small chins. They had the same coloring—his hair, of which he didn't have as much, of course, was a bit lighter. It lay smooth on his head. But he was very neat—exceptionally so. He made a very civilized impression. When he disappeared for a week, Galya's dreams were dashed. Every evening when she returned home from work, she looked for him in the courtyard, but he wasn't there.

Well, there went love, she thought bitterly, and lived through the entire week with the nagging feeling that nothing would ever happen to her, that her life in the semibasement would never end, although everyone else had been resettled, and her family was the last, and she herself was the last and the least, as her grandmother said.

Indifferent to everything, she was walking down Gorokhovskaya Street (now called Kazakov) from the institute to Kurskaya Station, where she would get on the metro and travel five stations to her home. The whole trip would take about an hour, including the time she would need to get to the metro and then to sprint home once she got off at Krasnopresnenskaya. In spite of the bad weather, and in a bad mood, she was walking along as though her muscles had been trained to do it, her back straight, her head, in a blue beret, held high, in an old raincoat Olga had given her the previous year. Suddenly, from behind, a strong hand grabbed her by the arm. First she thought it was one of her students. She looked around and saw that it was—him!

"Galya," he said, "I've been waiting for you for so long. Let's go to the movies."

How had he found her? It was obvious he had wanted to! Everything that followed was like the movies. And it flashed by just as quickly. The main thing was that it was exactly the way Galya wanted it to happen: at first he took her elbow, carefully, strongly, then by the hand, then he kissed her politely, without any pawing. He embraced her—again decently, without anything obscene or dirty. A month later he proposed to her. He wanted to visit her parents, with a cake and a bottle of wine, to ask for her hand. Galya warned her father before-hand:

"If you take out the vodka and get smashed, I'll leave home."

Her father made a dismissive gesture with his swollen brown hand:

"Oh, I'm scared! As though there's anyplace else for you to go to."

He was right, of course. But what he didn't know was that his Galya now had an actual shield against the misfortunes of life.

The formal marriage proposal did not go as planned. Her mother was called in to work to sub for someone else on that evening. Her brother and his wife had been skirmishing to the point of fisticuffs for the past week, so Galya had to come clean about all her family circumstances. Gennady was understanding.

"Galya, mine are the same. Never mind them, the relatives . . . they just get in your way your whole life. We'll just get married without telling them."

Everything about Gennady was to her liking. He was quiet, didn't ask questions, had a master's certificate in sports, by the way, with a college degree; and with a family like his, you could forget they had ever existed.

Gennady was eager to get married for his own reasons, which he informed Galya about. Through his job he was eligible to receive housing; they had promised him a one-room apartment, but if he married, they might give him a small two-room apartment, so he could start a family.

They filed the necessary papers, and set a date for the registration of their union. Galya went to Olga and told her she was getting married. She asked her to be a witness. Olga had by this time tied the knot with Ilya. Both her girlfriends were lonely and alone. Tamara at least had her hormones to make out with, but Galya was just plain alone and unloved.

Olga was happy for her, but surprised:

"What kind of friend are you! You didn't even tell me you had met someone."

Now she just had to marry Tamara off, and everyone would be settled.

Olga didn't suspect that she had also inadvertently decided

Tamara's fate. For a year Tamara had been seeing Ilya's older friend the brilliant Marlen. At Olga's birthday party, she had sat Tamara next to Marlen. They left the party at the same time, and Marlen walked her to the Molodezhnaya metro station. It turned out that they were practically neighbors. Tamara fell madly in love, igniting a mutual passion that was no laughing matter. For many years Marlen went back and forth between two homes (fortunately, only five minutes apart). In each home Marlen kept a toothbrush, a razor, and a clean pair of undergarments. He had always led a traveler's existence, though now the destination of his business trips was sometimes only as far as the neighboring house, where he hibernated in quiet retreat and in love. And, of course, in secret. Tamara took a vow of silence practically from the first day they met—not a word to anyone about Marlen, especially not to Olga and Ilya. Thus, Olga, the unwitting disposer of other people's fates, organized their lives and affairs but remained none the wiser about it herself.

Galya didn't have a wedding party. Gennady said that it made no sense to throw money to the wind, since they would have to buy furniture. Galya just nodded in agreement. She was disappointed about it, but Gennady was right, of course. About the furniture. They registered their marriage, and she went to live with her husband in his dormitory. The room was a decent one. He gave his old bed away to the supervisor of the dormitory, and bought a fold-out divan.

That first night on the new divan, Gennady accepted an unexpected gift from his wife, a gift that required painstaking effort from the receiver, no less than the giver. It turned out that Galya Polukhina was an upright girl; she had saved herself for her husband. Only one thing cast a shadow over this great day for Gennady: Galya's friend Olga. How on earth could he have let the wife of his target, Ilya Bryansky, whom he had been watching on and off for two years, appear as a witness on their marriage certificate? A personal connection was taking shape which was in part something of a nuisance, in part very promising.

While they were thrashing around on the new divan, while Gennady was carrying out his masculine duties and overcoming nature's difficulties, glad for the gentle participation of his wife, a small but insistent worry hovered in the back of his mind: Had Olga recognized him?

She had. After she returned home from the marriage registry, she told Ilya that Polushka had gotten married to the Rodent. That's what they had nicknamed Gennady when they discovered he was shadowing Ilya. The Rodent was one of the three outdoor surveillance officers whom Ilya knew by sight.

Ilya laughed at first—that meant he had married into the family! Then he started wondering. What was it you gave her to type?

In recent years Galya had often accepted work from them. She was a fast and accurate typist, without really understanding what she was typing.

"Oh, damn! I don't remember."

"Think! What did you give her to type?"

"Ah, now I remember! She has my Erika typewriter, and Solzhenitsyn's *Gulag Archipelago*."

"Get them back right away. Today."

Olga rushed down to the semibasement, and only remembered along the way that Galya had moved in with her husband. Her drunken father, Yury, hurt that his daughter hadn't included him in the marriage arrangements, but had done everything herself, was unwelcoming. Olga asked whether Galya had left her typewriter behind.

"She took every last thing with her and cleared out. Didn't even leave an address," her father said curtly, and slammed the door in Olga's face.

Olga went home upset, not knowing what to do next. Ilya lost no time in trying to comfort her.

"Never mind, Olga, things could be worse. Galya has been part of your family her whole life; she won't be in any hurry to denounce you. Wait awhile—before you know it we'll be drinking tea with her hubby," Ilya said with a crooked grin.

Ilya wasn't completely off the mark about the tea; but a friendly tea party was not in the cards for years to come. A good many of them.

They told Tamara about Galya's hasty wedding to the Rodent,

leaving out the part about the typewriter and the manuscript Galya
was working on. Even so, Tamara was horrified.

"Don't let her into your house!"

"Are you crazy? I've been friends with her practically since the day
I was born!" Olga was angry.

"It's too dangerous. How can you not see that yourself? You'll have
an informer under your own roof," Tamara said darkly.

"Nonsense! It's sickening, suspecting everyone in that way. Then
I might as well start suspecting you!" Olga burst out.

Tamara turned scarlet, began to cry, and left.

The next day, Olga called Galya at work. They told her that she
had gone on vacation that very day. Strange—Galya hadn't mentioned anything about a vacation. In fact, Galya herself hadn't known
about this surprise from her husband. A honeymoon! Galya's mother
confirmed the information, saying they had gone on a trip to Kislo-
vodsk. Olga asked about the typewriter, saying she had lent it to Galya,
and now urgently needed it back. Galya's mother, Nina, told Olga to
wait a moment while she looked for it. She came back saying there
was no typewriter in the house. She would have seen it—it was too big
to miss.

Then she wondered whether Yury might have drunk it away.
There was no telling.

The new Erika was worth a fortune, and they were nearly impossible to come by. And she needed it desperately! Olga was a good typist herself, but she didn't have the speed of a professional. She always
gave large projects to Galya and others to type.

Still, the missing *Gulag Archipelago* was a more serious loss by far.

Two weeks later, Galya came over uninvited, looking very fresh
and healthy, almost pretty. She was very perturbed, however. She cried
when she made the honest admission that the typewriter and the manuscript had disappeared from her parents' home without a trace, and
where they had gone she had no clue; she, Galya, would return the
money, it would take three months or so. Everything had vanished,
most likely, when they were on their honeymoon.

"No, it was before that!" Olga said. "I thought about it the day you

and Gennady got married, and I went over to your parents the very
next day!"

"It's impossible!" Galya said with a gasp.

The household investigation, which Galya immediately undertook, didn't yield anything. Her father was on a drinking binge, which
constituted indirect evidence of domestic theft. Still, her papa went
on these binges at regular intervals, right on schedule, and he had just
now gotten started after a bout of sobriety.

Her brother, Nikolay, whom she tried to interrogate, grew suddenly irate, began to shake, and screamed at her to leave him alone.
He wasn't quite right in the head, and the psychiatric clinic had had
medical records on file for him since he was a child.

Now Olga had to comfort Polushka and give her tea to drink. She
inquired about her married life. It was absolutely wonderful, her husband didn't drink and was very serious, had a good job, and even
promised to try to set Galya up in a good position as well. Then Ilya
and Kostya returned from the skating rink, both of them frozen and
encrusted with ice. They usually went to the one on Petrovka, but
this time they'd gone to a little patch of ice in the next-door courtyard, where they slipped and tumbled to their hearts' content. True,
when they were already tired out from all the fun, one of the other kids
pelted Kostya with an ice-filled snowball, giving him a bloody nose.
They quickly stopped the bleeding with more ice, though.

Galya always got scared and took to her heels at the mere sight of
Ilya, and this time was no exception. Olga laundered the bloody scarf
and handkerchiefs. Kostya, Ilya, and Olga had dinner together. Their
favorite days were like this one, when her mother stayed at the dacha.
Then Olga sent Kostya off to bed.

"Ilya, the typewriter and the manuscript have both disappeared.
No one knows where," Olga said with trepidation.

"It's the Rodent! We have to clear everything out of the house,"
Ilya said peremptorily.

He threw himself into the task, grabbing things off the shelves and
out of hiding places, gathering all the dangerous papers. Several onionskin pages bound together with paper clips he burned in the WC.
He collected all the most dangerous publications—issues of the *Chron-*

icle of Current Events. In her mother's bookshelves, behind the Romain Rolland and the Maxim Gorky, there were also some things stashed away. By three in the morning they had gathered up all the dangerous material and stuffed it into an old suitcase, which they stowed under a coatrack. They postponed the final decision, whether to take it all to the dacha or to Ilya's aunt's house in the country, out of harm's way, until the next morning.

They couldn't get to sleep for a long time, making all kinds of wild conjectures about what the near future had in store. They discussed whether they ought to inform the author, through Rosa Vasilievna, that the manuscript had possibly fallen into the hands of the KGB. They agreed to go to see her in the morning, to give her a detailed account of what had happened. Then Ilya discovered that Olga had fallen asleep, mid-sentence. And, like a bolt of lightning, it struck him: tomorrow they would be arrested! He even broke into a cold sweat. He had left so many tracks—his address books with all the phone numbers; and he would have to go to his mother's right away to rescue his photograph collection and hide it somewhere. And put the negatives in a separate place. No, best take it all to his aunt's in Kirzhach. If only he managed to do it in time! He'd have to get up at six and leave immediately for his mother's; and with that thought, he fell into a sound sleep.

At just after eight, Olya gave Kostya an apple and sent him on his way to school. Ilya was still asleep. Olga put some coffee on to boil. At ten after nine sharp, the telephone and doorbell rang simultaneously. Ilya woke up, looked at the clock, and realized he was too late.

"Go to the bathroom," Olga commanded. Ilya darted into the bathroom and latched the door. Olga went to open the front door, trying to decide what she should and should not say in the short space before she got there.

She had long known how these things happened, but her first thought was: call Mama for help. She immediately felt ashamed.

Six people barged in. Not one of them in uniform. A tall man, without taking off his cap, thrust a search warrant and an ID at her at the same time. He wasn't fooling around. They opened the door to every room except the bathroom.

"Is your husband in there?" the tall one asked, finally taking his cap off. A lock of hair from his toupee rose up with the cap, and he mechanically plastered it back down to his forehead. *He looks like Kosygin*, Olga thought. Suddenly her fear melted away.

"Yes, that's him," she said.

One of them went up to the door and rapped on it.

"Come out!"

"I'm coming," Ilya said.

He emerged a few minutes later in the general's old bathrobe with the patches on the sleeves. He had shaved hurriedly.

Good work, Olga thought to herself approvingly.

"You'll have to come with us to the residence where you are registered," said another one. He exchanged glances with the tall one. Meaningfully.

Ilya got dressed without any haste.

Three of them stood in a group by the bookcase.

"Your books?" the smallest one asked.

"Oh, no," Olga said. "Most of them belong to my mother. She's a well-known writer, of course. In the other room there are books on military construction. My father is a general and has a big collection of books on military subjects."

Olga's mood lifted. She could feel that her voice sounded fine, and betrayed no abject trembling. Ilya realized immediately that her fear had been replaced by some complex desperation that also contained an element of amusement.

Good girl, Ilya thought in his turn, taking heart. With that, he waved to her and went out, one goon on his right, another on his left.

Three stayed behind to search, and one more stood watch by the door.

The witness, Olga thought.

She had no firsthand experience of the KGB herself, but she had heard stories about how these searches were carried out. They were far more polite than she had imagined they would be. One of them had a pleasant face, like a tractor driver or a farmhand. Even his skin had something rural about it—it was chapped and reddish, as if he had spent a lot of time in the cold. He tapped the books perfunctorily, seeing right away that all suspicious papers had been carefully weeded out. Then he made a discovery. In the bathroom they found an ashtray full of dead matches and paper clips.

"What you were burning?" the one with the toupee asked. He introduced himself as Alexandrov, an investigator from the prosecutor's office, but Olga forgot his name immediately. She couldn't determine whether her guests were from the police, the KGB, or the prosecutor's office. She didn't know that there were subtle differences between these raids: some of them were only looking for anti-Soviet dissidents, or petition signers; others for books, yet others only for Jews.

"We burned toilet paper to cover up the stench in the bathroom," Olga said boldly.

"Do you wipe with paper clips?" Alexandrov poked around in the ashtray resourcefully. He had some idea about what those paper clips might have held together: protest letters with the names of signees attached, issues of the *Chronicle*.

"What do you expect? Our house is full of office materials. My mother's a magazine editor."

Arrogant bitch, Alexandrov thought. He had a great deal of experience.

Olga tried not to look in the direction of the worn-out suitcase standing under the coatrack, half-concealed by a long overcoat of her father's and her mother's fur coat. Would they notice? Or wouldn't they?

That's when they noticed. Alexandrov, the one who looked like Kosygin, asked Olga to open the suitcase. She opened it, and he glanced casually inside. He understood immediately; then relaxed.

"Now I see how well prepared you were."

They rummaged around for another hour and a half, just to keep up appearances. In addition to the suitcase, they took one of her mother's typewriters, her father's binoculars, Ilya's favorite camera, and all the address books, including her mother's. They even took the daily tear-off calendar from the wall. They impounded Ilya's "golden collection," photographs of the most brilliant personages of the time: Yakir, Krasin, Alik Ginzburg, the priests Dmitry Dudko, Gleb Yakunin, and Nikolay Eshliman, the writers Daniel and Sinyavsky, and Natalya Gorbanevskaya.

This photographic archive, the only one of its kind, would later come to be called "the dissident archive." It contained, among others, photographs that were published in the Western press. These were photographs that Ilya had sold to Klaus, a German journalist, and to one other American, as well as the photographs smuggled out through his Belgian friend Pierre, who then distributed them in the West.

When Alexandrov removed the folder containing this archive from the depths of Kostya's desk, Olga realized that Ilya was now exposed.

An official black Volga was waiting by the door, and another gray one was parked out on the street. They loaded the suitcase, the typewriters, and a sack full of papers into the gray one, and Olga herself into the black one. She sat in the backseat, two of the men pressed against her on either side. They drove her to a two-story building not far away, on Malaya Lubyanka. The building bore a sign that didn't mince words: "Office of the Committee for State Security for Moscow and the Moscow Region."

At three in the afternoon, the real interrogation began; or so it seemed to Olga. Alexandrov was sitting in the room, together with a nearly silent captain. He was the first person she had seen that day in a uniform. She didn't realize that this was merely a conversation, not an interrogation.

What should she say? What should she avoid saying? She wasn't in the habit of lying. Ilya had warned her to keep her head; that meant she shouldn't say anything. This, however, seemed like the hardest thing of all. And Olga, despite her best intentions, did start talking— for one hour, two hours, then three. The questions seemed random and insignificant—who are your friends, where do you go, what do you read? They mentioned her former professor, who had emigrated. They knew, naturally, that she had signed letters supporting him, and that she had been expelled from the university in 1965. They even expressed sympathy with her: this guy was spewing all that anti-Soviet nonsense, what use was it to you? You come from good Soviet stock—why did you get mixed up with that sort?

Olga played dumb, without going overboard, saying something about her girlfriends, most of whom she didn't really see anymore, since they almost all had families to take care of, children, work, and so forth . . . among her close friends she only named, out of spite, Galya Polukhina; she didn't think she mentioned a single other person.

Olga was surprised when Alexandrov asked her about Tamara Brin.

"No, we don't see each other anymore. We used to be friends, before science became her whole life. Now she doesn't have time for anyone."

"She doesn't have time for anyone? What about Marlen Kogan? She spends time with him. She's studying Hebrew."

Olga's eyebrows shot up.

"Really? I had no idea."

"I ask the questions here; you answer. You seem to consider yourself to be very smart and perceptive, Olga Afanasievna." He smiled, showing his large teeth, and for a moment Olga was overcome by something like horror. Suddenly she felt naked, vulnerable to a bite or a needle, as soft as a mollusk without its shell. At the same moment, she realized she needed to recover her composure, and she asked to go to the toilet.

Alexandrov made a phone call, and a heavy woman with a large rump came in, then led her down a corridor with unpredictable twists and turns to a WC. There were squares of newsprint hanging from a nail in the wall. Squatting over the toilet, which was clean but had no seat, she began thinking: *I wonder what the bathrooms in the FBI look like?* Then she laughed out loud, startling her chaperone. This little breather helped her. She was able to gather her thoughts, and even felt a bit stronger. Was he lying about Tamara? Probably not. Why hadn't Tamara told her anything about herself? Strange, very strange. Could she really have some sort of relationship with Marlen? She hadn't said a word about it. Silent as the grave. And him—going on about his family obligations, observing all those religious traditions, keeping kosher. All that stuff. She recalled that Marlen never ate anything at their house. He only drank vodka. He said vodka was always kosher. He had a scraggly beard and hair, and an unwieldy body—a big head with unruly curls, broad shoulders, and stumpy legs. But he had brains, that was for sure. It was like he had a whole library in his head, organized by shelves—history, geography, literature. Brilliant, absolutely brilliant; still, it was strange that Tamara had set her sights on him. It just proved that anything was possible.

Then the captain looked at his watch, went out, and returned fifteen minutes later. He looked at his watch again, and mumbled something to Alexandrov. Alexandrov's tone changed abruptly, as though a command meant just for him were written on the watch.

"Enough of that. Let's get down to business. Do these books belong to you, or to your husband?"

"They're mine, of course. I keep my own books at home."

"All of them are yours?"

"Well, a few of them may have been left behind by other people. Most of them are mine, though."

"Which of these books are not yours?"

"These are all mine," Olga said, correcting herself.

"Where did you get them?"

Olga had expected to be asked this question, and she had a ready answer.

"We buy books. We read a lot, and buy a lot of books."

"Where?"

"Well, you know there's a black market in Moscow, you can buy anything there: foreign junk, perfume, books . . ."

"Where is this market?"

"Different places. Some of them I bought near the Kuznetsky Bridge."

"Be more precise. Where exactly near the Kuznetsky Bridge?"

"There's a book market in Moscow. They sell all kinds of things there."

"You mean people stand right there out in the open by Kuznetsky Bridge and offer to sell you stuff like this, for example?" He pulled Avtorkhanov's book out of the pile. "*The Technology of Power?*"

"Yes," Olga said, nodding.

Then he pulled one book after another out of the pile until he lost interest. The captain went out twice; then he came back again.

"What can I tell you, Olga Afanasievna? All this book business qualifies as anti-Soviet agitation and falls under article 190 of the Criminal Code. It carries a penalty of three to five years. Perhaps you weren't aware of this?" He even seemed to express sympathy with her.

Olga, who had been showered with love, kindness, and understanding from earliest childhood, was more troubled by the ambiguity of her relations with her interlocutor than anything else. He was an unpleasant person, an enemy by definition, but she instinctively continued to rely on her own charms. Flirtatiousness and self-assurance kept breaking through the armor of restraint she had decided to adopt as her modus operandi. But the interlocutor was deaf and devoid of feeling, and she kept getting off track, catching herself in inconsistencies. It was tormenting, all the more because she had no idea how it would all end: whether they would let her go, arrest her, kill her . . . No, they wouldn't kill her, of course; but there were moments when she was plunged into fear, a physical, animal fear that exceeded human endurance. And it went on and on.

They questioned her repeatedly about Ilya. About his job. He had a more or less official cover—a document stating that he worked as a research assistant. He was already on his third patron. After his first arrangement with his father-in-law, an academic in the field of agriculture, he had a short stint with a cranky old man, a writer, who broke off relations with him after six months. Now he had an agreement with another writer, a decent sort, who lived in Leningrad. If a ruse became necessary, it was that he was carrying out research for him in the Moscow libraries.

Olga answered all the questions about Ilya with one phrase that was difficult to refute: I don't know, my husband never spoke to me about it. She gave the impression of an obedient, submissive wife.

"Think hard, Olga Afanasievna. It's probably best not to cross us. I'm sure your parents would be disappointed, too. Today we were just having a little talk, getting to know each other. Your books will remain here, of course. There are plenty of them—they'll suffice for five years of prison. Here's the list of the books. Yes, yes, I know you've already signed it. Think about everything we've discussed here. We'll meet again soon, there are still some things we need to talk about. We understand that your husband dragged you into this anti-Soviet activity. Now you must think about it, decide who you ... and sign here, too. A nondisclosure clause, about our little conversation."

Matters seemed to be drawing to a close. The clock on the wall read quarter to eleven.

Alexandrov scribbled something on a piece of paper, and gave it to a woman who had been sitting in the room for a long time. This turned out to be a permit for her to leave. The corridor was a veritable labyrinth, breaking off, turning, then veering off again at strange angles. The length of the journey to the exit didn't correspond to the rather modest dimensions of the building on the outside.

When she emerged onto the street, she wanted to get a taxi. Not a single car stopped, and she dragged herself, exhausted, through the whole expanse of Dzerzhinsky Square to the metro.

Her parents' house had been turned inside out, shaken down, violated. How had they managed in such a short time to destroy the propriety and dignity of their well-maintained household? There were footprints all over the parquet floors, books were strewn about everywhere in heaps, a trail of the general's underwear—piles of long johns and undershirts that had been accumulating on the shelves since the war—fanned out through the spacious hallway. It was a good thing that her mother was already at the dacha for the third night running and didn't have to witness any of this.

Ilya wasn't home. Faina Ivanovna, the housekeeper, had left a note on the table: "Olga! I picked up Kostya from school and took him to my house. He'll spend the night here. I'll take him to school in the morning. Call me when you get in, Faina."

If only she had had a mother like Faina—she always did just the right thing, no questions asked. She had raised Olga without a single extra word, and she was helping out with Kostya like no one else in the world knew how. What luck that her mother had gone straight to the dacha after work without stopping off at home!

She called Faina.

"Faina, you've been saving me my whole life. I can't thank you enough."

Faina grumbled a bit, and cursed under her breath, saying that if Olga kept this up she would leave them.

"If only for the child!" she said, before hanging up the phone. Pure gold. She was pure gold.

After some hesitation, Olga decided to call Maria Fedorovna, Ilya's mother. She dialed the number, but when no one picked up right away, she hung up. Her exhaustion outstripped her anxiety. She collapsed on the divan and fell asleep immediately. Fifteen minutes later she woke up, choking with fear. It was as though she hadn't slept at all.

At half past two in the morning, she began to clean up. By morning she had put the house in order.

What could have happened to Ilya? The question gnawed at her and gave her no rest.

She called Galya at work, saying they had to meet right away. An hour later, Galya was sitting in Olga's kitchen.

"Galya, our house was searched. Do you realize that this all started with the typewriter?" No sooner had Olga begun to talk than Galya broke into tears. "Tell me honestly, did you tell your husband what you were typing? That you had borrowed the typewriter from me?"

Galya swore that her husband knew nothing about the typewriter, nor that she earned extra money as a typist. Moreover, she hadn't told a single person in the world about it. She swore so vehemently that it was impossible not to believe her. It was a mystery how everything had ended up with the KGB. And why had they waited so long, why hadn't they come right away?

"Olga, please understand one thing; now I have to tell Gennady everything. Otherwise, it's as if I set everyone up: you, and Antonina Naumovna, and Gennady, too. He could get into trouble! What else can I do, go out and kill myself? Maybe you think I'm ungrateful—do you think I don't know how much your family has done for me? But Gennady doesn't know about that. It has nothing to do with him. He lives a completely different kind of life, his views on everything are different. He has strong ideological principles! Who was the secretary of the Komsomol organization at school, was it me? No, it was you! You were the most Soviet of all of us! Tamara, though she never said it out loud, was anti-Soviet. And I had nothing at all to do with any of that—after I turned twelve all I ever thought about were the uneven bars and the balance beam!"

At that moment, the lock clicked, and Ilya stumbled in. Ilya and Olga embraced as though after a long separation, then clung to each other in exhaustion.

Galya put on her coat and slipped out shrewdly.

"When did they let you go?" Ilya asked, still holding Olga to him.

"At eleven last night. Did they keep you all this time?"

"At first they drove me to my mother's, and they cleaned everything out. Everything. My darkroom is gone. Then they took me to Malaya Lubyanka. That's where I've been till now."

After Kostya had started school and they moved to Olga's Moscow apartment, Ilya had transferred the darkroom to his mother's, to the broom closet.

"That two-story building? That's where I was, too."

"Yes, it's the Moscow branch. To hell with them. They can all go to hell," Ilya muttered. And nothing mattered to him just then except his clear-eyed Olga, his wife, his beloved, who was worth more than all the world to him . . . he'd tried to keep Olga out of it, and to take all the blame upon himself. After all, he was the one who had brought the books into the apartment! He'd tried to extricate Olga from the mess. He could wriggle out of it somehow; if only Olga didn't have to suffer for it.

Now Olga, with her slightly chapped lips, her pale freckles sprinkled over her white skin, the center of his life, its very heart, stroked his face. He would still have to deal with the branch, but he was determined to keep Olga out of the affair at any cost.

When Antonina Naumovna returned home from work, she received a full account of what had happened from her daughter. Antonina clutched first at her heart, and then at the telephone receiver. She made an appointment the next day with General Ilienko, who was the Writers' Union liaison with the most vitally significant state organs. They had been on amicable terms since the thirties, when she was just starting her career. They survived the purges, then carried out purges themselves, making short shrift of the formalists, and working together on the Ehrenburg case.

It was hard work, and very unrewarding. Though of the utmost importance. Antonina had no doubts about that.

Ilienko always helped his own people, and now he helped Antonina Naumovna in her hour of need.

The general introduced her to another general, who spoke to her in what she could only feel to be a condescending manner; but in the end, her plea met with success. They returned her typewriters, the old Underwood and the new Optima, the address books, and the manuscripts that had been confiscated during the search. Among the things they gave back to her were some books of Ilya's—pre-Revolutionary religious texts that Antonina Naumovna was loath even to touch. Most unexpectedly, they even gave back Ilya's cameras and enlarger. Olga's Erika was the only thing that wasn't returned right away. She managed to get it back three months later, by special request. How it had ended up there, who had informed on them, she wasn't told.

Antonina Naumovna was not given to scandal and emotional upheaval. Moreover, after Olga's expulsion from the university, she had experienced the bitterness of rupture in the spirit of *Fathers and Sons*. For this reason she didn't reproach her daughter. Any hope of a meeting of minds had been uprooted from her heart long before, though she had raised the girl according to her own lights, her own best pedagogical insights. What would Olga say about her grandparents, those misguided religious fanatics?

Antonina's eyes burned with a dry flame; her lips pursed together once and for all—in her veins ran severe and obdurate Greek blood. When she was young, she had often been mistaken for a Jewess, which caused her a great deal of consternation. Now, later in life, she had acquired a likeness to a Byzantine icon: a fiercely spiritual countenance, devoid of pity or compassion. A Paraskevi of Iconium or St. Irene . . . though instead of a halo she wore a coarsely crocheted beret or an Astrakhan hat from the Literary Fund store.

Antonina Naumovna's first thought was to exchange her apartment for two smaller ones. Then she wouldn't have to see either her daughter or her son-in-law. She reconsidered, however: Would the second apartment go to the state after her death? What about her grandson? He was a good boy, and very attached to his grandfather. Why should he be cheated of his inheritance? No, that wouldn't do. Besides, someone had to keep an eye on them, the old writer decided. She had long known that the government was watching her lousy son-in-law and Olga at the same time.

After this, Antonina Naumovna changed her schedule. She went to the dacha on weekends and holidays, but not every weekday. Several times a week she visited the young family—always without warning, so that they knew she might drop in at any moment and wouldn't dare indulge in any anti-Soviet revels and mayhem at home.

Faina continued to work for them. She freed up the careless and irresponsible parents in the evenings, and even allowed them to stay out overnight. Olga and Ilya roamed around from house to house, visiting old friends and meeting interesting new ones.

Life drove a wedge between the old girlfriends. They saw one another now once a year, on Olga's birthday, June 2. They called one another rarely. This estrangement was natural: each of them had her own life, her own secrets to keep. Their school years were the only thing the girlfriends had left in common, and those memories became ever more faded and insignificant.

In addition to her beloved science, Tamara now had her beloved Marlen. And Galya, besides her husband and her job, had a secret pastime: she was getting treated for infertility, making the rounds of all kinds of medical clinics, homeopaths, herbalists, and even charlatans of every stripe and color.

These were the happiest years in Olga's life. It was like skating on thin ice: dangerous and exhilarating. The professor who had brought Olga and Ilya together outside the courthouse had served his seven-year prison term, had been released, and had then emigrated.

Neither Olga nor Ilya had been able to see him in the months before his departure, which they both regretted. But he had been inaccessible. Perhaps he didn't want to see anyone himself; perhaps his wife had erected an iron curtain around him. He left very quietly, almost surreptitiously—the authorities were clearly glad to be rid of him. Moreover, dark rumors about his involvement with the KGB were making the rounds.

During those years, members of the underground, readers and

creators of samizdat alike, had quarreled among themselves and broken up into small groups, into sheep and goats. True, it was impossible to distinguish between them, to decide who was a sheep and who was a goat. Even within the small herds and flocks there was no concord. Parallels with the "men of the sixties" of the nineteenth century— "Westernizers" and "Slavophiles"—were too remote to seek. Now everything was much more complicated and splintered. Some were for justice, but against the Motherland; others were against the authorities, but for communism; others wanted true Christianity; still others were nationalists who dreamed of independence for their Lithuania or their western Ukraine; then there were the Jews, who wanted only one thing—to leave the country . . .

And there was the great truth of literature—Solzhenitsyn wrote book after book. They came out in samizdat, passed from hand to hand in the time-honored pre-Gutenberg manner, on loosely bound, soft, hardly legible pages of onionskin paper. It was impossible to argue with these pages: their truth was so stark and shattering, so naked and terrible—truth about oneself, about one's own country, about its crimes and sins. And over there, already an emigrant, Olga's professor, an underground writer with a soiled reputation, but with Western glory, as shrewd, acerbic, and spiteful as a devil, made his damning, ignominious pronouncements, calling Russia a "bitch" and the great writer an "undereducated patriot."

Tea and vodka poured out in rivers, kitchens basked in the fervent steam of political dispute, so that the dampness crept up the walls to the hidden microphones behind the tiles at the level of the ceiling.

Ilya knew everything and everyone. He was calm and conciliatory in arguments, because he always had his "on the one hand" and "on the other hand" at his disposal . . . And he told Olga:

"You know, Olga, any position you take limits you, makes you dumber. Even this stool has four legs!"

Olga could only guess at what he was trying to tell her, but she agreed with him in her heart of hearts: the idea of stability appealed to her.

Meanwhile, Tamara, under Marlen's influence, had temporarily become a Zionist; but endocrinology prevented her from immersing herself completely in the Jewish movement. Her dissertation was al-most finished, and the results of her laboratory research were astound-ing. The hormones had been synthesized, and were working away like good little things in test tubes; all that remained was to test them on a living organism, if only a rabbit.

Vera Samuilovna was thrilled with her former graduate student, who, after graduating from the institute, took a lowly job as a senior lab assistant, with a likewise paltry income, but had nevertheless blos-somed into a full-fledged scientist.

Tamara stayed until late in the evenings at the laboratory, then met Marlen by the Molodezhnaya metro station. From eleven to twelve at night they walked together, while Marlen walked his beloved set-ter, Robik, whom he loved still more for the opportunity he gave him to go out in the evening.

Marlen and Tamara were in the throes of a great and secret love, with all the signs of its exceptional and divinely ordained nature: an abundance of every kind of intimacy, a burning sensation at the slight-est touch, an understanding beyond words, the bliss of mutual silence and the thrill of even the most ordinary conversation. Marlen was as-tonished by Tamara's magnanimity; she perceived even his failures as merits, never tiring of praising his mind, his erudition, and at the same time his nobility.

She based her judgment about the last quality on his devotion to his children, his family, and the Jewish traditions he had introduced into his home. For some time now his Russian wife had regularly set the table for the Friday night Shabbat ritual and had read the prayer in Hebrew above two candles. Marlen's Communist ancestors would have rolled over in their graves, but prisoners in Kolyma were not committed to graves. Only his mother, who had by some miracle been spared a fate in the camps, and had gone off her rocker from fear in-stead, had managed to lie down in a grave in Vostryakovo Cemetery.

The parents of Lida, Marlen's sweet wife, would have been very surprised about the "kikification" of their daughter. But they knew nothing about her Friday-night family entertainment; and, besides, they loved Marlen for his joviality, his affability, and his eternal read-iness to drink moderately, in a non-Russian way, while offering drinks generously to others. They were simple, unpretentious Soviet folk, an engineer and a teacher, who had not yet been informed that Marlen planned to move the whole family to Israel.

After the Shabbat meal, Marlen took Robik out on his leash and walked him to the nearby five-story building where Tamara lived, so that he could spend the Sabbath as the Talmud decreed. Robik lay on the doormat and also had his share of pleasure—he gnawed on a bone specially prepared for this occasion. Raisa Ilinichna sequestered herself in her hundred-square-foot room and didn't even dare come out to use the bathroom—it was as if she wasn't there at all.

Galya was coming up in the world. Her husband found her a suitable position working in the Army Sports Club. She had a job in her own field, and she received a good salary. As a husband, Gennady didn't disappoint. He was faithful and honest; he always carried out his promises. His own life was not easy. He worked long hours, traveled a great deal, and was enrolled in night courses, which he said were necessary for his professional development. He had been developing for five years already. And this development had already led to an apartment in a brick building in Kuntsevo, and to a good position. The exhortation of the Leader—to learn, learn, and learn—was not lost on him. He attended various courses to expand his qualifications, and he acquired a second higher degree along the way.

The only thing missing was progeny. It was as though fate were mocking them—in a country with the highest number of abortions per capita in the world, Galya happened to be the one whose ovaries backfired and defied the best attempts of all the little seeds, the one who was shunned by this most ordinary of miracles.

During these years of happiness for Olga, Tamara saw very little of her. The silence got in the way. Tamara's secret love was already common knowledge, but she never mentioned Marlen in her conversations with Olga. Olga was hurt; this was not the way a friend should behave, not the way women should behave. Female friendship that was not well oiled with exchanges of intimacies about life soon dried up and lost its charm. Even when Marlen and his family were unexpectedly bundled off to Israel, Tamara didn't say a word to Olga. And there was plenty to say.

After that, hard times began for Olga. Ilya emigrated and everything changed in Olga's life. All that had once held meaning for her was now meaningless, and nothing emerged to take its place. Ilya's absence proved to be even stronger than his presence. He became a fixation, and Olga's thoughts, like the needle on a crazy compass, continually pointed toward him. During these months, before Olga had recovered from the first blow, Tamara came to her side. At first Olga's illness appeared to be the classic symptoms of an ulcer. But Tamara saw all the signs of depression: Olga lay with her face toward the wall, silent, hardly ever getting out of bed, going without food and almost without water. With her medical acumen, Tamara sensed trouble ahead.

"Olga, it's like you've come to a standstill, you have to make an effort to save yourself. You'll lose your mind, you'll get ill! Get rid of it, root it out of your being—you can't live like this!"

Tamara tried to drag Olga out of her depression. First she took her to a psychologist who received patients in a clinic that was underground, in all senses of the word. Then she took her to a psychiatrist. Olga's natural resilience, Tamara's guidance, and antidepressants lifted her out of her doldrums. But soon she started bleeding. Tamara was almost glad, thinking that her bodily ills would save her psyche. But the obsessive thinking and talking about Ilya continued as before. The illness was snuffed out, but the flame of injury, jealousy, and animosity still burned bright. The former Olga, smiling and even-tempered, had nearly disappeared, and had given way to something else—tears, wailing, bouts of hysteria.

The girlfriends absorbed the fallout of these outbursts, taking the burden onto themselves. Galya visited Olga on a regular basis, sympathized with her quietly, and nodded mechanically in agreement. Ilya's cruel act, his abandonment of Olga, was perfectly in keeping with her view of the world, in which men were bastards, beautiful women were whores, bosses were unfair, and girlfriends were envious of each other. Olga, who was a girlfriend and also beautiful, was an exception. Likewise, Galya's own story: her husband was a decent man who didn't run after other women and who turned over his whole salary to his wife. From superstition, she held her tongue about the family happiness she enjoyed—she didn't want her girlfriends to jinx it inadvertently.

Tamara saw everything in a different light. Galya's simplistic notions inspired only contempt in her. Tamara didn't have time for Galya; she was busy rushing around to visit specialists of all kinds with Olga. The doctors had diagnosed cancer, which was progressing rapidly and seemed to be outpacing the medical examinations. The cancer had been caught in its early stages, but it was an aggressive one. It was possible that Olga's bitterness and hurt fed the illness; science was silent on the matter.

At times, Olga refused treatment. Once she even fled the clinic, the best one of its kind, to which Tamara, using all her own and Vera Samuilovna's medical connections, had managed to get her admitted. In the end, Olga gave in to Tamara's importuning and underwent a course of chemotherapy; her health began to improve.

The dynamics of the relationship between the friends changed: Olga lost the upper hand and seemed not to be aware of it. Now Tamara was in charge. Galya ignored this change in relative power and influence. She had perfected the art of keeping silent, observing pauses, not noticing questions, and nodding vaguely. Tamara, who had always considered Galya to be a nonentity, could hardly endure her presence.

Tamara was the only one who still remembered the incident of the typewriter.

The three girlfriends met for the last time on the occasion of Olga's birthday, at the general's dacha, in 1982. They were all thirty-eight. Galya and Tamara arrived at the dacha separately, one by bus, the other by the usual route—the commuter train from Rizhskaya Station. They ran into each other by the gates of the dacha. The gates appeared to be hewn from logs; they were ancient. The grounds were sprawling, and now seemed even more spacious. There was a pond on the property that hadn't been cleaned for ages and was overgrown with duckweed around the edges. The outlines of a half-rotted boat were visible in the middle of the pond. The two-story house was falling into charming decay. The general had died, Antonina Naumovna had been relieved of her high administrative post, and the dacha looked like a nobleman's dilapidated estate. Kostya came out to greet the girlfriends. He was already a tall young man with a shock of light hair like Esenin's, which he kept pushing off his forehead. Physically, he bore a striking resemblance to his father, Vova, but in his mannerisms and his speech he took after Ilya, though without Ilya's wit. They all exchanged kisses in greeting.

"Mama's over there," he said, and led them to the veranda.

Olga was sitting in a wingback chair, her head resting on a tapestry pillow, her little feet in thick knitted slippers, propped up on a low bench. Her hand, which looked more as if it were carved from ivory than like human flesh, lay on a side table that was next to the chair. Everything incidental had drained from Olga's face; all that was left was a sharp, naked beauty and the illness itself. Her small head was wrapped tightly in a silk kerchief. Then she pulled the kerchief off, revealing the sparse, uneven growth, resembling an auburn hedgehog, underneath. After the chemo, her hair was growing back like a child's, new and buoyant.

Half a year had passed since Olga had discharged herself from the clinic and had categorically refused any medical treatment. The letter from Ilya had done its work. Now everything was happening not according to science, but according to magic.

Kostya brought sandwiches with caviar and smoked sausage out to the veranda. Antonina Naumovna's supplies of provisions had not been cut off, Galya observed, accustomed to the government feedbag herself. On this day she had come to say good-bye to Olga, as it had seemed then, forever. But she couldn't find the words to communicate this: as usual, Tamara's presence daunted her.

Right before she left, she said she was saying good-bye for a long time, because she and her husband were going abroad. Olga, with seeming indifference, asked her where.

Galya grinned. "Just imagine, we're going to the Middle East. I can't say where exactly. Tamara would get too jealous."

There was no room for doubt about the precise destination. Tamara turned away her head, with its shapely afro. Tamara's neck was extravagantly long, even disproportionately so; Olga used to joke that she seemed to be able to turn it 360 degrees.

During their school years, Tamara had considered Galya to be a necessary appendage to her beloved Olga, or like a levy placed on her own friendship with her. She merely tolerated her. And she would never have admitted to Olga what she thought of Galya—that she was a lowly plebeian sort, a pest and a nuisance, lacking in wit and talent, and also unkind . . . not to mention a traitor. Tamara had never forgotten about the typewriter.

Tamara looked in the direction of the pond. *So they're over there, too, those KGB thugs. They're everywhere, there's no escaping them . . . not even in Israel! There's nowhere to hide from them.*

"Oh," Olga said. "The Middle East. You should learn French."

"Why French?" Galya said, surprised. "I'm studying English."

"Will you be gone long?"

"Three years, most likely."

Afterward, when she was home on leave, Galya visited Olga—both times during Olga's fantastical four-year remission, which lasted from the moment Olga received Ilya's letter until she received the news of his death.

She brought souvenirs with her: Jerusalem crosses, icons, amulets. Olga wasn't interested in these trinkets for the pious, and all of them migrated gradually into Tamara's possession. She was thrilled to have them. Olga had become her old self, cheerful and energetic.

The third time Galya came to Moscow, Olga was no longer among the living. Galya already knew about her death. She called Kostya and went to visit their home, which they hadn't changed or rearranged at all after Olga had died. The only difference was that now it was in complete disarray. Galya brought expensive gifts for Kostya's children: plastic soldiers with mechanical innards, battery-powered toy cars, and a long-legged doll with clothes that fit her.

When she got home, she cried long and hard over Olga, then called Tamara. It was early evening and they both wept into the telephone. Then Galya asked whether she could come to see her.

"When? Could you come over right now?"

Galya caught a cab and fifteen minutes later she was with Tamara. You couldn't say they talked—rather, they cried in each other's arms all evening, their tea growing cold on the table in front of them. They didn't even bother to turn on the lights. First they cried about Olga, whom they had both loved deeply, then about themselves, and about everything that life had promised and not given, interrupting their tears with silence, and their silence with tears. Then they cried about each other, sympathizing with each other about the things they could never say, and again about Olga. Then Tamara found half a bottle of cognac, and they each drank a glass, and Tamara finally asked the most important question—about the typewriter—for all the betrayal had begun with this machine.

"Didn't Olga tell you? I told her about it as soon as I found out. My brother, Nikolay, God be with him"—here Galya crossed herself with a sweeping gesture—"took the typewriter and *The Gulag Archipelago* to the district branch of the KGB. He would never have done anything like that himself. Raika, his wife, God be with her, too"—again she crossed herself, but with less vigor—"she had always hated me, and she talked him into it. They showed Gennady the text of his letter. 'To intercept an anti-Soviet conspiracy by enemies of the people and to evict my sister Galina Yurievna Polukhina from the apartment,' Nikolay wrote. The housing authorities were kicking them out of the basement and resettling them in a new apartment, and Raika thought they might end up with a bigger space if I was out of the picture. In the new apartment, they died in a fire that started when they were both drunk." Again she crossed herself ceremoniously.

Apparently, the mutual shedding of tears softened the invisible crust around Tamara's heart. She, too, told Galya about what she had kept to herself for so long. After telling her these things, she beseeched, under her breath: "Lord, Lord, forgive me!"

After Marlen's departure for Israel, and perhaps even before, Tamara had come to love Jesus Christ deeply. This had changed her in many ways.

Why have I hated this unfortunate little fool for so long?

Galya would have liked another drink, but she was too shy to ask.

For the first time, Olga's girlfriend, the clever Tamara, who had hardly paid the slightest bit of attention to her, was opening up to her.

It seems that Olga has brought us together, Galya thought tenderly.

Then Tamara showed her their new, but already aging, apartment. Galya had been to their old room in the communal flat on Sobachaya Square several times, but she had never been invited here. All the furnishings were from their previous life: the piano, an armchair, book-shelves, and photographs. Only the pictures were missing. Galya asked about them, and Tamara laughed.

"You noticed? The paintings are gone."

"I remember them. There was an angel with an enormous head, blue. Yes, Tamara, I was at your old house a few times. Olga took me with her. I remember the pictures, and I remember your grandmother."

When it was already after one in the morning Tamara walked Galya out to the taxi. Both of them felt like milk bottles in the hands of a good housewife, ringing with cleanliness after a thorough wash. They didn't yet know—they still had a great deal to share with each other—what kinds of strange paths had led them to this evening: Tamara, a Jew and former Zionist, who never did leave for Israel, was now a Russian Orthodox Christian; and Galya, the wife of an official at the Russian compound in Jerusalem, occupying what appeared to be a minor post, but which was, in fact, very significant. Over the past few years she had grown to despise everything that had to do with "religious leaders," priests, rabbis, and all other mullahs, and at the same time, the entire East, with all its stratagems, secrecy, and base insincerity. Still, she was steeped in a warm feeling for the person of Jesus Christ . . .

"Israel itself is a wonderful country. Too bad you never went there. If only it didn't have all those religions," Galya concluded.

Tamara laughed.

"Why do you make the sign of the cross on your forehead, then? You've always been a silly girl, Galya, and you still are! How can you acknowledge Christ, but not Christianity?"

Galya composed her poor face into a stern expression, then answered back for the first time in her life:

"You just can, that's all!"

After so many years of animosity, their relations had become easy and familial.

Galya, in no way offended, said defiantly:

"You're the silly one, even if you do have a Ph.D. You've got your head on backwards!"

Galya and her husband were supposed to be posted to Israel for three more years, but misfortune struck; her husband became very ill, and she returned home for good—wilted, washed out, and covered with tiny wrinkles from the dry sunny heat. Now there were no closer friends in the world than Polushka and Brinchik.

Their story must be told to the end, however. Tamara Grigorievna Brin, a doctor and an esteemed member of the scientific community, managed to talk Galya into getting an endocrinological examination, not in a polyclinic but in a scientific research institute, where they had discovered a substance—a hormone or something of that ilk—that they injected directly into a vein. They did it one more time, and Galya got pregnant. At the age of forty-six, for the first time. If the baby had been a girl, they would have named her Olga. But it was a boy, and they called him Yury.

Tamara had him baptized with the silent consent of the KGB-agent family. Every Sunday Tamara visited Galya to take her godson on an outing. He was a sweet boy, the offspring of two plumbers—fair of hair and blue-eyed. Tamara took him to church and to museums. He called her Godmama.

When they returned from their outings, Tamara would drink tea with Gennady. Just as Ilya had predicted. He had been, of course, the Rodent, and so he would remain. Never mind. God bless him. After his heart attack, he suffered a stroke and emerged from it only half-alive. His healthy side continued to drag his paralyzed side along. Poor Galya. But now Tamara would just murmur: *Lord, grant me the ability to see my own errors and not to judge my brother . . .*

And Tamara felt relieved.

THE DRAGNET

etting out of the taxi, Ilya glanced at his watch—three minutes past five.

Being late by three minutes is not being late, he said to himself.

By the hotel entrance he slowed down his pace. It was drizzling rain, and the air felt stuffy.

I've gone nuts! Since when did I ever worry about being late? He stopped directly in front of the doorman, who looked like an opera singer, with his double-barreled chest and muscular neck. The doorman eyed him suspiciously.

After the search, Ilya had been detained at Malaya Lubyanka for eighteen hours. The three interrogators took turns. First, two of them tried to confuse him, then the third crudely but convincingly tried to win him over to their side, to persuade him to become an informer. They parted with the understanding that they would meet again. Now, a week later, they called him on the phone and set a time to meet in a public building: Hotel Moscow, seventh floor, room 724.

Now Ilya bemoaned his own stupidity. He didn't have to answer the phone, he didn't have to show up for the appointment, he could have insisted they send a summons. And he definitely didn't have to show up right on time.

I don't owe them anything, Ilya thought, reasoning with himself. *They'll throw me in prison anyway, if they want to. I have to stop being afraid. It's essential. I'm carefree and unconcerned, I'm flighty, I'm lighter than air . . . and a bit thick in the head. Pardon me? What was that you said? No! It can't be! Really? I never would have guessed!* Ilya prepped himself for the meeting.

The doorman admitted him, but another person, a beanpole in a gray suit, bounded up to him.

"Excuse me, whom are you here to see?"

"Room 724."

"This way, please," he said too quickly, then grinned, baring his teeth.

Ilya, practicing being an idiot, replied jovially:

"Good day to you!"

There were two Frenchwomen in the elevator with him. One, a real *grande dame*, was wearing a luxuriant fur of some unknown kind that was inappropriate for the season. The other was younger, with a pale, narrow little face, also inappropriately dressed in some sort of white muslin raincoat. They chattered animatedly with each other, and every other word was *très bien, très bien.* Meanwhile, the younger one kept looking at Ilya with mild feminine interest. And he got so carried away by these glances that he forgot why he was going up to the seventh floor.

When he got to the door, he looked at his watch. He was ten minutes late, and now this fact buoyed him up: *Yes, what of it? I'm always late, and this is no exception. Or do you consider yourself to be more deserving than others?*

He knocked and opened the door to enter.

"Come in, come in. Good afternoon . . . or evening."

The man was sitting at a desk with his back to the light, his face a shadow.

"You're late, Ilya Isayevich, you're late. Like a debutante for a rendezvous," the man said patronizingly.

"I know, I know," Ilya said, smiling. "It's a bad habit of mine; I'm always late." He sensed that he had struck the right tone, one that betrayed no fear or servility.

"Well, a free spirit and artist can allow himself that luxury. I have

an official position. I'm beholden to both time and circumstance."
He spoke with irony and decorum, in an old Moscow manner rare
in a KGB agent. "Please, take a seat. Let's sit here, otherwise it's
all too formal." And he came out from behind his desk and pulled up
an armchair.

The room was known as a "semideluxe" variety; a Soviet invention, which featured two connecting rooms. The door to the bedroom
was slightly ajar. A stiff tapestry curtain hung in the doorway.

In the living room, besides the desk, there was a round table, two
chairs, and a painting. Ilya glanced at the painting. It was crude Soviet
art, with thick swathes of oil paint and a gilded frame, depicting two
boys up to their knees in water pulling a dragnet.

"Let's get to know each other," the KGB agent said, extending his
hand. "Anatoly Alexandrovich Chibikov."

Ilya shook the hand offered to him, sensing that he was beginning
to lose this game. He had not intended to shake anyone's hand.

Chibikov was thin, but his face was bloated, and he had bags under
his eyes. He grabbed an already opened pack of Bulgarian Suns. His
forefinger and middle finger were stained yellow with nicotine.

He's a smoker, and he smokes my brand, Ilya thought. *He doesn't look
Russian—black hair, shiny, falling onto his forehead; a cowlick on his crown.
His eyes look a bit Asian. It's an interesting face, as though it's been washed and
shrunk like a wool sweater. And he has some sort of pouch, maybe a goiter, under
his chin.*

"You and I share a common interest, Ilya Isayevich." Anatoly Alexandrovich said this perfunctorily, without any preamble. He paused,
assuming, apparently, that Ilya would be intrigued by this.

Ilya took the bait, but was quick to spit it out.

"I don't think so."

"Oh, but we do. Collecting. I'm not referring to your collection of
Futurism, a valuable collection, indeed. I'm talking about the field of
history. Yes, yes, modern history. I'm a historian by training, and I
have my favorite subjects, including those which exceed the bounds of
modern history. In the field of current trends, if you will!"

Ilya felt his head growing heavy. Something pulsed at the back of
his head, and his eyes seemed to tense up in their sockets. This had to

be about Mikha, or about the magazine they published with Edik. Or maybe it was about the *Chronicle*?

He forgot instantly about his intention to play the fool. They both lit up their unfiltered Suns simultaneously.

"Common interests, common tastes." Chibikov grinned, placing his pack of cigarettes next to Ilya's.

"As for tastes, that's open to debate," Ilya parried, and felt himself relax a bit. He felt satisfied with himself: it was a noncommittal, even bold reply.

"Have it your way," the KGB man said with a sigh. "You see, I occupy a position in my profession in which routine operations fall outside the purview of my interests. Nevertheless, the materials confiscated from you ended up on my desk."

He's a colonel, at least, Ilya decided.

"I read your juvenilia with great interest. I must admit, the history of the LORLs touched me. In a way, you're fortunate that times have changed, and that your preoccupation with literature didn't lead you to a deep place where one works with pickaxe and shovel instead of a fountain pen or quill.

"But these minutes of the LORLs' meetings from 1955 to 1957, the photographs, the reports, the essays—this is the work of a professional historian and archivist, and I can't help but admire the fact that it was all done by a child, a schoolboy. Remarkable! And your teacher— what a striking figure! I knew him slightly in my own youth. Do you continue to see him, to see your former classmates?"

"Almost never," he said, not so much warding off a blow as returning a ball. *Now he'll start in on Mikha.*

"It's actually very interesting to observe how the fates of people unfold. Even those who were in the same class at school, or lived in the same courtyard . . ."

He's definitely working his way around to Mikha. Or to Victor Yulievich, Ilya surmised. *Naturally, correspondence with a prisoner and packages sent in a prisoner's name . . .* but the agent continued to hold forth, never coming around to the subject of Mikha.

"All through 1956, your club studied the Decembrists. You boys wrote brilliant essays. Everything depends on the teacher, of course.

My daughter is now in her junior year of high school. Their teacher is an old woman who doesn't really have a grasp of these things. As a result, the kids don't have the slightest interest in the subject."

"Yes, a great deal depends on the teacher," Ilya agreed.

"But you were lucky with your teacher!"

Pause. Take a deep breath. Maybe I should ask about the typewriter? All the same, they'll never give it back.

The "colonel" looked pensive.

"In my time I also had a keen interest in the Decembrists. I was primarily interested in the investigation. The notes of the investigative committee are fascinating.

"In the Decembrists' own memoirs there's a great deal about their incarceration in Peter and Paul Fortress, about their transport to Siberia, about hard labor and banishment. But there's almost nothing about the interrogations. All the Decembrists, except perhaps for Trubetskoy and Basargin, are silent on the subject. Why do you think that is, Ilya Isayevich?"

Ilya wasn't in the least concerned about the Decembrists; his concerns lay elsewhere. He was wondering where all this talk about hard labor and banishment might be leading.

"And were many accounts left behind by those who were interrogated in the thirties?" Ilya said, trying to wriggle out of the first question.

"There is an enormous amount of material on the Stalin-era trials. And, by the way, the Decembrists were not required to sign nondisclosure agreements, a practice that became nearly universal a century later. I've read everything that is available in the investigative committee archives, and I can tell you why the Decembrists avoided mentioning the interrogations."

The bags under his eyes trembled, and he broke into a sad smile.

"They all testified against one another. Yes, it's true. And not out of fear, but out of a sense of honor. However strange it may sound in our day, they were governed by the belief that lying is dishonorable and wrong."

Son of a bitch, now he's telling me that lying is wrong! He's spinning these intricate tales and arguments just to throw me off.

But Ilya maintained his composure.

"In school we were taught that the Decembrists behaved hero-ically, that their conspiracy was doomed to failure because it was a palace coup, and none of the conspirators had any connection with the people, with the peasants . . ." Ilya said feebly.

Chibikov frowned.

"Yes, that's what the textbooks tell us. But that's not the point. Unfortunately, the results of all that heroism completely contradicted its intentions. The actions of the Decembrists delayed the very re-forms that the Tsar was already about to implement. Those who tried the Decembrists—and they were their own relatives, their fellow sol-diers, their friends—were trying to fortify the government, while the Decembrists tried to undermine it. Everyone knew that reforms were necessary. However, the ones who put them into practice were not the Decembrists, but their opponents. History is dialectical, like life itself, and at times even paradoxical. It was the conservatives who made government policy, not the radicals!"

Again. What is he driving at? Did he call me here to theorize about all of this? Be careful, be careful. Pay attention. Ilya's presence of mind didn't desert him.

"Russia has never been as strong as it is now, in our day. There is only one period of Russian history that stands up to comparison with our own: the Russia of Alexander the Second, the Liberator. At the be-ginning of the nineteenth century, Russia liberated Europe, as it did in the middle of the twentieth century. The uprising of the Decem-brists set Russia back decades. But history bestows glory on Muravyov-Apostol, while it reviles Muravyov the Hangman. Yet they were from one family, one social circle! Are you aware that Prince Sergei Bolkon-sky, the Decembrist, when he was an old man, after returning from exile and before he went abroad, went to say farewell at the grave of Benckendorff, his friend and comrade-in-arms, moreover the head of the Third Division, the Tsar's secret police?"

Chibikov's speech was refined and intelligent, his diction as well as his intonation. Could he really be a colonel? This was getting serious.

"You and your friends have misunderstood Russian history and the Russian state."

The history of the Russian state was the last thing that interested Ilya at the moment. He was thinking about the collection of portraits that had been confiscated. Some of these photographs had been sent to the West and published there in newspapers and magazines. If the KGB got their hands on these publications, his authorship would be revealed. Of the many photographs that had sailed or flown their way over, at least eleven had been published. Maybe twelve. There was no way he could deny it.

Ilya sighed.

The "colonel" seemed to read his mind.

"It's possible that the portrait gallery that was taken from you will be published in history textbooks a hundred years from now. Like the portraits of Karakozov and Kalyaev. Or maybe it won't. In any case, it all belongs to history."

It was still unclear whether they had traced the origin of the photographs in the Western publications back to his archive. *Fine, if you're so smart, see what you make of this . . .*

(Alas, Ilya had long forgotten his intention to play the fool.)

"History is one thing, and the KGB another. You can't just lump them together. It's my personal collection; and the portraits were not meant for the secret police, by the way," Ilya said.

"I'm afraid, Ilya Isayevich, that you don't have the slightest idea what the function of the secret police is. Exhibits disappear from libraries, personal archives, from museums. They are stolen, sold, exchanged, sometimes consciously destroyed. But I can assure you, in the archives of the secret police nothing is ever lost. True, the number of people granted access to them is extremely limited. But, believe me, there is no place more reliable for safekeeping. Nothing ever goes missing there! Moreover, it is the very place where historical truth is preserved."

"I'm sorry, but I would prefer to safeguard my collection in my own home."

"You should have thought of that before. Now it's no longer yours to safeguard." The "colonel" rose from the deep armchair with a painful grimace—radiculitis or hemorrhoids—and, flinging back the theater curtain, went into the next room.

Ilya looked at the clock. Almost two hours had passed without his noticing it. Between them they had smoked half a pack of cigarettes, and a cloud of smoke hung just below the ceiling. Poor ventilation. The boys in the painting, withdrawing further and further into shadow, were still pulling their net out of the water.

From the next room came papery sounds that were still not quite paper—and Ilya realized, somewhat belatedly, that someone else had been sitting in the other room from the very start. Lying in wait. After a minute Chibikov returned, carrying a file in his hands.

"Is this an ambush?" Ilya asked, suppressing nervous laughter.

Anatoly Alexandrovich smiled and shook his head.

"The police, Ilya Isayevich, are a vine with tendrils and runners reaching into every part of the government. A certain clever person decreed that the secret police would operate thus. And that, in there, is a little tiny shoot, one might say." He nodded in the direction of the bedroom.

Out of the file he pulled a copy of an émigré publication in Russian. On the first page was a portrait of Anatoly Marchenko.

"How interesting it all is! A photograph from your archive. One must admit, history is quite idiosyncratic. A very active girl managed to reproduce flyers in defense of this very Marchenko whom you photographed. She started a whole campaign to obtain the release of an ordinary criminal. But, just imagine, this nice young girl left her bag containing the packet of flyers and all her documents, behind in a taxi. She's the one you should have photographed. She was a formidable conspirator! But the picture of Marchenko is a good one. Have you known him for long? This photograph is quite an early one, isn't it? Between 1966 and 1968? He went into hiding after his first term in prison. A fine photograph! Of course, the quality of a newspaper reproduction leaves something to be desired. Here are a few other examples of your work, of varying quality. But there are no grounds for complaint, are there? In *Stern* magazine the quality is better."

This has nothing to do with Mikha. It's far worse. Novoye Russkoye Slovo *and* Stern. *What else does he have on me?*

The cover of the file was fairly stiff and thick, and it was impossible to see whether it was full, or whether it had contained only these two pages.

"In some strange way your photographs have ended up in Western publications. Perhaps your Belgian friend Pierre Zand was responsible for it? He's a very slippery character, by the way; he works for Western intelligence. And sometimes he lends us a hand, too."

I'm sunk! As for Pierre—he's lying, of course. But they've managed to connect all the dots, the bastards. Like an idiot, I thought they'd overlook things. Those guys in the Lubyanka were rank amateurs compared with this fellow. He's the cream of the crop.

"But no, that's not what really interests me. What concerns me is something else. These materials must be preserved at all cost. What has already been taken from you will remain safe. It will be preserved for all eternity. Or most of eternity, at any rate. But what will become of the work you do tomorrow, or the day after, or a year from now? Of course, if they don't throw you in prison tomorrow. I must admit that I like you, Ilya Isayevich. I wouldn't want you to have to experience prison, or the camps. But this is your own choice. In the space of a very short time it will be decided. It is, strictly speaking, already decided."

Ilya sat motionless. He didn't frown, but the back of his head was pounding again. He felt his heart stop beating, then scramble into motion with renewed force. *I must have a heart defect.* The thought flashed through his head. *They can pin anything on me, even espionage. And that gets you more than three years. What's the most incriminating thing there? Perhaps the portrait of Sakharov? I didn't keep it at home. When he sent out his* Memorandum *to the Soviet Leadership I gave the photograph to Klaus. It never made it into the German newspapers. But maybe it was printed somewhere after all?*

"But, I'll be honest with you, I have a few special means at my disposal. I'm going to make you a proposition that I want you to think about. It's possible that it will take you by surprise. I don't rule out that you may be offended by it at first. But think about it before you give me your answer."

Pause. For thinking?

"You have a wrongheaded view of our organization. It's no longer what it was during the thirties and forties. There are new ideas, new forces, new people. Profound changes are taking place in the country, which not everyone can sense yet. And the changes might be much more profound and radical than you imagine. Things aren't as simple as you imagine them to be. I don't want this portrait to be the last one you do. I'm talking about the portrait of Sakharov. I want you to continue your work. I'm prepared to back you up, to vouch for you. My conditions are that everything you do, you should do in two copies. One for yourself, and another for me. And, I stress, for *me*. Consider this to be my personal archive of your work. This is in the interests of history, if you will. Not to mention your own interests."

I'm caught. It's not about the typewriter anymore. It looks like they're not even interested in the manuscript of the Gulag. *It's me they're after, lock, stock, and barrel.*

His head was no longer pounding. He needed to have a clear head to find some way out of this. Ilya's face remained calm while he pondered these matters; but his palms were sweating.

"You are playing a dangerous game, and I respect you for it, though I've told you my views on the radical movements of our society. After the 1917 Revolution, all of them are doomed to fail, and, what's more, are devoid of meaning. This is simple dialectics. You'll understand it in time, I hope not too late. Frankly speaking, I'm not terribly worried about how you will go about your work in the future. As I explained, routine operations are not my domain. If you accept my proposal, you can do a great deal of interesting work. Moreover, I understand that a person who is able to create such a magnificent archive at the age of fifteen—I'm talking about the LORLs—is capable of working on a much more serious level."

He looked at the clock.

"I hope you understand that our conversation must remain strictly confidential. This is in your interests, as well as mine."

"It's hard to consider our conversation to be confidential, Anatoly Alexandrovich." Ilya swallowed, and gestured toward the slightly open door.

"Don't let that worry you. No one has seen you. And no one will see you. Stand up, please, and turn toward the window. Yes, that's right." Anatoly Alexandrovich, in a loud, commanding tone, said: "Vera Alekseevna, you may leave."

He heard the click-click of high heels, then the door to the corridor opened with a creak, and the lock snapped shut.

"It's not all as simple as it appears to you, Ilya Isayevich," Chibikov said sadly.

Ilya said nothing.

"You must decide today. Today I can still do something for you," the "colonel" said in a dark, velvety voice. "Tomorrow it will be too late."

So if I say no right now, they won't let me out of here. And they have all my things, anyway. If I agree, I can continue to live as before—but I will be working not for myself, but for them. No, I can't imagine this kind of life . . .

"Moreover—and here I just want to convey the full picture—if I don't intervene right now and the matter resumes its . . ."

Pause.

". . . former course, you and your wife will be held liable. We can say that you brought the books into the house single-handedly; but the typewriter is hers. And Solzhenitsyn's manuscript was in her possession. You're putting not just yourself in jeopardy, but her, too. Just between ourselves, you were the one who dragged her into this risky business. And that's a serious argument. While I still have the wherewithal to intervene in the matter."

They've got me. There's no way out. It's a Fool's Mate. My dear girl, I will never betray you.

"This is a gentlemen's agreement. I'll give you my phone number. At home. We won't keep up regular contact. You will call me when something interesting arises. You will print as many copies as you consider necessary for your work, and you will hand over the negatives to me."

"The negatives! That's asking too much," Ilya said sharply.

But the "colonel" already knew he had won. He laughed.

"You're twisting my arm!" he said.

"No, if we're talking about a gentlemen's agreement, I have to defend my interests," Ilya insisted.

Chibikov looked at him with new respect.

"All right. You keep the negatives. The last thing I need is your signature."

"But it's a gentlemen's agreement!" Ilya protested.

"I have to defend my interests, too," Anatoly Alexandrovich said, smiling.

Between them they had smoked both packs of cigarettes. The boys were still pulling on their nets behind the shimmering pall of smoke.

When Ilya left, it was already dark. And the autumn rain, an insistent drizzle, was still falling.

THE ANGEL WITH THE OUTSIZE HEAD

It's improbable, completely unlikely," thought Tamara early the next morning, before she had even opened her eyes, reflecting on the evening before. For so many years she had kept her rotten secret about her great and forbidden love to herself, like a jar of preserves, and now it had burst open. She had told all to the person whom she had her whole life considered superfluous, alien, a chance appendage to her existence. For so many years she hadn't breathed a word about it: not to her mother, so as not to disappoint her; not to Olga, so as not to break the ban; not to Vera Samuilovna Vinberg, her best friend and teacher, so that the secret wouldn't erupt into someone else's life and shake the happy equilibrium of another family . . . And suddenly, out of nowhere, she had gone and told everything to Galya, the wife of a KGB agent. Now it seemed that everything that had come before was no longer relevant.

No, that wasn't quite true—she had confessed the whole story once before, before she was baptized, to her priest. He had listened patiently, without betraying any emotion, and had then said, smiling:

"That's all in the past now. A new life begins with baptism; you will become an innocent babe again. This is one of the advantages of being baptized when you are older. It is a conscious choice. You are being offered a new purity, and you must look after it."

Her new purity faded rather quickly. Her former life didn't just disappear, and it cast a long shadow over the future. Until he died two years later, even the old Robik, whom Marlen had left behind, continued to sleep on the rug he had occupied every Shabbat eve for many years waiting for his master. The dog kept silent, and Tamara did, too.

But the evening before, the dam had broken and she had told Galya everything. Why? No, no—it was what it was. It had to happen the way it did, and she would have lived her life the same way again. She was sorry for her mother. Raisa Ilinichna had cried. No, not about the Korovin, nor about the Borisov-Musatov—but about the small, almost perfunctory study by Vrubel. It was a large head and a wing, contradicting all known laws of anatomy. Though who had ever been able to observe the anatomy of angels? All the paintings had belonged to her grandmother. They were originally from the Gnesins, and had been given to her over the years. Elena Fabianovna had been her best friend since childhood. Grandmother had devoted her life to this family, and there were still many traces and tokens of the girls' friendship in the house: teacups, postcards, feathers, books inscribed with loving sentiments in neat, small letters, with flourishes of signatures. But those three paintings were gone. Without a trace. No, no, she had no regrets about them. Far worse were the fevered years of eclipse, the burning passions, of which nothing remained but a feeling of bereavement. No, no, no—she wasn't talking about that.

Everything had already been terrible. Marlen was fired from his job. He had been denied a visa to leave the country over and over again. They had dragged him to the Lubyanka, threatened to imprison him. And at the very end, he confessed that his wife was pregnant and was just about to give birth. He always spoke so disdainfully about his wife and so warmly about his daughters that Tamara had formed a picture in her mind of a family life in which a new baby was somehow conceived out of thin air. He was so much her husband and hers alone. And, suddenly, here was another wife, a pregnant one . . .

He lost weight, and his skin took on a yellowish cast. Tamara even took him to the lab for tests. But his blood was in order, his liver just where it should be. And still they denied him the exit visas. The former obstacles had resolved themselves and vanished. His poor handicapped sister died, followed by his mother, who didn't want to hear a word about Israel. She hated that enemy country that caused so many so much grief. It was impossible to budge her from her position on the matter. And she would never have given her permission for her son to emigrate.

On the penultimate Shabbat of December, Marlen visited Tamara. His dog could hardly drag himself along for the visit. Robik, the only witness of their love, had grown old and decrepit. They were not embarrassed in front of him.

They had no reason to feel embarrassed in front of Raisa Ilinichna, either—in all these years she had never once laid eyes on Marlen. Before he arrived, she would sequester herself in her tiny room. They even resurrected her grandmother's chamber pot and put it under her bed.

The worse the circumstances, the hotter their embraces. Now, years later, Tamara began to feel a belated perplexity: Why had she been so completely taken over, to the exclusion of everything else, by this simple, mechanistic ritual, this here, there, and back again? How was it she had soared to such ineffable heights, when it was all just a matter of two steroid rings, one attached to the other, and one more on the upper right side, with a half-ring to the side, and a commotion of radicals forming around them? Who understood better than she the biological formula that dominates our bodies and souls so absolutely . . .

But now she felt awkward and even ashamed. And she was ashamed for him, too: Poor Marlen, why had he behaved so badly? He, too, had been ruled by hormones.

On that penultimate Shabbat in December, when their hearts were still pounding and his moist, hairy chest was still pressed tightly to hers, he had said matter-of-factly:

"On Wednesday they called me in for questioning again. They've thought up a new approach for nailing me: now I'm not just a Zionist, but a human rights activist. Their evidence is that I signed a petition on the right to emigrate. They went nuts after the demonstration, of course. The bald one who's always there says: You won't get off with just fifteen days administrative detention this time. Take a piece of paper and explain in writing how you ended up with the petition. Who brought it to you? Maybe it was Academic Sakharov? And there were about fifty names on it. I said I didn't intend to incriminate myself. Well, in short, they said they would give me three days to tell them who gave me the petition. If I don't tell them, they'll arrest me. So it might be a long time before we see each other again, Tam."

The weight of the broad-boned male body, being filled by it, becoming one with it... *Today I will get pregnant and then give birth... come what may... no more abortions... today... and if they throw him in prison, I'll do it myself... I'll raise the boy alone...*

"Then, you know, I learned of a new circumstance."

Propping himself up on his elbow, he wiped himself off with the edge of the sheet, then sat up, swinging his woolly legs down to the floor.

Tamara hardly heard him. She was listening hard to something else at that moment: how two microscopic but living entities, hers and his, were drifting toward each other slowly, but surely; it just had to be. Let that plump Lida of his bear him another girl, but she would give birth to a boy, and, all by herself, raise him . . . it was now or never. And she wasn't going to ask.

She lay on her back and stroked her belly. *What an idiot I was. What an idiot. I wasted so much time. He would already be starting school by now if I had made up my mind right off,* Tamara thought, imagining the life she wasn't destined to live.

"It's a very interesting circumstance. Long ago I had heard that these bastards let Jews out for a price. I found it hard to believe. It's just like it was in Germany in 1939: they used to let rich Jews buy their way out of the concentration camps. Later, even that became impossible. That's the way it works here now. Can you believe it?"

"What are you saying? Here?" Tamara said, astonished, forgetting momentarily about her imaginary embryo.

"Of course, here! Where else?" Marlen said, frowning. "Believe it or not, someone from my aunt's village told her. A tailor, you know, just as you'd expect. An excellent one, as a matter of fact. He outfits a very high-ranking official—I can't tell you his name." He knocked softly on the wall, then bent over to whisper in Tamara's ear.

"You're crazy! I don't believe it."

"Believe it! I'm not making it up. This tailor has been sewing for him since before the war. He sews for his whole family. The official even moved him to Moscow, and set him up in his own apartment. Well, not his very own—he has several apartments at his disposal, for people he needs around him. And he's a decent fellow, in his own way."

"The tailor?" Tamara said.

"Who cares about the tailor? No, the official! This man, Mister X, isn't a bad sort. He's not bloodthirsty; he just likes money. Well, actually, not money for its own sake, either. He collects art. Serious paintings, by famous artists. Serov, Perov, you know, those Wanderers, or whatever you call them. He had a whole trainload of them brought here after the war—German paintings. Now he's collecting Russian painters."

"An art collector?" Tamara couldn't quite grasp the notion of a bigwig official who was so devoted to art.

"Well, yes, a collector, if you like." Marlen grimaced slightly. "This tailor is a distant relative of ours. He says he has access to his boss. His boss doesn't want to get mixed up with just anyone, as you might imagine. So this relative of ours knows how to go about it. He's pulled it off before. They let out a family of four for a Savrasov. A rather small picture it was, too." Here Marlen demonstrated with his hands, just as the tailor had done.

Tamara understood instantly what he was asking her.

"Marlen, we don't have any Wanderers. The most valuable thing we have is a Korovin, and another by Borisov-Musatov."

"He didn't say anything about those. He said that the guy had his heart set on a Vrubel."

"Vrubel wasn't a Wanderer," Tamara said. "We do have a Vrubel, but it's not a painting; it's just a study."

"What difference does it make? The main thing is to act quickly. If they throw me in prison, no painting is going to help. That falls under another department."

Tamara turned on the light. The angel with the broken wing hung above the headboard of her bed. The head was outsize, the forehead too convex. The face was lacking in detail, all smears of paint, the strokes hurried and nervous. The wing, though, was bluish and softly feathered, shimmering and iridescent. It was a fine wing.

"Take it," Tamara said breezily. "Take all of them."

"But, you do understand—it might not work." He seemed to doubt himself whether it was worth the risk, but Tamara sensed that his eyes had grown brighter, and he was already thinking ahead—where to take the paintings, how to hand them over, and so on.

"Perhaps. But they may throw you in prison."

Without covering their nakedness—it no longer existed—they grabbed the pictures off the walls. They wrapped all three of them up in sheets, then got dressed.

"Please excuse me, Tam, but I've got to run. I'll catch a cab and take the pictures to my aunt. The tailor promised to come tomorrow at ten in the morning. He said we should have everything ready for him by then. I'll leave Robik with you till tomorrow."

After that, events unfolded at lightning speed.

Three days later, instead of being arrested, Marlen was called to the district office of the KGB, where he was given a document revoking his citizenship and permitting him to leave the country, accompanied by his entire family, within three days. The next Shabbat he didn't come to see Tamara; he dropped in on Friday morning. He brought Robik with him on his leash. He told her they were flying to Vienna the next day.

"I'm in your debt till the end of my life," Marlen said. "You're the best thing I've ever had. If you ever think about returning"—he always said "returning," rather than "emigrating"—"get in touch through Ilya. I'll send an invitation for you right away. I'm leaving Robik with you to remember me by."

Tamara didn't attend their send-off. Olga later told her about how many people showed up to see Marlen off, about how disoriented Lida's parents were about everything, about how unexpected it all was: emigration instead of the promised arrest. It was a celebration instead of a funeral. Still, there was something funereal about it.

"But you're not leaving, are you? Or do you think that all the Jews are going to leave Russia in the end?" Olga looked searchingly at Tamara's stony expression.

"No. As for me—no. Even if everyone else leaves. You can be certain of that."

So, at the very end of 1981, Marlen left. In November 1982, Brezhnev died. The bigwig official, art lover and friend of the much-decorated leader with the bushy eyebrows, was dismissed from his ministerial post. A case was opened charging him with brazen embezzlement and the abuse of power for personal gain. The tailor quickly moved out of the apartment that had been provided for him and disappeared. In bad novels, minor characters sometimes disappear in this way, a clumsy way of advancing the plot. The property of the former boss was confiscated, and he shot himself with a double-barreled Gastinne Renette hunting rifle. Or maybe his own people shot him, to close a case that could have resulted in a great deal of unpleasantness for all concerned

Tamara buried herself in her science and wrote her doctoral dissertation.

Marlen and his family now live in Rehovot, a research town outside of Jerusalem. Everything worked out well for him.

No one knows, though, who finally ended up with the blue-winged angel with the outsize head. Likewise the little Korovin and the Borisov-Musatov.

THE HOUSE WITH THE KNIGHT

By the time Ilya left, it was already dark. The rain was still falling. He felt strange. He had lost—dismally, irrecoverably. But he had also, inexplicably, won. Is it possible to win and lose at the same time? He walked slowly up Gorky Street. There really was no way out. Well, perhaps one: the record of his father's nationality on his birth certificate. His father had been half-Jewish. Ilya could recover the documents, haul out his one-fourth Jewish credentials, and try to apply for an exit visa on those grounds. But that was the very moment they'd try to arrest him.

He turned toward the Aragva restaurant; there was a pay phone there. He deposited a two-kopeck coin, and dialed.

"Katya! Hey, is Victor Yulievich home? On Bolshevik Lane? Thanks. How are things with you? Okay, see you."

He dialed the old phone number. Ilya knew that after his mother's death Victor Yulievich often stayed in his old apartment. The neighbor answered. Ilya waited a long time before Victor came to the phone. He asked whether he could visit right away.

He went to Eliseevsky's and picked up a bottle of five-year-old Armenian cognac. In the early days their teacher had treated them to good Georgian wine; now they treated their teacher to Armenian cognac.

At Pushkin Square he got in a trolleybus and went to Chistye Prudy. Then he walked to the house with the knight standing in a niche above the main door. It felt like coming home. The iron man underneath his pseudo-Gothic arch had outlasted the Revolution and the renaming of the street from Gusyatnikov to Bolshevik, and had no idea what lay in store for him—that he would return to his old address, Gusyatnikov, without budging from his niche.

Ilya went up to the fourth floor. The were five bells on the outside door; above one of them it read "Shengeli." He rang. There were six bolts on the tall door, placed at quite a height—had the people who lived here before been taller than they were now? All the locks but one were broken.

For how many years had he been coming here? Since 1956? Or was it 1955? Since they were all thirteen years old, at any rate. And now he was as old as his teacher had been then. Just about, anyway. Strange, it was taking him so long to open the door. A rotund neighbor woman in an apron came to the door.

"He's home. He probably doesn't hear you."

The bronze, asymmetrically rounded door handle, in the Art Nouveau style . . . how many times had he pressed it down until he heard the click of the latch? He entered. His teacher was asleep on the divan, snoring lightly, his head thrown back unattractively and his mouth slightly agape. The sleeve of his sweater was sewn shut from the inside. Ilya wondered what the stump looked like.

He looked like an unshaven, aging man with a yellowish complexion. The dark-red plush tablecloth was turned back halfway, revealing the table's stained surface, on which a thick notebook, a pen, and a glass of tea, as dark as iodine, were arranged. Of course, it would be impossible to write on that plush tablecloth.

Ilya threw off his raincoat and sat down at the table. He wouldn't wake the old fellow. Yes, he looked just like an old man. How quickly he had aged. And he was only fifteen years older than they were. Of course, it was not long ago that they had celebrated his forty-fifth birthday. Had a whole year passed already? Poor guy. He had been so brilliant, so elegant, a mix of both Don Quixote and Cervantes. The boys had followed him around in a flock. And the girls, too. He had cleared their minds, but had himself wilted. Gotten old. Katya had left him. Or maybe he was the one who had left her? They fired him from teaching. Then he had worked as a guard at the Museum of the Soviet Army for many years. He said he was writing a book. The museum had a marvelous collection—documents from World War II. He was preoccupied by a new idea: initiation by fear. Where there is no initiation into maturity through positive impulses, initiation through fear takes over.

The post-Revolution generations had been inoculated by fear at a very early age, and it had been so strong that other impulses were weak and ineffectual. This was Victor Yulievich's discovery. He discussed it with friends and with his former students. Mikha was completely enamored of the idea; it appealed to Ilya, too. They were eager to read the book. They offered to publish it in the West. Victor Yulievich never finished writing it, however. Perhaps he had talked about it too long, and it had become rarified; or perhaps it was now "in the air," become common knowledge for people who bothered to think about it at all.

In principle, the teacher was right about everything. Ilya closed his eyes. *Yes, he's an ingenious loser. And Mikha is a mediocre poet, an idealist. Sanya is a musician* manqué. *And now I've become a stool pigeon. What a bunch.*

Well, I'm actually just doing my job. I want to leave a legacy. If no one knows about it, then it will be like it never happened at all. My archive will preserve this entire pathetic, hopeless, plague-ridden era. And fear? It was, is, and will be . . .

He had a point; still, he couldn't understand what had happened to Victor Yulievich himself. He would have to ask him: Why he was lying there all alone, half-drunk, surrounded by the finest works of Russian literature? Maybe it was true that only beauty would save the world, or truth, or some other high-flown garbage; but fear was still more powerful than anything else. Fear destroyed everything: everything born of beauty, the tender shoots of all that was fine, wise, eternal . . . It was not Pasternak who would remain, but Mandelstam, because his poetry expresses the full horror of his time, and recoils from it. But Pasternak had always wanted to reconcile himself to it, to find a positive way of giving voice to it, of accommodating it.

Ilya was tired of sitting, so he began drumming on the tabletop with his finger. The sleeper was jarred awake, and his mouth snapped shut.

"Ah, I've been expecting you, Ilya."

Ilya pulled a bottle out of the pocket of his raincoat and placed it on the table. Victor Yulievich stood up, swaying on his feet.

"Yes, yes," he said, starting to bustle about, "just a moment."

He took two glasses out of a cabinet, smiling weakly.

"There's no food in the house."

Ilya dug around in his pocket and pulled out a lemon.

"Let's at least have some sugar."

"I do have that."

He poured them each a glass—round-bellied cognac snifters. The teacher's hand was beautiful and refined, with long, pale fingers and evenly trimmed nails. He held his glass tenderly by the stem.

"Well, my dear friend! You see what we've come to?" Victor Yulievich smiled. Two teeth on the left side of his mouth were missing. And what had Ilya wanted to ask him? What did he want to tell him? Nothing. This was just what he had wanted: to sit down and drink a glass together, to commiserate with each other, to feel mutual sympathy, compassion, love. They drank in silence. And Ilya felt better.

THE COFFEE STAIN

Irina Troitskaya, just over six feet tall, nicknamed Mile, with man-sized extremities, never told anyone that her father was a general. And definitely not which department he served in. She dressed like everyone else, even though her walk-in closet in the Generals' Building next to the Sokol metro stop contained everything a young girl could ever dream of.

She had everything a young girl could dream of, and more besides. But no one wanted to befriend her during her college years. When she approached, people would fall silent. And not only in the cafeteria; in the smoking lounge, too. They didn't mind bumming cigarettes off her; but they still wouldn't talk to her. Actually, not everyone avoided her—mainly the ones she would have wanted to be friends with: Olga, Rikhard, Lyalya, Alla, and Voskoboihikov. What hurt her most was that Olga's father was also a general, Rikhard's father was a government minister in Latvia, and Lyalya's was an ambassador to China. Why were they so haughty and contemptuous of her? She couldn't simply go around telling everyone right and left that although her father was a general in the KGB, he was a real heavyweight—he had been in foreign intelligence his whole life.

Her older sister, Lena, had graduated from the Moscow State University of International Relations. She hadn't experienced anything like the kind of contempt Irina endured there. On the contrary: children of bigwigs were highly respected. The girls all got married before graduation, to suitable young men of their own caste. This was encouraged. None of the girls embarked on independent careers, but for any diplomat, a well-prepared wife was an advantage.

The most eligible boys in Lena's year practically stood in line to ask for her hand; and students that were ahead of her in college as well. Her father joked: they're like Orthodox priests—they won't get ordained if they aren't married. And marriage was indeed good for their careers; they got excellent appointments.

Her father was very smart, jovial, and handsome. Her mother deferred to him in everything—except her height. Igor Vladimirovich always said he had married his wife, Nina, to improve his stock and produce strapping boys, but she brought him only girls. What use was their height to them? They might at least have played basketball.

Both his daughters were half a head taller than their father, and their shoes were two sizes larger. They adored their father, small of stature but always fascinating. He knew something about whatever subject one broached: history, geography, literature. Their home library was like that of a university professor. He wasn't a professor himself, but his grandfather had taught Roman law at the University of Kazan in those antediluvian times before there was any trace of Marxism-Leninism, and the founder of the backside of that future science sat on the benches among his fellow students, showing little interest in the subject.

Igor Vladimirovich insisted that his daughter study, arguing that life was far more interesting among educated people than among the uneducated.

He went up to the bookcase and pointed at the titles:

"If you can't read them, at least study the covers: Aristotle, Plato, Plutarch. Irina will study a smattering of these at the university; but you, Lena, should read a book occasionally—it won't hurt you."

Lena and Irina glanced absently at the valuable books. They had known which books stood where since childhood.

The bookcases were antique, of Swedish make. The lower shelves were enclosed, and the upper shelves were covered with glass panes. On the bottom shelves her father kept special books—they were in Russian, but had been printed abroad. He brought them home from work.

Lena had no interest in them whatsoever, but Irina sometimes read them. There were many interesting books that one couldn't find in the library: Gumilev, Akhmatova, Tsvetaeva, and Mandelstam.

It was these very books that changed Irina's status in her department. This poetry that had been out of print for ages was the bait that lured the whole group to her side. Then she began taking other books from her father's shelves, one by one. She didn't inform her father, naturally. He himself, by the way, loved this rare poetry, and knew much of it by heart.

Irina Troitskaya's prestige grew. She was clever and didn't reveal all her treasure to them at once, but apportioned it in measured doses. She brought dangerous publications and valuable rarities with her to the smoking lounge—all brand new, and published abroad. Most of them had been published by the YMCA Press. This was the first time that Olga had ever come across the name of Berdyaev; but back then she preferred poetry. By mistake she spilled coffee on the cover of a volume of Khodasevich—now it looked like a murky tree and a road, so indistinct you could tell your fortune in it. Olga was very upset about the incident, but Irina just shrugged it off and told her not to worry.

Then the first Nabokov arrived in Russia. It was *Invitation to a Beheading*. The group of friends read it and were completely beguiled by it. It was a tattered copy, published in Berlin in 1936. Inside the front cover was an inscription that read: "To my dear Edwin, on his birthday. Anna." It had been confiscated during the arrest of a German Jew who had emigrated to Russia from Germany in the thirties. The above-mentioned Edwin had studied Russian with this book; in the margins there were German annotations in pencil.

A friend of General Troitsky's had given it to him as a gift, also on his birthday, but many years later. These books met with various fates. Some of them were destroyed; others passed from hand to hand. *The Gift* was one of the latter. Its readers discovered a new writer who was not to be found in any library, nor mentioned by name in any textbook.

Olga was bursting with desire to show the book to her favorite professor. She asked him gingerly about Nabokov. He raised his eyebrows. "Which book?"

"*The Gift.*"

The professor had himself only recently become aware of it—one of his students, a Canadian of Russian descent, had brought him his first Nabokov.

"Yes, yes." The professor nodded circumspectly. "A remarkable writer. There has been nothing like it in Russian for many years."

He didn't ask: What else do you have?

Invitation to a Beheading was making the rounds of the young philologists. It put a dent in the Iron Curtain. Hands trembled, hearts skipped a beat. How to accommodate it? It required a complete revision of the entire hierarchy. A new heavenly body had appeared in the galaxy; the web of connections was disrupted, the celestial mechanism shifted before their very eyes. Half the literary canon underwent spontaneous combustion and turned to ash.

It was the purest diamond. And all courtesy of Irina Troitskaya.

By pure coincidence, that very copy of *The Gift*, which had passed from hand to reliable hand and had ended up in his, was confiscated from the professor during a search. Notes he had made during his reading were also found with the book. He had already begun writing an article on the book called "Return to the Homeland." He didn't manage to finish it. But even these hasty, incomplete notes were seized, to the professor's chagrin.

A scandal ensued, and the professor and his co-author were imprisoned—not for Nabokov, of course, but for their own books, published in the West under pseudonyms. A petition was initiated, heads flew, students were dragged in for questioning. Olga was expelled from the university for signing a letter in defense of the teacher. No one touched Irina Troitskaya. She didn't sign any letters, no one from Olga's circle of friends pointed at her as the source of anti-Soviet agitation.

Irina told her father, belatedly, about her enlightenment mission. Her father did not fear much in life, but he was shaken by this information.

Afterward, when everyone involved had been imprisoned, banished, or expelled, he replaced the lost copy with another. This was, however, an American edition. The general revered Nabokov as deeply as the professor did.

The general also duly read the books written by the imprisoned writers. He told his daughter: they're not bad, but they didn't warrant such a fuss. Irina agonized over these events, although she remained unscathed by them. She didn't see Olga anymore, and she regretted her disappearance. Now everyone was friends with Irina, although she no longer brought books with her to the university—her father forbade it.

Irina graduated, and she got an excellent appointment with the Foreign Committee of the Writers' Union. An old comrade of her father's was in charge of the union and fixed her up with the job.

In 1970, Igor Vladimirovich died suddenly of a heart attack. Not long before his death, he caught wind of a rumor that Solzhenitsyn had been nominated for the Nobel Prize. He was agitated by this news.

"What kind of outfit is this Nobel Committee, anyway? They didn't give it to Tolstoy, but they're giving it to Solzhenitsyn?"

After her father's death, Irina fell into a depression: everything made her feel sick, even her wonderful job. Her sister, Lena, lived in Stockholm, where her husband was a cultural attaché in the Soviet Embassy.

It was clear that the decision of the Nobel Committee was going to cause problems for him.

Something remarkable happened to Irina that year. An elegant middle-aged woman spotted her in a crowd and invited her to come in for an audition as a fashion model. The woman turned out to be the country's most famous fashion designer. The invitation lifted Irina's spirits. She went in for the audition, and they took her immediately. There were no tall fashion models at the time; she would be the first.

Thanks to her family's privileged position, Irina Troitskaya was allowed to travel abroad during the first year. She went first to Belgrade, then to Paris, and, finally, to Milan. In Milan she remained, having received an unexpected proposal from a journalist who wrote a fashion column for a provincial newspaper. He was neither handsome nor a millionaire, but they were supremely happy together in southern

Italy, near Naples, where he was from. Her Italian husband soon quit both the Communist Party, of which he was a member, and his journalism job, and opened a small restaurant. Later he became mayor of the tiny town they lived in. Irina did not become a Slavist, nor did she become a translator; she never again visited Russia.

The story doesn't end there, however—not for the rest of Irina Troitskaya's family, in any case. The scandal caused by the Nobel Committee would have been impossible for the young diplomat to manage single-handedly; but the foreign ministry liked to apportion blame not to the highest diplomats, but to those who occupied a lower rung. They claimed that Lena's husband hadn't tried hard enough. And then there was Irina's defection! The diplomat, Lena's husband, was put through the wringer for the Nobel Prize—a matter in which he had played no part whatsoever—as well as for Irina's defection and for his own lack of initiative. The young couple with brilliant credentials was recalled home from Sweden.

The unlucky diplomat returned home to Moscow with his family to live in the general's apartment. The children, twin boys, liked Moscow. Lena had soup waiting for her husband every day when he returned from the Ministry of Foreign Affairs, where he was the fifth deputy of the seventh assistant in a department that had been slated for dissolution for twenty years already. His salary was so poor that Lena finally went to teach English at a secondary school. Grandmother Nina, like an ordinary housekeeper, took the children for walks in Chapaev Park, until she came down with pneumonia and died. Everything was worse than one could have imagined possible, until Lena visited a fortune-teller. The fortune-teller was a real character, with a penchant for all things Indian. She instructed Lena to "purify her karma," but first she told her to clean up her house, in which a great deal of "filth" had accumulated. She recommended that they remodel.

Her husband was extremely dissatisfied. As it was they could hardly make ends meet, and now—remodeling!

To save on expenses, they completed the first stage themselves. To begin with, they removed all the books from Igor Vladimirovich's heavy bookcase before moving it away from the wall. They took the books with leather bindings to an antiquarian bookseller, who gave them a huge sum of money in exchange. He wouldn't accept all the books, however. It turned out that many of the general's books had library or museum stamps in them, and the booksellers wouldn't touch those.

Lena's husband found a large number of anti-Soviet books in the bottom section of the bookcase, including a collection of the works, complete thus far, of that very Nobel laureate who had caused him so much grief.

"Yes, Father collected books," Lena explained. "He had access to all the books that were seized during searches. Some books were brought from abroad by his friends. He was a great collector: of coins, paper currency, stamps."

Lena's husband did not occupy as high a position as his late father-in-law had, and couldn't allow such a collection to remain in the house. Late at night they took the dangerous books down to the garbage heap.

The next evening they were tearing off wallpaper when they dis-covered a safe in the depths of the thick supporting wall. There was no key. They were unable to open it with any household appliances, though it easily slipped out of its niche in the wall. The back of the smallish box turned out to be plywood. They ripped it off and discovered that the safe contained several stacks of old dollars, which still happened to be in circulation, and twenty-five pre-Revolutionary gold coins.

Her husband clutched at his head in consternation—but didn't take the safe down to the garbage heap.

This is where the story of Irina Troitskaya and her family ends.

What will now be related has nothing at all to do with them. Igor Chetverikov's shift at the boiler room ended at eight in the morning. He usually went trash-picking after six in the morning, making his rounds of the nearby garbage heaps. The Sokol district didn't yield much of value. There weren't many old buildings left. The houses in the neighborhood had been resettled just before and just after the war, so the local residents either threw away the Karelian birch and the

French bronze before they moved in or had never had them in the first place.

Here, in what was formerly the settlement of Vsesvyatsky, if something did end up in the trash it was usually vestiges and remnants of the petite bourgeoisie. Not long ago he had found a trunk full of mid-nineteenth-century women's clothes. Some of the contents had already been dragged off by some little girls, but Igor managed to salvage a brown frock with a crinoline, a fur wrap, and a girl's school uniform.

This time, what he saw made him gasp. Next to the wooden bin where the residents deposited their household garbage stood some neat piles of *tamizdat*, books in Russian published abroad. Without examining them too closely, he took them to the boiler room and ran to the metro to make a call from a pay phone. Ilya, his former classmate, was still asleep, and answered gruffly:

"Are you nuts? Do you even know what time it is?"

"Come to the boiler room immediately. In a car."

Ilya knew the boiler room well, since he had been responsible for getting Igor a job there after he had been expelled from the Kurchatov Institute under a cloud.

Half an hour later, Ilya arrived. They loaded the books into the car and drove them to the apartment of another general, who had at one time been enamored not of coins and books, but of old furniture. And he had preferred to live at his dacha, not in his apartment in the city.

Kostya had already left for school. Olga made coffee for the men and sat on the floor to go through the books. She had already read everything there. Among the small volumes she found a Khodasevich with a coffee stain on the cover—a sort of tree, and a road.

"Igor, is your boiler room at Sokol, in the Generals' Building?"

"Yes, why?"

"Oh, no reason. It's just that I read all these books in college. The owner has probably died. He was a general."

THE FUGITIVE

The storm took place at half past two in the morning. It was like an opera or a symphony—with an overture, leitmotifs, and a duet of water and wind. Lightning bolts flew up in columns, accompanied by incessant rumbling and flashes. Then there was an intermission and a second act. Maria Nikolayevna's heart pains, which had plagued her all day, stopped immediately, as did Captain Popov's headache, from which he had been suffering for the past twenty-four hours. He even managed to get some sleep before going to work. The only thing he didn't manage to do was put a stamp on the document. But he could do that later.

At nine o'clock sharp he rang the doorbell. No one opened for a long time; then he heard a commotion behind the door.

"Who's there? Who is it?" a tentative female voice called out.

Finally, the door opened a crack; but the chain was still secured. Sivtsev and Emelyanenko shuffled impatiently from foot to foot. They wanted to get this over and done with. Greenhorns. Popov showed his badge in the narrow space between the door and the door frame. Again, there was a commotion, and the door opened.

The witness, his man at the local housing authority, trotted up.

"Does Boris Ivanovich Muratov live here?"

Right then, Muratov appeared. A hefty fellow, about forty years old, with a beard. Wearing a blue robe that looked like it could be made of velvet.

We don't have robes like that, Popov thought suspiciously. *It's foreign. Where do they get the stuff?*

"Passport, please," Popov said with absolute civility.

Muratov went into the next room, from which his wife was just emerging. She was a real beauty, of course, also wearing a blue robe! Amazing—two of them, exactly alike!

When Muratov returned, Popov held out the search warrant for his perusal.

"Take a look at this, please," he said, standing some distance away, still clutching it in his hands.

"May I?" Muratov said, reaching out for it.

But Popov refused to part with it.

"What is there to read? It's a search warrant, you can see that yourself. I'll hold it, and you can read it if you think it's necessary."

"I can see it's a search warrant. But it isn't stamped."

"Oh, hell!" Popov grew irate. "That's unimportant. A warrant is a warrant; it'll get its stamp, don't worry about that."

"First stamp it, then you can enter," Boris Ivanovich said haughtily.

"If I were you, I'd try being more polite. Having words won't help either of us. Now let me get on with my work, please."

He moved deeper into the apartment, followed by Sivtsev. Emelyanenko stood in the tiny entrance hall, keeping an eye on the door and the living room.

"One moment, please," Boris Ivanovich said, going into the smaller room.

Popov knew the layout of three-room apartments like this like the back of his hand. First a tiny entrance hall, then a larger pantry space with built-in wall cupboards where they kept everything. He had seen plenty of them.

He blocked the door so Muratov couldn't enter the larger room. Muratov turned red, moved the captain aside, and went in to rummage through the top drawer of his desk. Popov lost his composure. In this petty struggle, Muratov was right. The warrant, strictly speaking, was invalid.

The captain couldn't admit defeat, however, and barked out: "Don't touch the drawers! We'll need to look through them."

But Muratov, apparently, had found what he was looking for. He unfolded a thick piece of paper, yellowed at the edges, bearing an official red letterhead and a profile of the "greatest of the great" leaders.

"My Certificate of Honor."

The artist thrust the paper at the captain, but at such a distance that he couldn't read anything it said.

Again, Popov's head started to throb.

"What is the meaning of this?"

The wife, blue-eyed, in her blue robe, her face pallid, looked beseechingly at her husband. Maria Nikolayevna, his mother-in-law, poured out tea for them as though nothing at all were happening.

Boris Ivanovich held the paper at a more reasonable distance: the captain could see it, but he couldn't snatch it from him.

"I'll hold it, and you can read it. I'll hold it."

The captain read it through. The captain heeded it. He turned around to go, his detachment following at his heels. They didn't say a word.

Muratov flung the saving document into a corner.

With a graceful flourish, Maria Nikolayevna placed a teacup and a sandwich in front of Boris Ivanovich.

Boris Ivanovich loved his mother-in-law; in her he saw Natasha, but with a more decisive character. In his wife, Natasha, he saw features of his mother-in-law—the first signs of a gentle fullness, small lines around the mouth, and a burgeoning soft pouch under the chin. Good, healthy stock. The generous plumpness of Kustodiev's women, but all the more alluring for it.

Natasha picked up the letter, which had been casually cast aside.

"What is this, Boris?"

Boris made a gesture indicating that walls have ears.

"Well, my dear Natasha, I got that Certificate of Honor after my Sculpture and Modeling Plant entrusted me with the task of manufacturing an object with the code name 'SL,' in two copies, as a matter of fact. This remarkable object represented, my girl, the sarcophagus of the leader and teacher of all times and peoples, Vladimir Ilyich Lenin. And just look at the signatures! The highest authorities express their gratitude to me."

After this booming announcement, he made an obscene gesture, visible though inaudible, at those very walls.

Maria Nikolayevna smiled. Natasha put her white hands on her still whiter neck.

"What's going to happen now?" she said quietly.

Boris picked up one of the pages of thin gray paper that were heaped about the room in multitudes, and wrote with a pencil:

"He disappeared to an unknown location."

And on that same piece of paper he drew his usual cartoon of himself—a large head hunched into his shoulders, a short, straggly beard, and a forehead framed by two bald patches on either side.

"Another cup of tea, please, Maria Nikolayevna!" he said, jangling his cup for effect.

Natasha sat rigid in her chair. Maria Nikolayevna went to put the kettle on again.

Boris embraced his wife.

"I knew this would happen. It's all so awful," she said.

Then she took a pencil and wrote in the margins of the page:

"They're going to arrest you."

"I'm leaving home in half an hour," he wrote back. And he drew himself somersaulting down the stairs.

The page was filled. He tore it up and burned it. He waited until the flame burned the entire page, nearly to his fingertips, then dropped the vestiges into the ashtray.

He took a new page and drew himself running down the street. At the top of the page he wrote "Train Station," and showed it to Natasha and Maria Nikolayevna, who had just come back. His mother-in-law grasped the situation faster than his wife, and nodded.

"Right now," Boris said.

"Alone?" Natasha said.

Muratov nodded.

Then he started rummaging around in those very walk-in cupboards that Captain Popov had been so eager to inspect, and pulled out a folder, in which he kept exactly what the captain had been looking for.

He took out a sheaf of pages, full of drawings, and went out to the kitchen.

Maria Nikolayevna watched him in silent sympathy.

Muratov pulled a baking sheet out of the oven, put several pieces of the paper on it, and lit a match. Maria Nikolayevna snatched the matches from him.

"How many times have I told you not to interfere in my household duties, Boris Ivanovich."

He was sitting on his haunches in the middle of the floor, looking up at her. Maria Nikolayevna pushed him out of the way, then squeezed past into the corridor, where she pried up the edge of the worn-out linoleum by the wooden threshold. Boris Ivanovich merely shrugged in amazement.

Deftly and in perfect concert, as though they had been doing this their whole lives, they stuffed all the drawings under the linoleum, then tucked the worn-out edge under the threshold again. Everything was just as it had been before, as though nothing at all had happened. Boris Ivanovich kissed Maria Nikolayevna's cheek gratefully. It would have been a pity to have to burn them.

Then he found some canvas trousers, short in the leg and loose in the waist, in the lower drawer of the dresser. From the cupboard he took out an old straw hat. Both had belonged at one time to his late father-in-law. He did all this without saying a single word.

"He's gone crazy. He's gone crazy," Natasha said. His mother-in-law, pointing to the telephone—she was as sure as Boris that their apartment was bugged—said in a loud voice: "Boris, shall I make meat patties for your lunch?"

"Meat patties sound good."

Twenty-five minutes later he left the house. He had shaved off his beard, but left a mustache. He'd cut his hair shorter. He walked through the courtyard, so full of rainwater that he could have floated across in a boat. Broken branches protruded from the giant puddle, like trees after a flood. Boris was lugging a big shopping bag in which he had a change of underwear, a sweater, and his favorite little pillow, as well as all the money he had been able to scrape together.

Sivtsev and Emelyanenko, who had stayed behind to keep watch, were lounging on a little bench in the courtyard, smoking. They were deliberating whether to go and get some beer.

Captain Popov arrived at ten fifteen with the required stamp on the warrant. Natasha Muratov, wife and officially registered tenant of the apartment, opened the door right away this time, and said that her husband had gone to work. Popov threw a furious glance at his blockhead underlings.

"He doesn't have a job!" Popov said. "What kind of work are you talking about?"

"He's an artist. He doesn't have a job, but he has plenty of work. You saw yourself: he worked on Lenin's sarcophagus," the mother-in-law piped up.

"He was fired after that," Popov said, offering a belated piece of evidence.

"That's right, he went out to look for a job," Maria Nikolayevna retorted.

"Wasn't he planning to come home for lunch?" the captain asked.

"Of course." They'd taken the bait about the meat patties, the damned eavesdroppers. They worked fast! "And he ordered meat patties. We're expecting him home for lunch."

The captain got down to work. He spared no effort in tackling the mountains of assorted papers. The samizdat were the run-of-the-mill variety that everyone had. The samizdat weren't what Popov was hoping to find, however.

What he was looking for was lying on his own desk in his office in the form of photocopied pages from *Stern* magazine. These were cartoons: gigantic letters spelling "Glory to the Communist Party of the Soviet Union," and under them a crowd of people and dogs trying to reach the sacred words. The words themselves were made of sausages: boiled salami, with circles of white fat where they had been sliced. They were strung together with rope, from which dangled a price tag reading "2 rub. 20 kop."

Another cartoon depicted a mausoleum made of the same kind of salami, with the word *Lenin* written in sausage links.

The third cartoon showed the Volga boatmen from the famous painting by Repin, harnessed together, and pulling, not a barge, but a rocket ship.

The agents had been searching for the malicious cartoonist for a long time, and had discovered him quite by chance. All that remained now was to find the original drawings, sketches, or something similar.

Captain Popov departed late in the evening. He took three bags of samizdat with him. The drawings that Popov had hoped to find were not discovered.

Boris Ivanovich, in the meantime, had taken refuge for the night with an old woman who had been hawking green onions and parsley on the Kimry docks, had sold nothing, but had somehow returned home with a wayfarer who had missed the last boat to Novo-Akatovo. For a ruble she allowed him to spend the night in her barn on a haystack covered with a sheet. At sunrise he washed at the well, and by six in the morning he was on the boat. The old woman was a godsend—she didn't report him.

On the evening of the second day he was sitting in the remote, nearly inaccessible village of Danilovy Gorki, in an old peasant cottage that belonged to his friend Nikolay Mikhailovich, also an artist. He explained the situation to him and asked permission to live there, in their summer hut, or in the bathhouse, for the time being, in the guise of a cousin or some such relative. Nikolay Mikhailovich shook his head and groaned, but didn't refuse him. And so began Boris Ivanovich's life as a fugitive.

Danilovy Gorki wasn't exactly a village, but a small settlement of five houses. One of them was Nikolay Mikhailovich's. Another stood empty, after the death of the owner two years back, and was awaiting a buyer. The owners of the other three hosted vacationers in the summer months. By the end of August, nearly everyone would return to the city.

Nikolay Mikhailovich's mother was from the nobility; his father had been a priest, and was executed in 1937. Thus, he was under no illusions about the relative seriousness of the situation. He said that until September, while there were still many strangers around the settlement, it would be safe to stay there. When the vacationers left, though, every person for five miles could be seen at a glance.

The cottage was full to the rafters. Children, the elderly, two spinster aunts, all manner of dependents and houseguests. Everyone lent a hand, but on a voluntary basis. They were all busy from morning till night, but all free and unencumbered.

For Boris, this country life was a novelty. He was a city man. His grandfather, who had been a serf, had started to work in Sytin's lithography plant after 1883. His father had been a typography engraver: a "proletarian of artistic labor," as he called himself. He settled in Moscow and lost all ties with his Ryazan relatives.

Boris Ivanovich didn't know much about country life, and was wary of it, but he didn't like the city, either. He had lived in the Zamoskvorechye district, not far from the typography plant, since childhood, and he and his wife moved to Kharitonievsky Lane when they married.

He felt happiest when he was on the Black Sea, and he vacationed in Sochi or in Gagra every year. He had never really seen the countryside before, and now, for the first time, he was discovering the charms of a secluded little village near a large river, among forests and swamps. He was also charmed by the descendants of this family of the nobility. They had never lived in palaces, or caught so much as a whiff of luxury. For half a century, between poverty and indigence, between banishment and prison, those who had survived had been honed and simplified. They no longer knew a single foreign language, but they had preserved some ineffable quality that Boris Ivanovich never managed to pin down.

Nikolay's daughters boiled kasha on the Russian stove, baked pies, worked in the vegetable garden, and washed clothing and linens in the river. The grandsons caught fish, the granddaughters and two aunts picked berries and mushrooms in the forest. All of them sang, drew, and put on children's plays.

Nikolay Mikhailovich's cousin, the vivacious and full-throated Anastasia, came for a three-day visit. From the moment she arrived, she began making eyes at Boris. She turned his head; he was an easy and quick-witted catch. They lost no time about it, and their first night together would have been longer if they hadn't sat around the table singing songs until all hours. And Anastasia sang remarkably well— with a kind of gypsy flair, sonorous and provocative. His own wife was more attractive than this Anastasia, with her small, childlike breasts and long nose, but Boris Ivanovich marveled about her long afterward: this woman, bony and angular, had been like the water of life for him. It was as though he had been cleansed from inside, picked apart bone by bone, ligament by ligament, then reassembled. He couldn't recall when he had ever been such a potent and untiring partner. Anastasia sailed away on a little boat on the fourth day of their romance. She was a doctor, moreover the head of her department, and had to return to duty. The whole family went down to the river to see her off, and when she was still on shore she began singing, "Marusenka Was Washing Her White Feet." For a long time, she waved her handkerchief from the boat that would take her to the big landing stage, where the regular ferry would pick her up.

She's such a cultured woman; but what a slut! Boris Ivanovich thought in rapturous bewilderment. He had never in his life met a woman like her.

Nikolay Mikhailovich, as though reading his mind, said quietly:

"It's in Anastasia's blood—her great-grandmother, or great-great . . . slept with Pushkin."

On Transfiguration Day the whole household went to church in Kashino. Starting out in the evening, they traveled first by boat, then by bus. It was an exhausting journey. They were cultured, well-educated people—but religious as well. Boris Ivanovich had never met people like this before, either.

"Your way of life is rather anti-Soviet," he said in amazement.

"No, Boris, it's simply a-Soviet," Nikolay Mikhailovich replied, laughing.

Boris stared wide-eyed at everything. He watched the rising sun, and the shallow water lapping the sandbars, where the minnows and tadpoles darted to and fro as though they had some great business to attend to. He saw the sandy shore with its empty mussel shells and ornately patterned grasses, which he had noticed on icons, but he hadn't known they really existed in the world. He saw all this, and felt a happy wonder. He and the others tramped into the woods to pick mushrooms, which were sparse in July but much more numerous in August, after the gentle, sweet rains.

Boris Ivanovich turned out to have a passion for hunting mushrooms, and for fishing. He even proved to be adept at peasant labors: he learned to wield an axe like the best of them, helping Nikolay Mikhailovich repair the barn and set the gate upright again.

The days were long, and the evenings, with their endless tea-drinking, were pleasant. The nights passed by in an instant: he would fall asleep and wake up again refreshed, as though no time at all had passed. And Boris Ivanovich felt an unprecedented calm and peace, something he had never known in his Moscow life.

A month and a half passed, and he still hadn't had any news from home. And, strange as it may seem, he didn't seek out ways to get in touch with his wife. On the face of it, this was because he didn't wish to cause her any trouble. But deeper down, he admitted that he felt more tranquil without her agitated caprices, her alarm and fears.

A relative of Nikolay Mikhailovich's tossed a single postcard in the mailbox from Boris Ivanovich upon her return to Moscow: Don't worry, everything's fine. I love and miss you.

In August, Nikolay Mikhailovich's wife arrived with their oldest son, Kolya. She was the daughter of a famous Russian artist. Both daughters hovered around their mother, pampering her like an honored guest, with a constant refrain of "Mommy, Mommy!" The son, a strapping thirty-year-old, trailed around after his father. Nikolay Mikhailovich's relationship with his wife was also unusual. They were tender and respectful toward each other, almost formal in their manners and forms of address. They spoke in quiet voices, attentive and courteous to each other. It was hard to believe they had ever made children.

The grown-up children still remained their children, and it was amusing to see how the grandchildren adopted the manners and habits of their parents—bringing them a pretty apple, or a bouquet of late-blooming wild strawberries. Boris Ivanovich, who was staunchly opposed to childbearing, even began to doubt his long-held theory—that producing new human beings in this country, ruled by an inhuman and shameless government, in which they would be destined to a life of poverty, filth, and meaninglessness, was wrong. This was the condition on which he married Natasha.

He and Natasha had been married for eight years already, and she had not yearned for children. But there was another circumstance that irked her. Whether it was because she lacked a sense of humor, or because her husband's views and ideas weighed too heavily on her, she began to recoil from the cartoons, which had become more strident and bitter with time. They lived very comfortably, compared with others. He had graduated from the department of applied arts and crafts at the Stroganov Institute, so he had never become a "proper artist." He carried out commissions, and earned more than the real artists at the plant, where he made up to a thousand rubles on a project.

Sometimes he took on private commissions for well-known people, or assisted in creating metalwork décor and panels for all manner of palaces of culture, whether railroad or metallurgical—but invariably socialist. This kind of hackwork filled him with spiteful rage, and he began making ever more acerbic cartoons about this socialist way of life that would any day now become full-blown communism.

He began to indulge his passion for drawing with greater intensity. By trade, he was a craftsman specializing in fine metalwork, but drawing became his source of joy and rest—and an outlet for his frustrations. Once he was invited to take part in an art exhibit held in an apartment, out of sight of the authorities, and after this he was welcomed into a select circle of underground artists.

His underground work even drew admirers. The first to attract attention were the laborer and female collective-farm worker made out of the coveted salami—but only on paper, naturally. Thanks to his friend Ilya, this salami even made it all the way to West Germany and was published in an evil anti-Soviet magazine (like all the magazines over there). After this taste of success, Boris even grew indifferent to large-scale commissions and spent most of his time scratching away with his pencil.

Here, in Danilovy Gorki, Muratov lost all interest in drawing salami. They didn't have it there, and no one missed it. Neither had he any interest in the quiet sketches of gentle nature that every member of Nikolay Mikhailovich's family, young and old, was so fond of making. So, during the summer, he refrained from drawing.

It was getting on toward September, and they began to prepare for going back to the city. They stuffed mushrooms, raspberries, and strawberries dried in the oven into pillowcases. They hadn't made jam that year—there wasn't enough sugar, and the jars were hard to transport to the city, anyway. They put away the salted cucumbers and mushrooms in the cellar, and buried the early potatoes.

During the winter, Nikolay Mikhailovich and his son always made a trip here from the city on "inspection"—to look at the house, and to fetch provisions to take back to Moscow. The route during the winter, in contrast to the summer "water" route, was far more grueling: first by train, then by bus, then four more miles through the forest. Cars weren't able to make it to Danilovy Gorki because there was no road; the only way to reach it was by tractor.

When their departure was imminent, Nikolay Mikhailovich said to Boris:

"Well, do you intend to winter here, Boris Ivanovich?"

Although he had lived there for nearly two months in placid tranquillity, he had nevertheless been contemplating the future, and so was quick to answer:

"I have some trepidation, Nikolay Mikhailovich. Not about the police—but about your stove, about your cottage. One has to know these things from childhood. I may be too old by now to pick these things up."

"True, our father was a parish priest, and we lived in a cottage like this from childhood. It's a simple science; but a science nevertheless."

Nikolay Mikhailovich scratched his scraggly beard, thought for a bit, then said:

"Old Nura's vacationers have all gone home, and she has been unwell for about a year. Why don't you stay with her, Boris; I'll talk to her about it. You can help her get through the winter. I'll come in December to check in on you. God willing, things will work out."

They had adopted a practice: If they called each other just by their given names, Boris and Nikolay, they used the formal address. If they used their patronymics, they addressed each other as "thou."

Muratov gave Nikolay Mikhailovich instructions about what to do once he reached Moscow. He wanted him to stop in at his home one evening without prior arrangement and hand over a letter, without revealing his whereabouts. That was all. And he wanted him to meet with his friend Ilya, convey his greetings, and tell him one word: "Forward." He would know what to do.

Before Nikolay Mikhailovich's return to the village in December, Boris requested that he meet with Ilya again, take the money he would have ready, give half of it to Boris's family, and bring the other half with him here. How much money there would be he didn't know: perhaps a lot, perhaps not much; perhaps none at all . . .

Nikolay Mikhailovich fulfilled these requests down to the last detail during the first week after his return to Moscow.

Muratov moved in with Nura. The old woman was shrunken and stooped over. She had a craggy face and gnarled fingers with huge, bulbous knuckles and joints. She held them perpetually in front of her, as though she were holding a cup or a saucer. Her joints no longer worked, and she manipulated her fingers as if they were claws.

She allowed Muratov to live with her in exchange, not for money, but for vodka. The old woman turned out to be very fond of tippling, and was quite a character. Early in the morning she would wake up and crawl out of bed, her bones creaking. Then she would cross herself in front of the holy place in the corner, where there was an icon completely covered in soot, and imbibe her first thimbleful. At noon she took another. At some indeterminate point during the day she ate porridge or potatoes. All the other fats, proteins, and carbohydrates a person needs to survive she would get from a further three thimblefuls of the potion. A bottle lasted her a week; she had established this for herself years ago. In the mornings she was barely alive, but by evening she was animated and cheerful, and even did some housework. But she mumbled more and more incoherently as the day wore on.

Three years before, the settlement had been furnished with radio and electricity. The old woman ignored the electricity. She never turned on the light, going to sleep when it got dark, and rising at sunrise. She took a liking to the radio, however. When Muratov learned to decipher the meaning of her mumbling, he would catch merciless and hilarious gibes at the radio broadcasts that she listened to in the mornings. That year, another campaign against drinking had been launched. They issued statements and decrees, and the antialcohol message was sent out over the radio waves.

"Now they're all worked up about vodka. Who can drink vodka, when there's not even any moonshine! We don't need anything from you, leave us to ourselves. You can keep your BAM,* but leave us the vodka."

When Boris Ivanovich started to understand her indistinct muttering, he came to appreciate the liveliness and wit of her repartee.

"Listen, lodger, that new Stalin, whatchamacallem, he'll be worse than the old one."

"Why is that?"

"The old one took everything, and this one is picking through the leftovers. Oh yes, they liberated us from everything, the dears—first they freed us from the land, then from my husband, then from my children, from my cow, my chickens . . . They'll liberate us from vodka, and our freedom will be complete."

Nura's husband had perished in 1930, during collectivization. Her three sons, who had come of age at the beginning of the war, had died in combat, one after another—the eldest in '41, the middle in '42, and the youngest in '45.

"And they liberated us from God, too." She peered through the darkness at the icon and muttered: "But maybe He Himself turned his back on us, who's to say . . ."

In the evenings there were sometimes visitors—Marfa and Zinaida, both a bit younger, but no less bitter than Nura. They drank Boris Ivanovich's tea, and Nura praised him:

"God sent me a good lodger. Sometimes he brings me vodka, and sometimes tea . . ."

Boris Ivanovich hadn't thought about salami for a long time now. It had completely lost its symbolic significance in these parts, having long ago been out of circulation, and thus forgotten. These women had no money to take a commuter train to Moscow to buy salami, and they

*Baikal–Amur Railroad.

would never have laid eyes on an orange if Nikolay Mikhailovich's family had not presented them with this delicacy from time to time.

Nowadays, Muratov drew only the old women's meager feasts. He discovered great riches amid the scarcity: small, crooked potatoes, boiled in their jackets, pickled cucumbers, disfigured from being crammed in their barrels, mushrooms—small boletes, stout milk caps, and saffron agarics. And the queen of the table was a turbid bottle of moonshine with a homemade stopper. And vodka, if they were lucky. In the winter, bread supplies were intermittent. They hadn't gotten any at the village store in the larger settlement of Kruzhilino, four miles from Danilovy Gorki, so the old women took turns baking it themselves.

Boris Ivanovich had quickly used up all the paper he found in Nikolay Mikhailovich's house. Luckily, he had found ten rolls of wallpaper that had been intended for the attic. The renovation had been put off for several years, and then forgotten. But the wallpaper was just what Boris Ivanovich needed. At first he drew on the back side, which was ash gray; then he started working on the right side of the paper, a lightly stippled yellow background that brought the old women's faces to life.

They were the last people in the village. The others had already died, as worn out as their ancient clothing, resigned and humble as the potatoes that were their only food, and free as the clouds.

When they drank, they would grow frisky and cheerful, rather than gloomy. They would strike up a song or lose themselves in reminiscences. They laughed, covering their toothless mouths with their blackened fingers. Among the three of them they had only a few teeth left. They cured the toothache with sage and nettles. The village shepherd, Lyosha, had pulled teeth, but after he died, all the teeth left in their mouths fell out by themselves, without any extra help.

The old women's stories were always the same. New ones were rarely aired. Boris Ivanovich sketched their gatherings with a fine pencil, along with their intriguing quips and words, which he inscribed on ribbons coming from their toothless mouths. And what words they were! There were stories about how, before the war, Party functionaries had come to the village to herd them into a collective farm. The people protested and shouted, but they had to join up, they had no choice. But Nura's eldest son, Nikola, was a daredevil if ever there was one. He found a rotten egg—they had a chicken who was such a schemer that you couldn't find where she hid her eggs, and when they would finally rot and explode, the stench was so bad it would hang around for a month. Nikola bent over backward to find a few that hadn't exploded yet, to put them in the wagon carrying the officials, so that they would break them with their fat behinds along the way. And what do you know, the first Party boss who sat in the wagon broke the rotten egg. There was a soft whistle—and the foul stink spread all over the place. Oh, what a laugh! Another time Zinaida's tooth was hurting, and Lyosha the shepherd was on a binge, so Zinaida went to Kashino to get her tooth pulled. The dentist sat her down in a chair, and she peed all over herself in terror . . . Imagine, from Kashino she ran all twelve miles to get home. When she got there, her toothache was gone: the abscess had broken along the way!

They recalled their husbands, and even argued a bit: Marfa remembered how Zinaida had seduced her husband in 1926. Zinaida, in her turn, reported that Lyosha the shepherd had stolen milk right and left from the entire herd. And Lyosha was Marfa's own brother. Words were exchanged, and they almost got into fisticuffs. But Nura saved the day by singing an off-color little ditty apropos of the situation, about who had sneaked into where and filched what, and they both started laughing.

And again they reminisced about things long past but not forgotten—about how the "Commonists" had starved the village and stolen its men. When they fell silent, they would drink a thimbleful. Then they'd burst out laughing and drink some more. But they didn't allow sad stories to creep in and put a damper on things. They derived pleasure from the most trivial matter; they laughed on the slightest pretext, or for no reason at all. They cracked jokes, mocked and made fun of one another, danced and sang, a bit for show, with Boris Ivanovich in mind as their audience, but mainly for one another, in the most candid and heartfelt manner.

Nikolay Mikhailovich's house yielded yet another gift to Boris Ivanovich: three boxes of children's colored pencils. He had no respect for his metallurgical hackwork, considering himself to be a graphic artist; but these simple colored pencils awakened the painter in him, and applying strokes alternately in blue, green, and black, he created something of strange, multilayered beauty.

Now he felt he was a scholar, a scientist, documenting a disappearing world in images. Laughing, the old women told their intricate stories, their wrinkled faces joyous, and Boris Ivanovich sat at the table, dashing off his marvelous pictures. He was already well into his supply of wallpaper.

The snow fell, and autumnal bleakness, the dreary brown wetness, gave way to the whiteness of winter. It stayed in Boris's memory as a brilliant, bright patch, a sunny clearing in the dull, gray background of his life.

Boris Ivanovich spent every daylight hour, which were few at the end of November, wandering around the village. The swamps were frozen over, and it was possible to walk out on them, but so much snow had fallen that it was already higher than the tops of his boots.

One day he returned home, frozen to the bone, and found all the old women scurrying around in the yard. They had decided to subject themselves to a major cleansing in anticipation of the next day's holiday.

"What kind of holiday is it? It's not November seventh, the reddest of red-letter days; and it's surely not the fifth of December, the day of the Soviet Constitution, is it?" Boris Ivanovich said.

"We call it the Great Presentation."

But who was presenting what to whom, they couldn't say. They all agreed, as one person, however, that they had to bathe. And it was time, in any case. The last time they had washed was for the Feast of the Intercession, when the first snow had fallen.

Only Nikolay Mikhailovich had a decent bathhouse. The old women's bathhouses had all fallen into disrepair long before. So much snow had piled up in Nikolay Mikhailovich's garden that it would have taken a whole day to dig a path through it. They decided to bathe in Nura's cottage, as they had done last time. If they had been younger, they could have bathed right in the stove, but now that they were old they were afraid they might burn themselves to a crisp.

Boris Ivanovich decided not to ask too many questions. He rolled the tubs from the outer entrance into the main room of the cottage. He hauled water from the well. He chopped wood for them, and brought it inside—the outer entrance was filled up with it. They began heating the water in the morning. It was so hot in the cottage that all the windows were steamed up, and tears ran down the panes, bathing them as well as the old women.

Everything was ready; they had even steamed the birch switches. Then they wondered: Where would they put the lodger? He would freeze outside, how could they chase him out of the house while they bathed? They couldn't hide him in the stove, he'd burn up. The cottage wasn't divided into separate rooms; there was only one place they could put him—behind the stove. But would he try to take a peek at them from there? Then they started laughing at themselves: Why would a young lad like him want to look at their old bones, anyway?

They put Boris Ivanovich behind the stove and pulled a curtain over it. He sat there with a book, but didn't read anything. The light from the lamp was as weak as candlelight, and didn't reach as far as where he was sitting. So he listened to the old women's conversation.

At first they giggled, saying that they had grown so dry the dirt wouldn't stick to them anymore. Then Zinaida said that she had already stopped stinking: when they were young they had smelled like pussy, but now they just smelled of dust and mold. Then the washing started. They groaned and whined, they poured the water and clattered the tubs. Then one of them slipped, fell down with a plop, and shrieked. Boris Ivanovich started, and jumped up to see whether she needed his help. He drew himself up to his full height and looked over the curtain. Zinaida and Marfa were picking Nura up off the floor, dissolving into childlike laughter.

Boris Ivanovich froze. He'd grown used to their wrinkled faces, to their dark, knotty hands and their blunt, shapeless feet, to everything that their ancient, faded clothing didn't conceal. But now—good God!—he saw their bodies. He couldn't take his eyes off them. Their long, loose gray hair streamed down over their bumpy spines. Their hands and feet seemed enormous and even more misshapen. Broken by working the earth, twisted like the roots of old trees, their fingers had taken on the color of the soil in which they had been digging for so many decades. The skin of their bodies, however, was so white it looked bluish pale, like skimmed milk. Marfa still had breasts, with dark animal-like nipples; but the breasts of the other two seemed to have evaporated, leaving only soft, translucent sacks that hung down to their bellies. Zinaida had long, shapely legs—or what remained of them. Their behinds had been rubbed away to a smooth flatness, and only the folds of skin underneath indicated where their round buttocks had once been.

"I'm telling you, Nura, I can't pick up anything heavy anymore; my womb starts falling out whenever I do," Marfa said, challengingly, and with some sort of secret pride. Just then, Boris Ivanovich noticed that a gray bag the size of a tobacco pouch was dangling down between her legs. He grimaced, but still couldn't tear his eyes away from these three cronelike graces.

Marfa squatted and nimbly pushed the little pouch back under the hairless, wrinkled mound, into the depths of what had once been a woman's body.

Boris Ivanovich was not an autodidact. He had graduated from art school, and his father had been, after all, an artist-engraver. From childhood he had been familiar with Doré's illustrations for *The Divine Comedy*. He had examined that book in the latter years of childhood and early adolescence, when the female body held a burning interest for him. But these crooked, bent creatures who were pottering about just six feet away from him were the living vestiges of bodies, and only with a great effort of the imagination could he discern a female form in their contorted bones, their drooping flesh.

"Old age is sexless," Boris Ivanovich thought, and felt a sudden horror: "And me? Will this happen to me, too? No, no, I don't want it to happen to me! I'd rather exit on my own than fall into this sort of decrepitude, this sort of nonbeing."

Just then, there was a screech of laughter; the old women had caught him in the act!

"Oh-oh, that lodger of yours, Nura, he's peeking at the girls!"

"Let's whip him with the birch switch so he won't be naughty again!"

Nura screamed. "Stinging nettles! We'll whip him with stinging nettles, since he peeked!"

"Oh, come off it, what do I need with a bunch of old grannies like you? I thought I might need to rescue whoever it was that slipped and fell. You should be glad!"

And he retreated behind the curtain again. He spent several days afterward drawing this "Bath of the White Swans," as he called it, in secret.

He filled up the last remnants of the wallpaper with this strange work. He remembered how he had been taught to do life studies in art school, but this quest for form by means of a child's pencil had nothing at all to do with that slavish shading, that endless struggle of light and shadow. The pictures that emerged were grotesque and terrifying—but for some reason, amusing at the same time.

He was able to draw about twenty of them before the paper ran out. Just when Boris Ivanovich was starting to feel bored, Nikolay Mikhailovich and his son returned from the city to inspect his household. He brought Boris Ivanovich a great deal of money from Ilya, more than he had ever expected. He also brought greetings and a letter from his wife.

Together they set out for a store in the neighboring village, a distance of about four miles.

Verka, the shopkeeper, knew Nikolay Mikhailovich well. She had great respect for him. She pulled out the hidden vodka from under the counter. Nikolay had brought two bottles from Moscow, but Boris Ivanovich couldn't pass up the opportunity to spend his newly earned riches. He had avoided going to the store, for fear of the locals: What if they informed on him, saying there was a stranger wandering around these parts?

They emptied out almost all the meager inventory of the store into two rucksacks: cookies, sticky candy without wrappers, sprats, vegetable oil, barley, a package of dried peas, briquettes of cherry kissel, cheese spread, and two packs of salt. Boris Ivanovich scoured the shelves in the hopes of finding some real food. Verka examined the customer, trying to size up whether he would do for any other kind of business. To all appearances, he would—but his eyes were roving over the foodstuffs, not over her, the beauty . . .

Nikolay Mikhailovich, after working his shoulders under the straps, gave them a good shrug to settle the purchases in the bottom of the rucksack; the bottles clanked together softly and invitingly.

"Have you come to stay for a while? Stop in and see us!" Verka propped her round cheek on her beet-red fist.

"No, Verka, thank you. I'm only here for a day. I didn't even bother heating the house, it would just waste firewood. We're going to stay the night at Old Nura's, then go home."

"Well, you could send your friend over to us," Verka said with a giggle. "Otherwise, we girls might get bored. He's been living here so long already, and he hasn't gotten to know anybody."

Ah, so the grapevine had been in good working order all along. They even knew in nearby villages that someone was living here who hadn't been accounted for. The artists exchanged a significant look.

"We're leaving tomorrow. You'll get to know each other in the spring, when we come back."

Upon their return, the men found that Nura had baked potato pies for them and had herself retreated behind the stove. Zinaida and Marfa stayed away, out of politeness.

"Maybe we should call them?" Boris Ivanovich said. He had made his decision: he would have to leave this marvelous place, where he had already stayed too long.

"No, they won't come today. They're well-brought-up peasant women. They would never come over on the first day. I don't know why—whether for fear of bothering someone, or not to seem to beg for gifts or favors. They had a sound upbringing, not like today's young local women. Verka, the shopkeeper, is just a broad, not to mention a thief. She's Zinaida's niece. According to the rules, she should come to visit her aunt and bring her gifts and provisions, but she doesn't. Zinaida's son has been doing time for two years already. His wife drinks. One of her grandsons drowned last year, and now there's just a slow-witted granddaughter left." Nikolay Mikhailovich gestured dismissively. "But what do our country dramas mean to you, Ivanovich . . ."

Kolya arrived, his arms full of supplies from the cellar.

"Everything's okay, Dad. Nothing froze. The potatoes are well protected. I don't think we could make it to the station without them freezing, though. I'd take the cucumbers and mushrooms, but I wouldn't touch the potatoes."

"Too bad. But you're right, Kolya. The frosts are getting stronger, and even in the bus the potatoes would freeze."

The three men sat around the table, talking companionably and eating the pies and all manner of country delicacies. To mark the occasion, they cleaned some potatoes to eat, and doused them in vegetable oil. They didn't open any of the canned preserves; they left them for the old women for their Christmas repast. The Nativity fast had just begun; but their fast lasted all year without interruption, not counting a chicken they might boil up now and then.

When it was already late, around ten o'clock, there was a knock at the door. Nikolay Mikhailovich leapt to his feet, thrust the plate and glass into Boris's hands, and bundled him behind the stove with the old woman. And it was the right thing to do: at the door stood Nikolay Svistunov, a distant relative and a policeman. Family ties weren't all that significant anymore, since half the people were Svistunovs, and the other half Erofeevs, in the three surrounding villages. And every other fellow was named Nikolay.

Svistunov took off his hat, then unbuttoned his uniform coat. Without a word, Nikolay Mikhailovich took a clean glass and filled it just over halfway for him.

"I stopped off in Gorki when I noticed that you weren't heating your stove and there was no light on in your cottage," Svistunov said.

"Well, you have to heat it for three days to get it warm. We just dropped in to look around and pick up some cucumbers and mushrooms from the cellar. We're staying here at Nura's, then heading back to the city."

There was no road out of Danilovy Gorki, not even a ski run. Nikolay and Boris had tamped down a fresh path, and this was what the policeman had followed. The newly fallen snow had already powdered over the recent tracks, however.

"It'll take more than an hour to get back," Svistunov said, and started hurrying. Wolves had been spotted last week in Troitsky. Svistunov didn't want to meet up with them, so he didn't stay at the old woman's for long. Never mind what someone had seen, or what some-one said. He had stopped by, checked documents; they were familiar vacationers, well known in these parts, lived in a house they had bought themselves, and he hadn't seen any strangers about the premises at all.

But, just for the record, he asked: "Nikolay Mikhailovich, you haven't see any strangers around here, have you?"

"Strangers?" the artist said. "No, no strangers. Only our own."

And officer Svistunov made his way back home along the narrow path through the woods. He ran into no strangers; he ran into no wolves.

Boris Ivanovich came out from behind the stove, where old Nura had been sleeping a childlike slumber; she was herself the size of a child. The men finished off a second bottle of vodka, and afterward drank tea. Then Boris wiped off the table and laid out three piles of his drawings. In one pile there were drawings of the old women's feast, with traces of their conversation. In another there were still lifes, with potatoes and salted cucumbers lying among curious nameless objects of questionable purpose, long ago fallen into desuetude: some sort of tongs, wooden pincers, little shovels, and clay vessels that could either be for drinking, or children's toys. In the third pile, the largest, were pieces of wallpaper covered with drawings on both the front and back. These were the naked old women, their bony protrusions, their sacks and pouches and folds of skin, their wrinkles. Only it wasn't "Hell" of any kind. They were laughing, smiling, guffawing. They were happy—from the hot water, from the ritual bathing.

Nikolay Mikhailovich examined them for a long time, groaned, sniffed, then said drily:

"Boris, I had no idea what a real draughtsman you were. Of course you can't remain here any longer. I don't know what you have in mind, how you intend to live your life further, but I'm taking these drawings with me to Moscow. I'll keep them safe until you return . . ." He smiled. "If I can stay safe myself."

"Do you really think they're any good? I wasn't thinking about that—whether they were good or not. Don't keep them at home, though. Give them to Ilya. Maybe he'll find a place for them," Boris Ivanovich said.

He was very, very happy. Nikolay Mikhailovich was highly respected among artists, known for his severity of judgment and his scant praise.

They left the next day, Nikolay Mikhailovich and his son in the direction of Moscow, Boris Ivanovich in the direction of Vologda.

Boris Ivanovich evaded arrest for four whole years. He had already grown used to the thought that they would catch him in the end, anyway, and he lived recklessly, frivolously, first in the Vologda region, then for three months or so in the city of Tver with the vivacious and full-throated Anastasia. Then, growing bolder, he moved back closer to Moscow and lived in a relative's dacha outside of town. Then it occurred to him: maybe no one was looking for him after all.

His friend Ilya helped him enormously—he kept his entire collection, except for the works he had managed to deliver safely to the West. Everything was going beautifully there. At the end of 1976, an exhibit was organized in Cologne with the title "Russian Nature Laid Bare." The old women, naked and terrible, frolicked. They were enjoying themselves.

And that's when it happened. They caught him, four years after his timely flight.

They only gave him two years, and they came up with an astonishing charge: pornography. They didn't nail him for the anti-Soviet salami, or for the sausage mausoleum, or even for the shocking portrait of the Leader made of ground sausage and holding a cut-off piece of ear on the tines of a fork. No, they nailed him for pornography! Considering that no one had ever been imprisoned in the USSR for pornography, it was some sort of record.

After spending two years in a camp near Arkhangelsk, he was released, and soon after that he emigrated to Europe with his new wife, Raika, a small Jewess, as agile, neat, and compact as a little boat, and somewhat reminiscent of the long-lost Anastasia. Until recently they lived there still.

The lovely Natasha also fared well. While Boris Ivanovich was on the run, she found herself a completely ordinary engineer, with whom she had a daughter of the same Kustodiev-type Boris Ivanovich had once liked. Maria Nikolayevna looked after her granddaughter and prepared their meager meals. She liked her current son-in-law—he was a decent person—but he didn't measure up to Boris Ivanovich!

All the old women in Danilovy Gorki died long ago.

Everything is just as it should be.

THE DELUGE

The girl, it seemed, had called from a pay phone near the entrance to the building, because she was at the door in the space of two minutes.

Ilya had been at their house a few times before her parents were sent to prison, but he either hadn't noticed her, or she hadn't been home at all. Or maybe she had already gone to bed.

Olga was certain that she was seeing the girl for the first time. She had the kind of face one doesn't forget—small and thin, with eyes that were pale and somehow flattened out, and too big for the rest of it, and a tiny nose with a collapsed bridge. A strange physiognomy! Ilya had once mentioned her, saying she had a vicious character, and that no one could handle her. Olga had heard a great deal about her father, Valentin Kulakov, however. He was a Marxist who proclaimed himself to be Marx's true successor, accusing all others who had entrenched themselves within the walls of the Institute of the Workers' Movement and the Institute of Marxism-Leninism to be falsifiers, if not downright traitors.

Olga didn't remember the details about where he had been expelled from, and why, before ending up in prison. He'd branded his enemies by any means available to him; he'd even written letters to the Central

Committee of the Party, but they refused to listen to him. Then Kulakov single-handedly multiplied his battle cries for truth on a government copy machine, and began writing daring and irresponsible letters to the International Communist Party, the Italian branch, or the Austrian—or maybe both at once.

It must be said that the authorities tolerated his escapades for a long time, but when they finally expelled him from the Party and his institute, he became unhinged. He started an underground Marxist magazine and even tried smuggling it abroad, which was completely unacceptable to the authorities. That was when they threw him in prison. At the same time, they imprisoned his wife, Zina, who, though she was all thumbs, somehow copied and bound the publication herself, and was not a whit less dedicated than her husband on an ideological level.

He was, as they say, a foremost specialist on Marx and Engels, and at the institute there weren't many scholars who could measure up to him. Inspired by Marx-Engels, he learned German. His goal was to read the *Paris Manuscripts of 1844* in the original before he died. There was something in them about which Marx didn't speak in his later years. When Hitler came to power, the German socialists had managed to smuggle these manuscripts into Moscow.

"What was the point? They're languishing there under lock and key, and they won't let anyone read them," Valentin complained to Ilya.

Those were the days when Valentin and Ilya communicated most often, usually in the smoking lounges of various libraries. It was also when Ilya visited their home for the first time, and photographed both Valentin and Zina. Olga remembered the photograph—it was in one of the folders of Ilya's archive. They made a funny couple. He had thick hair, parted in the middle and falling in two waves from the top of his head down to his ears. His wife had short, sparse wisps of hair, like a child after a long illness, and a doll-like face.

And now their scruffy daughter, wearing a child's jacket with sleeves too short for her and a threadbare collar, was standing at their door. A medium-size dog with thick, light gray fur, a curlicue tail, and a pleasant expression on its face (unlike his mistress) was sitting next to her obediently. It was a northern breed, a laika. Both the collar and the leash were made of good-quality leather.

"I'm Marina. Did Ilya tell you I was coming?" She kept standing in the doorway without trying to enter.

"Yes, please come in."

Marina made a little sound like a cough, and the dog went through the door ahead of her. The girl was carrying a rucksack.

Ilya came out into the hall and greeted her.

"Sit!" the girl said in a commanding tone. The dog sat and watched its mistress with an expression that seemed to say, Will there be anything else, ma'am?

Marina unhooked the leash and gave it to Ilya.

"Now she'll only go out with you. Not with anyone else. If you say the word, you know, *spazieren* . . . she'll come."

When it heard the German word, it pricked up its ears.

"I see," Olga smiled, "That's a smart dog."

"Hera? Smart? She's a genius. She's a laika. And laikas are the smartest dogs of all."

Olga offered her tea, and then remembered—a child bereft of her family needed to eat! She asked if she wanted something to eat.

"Yes, but I should warn you, I don't eat meat."

What cheek, Olga thought; but Marina smiled, showing her tiny pearl-like teeth, and turned the insolence into a joke.

"Hera and I made a bargain: she'll eat the meat, and I'll eat everything else."

And she launched into a story about what remarkable dogs laikas were, and how they had always had laikas at home, since before the war, because her grandfather had studied the northern peoples, and had brought home their first laika, a puppy, forty years ago, and ever since then . . .

Olga vaguely remembered something about her grandfather, a philologist who was compiling a dictionary of the language of a disappearing northern tribe . . . and then disappeared himself, into the camps.

Marina ate a bowl of kasha. She smeared a thick layer of butter on her bread. Her hands were scratched up, as though she had a litter of kittens in her care rather than a dog. Her fingernails were bitten to the quick. She ate the whole bowl of kasha, four pieces of bread and butter, all the cheese there was, and almost half a pound of smoked sausage, apparently forgetting that she didn't eat meat.

Poor thing, Olga thought, and sprang to her feet.

"Oh, do you like apricot jam?"

It turned out she liked it very much indeed.

The two of them ate more than half a jar of the jam. Then Ilya glanced into the kitchen, where they were eating, and, apparently feeling left out, said:

"What, without me?" Then he ate the rest of it.

Kostya came home from school, and was overjoyed to see the dog; but Marina warned him that it was a real dog, not a toy, and that he couldn't play with it. It would rip him to shreds.

Kostya was very surprised. What was the use of having a dog, then?

Olga grew alarmed—yes, the dog might actually bite her son.

"Not bite him; rip him to shreds," Marina said softly.

The dog was sitting stolidly in the same spot where he had been commanded to sit before they ate.

"Olga, will you give her something for a bed, a place she can lie down?" Marina said with easy familiarity.

After they had finished their tea, Marina said that she had to go out for a little bit. She ordered the dog, "Lie down!" and the dog lay on the old children's blanket Olga had given her.

While the girl was gone, Ilya told Olga about this Valentin Kulakov.

"Strange as it might seem, we have only one thing in common: Stalin. Though he doesn't hate him for the blood, for the Terror, but for trampling his own ideals. Kulakov had a rather complicated multilayered schema of consecutive betrayals: Stalin betrayed Lenin, but Lenin had already distorted Marx, though Marx had some sort of misunderstanding with Hegel, whom Marx didn't altogether understand correctly, at least as Kulakov saw it . . . and for life to unfold and develop as it should, in accordance with the laws of dialectical materialism, everything had to be brought down to a common denominator and adjustments had to be made everywhere, and Stalin had to be exposed as a criminal, an enemy of the idea of socialism. There is a whole group of them who are prepared to walk through fire over some quotation or other from *State and Revolution*."

"Oh, you don't have to explain. It sounds just like my mother."

"No, not at all! She's a completely different breed. She'll believe whatever they order her to believe. But this one uses his own brains; he's seeking the truth, comparing texts and checking them against one another," said Ilya.

"But my mother also believes in something," Olga said, trying to defend her mother's honor.

Ilya snorted dismissively.

"Sure, she believes. In directives issued from above. Everyone knows how she smeared Pasternak!"

Relations between the son-in-law and his mother-in-law were absolutely cut and dried: they felt a profound mutual aversion. Ilya couldn't forgive Antonina for having kicked Pasternak out of the Writers' Union. They had asked her to preside as secretary of that meeting, and she had agreed, whether out of foolishness or vanity— or perhaps fear. What a disgrace!

The mother-in-law couldn't stand her son-in-law, either. She considered him to be unsteady and ill-mannered. His laugh was loud and unpleasant, and even the smell in the WC after his visits there was particularly repulsive to her. "He smells like an animal. Some sort of Jewish smell." And each time she had to go into the WC after him, she would light a wad of newspaper to dispel the odor. "What a stinking stallion my daughter had to go and pick for herself . . ."

Olga, devoted body and soul to her husband, was disconcerted by the emanations of hatred that filled every space her mother and Ilya happened to occupy at the same time, and she tried as hard as she could to neutralize their interactions.

"All right, Ilya, I know all about my mother, it's all hot air. But what about the girl? How can we help her? Maybe the foundation will do something."

The Foundation for the Support of Political Prisoners, run by the most famous prisoner, the most controversial writer, and the most implacable émigré of all, was already transferring his royalties from the

West to Russia, and they were being distributed in the labor camps as food packages. They also went to other destinations as aid to the families of people behind bars, to facilitate their release, and to pay medical bills. And although all the people running the foundation were honest and upright, they were, in the Russian manner, disorganized and lackadaisical. Everything was carried out haphazardly, with blunders and mishaps—letters were mixed up, and money and packages had a habit of falling into the wrong hands. And the authorities weren't asleep at the wheel—Stop, thief!—so the game took on enormous dimensions, involving post offices, messengers, secret codes, and muddles throughout the country.

"Who should they help, if not this girl?" Olga said.

"No, Olga, you don't understand how it works. They do have money, and it's earmarked for the needs of political prisoners and for those who are being released. But, you know how it is, you first need to get the go-ahead from the Classic."

"So you need to get permission for every transfer or handout?"

"Not exactly. As far as I know there is regular distribution of, say, food, and the list of recipients is made up here. It's not monitored over there, but when there is some irregularity, they start asking questions."

"And who's in charge here?"

"What's the difference? Slava, Andrei, Vitya—they're all the same. The people change, but the job gets done. But when it comes to individual disbursements—questions always arise."

"You don't think they'd help a child?"

"How should I know? It's hardly likely the Classic would want to help any Marxists. He hates communism. On the other hand, she is the daughter of political prisoners, so . . ."

"Exactly. Someone needs to help her. I feel very sorry for the girl. She's raggedy, hungry—and she feeds meat to her dog and doesn't buy any for herself . . ."

Marina showed up again toward evening. She brought a "Prague" cake for them.

The vestiges of a good upbringing, Olga thought.

They drank tea together again, and Marina went to change her clothes. She was going to be taking a train trip. When she emerged from the bathroom, Olga gasped. The girl was wearing a light-colored raincoat instead of the child's jacket, and she wore high-heeled boots. Her eyes were made up like she was going to a drinking party in some workers' quarters out in the boondocks.

"You hardly recognize me, right? The watchers won't either. I've tested it out so many times. I go around in these rags on purpose. They're so used to them that when I get dressed up, they look right through me, like I'm not even there. Maybe I could leave this jacket with you?"

She stuffed the jacket, rolled into a ball, into her rucksack, along with her unisex sandals, and put the rucksack under the coatrack.

"Marina, why don't you let me take you to the station?" Ilya suggested.

"No, that wouldn't be right. Why do them any favors?" She shook her head, and her hair divided neatly into two parts. Marina pushed her splayed fingers through her hair, from her forehead to the back of her head, and tucked it under a barrette. Her bangs fell down to her nose. She blew them upward and shook her head.

Ilya looked at her in surprise: still just a kid, but she already understood a thing or two . . .

"Only you should take Hera out for a walk first. The first time while I'm still here, okay?"

Again she showed a remarkable perspicacity for her age. What a girl!

Ilya took the leash from the coatrack and gave the command: *"Let's go for a walk!"* The dog followed him out with a trusting demeanor.

Marina then turned to Olga.

"The thing is, you know, I've never been to Leningrad. One of my friends keeps telling me to come, saying it's great, with the white nights and all. I know the Leningrad scene a little—those guys came here once to visit. They promised they'd give me a place to crash."

How did Marina change her appearance in the space of a few minutes, from a gawky adolescent into a slutty-looking runaway who hangs around train stations? Olga wondered. Then she grew alarmed. *What if she gets lost in the role?* But Marina seemed to read her thoughts.

"Olga, I'm not the one you thought I was at first; or the other one, either. I'm someone else altogether! A third person!" She brayed with laughter. "Or maybe even a fourth . . ."

Without changing her tone, she gave Olga clear-cut instructions.

"I'll leave when they come back. You have to walk her twice a day, early in the morning and later in the evening. Early means about noon. I never get up before then. But you've got to give her a good run. Laikas aren't meant to live inside at all, really. The cold is good for them, and they need to be worked hard. There's a chance I may move away from the city altogether next year. We'll see . . ." And she looked at Olga secretively, as though expecting her to ask more questions, which she wouldn't deign to answer anyway.

But Olga sensed this, and didn't bother asking. She liked this Marina for her independence, but the effrontery of that independence irked her.

Then the girl left, and they all went to bed—Kostya in the little room next to the kitchen, Hera on the blanket by the front door, and Olga and Ilya in the bed of Karelian birch with the ornate headboard. This birch served Olga faithfully in both her first and her second marriage.

The night was not a quiet one. First Olga got the sniffles, then she started coughing. Toward morning, she woke up. Something strange was happening to her: her face felt heavy, and it had become hard to breathe. She prodded Ilya a long time before he would wake up. Then he opened his eyes and sat bolt upright.

"What happened to you?"

"I don't know, I'm having some sort of attack. Maybe we should call the emergency service?"

The medics came very quickly; they were there in only twenty minutes.

And they diagnosed Olga's problem quickly, too. They said it was Quincke's edema. They gave her an injection, sat with her for twenty minutes to make sure that the shot was working, and, before they left, said that it was most likely an allergic reaction to the dog. They should get rid of it immediately!

Olga waited until seven in the morning before calling Tamara and asking her, in a sniffly voice, to come over right away. In their school days it would have taken Tamara five minutes to run from Sobachaya Square to Olga's; now the trip from Molodezhnaya metro station took forty minutes. Tamara didn't deliberate for long, and didn't ask any questions. If Olga needed her, she needed her, and that was that. She quickly got herself ready, and in an hour she was with Olga.

When she entered the apartment she was greeted by a medium-size dog. Well, not exactly greeted—in the hall sat a dog that didn't so much as flick an ear upon the arrival of a guest.

Ilya was the one who greeted her. He took Tamara's raincoat and opened the door to the bedroom, where Olga was. The dog sat by the front door, like a stone carving.

Tamara looked at Olga and gasped.

"What happened?"

"Oh, it's Quincke's edema," Olga said casually. "Listen, Tamara, here's the situation. This is the Kulakovs' dog. You don't know them? No? But you've heard of them, of course? You really haven't? Valentin and Zina Kulakov? No, what does Red Square have to do with it? He's a philosopher, a Marxist, and he published a magazine. It's already been more than a year since they were both sent to prison, and their fifteen-year-old girl was left behind alone. Well, she's sixteen now; but just imagine . . . Thank goodness she wasn't thrown into an orphanage. At first they settled her with her aunt, but the girl has quite a temper. She ran away from her aunt after only a week, and started living by herself. We have some friends in common—not close friends, though. Since the girl was going to Leningrad for a week, our friends asked us if we would take care of the dog for a while. We agreed, naturally. Yesterday she showed up—right off the street. With the dog. And it turns out I'm allergic to dog hair. I guess it's obvious. We could have taken the dog to the dacha, but my mother would never allow it, that's for sure. Mother is from the country, you know, and a dog who lives indoors makes no sense to her. And outside—we don't even have a doghouse! It would run away and get lost. And we're supposed to be taking care of her."

Tamara didn't say anything. She wasn't from the country, and dogs living indoors made perfect sense to her—but she worked in a medical research laboratory, and she observed dogs either in cages, or in an enclosure and a vivarium. They had never kept any pets at home. Tamara's mother was mortally afraid of dogs, and she didn't like cats. When her grandmother was alive, she'd had an old cat named Marquise; but after her grandmother died, there were no more pets.

"So, Tamara, if you'd keep her at your place for the time being— her owner will be back before you know it. The dog's name is Hera."

"While Mama's still at the sanatorium, I'll keep her; but after she comes back, I really can't, Olga," Tamara said, surprisingly unequivocal about the matter.

"But for how long? When is your mother getting back?"

"In three days," Tamara said firmly.

Olga sniffed, and kissed Tamara's tight little curls.

"You're so dependable, Tam. You and Galya—there's no one else like you two. If you can just keep the dog until your mother gets back, we'll think of something by then."

"Maybe you could ask Galya? Maybe she'll take the dog?" Her eyes showed a glimmer of hope.

"As if! It's not just any old dog; it's a dissident dog! You might even say a Marxist dog! Take a dog like that into a KGB agent's den?" Olga laughed in what was almost her normal sonorous voice. "And besides, Galya's on vacation."

Transporting the dog was problematic. Hera was determined not to get into Ilya's car. She sat next to the open door with an imperturbable expression on her face, her translucent yellow eyes staring off into the distance. They were about to give up and take the metro when Tamara had an idea.

"Ilya, get into the car first, then command her to get in."

"Clever!" Ilya said. He got behind the wheel and, patting the seat next to him, said: "Lie down!"

The dog's eyes expressed momentary hesitation, but she stood up, sprang lightly into the front seat, and lay down, extending her paws out in front of her. Then she sighed, just like a human. The dog clearly didn't have enough room, but the look on her face showed only dignified submission.

Tamara sat in the backseat, and they drove off.

In the evening Tamara called Olga to say that the dog had run away. She had broken loose from Tamara's grasp, leash and all, and taken off.

Tamara had searched long and hard through the neighboring court-yards, asking all the dog owners whether they had seen the laika, to no avail. The next day they posted flyers around the neighborhood, and near the Molodezhnaya metro station. Then they waited. No one responded to their announcement.

In the meantime, Ilya had met with the director of the foundation and asked whether they could help a girl whose parents were in the camps. The director promised to look into it.

Three days later, early in the morning, Marina rang the doorbell.

Olga immediately told her about the missing dog. Marina sat down on the floor in the hall and put her face in her hands. Only when she took her hands away did Olga notice that her whole face was covered in red spots.

"Good God, what's wrong with you? Is it an allergy?" Olga said.

"No. I need a bath. I shouldn't have bothered going there. It's caused nothing but trouble." Marina sniffled, and rushed into the bathroom without taking off her raincoat.

She ran the water a long time, until Kostya woke up. He had to brush his teeth and get ready for school. Olga knocked on the bath-room door; it opened right away. Skinny as a fish skeleton, her body covered with red marks, scratches, and bruises, Marina stood there in front of Olga in her wet bra and underwear. All her clothes were float-ing in the bathtub, and the surface of the water was full of small, dark red globs. Heavens above, they were bedbugs!

Olga told Kostya to wash in the kitchen. She hurriedly fed him breakfast and sent him off to school. She found a nightgown for Marina to put on.

"Let's have some coffee."

Ilya was on a trip. If he had been home, they probably wouldn't have been able to spend this time together. They were like sisters: Olga the elder one, and Marina, confused and nearly eaten alive by bedbugs, the younger one.

"The first night was just an orgy of drunkenness. My friend was there, too—what a pig! He begged and begged for me to come, and

then, in the middle of the night, he went off with some girl and left me
alone with these complete strangers. In the morning I went out with
them to walk around town in the cold and rain. We were drinking
vodka in little dives and bars, and then we bought some kind of pastries
to eat and just wandered around all day. No one invited me to stay overnight. My friend had disappeared altogether. I called him at home, and
they told me they hadn't seen him for a whole week. What could I do?
I went to the train station, but they were completely out of tickets. I
called another girl, a friend of a friend, and she invited me to hang out
with her. I waited in the station for three hours before she showed up.
She looked like an awful person, but I went with her anyway.

"She took me to Saigon, some sort of café, like our Molodezhnaya.
I liked it there, and I got to know another bunch of people. We went to
Peterhof, outside the city, and wandered around there for two days. I
ran out of money. Everyone sort of left one by one, until there were
just two guys and me left. They took me to the university dormitories,
which were empty, since it's summer break, except for some sketchy
types, petty thugs and all that. Well, we ended up crashing there, sharing a room. I'm going to skip the next part, since I don't want to trau-
matize you. Right up until it happened, I didn't realize what was going
on; but I didn't scream. Why should I scream? It was my own fault. I
should have known I was just asking for trouble. And I got it. Well, I
tried to struggle a bit, but those guys were hefty, they pinned me down.
Then I just collapsed, like I was dead. To be honest, I was drunk. That
night I woke up feeling like I had been scalded with boiling water.
And it was light outside—those goddamn white nights and all that. It
was so disorienting. And I love the nighttime. But there, it's like there's
no real day or night, like some weird twilight, twenty-four/seven. And
my whole body was burning, like it was on fire. And then my eyes almost popped out of my head—the walls were covered with polka dots,
and the dots were moving toward me! I look down—and I'm covered
in bedbugs! I've never seen anything like it in my life. It was a swarm
of them, a whole army! There was no place to wash, just one small sink
in the WC at the end of the hall. Somehow I managed to get ready to
go. I noticed that one of the guys had left, and the other was still passed
out in the room. I went through his pockets and took all the money he

had on him. I thought it would be enough for a ticket; and even for two. Surprised? Yeah. Well, that's how it happened. Just like that. Which one of them screwed me, I wondered, this one or the other? Then I thought—both of them, most likely. I didn't remember. Anyway, what's the difference? So I split. Straight to the commuter train, then to the train station. There were no tickets, but I bribed the conductor, and she let me stay in her own little compartment in the front of the wagon. I slept the whole way. I kept scratching like a pig, though, I've got to admit. I only realized just now that the bedbugs had hidden in the lining of my raincoat, and crawled out on the sly to bite me. Don't worry, though. I drowned all of them, poured scalding water over them. Olga, what's wrong? Why are you crying? Don't, please, or I'll start crying, too. And now Hera's gone!"

Her tears streamed down her cheeks to her little chin. Olga and Marina grabbed hold of each other and cried in each other's arms. Their tears were as heady and salty as blood.

"Never mind, never mind, everything will turn out all right," Olga whispered. "We'll find Hera. Your parents will be released. Everything will be fine . . ."

Marina, who had quieted down a bit, began howling again.

"Fine? What could be fine about it? Those idiots will come back, and everything will start all over again. They're crazy, they belong in the loony bin, not in prison! The only good thing about my life is that they're not in it. I was ten years old the first time I ran away from home. I couldn't have told you why back then. But now I know why. They don't need me! I only get in their way. All the other kids had normal lives, but all I had were endless meetings and conversations in the kitchen. Marx, Lenin, Lenin, Marx! I hate them. I don't know how I'm going to survive now. But when they get out of prison, it will be the end . . ."

The coffee had long since grown cold.

"Warm it up, okay?" Marina said.

"I'll put on a fresh pot."

"Are you nuts? Just warm up this one. Have you got any cigarettes?"

Olga didn't smoke. Even after all her years together with Ilya, she had never taken up smoking. She looked around to see whether Ilya had left any behind. They drank the old, warmed-up coffee, then put on another pot. Olga wanted to keep Marina at home with her, but she couldn't. Her mother was going to spend the night at home, since she had scheduled some medical tests at the Writers' Union polyclinic that morning.

"I'll go home with you," Olga said. They got on the number 15 trolleybus and took it to Tsvetnoy Boulevard, where the Kulakov family lived on the first floor of a three-story building in the courtyard of the former Trubnaya Square.

The misfortunes didn't end there that day. When they arrived at Marina's, they found there was no electricity in the building. It was plunged in darkness, and there was a powerful stench. The wooden floor was full of puddles. When they entered the building, the door slammed shut with a bang.

"Olga, hold the door open, I can't see a thing."

Marina peered into the darkness: the door to her apartment had been forced, and a notice was stuck to the door frame.

"The KGB has been here again, Olga."

They went inside. Marina flicked the light switch—nothing. The whole apartment was underwater. It was clear that the flood had occurred several days ago already, because they could see where the water level had receded. Swollen books floated like victims of drowning. And the stench was commensurate with a disaster area.

Quite unexpectedly, Marina started laughing. Olga looked up in alarm: Had the girl suddenly lost her mind?

"Look, Olga! The four lower shelves of books are soaked! The water came all the way up to here! The divan is soaking wet—so are the pillows and the blanket! What a stroke of luck! Too bad it wasn't a fire! No, a deluge is way better! Olga, we're going to toss everything out right this minute. Get rid of everything! Everything the KGB didn't take! Plato! Aristotle! Hegel! And everything in German, too! And Karly-Marly! And Engels!"

She rushed over to the shelves and started pulling everything off, both the wet and the completely dry volumes, and they fell into the shallow, fetid water with a weighty plop, joining scraps of pictures, pieces of wallpaper, and little vases . . .

"'Over the gray expanse of sea, wind gathers the storm clouds. / Between the storm clouds and the sea the stormy petrel soars like black lightning! / Now with his wing he grazes the whitecaps, now like an arrow surges toward the clouds. / He screeches, and the storm clouds hear the joy of the bird's bold cries!'"

In clothes that were not her own (Olga's black sweater and trousers held up by Ilya's belt), given to her after the bedbug death bath, Marina swept through the apartment like a fury, throwing books from the shelves and yelling:

"'In his cries is the storm's wild thirst! In his cries the storm clouds hear / the power of his rage, the flame of passion, and sure victory! / Let the tempest rage and roil!' Fuck it, Olga, I'm a *Wunderkind*! Didn't you know? I've read every one of these books. I've even read Plato's *Republic*! I read Aristotle at fourteen! I never read Hegel, but I read the *Communist Manifesto*! Fuck it! It's the deluge! Finally, the flood has come! I'm going to throw everything out and renovate the whole apartment. All by myself! I'll scrub everything down, I'll whitewash it! Everything will be just like new, white and clean!"

Olga realized that this was exactly what would happen, and she started taking all the sodden books down to the garbage heap. The blue Lenin, and the red Stalin, and all the historical materialism, and the dialectical materialism, and the political economy . . . everything.

"Along with the bedbugs! We have them, too, you know! Not as many as in Peterhof—but plenty of them!" Marina shouted.

And Olga grew suddenly happy herself. This is it, the real *Fathers and Sons*! The Kulakovs would be released—Valentin in two years, Zina in a year. Then they would have three years of exile, and return home. And their lives would be pure and white.

Just one thing remained unclear—how she would survive all those years, this passionate, bold, desperate girl, covered with bedbug bites, raped by a pair of alcoholics, pitiless toward herself, pitiless toward her parents . . . a tender girl-child.

On her third run down to the garbage, a huge bin hammered together any which way out of rough boards, Olga discovered a medium-size dog sitting there. It was Hera. She had come back home, all the way from Molodezhnaya Station to Tsvetnoy Boulevard. A true dissident dog.

HAMLET'S GHOST

Ilya brought home a pass for the dress rehearsal a day before the opening night. Alik, a lighting technician at the theater and a longtime friend of Ilya's, got it for him. Getting a ticket for the premiere was out of the question—there wasn't a single seat left. The pass was for one person only. For Olga. Olga was beaming with delight.

The performance was for close friends and family, and the hall was filled to the rafters; people even crammed into the aisles. But the first two rows were nearly empty. They were reserved for the creators: Lyubimov, as magnificent as a commander going into battle, who was himself cut out for the role of a bold king, or a dastardly villain, or even the Lord Almighty; the gloomy artist with a wide, froglike mouth; the wiry young composer; the assistant director; and several other people of indeterminate function or position.

As she entered the hall, Olga felt a cold thrill of ecstasy, as though she were about to sit for an important examination. Everything seemed magnified, writ large with capital letters: Theater, Director, Hamlet, Shakespeare, and Vysotsky himself. She sat down in the next to the last row, on the side, and she swiveled her head around, craning her neck, because watching the audience was an integral part of the event—the spectators were personalities in their own right, and appeared almost beautiful on those grounds alone. Suddenly, she felt a hand on her shoulder, and heard a thick, pleasant voice say her name, half-questioning:

"Olga?"

She turned around. There was something familiar about the portly figure with an Eastern countenance.

"Karik? Mirzoyan?" She felt glad to see her former classmate, forgetting for the first moment that he was responsible for getting her expelled first from the Komsomol, and then from the university. Yes, in precisely that order.

He seemed to melt from happiness, and Olga understood immediately: *He thinks I've forgotten. And so I had, at first. Oh, what does it matter!*

Just then, the earth-brown curtain began to sway, then floated upward, raising a cloud of dust. Everything went still, and, suddenly, there was Vysotsky-Hamlet, a smallish figure wearing what looked like a black leotard. From the depths of the stage, not looking at the audience, he spoke, as though to himself:

"The din dies down. I enter from the wings . . ."

She felt goose bumps along her arms, her spine. And that's how it was until the very close, everything unfolded as though in a single breath, and the words of Pasternak's translation seemed newly fledged, as though they were being heard for the first time.

Olga completely forgot about Karik, and when she ran into him in the crush at the coat check, she was again taken by surprise to see him.

"Olga, you haven't changed a bit," said the heavyset, Eastern-looking man with a bald pate, smiling at her. He had liked Olga very much during their student days. He had even wanted to ask her out, but back then she had been completely out of his league. His fortunes had risen considerably, however. Now he found her even more attractive than he had in his youth. Her face was mottled with tears, her eyes were shining. She seemed as fragile as a young girl. In his youth he had preferred shapely women; the wife he had chosen was as spherical as a snowman. But recently Karik had developed an interest in just this kind of woman—fragile and shining. Very rare birds.

He took the tag out of her hand and fetched her coat for her. It was a jacket with a hood, too light for the season.

"I'll walk you home," he said, announcing rather than offering. She nodded.

"Thank you."

He took her by the arm.

"Shall we go straight to the metro, or walk a bit? You won't get too cold? You're very lightly dressed."

"I won't get cold. My father's from Vologda, I've got a hardy northern constitution."

"And I'm from Baku. I've been in Moscow for so many years, but I still can't get used to the winter."

"Oh, what a play! Absolutely brilliant. I love the Taganka Theater anyway, more than the Sovremennik. I don't even know what to compare it to, it was just . . . words fail me."

They walked a long time. From the Taganka they went to Kotelniki, crossed the streetcar tracks next to Ustinsky Bridge, and then went down Solyanka Street, talking all the while about Lyubimov, about Vysotsky, and about contemporary art, which was the only thing that breathed and moved in their stultifying existence.

Karik echoed her sentiments, then turned the conversation to more mundane topics: What, how, with whom?

"The same as before, only with a different husband."

"What about a job?"

"Hmm, that's more difficult. I have to chase around to find work, of course. I don't go to an office—I write reports, teach a bit, do some translation."

"Oh, what languages do you know? French, wasn't it?" Karik said.

"My French is decent; I can do simultaneous interpreting, and written translation. My Spanish isn't as good, but it's passable. And my most recent love is Italian. It's more like music than like language. I'm teaching myself. I mastered it in about a year. But you know how it is—I don't have steady work; it's either feast or famine."

"Do you know Spanish Spanish, or Cuban Spanish?" he said.

"My Spanish is Spanish," she said, and sighed. "But I don't have a diploma, Karik. Perhaps you recall that I was expelled in my fifth year?"

Karik laughed.

"How could I forget, when I'm the one who caused it. I was the

Komsomol organizer, and I was just in the process of getting admitted to the Party. You understand what I mean—I was about to defend my thesis, but I don't have five languages under my belt, like you do. In fact, I've always had problems with languages. Armenian is my native language, and I know some Azerbaijani from playing with other kids in the neighborhood. I learned Russian at school. And also in the neighborhood. But we Caucasians can never get rid of our accents. I'll be honest with you, I worked in England for a year, but nothing helped. They couldn't make a spy out of me."

"Well, never mind. You still became a good KGB man, didn't you?" Olga said, laughing.

"Olga, didn't your father work in the same capacity?" Karik said, smiling, not in the least put out by her comment.

"No, my father is a military man, in the construction department. He's retired now. My mother is active in the Party, though."

"Yes, I remember that someone in your family had a high position. My grandfather was a shepherd, and my father baked *lavash* at the market. There were eight of us children at home. Do you sense the difference?"

Olga felt uncomfortable. She did sense the difference between his background and hers.

"But I can help you out with work. I'm an administrative officer at the Writer's Union, on the Foreign Committee. I can't get you a staff position, but I can set you up with some freelance jobs. Our translator just resigned—you must know her, she was from your year: Irina Troitskaya. There is a Latin American writer arriving in two weeks. He's already almost a classic. The job will involve travel to either Leningrad or Tashkent. You'll have to accompany him, attend meetings with him, and so on. Would you be up to that? You won't let me down?"

Oh, so he does have a conscience after all! He's trying to make up for past sins.

They had already made their way to Dzerzhinsky Square. Olga was cold, and wanted to take the metro. He walked her to the entrance and they parted ways. They didn't exchange phone numbers.

Karik called her two days later, after Olga had already forgotten about their conversation. She still remembered everything about *Hamlet*, though; she couldn't stop talking about it. In fact, all of Moscow was abuzz with it. It was the premiere of the season, a major event. Everyone was in a hurry to see it, because Lyubimov's productions were always getting shut down, or even banned during rehearsals.

Karik asked her to stop by his office on the same day. Olga was just three minutes away by foot if she went through the main entrance. Even less if she went by way of the courtyard.

He was wearing a striped suit. Olga could tell immediately that it had been made by the Writer's Union tailor. His tie was also striped. Later, when they went down to the cafeteria, and he sat down, crossing one leg over the other, she noticed that his socks were striped, too. But she held her tongue and refrained from making any cutting remarks about it to herself, reminding herself again: his grandfather was a shepherd, and his father baked bread at a market . . .

"There will be two of them. One a writer, and the second a professor, both of them very well known. The writer is from Colombia, and the professor is Spanish. We'll draw up a part-time contract; I'll give you all the necessary instructions, and then we're good to go! They should arrive on February first."

That day there was a big hullabaloo at the Foreign Committee. The day before, they had received a West German poet, a young leftist who enjoyed great renown. It was a farewell party for him, since he was flying back to West Germany that evening. The writer, whose face had a provocative SS pallor, had been flown to a writers' conference in Baku. There he started an affair with the daughter of his translator, and now the entire Foreign Committee was at sixes and sevens.

On the previous evening, this young whippersnapper of a girl, whom he had brought along with him to the official farewell ceremony, had stuck to him like a burr. At the end, he sat her on his bony, five-foot-tall knee. Her mother, herself a poet and a recipient of the Stalin Prize, had translated his "Mayakovskian" verse into Russian from someone else's literal crib. Her face was an unhealthy beet-red color, and she was pretending not to notice anything.

In view of these upsetting circumstances, no one paid any attention to Olga. Olga, by the way, knew the daughter of this translator very well, first from the exclusive Artek Pioneer Camp, where privileged children of prominent parents were sent, then from the

Peredelkino dacha settlement for writers, and finally from the philological department.

Karik came back, accompanied by an older woman with a dissatisfied expression on her face.

"Olga, this is Vera Alekseevna, the goddess of our accounting department. She'll give you money for expenses and will explain everything. Come to see me afterward."

The following ten days shook up Olga's world and turned it inside out. The writer, a robust, bearded fellow, looked like a cross between Hemingway and Fidel Castro. He greeted her effusively, with a phrase Olga didn't understand until later:

"O Madonna! I thought we'd be in the care of some KGB agent, but they've sent us an angel instead! Too bad there's only one of you for both of us!"

Olga thrust a small, businesslike hand at him, and he kissed her on the forehead. The professor looked on disapprovingly, refusing to get into the act.

Olga took them to the Metropol Hotel in an official car. In the lobby, she asked them whether they needed anything, and handed them two folders and two envelopes with small sums of money for expenses. She asked them to put their signatures on some documents.

The writer whispered something into the professor's ear. He turned green and whispered back something that Olga couldn't make out. The only word she understood was *mierda*—shit.

The writer guffawed, and gently nudged the professor in the stomach with his elbow. Olga filled out the necessary paperwork at the reception desk, and they received their keys.

"I'll wait for you here, and then we'll go have dinner."

Olga sat on a velvet couch by the wall and reflected on the situation. It was all quite exciting, but she shouldn't have taken the job. It was ridiculous, sitting here and waiting like a servant, at their beck and call. There was something humiliating about it.

The first to come down was the bearded one. He immediately dispelled all these thoughts.

He smiled amicably, and bent down to her confidingly.

"Did you notice what a long face the other guy pulled? I told him that these were payouts from the KGB! And we had to sign that we had taken the dough. He's such a square, I love teasing him now and then."

Ten minutes later the professor came down. They went to a restaurant. The guests were agog at the decorative plasterwork and the abundance of mirrors, and the writer clucked his tongue, saying:

"Real Communist luxury!"

He turned out to be quite a glutton, ordering hors d'oeuvres, and soup, and two main dishes. He polished off one and a half bottles of wine, and demanded to know all about the local cuisine. The professor was more low-key, and looked tired. After dinner, the writer asked Olga to take them straight to Red Square.

"I wouldn't mind walking around a bit, either," the professor said.

"It's nearby, just a few minutes' walk from here," Olga said.

"No, in your case I'd advise against it. I was here in 1957, at the Youth Festival. There's a national custom—you can only approach the mausoleum on your knees."

The professor was filled with alarm, and started waving his arms.

"No, no, no, Pablo, I won't go. I'll stay in the hotel room."

Olga immediately picked up on the fact that this was a practical joke. The writer winked at her, as if urging her to get into the spirit of things. Which she did.

"No, they changed that custom! You don't have to approach on your knees anymore. That's only for the true diehards . . ."

The writer guffawed. The professor shook his head and started to laugh.

"Oh, go to hell! I should have known, you're always . . . me . . ." Olga didn't catch the expression, but she understood the gist of it.

The schedule was grueling. Every day there were two meetings with other writers, breakfasts, lunches, and dinners, trips to the Bolshoi and the Tretyakov Gallery. And with each passing day, the writer seemed to grow more bored, as though he had expected something completely different from this trip.

Then they went to Leningrad. In Leningrad, the writer cheered up. He had never been there before, and he was delighted with the city, which he justifiably compared with Amsterdam and (though it was a stretch) Venice.

Olga was unable to offer any views on the matter, since all cities beyond the boundaries of the USSR existed primarily in the realm of her imagination, as a literary mirage, while this South American writer from some banana republic in the back of beyond was a citizen of the world. He had studied in Paris and New York, and had traveled throughout Europe. He ate and drank copiously wherever he went, read and wrote whatever he wanted, and lived life to the hilt, everywhere, without respite. Even the "snain," the snow mixed with rain that fell unabated the whole time they were in Leningrad, pleased him. In the morning, in the corridor of the hotel, Olga noticed a powerfully built hooker, with the face of a grenadier, leaving his room.

It's none of my business, she thought on her way to the elevator.

The last stop on their itinerary was Tashkent. The journey was exhausting, with a layover and a delay The airports were freezing. Finally, they arrived at their destination. When they came out of the airport, it was dawn, and the air was warm. The sun was floating up over the horizon, right in front of their eyes.

Olga had never been to Central Asia, and she had long wanted to see this part of the world. Ilya was very partial to it. They had planned to travel here together, but it had never worked out. The Baltic countries were as far as they had gone together.

Unfortunately, they didn't get a chance to see anything. They flew out of Tashkent on the evening of the following day, hastily and under a cloud.

On the first morning, they were taken to a government building in the style of Stalinist barracks and ushered into a long hall with a table covered in Central Asian dishes. Along the entire length of the table, on both sides, sat middle-aged men in identical suits and ties— the Eastern men with skullcaps, the non-Eastern men without. It was a warm, almost hot February day, and the hall smelled of last year's sweat. The reception was a red-carpet welcome; Party heads, municipal authorities.

Evidently there had been some kind of misunderstanding. For

some reason the local bigwigs thought they were receiving a government delegation from a friendly nation.

Chile, Peru, Colombia—they were all the same to the Party functionaries. They had a job to do. And their job consisted in making speeches.

From the very start of the first speech, Olga fell into despair: it was untranslatable. Olga leaned over to Pablo and told him this. He nodded and requested that she recite some Russian poetry—the sounds of the Russian language were very pleasant to his ear, and he easily committed the sounds to memory.

"All right, I'll recite *Eugene Onegin*, Pushkin's novel in verse."

And Olga launched into a recitation from memory, echoing the cadences and intonations of the orator's words. She inserted pauses and line breaks that coincided with the periods of speech and the expression of the orators.

Pablo grew tired by the fourth chapter. The professor looked like he was about to fall into a dead faint.

"All right, that's it. This nonsense has to stop. José, I beg you, play along with me, just this once!" said the writer.

When the next (but not meant to be the last) orator had finished making his speech and everyone was clapping, Pablo jumped from his place of honor, pulling his comrade, who was balking, and Olga, who needed no coaxing, in his wake. He stopped next to the tribune, festooned with red plush, and intoned in a deep, sonorous voice:

"In my homeland, we have the custom of singing a song of gratitude to our friends. And so I will sing you our favorite song, which Christopher Columbus brought to America from Spain five hundred years ago."

And he began to sing. The song was "La Macorina," a top-ten pop hit that had not yet reached Moscow, not to mention Tashkent. He galloped around, flailing his arms and pulling José toward him. This time, weary of the role that had been forced on him of older and wiser friend, an easy target for mockery, José gave himself over completely to the singer's instructions.

The refrain of the song, "Put your hand on me here, Macorina!," was repeated about ten times, during which Pablo placed José's hand on various parts of his body, gradually inching toward the locus of maximum masculine vulnerability.

When he had finished his performance, Pablo raised his clenched fist in an archaic gesture completely unknown in this part of the world, and said to Olga, "And now, translate! Long live the teachings of Marx-Engels-Lenin-Stalin! Proletarians of the world, unite!"

And he began applauding himself, after which the skullcaps, completely baffled, joined in good-naturedly. Next to Olga stood the official who was responsible for leading receptions at the highest level. His face was as pale as it was possible for a face burned day after day by the Central Asian sun to be, and he whispered:

"Olga Afanasievna! What is the meaning of this? What is he doing? It's our heads that will roll for this! He's ruining the entire event!"

"Olga, tell him that we are leaving today. Have him change the tickets. Tell him to go to hell, that we have a meeting tomorrow at the highest levels!" The Colombian writer rolled his eyes in indignation, and, inflating his fleshy cheeks so that his thick mustache twitched, he blew out a stream of air. "Say whatever you want!"

Olga translated.

"What about Central Asia? You were so eager to see it."

"I've seen enough. Screw it!"

"We haven't booked a hotel room in Moscow for tonight!" Olga put forth a rational argument against their headlong departure, but Pablo would have none of it.

"We'll sleep in your kitchen!"

"Are you crazy, what do you mean, sleep in my kitchen?"

He looked around; fifteen or so functionaries stood around, uncomprehending but expectant.

"Our guests would like to express their deepest apologies, but they must fly out today, since tomorrow the Central Committee of the Party will be receiving them."

"This is an outrage! Does he have any idea what he is doing?" the official in charge whispered to Olga.

The final scene took place three days later, when Olga handed in the record of expenses to the accountant. The telephone rang.

"Karik Avetisovich would like to see you," the accountant told Olga.

Karik was sitting behind his desk with an imperious air:

"Would you care to explain to me what happened there?"

Olga told him, being honest and forthright about it.

"Um-hmm. Well, take out a piece of paper and write a report."

"Another report? I already submitted one."

"That was a financial report. This one's for the KGB," Karik said coldly.

"What do you mean?" Olga said indignantly. "I won't write any report! We agreed."

"What did we agree?"

Olga put her head in her hands. What a fool she was! Now she would have to write a report, compromising her good name forever. This was how informers were born.

From her purse she fished out the sizable packet of money she had just received from the accountant. A clear conscience was worth more to her.

"Let's just agree that I never worked here. Here's my honorarium. Case closed."

"Let's go out and get some fresh air, the weather's nice," Karik said, pointing at the ceiling with his thumb.

Ah, so even you are afraid of listeners! Olga thought spitefully.

They went out without talking. She went first, and he followed behind her. They crossed Vorovsky Street, and turned into the first courtyard they saw on Trubnikovsky Lane. They sat down on a bench.

"What are you afraid of? These are the rules of the game, and you have to play by them. The main thing is to remain a decent person. I've never harmed anyone in my life. I've helped many. But always playing by the rules."

Olga cursed herself under her breath: *Idiot! Cretin! Sellout!*

"But this Pablo has different rules, doesn't he? Yes, he says he's a Communist; but he fell out with all the others back home, and there are no consequences for him. He's not afraid, because no one beat him up, no one tried to kill him. But my family had to flee Turkey; all the Armenians there were slaughtered. Do you want to know what really happened? The rich all escaped, and the poor remained. Money saved their lives. Now it won't save them anymore. Now it's only the authorities who can protect you and save your life. Who is this Pablo, anyway? He's an ordinary hooligan, a con man. Morally corrupt. That's a fact! He's been married three times; he took prostitutes to his room in Leningrad! If you didn't see it, you don't have to report it! Politically, he's sound, yes. But what kinds of sounds does he make? He hops around onstage, singing little ditties! Am I right or not? So that's what you write—"hops around, singing little ditties." Just stick to the facts. Well, maybe you don't have to report the whole story, but you have to be truthful. Am I too ideological? Ideological, yes, I admit—but I don't betray my friends. You're silent; you're thinking about how I had you expelled from the Komsomol? The mistake was your own. Why did you get mixed up in defending your professor, why did you sign the petition? He broke the rules, he set everyone up! How many people lost their jobs because of him, just like that . . . and where did he come from? You probably don't know this, but he was working for us. He'd been working for us since the fifties! He wrote reports I've seen them with my own eyes. I swear by my own mother! And where is he now?"

Olga knew that rumors like this had been making the rounds. She shrugged; she didn't know.

"He's been released, and is living in Paris! Because those are the rules—you can't betray your own kind. They punished him so that justice would be served, then let him go. And so many are sitting in prison because of him to this very day! He's a scoundrel! I have no respect for him whatsoever. You should be thankful that they stopped you before it was too late. I have no idea, perhaps at this very moment your beloved Pablo is sitting somewhere writing a report about how he was received, about who said what to whom. Because everyone lives by rules, and that's the most important one: live by the rules."

He actually means what he's saying; he's staked his life on it. Poor guy, he could have been selling vegetables or carpets somewhere—but he got caught up in all this, and this is the result. Olga observed his deeply flushed face. He wiped the sweat off his forehead, though here, on this snowy bench, it was anything but warm.

"I don't need anything from you but a report. You were in such-and-such a place, you saw this, you said that. And that José is a sly one, too. His brother's family lives in Russia. His brother died in the Spanish Civil War, and his nephews were evacuated, ending up here. He saw them in Moscow. You didn't know that? Well, I'm not asking you to write about anything you haven't seen with your own eyes. And a man came to see him in the hotel before their departure. You didn't see him? It was his nephew. José brought money for him, and gave him his own things. You didn't see anything? I'm not telling you—write that . . ."

So they knew everything. José hadn't concealed the fact that his nephews lived in Russia. Olga had even called one of his nephews at his request. Pablo had organized this whole trip to take his Spanish friend to Russia to visit his relatives.

But Karik was telling her in no uncertain terms that he knew that she knew, and that he was not requiring her to divulge everything she knew in the report.

"Let's go. You'll just write one page, relating exactly what happened. Whatever you consider necessary. I won't give you any more work if you don't want it. If you do, I'll keep you in mind. But you have to write a report."

They walked down the empty corridor to Karik's office. Everyone had already left. And no one saw her. And no one ever found out about anything. But the main thing was that Ilya should never find out.

A GOOD TICKET

By the time she was thirty, Lyudmila had come to terms with being an old maid, and even found many advantages to this state. Her married girlfriends, having given birth to children and now divorced, or joylessly bearing all the burdens of running a household, did not inspire envy in her. The years when she wanly expected first a prince, then some kind of lover, any kind at all, and, finally, just a decent man had given way to a measured, rather tedious, but completely calm existence.

Ilya had appeared gradually. She began to recognize his lanky figure and curly head of hair among dozens of regular readers at the library. Glances of recognition were replaced with nods. Once, right before the library closed, they ran into each other next to the cloakroom, and they went out together—unintentionally. They went toward the metro, conversing politely. They exchanged names: Lyudmila, Ilya.

Six months later, Ilya walked Lyudmila home. She was lugging five rather thick books home for her father. He was an academic—not a bona fide one, in Ilya's view, since he was an agronomist. Lyudmila's family also lived in the vicinity of Timiryazevsky Academy, which took an hour to reach by bus from the Novoslobodskaya metro station. It turned out that they lived not in an ordinary building or house but in a large old dacha, built at the end of the nineteenth century for the agriculture professors.

It was already late evening. The buses had abandoned their routes, heading back to the bus depot for the night, and Lyudmila suggested that Ilya stay the night. The professor, never having lost his rural habit of turning in early and rising at the crack of dawn, had gone to bed long before. Nanny Klava, who had raised Lyudmila after her mother died when Lyudmila was still a child, had left that day on a visit to her sister. If Nanny Klava had stayed home that day, things might have gone in quite another direction.

After a simple meal, which was served in the dining room—featuring a small table for the samovar, a sideboard with colored glass, an étagère, and napkins—Lyudmila showed Ilya to the divan, pointed out where the bathroom was, and left him, wishing him good night. After some time, she returned with a towel.

"I forgot to give you this," Lyudmila said, smiling.

She had already changed for the night, and was wearing a blue flannel robe, from under which peeped a blue nightgown with a fancy ruffle. She had already loosened her hair from its bun, and her messy plait fell against her chest when she bent over to place the towel on a chair next to the divan. The light from the full moon, blue and intense, the gleaming snowdrifts outside the window, and the old-fashioned coziness (*Like an aristocratic home*, Ilya thought in passing) awakened romantic impulses in him. He pulled Lyudmila toward him, and she clung to him compliantly.

In the morning, Ilya left, not in the least troubled about the adventures of the previous night. At the end of the week, he met Lyudmila in the library, then accompanied her to Timiryazevka. Again he stayed overnight. Nanny Klava was absent, as before.

They were not having a relationship. That, at least, was Ilya's view of the matter; and he knew a thing or two about romantic entanglements, falling in love often with pretty girls, and even enjoying a reputation among his friends as a skilled ladies' man and seducer. But in this case, getting the girl—unprepossessing, and already wilting, without ever having bloomed, it seemed—did not require any effort. She fell out of the blue into his embrace.

Ilya had no thought that these chance meetings, devoid of any festive brightness or intensity, would turn into a dull but tolerable marriage.

In the third year of their uninspired relationship, Lyudmila got pregnant. She was thirty-four years old, ten years older than Ilya. They registered their marriage not long before the birth of their child—and, it must be said, without any special urging on Lyudmila's part. When Ilya suggested they should get married, she was not over the moon with joy, which disappointed him somewhat: he was rather proud of his noble gesture.

After the birth of their child—named Ilya, whether after his magnanimous father or after Ilya Ivanovich, his indifferent grandfather, the professor—Ilya moved in with Lyudmila more or less for good. He even moved the most valuable part of his book collection out to the dacha. Nanny Klava, whose small room was right next to Lyudmila's, did not give it up for the young husband. He was given a room on the second floor, which was rather chilly, but spacious.

Lyudmila was in charge of some sort of agronomy research laboratory. She had long before finished her master's thesis and qualifying exams, and would have gotten her doctorate had it not been for her pregnancy. But the baby, although quiet and uncomplaining, and almost wholly in the care of Nanny Klava, seemed to sap Lyudmila's enthusiasm for science, and she never managed to defend her dissertation.

Ilya grew to like living at Lyudmila's more and more. The city was encroaching on one side of the dacha community, but on the other side it was adjoined by fields for research experiments. Beyond that stretched Timiryazevsky Park, with its ancient lime trees and avenues of pine, its ponds and old feeding troughs for hoofed wildlife, which hadn't been seen in those parts for a long time already.

Sometimes Ilya would stay home without going anywhere for a whole week; then he would leave for several days. Lyudmila never asked him to account for his comings and goings, neither did she ask him for money. He would arrive, and she seemed happy; he would leave, and she didn't reproach him. She simply asked him to warn her beforehand, if possible.

The boy took after Ilya, with his curly hair and narrow face. He rarely cried, and rarely smiled. Ilya thought the child had inherited his mother's character. By the time he was three, they began noticing peculiarities in him. He had a large passive vocabulary, and had even learned by heart some difficult poems that they read to him. But when they would ask him, "Do you want it?," he would answer "You want it." Nanny Klava thought he was fine, and the only unusual thing about him was that he was smarter than other children, and that he was destined to become an academic. By the time he was five, he could recite all of Pushkin's rhymed fairy tales aloud, to Nanny Klava's delight; but the small aberrations in his speech remained. A specialist was consulted, and he was diagnosed with autism. This explained his peculiarities of speech and the developmental abnormalities: gloomy concentration, incommunicativeness, inability to converse. And, according to the doctor, the prognosis was not promising.

In the year that little Ilya was supposed to begin school, his father stopped showing up at the house at Timiryazevka altogether. Just as gradually as he had appeared, and then married, he gradually left them.

That same year, Lyudmila's father, Ilya Ivanovich, died. A new professor was appointed, and he expressed the desire to live in the house of his late predecessor. After a short legal battle—although Lyudmila was the head of a laboratory, her rank didn't qualify her for a dacha—she was awarded a three-room apartment not far away, on Krasnostudenchesky Lane, in exchange. Ilya helped her with the move, wrapping up the books in small bundles, packing dishes into boxes, then loading everything into a truck.

But he didn't even stay for one day in the new apartment. He took the suitcase with his collection, intending to transport it to the apartment of his new wife, about whose existence Lyudmila had a vague suspicion. At the door, when he was ready to leave, Ilya kissed his son on the head.

"Be good, don't upset your mom," he said to his son.

"Don't upset your mom," his son replied.

Ilya cringed inside. This trivial parroting of other people's speech, weak echoes of other people's words, sounded all too often like mockery.

The heavyset Lyudmila, covered in dust from the move, her hair suddenly gray, stood in the doorway. Ilya, who was abnormally large for his age, pressed against his mother.

"Next time you come, you wouldn't hang up the shelves for me, would you?" Lyudmila asked.

"Wouldn't hang up the shelves, wouldn't hang up the shelves," the boy repeated.

Olga was like a pink-and-yellow flower bulb, with laughter always playing around the corners of her mouth, and dimples in her childlike cheeks. By bus to Novoslobodskaya, from there to Rizhskaya, and by commuter train to Nakhabino. Then, the final leg of the trip, a packed bus to the dacha, where his beloved, and a squealing puppy, snowball fights, skiing, hills and slopes, and talkative Kostya, all awaited him . . . and the typewriter tapping away till all hours of the night, and the closet with the red lights and the black cuvettes, and Olga's laughter, and tickling, and heat and love . . .

Ilya visited his son only occasionally. With books and building blocks. And each time it was the same, but worse: the full-figured, silent Lyudmila, the shriveled-up, spiteful Nanny Klava, and little Ilya, whose curly head was shooting upward, but whose body was long and feeble, like a plant growing in a pot too small for its roots. He sadly repeated fragments of everyone else's sentences. His favorite toy was a tape recorder. He listened to verse, and the lines lodged effortlessly in his memory. But what he understood them to mean, no one knew. When asked, he could declaim poetry for hours on end, reproducing the intonations of the narrator. He never learned to read, but he could do calculations in his head very quickly. He was always happy to listen to music on the radio, and he loved programs about animals. He was afraid, however, of the real live cat that lived with them, as well as the dogs he saw on the street when he went out walking with Nanny Klava.

Ilya and Lyudmila divorced. Soon afterward, Nanny Klava died. Six months later, when Ilya was visiting for only the second time since the divorce, Lyudmila requested his permission to take the child to Israel. This was just the time when everyone in Ilya's circle was trying to emigrate; but, coming from Lyudmila, it was a shock.

"Lyudmila, why Israel all of a sudden? I don't understand."

"My mother was unbelievably fastidious, you know. She never lost track of a single piece of paper or document. After her death I had already found the death certificate of my maternal grandmother. She died in 1922. Her name was Barbanel. Alta Pinchasovna Barbanel. Her father was Pinchas Barbanel, from a famous line of rabbis. My mother saved all the papers—my grandmother's birth certificate, and a note about the change of her family name after marriage. She became Ki-taeva after she got married. And my mother's papers have all been preserved as well. When Jews hear the name Barbanel, they nod their heads and cluck their tongues in recognition." She spoke, as always, in a listless, expressionless voice—only her face was sweet and soft, with a perpetual half-smile.

A Proto-Slavic face, rounded mouth and brows . . .

"Why Barbanel? Where is it from?"

"It's a distortion of the name Abrabanel. I discovered that it's a well-known, ancient Sephardic family of Talmud scholars."

"Amazing! I can't wrap my head around it. You—in Israel! It's all so unexpected. What are you going to do there?" Ilya said, incredulous.

"It's all the same to me—maybe I won't even stay there. I have an invitation to go to Israel, but where I'll end up I have no idea. Maybe America."

"All right, all right . . . but how in the world did you come up with the idea? Can you just explain that to me?" Ilya was terribly agitated.

"What is there to explain, Ilya? I'm nearly fifty, my heart isn't very good. My mother died of a heart attack at forty-three. I have no one to leave Ilya with. And they have good medical facilities there. They'll take care of him; he won't perish. But here—can you imagine what would happen to him without me?"

Little Ilya came into the room. He was enormous for his age, and deformed from illness: his arms and hands were elongated, with thin, dangling fingers; he had a tiny chin and sunken eyes . . . poor, poor thing . . . In addition to autism, they had discovered another syndrome; but autism alone would have been bad enough . . .

"Without me, without me, without me . . ." He uttered the words almost threateningly.

Lyudmila sat him down and gave him an apple.

"Good clinics, humane interaction and care, the best possible treatment—it's our only choice," Lyudmila said calmly.

"Our only choice, our only choice," little Ilya said with an absurdly happy intonation.

That same evening, Ilya signed the document that Lyudmila had already prepared. He didn't raise any objections.

He saw his son a few more times after that. The last time was when he took them to the airport.

Before he left for the airport, Olga thrust an enormous stuffed teddy bear into Ilya's arms.

"Give this to your little boy so he has something to remember you by."

"It's a pretty hefty bear," Ilya said, feeling the weight of it in his arms.

"Like your son. He's rather large himself, from what I know."

Ilya had never given any stuffed toys to his son, and he was already getting too old for them. But little Ilya beamed when he saw the bear. He ripped off the cellophane wrapping and pressed his prematurely old face into its soft belly.

"Olga and Kostya asked me to give you this teddy bear," Ilya mumbled, and was surprised at himself: he had said the names of his other family, names his unfortunate son was hearing for the first time.

"Teddy bear, teddy bear," young Ilya said joyously, while his father frowned from embarrassment and pain.

Ilya was already approaching Rechnoi Vokzal metro station at the same time that Lyudmila was asking the flight attendant to move them to the front row, where the boy's long legs would have more room.

Young Ilya settled in to his seat, repeating the last words he had heard in his homeland:

"A good ticket, a good ticket..."

In America, Lyudmila agonized for a long time before placing Ilya in a home. She might not have done it, had it not been for the fact that he had become more aggressive with time, and she found it increasingly difficult to manage him. He stayed in the home for two years. Then they transferred him to a special institution, where he was given job training so that he had skills for doing some limited but useful tasks.

Lyudmila visited him on Sundays. She brought him white chocolate, which he loved, and a big bottle of cola. It took her two hours, one way, to get there—from Brighton Beach, where they had settled her in low-income housing, to a distant part of Queens. Six hours every Sunday she devoted to her son, and each time, after she returned home, she would collapse onto the double bed given to her by a charity organization, close her eyes, and give thanks to God that the boy was well nourished, warm, and receiving good medical care. One Sunday she didn't show up, but he didn't seem to notice.

The socialization program went very smoothly, and a year later he received his first job: twice a week he sold papers in a kiosk one stop from his institution. He got ten dollars for the work he did, and in a tiny store where they already knew him, he bought some treats for himself—a bar of white chocolate, a bottle of cola, and a lottery ticket. He pointed his thumb at the candy bar, and the black salesclerk said:

"Chocolate?"

"Chocolate, chocolate," Ilya replied.

Then he pointed to a lottery ticket, and the salesclerk held out the printed paper to him, saying, "Here's a good ticket for you..."

"A good ticket," Ilya replied.

His whole life seemed to fall in place. He had friends that he could watch television with. After Lyudmila stopped visiting him, Russian words seemed to evaporate completely from his strange memory, which still contained many verses, however. Now they had become foreign to him.

During the last week of May, Ilya worked in the kiosk until noon, received his ten dollars, and bought a bar of chocolate, a cola, and a lottery ticket. The ticket turned out to be better than just good—he hit the jackpot, winning $4.2 million.

His residence was intended for low-income people. They didn't keep millionaires there.

The millionaire couldn't quite fathom the complexity of the new situation. According to the law, Ilya was considered incompetent to deal with it. His mother had died. They tried to find his father, Ilya Bryansky. After lengthy correspondence and numerous inquiries, they established that his father lived in Munich. When they tracked him down, it turned out that he had died not long before. Then the lawyers contacted his stepbrother, Konstantin (Kostya).

Kostya was summoned, and he flew to New York. He remembered dimly that Ilya Isayevich had a son from his first marriage. The doctors warned him about his newfound brother's illness. On seeing Ilya, Kostya was taken aback—but the expression on his face didn't betray his shock. He clapped the skinny giant on the shoulder and said in Russian:

"Hey, brother!"

Ilya broke into a grin.

"Hey, brother!"

Kostya pulled a photograph of his stepfather out of his wallet.

"Here's Ilya."

Ilya took the photograph, and his face lit up.

"Ilya."

"And I'm Kostya."

Ilya dimly grasped who he was, and said with some effort:

"Teddy bear."

But Kostya knew nothing about Olga's parting gift.

Ilya repeated "teddy bear" a few more times, and then began reciting Pushkin:

> "When in the country, musing, I wander
> and, stopping off at the public cemetery,
> survey the gates, small columns, and the decorated graves . . ."

He recited it to the end.

"More," Kostya said.

And Ilya, furrowing his brow, fished out another from his afflicted but boundless memory.

He recited for a long time—all the favorite verse of his dead father, with the same intonation, and in a voice that very much resembled his.

Kostya looked at this sick, no-longer-young boy, and remembered his stepfather—quick-witted, lively, talented—and at the same moment realized that he would have to find a similar kind of institution, not public, but private, for the well-off, apply for guardianship, make calculations, and set this strange and uncanny life to rights again.

Then Kostya took his newly discovered brother to a diner. Ilya pointed to a big apple pie.

"Do you want one piece or the whole thing?"

"The whole thing," Ilya said, looking down shyly.

Kostya thought for a minute, and asked again.

"Do you want the whole pie, or just one portion?"

Ilya, even more shyly, stared down at his enormous sneakers. He didn't say a word.

"I see. You do follow a certain logic."

"Logic," Ilya answered happily, and sat down at the table like an obedient child.

The waitress brought the pie and a cola for Ilya, and mineral water with ice for Kostya. It was only the middle of June, but the New York heat had already set in, and there was no air-conditioning in this run-down little place.

Ilya consumed bite after bite with a plastic spoon, eating with intense childlike pleasure. His head was exactly like his late father's—

curly chestnut-brown hair, with a sprinkling of premature gray. Even his face resembled his father's, in a slightly caricatural way.

Kostya recalled with cinematic clarity how, when he was around eight, the three of them were sitting on the shore of a lake—Valdai? Ilmen? Pleshcheyevo?—at sunset in front of a campfire, and his stepfather's long, dirty fingers had cleaned the ash from the baked potatoes. And all along the lake horizon there were ribbons of color—pink, raspberry, yellow—from the setting sun, and Mama, the red highlights in her hair aglow, was laughing, and his stepfather was laughing, and he, Kostya, was happy, and would love them forever and ever.

Poor Ilya! Poor Olga!

POOR RABBIT

When it came time to look back on his life, Dr. Dmitry Stepanovich Dulin was inclined to think that it had been a good one, maybe even undeservedly so. But he rarely thought about such abstract matters. Still, on Saturdays, when his daughter, Marinka, jumping up and down with excitement, pulled a little bunny wrapped in an old towel out of his briefcase, he felt a grateful satisfaction. His daughter looked like a little bunny herself—soft and gray, with an upper lip like a rabbit's. Where the rabbit's white ears stuck out, she had blue ribbons hanging down. Too bad he hadn't taken a photograph of Marinka with the rabbit.

Dmitry Stepanovich gave the rabbit to his daughter, and handed the towel with the hard, dry little pellets to his wife, Nina, which she then shook off into the trash pail before taking the towel into the bathroom to wash. This was the special rabbit towel, in which the little creature traveled home each Saturday, and in which it was wrapped again each Monday to go back to the laboratory.

The little rabbit was a different one each time—whichever one he happened to grab out of the cage where the test animals lived. Dulin, of course, brought home not those that were undergoing testing, but those from the control group. The test rabbits were more or less healthy, but they had been born from alcoholic mother rabbits. The doctor had plied the mother rabbits with diluted spirits from a young age, then mated them with alcoholic father rabbits, after which he studied their offspring. This was the subject of his dissertation—the influence of alcohol on the offspring of rabbits. The effects of alcohol on the offspring of humans was already well known, of course. Masha Vershkova, the lab assistant, who was at his disposal on a part-time basis, was a representative of this sector of the population: her irises trembled—she suffered from nystagmus—and her fingers shook with a tremor as well. She had been born prematurely, at seven months old. Both her parents were alcoholics, but fortunately she was not mentally impaired. Proof that even alcoholics have a stroke of luck now and then.

Marinka had never been in any such danger. Her father could not tolerate alcohol. He didn't even drink beer; nor did he smoke. He led a healthy life in all respects. Her mother drank about three small glasses a year, on holidays.

Marinka would take the Saturday bunny to her own little corner, put it into her doll's bed, pretend to wash it, squeeze and cuddle it, and feed it carrots.

Dmitry Stepanovich had been born in the country, and was used to animals. He had remained a country boy until the urban sprawl of the city of Podolsk had swallowed up his unlovely little village and destroyed its rural ways and practices. Still, Dulin's urban existence hadn't begun immediately. The new five-story buildings were constructed according to some whimsical plan, by which they didn't tear down all the peasant cottages at once, but only those that occupied the plots scheduled for construction. The Dulins' home was one of the houses that remained standing for some time; but their farming and animal husbandry collapsed. The chickens, a cat, and a dog were the only animals left. The goat and the pig were given to his grandmother's sister in a more remote village.

By that time, they didn't keep a cow.

For some reason, the well next to the house was filled in, but plumbing was not installed. After that, they had to walk almost a mile to reach a water pump. Thus, the boy Dmitry lived between city and village. He wore raggedy country clothes to a city school, was a poor student, and was despised by the urban majority for being the "country" minority.

His mother punished him for his bad grades. When she wasn't too tired and careworn, she would thrash him, letting her bony little fists land where they might, and she would shriek in a high, piercing voice until she fell down in exhaustion. Many years later, after Dmitry had become a doctor, he diagnosed her disorder ex post facto as "hysteria." And her thyroid was involved. But by the time Dmitry made the diagnosis, she was already dead.

Uncle Kolya also gave him a hard time. True, he didn't hit him; instead, he dragged him by the ear, squeezing the top of it painfully between his thumb and forefinger. Dmitry was hurt that his mother allowed this to happen, and didn't intervene. Dmitry's grandmother defended him, however. Uncle Kolya, a country fellow who was desiccated from drinking, paid visits to many of the single women around, Dmitry's mother among them. Grandmother called him the "traveling ladies' man." She despised him, but at the same time feared him. They died at almost the same time—Uncle Kolya of drink, and his grandmother of old age.

In contrast to Dmitry, his mother was a complete failure. When it came time for their house to be demolished and for her to get an apartment in a new building—the one-room apartment with gas and hot water seemed like heaven to her—his mother took a spill and died instantly, as had her mother. She was awarded her heavenly dwelling, not as a result of all the tedious paperwork necessary for the transaction— as a soldier's widow, an invalid of the paltry third class, and a high-achiever of Communist labor—but just like that, without lifting a finger. The upshot was that Dmitry's dream of moving his mother to the capital, of shrewdly exchanging the apartment in Podolsk (which she never received) for a single room in Moscow, was all for nought. Through her bad luck, his mother had liberated her son from the fuss and bother of an apartment exchange and a move.

He had always pitied her, poor thing. Very early on, however, he had decided that he would not be like his mother—he would leave and make something of himself, he would cut the contemptible country hick out of his very being. After seven years of primary and secondary school, he enrolled in nursing school. There were few men there. His presence was valued, and he applied himself to his studies. Then came the army, where he was assigned to a medical unit, thus making using of his education. After the army, he didn't stay in Podolsk, but entered medical school in Moscow, where he was accepted on the strength of his army service, without having to compete for a spot. Since that time he had been a true city man.

All that remained of Dulin's rural childhood was the habit of working with animals. Sometimes he even missed having a cat in the house, and he brought home Marinka's Saturday bunny because he liked feeling the creature's animal warmth in his own, human, hands. But Nina didn't want animals in the house, not even a cat. And what Nina did not want, Dulin did not do.

They got married in the third year of medical school. Dmitry was older than Nina by six years. She was rather stunted, and he enticed her with his height, his seriousness, and his modesty. She was not mistaken in the least—nor was he. Dmitry owed everything to his wife: his residence permit in Moscow, and his internship in neurology, and then his graduate studies. He had not aspired to that himself; but through her friends, Nina secured him a place in a research institute. She herself worked as a doctor at a local clinic, for which she was given an apartment, thus bypassing the waiting list.

Dulin initially resisted the idea of graduate school. He couldn't understand why it was necessary. If it was so important to her, why shouldn't she enroll in graduate school and defend her dissertation? But Nina had decided otherwise. Since the institute he entered for graduate studies specialized in psychiatry, and Dulin's particular field was neurology, he had to dip into some psychiatry textbooks to pass the entrance exam. He was assigned the topic of alcoholism—and he learned everything there was to know at the time: about changes in the psyche, behavioral responses of alcoholics, delirium tremens, and other fascinating things.

For three years Marinka played with the rabbits, while Dulin forced his rabbits to drink diluted spirits, pouring it into them through a funnel since the test animals refused to drink it on their own. Then Dulin defended his dissertation and became a junior researcher. He no longer brought the baby rabbits home, but now Marinka sometimes accompanied her father to the institute's vivarium. In addition to rabbits, there were also white rats, and cats and dogs. At one time there were even monkeys.

When Dulin finished his dissertation, he was suddenly filled with uncertainty: the results of his research were exactly what he had expected them to be, and his work had not yielded anything even remotely resembling a discovery. Karpov, his academic adviser and the head of the department, reassured him:

"Expecting a great deal of oneself is a fine quality in a scientist. I assure you, however, you can live a worthwhile life in science without making any discoveries. We are the workhorses of science. We are the ones who move it forward, not those who make discoveries, some of them quite dubious. And as for geniuses . . . we know what these geniuses are like!"

Dulin understood perfectly well that his adviser was referring to Vinberg. Dulin had become acquainted with him by chance, on account of a fire that broke out in Vinberg's laboratory. Two years before, when Dulin happened to be the only one on that floor, he was busy with his calculations when a wire shorted out and caught on fire. His keen sense of smell sniffed out the fire in Vinberg's lab, and he called the fire department; but even before they arrived, he managed to switch off the fuse box and put out the fire. And he prevented the firemen from even entering the lab, since he knew they would only cause chaos, and would steal things, besides. He spoke firmly to the fire chief, let him have a look around, and signed the protocol. Vinberg was grateful; and Dulin had been on friendly terms with him ever since.

Edwin Yakovlevich Vinberg was a real professor, with a brilliant education. And he was a rarity: he loved to talk about science. There was nothing he liked more than a question, in answer to which he would deliver a whole lecture. Because of his modest position and intellectual innocence, Dulin could never have expected to find any grounds for communication with this stellar individual. But the fire had afforded Dulin the right to visit the Vinbergs in the evenings for a chat over tea.

From him, Dr. Dulin learned things that never appeared in Soviet textbooks: about Dr. Freud, about archetypes, and about the psychology of the masses. Vinberg himself studied gerontology, forms of dementia in old age; but he seemed to know everything about everything, and had fascinating theories on every subject, including alcoholism.

Many people were suspicious of Vinberg. He had fled from the Fascists in Germany to the USSR even before the war. In Russia, he was arrested a month later. They protected him from the Fascists for nearly twenty years in the labor camps. After the death of Stalin, he was "rehabilitated"—it turned out he had been arrested by mistake. He was released, and very soon, in a matter of a few years, he assumed his rightful place—not in a career, of course, but in science. How many years he had spent in the camps! It would have been natural to suppose that there, as a doctor in the camp dispensary, he would have been unable to continue his work as a scientist. It turned out, however, that not only had he kept up with modern science, he was even in the forefront of it: he wrote two monographs right away, and he was awarded a doctorate without having defended a dissertation. Psychiatrists flocked to him for consultations from every corner of the land. His authority was undisputed, though he still had a fair number of detractors. Not everyone liked the fact that this quintessential stranger, moreover a Jew and a German to boot, was developing his legendary teachings and comporting himself with a European self-respect virtually unknown on our native soil.

"Dmitry Stepanovich!" he said to Dulin, in his heavy German accent, with irreproachable Russian grammar. "No one has yet studied the social nature of alcoholism, and the patterns of social behavior specific to alcoholics. There's no better place than Russia for studying this subject. Here, the entire country could serve as a platform for laboratory experiments. But where are the statistics about the relationship between alcohol use and aggression? They don't exist. If I were younger, I would certainly take on this topic. You ought to work on it, it's very promising! As for the somatic view, it's not terribly interesting. It would be fruitful, however, to work at the genetic level. But those rabbits of yours—they're not viable objects of study. They aren't drosophila! And alcohol dehydrogenase is the same in everyone, it's a simple fermentation process. No, no, if I were you I'd study alcohol and aggression."

But Dulin didn't observe any alcohol-related aggression in his objects of study. The tipsy rabbits began to exhibit signs of tremors, then just fell asleep. Their appetite diminished, as well as their weight, but they remained peaceful creatures. They didn't bite, and they didn't attack humans. In short, there was no protest activity on their part. Moreover, the professor's arguments notwithstanding, the primary male, head of this alcoholic harem, not only did not become more aggressive, but actually lost his renowned rabbit potency. Every three months, one of his own sons took over where he had left off.

When Dulin worked up the courage to challenge Vinberg, saying that his research in no way confirmed the aggression of alcoholics, the professor only laughed.

"Dmitry Stepanovich, what about the workings of the higher nervous system? A human being is not a rabbit, of course, but a highly organized, complex being! Moreover, I would draw your attention to the fact that rabbits are vegetarians, and people, for the most part, are predators. In their eating habits people are closer to bears, which are omnivorous! Keep in mind that not a single species is comparable to *Homo sapiens* in the variety of its diet. Northern peoples are carnivorous, while in India, for example, there are huge swathes of the population that are exclusively vegetarian. As far as can be observed without scientific study, neither group outdoes the other in displays of aggression."

The professor enjoyed his musings, rubbing his dry, cleanly scoured palms together in a gesture that suggested he was about to examine a patient.

"Very curious. Very curious. One must begin with biochemistry, I believe. *Der Mensch ist was er isst.* And what he drinks!" And just like that he laughed, showing his mouthful of pure metal teeth, which a local dentist, originally from Vienna, had fitted him with in Vorkuta. Dulin either recalled from the German he had managed to pick up at school, or simply guessed, that what Vinberg had said was: You are what you eat.

Vinberg knew everything there was to know in the world, or so it seemed: anthropology, Latin, and even genetics. But he hadn't been able to take care of his teeth. He was in a hurry to live, to read, to think; he had been in a hurry to write down all the idiosyncratic and untimely ideas that had descended on him in the northern latitudes.

He talked a great deal to whoever would listen, including Dulin. But there were some things he kept to himself, telling only those closest to him.

"A land of children!" he would say to his wife, whom he'd acquired through the camp dispensary. "A land of children! Culture blocks the natural impulses of adults; but not of children. And where there is no culture, blocking is absent. There is a cult of the father, of obedience, and at the same time an unmanageable childish aggression."

Vera Samuilovna brushed this off disdainfully. She was the only one who would permit herself such a gesture.

"Edwin, what nonsense! What about the Germans? The most cultured country in Europe? Why didn't culture block their primitive, natural impulses?"

Vera Samuilovna attacked her husband with youthful passion, and Edwin Yakovlevich, as usual, fiddled with his nose, as though it were precisely in that organ that his intellect was concentrated.

"Another mechanism was set in motion, Vera, another mechanism. *Das ist klar. Selbstverständlich.* This can be proven. Levels of awareness—this is what we must consider."

And he would fall silent for a long time before offering this theoretical proof.

They had no children. One boy had been born to them in the camps, but they had been unable to save him. All their energy, their entire store of talent that had remarkably survived and flourished, was invested in their profession. Vera Samuilovna was obsessed with her endocrinology. She synthesized artificial hormones, which she nearly believed could guarantee human immortality. Edwin Yakovlevich did not endorse his wife's views. He was not attracted by immortality. Their scientific interests converged in this fundamental conflict: gerontology by definition flew in the face of the idea of immortality. Vinberg was certain of this. But Vera believed in hormones.

The couple had plenty to discuss in their late-evening soirées. After the loss of their whole prewar way of life—conservatories, libraries, science and literature; after the camp barracks, the dispensaries, the necessity of curing every possible illness with no medicine at all; after all that, sitting in the nighttime stillness of their own tiny apartment, stuffed with books and records, in the warmth, with plenty of food, just the two of them, was their source of joy.

Dulin continued to study alcoholism, now not only from a scientific perspective, as theory, but in an applied, practical context as well. His department started a treatment program, which, unfortunately, didn't meet with any particular success. The salary was good, though—he received 170 rubles a month, plus a bonus.

Three years went by. Again, he got lucky, this time without Nina's influence. A position for a senior research fellow opened up when an elderly colleague retired. At the same time, quite unexpectedly, Dr. Ruzaev, the most promising doctor in their institute and one who had already defended his dissertation, was lured away by the Kazan Medical Institute.

A search was begun to fill these two positions. Dulin would never have considered applying on his own initiative, but the head of the department urged him on, telling him to get all the necessary papers in order. And in the autumn of 1972, Dulin was promoted to the position of senior research fellow! This was a stunning coup in the unfolding of his career. It took all winter for Dulin to get used to it. In the mornings, while he was shaving in the bathroom, as he scraped the foamy hillock covering his dark brown whiskers from his cheeks with a safety razor, he would look at himself in the mirror and say: "Dmitry Stepanovich Dulin, Senior Research Fellow." He had expected it to take ten or fifteen years to reach this position, but suddenly—there it was!

And he felt pride, and uncertainty, all at once . . .

Things were going very well in the department. Now he had a new subject—alcohol-related paranoia—and two wards of patients whom he studied and treated. Gripped by fits of jealousy, inflamed with hallucinations, tormented by persecution manias, overwrought and excitable, or, on the contrary, listless and depressed, devoid of any sense of self-worth, pumped up or deflated by neuroleptic drugs, they bore very little resemblance to his soft, warm-eared rabbits. Aggression was always hovering just below the surface.

Some of them were tied to the bed, others were sedated with drugs. On occasion, a particularly ungovernable patient would break the windowpane and fling himself out, trying to escape his illness straight into the arms of the Lord God. All told, there were only two windows without bars in the entire department: one in the department head's office, as well as a tiny one in the examining room. At the beginning of spring one such patient took the leap from that very window. Luckily, the ward was only on the second floor; still, he broke his arm. It was very unfortunate for all concerned. The patient was a celebrated actor, beloved by the whole nation. And his form of delirium was also deeply rooted in the people: he believed that tiny men were after him, and he had to keep picking them off, shaking himself free in squeamish terror.

Dulin chased off the tiny men with the help of Amytal and haloperidol.

Then the artist recovered, and his beautiful wife, also an actor, came to fetch him. She gave the nurses six boxes of chocolate, and the department head a portrait of the patient. Now it hung in his office, adorned with the artist's autograph. For the teetotaler Dulin, they brought a bottle of cognac. Dulin was very happy—not about the cognac, of course, but that no scandal had ensued. The actor had arrived all in one piece, and he had left with a broken arm in a cast. They should have been more careful.

Dulin didn't like his paranoiacs. In fact, he felt a deep contempt for them. He considered them all to be lost causes, and deep inside he viewed alcoholism itself not as a true illness, but as an ordinary human failing. His wife, Nina, from morning till night, made her rounds of the district, listening with her stethoscope, palpating stomachs, writing out prescriptions and sick-leave certificates, and carrying out what he considered to be true medical work. What went on here, Dulin suspected, was just academic rigamarole. But, on the whole, he was satisfied with the job. It was a good one.

One day, in the middle of summer, when vacation season was in full swing, Dulin was summoned to the administrative office. Eleonora Viktorovna, the secretary, a mature black-haired beauty with luxuriant, immobile eyebrows and unbridled power at the institute, nodded to him and smiled sourly:

"Dmitry Stepanovich, you are being asked to give a consultation in the Special Division, in your area of expertise."

Dulin was alarmed. This request was, in fact, an order. It was common knowledge that the Special Division was where "politicals" were kept, and the people who worked there had "clearance"—they were special people, secretive people who kept quiet. No one else wanted to have access to it. Ordinarily, if they needed to consult someone, they invited Karpov, the department head; but he happened to be away on vacation. Kulchenko, another distinguished senior research fellow, had gone to a conference in Leningrad. Dulin tried to wriggle out of it.

"Eleonora Viktorovna, I would be honored, of course, but I'm afraid it's impossible; I don't have clearance."

Eleonora Viktorovna adjusted her hair—a fashionable bun that added volume to her head on top and in back—and smiled:

"We have already arranged for clearance. Just sign here."

And she held out to him a malachite pen sticking out of a malachite stand. Dulin took the pen, still protesting:

"But I've never taken part in this kind of consultation. Karpov will be back in two weeks, and Kulchenko will already be back at work on Monday."

Eleonora Viktorovna's mouth expressed dissatisfaction.

"Are you not aware that any specialist with a diploma can be called in to offer expertise? It's your duty! Those are our laws. And this is just such a consultation." Eleonora paused; the pause lasted just long enough to give Dulin to understand that resistance was futile. He signed the document.

"Please report to the Special Division at eleven o'clock on Thursday. They'll provide you with a pass. Professor Dymshitz, head of the Special Division, would like to have a little talk with you now. Wait for him here. He's in the director's office."

"Yes, of course," Dulin said, with a sense of foreboding.

He sat on a chair, taking note of its alarming crimson upholstery. He had already heard unpleasant rumors about this Dymshitz, but he couldn't recall precisely what they were.

He waited for quite a while. Finally, the door opened, and a fat, stumpy fellow with a few thin gray hairs combed over his bald pate, from the right side to the left, emerged from the director's office.

"Efim Semenovich, Doctor Dulin is waiting for you. You wished to see him," Eleonora said, rising to greet him.

A head taller than he, the older beauty had to bend down to communicate with this gnomish creature; still, she exuded fear, and he menace. Dulin's agitation grew more and more pronounced. He couldn't quite grasp what was happening, as though he were witnessing a play performed in a foreign language.

No one explained to Dulin that Eleonora had been married to Dymshitz before the war, and that she had left him for a younger man who went missing in action during the war. In 1946 she returned to Dymshitz again, and after living with him for a short while, abandoned him again. Thus, Dulin was a chance witness of their strange and convoluted relationship.

Dymshitz turned his gaze toward Dulin.

"Yes, yes. Very good. Have you ever taken part in a psychiatric expert review?"

Dulin had done this hundreds of times for cases of alcoholism, naturally. But he suddenly grew confused, and something so frightened him that his underarms, as well as his back and chest, broke into a sweat.

"Yes, of course," he said.

The gnome was sizing him up. And not very highly.

"I would like to talk with you beforehand, but I'm in a hurry at the moment. Come to the Special Division at eleven, and before you see the patient, look in on me."

And Dymshitz went up the stairs to the third floor, his little ankle boots clattering noisily on the steps.

He probably buys his shoes in Children's World, Dulin thought irritably. And he wasn't wrong. The professor wore a size 4.

Leaving the institute at eight o'clock in the evening, a vapor of dried, malodorous sweat trailing behind him, Dulin ran into Vinberg. Erect, lanky, and thin, in a worn-out gray suit with a striped silk tie, and smelling of eau de cologne, he was elegant, as always.

It's not just the tie, of course, Dulin thought to himself. *It's his nature, his character. He's dry as a biscuit.*

Dulin himself had put on weight in the last two or three years. He ate a lot: for his mother, for his grandmother, for all the years he had gone hungry in childhood, which had settled into depths known only to psychiatrists.

They walked to the metro together.

"They called me to give a consultation at the Special Division," Dulin reported without any hesitation.

Vinberg raised a neatly trimmed eyebrow.

"Really? They must trust you. Are you a member of the Party, Dmitry Stepanovich?"

"Of course I am. I served in the army after college. They took everyone back then."

"Ah, yes. Party discipline. You have a duty to take part, then," Vinberg said drily, clearing his throat.

"Usually, Karpov . . . he's on vacation," Dulin said, trying to justify himself, and was taken aback by his own behavior. "They obviously have an alcoholic there, or there's at least an episode involving alcohol in the case. But in our country, Edwin Yakovlevich, everyone drinks: actors, academics, and cosmonauts. Recently we had . . ." And Dulin told him about the celebrated actor.

"Back in the camps, there was a certain talented writer, an exceptionally erudite man. He translated Rilke in prison so as not to be degraded by the circumstances. Well, it's unlikely that you've ever heard of Rilke. Right here, in the Serbsky Institute, that very writer underwent a psychiatric expert review at the beginning of the 1930s; he hoped to be diagnosed as an alcoholic (which he was not). And for the time being he wasn't sent to prison, but for treatment. He spent three years in treatment. He praised God and read books. But they sent him to prison in the end anyway. Yes, Rilke, Rilke . . . That's the paradox of our time: before the war, people evaded persecution in psychiatric wards, and now it's precisely psychiatric wards where—"

"Dymshitz asked me to drop by for a talk with him," Dulin said plaintively, his voice lowered. But Vinberg seemed not to hear. He suddenly turned away.

"Excuse me, I completely forgot. I have to run into the bookstore. Good-bye!"

And he strode off in the direction of Metrostroevskaya Street. Vinberg had been taken off guard. This decisive young man who had single-handedly managed to quell a fire, unsophisticated and somewhat limited, but conscientious and decent, in his own way, seemed to be asking for his advice.

What could he say to a simple-hearted and conscientious fool? Even a wise man wouldn't be able to extricate himself from this one. Vinberg walked right past the bookstore. He hadn't really needed to go there.

When Hitler came to power, Jacob Vinberg, his father, a well-known Berlin lawyer, had said: "As a lawyer, I always find a way out. I know that in every situation there is at least one exit. Usually several. Under Hitler's regime, there are none." Jacob Vinberg died without realizing how right he was. *This regime doesn't allow a man any way out, either. Not one. They always get the better of those who have a conscience*, Vinberg thought.

The Special Division was located in a separate building, three trolleybus stops away. At half past ten on Thursday, Dulin rang the stern bell, which seemed to be calling him to account. A female porter in a white robe opened the door.

"Whom do you wish to see?"

Dulin showed her his pass. "I'm here for a consultation. I need to see Professor Dymshitz."

"One moment," the woman said, and, with a brisk nod, shut the door in his face. A few minutes later another woman, taller, with a fancy hairdo, opened the door. Instead of a robe she was wearing a pink dress.

Jersey knit, Dulin noted. *Nina is dying for one. I feel awkward asking her where she got it.*

"Good morning, good morning! We've been expecting you." She extended her hand. "Margarita Glebovna. I'm the doctor in charge of the case. Efim Semenovich is waiting for you. Then I'll show you to the patient."

A corridor, doors—it looked just like an ordinary hospital ward. Only the corridors were absolutely empty.

Then they came to some heavy double doors adorned with a brass plaque. He was surprised by the spaciousness and the complete sterility of the office. There was not a single piece of paper or a single mote of dust on the sleek tabletop. The gnome, who was sitting behind the desk, was almost affable this time.

"Please, come in, Dmitry Stepanovich."

Dulin sat on an uncomfortable chair in the middle of the room. A sea of gleaming parquet separated him from the professor. About ten feet of it.

Like an investigator, Dulin thought. He had once found himself sitting in just such a lone chair in the district KGB office. One of his classmates had gotten up to no good, and Dulin was called in for questioning. But the fairly canny functionaries realized very quickly how remote Dulin was from all that business, and let him go.

At various points in his life, Dymshitz had also had to occupy a faraway chair like that one. He didn't like it; but it had made a deep impression on him.

"So," Dymshitz said, barely parting his lips. "We have a very interesting patient on our hands."

Seemingly out of nowhere, a cardboard file appeared. From afar, Dymshitz waved it around invitingly.

See that? He's taunting me, Dulin thought, annoyed.

"A distinguished man. Was once a brigadier general," Dymshitz said ponderously, emphasizing every word. "Fought at the front. Wounded twice; a concussion, mind you. He received honors and awards galore. Lost it all. His behavior is aberrant. He's a drinker . . . his mind is shot. He suffers from delusions of grandeur. This contains the findings of the outpatient commission. I don't think they were able to get to the bottom of it. You, however, will—I hope."

He spoke these last words emphatically, articulating every syllable.

Anxiety gripped Dulin, so deep-seated that a wave of nausea rose up in him.

Why in the world am I so on edge? Dulin asked himself. But there was no time to come up with an answer.

"Here is the case history; and here is the epicrisis. Here are the findings of the commission. In making your diagnosis, you must take into account the role that alcohol plays in the illness, and make an annotation to that effect in the patient's medical history." Dymshitz opened the file and began to sort through the pages. "Here is a summary of a previous expert review, which was carried out under outpatient circumstances. There it is. Nineteen sixty-eight. We have our doubts about it. We would like you to examine the patient and then substantiate your opinion. We have reached the provisional conclusion that . . . Well, have a look at it."

He approached Dulin, who stood up to take the file from him.

"The opinion of the commission is unfavorable . . . a number of paranoiac traits. Could these be alcohol-related? You have the last word, you're the expert. We ourselves have come to a provisional conclusion. In short, examine the patient. Margarita Glebovna!"

Margarita Glebovna seemed to take shape out of thin air.

"Have there been alcoholic episodes?" Dulin asked timidly.

"Hmm. Well, yes," Dymshitz said vaguely. "At least one unquestionable episode is present: he was under the influence when they arrested him."

Dymshitz stood up again, a sign that the audience was over.

Margarita Glebovna ushered Dulin out into the corridor.

She wiped the corners of her lips with her fingertips, as though removing extra lipstick.

"You can look over the records here in the doctor's lounge. Then I'll show you the patient."

Dulin opened the file and began studying the papers. Patient: Nichiporuk, Peter Petrovich, sixty-two years old. Wounded twice, one concussion, physical disorders. Who doesn't have those? Record of a conversation with the psychiatrist . . . protocol. Dmitry Stepanovich couldn't believe his eyes: even reading what the general had said was terrifying! Some sort of craziness! "What was your goal in creating an underground organization?" An anti-Soviet—he was a true anti-Soviet! And further: "The organization is called UTL—the Union of

True Leninists." Oh, so it turns out he's not anti-Soviet, but the opposite . . . The opposite? What could that be? "What was your salary, Peter Petrovich?" A strange question for a psychiatrist. Oh, I see . . . I see. Seven hundred a month. Dulin didn't even know that it was possible for someone to earn that much . . . And further: "So what was it you were lacking, Peter Petrovich, with a salary like that? The authorities provided you with everything you needed." Yes, he's absolutely right. It doesn't make sense. Really, with money like that, why would you bite the hand that feeds you? Ah, that's what it was . . . Czechoslovakia. He didn't like the Soviet troops marching into Czechoslovakia . . . He denounced it publicly . . . slander against the state . . . now it all makes sense. But why would he tell a psychiatrist things like that? Of what interest would they be to a doctor?

The terms "spiritual brotherhood," "moral perfection," "anti-populist power of the Party-ocracy," and, finally, "the sacred task of socialism," underlined in red pencil, flickered in front of him. *He's a strange old geezer, not crazy, just eccentric.* This was Dulin's preliminary conclusion. He spent forty minutes poring over the records.

Then they brought in the patient—a tall, thin man in hospital pajamas and felt slippers. He stood close to the door, holding one hand behind his back and hanging his head slightly. Another man, shorter than the patient, came in with him; he sat down on a chair by the door.

"Good day, Peter Petrovich. I'm a psychiatrist, Candidate of Medical Sciences Dmitry Stepanovich Dulin. I would like to examine you and have a chat. Come over here and sit down, please." Dulin indicated the chair next to him. "How do you feel? What symptoms do you have?"

The former general smiled and looked at Dulin. His gaze was too long, and too attentive.

"Only those corresponding to my age. Nothing in particular to complain about." He gripped his knees with his large hands, which were covered with red spots.

Dulin asked, "How long have you had psoriasis?"

"From a young age. It began after the war. During the war, people didn't suffer from ordinary human illnesses. It wasn't the time or place for that. After the war it all started: heart, stomach, liver."

He pronounced "liver" with a mocking drawl. Dulin examined Nichiporuk as they had learned to do at the institute: the sclera, the condition of his skin, mucous membranes . . . poor nutrition, most likely anemia . . . blood samples . . . it was anemia, of course . . .

"What day is it today, Peter Petrovich?" Dulin said quietly.

"A lousy one," he replied briefly.

"Can you remember the date?" Dulin said.

"Ah," the patient said, laughing. "You mean like Marchember? Today is July 22, 1972. Exactly thirty-two years and one month after the invasion of the German Fascist troops into the territory of the USSR."

He seemed to be making fun of him, this former general. No, he was no doubt just trying to be funny—alcoholic wit! Actually, Dulin quite liked him. Dulin placed him on the examining table, palpated his stomach. His liver was enlarged. *Let's assume it's alcohol-induced fatty degeneration. With significant malnutrition.*

"What is your height? Your weight?"

"I am exactly six feet tall. I don't know my weight."

Margarita Glebovna and the one by the door didn't budge. They were planted there like stone statues.

"Good! Now, close your eyes and place the forefinger of your right hand on the tip of your nose. Now your left . . . What is the year of your birth? Your birthday?"

The patient smiled.

"September tenth, one thousand, nine hundred, and ten years after the birth of Christ. According to the Julian calendar, naturally."

"Very good," Dulin said with alacrity. "And do you always live by this calendar?"

"No, of course not. The USSR shifted to the Gregorian calendar in February 1918, and all dates after February fourteenth were most reasonably calculated according to the Gregorian calendar; before that, according to the Julian. Quite logical, isn't it?"

"Yes. Perhaps," Dulin said. He would have to look up in the encyclopedia what they said about calendars. The old geezer was, of course, highly educated, and there were always additional complications with well-educated people. He had, naturally, a dilation of the reflexogenic zones; this could be interpreted variously as alcoholization, right up to the possible onset of alcoholic paranoia. It depended on how one looked at it.

"Your place of birth, Peter Petrovich?"

"The village of Velikie Topoli, in the Gadyachsky Uyezd, Poltava Gubernia. My father belonged to the local intelligentsia. He was a teacher in a public school."

"I see, I see. What about heredity, Peter Petrovich? Did your father drink?" Dulin said, introducing the subject at hand.

"I see what you mean, Doctor. That is, it is impossible not to see. Yes, he drank. My father drank. And my grandfather drank. And my great-grandfather. And I drank, when they let me." He smiled, and his smile was simply radiant. He had a good smile—absolutely devoid of mockery or hidden malice.

"And when did you begin to indulge, Peter Petrovich?" Dulin said politely.

"Now that's something I don't quite remember. Everyone drank on holidays, children, too. My father always drank with dinner, that was a sacred ritual—a glass of vodka with the meal. I still honor this custom, I admit."

"And do you drink alcohol now?"

Peter Petrovich suddenly let all his defenses down.

"Dear Doctor! They don't offer you any here! I have to admit that since the beginning of the war, there hasn't been a single day that I didn't imbibe spirits of some sort—vodka, or whatever else God provided. I miss it badly!"

Dulin suddenly felt quite awkward: Peter Petrovich was so very trusting and confiding.

"Do you have a need for it? A dependency, I mean." Dulin probed deeper.

"A dependency—not in the least. But a need—certainly. A reasonable need."

" 'In the words of the patient, he has abused alcohol regularly for many years, without excess,' " Dulin noted down in good conscience.

Margarita Glebovna, who continued to stand by the door in silence, was clearly dissatisfied. She whispered something to the person sitting in the chair.

"A Russian man, Doctor, can't do without it. Vodka quiets the soul. It softens the edges of life. Don't tell me you don't know that?"

And then Dulin understood: Peter Petrovich himself wanted to be sent into treatment. Dulin looked through his file again. The doctor's notes indicated that Peter Petrovich had spent four years, from 1968 to 1972, in prison, and his physical condition at the time had been poor. Dulin also came across an old outpatient record from Riga, in which it was written, in black and white: "Mind clear, correct orientation, comports himself well in conversation, speech coherent and to the point." He was declared fit and mentally sound. And the most recent record, as yet inconclusive, which he himself was expected to sign, ascertaining alcohol-induced paranoia. Followed by a fat question mark.

This was something Dulin was unable to do in good conscience. He exerted himself like a schoolboy at an exam. Finally, groping beyond the limitations of his own mind, he came up with the right answer. He inserted a single word in front of "alcohol-induced paranoia": *atypical*. And this set everything to rights! It was an atypical case. This Peter Petrovich was not insane, he was merely eccentric. But it wouldn't be a bad idea to send him in for treatment.

In any case, the hospital would feed him. Now Dulin understood why the patient had confided to him so candidly and happily about his use of alcohol. This was his way of hinting that he wouldn't mind undergoing treatment. And Vinberg had just told him about some Rilke or other who wanted more than anything to be declared mentally unsound and to be hospitalized.

They chatted a little longer, and Dulin, with a light heart, wrote down his diagnosis: "Alcohol-induced deterioration of the internal organs. Changes in the central nervous system: the presence of alcohol-related encephalopathy and retrograde amnesia. Diagnosis: atypical alcohol-induced paranoia."

Dulin graced it with his beautiful signature.

And he looked at the clock—half past two.

Half past two, Peter Petrovich thought. *I missed lunch because of that quack. Maybe the nurse left it there for me?* thought the hungry general, with perfunctory agitation.

Dulin went back to his department, took the sandwiches Nina had made him out of his briefcase, and drank a glass of milk. The cook at the institute always left him a pint. He ate and glanced through two journals that had been lying on his desk for a long time and needed to be returned to the library. Then he went to see Vinberg, in the former linen storeroom, which was now a cross between an office and a pantry, piled high with books, most of them foreign publications.

This is how Vinberg acquires his erudition. He has an advantage, since he knows other languages, the ingenuous Dulin thought.

It was already getting on toward evening. The working day for the doctors was over. On Vinberg's desk, on top of a sheaf of journals and letters in gray envelopes covered with handwriting that had a Gothic cast, lay a vinyl record in a white paper sleeve.

"Someone brought me a Daniil Shafran. A unique piece—Shostakovich's 1946 cello sonata. The first performance of it. Shostakovich himself plays on it." The professor stroked the record gently with his dark hand. His fingernails were long and well tended. "And Daniil Shafran was only twenty-two years old at the time. Brilliant. An absolutely brilliant cellist . . ."

They're always like that. Jews always prefer their own, Dulin thought disapprovingly, then caught himself: *What's wrong with that? That's what all people are like. Everyone prefers their own kind.*

"I held my consultation," Dulin reported to Vinberg.

But Vinberg didn't seem to remember about their earlier conversation. The expression on his face was vacant.

"I diagnosed him with alcoholism. They'll most likely send him in for treatment now."

"*What?*" Vinberg said. "What did you say? You sent him to a treatment facility?"

"Well, what does it matter, Edwin Yakovlevich? He's emaciated, I thought that if he were admitted for treatment they'd at least feed him. Anything's better than the camps." Dulin's spirits, boosted by doing a good deed, suddenly started to sag.

"Are you just playing the fool, Dulin? Or are you a bona fide idiot?" the well-mannered professor said.

At this Dulin became distraught. He had always considered it an honor that Vinberg wanted to spend time with him, to discuss things with him—and here he was, all of a sudden, out of nowhere, calling him an idiot. Dulin felt deeply injured.

"What do you mean, Edwin Yakovlevich? You yourself told me about Rilke, that he dreamed only of being declared insane so he wouldn't be sent to the camps . . . you said it yourself . . ." Dulin pleaded in his own defense.

"Me, myself, and I what? In the thirties they didn't have any haloperidol! Aminazin! Stelazine! It didn't exist yet! You've consigned him to the torture chamber, Dmitry Stepanovich! You can go and denounce me, now, if you like."

He lowered his head and stared at the record. *Daniil Shafran Performs* . . .

He said nothing, his mouth twisted into a grimace. What baseness . . . what baseness everywhere one looks . . .

"What should I have done, then? Tell me," Dulin asked in a quiet voice. "He really was . . . well, not completely, but . . . what was I supposed to do?"

Vinberg, spinning the record absently, then put both his hands on the desk.

Leave this place, leave this place. As soon as possible, leave this place, he thought. And also: *What a people! How can they hate themselves so?*

Then he smiled a bitter smile, and said something incomprehensible:

"I don't know. A Chinese sage once said that for every question there are seven answers. Everyone has to answer this question for himself. Please forgive my rudeness, Dmitry Stepanovich."

———

Vera Samuilovna understood immediately that her husband was agitated and dejected: by the brusque way he took off his coat, by the gloomy expression on his face, and the nod and a wooden *"Danke,"* when she put his soup in front of him. A tactful, clever woman, she kept silent and didn't ask him any questions. He was always grateful to her afterward for her aristocratic silence and self-possession.

Edwin Yakovlevich felt his own failure keenly, and experienced a belated remorse: How could he have let himself humiliate this sweet, dim-witted, and diligent person? Had not he, Vinberg, taken part in a psychiatric expert consultation several years back, in the same Special Division? Had he not offered his conclusion about the mental unsoundness of a prisoner whose political beliefs about the nature of this regime he completely shared? But from a clinical point of view, his illness was undeniable. It was a clear and detailed picture of manic-depressive psychosis. Vinberg, the former prisoner, could do nothing about it. Almost all the freethinkers, the petition signers, the home-grown rebels were mad in both the everyday and, partly, the medical sense of the word. *This is the nature of Russian radicalism, of course. It is never grounded in common sense*, Vinberg mused, feeling gradually more calm.

Vinberg wasn't even aware of it himself when he began voicing his inner musings out loud:

"When Hitler came to power, all of the intelligentsia who had their wits about them emigrated, but the loyal ones ... There's no way out, no way out. But a doctor is in a unique position—he's only supposed to heal, to treat illness. The way out, or through, is through his profession. The prison camp hospital. Physical injuries, ulcers, tuberculosis, heart attacks. The honor of the profession is the highest value. Higher than politics, undoubtedly. Undoubtedly. However ... Vera, Vera! Every single person I've seen who is struggling against the regime in our time is on the border, on a very thin boundary, between health and sickness. Do you remember the woman who went out onto Red Square with her baby in a baby buggy? There is such an instinct as self-preservation. There is such a thing as maternal instinct, which forces the mother to protect her child. But there is no instinct for social justice in nature! Conscience militates against survival, Vera!"

His wife sat opposite him on a stool, in their fifty-square-foot kitchen, where a second chair wouldn't even fit. Still, there was a table, a cooker with two burners, warm radiators in winter, and the luxuriant growth of some nondescript weed under the window in summer.

Vera peered into the black glass of the window, behind which nothing was visible except her own blurry reflection. She, too, knew that conscience worked against survival. Yes, biological evolution wipes out the species of those with a conscience that lives and breathes. The mighty survive. But she didn't want to revisit that subject: the camps, starvation, humiliation, hell.

"Edwin, tell me, did Grachevsky bring you the record?"

Edwin Yakovlevich broke off, burst out laughing, and left the kitchen. Yes, they had talked it over; enough of that.

He took the cello sonata out of his briefcase and put it on the turntable. Vera was already sitting in an armchair in the room they referred to as the "living room" for propriety's sake.

It was the earliest performance of the piece. Later, in 1950, Shostakovich recorded it with Rostropovich, and even modified the original version.

Vinberg's large ears, with their tufts of hair, inherited from distant ancestors, seemed to quiver from tension. Vera Samuilovna, a qualified listener herself, had always considered Daniil Shafran to be a more versatile and gifted performer than Rostropovich. But here was Shostakovich, who seemed to her to be dry and severe. Her husband heard the music differently: there was a refusal to compromise, a drama of inner struggle and confrontation. The piano cadenza in the third movement recalled Beethoven's late sonatas.

"Hopelessness. Cosmic hopelessness. Don't you think, Vera?"

Dulin went straight to the vivarium after talking to Vinberg. He had a cabinet there in which he kept a secret stash of medical spirits under lock and key. He removed a half-liter vessel and poured some of it into a measuring beaker, to which he added tap water, half and half, as he did for the rabbits. Then he drank it down, all 200 ml of it straight from the measuring beaker. He put the vessel in his briefcase. It didn't quite fit, but the cork was sturdy and snug, so he lay it on its side. And he went to get the trolleybus. He began feeling drunk only once he was inside the bus. When he got home, no one was there. Nina had gone to pick up Marinka from the biology club at the municipal House of Pioneers, which she took part in even though she was too young to join the Young Pioneers organization. She had an avid interest in biology.

At home, Dulin diluted more of the spirits, and drank another 200 ml. Disgusting stuff. How do they drink it? Now he was already feeling woozy. The room was spinning around his poor head. He couldn't fall asleep, though. One thought, like a splinter in his brain, kept jabbing and jabbing away at him: What were the seven answers? What answers could there be, besides yes and no?

Then Nina came home. It took a while for her to realize that he was stone drunk. At first, she started to laugh:

"Poor little drunken rabbit!"

She tried to sober him up with strong tea, to put him to bed; but he refused to go. He kept babbling on and on about seven answers, or seven questions, and only late at night did she understand the cause of his torment.

By that time, Dulin had diluted the rest of the spirits, but he couldn't drink it. He vomited, and began having severe stomach spasms. Then he lay down, shaking with chills.

Nina was already tired of looking after him. She sat down in a chair, muttering something angrily under her breath. She didn't get into bed herself. Then Marinka came in in her nightgown, complaining that her head was hurting. At that moment, Dulin recalled all the bad things that had ever happened to him in his life: how the local kids had teased him at school, how Kamzolkina, the teacher, had yelled at him, how his mother had beaten him, how Mama's drunken "suitor," Uncle Kolya, had pulled him by the ears . . . And he began to weep.

Dulin wept—because he was a rabbit, and not a man.

That's what Nina told him, anyway.

THE ROAD WITH ONE END

A camera without film dangled from Ilya's neck. The film had been confiscated and exposed by the border guards. A half-empty camping rucksack was slung over his shoulder. In it he had a change of underwear and an English-language textbook that he had carried around with him constantly for the past two years. He was wearing a new jacket and old jeans. A scarf was wrapped around his neck. Olga had knitted it out of black and gray yarn, and it resembled exactly his already graying hair.

There was a line of people leading up to the mobile staircase used to enter the plane. The former Soviet citizens, a good half of them, were easily distinguishable from the non-Soviets by their heavy, poor-quality attire and varying degrees of bewilderment. An old man in a sheepskin hat standing next to him hiccuped, and some woman whom Ilya couldn't make out in the midst of the throng of people giggled nervously. Ilya was eager for the moment when he would finally board the aircraft, take a seat, and the plane would take off. Although it was already obvious that he had crossed some irrevocable boundary, he wanted to leave the ground. And he wanted even more to go to the restroom.

He knew that Olga and Kostya and the other well-wishers were standing behind some window, waving good-bye, and that they were probably waiting for him to wave back when he ascended the steps to the plane. He didn't even try to seek out with his eyes the glass passageway where they were most likely standing. He couldn't have made them out in the crowd anyway. Nevertheless, when he was on the very top step, he turned around and waved his hand vaguely in an indeterminate direction, like Brezhnev on the rostrum in a Party greeting.

This was it—the cinematic moment of his life, Ilya thought, smiling to himself and relaxing. His seat was in the second-to-last row, by the window. The plane was full to bursting.

When the cumbersome aircraft finally left the ground, Ilya said to himself: *Free! From everything—I'm free!*

The plane seemed to gain altitude with difficulty, pressing everyone downward; but Ilya felt himself becoming weightless. He felt he could have flown all on his own, without a motor, just on the strength of his sense of limitless freedom.

The woman who had been giggling by the steps, who was sitting somewhere in front of him, near the aisle, started laughing and sobbing out loud, both at the same time. A stewardess the height of a basketball player brought her a glass of water.

Yes, yes—a tall woman . . . that's good, a tall woman. But he didn't think through to the end the thoughts that flashed through his mind.

The gray mist beyond the window grew brighter, and the plane broke through finally into a clear blue sky. Underneath were thick white clouds, dense as thick porridge, and as crude as theater props. The plane gained altitude steadily, and lunged westward, leaving behind the ruins of a cursed life, a viscous confusion, fear, shame, deceit. He breathed the artificial airplane air—the air of freedom and high altitudes. Ahead of him a captivating emptiness beckoned. Life turned over a new page, and all the blots and mistakes were wiped out, as though by an eraser. His neighbor in the seat next to his tugged at his sleeve—an old Jewish woman with a new set of gold teeth.

"Excuse me, please, would you mind changing seats with me?"

Certain of his answer, she tried to unfasten her seat belt, but pulled it from the wrong end.

"No," Ilya replied curtly.

"Why not?" she said, offended.

"I don't want to," he said, not even turning his head.

"But why not?" She couldn't believe her ears.

He didn't deign to answer. She was a piece of the past, which he had turned his back on.

"But I'm stuck here right in the middle," said the woman plaintively, and turned to her neighbor on the other side. "Excuse me, could you please change seats with me?"

"I'm sorry, I didn't understand what you said. What do you want?" said the man, with a noticeable accent.

Ilya looked over at him. An old man with gray hair, holding a German newspaper in his bony hands. Intriguing. This was what Ilya liked more than anything: a question, a mystery, details, details . . . The striped silk tie, the white shirt made of some unfamiliar ribbed fabric, the worn-out blazer, and, particularly, the German newspaper— it all captured his attention.

"Well, I wanted to sit by the window. This man here wouldn't let me, so I'd at least like the aisle seat." She kept tugging fruitlessly at the seat belt, but Ilya didn't offer to help her. He looked at her askance: What a pushy old bag!

The old man stood up. He was very tall and thin, and, judging by his appearance, he was a foreigner. The blazer, though . . .

"Just a moment, I'll help you unfasten it." The man released the woman as though from captivity, and stepped out into the aisle. She immediately plunked down in his seat.

"You can always judge a person by his manners," she said loudly, reproaching Ilya and praising the old man.

"Excuse me, but allow me to sit down in your place first, before you take mine." He stood in the aisle, his head hanging down, in an expectant pose.

"Oh, sure," she said with a nod, and unpeeled her behind from the seat.

Ilya grinned, his eyes meeting those of the old man—a delicate visual touch, without words, as if to say: How amusing; the nerve of the old fool! But the old man's eyes registered no response.

They changed places. The old man sat down and nodded to Ilya.

Then he opened his newspaper again. The name of the paper wasn't visible.

The woman wouldn't leave him in peace.

"Oh, so you can read a foreign language?"

He nodded yes.

Ilya turned back to the window. The sky was brilliant and bright, but his sense of elation had plummeted. He wanted to talk to this unusual neighbor, but now, after the impositions of the woman, he felt awkward.

The woman refused to give up.

"Hmm, I see. Which one?"

"In this case, it's German," the old man said with a smile, his gaze still trained on the paper.

After a short pause, she asked him another question, in a loud whisper.

"Tell me, are you Jewish?"

"Yes," he said. He smiled.

"And where are you going—to Israel or America?"

She's a real pain in the ass! Ilya thought. He was relishing this little scene.

"I lived in Germany until '33. I'm returning home. I lived in Russia for a very long time."

"So you're a foreigner?" The woman was fascinated.

He smiled again.

"Now I am."

"That's what I was thinking. You don't really seem like one of us. I'm going to Vienna, and then to America. My son is there already. At first I didn't want to, but then I thought—okay, I'll go. It's too bad I have to leave everything behind, of course." She wanted to talk, and her neighbor satisfied her purposes.

The German was a polite, considerate man. He answered all the silly questions of this silly woman. Ilya did the calculations in his head—he had left in '33, when Hitler had come to power. He was probably a Communist. He had done time in Russia, of course. Now, that's a biography. He had most likely reclaimed his German citizenship. It would definitely be worthwhile talking to him.

Ilya turned to the window again, but the rapturous feeling that had filled him on takeoff had vanished completely. He already felt earthbound, and was wondering whether Pierre, who had promised to fly to Vienna to meet him, would be there, or whether he would have to go to some transit camp—a dormitory stuffed with immigrants.

No, no, he'd break out of it. After all, he had acquaintances, even friends. He'd call them; maybe they'd send money. And Pierre would help him, of course. He wanted to go to Italy. But France appealed to him, too. Nicole was there, a good friend of his. He had people he could turn to. And at some point, at least part of his collection would sell. The elation he had felt at first began to revive.

The meal was served—delicious! An hour passed.

Mountains were visible from the window. Could they really be the Alps?

He even said it aloud: "The Alps."

The old man, who seemed to be dozing, suddenly threw his head back and turned to Ilya:

"Call the stewardess, please. I'm feeling unwell."

Ilya pressed the call button. The old man closed his eyes. He was yellowish-white, and his open mouth was gasping for air.

"Hurry . . . a doctor . . ." he wheezed.

Spasmodically, with deep, hoarse gulps, he sucked in air, then threw himself against the back of the seat. He froze, his mouth agape.

The woman next to him stared at him in horror.

The stewardess came up. She took his hand and felt for a pulse.

The woman, who was now standing in the aisle, was first to understand, and she set up an urgent peasant wail of despair: "Aaaaaah!"

Then Ilya realized that his neighbor was dead.

Edwin Yakovlevich Vinberg's emigration was over.

DEAF-MUTE DEMONS

There is a year, or perhaps a season, in almost every person's life, when the buds of possibility burst open, when fateful meetings take place, when paths cross, when courses and levels shift, when life rises from the depths and ascends to the heights. When Mikha was twenty-one, he met Alyona and fell in love with her so profoundly and so hopelessly that his entire former life, full of sweet girls, light-hearted and noncommittal rendezvous, and earnest, energetic nights in the dormitory, shattered like glass. Only meaningless shards and slivers of his former enthusiasms remained.

The second event that shook the foundations of his life, one no less significant, occurred a bit earlier. It involved his professional interests. At the beginning of his fourth year, Mikha didn't exactly renounce his love of Russian literature, but he did discover one more strong attraction. Every day he rushed off to the department of defectology, where he audited classes on pedagogy of the deaf-mute taught by the renowned specialist Yakov Petrovich Rink. Rink represented a whole dynasty of specialists who had been developing speech therapies for the deaf, deaf-mute, and hard of hearing over the past century.

A friend of Mikha's took him to Rink's first lecture, and after several weeks Mikha was determined to devote himself to studying the

pedagogy of the deaf-mute without having to abandon the department of philology. With Rink's permission and encouragement, he
took several preparatory exams and declared a double major in deaf
education and philology.

At first he rushed from one department to the other, but with time
he gravitated more and more toward defectology.

Perhaps an astute psychoanalyst could have ascertained the true
motivation behind Mikha's new interest, but this did not happen. The
shade of the inarticulate Minna did not trouble him, and the universal
sense of guilt that plagued him did not enter into it. Alyona's arrival in
his life swept away all thought of his minor amorous triumphs of the
past three years, as well as his memories of this adolescent trauma.
And what was there to remember, anyway?

A slow-witted, barely articulate creature, Minna had lived her
twenty-seven years almost unnoticed. She never burdened anyone
with her presence, and she died just as inconspicuously as she had
lived. Aunt Genya viewed the death of her daughter almost as though
she had been a household pet. Other people didn't even notice that the
timid, gentle creature with the weak smile, who never caused anyone
any harm, had died. And Mikha recalled Catullus's sparrow, how—
what was her name?—Lesbia had wept for it.

Soon after Minna's trestle bed and the child's chair she always laid
her clothes on before going to sleep were removed from the house,
Aunt Genya was liberated from heavy cares, and with deep satisfaction and a shadow of pathological pride, she would lament from time
to time, like a litany: "How much misfortune! How much misfortune
has fallen on me to bear! I have been the butt of misfortune!"

Mikha had been a boon for her. From the time he moved in with
her at the age of twelve, he had been tasked with going to the store,
tidying the room, cleaning the communal facilities and the kitchen, as
well as—and this was the most unpleasant task for him—carrying out
random trivial errands for Aunt Genya, such as rushing off to the
drugstore for medicine, taking half a pie to her sister Fanya and picking up a saucer of meat jelly from her other sister, Rayechka.

For almost ten years he had carried out his familial duties, uncomplaining and with a light heart. His aunt, insofar as she was able, loved

her charge, and did not intend to part with him if she could help it. But, obeying her Jewish instinct for matchmaking—joining up two free valences so they wouldn't end up in the wrong place—she occasionally introduced him to nice Jewish girls from her wide circle of family members. Her greatest misfire had occurred on this front: her own son Marlen had slipped out of her fingers and married a Russian girl. She had never been able to reconcile herself to this fact, though she admitted that "this Lida girl" was "quite suitable and decent."

At the beginning of October, Aunt Genya invited her distant niece Ella to visit. Quiet, as curvaceous as a bottle, with bottle legs, Ella brought with her a large oval box of chocolates. Aunt Genya wouldn't touch them, for fear of diabetes. Among her other firmly held beliefs was this one—that diabetes is caused by indulging in chocolate. She placed the box adorned with a running elk on the buffet and served bouillon.

Mikha sat submissively through all three courses of the meal, praising each of them, while the downcast Ella pushed her food around with her spoon silently. It was evident that she, too, suffered through the forced spontaneity of these meals with eligible distant male relatives, none of which culminated in the engagement that was sought. After dinner, Genya raised an eyebrow signaling that it was time for Mikha to take Ella to the metro. When he returned, his aunt, crossly shaking her doll-like head with its narrow part down the middle, said:

"You should have paid more attention to Ella. She has a good education, and she's an only child. They have an apartment in Maryina Roshcha that you wouldn't believe! Yes, she's a bit older than you are, I won't deny it. But she's one of ours!"

Still, the last thing she wanted was to be left alone in the communal apartment with the neighbors, who used to be decent, but who had all been replaced by anti-Semites and thieves, as if they had been handpicked exclusively for her.

But at that moment Mikha was thinking only about the box of chocolates. A beautiful girl named Alyona, a first-year student from the department of graphic arts, had invited him to her birthday party. As soon as she had arrived at the institute, she began to attract attention, not so much for her beauty—her face was like those Botticelli had loved, full of bright silence and youthful androgyny—as for her remoteness and haughtiness. Everyone wanted to be friends with her, but she was like water: she slipped out of one's grasp. Yet the previous evening, she had approached Mikha herself and invited him to her birthday party!

Mikha was not the most eligible young man in the department, since there were also several singer-songwriters, whose fame as wildly popular youthful bards was just beginning. Mikha couldn't compete with them. He wrote poems, too; but he certainly couldn't sing and accompany himself on the guitar. Still, he was a striking redhead, exceptionally conciliatory, who enjoyed great success among the girls, in particular those from out of town. His presence was indispensable at every student gathering or party.

Oh, he would have jumped at the chance to go to Alyona's birthday party; but he didn't even have the money to buy her the most modest gift. So, out of a sense of pride, he decided not to go. He had no one to borrow it from. Ilya was out of town, and he still owed Anna Alexandrovna fifteen rubles from the month before. He hadn't taken any money from Aunt Genya since he had started receiving a student stipend. This month, he had run through his funds early.

This fancy box on the buffet was just the thing, though! A dull-enough present, of course, but one couldn't arrive empty-handed . . .

He listened to his aunt's exhortations about marrying a Jewish girl. Then he asked whether he could take the box of chocolates to someone as a gift. His aunt had other plans for the chocolates, but Mikha turned on the charm and reminded her, as if by chance:

"The day after tomorrow I'm taking you to the cemetery; I haven't forgotten!"

The trip to Vostryakovo Cemetery took precedence over all other forms of entertainment for her, including the theater, movies, and visits to living relatives. She had never traveled to the distant cemetery alone, however.

His aunt understood the trade-off. Mikha got the box of chocolates and ran off with the elk under his arm to Pravda Street, where Alyona lived. He arrived—and it transpired! He was in love. Helplessly and inextricably, as had happened to him once before in his childhood, when he went to Sanya's for the first time. This time he fell in love with the household: with the head of the household, Sergei Borisovich Chernopyatov, Alyona's father; with his wife, Valentina; with the cabbage pies, the beet salad, and the "music on the bones"—records pressed on old X-ray film. Imagine, a rousing Gershwin number resounding from a hipbone! But, most important, of course—he fell in love with Alyona, who was not at all haughty or arrogant at home, but, on the contrary, quiet and sweet, embodying all the feminine charm the world had to offer.

They lost themselves in kisses on the balcony, and a mad tenderness held in check the mad passion that flared up in Mikha at his first touch of her fragile collarbone, her delicate wrists, her limp, childlike fingers.

Some people have talents as straightforward as apples, as obvious as eggs—for mathematics, for music, for drawing, even for mushroom-picking or table tennis. Mikha's talents were more subtle. In fact, at first glance, he seemed to have none. Rather, he had abilities: poetry, music, drawing.

His true talent was not visible to the naked eye. He was endowed with such emotional sympathy, such an unbridled, absolute capacity for empathy, that all his other qualities were subordinated to this "universal compassion."

He fulfilled the requirements of his studies in the philological department with pleasure and ease, but his interest in defectology arose from the very depths of his personality, from his gift of empathy. From the beginning he had set his hopes on teaching literature. He hungered to continue the tradition established long ago by Victor Yulievich, and he already saw himself entering the classroom and declaiming the greatest lines of Russian poetry . . . into the air, into the world, into the cosmos. And the boys and girls sitting around him—some of them! some of them, at least!—would be receptive to these sounds, and the kernels of meaning they contained.

Before getting his work assignment, Mikha went to see Rink, to ask his help in finding an appointment in a school for the deaf. For who else would bestow the treasures of poetry and prose on them?

Yakov Petrovich studied Mikha through his glasses, and asked him more questions about his life than about his profession. He concluded that this was the first time in his experience that a philology student had wished to work in the area of defectology.

"There is a very good boarding school for deaf-mutes where you could be of use, and where you could broaden your skills. It's a wonderful corrective learning institution, just outside of Moscow; but you would have to live there yourself. They need a good Russian literature and language teacher. Go there and have a look around. If you like what you see, come back and we'll continue our discussion," Yakov Petrovich suggested.

It took Mikha three hours to reach the school—he traveled first by commuter train to Zagorsk, then by bus, which he had to wait for, and then a half hour by foot along a forest road. It was early spring, and a light rain was falling, through which the woods showed a pale green. The rain whispered in last year's grasses, and the new growth was already pushing up through the dead foliage. It seemed that the rustling was the delicate sound of its growing. A bird screeched at regular intervals. Perhaps it wasn't even a bird, but a wild animal. It occurred to Mikha that the residents of this place couldn't hear these living sounds. On the other hand, city dwellers didn't hear them either, since the urban noise drowned them out. And a poem began to take shape in him already:

> Out of silence, rain, and growing
> grasses, sounds are born midst tender
> da-da. Music, da-da, da-da
> da-da, da-da harks the sender . . .

No, it wasn't coming together.

> Out of silence, rain, and growing
> grasses, hark!—from embryos spring
> symphonies so wild and tender,
> da-da music floods surrender . . .

Well, it had promise. He liked exact rhymes and regretted that all of them had been used many times before. This is what he said about the well-worn railroad ties of poetry that had been laid down long ago. He enjoyed the process of seeking them, but realized that one couldn't get very far on them. Brodsky had not yet begun his triumphal conquest of the world, compelling, through his long lines and his absolute contempt for this "tic-toc" and "da-da," the impoverished but inspired doggerel to cease.

Now the forest ended, and the grounds of the school began. A two-story wooden house stood on a small rise surrounded by dozens of small, cottage-like structures. There wasn't much left of the ancient fence—squat columns crowned with spheres eaten away by time were interspersed with worn gray palisades. The gate had long since vanished. Fat linden trees grew at uneven intervals—the remnants of a tree-lined avenue. It was already past lunchtime, and there was no one to be seen. He walked along the soggy, still bare earth toward the porch and knocked on the door. No one opened. He waited a bit, then the door flew open. A woman with a bucket of water and a dirty rag floating on top was standing in front of him.

He laughed and introduced himself to her. Aunt Genya, a slave to superstitions, signs, and portents, would have deemed this an auspicious beginning: the bucket was full of water, albeit dirty.

And, truly, it would have been hard to imagine a better beginning. In the director's office three women and an older man with a small mustache were drinking tea with jam. Mikha knew the director was a woman, and he concluded that she must be the Armenian woman, who also had a small mustache.

"Hello. I'd like to talk to Margarita Avetisovna. I'm here on the recommendation of Yakov Petrovich . . ." Before he managed to say the last name, they all broke out in smiles, and hurried to pour him tea and serve him jam in a little dish.

Suddenly there was a knock at the door and a boy of about twelve came in. He reported something, speaking only in a language of gestures.

"What happened, Sasha?" they asked in a chorus. "Well, tell us, you know how. Speak, speak, you can do it."

"Da dag wan awa." He struggled to articulate the sounds.

All four of them surrounded him, and a short woman with a thin plait wrapped around her head asked him loudly, stressing every sound: "Which dog? Nochka or Ryzhik?"

"No-ka," the boy said.

"Nochka. Don't worry, Sasha. She'll come back."

The boy made another gesture—placing one hand on another, and making an upward movement. This was a question.

"She'll get hungry and come back for food," the woman with the mustache said.

That has to be the director, Mikha thought.

The boy said something else with his hands.

"Listen to me, Sasha. She'll get hungry and come back for food."

When she made the sound "oo," she pursed her lips, pushing them as far forward as she could.

The boy nodded and left.

"Sasha has only been here six months. And he began learning very late," the woman with the plait said.

"Yes, it's only six months," the one with the small mustache confirmed.

"Five months, Margarita Avetisovna," Gleb Ivanovich, who had his own mustache, said. Very politely, so Mikha knew that she was indeed the director.

Ten minutes into their little tea party, Mikha knew that if they wouldn't take him on as a teacher, he would stay here and work in any capacity: whether as a janitor, a stoker, or a gym teacher.

They showed him the classrooms; there were four of them. And only forty-two children in all.

In one of the classrooms a girl was standing at the chalkboard and communicating something with her hands. The others listened to her—by watching.

"We don't renounce sign language completely. But we feel that if one begins teaching our methods early enough, most children can learn to speak."

"I would like to work here. I lived in an orphanage until I was seven, until my relatives took me in. I know I'm probably not the sort of person you're looking for . . . I've already begun studying sign language, but I'm not proficient yet. But if you would agree to take me on . . ."

They welcomed him with open arms.

He signed a contract that no one else would have accepted, and started work without even taking the vacation that was his due as a recent university graduate.

Everyone was dissatisfied with Mikha's departure for the boarding school: Aunt Genya, who cried on the day he left as though he were departing for the next world, although he would return again the following Sunday; Marlen, who would inherit some of Mikha's responsibilities for looking after his mother; Alyona, with whom his on-again, off-again romance was at a low point, but who shrugged her shoulders in consternation nevertheless, saying, "Why a boarding school? Why?" Alyona's father, the extremely clever Chernopyatov, felt that the closer one's job was to the city center, the better the job. And the provinces, anything beyond the capital city limits, were not even fit for living.

Even Anna Alexandrovna expressed concern—not about his career, but about the hygienic conditions there. She believed Mikha would be lice-ridden and dirt-encrusted in no time. Sanya thought about how long it would take to travel from that back of beyond to the Conservatory, but he didn't say anything. Ilya was upset that he was losing his friend just at the moment when they might have been able to earn a decent income working together.

Mikha was now teaching Russian language and literature to deaf-mute children. He worked alongside a speech therapist, and things were going very well. Mikha developed an approach that even earned the praises of Yakov Petrovich. He introduced rhythm exercises into the lessons. He clapped out the various poetic meters, and the children hummed their iambs and trochees. How happy they were when he expressed his delight with them; and how generous he was with his praise!

The school was unique in both its poverty and its plenty. The government subsidies were paltry, and even with extra compensation the salaries of the staff were incommensurate with their qualifications and with the time they invested in their work. The materials they had at their disposal were insufficient. But the absolute dedication of the teachers, their selflessness, and their pride in the results of their efforts, which were evident to all, outweighed all these other factors. Not to mention the atmosphere of creativity and love.

Almost a third of the children had been chosen from orphanages. The rest had been brought by their parents, who hoped that the school would enable them to communicate with the world more easily. The children from orphanages had an easier time than the others, since they were already used to life in an institution. The children with families usually stayed for only a year or two, at most.

Almost every Sunday Mikha returned to Moscow. He visited Aunt Genya and caught up on all the chores and errands he had missed during the week—from washing the floors and windows to buying groceries. Since the time Mikha had started college and the financial help from his relatives to his aunt had stopped, she had become tight-fisted and capricious. The sausage had to be Mikoyan, the cheese had to be Poshekhonsky, the milk Ostankino, and the fish—fresh carp or frozen perch—from a store that was closed on Sundays. So Mikha occasionally came to town on Saturdays just to buy this carp, if it was available.

After finishing his household chores and errands, he flew over to Alyona's. She would either be waiting for him with mascara on her lashes, which meant that she had turned her face toward him that day, or without any makeup at all. This suggested that her thoughts were elsewhere. Why her moods were so volatile he didn't know. He would try to find out from her, but she would just shrug her hair off her shoulders and slip away without explanation.

Then he would sit down with Sergei Borisovich in the kitchen and drink tea or vodka, depending on the time of day, the presence or absence of guests, and the mood of the host.

What an incredible human being! What a life! Mikha marveled at Chernopyatov. Sergei Borisovich Chernopyatov's father, born in Batumi, had been one of Stalin's closest companions. He was killed later than all the others, in 1937, when the leader had already done away with most of the friends of his youth. Sergei Borisovich was still just a boy the first time he was imprisoned, several weeks after his father's arrest. This was just a trial run—a children's penal colony. When he was eighteen they transferred him to a prison camp. In 1942, he was released from the camp and sent into exile. In Karaganda he met an "Algerian"—his future wife, Valentina. That was when he learned the meaning of that satanic geographical moniker, ALZHIR. It meant: Akmolinsky Camp for Wives of Traitors of the Homeland. Among the thousands of women were the mothers of Maya Plisetskaya, Vasily Aksyonov, and Bulat Okudzhava. Alyona's grandmother on her mother's side was the widow of a prominent Party member from Ryazan.

Valentina fell under the "FMTH" category: Family Members of Traitors of the Homeland. She was seventeen when they executed her father and arrested her mother. She managed to escape the fate of 25,000 FMTH minors who were sent to orphanages. She followed her mother, and ended up in the village of Malinovka, a forced-labor settlement. Her mother died a year later.

That was where she met Sergei. They were both twenty years old, and both of them dreamed of having a family. They married young, thus saving each other's life. Alyona was born in 1943. In 1947 they received permission to return to Russia, and they moved to Rostov-on-Don, where they found Valentina's relatives. Sergei Borisovich passed his high-school graduation exam, then entered college. The life about which they had dreamed began. In 1949, he was sent to prison again. Stalin's hand refused to loosen its grip. He was released in 1954; and his life began again for the third time . . .

Alyona was sick to death of hearing these stories. She would lock herself up in her room and turn on loud music. Sometimes she sat in her room for hours on end, scribbling with a slate pencil on rough paper: whimsical patterns of curlicues and cascades. Sometimes she simply left, without saying a word, ignoring Mikha altogether.

Mikha sat with Sergei Borisovich, picking up commonsense wisdom. And what a talent he had for sharing it! You would say something to him, and he would hold it up to scrutiny and then reveal its full significance to you, like a picture that blossomed into color when you held it underwater. He had such a deep understanding of life, of its inhumanity and absurdity and cruelty!

And the people! The guests who visited Sergei Borisovich, for all their diversity, had one thing in common: they were inveterate, implacable enemies of the authorities. They understood the nature of the system, its deep-rooted injustice. One was a geneticist, another a philosopher, yet a third a mathematician. And at the very center of all of them stood Sergei Borisovich—hardheaded, astute, clever—actively committed to the public welfare.

Mikha loved him, too, because he was the male embodiment of everything that attracted him to Alyona: barely discernible wrinkles in the corners of the eyelids that rose slightly upward, small folds pointing downward at the corners of the mouth, the small bones and lightness of movement characteristic of dwellers of the Caucasus. True, Alyona had inherited a delicate pallor from her mother, but Sergei Borisovich, with his admixture of Circassian blood, was dark-haired and swarthy. He was a real man—a father, brother, friend. An antidote to Mikha's fatherlessness, something he had never yet managed to come to terms with. Sergei Borisovich treated Mikha with kindness, but too much condescension. That was, in fact, how he treated most people—he seemed to look down on them slightly.

Sometimes Alyona, having done her eyelashes, seemed kindly disposed toward Mikha. At those times he would follow her wherever she wished; they would walk around Moscow, her limp, fine-boned hand in his—what intense joy!—and he would touch her hair, breathing in its pungent, feathery scent. He would speak off the top of his head, and from the bottom of his soul, reciting poetry. He had already gone through Mayakovsky, had absorbed Pasternak, and was in those days brimming over with Mandelstam. Brodsky began a bit later with him. She listened, fell silent, hardly deigning to respond. Also with condescension.

Sometimes, during these felicitous periods—there were three such during Mikha's life in Milyaevo: the winter of 1962, at the very beginning of Mikha's stay in the boarding school; then in the spring of 1963; and at the end of 1964—she suddenly came to him in the middle of the week, and stayed overnight with him in the utility room that had been allocated to him. Mikha was nearly beside himself with unexpected joy.

The greater these intervals of happiness, the more bitter were those periods when she would cool toward him and withdraw her affection. At those times he would throw himself into his work. His commitments to the deaf children filled his life to the point of overflowing, so that he had almost no time for misery and longing.

The boarders were also lacking fathers, and they clung to the male teachers—Gleb Ivanovich and Mikha—vying for their attention and affection. The older ones were more restrained, but they also gravitated toward the male teachers.

Yakov Petrovich Rink invited Mikha to participate in seminars once a month, trying to involve him in the project to which he had devoted the better part of a decade. He was engaged in a struggle to found a deaf children's learning center in Moscow, either at the pedagogical college or at the Academy of Medical Sciences. The authorities had already approved the project in principle, but the inertia of the government machine was so great that the span of one human life was simply not enough to create something new, unless it concerned either the military-industrial complex or the cosmos. Rink was counting on Mikha becoming one of the handpicked protégés who could continue his life's work.

Yakov Petrovich mentored Mikha, gave him studies to read by contemporary French and American researchers, and, finally, advised him to write an article himself—which Mikha did with great enthusiasm. Yakov Petrovich read through the industrious scrawl—the boy could write!

He had bred his students and assistants over the decades for quality—selecting them for size, taste, shade . . . After three years of voluntary slavery in the boarding school, Rink broached the subject of graduate studies to Mikha—albeit in absentia. But Mikha himself preferred this. He had no intention of parting with his charges.

Mikha passed the qualifying exams for graduate school with flying colors, and was waiting for his enrollment papers. This was in fact just a formality. He was not interested in abstract, theoretical scholarship. Rather, he was looking forward to real, applied scholarly research, such that the results would be immediately evident after several years of implementing the proper methods. The blind did not yet see, the deaf did not hear, and the dumb did not speak; but some of them were learning little by little to articulate words and to enter a world that till then had been closed to them . . . and what a joy it was to lead them by the hand!

Contrary to all expectation, Mikha seemed to be the most successful of the Trianon members. Sanya had dropped out of the Institute of Foreign Languages and begun his studies at the Conservatory again. Ilya had forgotten all about his intention to study at the Leningrad Institute of Cinema Engineering, assuming that he could teach photography himself if he wished and that there was no need for him to continue his education. He had accumulated friends and acquaintances, and interesting connections, especially in the new democratic human rights movement. Ilya and Mikha continued to share a common interest in poetry. Ilya still made the rounds of antiquarian booksellers, and his collection of rare and valuable books was growing apace.

Ilya was the one Mikha chose to confide in about his fantastic new prospects. Ilya's reaction was tepid. He had been lucky that day, too. He had a new acquisition. It was an absolute rarity—one of the few remaining copies of Vladimir Narbut's collection *Alleluja*, which had been published in St. Petersburg in 1912 and immediately banned by the Holy Synod, condemned to destruction "by means of rending and tearing."

Mikha opened to a random page—it was indeed "Alleluja," Psalm 148.

> Praise the Lord from the earth, ye dragons, and all deeps:
> Fire, and hail; snow, and vapor; stormy wind fulfilling his word:
> Mountains, and all hills; fruitful trees, and all cedars:
> Beasts, and all cattle; creeping things, and flying fowl . . .

Ilya took the volume from Mikha gently.

"That's a well-known psalm. Let me show you something else. Here."

> It's a standing bog that sings,
> and not a murmuring river!

A rust of ancient red gilding
settles on him. Light is
the long-legged spider's flight
across the rippling water.
Green roads float away—
but blood flows nowhere.

"But who knows Narbut now? He floated away! And how much else has floated off! Do you hear anything that's going on, out there with your deaf ones?"

"What are you talking about?" Mikha felt a vague sense of alarm, as though he had missed something important.

"They've arrested two writers."

The inquisitive Mikha was already aware of this arrest, having heard about it on a nighttime radio broadcast. He had forgotten their names. Ilya reminded him. They had sent manuscripts of their books to the West, and they had been published there.

Mikha expressed an interest in reading them. Ilya told him that he didn't have them, but his friend had a photocopy. Ilya had made the photocopy himself; but he didn't tell Mikha, just to be on the safe side. He was sitting on a powder keg. He had removed everything from his house, and stored it with friends.

"Only you'll have to get it from him yourself. You can take it and keep it for a while. I'll pick it up later, when things simmer down."

On conspiracy alert, they went outside and called the friend, whose name was Edik, from a pay phone on Pokrovka. Ilya spoke into the receiver in a loud, careless manner:

"Hey, Edik, I left a sausage roll over at your place yesterday. A friend of mine is stopping by to pick it up. Thanks. See you!"

The unmasked writer, who had gone under the pseudonym Nikolay Arzhak, was actually Yuli Daniel, a literature teacher in a Moscow school! Amazing—just like our Victor Yulievich! A literature teacher! And he, too, had fought on the front and been wounded, and was also a philologist!

Mikha was already impressed by the coincidences before he read the manuscript. He went over to get it from Edik, a comical, long-legged fellow. There turned out to be two sausage rolls. One was called *This Is Moscow Speaking*, and the other was *Redemption*.

Mikha picked up two fat manila envelopes. He began to read the first one.

It scalded him like boiling water, even though he had already read Orwell's *Nineteen Eighty-four*, a brilliant, horrifying book. *Nineteen Eighty-four* was an invented country, neither here nor there—but this one was about Daniel's own circumstances, his own time. It took place on Russian soil, which made everything that much more urgent and immediate. For this reason *Moscow Speaking* was even more terrifying than *Nineteen Eighty-four*.

And it was unclear which was worse: the right, bestowed by ukase, for each to kill any on a certain day; or the same right arrogated by the government to kill any citizen, on any day of the month, for years to come.

Redemption was perhaps the most frightening of all. It turned out you could not only kill, but destroy a person by the most subtle and ingenious methods—accuse an honest man of being a stool pigeon, an informer, to make him lose his mind. And the worst thing was that one couldn't prove anything to anyone, and there was no way of vindicating oneself.

This Victor Volsky was a wholly sympathetic and believable character, slandered and driven out of his mind by his friends, who chose to believe the false accusations about him. When he was locked up in his psych ward, he no doubt recalled Pushkin:

> Let me not go mad—
> Better a beggar's crook and pouch;
> No, hard labor and hunger...
>
> This is the curse: go mad,
> and, as though you suffer from the plague,
> They'll lock you up, banish you for good...

How had Pushkin known? Could it be that even then ... Oh, of course, the Decembrists! The same thing had happened back then already— denunciations, betrayals. Maiboroda, the informer. And he had taken

his own life many years after the trial. He had probably suffered all
those years. He really had signed a letter of denunciation; but Victor
Volsky was not guilty of that act. No, it was better to forgive a true
informer than to ruin an innocent man that way.

Mikha read the whole night through. He was so engaged, so lost in
the book, that in the morning he was disoriented and didn't quite realize he had to be at the boarding school at eight o'clock.

His recent successes suddenly seemed insignificant, and the future
didn't beckon quite so brightly. It all seemed trivial and unimportant.
He even felt ashamed. Yes. He felt guilty for merely living, while
Daniel, this marvelous writer, had penetrated to the very essence of
their current life, and was now being held in solitary, undergoing interrogation. God knew what was in store for him.

Mikha, snapping out of his reader's reverie, realized that he was
already late for work, and that if he really hurried he would only make
it for the fourth lesson. But soon the two-hour lunch break between
commuter trains would begin, so he would most likely arrive too
late, and the day would be a total loss. He tried to call the school to
inform them, but the telephone line was down.

His colleagues rose to the occasion and covered for him. Katya, the
speech therapist, called off her individual tutoring and took over two
of Mikha's lessons. Gleb Ivanovich stepped in to teach the other two.
But when Mikha arrived, the classes had already ended. The children
had eaten their midday meal, and had been sent off for their "dead
hour," a postprandial rest period. It was so late that by now they had
already eaten their afternoon snack. Gleb Ivanovich was sitting in the
cafeteria drinking the last of the fruit compote and eating it with
white bread—his favorite treat.

Mikha rushed over to thank him. Gleb Ivanovich didn't view his
actions as heroic in the least. It was just what one did. But Mikha insisted on trying to account for his lapse. He told him that he had
stayed up the whole night reading. When he was finished, he looked at
the clock—and it was already after ten in the morning!

"But the books, the books! What books they were . . ."

"What were they?" Gleb Ivanovich asked between his second and
third glasses of compote.

And Mikha immediately pulled out the two manila envelopes containing the photocopied pages. The print was very small.

The children were doing their lessons in study hall. A young teacher was sitting with them. It was her first year of teaching, and Gleb Ivanovich was supervising her, just in case she had any difficulties. She was a nice young woman. Gleb Ivanovich glanced into the classroom, sat down in the back row, and put on his reading glasses.

Fifteen minutes later, he woke up Mikha, who hadn't been able to sleep on the commuter train and was dozing in the utility room.

Gleb Ivanovich sat down next to him on a stool and said, in a frantic whisper:

"Do you have any idea what you just gave me to read?"

Mikha felt like he had been caught out. He tried to extricate himself from the awkward situation by mumbling some nonsense about the profound truth he had discovered in these books, at the same time offering his apologies for having alarmed Gleb Ivanovich with such dangerous literature.

Gleb Ivanovich's whispers became ever louder, until he was actually shouting. He accused Mikha of every kind of transgression: lack of gratitude to the authorities who had rescued his Jew-face from fascism; treason; hostility to the state; and taking part in criminal anti-Soviet activity.

It was all extremely awkward and idiotic. Five minutes later they were already locked in a shouting match, banging their fists on the table and itching to bash each other's face in. All the sympathy that they had felt toward each other had vanished. Now each of them considered himself to have been cheated and robbed, having wasted so many good feelings on such a worthless nonentity. In an instant, the sense of camaraderie, which had bound them together in their shared joys and misfortunes, had collapsed. Mikha, who was by nature mild-mannered, had rid himself of his anger by shouting and waving his arms around. He was ready to return to their original state of mutual peaceful misunderstanding, to consider, calmly this time, all the ridiculous arguments that Gleb Ivanovich had put forward. But Gleb Ivanovich was not agreeable to this. He was primed for battle. Now he began enumerating a long list of Mikha's mistakes and transgressions—which, according to him, were just short of criminal acts.

Gleb Ivanovich turned out to have greater endurance and strength in verbal warfare. The voice that rose out of his scrawny neck was strong and low, more like that of a big potbellied man than the undersized weakling he appeared to be.

Mikha was tired. He let Gleb Ivanovich shout his fill, and then tried to reclaim the manila envelopes with the photocopied books.

"You leave those pernicious things right here with me! I'm not letting you take a single page out of here, not a single line!" Gleb Ivanovich screamed when he saw Mikha reaching for the envelopes, and grabbed hold of them himself.

There was a tug of war, each of them gripping a side of the envelopes. Under other circumstances, Mikha would have burst out laughing long before; but for laughter, one needs to be met with a favorable disposition. And what he witnessed here was some sort of madness. Gleb Ivanovich began barking out words and phrases that had no relation whatsoever to what was happening.

"Up against the wall! Forward! Kosachev, move it! Kosachev, get back! Motherfuckers!"

Most surprising were the exhortations to Kosachev, since Kosachev was Gleb Ivanovich himself.

Polina Matveevna, the cleaning woman, looked in when she heard the shouting, then backed out again. A minute later she returned with a white cup, which she pressed Gleb Ivanovich to drink, clutching his unevenly balding head in her gentle hands.

"Careful now, careful. Take a little sip of this, Gleb Ivanovich, and watch out that you don't spill water all over yourself," she urged him.

At last, Mikha realized that he was dealing with a mad person, and that Mikha himself had provoked the outburst when, unbeknown to him, he had pressed some psychological trigger.

Polina Matveevna made signs at Mikha, which all the residents of the boarding school knew immediately how to interpret, signifying that he should clear out. And Mikha, grabbing up the envelopes, did.

Volsky! Volsky! Daniel's protagonist, dying in a mental hospital! But Gleb Ivanovich was a victim as well! And the very same forces had driven him mad. Demons, demons. What had Voloshin said? "They walk the earth, blind, deaf, and dumb, and draw fiery signs in the spreading gloom ..." He repeated it to himself, noting an irregularity in the stress pattern. Nevertheless, it was a great poem.* And he went back to thinking about Gleb Ivanovich. He wasn't really to blame for anything, either. During the bus ride to the commuter train that would take him home, he pondered all these things with a heavy heart.

Gleb Ivanovich had been hospitalized for psychiatric disorders, and was on the registry. He had a checkered past. He had been fired from SMERSH, the counterintelligence organization, during the war. At the boarding school his official job description was physical-plant manager, not teacher. This was not merely for the sake of convenience. Because of his medical history, he was barred from working with children. He was a good man; he loved children, and he was honest and upright almost to a fault, with an almost German ardor and fastidiousness. Perhaps this was the quality, which bordered on the extreme, that led him to write a denunciation of Mikha the very next day.

Mikha had no idea that Gleb Ivanovich's denunciation was already crawling, slowly but surely, to the place where all waterways cut off and all roads ceased.

Due to the general laxity of Soviet life, as well as the law of coincidence of misfortune, Mikha's application for enrollment in the graduate program in absentia matched the unhurried progress toward the institute of the denunciation against him. When, two weeks later, two documents landed simultaneously on the desk of Comrade Korobtsov, head of the first section, he called in Yakov Petrovich. The seventy-eight-year-old corresponding member of the Academy of Pedagogical Sciences trotted down to see Comrade Korobtsov, already a captain at the age of thirty-six, who gave him a proper dressing-down.

*See the full translation of Voloshin's poem in the Translator's Note on page 578.

Though Yakov Petrovich Rink was fairly old, he looked younger than his years. He had been dressed down over and over again. He had devoted his entire life to deaf-mute pedagogy. He had helped the hard of hearing; and the deaf had, in turn, been his salvation. In the offices where semiliterate lieutenants and poorly educated captains decided the fate of science, the professor's work seemed so innocuous and absurd that they left him alone. He was German—but a Russian-German. His ancestor had been invited into the Russian Academy of Sciences one hundred fifty years before, and the family had been firmly settled on Russian soil ever since. Luckily, his nationality was registered as Russian in his documents. Unlike his cousins, who had been banished to Kazakhstan at the beginning of the war, he had never been subjected to political repression. He was well aware that this was a gift of fate. Each time that Yakov Petrovich was summoned to the offices of the lieutenants and the captains, he expected to be unmasked. Even now, twenty years after the war had ended.

Pursing his lips in the tight, straight line that signified a smile, he told his close friend and associate, Maria Moiseevna Bris:

"You have it good, Maria Moiseevna. You are a bona fide Jew, and there is no need to unmask you. Half my life I feared being taken for a Jew, and now I live in fear that they will unmask me as a German. And all the while, you and I are just ordinary Russian intellectuals."

"Who are these people you're taking on as graduate students this year, Yakov Petrovich?" Korobtsov said, not offering him a seat.

How sick I am of him, how sick I am of him, how sick I am of all of them . . .

"Are you lacking some documents, Igor Stepanovich? There's a student named Sasha Rubin, and an in absentia student—one Mikha Melamid. They're good kids, both graduates of our institute."

"Sit down, sit down, Yakov Petrovich. We have some things to talk about. Sasha Rubin is fine—good recommendations, he's a Komsomol organizer. But how well do you know this Melamid?"

It was plain as day. They didn't like Melamid. There was something about him that gave them pause. Maria Moiseevna had been right: he shouldn't have allowed Jews to take two spots in the program. They'd seize upon it. There was one young man from Moldavia, but he didn't have a very strong academic background. They would have accepted him, but he hadn't passed his entrance exams . . .

"He just published a very interesting article. He's already working in the field. Well-read. Keen on his subject. He has all the makings of a scholar," said Yakov Petrovich.

"Um-hmm . . ." Korobtsov paused. "And why him in particular? Other kids took the entrance exams, too. Take a look . . ." He rifled through some papers, and read out a name syllable by syllable: "Pe-re-po-pes-cu, Ne-do-po-pes-cu, something along those lines. From Moldavia, an ordinary fellow. And you give us these Melamids, Rabinoviches . . ."

How I hate you, how I hate you, how I hate you . . .

"Melamid is one of our own graduates, and he has a job we recommended him for. He's a talented and serious young man!"

"Umm. Well, Yakov Petrovich, you tell this serious young man that the first section wouldn't let him in. If he has any questions, he can come to me, and I'll explain."

"Do you mean to say that you won't okay the application?"

"Exactly. Why are you looking at me that way? We're looking out for your interests, the interests of the institute, and the country as a whole! Are you willing to answer for him, Yakov Petrovich, if he gets mixed up in some sort of trouble? Personally vouch for him?"

Go to the devil, go to the devil, you can all go straight to the devil . . .

"I'll think about it, Igor Stepanovich. I'll think about it."

In fact, there was nothing to think about. Financial backing for the laboratory, Maria Moiseevna's doctoral dissertation, which she hadn't been able to defend since 1953, the opening of the learning center, colleagues and associates, students and graduate students—Yakov Petrovich couldn't afford to beat his head against a brick wall.

———

In the fall, so many things happened in Mikha's life, both good and bad, almost simultaneously, that they all blended into one patchy, vibrant mass. Alyona's behavior toward him suddenly changed, and their nervous relationship, with its thaws and its cold snaps, accompanied by Alyona's constant emotional fireworks, suddenly grew calm and close. Mikha didn't understand why the change had occurred; Alyona didn't consider it necessary to explain to him that she had broken off with a married man she had been in love with since the age of sixteen. She put him out to pasture and decided to marry Mikha. Mikha was overjoyed.

He hadn't yet managed to come to terms with all the implications of this imminent change in his life, to think through the myriad quotidian issues it raised, and to which Alyona was oblivious, when things were resolved in a very unexpected way: Aunt Genya died suddenly and without any fanfare.

She had planned on living a long time, and getting properly sick before the end. She had already accumulated a sizable list of illnesses; but she was deceived. She went to bed in the evening and died in her sleep, thus magnanimously resolving, in a way completely uncharacteristic of her, Mikha's greatest worry—where to live.

It so happened that on the day of Aunt Genya's death, Mikha didn't spend the night at home. He and Alyona had gone to the dacha of a girlfriend of Ilya's. It was a small gathering of friends against the backdrop of nature. When Mikha returned home late in the evening of the following day, Aunt Genya didn't greet him with her usual reproaches or complaints. She was, rather, completely cold and calm.

Now he was the only registered person in that home, master of a 150-square-foot room in the center of town. Marlen had been registered at his wife's address for a long time already. The room was supposed to have been left to Minna, and Mikha, according to the same strategic family plan, was supposed to receive a job appointment and go live somewhere else.

Marlen was a pragmatic man. Three years before he might have been distressed about losing the room and not carrying out the family plan, but at this point everything in his life had changed. He had taken the plunge into Judaism. He had started studying Hebrew, reading the Torah, corresponding with Zionists, and preparing himself for a long struggle for the right to be repatriated to Israel. The biggest obstacle for him on the path of his journey was his mother. Aunt Genya hated Israel, which, according to her, was the cause of all Jewish suffering. She had already informed her son that she had no intention of leaving her homeland and would never grant him permission to leave himself.

The death of his mother hastened Marlen's reunion with Zion.

When Mikha asked Marlen what to do with Aunt Genya's belongings, he merely shrugged:

"Ask the other aunts. They can take what they want. Throw everything else away."

But by this time the aunts had already taken everything that was worth anything.

Alyona came to Mikha's house for the first time after Aunt Genya had died. She walked through the door, paused on the threshold, and looked around her. She saw a crystal chandelier with missing baubles, and other luxuries amid poverty: broken vases; two paintings in thick, gilded plaster frames; a potted geranium; an aloe plant; and a three-quart jar with a Japanese mushroom purported to aid digestion sitting on the windowsill. There was a photograph of a fairly pretty woman with a permanent wave and two children—an intelligent-looking adolescent boy and a plump, smiling little girl. The girl looked about three, and her fat tongue was protruding from her mouth.

"Is that Aunt Genya and her children?" Alyona asked.

Mikha nodded. He suddenly felt ashamed of the squalor of his home, and, at the same time, uncomfortable that he was betraying his poor aunt by feeling this shame.

"Was the little girl sick?" She indicated with her eyes that she meant little Minna.

"Yes, she had Down syndrome. It was only when I went to the institute that I understood. Aunt Genya was told it was some kind of endocrinological disorder. She died."

Alyona nodded, and remained silent for several minutes. Then she said:

"What a sad, awful home. This was just how I imagined it. Well, not exactly, but almost."

She entered the room, sat down at the table covered with maroon-colored plush. She ran her finger over the dusty nap and said plaintively:

"Mikha, this is no place to live."

"It will be fine, Alyona. I'll renovate it. The other guys will help me."

"No, it's not about the condition of the room . . ." Alyona sighed, and sank into a heavy despondency that covered her like a rain cloud.

Her married lover had received her in just such a room. The same round table with a plush tablecloth, the same kind of chandelier with missing crystal baubles hanging above it, the same photograph of a pretty woman with a permanent wave—but in that one she had been holding a fan. Alyona looked at the two shelves with books. Even the books were the same, though the married man had had far more of them. And that room had been three times bigger than this, and partitioned with a curtain.

Mikha wanted with all his heart and soul to reach out to her, but he was afraid to touch her. He couldn't summon up the courage, and he waited for a sign from her. She came to him, and ran her fingers through his thick red locks. And he took heart; because just a moment before he had been certain that he was such a blockhead, that with all his shortcomings and disadvantages he was no match for Alyona, and that not only would she never agree to marry him, she wouldn't even want to look at such a nonentity anymore.

Something of the sort had occurred to her; but she stroked his hair, and said over and over again:

"Mikha, you're so good. You're too good for me, you know."

She already knew in advance that all these qualms, these second thoughts, would disappear, that Mikha was not only a sweet and pure human being, but also the most reliable, and loyal, and the finest of the lovers she had known till then. The married man, though, always a bit tipsy and coolly relaxed—she couldn't quite shake him. What was it that bound her to him? She had an inkling, but she was unable to express it, to fathom it completely.

The springs in the lumpy divan creaked wildly, but it held out the entire night and half the following day. All the oppressive, alien thoughts fled from their young heads, and when they awoke, both of them felt giddy, weightless, and empty, and basked in the triumph of a battle won.

Mikha's happiness knew no bounds. He felt it would last him the rest of his life. In the daytime, when Alyona was with Mikha, she felt fine, but she dreaded the evenings. She would fall asleep instantly, but an hour later she would wake up in unendurable nocturnal torment. Toward morning she would fall asleep again, and when she woke up, her pain would leave her, and she would even marvel at the depth of the anguish she had felt the night before.

They had to do something about this, and one day, after a typically sad and exhausting night, she and Mikha went to file for a marriage certificate. Then they went back to Mikha's, on Chistoprudny Boulevard, and threw out all that remained of Aunt Genya's junk, which even her sisters had rejected. It was the sad dust and clutter of an ordinary life: plates held together with yellowing glue, pots and pans with missing handles, half-used lipstick tubes, old newspapers, tatters, rags, and scraps, half a porcelain bear, and a little May Day flag.

In the evening Ilya and Sanya came by to help Mikha drag out the heavy furniture: the buffet, cupboard, wardrobe, and Aunt Genya's divan.

Alyona washed the floors and felt that in this empty room she would be able to live. They slept on the floor for several nights on a spread-out sleeping bag. Alyona slept deeply and soundly, without dreaming, in Mikha's embrace, and it seemed to her that he would hold her safely in his arms forever.

While the renovations were in progress, they went to stay with the Chernopyatovs for a few nights. Sergei Borisovich, who adored his daughter, grieved that she planned to move away from home. Valentina even started talking about an apartment exchange—their two rooms and Mikha's one room for a three-room apartment where they could all live together. But Alyona didn't want this.

She wanted to move into Mikha's renovated room as soon as it was ready. When the smell of paint had finally dissipated, they moved into the clean, empty room, which already seemed to have no past, except the view from the window: a littered courtyard, visually transfigured by the sixth-floor vantage point.

All that remained of the past were two cardboard boxes, a pile of books, and bundles of old letters that had been discovered at the bottom of the listing old wardrobe. Marlen had asked that they be saved; he intended to come by to fetch them. Alyona moved her easel into the room, which stood by the window and gave the place an artistic air. They also moved in a drafting table that Sergei Borisovich himself had made for her, and five large portfolios with old (which meant three years ago) work, almost all ornate, abstract designs.

The young couple didn't have a wedding celebration, but they received presents from Marlen, from Alyona's parents, and from an aunt—in the much-maligned but much-needed form of money. After her classes Alyona would scour the stores, buying new plates and pillows, taking quiet delight in her new life. Under the influence of Mikha's inexhaustible tenderness and active passion, her heartsickness began to retreat, if not altogether heal.

And at that very moment their luck ended. Yakov Petrovich called Mikha in to inform him that his graduate studies were not going to work out. The personnel office had blocked his application. Their collaborative work would continue, however.

"We won't abandon the dissertation, but, frankly speaking, the road ahead will be a long and fraught one." Thus the discussion ended not with a period, but with an ellipsis.

At the end of the same month, upon the request of the director, Mikha resigned from the boarding school. She begged forgiveness, she wept, and she tried to justify her actions by saying that her first priority was to keep the boarding school open and not to put the forty-some children in jeopardy.

Mikha, who had caught the drift, said: "They called?"

Margarita Avetisovna nodded.

There was only one possible explanation: he was now in the crosshairs. Mikha resigned "for personal reasons." Since he needed to give them two weeks' notice of his resignation, obligatory in this case, the director suggested he spend the time looking for a new job. Two weeks later, he returned to pick up his employment records and to say goodbye to his colleagues. Everyone looked dispirited and upset. Gleb Ivanovich wasn't there.

When Mikha asked about him, he was told that Gleb Ivanovich had been admitted to a psychiatric hospital.

Mikha felt an enormous void opening before him. He sensed a great change coming in his life: something completely new would now take root and grow out of this emptiness.

MILYUTIN PARK

N o one knows the secret of irresistible attraction, the law that draws a particular man and a particular woman together. Ecclesiastes, at any rate, didn't know. Medieval legend tries to account for it in the guise of a love potion. Poison, in other words. No doubt the same poison in which the omnipotent Eros soaked his operatic arrows. Modern people find the answer in hormones serving the instinct to preserve the species. Clearly, between this pragmatic goal and platonic love there is a significant gap, even a cognitive dissonance, as a more contemporary idiom might have it. The earnest task of continuing the species takes refuge in all kinds of ritual embellishment— orange blossoms, priests, seals graced with eagles, and so forth, right down to the bloody sheet hung out in the courtyard for public inspection. This aspect of love is more or less straightforward.

But where does that leave friendship? Not a single major instinct supports it. All the philosophers (men, of course—before Piama Gaidenko there were no women philosophers, unless you count the legendary Hypatia) considered friendship to be at the very pinnacle of the hierarchy of values. Aristotle provides a wonderful definition, which still rings true right up to the present, in contrast to many of his ideas, which are so quaint and anachronistic as to sound ridiculous. Hence: "Friendship is a specifically human fact, the explanation and goal of which must be sought without recourse to the laws of nature or a transcendent Good extending beyond the framework of empirical existence."

Thus, friendship is not conditioned by nature, and has no apparent goal. It consists in the search for a kindred spirit with whom to share one's experiences, thoughts, and feelings—right down to "sacrificing one's life." But in order to achieve this happiness, one must feed friendship with time, time that is part and parcel of one's own, and only, life: going for a walk down Rozhdestvensky Boulevard, for example, and drinking a beer, even if you'd prefer another beverage, since your friend likes beer; or going to his grandmother's birthday party; or reading the same books and listening to the same music—so that eventually you create a small, warm, enclosed space together, in which jokes are understood by a single word or gesture, opinions are exchanged through a mere glance, and interaction is more intimate than anything one can achieve with someone of another sex. With rare exceptions.

But there was less and less time for friends. There were no more school breaks, walking excursions through Moscow with a favorite teacher on Wednesdays—the sublimely obligatory school-day camaraderie had ended. They came together from time to time out of the inertia of habit, but they dove into their little coves of friendship less and less often. Suddenly they discovered that life had forced them apart, and the need to share their daily experiences and events—whether large, small, or completely trivial—had exhausted itself. A telephone call once a week, once a month, or on holidays was sufficient.

Of course, this growing apart happened gradually. The history of the friendship the three friends shared had an irrevocable significance; but five or six years after graduating from school, it was possible to look back and identify the points or moments when the divergence began. Take Mikha, for instance.

Ilya could remember Mikha's personal evolution—how he followed a trajectory of enthusiasm for the revolutionary Mayakovsky, the magical Blok, and that Pasternak who could write:

Eight volleys from the Neva,
And a ninth.
Tired, like glory.
Like—(from left and right
They lurch headlong).
Like—(the distances shout out:
we'll get even with you yet).
Like the straining, bursting
Asunder of joints
Of oaths
Once sworn
To the dynasty . . .

Ilya tolerated Mikha's revolutionary sympathies. Sanya smiled wanly. Their friendship easily withstood minor differences, divergences in the placement of accent and tone. Pierre Zand, the festival visitor they befriended, a young Russian-Belgian, troubled Mikha to the depths of his soul with his antagonism toward the Revolution. Mikha decided to establish a personal and dispassionate perspective on communism. This took more than two years. First he read Marx, then he reversed his steps, beating a retreat into the past to read the early socialists, who were all fairly accessible. After that he stumbled over Hegel, and, executing a pirouette, made a beeline for Lenin.

Marlen, his uncle (they had grown steadily closer over the years), viewed his interests with suspicion:

"You're reading the wrong stuff, Mikha. There were many revolutionaries in our family, and they were all executed, except for Mark Naumovich. And Mark Naumovich survived because he first volunteered to serve in the NKVD, and then hightailed it out to the provinces just in time, as some sort of consultant. A very clever fellow, and a bastard if ever there was one."

"I need to figure it out on my own," Mikha said in his own defense.

"Well, figure it out then, figure it out," Marlen said, conciliatory. "If you want to reinvent the wheel, it's your business."

Aunt Genya put a bowl of borscht in front of each of them, then served the main dish: meat patties with potatoes. Her son got three, Mikha got two, and she herself got one.

Marlen laughed, pointing at the meat patties.

"There's your socialist equality! And everywhere you look, it's always the same!"

Mikha racked his brains, trying to get to the bottom of things. He read and read; what he read generated many questions, and few answers. He tried to talk about socialism with Victor Yulievich, who just grimaced and said that he had no predilection for social science.

Ilya, who had one of the most inquiring and informed minds of all the people he knew, threw fuel on the fire. The most combustible, in his view, was Orwell's *Nineteen Eighty-four*, the samizdat they had lost, without ever knowing what it was, in the briefcase of Pierre's uncle Orlov, the French diplomat, in 1957. *Nineteen Eighty-four* made a deep impression on Mikha. He was far more receptive to the artistic word than to the dry erudition of socioeconomic scholasticism.

Ilya could boast of a small victory, at least: Mikha's revolutionary ardor had cooled. Nevertheless, they began spending less time together. And Sanya was off in his own musical universe. He was up to his ears in arcane theories of scales, and his best friends could never have been interlocutors on this subject.

It was Mikha's affinity for literature that had led him to the difficult and sad situation in which he found himself in the late autumn of 1966, unemployed and barred from graduate studies.

His would-be adviser, Yakov Petrovich Rink, was distressed about what had transpired and tried to help Mikha. Within the bounds of reason. Yakov Petrovich was unquestionably decent, but he was also pliant and adaptable. And so clever that he understood perfectly well how complicated and difficult it was to combine decency and pliancy when faced with the powers that be, with whom he had successfully negotiated his whole life. In Mikha Melamid's case, however, he had not managed. It was a great disappointment, and it grieved him; but it hadn't prevented them both from continuing work on their very important common cause.

Yakov Petrovich had made several attempts to help the young man find employment. Yakov Petrovich had countless connections in the pedagogical world, but even he wasn't able to find a job that would allow Mikha to carry out his experimental research: implementing new methods of speech therapy.

Thus, every avenue of scholarly work was closed to Mikha.

The only thing Rink, corresponding member of the Academy of Sciences, was able to do was arrange for the unsuccessful graduate-school candidate to teach literature in a night school—and only on a part-time basis. The eight hours a week he taught offered them meager sustenance for only eight days—and there were at least thirty days in a month. Alyona was still going to college, and her studies completely exhausted her energies, which were not very ample to begin with.

Mikha became convinced that he would never be able to find work on his own.

At the local Board of Education, where he went to inquire about a permanent job as a teacher of Russian language and literature, he was told there were no vacancies in Moscow, and that he would have to go to the Ministry of Education—maybe they would have something on offer in the provinces. They told him to leave his résumé and contact information with them just in case; sometimes there were temporary vacancies.

Mikha didn't go to the ministry. Alyona was a young wife and still a student; nothing could have induced him to leave her behind in Moscow to go it alone.

Victor Yulievich, who had left teaching, felt that Mikha didn't stand a chance to find a job as a schoolteacher. Tutoring was his only hope. And he gave him a student right away. But none of that—work by the hour, private lessons—could really satisfy him. He missed the boarding-school children!

By this time Mikha had taken on the dullest and most strenuous job of all—he was loading and unloading cargo at night at the Moscow-Tovarnaya railroad station. The work wasn't terribly difficult for him, but Alyona objected. Mikha's eyesight had never been good, and it put too great a strain on his eyes, she said. And she was right.

Another regular source of income was blood donation. He became a donor, but there were limits placed on how often one could do this—only once a month.

Finally, Mikha decided to talk to Ilya about more unconventional ways of earning a living. They planned to meet at the Pokrovsky Gates in breezy Milyutin Park, which had once belonged to the Office of Surveying and Land Management, on a park bench with two broken slats. Each of them had a bottle of beer in his hand and a briefcase at his feet. Sanya wasn't there. They had decided not to include him in their deliberations.

After they graduated from high school, Ilya was the first of them to realize that he didn't wish to work for the state—whether on a nine-to-five, or an eight-to-eight, or a three-days-on, three-days-off schedule. He also had no desire to go to college, because everything that truly interested him he could learn without disciplinary regimentation and coercion. He was adept at various means of avoidance, evasion, and disappearance.

The best option was a fictitious hire as an assistant to a scientist or a writer. This kind of opportunity was not easy to come by, but it had guaranteed Ilya virtual independence from the state. A more reliable, but less attractive variant required real input of one's own time and effort: working in a boiler room, as a concierge, or as a security guard. When it came to earning dough, Ilya knew plenty of ways.

Ilya expounded on this to Mikha, yet again demonstrating his long-acknowledged intellectual superiority.

"You see, Mikha, we're really talking about two different things here: fulfilling, interesting work, and making money. But I still think that you have to know how to combine them. Let's take samizdat. The phenomenon itself is remarkable and unprecedented. It's vital energy that is spread from source to source, establishing threads, forming a sort of spiderweb that links many people. It creates passageways that conduct information in the form of books, magazines, poems, both very old and very new, the latest issues of the samizdat *Chronicles*. There are streams of Zionist literature printed in Odessa before the Revolution, or in Jerusalem last year; there is religious literature of both émigré and domestic manufacture. The process is in part spontaneous and natural, but not completely. This is a conscious undertaking for me, and, in a sense, a profession. This is the work that earns me a living. And, of course, the cause needs to be developed and expanded."

Mikha sat rapt and openmouthed, quite literally. A small trace of saliva had even gathered in the corner of his mouth, as happens with a sleeping child. Ilya held forth in an unusually solemn, serious tone. Mikha was completely enraptured with the contents of the lecture, and at the same time filled with pride: that's our Ilya!

"It's a fine thing!" Mikha said quietly, somewhat overwhelmed with the greatness of his friend.

At that moment Ilya was himself enamored of his role in further-ing world progress. The grandiose picture that he painted did not completely jibe with reality, but it wasn't pure invention, either. The petty demons of the Russian Revolution—the very ones Dostoevsky described—haunted the darkening recesses of the forlorn, overgrown garden. The long shadow of the completely ingenuous Chekhov was moving in the direction of Immer's garden store, where the writer had stopped in to buy seeds now and then, and in a neighboring wing, in about the same years, under the patronage of the not completely in-nocent Savva Morozov, died Levitan, the gentle Jew who sang the praises of Russian nature with his paintbrush . . .

On this very corner, a few steps away, twenty years before, a tram came to a screeching halt . . . Yes, Murygin.

But on the whole, progress was on the march; of that there could be no doubt!

Ilya had an intriguing proposal at the ready. Samizdat had become a widespread social phenomenon, and demand for it was growing steadily. By the mid-sixties, the provinces had come alive. Not all samiz-dat was produced by idealistic enthusiasts. A real market was taking shape, and the most diverse kinds of people were active in it, includ-ing those with purely commercial interests. In addition to publica-tions, the cost of which was determined solely by the price of paper or film, new merchandise was appearing that was meant to be sold for profit. Something akin to a trading network was coming to life. One of the key figures in this market was Ilya. Mikha could help with the distribution.

Mikha would never make a stellar distributor, Ilya knew this already. He was too noticeable, too friendly and open, too imprudent. He was also trustworthy, loyal, and responsible, however. Ilya might have thought twice about making such a proposal to Mikha; but he needed to have some means of survival. And besides, he had a wife!

Mikha was appointed as a traveling salesman.

The first trips didn't take him very far afield. Stuffing his backpack with samizdat, he set out on the commuter train or the bus for a nearby station: Obninsk, Dubna, or Chernogolovka. He would meet other young research associates, hand over the literature, take the money in exchange, and return home on the same day.

Getting acquainted with them was strictly forbidden. Mikha introduced himself as Andrei, and the counteragent didn't introduce himself at all. He usually said something like: "Alexander Ivanovich sent me."

From the money he received, Mikha would get five honestly earned rubles each time. The money stung his hand a little.

Working in the boarding school for the deaf-mute had been so much better. It had satisfied in some ideal way everything Mikha needed and wanted—a modest but sufficient income; absolute pleasure and satisfaction from the creative, useful work he did; a rare feeling of being in just the right place, at just the right time. That work, and the money he earned, had never stung his hand!

After two months, Mikha admitted to Ilya that he wanted more meaningful work than merely delivering goods in a backpack to different addresses. He was well versed in the ins and outs of samizdat, and he considered himself to be entitled to something more creative ...

"Fine, all right. I knew this was bound to happen." Ilya looked somewhat dissatisfied, though he usually swelled with pleasure when he could solve other people's problems. "Edik is the one you need. Edik! You know, the tall fellow," Ilya said.

Mikha remembered. He had delivered some books to him. And he wasn't someone you could easily forget. He was nearly six feet six, and had a pink baby face with nothing growing on it but thick, bushy eyebrows.

Ilya took Mikha to meet Edik. Edik lived with his mother and his wife, Zhenya, in a separate two-room apartment. Looking around, Mikha again grew enamored of someone else's home, which didn't resemble anything he had seen before. Edik's mother was a specialist in Buddhism. The walls were covered with Eastern paintings and images, which were, as Edik explained to him, Buddhist icons. Edik's wife was an archaeologist, and she had left traces of her profession in their home: three unprepossessing earthenware pots. The women were not home at the moment.

Edik published the samizdat magazine *Gamayun*. It consisted of twenty pages of onionskin paper, crudely stitched together between two pieces of blue cardboard. It was a literary and social-commentary journal that thus far existed as one copy of the first issue. Mikha grabbed the magazine and examined it from cover to cover.

"Interesting! But why *Gamayun*?" he said.

"*Alkonost* and *Phoenix* were already taken; I don't like *Sirin*. *Gamayun* was just the thing."

"Yet another bird from Slavic mythology?"

Edik explained:

"Sure. But this little bird is a great intellectual. It knows all the secrets of the universe. It also has the gift of prophecy. We initially thought we would call it *The Historical Project*. But we decided that was too dry. It's an educational journal. With modern poetry, naturally."

Mikha was more than ready to take part in the publication of a journal that would open the eyes and ears of the unenlightened.

Ilya left Mikha at Edik's, and the new friends shared a dinner of grayish macaroni. After the macaroni they agreed fairly quickly that the magazine should concentrate on literary and social commentary, rather than political. That is, politics would be kept to a minimum. Edik was interested in historical prognostication, and the analysis of social trends, tastes, and preferences—sociological subjects, in other words.

"As far as literature goes, I am most interested in poetry and science fiction. Science fiction is able to generalize the processes under way in the world and offer interesting prognoses. Nowadays, Western science fiction functions as futurology, the philosophy of the future. I simply don't have time to take it on, though. If you would answer for it, it would be fantastic."

Mikha thought about it: he had never been exposed to any science fiction. He promised to keep it in mind.

Right on the spot they decided on the contents of the poetry section for the next issue. There would be a large selection of works by one poet, and one or two poems each by five to eight other writers. Mikha suggested Brodsky as the featured poet, and began murmuring rapturously:

> "General! Our maps are crap. I pass.
> The north is not here at all, but at the North Pole.
> And the equator is broader than the side stripes on your trousers.
> Because the front, General, is in the south.
> At such a distance a walkie-talkie turns any command
> Into boogie-woogie."

"Who are you going to surprise with Brodsky? Listen, there are new poets, nearly unknown:

> 'Memory is an armless equestrian statue
> You gallop wildly, but
> You have no arms
> Today you shout loudly in the empty corridor
> You flicker at the corridor's end
> It was evening and tea swirled aromatically
> Ancient trees of steam grew out of the cups
> In silence, each admired his life
> And a girl in yellow admired it most of all . . .'"

"Yes, it's really good. Who wrote it?"

"Who? A nobody. Young fellow from Kharkov. Came to Moscow not long ago. No one knows him. But in five years they will. Like everyone knows Brodsky now. I'm willing to bet on it. He's the one we need to publish."

"I'm not so sure. I think we should take Khvostenko," Mikha said.

"I love Khvost, but what is he without his guitar? This other fellow will make a stronger impression . . ."

"What's his name?"

"What does it matter? I'm telling you—everyone will know him in five years. And you want Khvostenko?" Edik was getting angry, and the good-natured Mikha began feeling uncomfortable.

"This is absurd! We haven't even started working together, and we're already quarreling."

Edik laughed. "That's what always happens. I'm constantly falling out with my friends. It's just my character."

"What idiots we are!" Mikha said. "Gorbanevskaya! Natalia Gorbanevskaya! She's the one we need! She'd be ideal." And, his voice full of pathos, he began to recite:

> "It will not perish in our wake—
> The dry grass smolders.
> It will not perish in our wake—
> The millstones are still.
> In our wake not a step, not a sigh,
> no blood, no blood-soaked sweat,
> No blood-sealed debt,
> will perish in our wake.
> The fire runs through the grass,
> The fire presses to the trees,
> And for those reclining in the foliage
> A day of reckoning will come . . ."

"Done! There can be no objections to Gorbanevskaya! We just have to ask her," Edik said.

"But it's samizdat! Why ask permission? We'll take these three poems, addressed to Brodsky."

With his passion for the literary classics—the poetic correspondence between Pushkin and Vyazemsky, or the epistolary exchange of Herzen and Turgenev, Turgenev and Dostoevsky, or Gogol and his chosen friends—he wanted to elaborate on the subject immediately.

"It would be good to find poems of Brodsky's addressed to Gorbanevskaya, or, for example, poems of Gorbanevskaya addressed to someone else!"

"To Pushkin, for instance! Go ahead, commission her to do it!" Edik said sarcastically.

But Mikha was supremely serious.

"No, that's not what I mean. You know, it's a good idea to look for poems addressed to friends. A poetic conversation between fellow poets. This one, for instance:

> 'In the madhouse
> Crush your palms,
> Smash your forehead against the wall,
> Like smashing your face in a snowbank . . .' "

"I remember that one. It's to Galanskov," Edik said.

"Here's another one. Listen.

> 'Brush the bliss of half-sleep from your cheek
> And open your eyes until the eyelids cry in pain.
> The filth and whitewash of the hospital—
> A volunteer's flag of your captivity.' "

"I know that one, too. It's to Dimka Borisov. How do you know her poems so well?"

"I heard her read her poems twice at my father-in-law's house. And I memorized them. She seems rather gloomy and unapproachable; but her poems are full of tenderness. I can't say I liked her as a person. But she writes the kinds of poems I would like to have written myself."

They decided that Mikha would go to Natalia and ask her for some new poems.

Then Edik remembered about some high-flying intellectual from the philosophy department at Moscow State University. He could write an article about contemporary American science fiction.

The third part of the magazine was a large section entitled "News." And there was plenty of it. A large number of independently thinking people first whispered in corners among themselves, then spoke half out loud, and, finally, went out and joined demonstrations, protesting ever more boldly and conscientiously. They were detained, tried, sentenced to prison, and set free again, and life was full of daily events that people found out about from one another, or from Western radio stations: everyone picked up some bit of news or other.

Along with the human rights activists, there were also the Crimean Tatars who had been expelled from Crimea twenty years before and now wished to return; Jews who demanded the right to emigrate to Israel, from which they had been expelled two thousand years before; adherents to many kinds of religions; nationalists, from Lithuanians to Russians; and many others. All of them were at odds with the Soviet authorities. And things were happening at every turn.

Edik was not a member of any particular group. He considered himself to be an objective journalist, and his point of departure was that society had to be informed about what was going on. Mikha was prepared to facilitate this in every way he could.

Suddenly, they realized it was already past one in the morning.

"Where's Zhenya, I wonder?" Edik said. They were not in the habit of keeping tabs on each other, but they usually told each other of their whereabouts.

Mikha gasped, then set out for home in haste. It was too late to get public transport. A chance trolleybus took him to Rachmanovsky Lane, where a herd of trolleybuses converged to spend the night. He ran the last twenty minutes home. Alyona was asleep, and didn't ask Mikha to account for himself.

Life rolled along steadily and pleasantly. After Aunt Genya's death, her old room crammed with dusty junk and bric-a-brac seemed to have dissolved into oblivion. In the new room that took its place, everything was clean, white, and new. Alyona's drafting table, with Whatman paper clipped to it, stood next to the window. She was about to graduate from the graphic arts department, and her graduation project was to illustrate Hoffman's fairy tales. A wide, intricate border with Masonic motifs wound about the margins of every page.

Instead of the weekly watch at the boarding school, Mikha's days, from morning till night, were now filled with any number of activities. He was surrounded by new acquaintances. Their most frequent visitors were Edik and Zhenya. Although Zhenya was plain, her mouth was full of infectious laughter (though not many teeth), and she was an attractive, sweet person. Alyona, to Mikha's delight, would smile weakly at Zhenya's straightforward jokes. The four of them became good friends, and often spent time at one another's houses, talking and drinking tea and wine.

Alyona seemed to come to life, to awaken. Her usual expression—like a child just getting up from a nap who hasn't quite decided whether to laugh or cry—became more defined: not yet laughing, but certainly not crying. She even became more responsive to Mikha's conjugal expectations. Since they had gotten married, Alyona had seemed even more unavailable than before, when she would now and then come to him in Milyaevo without being asked, and stay overnight, tender and complaisant.

In their married state, things seemed to get in the way, each obstacle more awkward and absurd than the one before. Either their sexual activity wound her up so much that she couldn't sleep afterward, or, on the contrary, it wearied her so much that she couldn't get up in the morning and would have to sleep the entire day.

It was, most likely, a slight sexual pathology—perhaps a consequence of traumatic premarital experiences. Feeling desirable, sought after, an unattainable object—this was for her the epitome of pleasure in sexual relations. She hungered perpetually for affirmation of Mikha's ready desire, and was adept in the subtle art of keeping her husband interested and aroused, but avoiding sexual contact. The less frequently Mikha was able to indulge in the full-fledged conjugal rite, the sharper and giddier were his feelings for her.

As Alyona became more inaccessible to him, love raised him to unprecedented heights of feeling. In a secluded nook of his consciousness, he was constantly at work writing poems. He had long before stopped sending her love poetry, which Alyona had greeted with a set mouth. That didn't prevent him from writing it, however.

> Love is the work of the spirit.
> Still, the body
> Does not hold itself aloof from it.
> A hand resting in a hand—
> What joy!
> For degrees of spiritual fire
> And the white heat of corporeal passion
> There is a single scale of measure.

Among the new friends who were always coming around to their "grown-up home" *sans* parents, which was moreover in the center of town, were admirers of Alyona. When men would show up, she grew animated, sitting up straight and smiling vaguely. Mikha felt fresh pangs of male jealousy; Alyona experienced a complex satisfaction. Their home began to exhibit all the hallmarks of a literary salon: the canonically prescribed love for the hostess, tea drinking, cakes and cookies, conversation about art, reciting the latest poetry, and guest lecturers on intellectually stimulating topics. In this way Alyona reproduced (with allowances for another generation) her parents' home, but with more refined tastes.

At about that time, traveling through Russia came into vogue. Backpacks, canoes, trains, risky hitchhiking, spending the night in tents or in abandoned villages—Ilya, of course, was the first in their group of friends to experience all this. He adored these trips and often went without any companions, returning home with rarities fit for a museum: books, icons, objects of peasant life. He made friends in far-flung parts of the Russian north, Central Asia, the Altai.

Mikha never joined Ilya in his travels; he would never have left his aunt for long while she was still alive. Early in the spring of 1967, two young couples—Mikha and Alyona and Edik and Zhenya—

seized by a new passion for traveling, went to Crimea for the first time, to Koktebel. The genre of their journey was a pilgrimage—to the grave site of a poet Mikha revered.

It took them two days and nights to get to Feodosia. There was still snow on the ground in Moscow. In the morning, as they journeyed southward, they passed through warm rain, having already gone through floating remnants of snow, and through fogs and mists. After midday, entering another climatic zone, through the train window they observed roadside willows up to their knees in water, with swollen joints and straining branches. In Feodosia it rained on them again—gray and pearly iridescent. They got on a bus and, bumping and jostling all the way, continued on to Planernoe—where the poet Maximilian Voloshin had lived. The landscape—smoky, quivering, milky, and opaline—riveted their gaze. Columns of trucks were coming toward the bus from the other direction. They were excavating one and a half million tons of Koktebel sand, urgently needed for the purposes of the national economy. But what the travelers didn't realize was that before their very eyes the treasure of the ancient shoreline was being destroyed. The people who might have realized this were almost all gone by now.

When they got out of the bus, they heard the roar of the Black Sea for the first time, and began moving toward the captivating sound. The sea was raging for the second week in a row, in accordance with its seasonal mandate. It was even harder to accommodate the sea with one's vision than one's ears. Mikha and Zhenya were experiencing the sea for the first time. Alyona's parents had once taken her to the seaside by the Caucasus Mountains, and Edik knew the sea—albeit a different one altogether: the Baltic.

They turned to walk along the shore in the direction of Voloshin's house. They didn't ask anyone the way—the road simply beckoned them. They recognized the house immediately, by its eloquent appearance, its tower, its contrast with everything else that was built here after the Revolution, after the war. They sat on some rocks below the house. They pulled out a bottle of wine and the remains of their Moscow rations.

Mikha couldn't contain himself and began reciting poems. He had already burst out in a fit of lyrical passion on the train, but they had squelched it.

> "As in a small seashell, the Great
> Ocean roars its breath,
> As its flesh shimmers and burns
> with tides and silvery mist,
> and its curves repeat
> in the motion and scrolls of a wave—
> Thus, in your coves,
> O dark land of Cimmeria, my soul
> is imprisoned and transfigured."

The wind tore at their jackets and carried off their words. They huddled together, but Mikha couldn't stop. He didn't even notice when a flabby old woman with an ornate walking stick in her hand, wearing a huge, tattered raincoat and turbid glasses, glued together at the bridge, appeared in their midst, listening intently.

"Let's go into the house," she said. The hospitable invitation contradicted the severity and gloom of her expression. She led them to a house they could not have imagined in their wildest dreams . . .

This was Voloshin's widow, Maria Stepanovna. She gave them a personal tour of her home. On the first floor, which at that time was called "Corpus 1," vacationing miners working in the Donbas region were usually housed; they hadn't yet arrived on their local Communist Party tourist vouchers. The widow tried to fend off this invasion as best she could, but there was little she could do. She opened up two rooms for the young people on the lower floor.

"You can live here, until the strangers arrive."

They spent several happy days under Maria Stepanovna's wing. Mikha and Edik undertook some urgent household tasks and repairs, of which there were many. Zhenya and Alyona washed floors, dusted the books on the tall shelves. They spent one whole day tidying up

Voloshin's grave. Mikha and Edik restored the path leading to it, which had crumbled during the winter.

In the evenings they sat in Voloshin's freezing study, drank tea, and talked under the huge sculpture of Queen Taiakh, which was described in almost all the memoirs of his friends. Sometimes local inhabitants in their declining years would stop in—old ladies, some of them girlish, some of them like reptiles, as well as young writers from the House of the Arts. Once a famous young poet came over with a can of unbottled wine; another time his rival visited. They hated each other with a vengeance, but, in the tradition of the house, they refrained from quarreling when they both turned up at the same time.

They were both too Soviet and official for Mikha's and Edik's taste. But, as soon became clear, they were no better, nor worse, than those who congregated around Mayakovsky's statue.

At the end, when the young people were preparing to go home, Maria Stepanovna commanded them all to go to Staryi Krym. The way was not short—about ten miles—but unless they took this little detour, they could not be considered "kin."

"You'll be able to rest up a bit there, my friend will feed you."

Maria Stepanovna wondered whether she should send these young people to a rival widow. Assol, as she was called, had already done time in prison and returned to Staryi Krym, to fulfill her duties as the writer Grin's widow. *Perhaps Faina Lvovna would be better*, Maria Stepanovna thought, and gave them a note for a local lady whose husband, a dentist, fixed all the teeth of the elderly inhabitants.

They decided to go home by way of Simferopol, with a trip to Bakhchisaray. Maria Stepanovna explained that it was inadmissible not to go there—it was the very heart of old Crimea. The route was a bit convoluted: from Staryi Krym, bypassing Koktebel, to Bakhchisaray, where they would stay overnight, then go directly to Simferopol, to the railroad station.

Real spring had already begun in Staryi Krym. The leaves on the trees looked like delicate green lace. People sat in their gardens, prepared the beds for planting, or rushed about, setting out seedlings. The almond trees had blossomed.

The whole way, Mikha and Edik debated the nature of Soviet power, which, in Mikha's view, was weaker on the periphery of the empire than in the center, and more humane as well. Edik did not agree. He even claimed that in some places they were crueler and more stupid, citing Voloshin as an example: if he had lived closer to the center of power, they would have executed him by 1918.

Zhenya and Alyona walked behind their husbands, like Eastern wives, and talked about art. Alyona didn't approve of Voloshin's watercolors, which were all over the house. Zhenya argued hotly that one couldn't judge this artist by the immediate fruits of his activities—paintings or poems. His greatness was spiritual in nature, and when the specious verdict made way for a lasting, authentic one, the true scale of his greatness would become clear. Zhenya was a well-educated young woman. She read both French and English, and even knew a thing or two about anthroposophy. This irked Alyona somewhat.

In Staryi Krym, they had dinner at Faina Lvovna's. She received them with great solemnity, like visiting dignitaries from a friendly kingdom. She was wearing very long beads, and a dress with a dropped waist from the NEP period in the mid-1920s, as well as a flirtatious tendril pasted to her forehead. She fed her guests a modest but fashionable meal—bean soup and patties made from some indeterminate kind of grain, with kissel gravy.

They walked around the local cemetery, and strolled past the house of Alexander Grin. It was closed, but it felt like the residents had just stepped out and would be back any moment.

They arrived in Bakhchisaray in early evening—they were able to hitch a ride just in time. Again on the recommendation of Maria Stepanovna, they went to see a curator at the museum of local history. They immediately hit it off, and soon it seemed they had known each other their whole lives. Here, in the Crimea, there seemed to be a secret society of "former" people. They were privy to some arcane secret of the Crimea, but, however much they revealed of it, the secret remained intact. The curator turned out to be not Crimean at all, but from Leningrad; still, she seemed to be a keeper of secrets. She showed them wax figures of harem wives and eunuchs, bronze vases, a fountain that recalled Pushkin, "the tomb of khans, the final home of sovereigns . . ." The woman from the museum said that she would take them to Chuft-Kale the next morning, but that they couldn't stay overnight at her house, since her aunt had arrived that night from Petersburg for a visit.

In the evening they went to a hotel, in which they found the ordinary provincial squalor. They stowed their rucksacks in the storeroom, a small closet next to the reception desk. They agreed that the rooms would be waiting for them later in the evening, and they would register then. They went out to walk through the dark town, and to have a meal in some eating-house somewhere. They couldn't find any place to eat, but they did find a grocery store that was about to close in five minutes.

Mikha went to get their rucksacks out of the storeroom, and began digging around for their passports. He found them, and put them on the desk in front of the receptionist. She began inspecting them diligently, looking in the last pages for their officially registered addresses, and the stamp proving they were legally married.

Just at this time, a family entered the hotel. It was a husband and wife, who were getting on in years, and a daughter who looked about fourteen. They were Tatars from Central Asia. This was evident from the Uzbek *tubeteika* on the man's head, from the woman's striped dress, from their high cheekbones, from the silver bracelets studded with red carnelian on the fragile wrists of the girl, and from the anxiety written on their faces. The man pulled two passports out of the inner pocket of his suit coat and placed them in front of the receptionist.

The jacket was not new; the back of it was faded. Nearly the entire front, however, from his shoulders to his waist, was covered with military decorations and orders.

The sullen receptionist put the passports of the Moscow travelers aside, and opened their passports. She shook her head.

"There's no room."

"What do you mean, there's no room? You're lying! There are vacancies!" Mikha objected. "We have booked two rooms. Please give this family one of ours."

"We don't have any for you, either," the woman said, pushing the pile of passports toward Mikha.

"What? We made an agreement!"

"Our first priority is to serve business travelers, and only then to accommodate 'savages.' There's no room here."

"We traveled more than a thousand miles to look at the graves of our ancestors. Here are our return tickets. In two days we are flying back to Tashkent," the man said, still holding out some hope.

"Don't you understand Russian? I said there's no room here!"

"I understand Russian. Perhaps in the private sector it would be possible to stay for only one night?"

"Stay wherever you want. It's not my concern! But just remember—you'll be answerable for violating the passport rules."

Mikha was boiling with anger. His response to injustice was instantaneous and passionate, even corporeal. It felt like a hammer pounding in his temples. His hands spontaneously curled up into fists.

"Bastards! What bastards!" he whispered to Edik. "Do you realize what's happening? This is a Tatar family that was deported . . ." Just a few days before, their friend Maria Stepanovna had told them about the events of May 1944. This information was still fresh in his mind, and the injustice of it still rankled. "While this man was fighting at the front, they evicted his family from their home and deported them!"

"Take it easy," Edik whispered to him. "We'll think of something."

The much-decorated Tatar wrapped up the passports in a silk handkerchief, and put them carefully back into his inner pocket.

"Let's get out of here. They'll call the police any minute now!" Edik bent down nearly in half to whisper to the Tatar.

He nodded, and they all made their way to the door, onto the street, where it was already pitch-dark. The darkness seemed peaceful and safe, in contrast to the loathsomeness of the reception area, albeit illuminated by electricity.

Natasha Khlopenko, the receptionist, was already dialing the number to contact the police. This was her duty—to inform them about Tatars arriving in Bakhchisaray. But the officer on duty didn't answer the phone, and she threw down the receiver in relief: her mother was a Karaite Jew, and her father a recently arrived Ukrainian. It wasn't that she felt any special sympathy toward the deported Tatars, but more that she didn't want to be an accessory to this long-standing war of nationalities and peoples, which involved her to a degree. To a very small degree.

Seven people left the hotel, and the Tatar man silently headed up their exodus.

"Let's go. I know a place where we can find shelter for the night. You're not afraid of cemeteries, are you?"

"No, let's go," Edik said.

Although it was completely dark, the Tatar walked confidently westward, and up a hill.

They walked about a mile and a half, and came to an ancient Tatar cemetery.

The ruins of a small mausoleum seemed cozy, rather than threatening. And perhaps the Tatar's trust in this place was so great that it communicated itself to the young people. They sat on a slope—or reclined, as it were. The slope was as comfortable as a floating pillow. Edik pulled out a bottle of Crimean port from his rucksack. The domestic Zhenya took out the feta cheese they had bought in the store, some salted tomatoes, and bread, which they had planned to eat in their room at the hotel.

They didn't light a fire. A full moon suddenly rose in the sky, illuminating the landscape with an intense brilliance: every stone, every branch, became visible.

The two fat braids of the Tatar girl gleamed in the moonlight with an oily sheen, and her silver bracelets shimmered. Her mother unfolded a muslin napkin and took out some dry Tatar pies, and they all partook of their feast in solemn silence and spiritual concord.

After the meal a conversation got under way, little by little—curiously disjointed, not following any particular path, but somehow concerned with everything at once—about the strange circumstances that had brought them all together, seemingly random, disparate people, unrelated through the past or the future, unconnected by blood or by fate . . . about the beauty that seemed to have dropped down from the heavens . . .

The moon retreated, slipping down to the edge of the sky, and an hour later a rose-colored ribbon of light appeared in the east, brightening the comforting darkness. The Tatar man, whose name was Mustafa, said:

"I've remembered this dawn so many times, through so many years. As a boy, I herded cattle here. I looked at these mountains thousands of times, always waiting for the first ray of sunlight. Sometimes it seemed to just shoot out. I thought I would never see it again."

When it was light, they parted ways. The young people went to Chufut-Kale, and the Tatar family stayed in the ancient cemetery. Mustafa wanted to find his grandfather's grave.

They agreed to meet at two o'clock at the bus station, and to travel to Moscow together.

At the bus station, it was impossible to avoid the police. The young people surrounded "their" Tatars, and began making a happy commotion. Zhenya waylaid two policemen, flirting with them and babbling away to them about nothing. Eventually Edik pulled out his press pass, long expired, and waved it in front of the lieutenant's face. The provincial police turned out to be shyer than their Moscow counterparts. Or perhaps Edik's towering height and horn-rimmed glasses threw them off. In any case, the bus opened its doors, gave an impatient roar, and all seven of them packed in and drove off. Or maybe these servants of the law just didn't want to take on any extra trouble for themselves.

After that everything went like clockwork. The train staff turned out to be from Kazakhstan, and they put the "illegal" passengers in "illegal" seats, shielding them from the conductors and guards the whole way, until they finally arrived at Komsomol Square two days later. A half hour later, Mikha and Alyona and their Tatar guests were already in the long-suffering Aunt Genya's room. In another twenty-four hours, the former Hero of the Soviet Union and former captain Usmanov, one of the initiators of the movement for Crimean Tatars to return to their homeland, with his wife, Aliye, and his daughter, Ayshe, took a flight from the capital of our homeland to the capital of Uzbekistan, and finally sat down in their Tashkent home, where their friends and relatives were waiting for them. Usmanov, a Communist and a hero, placed a handful of stones from the ancient Muslim cemetery of Eski-Yurt on a tray.

"Here. Look at them. Our stones have come back to us; now it's our turn to go back to our stones."

Henceforth, young Tatars would frequent Mikha's home. They came with petitions, with letters of protest, with requests and demands. They stayed overnight, sleeping on air mattresses on the floor. The cause of these Tatar strangers was closer to Mikha's heart than the efforts of Jews to return to Israel. After all, the Jewish exile had lasted for two thousand years already; it was ancient history, while the Tatars' was still fresh. Their homes and wells in Crimea had not all been destroyed. The Tatars still remembered the Soviet soldiers who had evicted them and then deported them, and neighbors who had occupied their homes.

Mikha got caught up in this cause which was not directly his own, drawn in by his characteristic unflagging sympathy and warmth. He helped them write letters, distribute them, and establish contacts. Several times at the behest of his Tatar friends he traveled to Crimea, and he and his friend Ravil collected memoirs about the deportations of 1944.

He and Edik published their magazine, but, quite predictably, the literary section shrank and the political section grew. They also added a new section called "The Periphery," in which they discussed the plight of various ethnic minorities and nationalities, the extinction of the smaller peoples, their forced assimilation. Edik, with his characteristic academicism, wished to stay within the framework of anthropology and demographics, which lent the magazine an aura of scholarship. This did not diminish its anti-imperialist bent, however.

Ilya made photocopies of all eight issues. The editions usually numbered about forty copies. A full collection of all the different issues has not been preserved, but individual issues may still be found in various archives, both Western and KGB.

Mikha hadn't seen Sanya in nearly a year, and met with Ilya only on matters of business.

On the night of August 21, 1968, an event took place that would change everything: Soviet troops entered Czechoslovakia. Actually, this was a coalition of troops from five countries, but the initiative was indubitably a Soviet one. They called it "Operation Danube." Russian tanks rolled into Prague, dealing the strongest possible blow to the global Communist movement.

The whole night through Mikha fiddled with the corrugated knobs on the old Telefunken, his only legacy from Aunt Genya, listening to the Western news reports. Dubcek's "socialism with a human face" lay in pieces, and the last illusions were shattered.

For so many years Mikha had studied Marxism, trying to work out how such wonderful ideas about justice could become so misshapen, so distorted, in their implementation; but now the truth was laid bare— it was a grandiose lie, cynicism, inconceivable cruelty, shameless manipulations of people who had lost their humanity, their human dignity and self-worth, out of fear. This fear enveloped the whole country like a dark cloud. One could call this cloud Stalinism; but Mikha had already understood that Stalinism was only a singular instance of the evil of this enormous, universal, timeless political despotism.

Mikha was prepared to rush out onto the square to share his anguish and horror. But first he went to grab a pencil. He wanted to write a poem; but what came out instead was a vehement tract. For three days Mikha wrestled with the words, but they never seemed as elegant and convincing on paper as they were when they originated in his heart. What he was feeling was a desire to find the right words, and to express them, so that everyone would read them and understand, and everyone would agree . . .

On Sunday the twenty-fifth, Sergei Borisovich called and asked the young people to come by immediately. From him, they learned the latest news: that on Red Square, next to Lobnoe Mesto, also known as the Place of Skulls, there had been a demonstration against the invasion of Czechoslovakia. The names of seven people who went out onto the square were already known. All the demonstrators but one had been arrested. Next to the former site of public executions, she had sat down with a three-month-old baby in her arms, holding a Czech flag.

"Gorbanevskaya!" Mikha said.

Chernopyatov confirmed it. His house was full of people. They were already discussing who would write a letter of protest, and to whom it would be addressed. Mikha shut himself up in Alyona's room and finished the piece that he had been working on all those days, without being able to finish it. Now, after the demonstration, he reworked it, shifted the accent of the argument, and titled it: "The Five-Minute Demonstration of the Magnificent Seven on Lobnoe Mesto." He handed it to Chernopyatov, who frowned,

"As usual, too much pathos, Mikha!"

In the evening he showed the piece to two more people: Edik and Ilya.

Edik considered it to be too wordy and vague. Ilya took the piece of paper without saying a thing.

Twenty-four hours later, the Voice of America was reporting what had happened on Red Square—about the five-minute demonstration and about the magnificent seven. The text had been edited and shortened. Still, there could be no doubt, it was Mikha's piece!

So someone must have passed it to them! One of two people: Ilya or Edik. Unbelievable!

Everyone was nervous, and tried to keep a low profile. Searches and arrests were taking place throughout the city. In contrast to what the century had seen prior to these events, the numbers of human casualties were small: around a hundred civilians killed on the Czech side, and nineteen Soviet troops. After the successful completion of the operation, about two thousand people were arrested in Czechoslovakia. In Russia, the numbers were negligible: the seven demonstrators on Red Square and ten more demonstrators, unknown and unsung, in the provinces.

A major trial was being planned for the protesters. Chernopyatov knew them all, and all the information about the trial filtered down to him.

Mikha and Edik were planning to publish a new issue of *Gamayun* devoted entirely to the Crimean Tatar movement before the New Year holidays. Putting together a literary section was proving to be the most difficult part, but with the help of his Tatar friends, Mikha was able to find a Crimean Tatar poet living in Uzbekistan. His name was Eshref Shemi-zade. The Tatars did a word-for-word translation, and Mikha translated excerpts from the semidestroyed poem. The excerpts were written with the poet's lifeblood, and Mikha, in anguish himself, somehow managed to make a rendering:

> It's not a dog that sets up a terrible howl
> In the icy Moscow night.
> It's the Kremlin leader, craving blood,
> Insatiable. He howls and snarls . . .

Just before the New Year, Mikha had his baptism by fire. His house was searched. Four men scoured the empty room, taking a long time, then, bewildered by its unyielding transparency, they began to knock on the walls to see if they could discover something that way. On a bookshelf, among the books, they found a packet of letters that had belonged to his late aunt Genya. The letters were wrapped in gray paper and bound with coarse string into smaller bundles, according to year. On every bundle there was a date: one bundle per year, dating from 1915 to 1955. There were forty in all. It was family correspondence with relatives from Arkhangelsk, Karaganda, and the Urals. Mikha had found the letters not long before, when they were discarding the wardrobe. He had kept them at the request of Marlen, but he hadn't even thought to read them, out of a sense of delicacy and tact. Now the police were hastily untying the string; but when they saw the dates, they lost interest. That was unfortunate: among the letters was, among other things, correspondence between the legendary Samuil and Lenin, as well as between Samuil and Trotsky. There was also an extremely interesting letter in which Lenin tried to persuade Samuil to find a secret source of financing, independent of government, to develop the world Communist movement . . .

"Those letters belonged to my aunt. Her son was planning to come by to take a look at them," Mikha said by way of explanation, taking possession of the letters again.

"Too late now," the senior officer said gruffly, and grabbed them out of Mikha's hands.

The whole operation lasted about two hours. There was nowhere to search, and nothing to search for.

They impounded the family correspondence, more out of a sense of professional duty, along with ten pre-Revolutionary poetry collections, almost all of them given to him by Ilya, a rephotographed book by Berdyaev that Mikha kept intending to read, but never got around to, and a small-format, two-volume copy of *Doctor Zhivago* from Pierre Zand.

All the materials for the journal had been deposited with Edik immediately. Nothing remained in the house. Nonetheless . . . nonetheless, when he saw the two-volume Pasternak in the hands of the searchers, he felt a hot wave of panic wash over him. He remembered a single page, completely filled with very small handwriting. He remembered where he had put that page—in the first book that came to hand—just after the neighbor had called him to the telephone that was affixed to the wall in the main corridor of the communal apartment.

After he came back to his room, he looked around for the paper, couldn't find it, and so reconstructed it from memory. And now Mikha remembered—he had put the little piece of paper in that very two-volume copy of *Doctor Zhivago*.

The paper was valuable. For the next issue of the magazine, Mikha had prepared a demographic rundown of the deportees from Crimea during the war. The Crimean Tatars had conducted a poll among the deportees and their descendants in Central Asia, collating the information with old, long-forgotten data. It was a huge project, in which hundreds of Tatar deportees took part.

On the page, in minuscule calligraphic handwriting, under a heading in red ink that said, simply, "The Tatars," was the following text:

1783—around 4 million Tatars in Crimea when it was annexed by Russia
1917—120,000 Tatars
1941—560,000 Tatars in Crimea
1941–42—137,000 Tatar men mobilized, 57,000 of whom were killed

1944—420,000 Tatar (200,000 children) civilians
1944, May 18–20—32,000 NKVD officials took part in the deportation
1944, May 18—200,000 Tatars (official figures) transported to Central Asia
1945—187,000 deportees died (official figure 80,000)
1956—deportee status of Central Asian Tatars revoked, but return to
   Crimea forbidden

At the bottom there was a note written in blue ink:

Red: Note that the official figures (the number of deportees, for ex.) are
artificially lowered; according to our data, 42 percent of the deportees
perished in the first year and a half. This doesn't correspond to official
figures, which were all falsified. Ravil is preparing a table from 1945 to
1968. Musa.

There was still hope that they wouldn't open the Pasternak and find the piece of paper. Mikha was glad that Alyona was staying late at the institute and wouldn't find the KGB at her home when she got there.

Mikha tried to call Edik immediately, but no one picked up.

The next morning Mikha and Alyona went to Edik's house. A tearstained Elena Alekseevna told them that the day before, at the very same time, they had also been searched. But things had ended far worse. They had taken Edik away with them, and he had not yet returned. They had found many rough drafts, materials from the last issue of the magazine with corrections marked in pencil. They also took five issues of the publication *Vestnik*, the journal of the Russian Christian Student Movement, and a pile of other samizdat publications. Finally, they had confiscated photocopies of what was perhaps the most damning anti-Soviet book, published for the Party elite in a small edition, stamped "Top Secret"—Avtorkhanov's *Technology of Power.*

Elena Alekseevna's room was also subject to unsolicited "cleansing." They took away two copies of the Bible, a statue of the Buddha, prayer beads, and a photocopy of Buddhist texts. They asked her what language all this anti-Soviet junk was written in. She tried to explain to them that she was a specialist in Buddhism and Eastern studies, and that the two languages she worked in most often were Sanskrit and Tibetan. Also, that the paper they were holding in their hands was a copy of a document written in the seventh century.

There was something almost touching about their fabulous ignorance. When one of the uninvited guests told Elena Alekseevna in a whisper that he knew all about the Buddhist blood sacrifices, she couldn't contain her laughter, in spite of the fear she felt under the circumstances. Even when she was telling Mikha and Alyona about it, she had to laugh. She knew that the copies would be returned—and even if they weren't, it wasn't the end of the world. But she regretted the loss of the family Bible, on the last page of which was written the name of its first owners.

They decided to go see Sergei Borisovich and ask his advice, as someone with a great deal of experience in these matters. His house was, as usual, full of people: some newly released prisoner on his way to Rostov, a man from Central Asia, an elderly woman with the botanical-sounding name of Mallow, whom Mikha had already met before, and Yuly Kim himself, with his guitar. Some people drank tea or coffee, others wine or vodka. Alyona frowned in displeasure. She was always annoyed by these gatherings that smacked of a street fair, a station, or a flophouse. Mikha drew his father-in-law into a corner and told him about Edik. Should he go to the KGB district office and inquire? Perhaps to the central headquarters?

"Well, whether you go or not, they have the right to detain him for up to seventy-two hours without charging him with anything." Sergei Borisovich knew all of this from personal experience going back to his childhood. "Most likely they won't tell you anything now. But you need to take some action so that they know there are people looking after his welfare. It will all become clearer in three days."

Mikha went to see Ilya, and Elena Alekseevna went with Zhenya to Kuznetsky. Most, to the KGB headquarters.

Ilya told Mikha that there had been seven or eight searches of various people that night. Four of them had been detained, but two of them had been released already. He knew nothing about Edik.

Edik Tolmachev was not released three days later. He was charged with "Distribution of False Information Defaming the Government and Social Structure of the USSR," under Article 190 of the Penal Code.

Again, Mikha went to see his experienced father-in-law, this time about the magazine. He wanted to continue to publish it, but he was uncertain whether he could manage such a complex and important task on his own. Moreover, all the materials for the next issue had been confiscated; he did know how to restore them, however.

Sergei Borisovich was categorical in his answer: no, now was not the time. Mikha was sure to trip up.

As far as Mikha himself was concerned, he began to relish the situation. In the same way that he had once been completely consumed with methods and approaches toward developing the faculty of speech in the deaf, he now felt he was performing a very significant task, playing a crucial role. It seemed to him the future of poetry was in his hands. It was as though someone was instructing him from on high to preserve for posterity everything with intrinsic worth, everything that lived spontaneously, all that escaped the scrutiny of the authorities.

Ilya gave him some wise advice.

"Don't continue the magazine; make a new one, Mikha! Change the name. Think up some sort of bird, it could even be fun. You'll be able to manage the poetry yourself, and I'll introduce you to some artists. I know some art historians; they're really great. It's the new avant-garde. I'll help you make new connections. I know many amazing people. It will be an arts journal. As for politics, it will take care of itself."

Three months passed. Just when Mikha had grown tired of waiting to be called in by the KGB for his activities surrounding the magazine, he found a summons from them in his mailbox.

Alyona wasn't feeling well. She suspected she might be pregnant, but she decided not to tell Mikha for the time being. She had been silent for days, which was not unusual for her. He, on the other hand, talked nonstop: about Edik, about the lawyer some friends had found, about the magazine, old version and new, about Sanya Steklov, who had suddenly turned up and invited them to the Conservatory, though they hadn't heard a word from him in six months . . .

He babbled on about everything under the sun, but didn't say a word about the summons from the KGB in the pocket of his checked shirt.

There were two possible reasons that they wanted to see him. One was that they had given *Doctor Zhivago* a good shake, and the piece of paper with the Tatar demographics fell out; the other was that Edik had informed on him as an accomplice, which seemed improbable to Mikha.

He was not vexed by the summons. What he felt was closer to embarrassment that he had managed to do so little: nothing, really! He had only written a few articles, and selected and edited some poetry.

When he told Ilya about the summons, Ilya was very upset.

"It was to be expected. I was actually surprised that they had left you alone for so long. And I'm at fault for dragging you into this magazine business. We'll have to figure out how to extricate you from it now. Edik has a strong character, I don't think he'd set you up. They're going to put you through the wringer for those Tatar statistics. You've got to think up a good alibi—you bought *Zhivago* a long time ago from a street vendor, because you'd heard a lot about it. But you hadn't had time to read it, or even look at it, yet. You don't know anything about any sheet of paper covered with numbers. And anyone in Moscow can buy the book near the secondhand bookshop on Kuznetsky Bridge; by Pervopechatnik there are street vendors, and it's even easier at Ptichka, by the entrance. And describe the guy who sold it to you in detail. Say he had long hair, with greasy long locks hanging down from the sides of his head, and a really long nose that reached right down to his lip. And black eyes. And he spoke with a Ukrainian accent. And he wore a vest with spangles . . ." Ilya looked at his friend searchingly. "Or, let's say, he was really small, with curly hair and curly sideburns. He had a down-turned nose, light-colored eyes, and small, womanish hands . . . and he spoke with a burr. Or how about this: He was a nervous, high-strung type, skinny, rather tall, yellowish, with a high, balding forehead, a scraggly beard. And he seemed to walk like a wind-up toy . . ."

Then Mikha jumped in:

"No, he was a big, burly guy with a massive beard, dressed like a peasant. And a mustache. I'd say he was kind of a slob; an old-timer. And he carried his books in a sack, and wore felt boots with galoshes over them! A giant of a man, indeed!"

They were almost rolling on the floor in laughter.

"No, a woman would be better. A tall, elderly, buxom lady, aristocratic-looking. Wearing a hat and carrying an umbrella. She took the book out of her handbag, and she was wearing gloves. And the strange thing was that it looked like she was wearing them on the wrong hands . . . The gloves are what made me remember her . . ." Mikha was getting completely carried away by the game.

"Well, Mikha, what can I say to you? Just say no to everything they ask you. That's the best way to deal with the situation. I know from experience."

"You've been there?"

"Yes. But I got out. The best thing is not to say anything at all. Remember, every word you say will work against you. No matter what it is. We're just amateurs—they're professionals. They have their methods, and they know how to make you take the bait, how to trip you up. The best thing is not to talk. But I've heard from other people that this is nearly impossible. They could make a deaf-mute talk."

The mention of a "deaf-mute" seemed to sear Mikha. It was January. For three years in a row he had been with the boarding-school kids, with his deaf-and-dumb children, during these deep-winter days. They had gone cross-country skiing, first departing from the school gates and walking about a hundred yards into the forest, where a ski track had been made the night before. Usually he went first, followed by the children, with Gleb Ivanovich bringing up the rear. How long had it been since he'd visited them? A year? Two? Suddenly, he wanted desperately to see them. It was urgent. And he spontaneously signed the word to himself with his hands—urgent!

He didn't say anything to Ilya. There were still two days until Monday, and he decided that on Sunday morning he would get up early and go to the boarding school to spend the day with the children. After all, they let parents visit. He had worked with them for three years. Who would dare try to stop him?

They arrested Mikha at Yaroslav Station when he was getting on the commuter train. He already had one foot in the train when two men yanked him off so adroitly that it seemed at first as if he had stumbled and fallen off the steps himself.

"Easy now, keep quiet!" one of them, wearing a rabbit-fur cap, barked in his ear.

"Quiet—if you know what's good for you!" said the second one, wearing nutria.

Mikha had a cold. He wanted to reach into his pocket for a handkerchief, and he jerked his hand. He felt a sharp pain in his wrist.

Only then did he understand fully what had happened to him: they were afraid he would take to his heels, so they had intercepted him. That meant they had been following him.

He sniffed loudly.

"Let me just wipe my snot," he said, and laughed.

"You're fine the way you are!" roared the rabbit-fur hat again.

"What do you need with a snot-nosed wimp?" Mikha said, and seemed to grow completely calm, even apathetic. He was under arrest.

The first days were the hardest. He was determined to carry out to the letter all of Ilya's urgings. On the third day they charged him, and he realized it was all over. The mousetrap had snapped shut, and he couldn't get out. He fell into a depression then. All his thoughts were with Alyona, and an enormous sense of guilt, one he had known since childhood, gripped him. He didn't know how she was; he had no connection at all to his life outside prison. The first familiar face he saw, in the second week, was the pale, haggard face of Edik Tolmachev.

They hadn't agreed on a common strategy, but their actions in prison coincided remarkably. Edik denied Mikha's participation in the magazine, Mikha refused to answer any questions at all. The only evidence they had against Mikha was the sheet of paper in the volume of *Doctor Zhivago*, or, more precisely, Musa's addendum at the bottom addressed to "Red."

It turned out that this was enough. Besides Edik Tolmachev, two more people, whom Mikha truly didn't know, had been brought in about the case of the unsanctioned journal *Gamayun*. Despite some shortcomings in his management, Edik knew the basics of conspiracy— not all the participants in the publication of the magazine knew one another.

The investigation and preparation for the trial took a little over three months. Mikha was held in a KGB detention cell in Lefortovo Prison, in the most secret and cut-off quarters—a whitewashed cell with a sealed-off window that blocked out all light, and the outside world. Every day, to the sound of a metallic clip-clop, clip-clop, the guard would lead him down the long, labyrinthine corridors, and up and down narrow stairways, where one could only walk in single file. Twice, when they met a prisoner being led toward them from the other direction, they shoved Mikha into a recess, like a side closet. Then they resumed their journey through the tangle of nightmarish, seemingly endless corridors, until, finally, they deposited him in the investigator's office. Now the interrogators didn't alternate. There was just one heavy-set, gloomy officer, who always began their hours-long interaction with the words:

"So, are we still refusing to speak?"

He had absolutely no imagination, and always repeated, in the same soft, hoarse voice:

"We don't have anything on you. You could be out of here tomorrow. You're pushing up the length of your own term. We want to get rid of you."

Mikha repeated, in a bored monotone:

"I even address my young students with the formal 'you.' Please be so good as to address me the same way."

The investigator's name was Meloedov. Mikha, with his keen ear, was immediately alert to the echo in their names: Meloedov and Melamid. But apart from the first two syllables of their surnames, they had nothing in common. True, Meloedov was no man-eating monster. He even had the reputation, in his own circles, of being almost a liberal (among those who knew words like that, at least). And, to the investigator, this redheaded fellow seemed at first like a chance character who had wandered into the wrong play. His dossier contained Gleb Ivanovich's already old denunciation, and a piece of paper of indeterminate origin, testifying to his links to the Tatar right-of-return movement. Article 70—agitation and propaganda—was clearly not relevant here. And Article 190—the distribution of intentionally false information harmful to the Soviet authorities—would have to be proved, before it was imputed to him. A single denunciation by a single loony was a bit flimsy as evidence. Moreover, the fellow's defense wasn't half bad.

Mikha had no way of knowing that the decision to isolate him had been made beforehand, and that the powers-that-be were leisurely trying to come up with a case they could slap on him.

Finally, the decision came down from above, and the interrogation became more pointed and expedient, and Mikha realized that the case they were building was not related to the journal activities. Rather, the focus had been narrowed to his involvement with the Crimean Tatars. By this time, Edik had already been sentenced.

Mikha did not give any testimony, didn't sign anything, and answered some mundane, insignificant questions, and only off the record. He was amiable enough, but he firmly denied having any part in the right-to-return movement, and insisted that he knew nothing about the Tatar demographics paper.

Meloedov, certain at first that it wouldn't take much to make Melamid talk, grew progressively more agitated at Mikha's recalcitrance, and resorted to ever more convincing threats. He raged and fumed at Mikha's stubbornness, but nothing could make him give evidence. And to think that at first the investigator thought it would be enough to scare him a little, give him a light kick in the behind . . .

By the end of the month, Meloedov had left Mikha in peace and stopped calling him in for questioning. The interest of the investigative committee had shifted to the Tatars. One of them revealed that Mikha had helped them to write letters.

But Mikha knew nothing of this. Now he shared the cell with two other men. One of them was completely mad, and constantly muttered either prayers or curses under his breath. The other was a discharged military man, a procurement officer who had been caught stealing. These cellmates inspired no desire to socialize.

Then they transferred him to another cell, which he shared with a Tatar who was involved with the Crimean Tatar movement. It turned out that he was friends with Mikha's acquaintances Ravil and Musa. It was only on the third day, when they removed the Tatar from Mikha's cell, that Mikha realized he had been planted there. He was an informer. Now Mikha was even more adamant about not saying another word. After some time, Meloedov started calling him in for questioning again; now Mikha really did keep silent, like a deaf-mute.

In the middle of February, Mikha was formally charged, and he was allowed to see a lawyer. The lawyer was one of their own, not someone assigned by the state. Sergei Borisovich had seen to this. Her name was Dina Arkadievna, and she had the first intelligent and attractive face he had seen in a long time. She took a chocolate bar out of her pocket and said:

"Alyona says hello. And there's another piece of good news: Alyona's pregnant. She's feeling fine. Now we'll try to figure out how we can get you home before the baby is born. Eat the chocolate here. I'm not allowed to give you anything."

She was one of the lawyers who took on political cases—the "magnificent five." This was the third trial of its kind. It was also the trial that got her kicked out of the Collegium of Moscow Attorneys. After the prosecutor's statement demanding the application of Article 190, Part 1, of the Penal Code—the dissemination of false information defaming the Soviet authorities—she committed the rash act of not requesting that the sentence be reduced, instead insisting on the absence of grounds for indictment. In other words, she claimed the defendant was innocent.

Alyona, whose face had grown thinner as her belly grew, was sitting in the last row of the small, packed courtroom. On her right was her mother, Valentina, and on her left, Igor Chetverikov, one of Mikha's classmates from school, though not a close friend. Ilya and Sanya, along with many others, were not allowed into the courtroom, and stood outside the door.

Marlen, who was also present in the crowd outside the door, his face contorted with helpless anger, whispered fiercely in Ilya's ear:

"He's simply mad! What was he thinking? It's just beyond me! Why the Tatars? Why the Crimea? He should have been thinking about himself! For a Jew to get mixed up in the right of return of the Crimean Tatars! He should have been organizing his own right of return to Israel!"

Mikha was sentenced to three years in a medium-security prison camp, after which he was allowed to make a final statement. He spoke better than the judge, the prosecutor, and the lawyer put together. In a clear, rather high voice, calm and confident, he spoke about the justice that would ultimately prevail in society, in the world; about those who would feel ashamed of themselves; about the grandchildren of people alive today who would find it hard to believe the cruelty and senselessness of the past. What a wonderful literature teacher he made, and how unfortunate that the deaf schoolchildren had been deprived of his rare gifts!

After the trial, Alyona's parents took her home to their house. She spent two days there, quarreled with her father, then returned to Chistoprudny Boulevard.

Sanya, who turned up at Alyona's on the day he found out about Mikha's arrest, went to see her every day now. The years of mutual coolness in his relations with Mikha seemed to have evaporated overnight. Their friendship, it turned out, was alive and well, and didn't require any special nourishment in the form of frequent telephone calls, status reports, or drinking beer together.

A week after Mikha's arrest Ilya and Sanya were sitting one evening in Milyutin Park on the bench with two broken slats. Sanya stared at the toes of his boots: Should he say it or not? Either way it was lame; but not saying anything at all was wrong. He said it, without looking at Ilya's face.

"Ilya, you're the reason Mikha's in prison, you know."

Ilya spat out defensively: "What are you talking about! Are you nuts?"

"You tempted him. Don't you remember what it says in Matthew about causing the little ones to stumble?"

"No!" Ilya insisted. "We're all adults, aren't we? Well, aren't we?"

But in his heart of hearts he felt uneasy. He was the one, after all, who had introduced Mikha to Edik, and he was responsible for what had happened in an indirect sense. But only indirectly!

The vindictive Meloedov did everything in his power to prevent Mikha from seeing his wife before being sent away under armed guard to the prison camp. Only the persistence of his father-in-law, an experienced ex-con himself, who managed to get an appointment with the deputy security officer of the prison, foiled in the end the machinations of the investigator.

On the eve of his departure, Mikha was granted a meeting with his wife. She had grown plainer, as some pregnant women do, especially (according to folk legend) if she's carrying a girl. To Mikha, her beauty was angelic, but he was unable to express what was boiling and seething inside him. He was unable because of his habitual, innate sense of profound guilt toward every living being, which was magnified even more by the circumstances. The only thing he managed to say was some sort of nonsense that sounded like Dostoevsky: "I am guilty for everyone, for everything, before all people . . ."

That was what he was feeling as he left under convoy to the prison camp: guilty, guilty for all that had happened . . . Guilty before Alyona, since he had left her alone; before his friends, for not being able to do anything that would change the disposition of things for the better; before the whole world, to which he was indebted . . .

It's a strange, inexplicable law that the most innocent people among us are the ones predisposed to the greatest sense of guilt.

FIRST IN LINE

It was completely natural that the powerful musical ideas that pre-occupied Sanya rendered him completely oblivious to domestic political events, large and small. They seemed as distant from him as revolutions in Latin America, crop failures in Africa, or tsunamis in Japan. Even Anna Alexandrovna, who was apt to admire her son uncritically, would sometimes remark, with a tinge of perplexity:

"Sanya, dear, we live here. It's our country, after all. But you're almost like a foreigner in your own country."

Early one morning in January 1969, Alyona rushed over to see him and to tell him about Mikha's arrest. It was Sanya's first personal contact with politics. It left him shaken and crushed. Mikha had shown him his magazine, and it was amusing. But it was impossible that a self-published collection on onionskin paper, consisting half of news that was usually heard on Western radio broadcasts, and half of poetry—some good, some indifferent, but still just poetry—could land someone in prison. It wasn't *The Bell*, not at all. It was homegrown. Sanya didn't know about all Mikha's activities, however. He was unaware of the Tatar connection in Mikha's life.

Ilya was exceedingly well informed about the progress of the investigation and trial; they summoned him to the KGB headquarters about the case of Edik Tolmachev. They didn't ask a single question about Mikha, and this surprised Ilya. He was even more surprised when Mikha was arrested three months after Edik.

Alyona came down with strep throat just after Mikha's arrest. Then and there she chose Sanya as her "girlfriend," and, somehow, all the responsibility for taking care of her fell on his shoulders. Alyona had never been overfond of Ilya, and she avoided having any dealings with him.

Alyona had all but broken off relations with her father. She suspected him of some kind of foul play, and once she even burst out with the accusation that he was to blame for all their misfortune. She rarely allowed her mother to visit her at home, as though she were trying to punish her for something. Alyona wept a lot at first, and didn't want to see anyone but Sanya.

Sanya was the first to know about her pregnancy. He had agreed to accompany her to the gynecologist who was supposed to carry out the Soviet woman's favorite operation. Halfway to the doctor, who was ready to perform the procedure, they turned back, after he persuaded her not to go through with it. Alyona was often offended by something Sanya said or did. She sent him away, made scenes, and kicked up a fuss; and he put up with everything patiently. Alyona rarely left the house all winter—either she was sick or simply didn't feel up to it.

She's so cantankerous and bad-tempered! he would think. But he couldn't resist her capricious charms. Up to a predictable point.

Ilya brought Sanya money to give to Alyona regularly. Alyona didn't refuse the money, but she didn't particularly need it. Anna Alexandrovna put together care packages and sent them to her through Ilya. Throughout her pregnancy, Alyona either lay in bed or drew her enigmatic ornamental patterns. During the final months she learned how to draw lying prone on the bed.

When the time came, Sanya took Alyona to the maternity home, then fetched her, now with her newborn daughter in her arms. With a bouquet of carnations in hand, he played the role of husband and father for the nurses. This set a precedent, and afterward he accompanied Alyona and her daughter to consultations at the polyclinic, bathed the baby, fed her . . . He even liked this intimate bustling and pottering about. At the same time, however, he felt uneasy for his own safety and well-being. The whole time that Mikha was in prison, Alyona was half-unconsciously trying to seduce Sanya. He would adopt a high guard, like a boxer; or simply let the feminine signals pass over him, like air or steam; or quickly make himself scarce, like water running down a drain. Occasionally, Alyona had hysterics, or went into a sulk with him. Several times she even chased him out of the house; but either she would start missing him and call him up, or he would come over without warning with a toy for the little girl, or pastry eclairs for Alyona. In fact, she ate almost nothing the whole three years that Mikha was gone. It was some sort of metabolical hunger strike. She was able to drink tea with bread or sweets, but she couldn't stomach meat, or cheese, or even soup. It was strange that the more emaciated she became, the more beautiful and ethereal she seemed. Sanya felt this, and feared her morbid attractiveness. It was Sanya who had taken her to see Mikha, before he was transferred to a prison camp. Sanya was the only one who wrote Mikha long letters. Alyona wrote short letters, very beautiful, sometimes even with little drawings. Mikha would write Alyona an open letter once a month—one for everyone, but with a specific message for each person individually. All the people who corresponded with him would gather at Alyona's for the reading. Alyona usually sat in an armchair with the sleeping baby on her lap, and Sanya set out tea with cookies. He gave the impression of being Mikha's replacement. This occasioned rumors about a romance between Alyona and the friend of her imprisoned husband. There was no romance. But a tension hung in the air nevertheless.

Sanya, perhaps more than Alyona, was anxious for Mikha's return. He sensed her psychological volatility and was afraid—what if her strength gave out suddenly before he came back or his own well-trained resistance failed him? Alyona was perhaps the most attractive of all the women he had ever known: she seemed nearly disembodied, with the long, slow turns of her swanlike neck and head, to the point of conclusion made by her chin, upraised. Or the slow, gentle sweep of the fingers that grazed her temples, and the fingertips coming to rest at the edge of her hairline, pulling slightly at her almond-shaped eyes. It was almost as though her head were hanging on her fingertips, frozen in midair.

Mikha's family took up a great deal of Sanya's time, and cut into his musical activities. He suffered over this, and had difficulty concentrating. Preoccupied with household worries and chores, he was forced to find a time and place in which to seclude himself with his beloved music, fleeing his family obligations.

He taught at the Conservatory. He didn't have a heavy teaching load—it never exceeded twelve hours a week.

Thanks to Alyona, he had stopped being a foreigner in his own country. In any case, now he knew the address of the infant feeding center, and all the surrounding pharmacies and polyclinics. He began his mornings with a run to the infant feeding center, and the evening closed with a scheduled visit to Alyona. He knew he had to force her to swallow at least a spoonful of some sort of nourishment. Without Sanya she never sat down at the table at all. She spent the greater part of the day in bed, with her daughter. When the baby, Maya, got a bit older, Alyona, who was afraid of the people and noise out on the streets, began going out into the more secluded courtyard to walk with her, but only if Sanya accompanied them.

Late in the evenings, Sanya took out a musical score from a pile lying on the floor next to his bed. He lay down and leafed through it. Beauty and wonder. Mozart's Concerto no. 23 for piano and orchestra. Evgeniya Danilovna had once told him a story about this concerto.

Stalin heard a performance by Yudina on the radio and demanded the record. There was no recording of the concerto on the face of the earth. That very night, they roused Yudina, the conductor, and a dozen members of the orchestra, and took them to the House of Sound Recording, duly recorded it, and by morning the only copy of the record was ready. Stalin generously rewarded Yudina. It is said that he sent her an envelope containing 20,000 rubles. She answered the leader with a letter: she had sent the money to a church, and she would pray for him that God would spare him despite his evil deeds. Stalin forgave her. He said she was a Holy Fool . . .

Sanya studied the Mozart concerto, and happiness broke over him like a wave, from his head to his feet. Stalin wasn't the only one to have been overwhelmed on the spot by this piece. Sanya smiled, and closed the text. He turned out the light. Mozart himself was conversing with him. What more could he dream of? What better interlocutor, friend, confessor could he find? And he realized that he could endure Alyona after all.

Sadly, Sanya's relations with his grandmother were unraveling. She never asked any direct questions, and Sanya didn't consider it necessary to enter into explanations. Anna Alexandrovna was convinced that Alyona had lured her boy into an indecent romance with her, and was disappointed in her beloved grandson. At the same time, she saw the burden of care and responsiblity her spoiled Sanya had taken upon himself, and she admired his heroism. She suffered in the knowledge that Sanya was sinking ever deeper into the affairs of Mikha's family, and was bitterly jealous of the unhappy Alyona, for whom she had so little sympathy. And, however irrational and ridiculous, she was jealous on Mikha's behalf, considering him to be a deceived husband . . .

By virtue of the sins she ascribed to Sanya, Anna Alexandrovna felt a share in his guilt, and she didn't write Mikha a single letter in three years, but sent him food packets and greetings through Ilya. She knew exactly what one needed to send to the prison camps, and she even baked special cookies in which she secreted fat and bouillon cubes, and then wrapped them in paper from the official Privet baked-goods brand. They didn't allow anything homemade into the camps, but these fake Privet cookies contained an unheard-of number of calories. From time to time, she also sent money for Alyona.

She remembered very well how she had tenderly tried to dissuade Mikha from this marriage. And also: she was the only one who feared Mikha's return. She anticipated scandal, revelations, unmasking, indecency. No, even more than that, she feared a catastrophe. What did she know, and what was presentiment?

Mikha forbade himself to count the days until his release; but he couldn't help it. The fewer that remained, the stronger was his anxiety that they wouldn't let him go. His friends were also counting the days.

It was, of course, very silly of them to assume that Mikha would be released in precisely three years, at exactly midnight on the day he was scheduled to go free. They already knew that he had been brought under convoy to Moscow, and that he was in Lefortovo Prison. They assumed, not without reason, that this was connected with the arrest of Sergei Borisovich, who, as they also knew, was in Lefortovo as well.

Three of them arrived at Lefortovo toward midnight—Ilya, Sanya, and Victor Yulievich. Ilya had an old jacket and new jeans in his rucksack. Ilya also brought a new pair of shoes for Mikha—true, they were one size too big, but they were fine ones.

There were three places from which Mikha might have been released: through the central entrance, the investigative offices, or the service entrance. The friends kept watch at these doors throughout the night and morning, until noon the next day. Then they went to inquire. A militarized-looking woman at a small window told them that Melamid had already left.

They rushed to call Mikha at home. Alyona came to the phone, and said in a quiet, remote voice:

"He's home. Come."

It turned out that they had released him at eight in the morning through the investigative offices, and his waiting friends had simply missed him. They got a taxi, and twenty minutes later they all tumbled into Mikha's front entrance. The elevator was out of order. Sanya and Ilya flew up to the sixth floor via the stairs, and an aging Victor Yulievich, panting from exertion, followed, two floors behind. They waited until he caught up with them, then rang the doorbell. Mikha himself opened the door. Rather, it was a gaunt, colorless ghost of Mikha . . . Ilya lost no time remarking on this, trying to avoid any outburst of feeling the situation might otherwise have inspired.

"Well, you're nothing more than a shadow!"

And Mikha laughed, suddenly himself again.

"I'm no shadow! I'm the skeleton of a shadow!"

Victor Yulievich raised his hand in a gesture familiar to them since childhood, and said:

> "This to me
>   In dreadful secrecy impart they did;
>   And I with them the third night kept the watch;
>   Where, as they had delivered, both in time,
>   Form of the thing, each word made true and good,
>   The apparition comes..."

And everything seemed to fall back into place. They slapped one another on the back, pestered Mikha, and barged into the living room in a tumult. In spite of the former ideals of severity and asceticism, it was crammed with knickknacks and junk—a chair, a child's bed, and even a curtain that partitioned the child's sleeping corner from the rest of the room. The place was fast reverting to the appearance it had had during Aunt Genya's time.

Maya, who had just been put down for her nap, woke up and began to howl. Alyona darted into the sleeping nook to comfort her, then brought the little girl out to see the guests. Maya stretched out her arms toward Sanya, the only one of the guests familiar to her. Sanya took her in his arms, and jiggled her gently up and down. She threw her arms around his neck, hugging him.

"What did you bring me?" she asked in a voice raspy from sleep.

Then he murmured something in her ear, and she smiled.

"Where?"

Sanya took a bright glass marble out of his pocket, and rolled it around on the palm of his hand. The girl snatched it like a little monkey.

Mikha watched the two of them jealously. The girl didn't recognize her shy father. He was seeing her for the first time in her life, and he couldn't yet grasp that this small creature, a living being with curly hair, big eyes, and busy little fingers, had come from him, from his great love for Alyona. It was still not completely comprehensible to him how these two things, the most important things in his life, were connected.

Mikha had already taken a bath before they arrived. He scrubbed the three years of vileness off his skin. He wanted to wash himself from inside out, to clean the prison air out of his nose, his throat, and his lungs, to purge the foul prison food and water from his mouth, his intestines, his stomach . . .

Seven years! It would take seven years. In seven years, all the cells in the human organism are renewed. Who had told him that? But how long would it take to cleanse the soul of prison filth? Oh, if he could only wash his brain in liquid nitrogen, in hydrochloric acid, in lye, to expunge those three years from his memory! Let it all be washed away, so that he would forget everything that he knew and loved, everything he revered, as long as all trace of these three years would vanish.

His friends stayed a short while, less than an hour, then left. The three of them, their small family, remained. There was a lot they had to talk about. The little girl clung to her mother, pushing her father away. Mikha frowned and wrinkled his nose; she was afraid, and turned away from him.

What a high price to pay. The child doesn't recognize me, she'll never recognize me. Mikha didn't feel things by halves, and he suffered from an acute sense of rejection.

"Let's all go for a walk. Maya, want to go swing?"

"Yes. With you," she said, and took her mother by the hand.

"We'll take Papa with us, too." And they went outside together.

Maya sat down on the swings, and Alyona pushed her gently.

"They dragged me back here under armed guard five weeks before my release was scheduled, and I realized that they were planning to pin something else on me. It turned out to be the case of Chernopyatov and Kushchenko," he told Alyona, through Maya's interruptions. "They didn't let us meet face-to-face for a confrontation for a long time, but they let me read their testimony. The testimony was dreadful; I didn't believe a word of it. I thought they were just planting false evidence cooked up by some agents. They named more than thirty names, including that of Edik Tolmachev. But this case wasn't about *Gamayun*, but about the *Chronicle*, about all possible human rights cases. The protocols ran the gamut—sincere confessions, repentance, you name it."

"I know all of this already," Alyona said drily, nodding.

"I didn't believe it until the very end. Actually, I still can't believe it. But we met face-to-face. And what I heard was an echo of the protocols. What they did to them I don't know. Maybe they beat the confessions out of them. I denied everything. Except that Sergei Borisovich was your father and my father-in-law. I was sure they were going to tack this case on me, too. Until the last day I couldn't believe they would set me free. I still can't believe it, really."

Alyona didn't raise her eyes to him. The expression on her face didn't even seem to register his presence. Mikha put his hand on top of hers.

"I just can't wrap my head around it, Alyona. Sergei Borisovich couldn't possibly have said all that. But I heard him say it with my own ears. Don't think that I love him any less, Alyona. I'm just terribly, terribly sorry for him."

"I don't know, Mikha. I don't think I am. Since childhood, I always believed I had a hero for a father." Alyona did lift her eyes, but stared at one place under the swing, at the confused shadows made by the seat that carried her daughter back and forth, back and forth.

"You're not swinging me right, Mama!" the little girl said sternly. Mikha grabbed hold of the chain of the swing.

"Don't touch it!" she said even more sternly.

Toward evening Zhenya Tolmacheva and an acquaintance from Alyona's institute stopped over and stayed for a long time. They sent them away at nine, saying the little girl needed a bath.

In the communal bathroom, they placed the children's tub on a stool, filled it with warm water, and placed Maya in it. She washed her dolly and her rubber dog diligently, then just splashed around. Mikha watched from the doorway and was filled with an unparalleled new love for the wet child, her darkened curls sticking to her forehead.

"Get the towel," Alyona said, and he took the fragile back into the large towel. It was the first time he had held his own child in his arms. She was very light, but weighty. Small, but enormous; bigger than Mikha, bigger than the whole world. And that's what she was—the whole world.

My little world, my giant world,
A world all eyes, light-brown, and moist,
One sleepy green eye, shade unfurled,
Ta-dum, ta-dum, ta-dum, ta-dum . . .

The little girl had fallen asleep. Mikha embraced his wife. She covered his lips with her hand and said:

"You haven't told me anything I wasn't already aware of. I know everything. I spoke to his lawyer. You don't know her, Natalia Kirillovna. She's wonderful. I asked her to tell him I didn't ever want to see him again."

She didn't say the word *father*. She said "him." Mikha took her hand away.

"Alyona, that's crazy. You can't do that to him. He deserves only pity . . ."

Everything was just as it had been before—the courtyard, the neighbors, the broken floorboard in the corridor, the poplar trees outside the window, the ancient curbstones that marked out what had once been a flower bed, the former skating rink . . . the saleswomen in the bakery and the fish store, the building manager. Yet it seemed as though thirty years had passed, and not just three. One false move and everything might split open with a resounding crash—the house, the courtyard, his little daughter, his wife, the whole city. And April, so warm and welcoming this year.

Anna Alexandrovna was the first person Mikha visited after his release, in the evening on his second day of freedom. She was the one he told, on that same day, that Alyona's father was giving evidence and that he was afraid it would land him back in prison.

Anna Alexandrovna had prepared for Mikha's arrival: she had spent the whole day before his visit in the kitchen.

"You know, Mikha, there's nothing new under the sun. My husband's own brother sent him to prison. They both perished. It's fate that decides, and not our own actions or behavior, whether good or bad. Please eat, I made it for you."

Three years in prison camps had changed him beyond recognition: a dark, haggard face, thinning hair, eyes faded almost to yellow. And the way he thought about everything seemed to have somehow shifted.

Anna Alexandrovna had not changed in the least. Her face was overlaid with a dense, fine net of wrinkles, as though carved with a burin. It had appeared very early and had frozen in place, without disfiguring her in the least. Now, when she was nearing eighty, she appeared to be very youthful. Looking at her, pondering her enigmatic words, Mikha realized that Anna Alexandrovna was a strikingly beautiful woman. And much more than beautiful. Through the veil of wrinkles, through the abyss of years, he saw her face suffused with light and loveliness.

"Anna Alexandrovna, I've so missed your home . . . If you only knew how much I love you . . ."

She laughed.

"Well, it's about time! Mikha, I prepared you a 'Jewish-style pike.' That's what Molokhovets calls it in her cookbook. I just threw it together, never having made it before. Taste it and tell me what you think." And she placed an oval dish with pieces of pale fish in front of him.

"It's delicious! Especially considering I've never eaten such a delicacy in my entire life!" At that moment, Mikha realized he was truly home. He beamed, smiled, talked, and ate all at the same time, forgetting for a time about the constant gnawing pain in his stomach.

Anna Alexandrovna, on her part, felt relieved. Perhaps everything would fall back into place. Mikha would assume his rightful role as father of his family, and Sanya would return, freed from his worries and cares about Alyona. Everything would go back to the way it was before, and all the complications, real and imagined, would disappear of themselves.

For the next two weeks, Mikha was often at the Steklovs'. Everything seemed fine with Alyona, and their daughter was for him a miracle from above. Still, everything else that surrounded him was bad, far worse than before he was sent to prison.

Nevertheless, in Anna Alexandrovna's home, he was happy. As before, Sanya was rarely home, but his absence was comforting. It meant that Sanya was gradually returning to his element. He again spent his evenings at concerts, and in the Conservatory dorms, where he had many friends. It seemed that the electrical charge that had been building up during the years when Mikha was in the camps had been defused.

In the first weeks after his release, Mikha managed to stop by to see Anna Alexandrovna several times. Two of those times Sanya was at home, and the aura of closeness that they had shared in childhood and youth returned. They understood each other implicitly; and what they didn't understand about each other inspired interest and sympathy.

Mikha was also happy that Anna Alexandrovna was, as before, the grown-up, and he was still the child. And, like a child coming home from a walk, he brought Anna Alexandrovna little tributes from his excursions: a pine branch with a cone still on it, a funny drawing of Maya's.

One evening he dropped in to see Anna Alexandrovna after returning from Tarasovka, where he had visited his old friend Artur Korolev, the bookbinder. He and Korolev had drunk vodka together, but the visit hadn't lasted too long, and Mikha returned to the city before nightfall. He had nothing special to give Anna Alexandrovna, so he bought some lollipops in the shape of roosters from a gypsy at the train station. He presented the handful of fiery roosters on sticks to his elderly girlfriend like a bouquet. She placed the roosters in a glass, and they gleamed with festive brightness. Mikha suddenly noticed that the whole house had become rather old and shabby.

The heart is home. The heart is glad. For what?
The shades of home? The garden shadows? I don't know.
The ancient garden, all the aspens bent and withered. Horror!
The house in ruins . . . the scum that lines the ponds . . .

So much is lost! Brother against brother . . . what wrongs!
Decay and dust . . . it lists and crumbles; but still stands . . .
Whose home is here? Whose ashes on the ground? . . . Whose corner, this?
Dead pauper's lair, without a hearthstone or a stove . . .

The hands of the old woman, as fragile and thin as porcelain, poured the weak tea into semitransparent cups. "You remember Annensky . . . It's so very sad . . . Look how plain our tea ceremony is today—just tea with sugar and lollipops. Sanya will be coming soon. He promised to go to the store on his way home. Can you wait?"

She stood up and pulled out the potbellied sugar bowl and tongs from the cupboard—the sugar was cubed.

Anna Alexandrovna and Mikha sat in front of their weak tea. There were no cookies, no gingersnaps, not even dry crusts of bread. For the second week in a row Anna Alexandrovna hadn't left home because of the unusual fatigue that had come over her. She hadn't taken sick leave, but asked a teacher who taught only part-time to take over her lessons. A week had already gone by, and she didn't feel any better. She complained to Mikha that she felt terribly lazy: she didn't go to work, and she was letting things slide at home, too—she didn't even have anything to offer him to go with his tea.

"Tomorrow I'll pick up my old bones and go out. But Sanya's not pulling his weight either—he couldn't even bring home a loaf of bread! And I won't even start in on Nadezhda. Ah, you haven't heard the news! My daughter has gotten herself involved in a romance. She doesn't sleep at home these days. Imagine! It's indecent." She laughed, as though she were talking about a fifteen-year-old scamp of a girl, and added, with her characteristic directness:

"She's going to marry him. What idiocy . . ."

And she frowned.

It seems like she's not feeling at all well, Mikha thought. He was used to Anna Alexandrovna always serving fresh tea. Even if the old pot had just been brewed a few hours before, she tossed it away without a moment's hesitation.

"Well, how are things going with you?" Anna Alexandrovna said. Mikha began telling her about what pained him the most: he couldn't find a job. He had looked high and low. No one would hire him. "The local police keep coming by and asking me when I'll start working . . ."

She listened to him attentively, mechanically kneading her self-rolled cigarette and thumping the empty mouthpiece against the table-top. Suddenly, she dropped it, leaned back against the chair, and, looking somewhere into the distance, said:

"Mikha, I don't feel well . . . I'm unwell."

She opened her mouth and let out a few spasmodic gasps, one after another, through tensely drawn lips. Her hand scrabbled across the table, knocking over the red roosters. Her eyes stared so intently and fixedly at a place somewhere behind Mikha's head that he turned around to look. No one was there. The gold spines of the Brockhaus and Efron encyclopedias gleamed on the bookshelf.

Mikha caught her and carried her to the divan. She was light, and hung over his arms like a down comforter. He laid her down, propping two cushions behind her back. She continued to stare straight ahead—not at him. He pressed her wrist in the wrong spot, where there's no pulse even among the living.

"Just a minute, just a minute . . . medicine . . . an ambulance . . ." Mikha mumbled, already fearing it was too late.

He dashed to the telephone. The Steklovs were the only ones in the communal flat with a telephone in their own room, though they shared the line. He picked up the receiver and heard a snatch of the neighbor's conversation:

"How many times did I try to warn her, you've got to keep your eye on him! She just laughed; and now she's had her laugh! He's a respectable man, which is rare in our day and age . . ."

Mikha rushed out into the corridor:

"Quick! Anna Alexandrovna's ill! Call an ambulance!"

The neighbor, Maria Solomonovna, a pharmacist with gold teeth spotted in red lipstick, greatly admired and respected Anna Alexandrovna.

"Well, that's all for now. The neighbors need the phone. It's an emergency. But don't forget to remind her: how many times did I warn you . . ."

The latch on the entrance door to the flat rustled, then clicked open. Sanya walked in. He was carrying a bag of groceries. On the way he had stopped in at the store and bought everything they needed, even a chicken, and was proudly bringing home the provisions to his grandmother. Perhaps for the first time in his life . . .

"Anna Alexandrovna is unwell . . . the ambulance . . . it seems very bad . . ." Mikha mumbled. Sanya tore into their room, with Maria Solomonovna waddling right behind him.

Fifteen minutes later, before the doctors had even arrived, Vasily Innokentievich called. It was his daily call and mantra—"How's life?"—

which was a source of slight annoyance to Anna Alexandrovna. He rushed over immediately. Their lifelong romance, which had lasted for nearly sixty years, with breaks and interruptions for Nuta's marriage and infatuations, was coming to an end. Rejected countless times and returning to her over and over during the most difficult times of her life—when her husbands and lovers were imprisoned and shot—now he had to bury his great love, without hope for another resurrection. It was over.

Ilya arrived simultaneously with Vasily Innokentievich. He was an infrequent visitor. Thus, all Nuta's favorite people had gathered around her body, already growing cold, before the doctor had even come to pronounce her dead. Only Nadezhda Borisovna was missing—she was spending the night at a rented dacha, where there was no telephone. She found out about the death of her mother only on the morning of the next day.

The body was removed later that evening, and the three grown boys sat together. It was almost as if they fused into a single being—with their shared thoughts, feelings, and memories, similarly devastated, similarly forlorn. In the presence of Sanya and Mikha, Ilya's third eye, or fourth, or whichever one it was—the organ of warmth and sympathy—opened up in him, and they all seemed to breathe the same air, to suffer the same grief.

The funeral was strange in its unevenness and incongruity. A will was discovered in which Anna Alexandrovna gave very precise instructions about how she wanted to be buried. She wanted a funeral service to be held in the Church of Peter and Paul by the Yauza Gates.

There were many people. They distracted Sanya from Anna Alexandrovna, who lay like a white island among the black human waves.

Along with friends and family, the academy directors were present, too—looking puzzled and out of place in their uniforms with blue shoulder straps. Students also came. In those years, they were no longer Chinese, but Cubans and Africans. Anna Alexandrovna had taught them Russian very well. They brought her a pine wreath with a black-and-red ribbon. The wreath chafed Sanya's eyes.

At the head of the coffin stood Vasily Innokentievich, his gray hair giving off sparks, his face crumpled. Liza was not with him. She was on a concert tour in Germany. Ten or twelve old-lady friends—Evgenia

Danilovna, a couple of her gymnasium friends, Eleonora Zorakhovna with two aristocratic white roses—mingled with former colleagues from various walks of life and with Sanya's friends. Ilya brought Olga. Near them stood Tamara Brin, granddaughter of Nuta's late girlfriend. Tamara's face was a rare Levantine type that was instantly recognizable. Sanya remembered her—she had been invited to one of his birthday parties in childhood.

The pallid Mikha stood next to Sanya, and quietly wept into the mohair scarf that Anna Alexandrovna had given him long ago for one of his birthdays. Next to Ilya stood his wife—pale, strawberry-blond, holding hyacinths in her hand. From time to time Sanya's gaze would come to rest on a thickset man with bushy eyebrows and a broad face. He stood by Sanya's mother, and for some reason gripped her arm possessively. It was her intended, whom Sanya was seeing for the first time. Why had his mother brought this man along?

Sanya observed everything happening as if at a remove, like watching it through thick glass. The dead face of his grandmother seemed like an artist's forgery. Her beauty had taken on a kind of ultimate form, and this absolutely superfluous beauty inspired uncertainty about the world of the living, so bustling and unattractive.

From a side recess, a priest emerged and began the service. Evgenia Danilovna thrust a burning candle into Sanya's hand. The voice of the priest mingled with the voices of the choir, a music that Sanya had never heard before. It commanded attention, because it contained something very significant, but ineffable.

The priest, who looked Greek, offered prayers with profound attention and without any shortcuts. The whole funeral mass seemed interminable. Sanya noticed that the voice of the priest blended in beautifully with the singing, and the subtle sounds—the crackle of the candles, coughing, soft sobs—also enhanced it. The instrumentation was exquisite. When the candles were extinguished, Sanya thought that the service had ended. But the priest again began reading something out loud, and the choir began to sing again. Sanya was transported by the sounds, the smells, and the sheen of light on the icon settings to a place that, until now, only music had been able to take him.

The choir fell silent, and the priest said that the close friends and relatives could take their leave of the departed. Everyone began to move, forming a line to the coffin.

Anna Alexandrovna hated lines. She said that half her life had been spent standing in line: for bread, milk, potatoes, soap, tickets, letters. She had even perfected a means of defense: she repeated poetry to herself that she knew by heart.

She would say, laughing, that the Soviet authorities had helped her train her memory, forcing her to stand in line so long. She had no doubt never imagined that on her final day on earth there would be such a long line of people waiting to bid her farewell.

Anna Alexandrovna had requested to be buried at the Donskoi Monastery, at her grandfather's grave. The body was cremated at the Donskoi Crematorium. The monastery cemetery had been closed for a long time already, and it was only possible to bury the urn two weeks later.

It was not a grave, but a crypt; but it had collapsed so long ago that it was only possible to bury her on top of it, next to the listing tombstone. Her grandfather's name was an aristocratic one, but not very well known.

Unlike the funeral service, there were few people at the burial— only the closest friends and relatives. Vasily Innokentievich stood next to Sanya and kept wanting to say something to him, but couldn't find the right moment. When everything was over and they were all walking out of the monastery gates, he caught Sanya by the hand and said, very quietly and clearly:

"Sanya! We've lost Liza for good. She's not coming back after her tour. She's staying in Austria. She called me to say that we would all understand in time, that everything was fine, that she was happy and asks everyone to forgive her. And she loves us all. I told her that Nuta had died, and she cried and asked whether she could call you. I said I'd ask you."

"Oh my God!" was all Sanya could get out.

"She's planning to marry a conductor there. She met him on her first tour, and they performed together. He's an old man! A terrible loss. The people we love most are all abandoning us. We'll never see Liza again. Maybe you will; but I won't."

"Vasily, how sad it is! Women always want to get married for some reason; look," and he gestured with his eyes toward his mother, who was being led by the hand by a man with a hat like a furry pastry on his fat head. "Your son-in-law is an Austrian, and not a German?"

Vasily Innokentievich nodded.

"I just didn't like that fat Boba fellow, and I was glad when they divorced. This new son-in-law, by the way, is a handsome guy. He has a wonderful face. I have a record with his picture on it. Why do women do what they do? Take a look at that . . . janitor," Sanya said, looking over at his mother and her fiancé. "Nuta knew everything."

Mikha came up to them. He gripped Sanya's maimed hand, and bent right down to his ear:

"Your mother is alive, but I have no one. Anna Alexandrovna was closer to me than my whole family put together. I only just now understood that. She's gone away, and now I'm first in line."

"What? What do you mean?" Sanya said, not hearing or understanding what Mikha said.

"There are no more grown-ups ahead of me. It's my turn next," Mikha explained.

Two weeks after Anna Alexandrovna's death, the thickset gentleman in the pastry hat who was holding his mother's hand moved into their apartment. His name was Lastochkin, and the name didn't suit him in the least. In no way did he even remotely resemble his namesake, the swallow. They rearranged the furniture, took down the dividing screen, and partitioned the room with a wardrobe and a bookcase. They nudged Sanya over a bit, depriving him of the geometrical security to which he was accustomed.

Anna Alexandrovna's death, sudden, easy, and completely spontaneous, could not be reconciled with life. Sanya awoke in the mornings, heard the unbearable sounds of alien everyday existence, and wanted to fall asleep again, in order to wake up in his normal, habitual home.

But that former home was gone; his grandmother was no longer there, and his mother had undergone some strange transformation, like children under spells in fairy tales. She had changed in a single moment into the opposite version of herself. Whereas before she had been soft and plump, now she was sharp and hard; before she had had light-brown hair mixed with gray, and now she had become a brunette. She began to use lipstick and wear a new astrakhan fur coat, black and unruly, instead of the ancient gray rabbit fur in which they had wrapped Sanya as a baby.

But most intolerable of all was the new voice of Nadezhda Borisovna: sonorous, fawning, with a giggle at the end of every phrase. No, even more unbearable than that were the nighttime sounds of coupling, of bedsprings, panting and groaning . . .

It was as though the janitor's quarters on Potapovsky Lane had encroached on the very place where once Nuta had read her favorite Flaubert and Marcel Proust during sleepless nights.

He couldn't sleep. He caught small snatches of slumber, but he would start awake and return to the obsessive thoughts: *Nuta is gone. Nuta will never come back. Nuta is no more.*

He slept at intervals. When he woke up for good, he would fall into his usual despondency. He washed and left the defiled house. If he didn't have class, he went to see Mikha.

Mikha's mood was no better. He still couldn't find a job—no one would hire an ex-convict—and they were broke. Alyona tried to teach some classes. Their friends chipped in to help, and Mikha accepted these alms unwillingly. Marlen finally left for Israel—hurriedly, unexpectedly, and inexplicably—and wrote Mikha letters, trying to persuade him to follow him there. But Mikha rejected the idea of emigrating out of hand.

"Everyone keeps repeating the same thing: emigration, emigration. Everyone has an opinion on the subject—for or against it. I can't even consider it, Sanya. I'd die there."

Maya, who adored Sanya and still hadn't come to trust her newfound father, climbed into Sanya's lap and tickled him behind the ear. That was a little game they had.

"Mikha, we're going to die anyway. And music and poetry are everywhere, not only in Russia," Sanya said.

"Music, yes. But poetry—no. Poetry has its own language, and that language is Russian! I'm a poet—perhaps a bad one, but still a poet!" the usually gentle Mikha burst out. "I can't live without Russia!"

Sanya was unable to counter this. He couldn't say: yes, you're a bad poet. And was it any better for the good ones? Khodasevich? Tsvetaeva? Even Nabokov, for God's sake?

But Mikha, like a pendulum, kept returning to the same point: Russia, the mother tongue, Russian metaphysics . . . Russia, the Lethe, Lorelei . . .

Sanya attempted to lower the level.

"Well, my friend, leave Russia with your Lorelei, otherwise you'll drown prematurely in our river Lethe . . ." And he frowned from the awkwardness of his own joke. "Leave, Mikha. It's a lost cause. And Nuta is dead."

He thought about Liza. She had left, abandoned her grandfather, who doted on her, and lived now on the other side of the looking glass. In Vienna, Mozart, Schubert, and the entire Viennese School promenaded along the Ringstrasse.

Going down the stairs, Sanya began composing in his mind a long, meandering phrase, words set to music—the strings resounded plaintively, the brass crashed, the alto saxophone crooned in a soulful voice. The words were almost lost, but still they surfaced, indistinct but indispensable.

Nuta left, died, flew away, poor thing, her thin fingers, the rings no longer ringing . . . even her smell is gone.

A short sprint through Mikha's courtyard, past the corner house, from Chistoprudny Boulevard to Maroseyka.

Mikha, orphaned, kin, terrible childhood, the transparent Alyona, my God, it reeks of madness, it reeks of the mewling of the deaf and dumb, poor, poor everyone.

Woodwinds, advance! The clarinet sobs, and the flute weeps . . .

Crossing the streetcar rails, where an invisible monument to underage hooligan, killed on this spot twenty years before, stood.

Fortissimo, percussion.

Brass, brass, brass . . . and the screech of brakes.

Unhappy boy in a padded cotton jacket, in a soldier's cap with earflaps, running, running, cold metal clenched in his fist.

Turn left on Pokrovka, home to the Vanity Chest House.

Poor fingers, poor fingers, perished forever. For violin, viola, and clarinet, for bayan, accordion, for the baneful balalaika. Oh, piano!

Piano duet! For four hands! The right piano Liza, the left one me. Liza begins the piece, I join in.

And a right turn home to my building, to my side wing. String section. The violins begin. Tipsy, pianissimo. The piano theme builds and develops, attenuates in the string rendition. Rises. And everything concludes in the deep, sad voice of the cello.

Some carry skates in their hands, some shopping bags, briefcases, musical scores, boots from the shoemaker, repaired and repaired again. They carry illnesses, misfortunes, summonses, blood test results, garbage, a dog, a bottle.

And right in front of his door, his fingers already touching the only remaining bronze door handle in the whole building, he lifted all the music up, then dashed it with all his might to the ground, so that it shattered and rolled away.

If you exist, God, take me away from here and put me in another place. I can't go on here. I can't go on without Nuta . . .

He entered the building. He went up to the second floor. He went into the apartment, and paused. Lastochkin had wrapped Nuta's blouse around the handle of a gigantic cast-iron frying pan filled with hash browns cooked in lard. He was carrying it from the communal kitchen to their room. It stank.

THE DECORATED UNDERPANTS

In 1961 Peter Petrovich Nichiporuk addressed a Party conference, saying exactly what was on his mind: Stalin's personality cult had been exposed for what it was, and now, slowly but surely, a new cult was growing up around Khrushchev. Lenin's precepts had been forgotten, and they had to return to them, to strengthen democracy and the responsibility of elected officials to the people. To achieve this they had to abolish the high salaries of government officials and introduce limited terms in office. He told them exactly what he thought.

He had already "rolled out" all these thoughts for his friend Afanasy Mikhailovich, one of his former college buddies from the General Staff Academy, where they had both studied before the war. Afanasy didn't approve, though he shared all of his ideas. He didn't approve, specifically, of the plan to introduce these ideas at a Party conference.

"It won't have any positive effect, Peter; but the consequences could be dire," Afanasy said of this harebrained plan.

Peter reproached Afanasy as a coward. Afanasy, usually restrained, suddenly flew into a rage and sent his friend to the place that the old friends were not in the habit of sending each other.

Then Peter Petrovich announced something very unpleasant to

his friend's ears: there is no greater coward than a soldier. And the higher the rank, the more cowardly they are.

Highly trained professionals who had gone through the war, fearing neither enemy fire nor the foe himself, never taking cover behind someone else's back, were deathly afraid of the powers that be and were now defending, not the Motherland, but their own fat backsides and their own cushy armchairs.

Since this discussion was taking place at Afanasy Mikhailovich's dacha, he showed his friend the door. Discord arose between them, of the kind recalling Nikolai Gogol's two Ivans. In this case, however, it was not a "pig" or a "goose" that set it off, but Peter's "coward," which had offended Afanasy Mikhailovich to the bottom of his soul.

Peter Petrovich was punished for his scandalous speech. They gave him a new job and transferred him to the Far East—basically sending him into exile—where he was less likely to cause trouble. At first he pined, and life in the remote provinces bored him; but then he resumed his activities. He organized a union of like-minded people who, like him, wanted to get the entire lopsided, meandering country back onto the straight and narrow (as Lenin had envisioned) again. This underground activity, with secret meetings, and even leaflets, didn't last long. Peter Petrovich was arrested. First he was kicked out of the Party, then he was tried in a closed court and given a paltry three years. By way of additional punishment, he was demoted to the rank and file. The condemned general was stripped of his title, his military decorations, his pension, and all privileges conferred on him by dint of his former services, now rendered null and void.

And so began Peter Petrovich's new biography. He gradually shed, along with extra pounds, his ramshackle, down-at-heel notions about life. He spent three years in prison, was released, and was thrown in prison again. He recalled his former, "academic" life, as he now mockingly termed it, and deemed it juvenile.

The general had a good head on his shoulders. It was not for nothing he had once headed the Department of Military Tactics at the academy. But he had entered into an unequal battle with the authorities, which fought not with brains, but by brute strength. What use were tactics, not to mention strategy, here? Wherever the authorities, humiliated and scorned by a former general, sent him—prison, the labor camps, exile, a psychiatric institution—he always emerged from the ordeal and picked up where he had left off.

In the spring of 1972, he was given a little respite—he was freed. By this time, he was no longer part of the rank and file, but had become a true general of the small army of dissidents. Some people are born generals.

Nichiporuk knew that the authorities never forgave domestic enemies, and realized that he didn't have long to kick up his heels in freedom. He enjoyed to the hilt his home life, socializing with people, even a little stroll through the city. Freedom! Sweet freedom!

But this freedom was an illusion. All the while his telephone was tapped, and the shadowing had never stopped. Peter Petrovich decided to go to Minsk. He had business to attend to there. He didn't tell his wife, Zoya, what kind of business it was—and she, an experienced friend, didn't ask.

He bought a ticket for the evening train, came home, and packed a few things—a change of underwear, shaving kit, the two last issues of *Novy Mir,* already dog-eared, and a stuffed animal for the granddaughter of a friend.

They had just sat down to dinner when the doorbell rang. It was Zoya's friend Svetlana, dear to both of them. She came bearing news: yesterday there had been a search at Kharchenko's, and at Vasilisa Travnikova's. They had taken Kharchenko away but left Vasilisa behind.

Peter Petrovich shrugged; there was nothing at home to incriminate them.

"They don't know that. They'll come and turn the whole place upside down," Svetlana said.

"Oh, wait!" Peter Petrovich had just remembered something. "My decorations! They stripped me of them on paper, but all the medals are still here. I don't want to give them away. We'll have to do something about it, Zoya. Could you get them out of here, Svetlana?"

"We'll get rid of them. But I'd rather send my girls. It's safer. This evening."

And, true to her word, that evening, after Peter Petrovich had already left to catch his train, two girls, both of them about fifteen, arrived. One was called Tonya. She was plump and had chubby cheeks. The other was called Sima, and she was very plain. Both of them were wearing identical caps and scarves. Svetlana was a teacher, and these were her pupils.

They shuffled awkwardly in the doorway. Zoya Vasilievna told them to take their coats off, and she prepared tea and cookies. They sat in the kitchen, both of them still in their blue caps, and didn't say a word. Zoya Vasilievna placed a heavy bundle on the table. The soft fabric parcel was wrapped with newspaper and tied up with string. She put the parcel in a homemade fabric grocery bag as they watched. Then she placed on the table a note, which read: "These are military decorations that need to be kept safe." The girls read it and nodded amiably. Then Zoya took a match and set the note on fire. She put the remains of the paper under a stream of water, and threw it in the garbage pail.

The girls exchanged glances: this was serious.

They went out the main door, and looked around. Outside it was quiet and deserted, and a vacillating April ambiguity reigned. They walked to the metro, not talking. They arrived at Belorussky Station, and Tonya walked Sima to the metro entrance. Next to the entrance Sima held out the bag to her friend.

"Listen, I'm scared. What if Mama finds it? You take them home to your house, okay?"

"All right," Tonya said agreeably. "But where should I hide them? Maybe in the broom closet? We have one under the stairs. Though the lock gets broken off pretty often, so people can steal firewood."

"But what's the firewood for?" Sima said, surprised.

"Nothing. No one has stoves anymore, but the firewood's still there. And people steal it."

"But it's almost summer now . . ."

"Yeah, that's true."

Tonya took the trolleybus from Belorussky Station almost to her front door on Dzerzhinsky Square.

As if on cue, she arrived when there was no one home. Vitka, her nephew, was at the neighbor's; his mother, Valka, was out living it up; and her older brother, Tolya, was doing time.

Her mother wasn't home, either; she was working the night shift.

Pressing the parcel to her stomach, Tonya walked through the apartment. Should she put it in a box on top of the wardrobe? There were no empty boxes—only three, stuffed full. In the lower drawer of the wardrobe there were tools. Sometimes her mother opened it to get out a hammer or some nails. They were left over from her father. The underwear was all folded in little piles; only on the bottom shelf was there a messy clump of them. There were old underpants with a nap, at one time blue and peach-colored, and with faded, worn-out crotches. Her mother had cut pieces of fabric that was a bit sturdier, and, in multiple layers, from the inside, had patched the ones that still had some life in them with crude hand-stitching. Tonya took the most ragged pairs and wrapped them around the parcel, then stuffed them right up against the back wall of the wardrobe. The parcel took up almost half the drawer. She took the parcel out again and unwrapped it. There were eleven fancy boxes inside. They contained military decorations of enamel and gold, very lovely to look at, and surprisingly heavy. Tonya decided to get rid of the boxes, since they took up a lot of room. She removed the decorations, and hooked or pinned each piece to the fabric, then rolled it up into a large sausage and again stuffed it into the drawer, right up against the wall. She decided to store the boxes separately, in her own little corner on the top shelf. Empty boxes— what did they matter? The decorations were the important thing.

Early in the morning on May 9, Vitka, Tonya's pesky nephew, discovered the parcel in the wardrobe. The other kids in his courtyard had told him that moms hide money in the wardrobe, in the underwear. You just had to look hard for it. He started with the lower drawer. He didn't find any money there, but his hands felt the lumpy parcel by the wall right away. He pulled it out and unwrapped it—and what did he see there but decorations and medals pinned to his grandmother's old underpants! What a find! And it was just the right day for decorations and medals: Victory Day. He unfolded the underpants, full of amazement. There were lots of decorations and medals. He counted five; then five more. And there was still another one. They were pinned and hooked every which way, and he slowly and methodically freed them all from the worn-out rags. Then, not worried in the least about his own shirt, he began sticking them on both sides of it, from the shoulders down. Their weight pulled down the fabric, and they sparkled with gold and silver and Kremlin stars. He went out into the courtyard to show the other kids. He had forgotten all about the money he had promised to look for in the underwear in the wardrobe. But the kids had forgotten about it, too, and had already left. While he was wondering where to find them, three big boys appeared out of nowhere: Artur the Armenian, Sevka, and Timka the Stump. They immediately descended on him and started ripping off the decorations. Vitka hollered and made a dash for the gates.

The fortieth day after Anna Alexandrovna's death fell on May 9, and Vasily Innokentievich, retired colonel of the Medical Corps, rather than meeting with his fellow officers from the regiment, went to attend a memorial service at the Church of Peter and Paul by the Yauza Gates. There was still a whole hour before the service was scheduled to begin, and he decided to go on foot from Dzerzhinsky Square. He walked along the western wall of the Polytechnical Museum, but on the opposite side of Serov Passage. A bevy of boys rolled out from under a gate and collapsed in a thrashing, kicking heap at his feet. One of them, the one being pursued, and the smallest, screamed loudly. The old man picked him up off the ground. The boy looked like he was about seven, with crooked teeth, and large gaps where they hadn't grown in yet. The three older boys scrambled back under the gate, and spied on them from around the corner. The little boy squirmed in Vasily's arms like a fish on a hook. His shirt was clanking with brightly shining metal . . . military decorations.

Vasily Innokentievich set the little fellow down on the ground. Holding him by the shoulders, he examined the military iconostasis.

In addition to the ordinary decorations being paraded about by elderly veterans on this holiday, on their old uniform jackets or new suit coats, Vasily Innokentievich noticed some very special ones: For the Defense of the Soviet Polar Circle; For the Capture of Königsberg; and, very rare indeed, an American one, on which there was a laurel wreath, stars, and rays of light. This was the Legion of Merit. The American Allies had conferred this medal on the highest-ranking Soviet officers after the fall of Berlin, in 1945.

Vasily Innokentievich knew only one person who had received this honor. General Nichiporuk had lain in his hospital in 1945. In the evenings the hospital head had visited the general. Several times they had drunk and conversed together. The general had gone straight from the hospital to get his decoration, and they drank to the honor together the same evening. There was no doubt in his mind that these decorations belonged to General Nichiporuk—the proof of this were the others, much more common, for Königsberg and the Arctic Circle. This geography corresponded exactly to the war biography of Peter Petrovich.

Were these stolen? Vasily Innokentievich wondered, and immediately remembered that someone had told him General Nichiporuk had lost his mind, or was in prison for anti-Soviet activities. Vasily Innokentievich didn't remember the details.

"What's your grandfather's name?" he asked the boy sternly, gripping his bony little shoulders.

"I don't have any grandfather! Let me go!" the boy shouted.

"Where did you get these medals?" The old man shook him by the collar.

"I found them in the wardrobe, at my grandmother's! My grandmother gave them to me!" He was an energetic little fellow. He twisted and turned, trying to slip out of the old man's grasp.

When he finally wriggled free, he bit Vasily Innokentievich's hand.

"You little stinker!" the old man said angrily. "Let's go see your grandma!"

"She's not there! There's no one home!" he said, turning to go.

"Well, take me to your mother, then. Come on, let's go!" the old man insisted, clutching the little boy by the back of the neck with his steely grip.

"No! I won't go! I won't take you there!" little Vitka screamed.

Then he fell silent, and, in a grown-up, serious voice, offered him a deal. "You might as well take them; the big boys will take them away from me, anyway. Only I don't want to go home." He could just imagine how his grandma would shout at him, what a whipping his mother would give him. It was better just to surrender now.

"Take off your shirt," the old man commanded.

He had intended to take the decorations and medals off the faded blue shirt and return it to its rightful owner. But as soon as Vasily Innokentievich held the shirt with the decorations and medals in his hands, the boy slipped away, like a bar of soap, and disappeared under the gate.

It was stolen—there's no doubt about it. Stolen, Vasily thought. He folded up the child's shirt without unpinning the medals, and stuffed the whole thing in the pocket of his suit jacket, not without difficulty. His jacket was sagging, weighed down on one side.

Strange, strange incident—funny, in a curious way.

Vasily Innokentievich hadn't seen General Nichiporuk since the war. After that, it was rumored that Nichiporuk was teaching at the Military Academy. He was no longer in touch with the general, but finding him would be easy enough—through Nefudov or Golubeva.

Pondering all of this, he walked to the church. Nadezhda was standing by the door. She looked like a forty-year-old Nuta, though completely ordinary. Nuta, of course, had been magnificent, incomparable, peerless. There was no one like her.

Two old women he didn't know, and two young men—Sanya and his friend, the red-haired, bearded Mikha—were chatting with Nadezhda.

Anna Alexandrovna's friend Elena ran up and stood next to him—her face was scarlet, and she was out of breath. She was a witness, a trusted companion, nearly a participant in their lives.

High blood pressure, Vasily Innokentievich noted to himself. He kissed Elena, but didn't mention her blood pressure. What would be the point?

A church attendant came out.

"Father is calling you inside to the service."

Vasily Innokentievich stood between Nadezhda and Elena, the old women he didn't know stood at the sides, and behind them, Sanya and his friend.

From a side door a small, desiccated priest came out, swinging a smoking censer.

Vasily Innokentievich was in a church again for the second time in two months: first for Anna Alexandrovna's funeral service, and now for the forty-days memorial service. Before this he hadn't set foot in a church for about forty years. He had to admit, it stirred something in his soul that had stayed with him since childhood. How strange . . . Perhaps he was feeling his age. The elderly women sang magnificently, and he suddenly recollected all the words. Some men's voices from behind joined in. He turned around to look. Sanya, Nuta's grandson, a sweet boy, was singing: "O Thou, Who with wisdom profound order all things with love, and Who give to all what is needful, O only Creator, give rest, O Lord, to the souls of Thy servants, for on Thee have they set their hope, our Maker and Builder, and our God."

How can he know this music? Vasily Innokentievich wondered.

In truth, forty days before, Sanya had not known it at all. But now he did.

Sanya's red-haired friend was weeping like a child. Both of them were holding burning candles.

Vasily Innokentievich felt an indeterminate sense of guilt, longing, and sadness. Nuta, his second cousin, his first love and the love of his life, a romance that had lasted, with interruptions, since childhood—a parallel life, flickering, fading in and out, and most precious. How pitiless fate was . . . Her whole life she had tried to fend him off, but he pursued her insistently, stubbornly, making his presence known almost by force. She responded reluctantly, it seemed . . . and said with a smile, mysterious and melancholy, that had an air of the early twentieth century about it:

"Vasily, you always appear in my life when it is falling to pieces; you are my rescuer. But, forgive me, you are also the sign and the embodiment of my failure and misfortune . . ."

This is what Vasily Innokentievich recalled in the midst of the wondrous chorus of voices. He didn't give a single thought to the military decorations belonging to someone else that were weighing down his pocket. He had completely forgotten about them.

Peter Petrovich was arrested in Minsk on the day after his departure. On the same day they came to his house and searched it. There was nothing in the house, but they ransacked it, nevertheless, turning everything upside down. They took away some small tokens—autographed books from experts in his field from before the war, lecture notes.

Zoya was glad that the military decorations had been removed from the house. In fact, the medals were not really even valid. It had been one thing after another: the general had been reduced to the ranks, stripped of his military honors, he was an ex-con, and had been pronounced insane. She knew, of course, that there was nothing wrong with Peter—it was the country that was insane.

As for Tonya Mutyukin, it was a long time before she realized that she was only keeping watch over empty boxes in her house, and that the decorations had disappeared. This was revealed when her older brother, Tolya, came back from doing time with a pile of money, bought everyone presents, and gave the rest of the money to his mother. His mother bought a new wardrobe with it. She began throwing out junk from the old one, and that was when Tonya realized that the military decorations were missing. She was beside herself. First she suspected Tolya, since she knew that those medals were worth a lot of money.

But Tolya had had nothing to do with it.

Anyway, why even bring him into it—two months later he was picked up again, because the money for the presents was stolen after all.

Vitka was the one who suffered most. He hardly remembered his father, and now, just as he was starting to get used to him, he disappeared again.

The decorations were returned to the general's home again through a chain of acquaintances and half-strangers. "Naked," deprived of their little handcrafted coffins, they were wrapped up in cellophane and placed in an iron skillet for safekeeping. Then they were committed to the ground, buried at the dacha of Zoya's niece near Kratovo Station, on the Kazan railroad line, behind two pine trees holding up a child's swing. Awaiting better days.

And better days did, in fact, come. In the end, the general was reunited with his decorations. The general lived in a country where you have to live for a long time. He lived until he was ninety, and thus managed to die a hero. He was buried in 1991, and all his medals and decorations, once wrapped up in worn-out underwear with a nap, even the American medal, were displayed on a pillow in front of his coffin. And the pillow was red, just as it was supposed to be.

THE IMAGO

Everything was just as it had been before—the courtyard, the neighbors, the broken floorboard in the corridor, the saleswomen in the bakery and the fish store, the building manager. Yet it seemed to Mikha as though thirty years had passed, and not just three. One false move and everything might split open with a resounding crash—the house, the courtyard, his little daughter, his wife, and the whole city, and April, so warm and welcoming this year. Cautiously, gingerly, he made his way around the room, the apartment, and his surroundings, doing what he had to do.

He first went to see Anna Alexandrovna. Then to the police, to have his passport registered. They said he had to find a job within thirty days.

Then he went to the History Library, almost certain they wouldn't admit him. But they just told him he needed to reregister his library card.

Several weeks later, after Anna Alexandrovna's death, he went to see Ilya and Olga. He rarely visited this strangely eclectic apartment—an admixture of Communist asceticism and Russian Empire style—on Vorovsky Street. Olga had never really warmed up to Alyona, but she adored Mikha.

Olga kissed him, and pulled out of the refrigerator some parchment paper bundles of pâté, Wallachian salads in little tartlike pie crusts, cold cuts, herring, and who knows what other marvels, all from the Prague confectionery and delicatessen. She laid it all out on translucent plates, and, blowing a kiss good-bye, ran off to finish a translation that had to be completed by the morning. Ilya took out a bottle of Armenian cognac. Mikha could hardly drink a thing, and he ate sparingly as well, expecting the pains in his stomach to start up again at any moment.

They sat down and looked at each other closely. Ilya was afraid to say anything out of place or unnecessary. He wasn't terribly sentimental, but he was overcome with a feeling for Mikha that he had rarely even felt toward his disabled son. His eyes and nose stung.

"Did you see it last night?" Mikha asked.

Ilya nodded.

"Of course. All of Moscow watched it. Everyone was expecting something like this."

"Expecting it? And I could never have imagined that he would do anything of the sort . . ."

"Ingenious, in its own way," Ilya said.

The trial of Chernopyatov and his two closest friends had ended the night before. There had been an unprecedented television broadcast—a press conference with Chernopyatov. Sergei Borisovich had repented of all his sins against the Soviet authorities for an hour and a half. And he did this with real talent—if one can be said to have a talent for baseness and treachery. The most surprising thing was that he introduced himself as the head of the "Democratic Movement," its leader, and its main ideologue; and as self-proclaimed leader of the movement he called upon his followers to reexamine their actions. Everyone who was even remotely involved understood very clearly that there was no unified movement to speak of, that there were various groups of people with their own concerns and "interests," which sometimes coincided and sometimes did not, who were united only in their rejection of the current authorities and their hunger for change. And the change they wanted varied from group to group, person to person . . .

Many people discussed the previous day's broadcast. The similarity with Dostoevsky's *The Possessed* was not hard to see. People with a pragmatic bent feared an unleashing of wholesale repression against any nonconformist thinker. People who took a more philosophical view asked more abstract questions: Had the great Dostoevsky discovered a particular elemental force in the Russian character, this possession by revolutionary fervor, or had he unwittingly created it, along with his literary protagonists Stavrogin and Pyotr Verkhovensky?

He and Mikha talked about this all evening, without coming to any hard and fast conclusions. There was too much of the story that still remained obscure.

It was impossible to fathom what had happened to Chernopyatov himself. He had been the most steadfast of them all, wise and experienced. He had survived the children's penal colony, Stalin's labor camps, and exile . . . And he had a clear-cut enemy: the Soviet authorities, Stalinism. What could have happened to him to make him turn around so abruptly, so radically?

"Ilya, a month and a half before my release they brought me face-to-face with him. I didn't know that he had been arrested and was naming names. A frank confession, they call it. Dozens of names. He betrayed nearly the whole *Chronicle*: editors, writers, compilers. This was the last thing I expected. Sergei Borisovich told me that I was making a mistake, that I needed courage to admit my mistakes, that I had to seek a new path. They tried to pressure me into going down that path with him. I refused. They told me they would send me up for a second term if I didn't cooperate. I was certain they would never let me out after that. But they did. They made me sign a paper saying I wouldn't engage in anti-Soviet activity, and let me go. What happened to him I really don't understand. Maybe there is something we don't know. They have so many methods at their disposal, besides beatings."

"I was told they have some sort of 'truth serum' that they sprinkle in your food," Ilya ventured.

"I could believe that. You know yourself that they're professionals, and we're absolutely defenseless against them. And we're just as defenseless against the common criminals. I thought about Mandelstam a lot when I was inside. What it was like for him . . . to die there.

"But don't imagine that they feel any lack of moral justification! In fact, they feel they are morally superior. For them, breaking a person with ideals is a special pleasure. It's like we all have the same face to them. Like we're all Chinese; or like we're all weaklings who wear glasses. Before I was transported from prison to the camp, one of the jail bosses smashed my glasses. He got such a charge out of it, it was such a thrill to him to hear them crunch underfoot. I really can't see a thing without them, as you know. I only received a new pair three months later—Anna Alexandrovna sent them to me. Chernopyatov, by the way, also wears glasses."

"Yes, I photographed Chernopyatov a few years ago. It was a good portrait."

No, Ilya didn't feel any guilt about that whatsoever. *What a bunch of motherfuckers* was what he was thinking.

"Well, I'm just thinking about the ways in which he was vulnerable, that's all," Mikha said, explaining something that Ilya already knew perfectly well. "Maybe they made him drink something, or broke him in some other way . . . I just don't want you to say anything bad about him. One has to feel sorry for him, on top of everything else. He wasn't thinking of Alyona. How will this affect her? And all the people who've surrounded him all these years.

"I think the price he has already paid is so high that he is worse off than everyone else. How will he ever live this down?

"You helped me so much, Ilya, before my arrest. I'll always remember what you said to me: 'Every word you say will work against you. Keep silent. The best thing is to say nothing.' And that's what I did. But you know yourself, Sergei Borisovich is a big talker—an orator, even. He said too much, and then there was no going back. Or maybe his strength and willpower gave out. I'm not going to be the one to judge him."

Mikha's words were feverish and disconnected, but Ilya understood everything. In silence, Ilya poured them each another glass, and then drank, saying: "Me neither."

"I don't know what I'm going to do for work now. It turns out that working with the deaf children was the best thing I've done in my life."

"We'll think of something," Ilya said, with less confidence than usual. "Have you ever thought about emigrating?" This was the first time Ilya had ever brought this up directly with Mikha.

"Emigration—only to save my skin. The most terrifying thing for me is the prison camps, Ilya. I won't survive them a second time. But emigration . . . I'm from here, everything I know and love is here. Friends, Russian, my work."

"Work? What kind of work?"

Mikha seemed to wilt.

"But how—without work?"

Ilya didn't know either. For him it wasn't a matter of a single job, but of various kinds of work. A multitude of tasks.

"You know, let's take one step at a time. First we'll find a job for you. Then we'll try to take stock of the situation, and think about where to go from there. I've already asked around. My friends are keeping an eye out for some kind of job for you. Start with your personal life, putting your own house in order."

"That sounds like one has to make a choice—between one's personal life and society."

"Your head's full of romantic rubbish. Why a choice? What kind of choice? That's just childish thinking. There's no choice—you wake up in the morning, brush your teeth, drink your tea, read a book, write your poems, earn your money, gab with friends—what kind of choice does that involve? At a certain moment, you start to feel—there's something dangerous here. So you don't touch it. You stay away from it. There's always a boundary line. But we'll figure that out when we come to it. You're not going to go around asking for trouble! Sometimes you can't help it. But you learn to move to the left, move to the right, so they don't grab your ass. Of course, there are those who love to bask in glory, to be in the limelight. Sergei Borisovich is ambitious that way. He wanted fame, influence. He wanted to play a role. But there are others—Vladimir Bukovsky and Tanya Velikanova, for example. Sakharov. Valera, Andrei, Alik, Arina . . . many of them! They never choose between personal life and social life. They just live how they live, from morning till night. They don't play at life . . ." Ilya said, sounding certain and knowledgeable. It was difficult to counter him.

But there was something in his reasoning that didn't add up. Mikha jumped on it.

"You've got to be kidding! You've just named all the ones who actually did make a choice. Not all of them have served time in prison yet, but their time will come, you'll see. And I won't survive another term in prison. I know that about myself. I won't make it."

But, as it turned out, Mikha didn't have to make a choice after all. Everything happened of its own accord.

There were bad days and good nights—so bright and brilliant was the unprecedented love that finally took hold between Alyona and her husband that it illuminated the gloomy days. Only now, Mikha sensed, was Alyona finally able to respond to his loving ardor. They were in corporeal dialogue with each other, something that had never happened before now. Something had shifted in the depths of her body—or was it her heart? Or perhaps the birth of their child had opened something like a sluice gate? And some natural gravity drawing a woman toward a man had fallen into place. Their sleeping daughter warmed them with her presence, and she gave great meaning to their unfolding happiness.

Their intimate life flourished and filled the gaps of their impoverished existence. But what happened in the world outside the small circle of their love for each other gave no cause for comfort or hope. There was no job, no money, no meaningful activity of the kind that had occupied him before he was imprisoned. Their home, which had always been full of friends, both Muscovites and Central Asians, was now empty. Either they were afraid for themselves, or they were staying away because they feared for Mikha and Alyona.

Even Sanya almost stopped dropping by. He was feeling both relieved and slighted: Alyona had seemed to have dropped him like a thing she no longer needed. Now he was perplexed. Had he imagined all the emotional pressure that Alyona put him under during the three years that Mikha was gone? He was hurt that Maya so easily and quickly withdrew her affection from him. She no longer clung to his neck or tickled his ears. Were all women in it together?

Sanya even began to think vaguely about some colossal struggle of women against men, similar to the class struggle. Only Nuta never took part in that struggle: she loved boys. Most of all she loved her own grandson, of course; but she had also loved Mikha and Ilya. He wondered how it had been with her husbands and lovers—but it was unlikely she had waged war on them.

Perhaps the problem was one of age? In youth, there is conflict; then a truce is declared; and, finally, in old age men and women become invulnerable to each other.

I should discuss it with Nuta, he thought by force of habit. But this thought came up against the feeling of injury toward Alyona and Maya, who (both of them!) had loved him so importunately, so onerously, for three years; and then, after Mikha's return, within a matter of a few weeks all that love had dried up and disappeared, as though it had never been . . .

Sanya would never know what Nuta thought of all of this. And Mikha would never know that Anna Alexandrovna couldn't stand Alyona—or any others of that subtly drawn type: weak, demanding, despotic, feeble women, with a gift for inspiring tenderness, passion, and love, but who were nearly incapable of responding to it with gratitude and sympathy.

After her death, all Anna Alexandrovna's close friends were always trying to gauge what her reactions might have been, to reconstruct the words she might have said, apropos of one thing or another.

Nadezhda Borisovna tried to push away her knowledge of the aversion her mother would have felt toward her fiancé, Lastochkin. Only six years later, after their divorce, when Lastochkin would begin the process of trading their large room in a communal flat on Chernyshevksy Street for two smaller apartments, and, to complete the absolutely fair transaction, would do an inventory of Nuta's property, from the spoons to the bed linens, and then divide it all into two absolutely equal parts, did she shiver, thinking how lucky it was that Mama didn't live to see this, and that Sanya had left for good . . .

But Anna Alexandrovna had also done something terribly cruel, something no one would have expected of her: she had left them all, abandoned them—Sanya, Mikha, Vasily Innokentievich and her daughter, Nadezhda, who had never learned how to move through the world on her own. She had not provided them with any explicit instructions for how to go on living. She had told them how and where she wanted to be buried—but what happened after the funeral? The next day? A month later? A year?

All the boys and girls whom Anna Alexandrovna had guided so tirelessly through life, without their even being aware of it, were suddenly deprived of that light and lighthearted guidance, in which there was a golden mean of wisdom and whimsy. She had both common sense and a sense of contempt for it; a trust in life, and a sharp, critical vision that could size up a new person after only a single, fleeting encounter.

While Sanya sank into a depression after his grandmother died, Mikha underwent, like an insect, the final stage of metamorphosis: the death of Anna Alexandrovna forced him to grow into an adult.

Now, without Nuta, Mikha tried to understand why he had been the one to witness her last minutes on earth. He kept waiting for the mystery to be revealed, so that he would know how to live, how to go on in this world; for he was now the eldest, and there was not a single person on earth who could advise him on difficult questions and quandaries of existence.

There was something very important that Anna Alexandrovna had not had time to tell him, and now he had to find out what it was for himself.

Quietly, fearing to startle away the improbable happiness, Mikha delighted in his blossoming family life, adored his daughter, and trudged around to various places trying unsuccessfully to find a job. The deadlines imposed by the authorities had all passed, and he now ran the risk of being accused of "parasitism," punishable by banishment from Moscow.

Kusikov, the neighborhood parole officer, came by to urge him on in his search for employment. He was a country boy, with the vestiges of a rural ruddiness and with glimmers of humanity left in his face.

He took a good look around him. He examined Alyona's graphics for a long time. They were marvelous. Mysterious and enchanting. Noticing his curiosity, Mikha explained that his wife was an artist. The policeman was impressed, and filled with respect for the wispy girl. They may have been poor, but you could see they were cultured. He even wanted to help them out. As if from nowhere, Kusikov was filled with a sense of pity for Mikha and his spindly wife.

He offered to help him get a job as a loader in a fish factory. The manager was a friend of his. Mikha shrugged uncertainly. He'd worked as a loader before, but his eyesight had gotten so bad that more of that kind of work—loading and unloading things in the dark—could do untold damage to his vision. His hand strayed mechanically up to the metal frames of his glasses. Alyona offered the policeman tea. He sat down, his legs spread-eagled on the chair, his sturdy boots planted on either side of it. Maya stared transfixed at the policeman's cap lying on the table. Alyona placed two pastries on a plate in front of him. He ate only one of them, evidence of his good country breeding.

When he was leaving, Kusikov said he knew of another good job opening for Mikha, working somewhere as a guard. He lamented that the personnel office might not approve it, though, with Mikha's criminal record.

"How strange our Soviet—or maybe Russian—life is: you never know who will denounce you, report you to the authorities, or who will help you out; or how quickly those roles might reverse. Isn't that true, Alyona?"

Alyona nodded, her hair falling over her face.

"Yes, I think about that a lot. Everything is so mutable, so unpredictable. There is warmth and sincerity in abundance, and so many good intentions; but they never amount to anything."

"That's not what I meant," Mikha objected.

"But that's what I mean," Alyona said, smiling a clever smile. Lately, she had acquired a new, clever smile—much cleverer than she really was.

Two days later, Kusikov took Mikha to a curious establishment, where they hired him as a forwarding agent. He was in charge of sorting and sending out samples sent in by geological expeditions to several other establishments.

In comparison with his work at the school for the deaf, which required all his spiritual and emotional energy, or the camps, which drained him of all his physical strength, this almost meaningless work was remarkable in one sense: it lasted from eight to four; sometimes he was even able to leave earlier in the day. The workday ended when it ended, until the next day. He didn't have to think about it; his mind, his heart, were free, and he had strength left over. There was an enormous expanse of time that he could spend with Alyona and his daughter. Sometimes he went to the library, where he read up on every possible subject, without his former greedy hunger, allowing every word to penetrate his being—Montaigne, Madame Blavatsky, Lao-tzu . . .

Then he returned home for a late dinner. Maya would already be asleep. Alyona would be wearing her lime-green sheath dress that outlined her slim body, but had generous bell sleeves. In her fragile hands she would bring in from their communal kitchen a heavy cast-iron skillet loaded with fried potatoes.

The room smelled of cooking oil, a sleeping child, freshly mopped floors, and Alyona's special scent—cool, and a little sweet. These were the smells of home life, of family and love.

Mikha ate his potatoes in a hurry, while Alyona slowly drank her herbal tea, drawing out the end of the day and keeping the arrival of nighttime at bay.

His former life, with its wrongs and injustices, its stale ideas, and its notions of reform and change, drifted away from him. Sergei Borisovich's public repentance, though it threw into confusion all of his previously held ideals, to a certain extent justified Mikha's capitulation. Having chosen between the valorization of some and the betrayal of others, he lived his life in quiet and somewhat shameful disgrace. The act that several months before had tormented him as defeat and apostasy—signing the humiliating document renouncing all social and political activity—now seemed to him to be his only means of surviving and protecting his family.

Everything fell into place again, and even the job as a forwarding agent—a mind-numbing, alienating task—had its advantages. Mikha sometimes had to sort the contents of parcels with all manner of samples: colored clays; sharp, translucent crystals; stones gleaming with veins of metals. The marvelous names of the places where these samples had originated—Maly Storozhok at a tributary of the Lenochka stream; Matiukovka Mountain, part of the Vsevolod-Vilvensky deposits; the Shudi river basin in the northern Urals—caressed his tongue. Mikha once even wrote a poem full of these enchanting geographical names.

Life continued on its quiet way, as though on tiptoe at twilight, and despite the lack of money, the material scarcity, and Mikha's deeply hidden shame for renouncing his former existence, daring and vivid, domestic happiness brightened their 150-square-foot room, and everything seemed larger than life, like the best films, like his favorite lines from Pasternak:

> Shadows lie upon
> the glowing ceiling.
> Crossed hands, crossed legs,
> Fates entwined.
>
> Two small slippers
> clatter to the floor,
> and tears of wax drip
> from the lamp onto the dress.

Just around the corner, a three-minute walk, was Potapovsky Lane, where Pasternak's last love, no longer young and gone to fat, who had done time in the camps for this love, and her daughter, who had also been imprisoned for complicity and knowledge of the affair, stopped into the same bakery or grocery store that Mikha shopped in. When he saw them on the street, he would whisper to Alyona: "Look, there's Ivinskaya, there's Ira Emelianova, she went to our school."

Alyona turned around to look—she saw a heavy older woman wearing too much makeup, without a trace of her former beauty, in a tattered coat. Could it really be her? Was it possible? And to think that at one time she had been compared to Simone Signoret.

Alyona and Mikha exchanged glances: we live not in nature, but in history . . . And Pasternak walked down this very lane twenty years before. And one hundred fifty years ago—Pushkin. And we are walking down it, too, skirting the eternal puddles.

In the spring, in the middle of May, something unexpected happened. At two in the morning, the elevator door banged shut, then the doorbell rang four times—the Melamids' ring. Mikha and Alyona, sleeping in each other's embrace, startled awake simultaneously. Through their confused, nighttime stupor, they thought: *They've come!*

They hugged each other more tightly, pressing together their cheeks, their breasts, their knees, bidding farewell with their whole bodies, and got up, pulling on their clothes. The bell—four rings—resounded again, but this time less urgently. Now they embraced again, this time not saying good-bye, but expressing hope that misfortune would pass.

Hand in hand they walked down the communal corridor toward the front door. Mikha opened it without asking who was there. Instead of three, four, five security thugs, they saw a small girl in a green silk dress, with a thick braid of hair as coarse as a horse's tail hanging over her shoulder. They recognized her immediately.

"Ayshe! Ayshe!"

The Tatar girl they had met in Bakhchisaray, daughter of Mustafa Usmanov, hero and leader of the banished Tatars, was standing in the doorway. Only she was now no longer a small girl, but a young woman. "Come in, come in! Why didn't you call? We would have met you at the station . . ."

A small suitcase, a cloth-lined basket, her gloves fall to the floor. "Don't take off your shoes! In our room, you can take off your things in our room. Why didn't you call, how many years has it been? Yes, four, five, at least, you have a daughter; and we do, too! We have a daughter, too. You got married, yes, tell us, tell us everything! Tell us . . ."

"I couldn't call. I was too scared. They arrested Father. He has a good lawyer, who told me to come to Moscow. He said I needed to find Academician Sakharov, so that he would write a letter. But how can I possibly find this Sakharov? The lawyer said we need foreigners to make a fuss about it, on the radio, or however they do it there. From

America! It's urgent—Father has shrapnel in his chest, and if it moves, he'll die. And our Tatars are all quarreling. Father is a Communist. Although he was expelled from the Party ages ago, he still keeps talking to them about Lenin. And those evil devils will destroy him in jail! The lawyer sent me—you need to leave immediately, he said, otherwise your father won't survive until the trial . . ." And she cried through her garbled words, and her tears were as blue as her eyes, and fell thick and fast, like the tears of small children.

"Ayshe, don't cry, please. There, now, don't cry . . ."

There was an extra place to sleep in the room on a folding cot, if her head was pushed right up against the wall under the windowsill, the table was shoved about eight inches to the side, and the child's high chair was put away. They drank some tea, put Ayshe to bed, and went back to sleep themselves for another two hours. Mikha got up at seven, and by eight he was already at work.

He called Ilya from work to say that they needed to meet. Where? Same place as always. Milyutin Park, in other words.

"You mean she's at your house right now?" Ilya asked, frowning. "That's dangerous. Someone's sure to be shadowing her. You have to move her somewhere else."

"No, that's impossible. That night in the cemetery, in Bakhchisaray . . . And Mustafa is a remarkable human being. What will be, will be. Can you find Academician Sakharov for me, Ilya?"

"Give me one day," Ilya said.

Ilya's circle of friends and acquaintances was enormous. He even boasted a bit about the variety of his connections, and joked that if you didn't include the Chinese, common laborers, and peasants, he knew everyone in the world, either personally or through someone else. That's exactly how it was with Academician Sakharov. A certain Valery, an old acquaintance of Ilya's, worked closely with the academician: both of them were members of the Committee for Human Rights. After a few phone calls back and forth, Sakharov agreed to meet with Ayshe.

Three days later, Mikha took her to Chkalov Street. They walked the distance, since it was twenty minutes by foot from their house to his.

The whole way, Ayshe couldn't stop trembling. Her head ached from agitation and worry, and she broke down in tears when they were at the door. While Mikha was trying to comfort her, the door opened, and an adolescent carrying a garbage pail asked them who they wanted to see. When they told him, he let them in, and asked them not to slam the door behind them.

From that moment on, everything that happened seemed to Mikha and Ayshe to be completely improbable. Ayshe even began thinking that someone had played a trick on them. A thin, ordinary-looking man in an old cardigan, who did not in the least conform to their idea of an academician, received them sitting on a bed in a small, cluttered room. Ayshe was hiccuping so strongly after her bout of tears that Mikha had to tell the whole story of Mustafa himself, beginning with their first acquaintance in a hotel in the city of Bakhchisaray.

The academician—or the impostor who called himself an academician—listened attentively, nodding, his head inclined forward. He made a few replies that revealed a detailed familiarity with the case, noted down the name and surname on a scrap of paper, then offered them tea.

They moved into the kitchen, where a middle-aged woman in thick glasses was presiding.

An old woman in a soft cap was sitting in a corner, and the adolescent whom they had met when they arrived took a glass of tea and a few cookies, then disappeared into the dark corridor.

Ayshe touched the cheap teacup decorated with polka dots and said frankly what had been on her mind for the past half an hour:

"Andrei Dmitrievich, I could never have imagined that academicians lived so modestly."

Mikha blushed from embarrassment. What a country bumpkin!

The older woman in glasses laughed:

"My dear child, only academicians who write letters in defense of exiled Tatars live like this!"

Then Ayshe realized what a foolish thing she had said. Her cheeks turned crimson, and her face began perspiring profusely. "I'm sorry,

please forgive me! I understand everything. I just hadn't expected it—
no one ever told me that this is how it is."

Then a young couple came in—the middle-aged woman's daughter and her husband. They wouldn't all fit into the tiny kitchen, so Mikha and Ayshe went out, freeing up some stools.

The academician promised to write a letter about Mustafa Usmanov, and advised Ayshe to give an interview to one of the American journalists accredited in Moscow. He said he would organize it.

The most remarkable part of the story was that Academician Sakharov really did write the letter, and not to the American Congress, and not to some Western newspapers, but to the Ministry of Internal Affairs. Two weeks later they invited him to a reception on Ogarev Street, and there he discussed the matter of Captain Usmanov with a couple of officials. It was still the time when they talked seriously to him, and didn't just chuck him out with a respectful expression glued to their faces. The academician did truly achieve something: not long before, a Tatar family had been granted a residence permit in Crimea. One family out of many thousands. And he continued to make the rounds, to submit requests, to petition, to write letters.

Only in Mustafa's case it was impossible to determine whether his words had an effect or not, since Mustafa Usmanov died in solitary confinement in a pretrial detention cell in Tashkent a month and a half later. Perhaps the academician's letter pleading the case of the former Tatar hero, defender of the Motherland and special deportee, had not arrived in time, because the postal service of our country is known to be very slow.

But, for the time being, Ayshe was glad that she had had an important meeting, and she was hoping for the best. Mikha led Ayshe by the elbow. She could hardly stand on her own two feet, and kept thanking Mikha in words that were both too direct and too wooden. Only when they were right in front of Mikha's house did he realize that they were being followed by someone with such an ordinary, unprepossessing face that there could be no doubt about where he had come from.

Two days later, in the evening, a foreign correspondent by the name of Robert visited them at home. He had been sent by Academician Sakharov. He wore a long Soviet coat and a fur hat with three flaps. He resembled more closely a Russian truck driver than an anti-Soviet Slavist from Washington, with Polish roots thrown into the combustible mix. They drank tea and talked. A small tape recorder, a miracle of Western technology, was placed on the table to record Ayshe's words. The former Pole was wont to be a skirt chaser. He stared at Ayshe with a sweet expression on his face, and paid her compliments. She basked in the attention and bloomed. Smiling, she straightened her shoulders and spoke freely and even boldly, not at all shyly and haltingly, as she had in Sakharov's kitchen.

Then Robert left, got into the cab that had been waiting for him the whole time, and went to his house on Leninsky Prospect. When he got out of the car, two thuggish-looking young men jumped him. He got into a fight with them, though he knew perfectly well that he shouldn't have done that, and that the best thing to do was to make a beeline for his front door. As a result of this tussle, all three of them were taken down to the police station and charged with hooliganism. Robert got off fairly easily. They held him there overnight, and in the morning the American consul came to liberate the idiot. Unfortunately, in the midst of all these vagaries the tape recorder disappeared, never to be seen again.

The following day, toward evening, when Ayshe had gone to Children's World to shop for her daughter, the neighborhood policeman, Kusikov, looked in and saw both the basket in which Ayshe had brought a melon and grapes, and the cheap suitcase. He hemmed and hawed a bit, then led Mikha out to the staircase landing and said:

"Hey, Mikha, it'd be better if you would, you know . . . They stopped by asking about who was living at your place. They really let me have it. You—well, you know, she's gotta get out of here . . ."

That same evening Mikha took Ayshe to Kazan Station, and early in the morning, she left for Tashkent, after Mikha arranged for her to travel in the conductor's compartment, without a ticket, in exchange for some hard cash.

Three days later, Mikha found a summons in his mailbox. It was an invitation to the Lubyanka, to a meeting with Captain Safyanov.

Mikha never told Alyona, but he showed Ilya the piece of paper when they met at their regular spot.

"I warned you. You shouldn't have let Ayshe stay with you at home. You're in the crosshairs now."

Mikha blazed up all of a sudden: "What the hell should I have done, chase a young girl out onto the street in the middle of the night? In some situations you just can't say no."

"My God, Mikha, you're such a child! You could't afford to say yes, either! I warned you! And I told you that she should go to Sakharov's alone, without you! How could you have agreed to allow someone from the foreign press corps into your home? You've made so many mistakes acting on someone else's behalf, and now you're going to be the one to take the rap. These are serious times we're living in, things have never been worse. They've rounded up almost everyone. The Tatars, the Jews. The *Chronicle* isn't even coming out anymore—there's no one left to publish it. You picked a bad time to be noble and high-minded."

Mikha relented.

"I know, I know. But there was no way I could act otherwise. I couldn't chase her out onto the street; I couldn't send her off to Sakharov's alone. As for Robert coming over to my place—I could have avoided that, I suppose. But the rest of it—there was no other choice, Ilya. No other way."

Ilya grew morose and silent. What could he do for his friend now?

"Listen, I know a man, a geologist. Maybe you could take off for the Far North, on an expedition? Conditions are harsh up there, of course. Yakutia is a long way off."

"No. I can't. Alyona. Maya. Anyway, you know there's no hiding from them, once they set their sights on you!"

"Well, what if I went to Yakutia with you?" That was the most Ilya could offer. And there was no one who had anything else to offer him. Ilya recognized the familiar hand of fate, and knew deep down that Mikha could not extricate himself now.

Captain Safyanov wasn't suited to outside surveillance—he had a large purple birthmark on his right cheek, which may even have been a growth. It was visible a hundred yards away. The birthmark didn't interfere with investigative work, and Safyanov rose steadily in the ranks, not overtaking anyone else, completely satisfied with his salary, his bosses, and his family life. The most unpleasant part of his work was questioning those under investigation, but he tried to keep good relations with them insofar as it was possible. Which wasn't always the case.

Melamid, the citizen who had been summoned for questioning today, had been handed down to him by another colleague who had just been promoted. The captain familiarized himself with the contents of the thick dossier beforehand, and was distressed—judging by the documents, this was someone with experience. He would have to work on him a long time.

The experienced citizen came right on time, not a minute late, and he looked like he had been around: a skinny neck, pale red hair, almost yellowish, sticking out in tufts, and cheeks covered with the beginnings of a beard. There was no beard to be seen on the photograph.

Well, we'll need a new photograph for the file, Safyanov decided.

The captain began the conversation obliquely, reminding him of the document he'd signed last time, asking him about his employment, about his future plans. Then, out of left field, he asked:

"Are you acquainted with Ayshe Mustafaevna Usmanov?"

But this Melamid character clammed up, then denied it. This was just how he had behaved during the last interrogation, when he had been brought face-to-face with Chernopyatov—which the captain was able to gather from the documents. For an hour and a half they circled around and around the issue, and then Safyanov, the first one to grow tired of this game, pulled out a piece of paper covered with foreign print and said with feigned chagrin:

"Well, Mr. Melamid, I can't see that you have any interest or desire to help us in our work. This is most unfortunate. We conferred about your case, considered your situation, and decided that, from our side, there wouldn't be any objections to your leaving for somewhere beyond the boundaries of our homeland. You are not one of us, Mr. Melamid. Which is astonishing—your father died on the front lines, but you have no respect for . . ." Safyanov did not find it easy to say these words. "In short, I won't hide from you the fact that an invi-

tation has been sent to you and your family from the state of . . ." Here
he inserted a pregnant pause, cleared his throat, and pronounced, with
repugnance, "Israel." He placed the stress on the final syllable, which
made it sound even more sinister.

"Your relative Marlen Kogan—you know someone by that
name?—has interceded for you, to reunite the family. The invitation
is for you, your wife, and your daughter. Have a look."

He held out a beautiful letter. Mikha took it, and held it up close
to his nose. The invitation had been issued three months before. All
that time it had been languishing somewhere in the Foreigners' Registration Office or the KGB, and they had decided that now was the
time to put it to use.

"It's expired, Comrade Captain," Mikha said.

"Well, we'll take care of that. It can be extended," he said, tapping
his finger on the telephone. "It's in our hands . . . we won't object.
Think about it. You have many things to consider, too. You haven't kept
your word: you signed a document stating you wouldn't get mixed up
in any of these kinds of activities. And what do we see? You allow un-
desirable people to live under your roof, with no residence permit, no
passport records; you go to Academician Sakharov, and he writes all
kinds of libel that he distributes abroad. You invite foreign correspon-
dents to your house. And who gave you permission to engage in these
activities? Leave the country! It will be better for you. If another
case against you is opened, you won't get off with only three years,
Mr. Melamid. Why are you dawdling? All your people are champing
at the bit to get to Israel! They would give anything for an invitation
like this. All right, all right, think about it. You won't have a lot of time
to think, but we'll give you three days or so. If you don't leave, we'll
throw you in prison. Although there are other possibilities . . . Take a
pen and a piece of paper and write a frank confession: about your connections with the Tatars, about Mustafa Usmanov, and about this Ayshe. How you went to see Academician Sakharov, and what you did
there. And about what Robert Kulavik, a fake American, was doing at
your house. Write it all down in detail, take your time, and we'll be
able to part on good terms. I can't promise anything, though. I'll do my
best. You do your best, and we will, too."

He rubbed his purple birthmark with the back of his hand. Mikha decided the captain must be a nervous sort. *And I don't have any nerves at all, it seems.*

Mikha smiled and put the invitation on the table. He pressed it to the tabletop with his palm, as if it might fly away.

"I understand you, Comrade Captain. I'll think about it. May I leave?"

"Go, go. I'll expect you on Monday at three." He signed Mikha's pass. "Personally, I think you should seriously consider this proposition. Such an opportunity will not present itself again."

He went outside. Winter? Spring? What time was it? Late morning? Early evening? Was he in Kitai-gorod? The Boulevards? The Lubyanka?

O God, don't let me lose my mind . . .

No, no, not that one.

When will the pall on my
Ailing heart disperse?
When will the tangled nets
I'm caught in set me free?
When will this demon that
Commands my mind's dark dream . . .

He forgot. He forgot what Baratynsky wrote next.

He walked in circles, first away from home, then approaching it again; but he couldn't find the strength to go home and say that single word to Alyona: *emigration.*

Finally, he mustered his courage and told her everything: about the summons, about the unexpected offer. Alyona heard him out. Her face went dark. She averted her eyes, dropped her lashes, bent her head down so her hair fell over her face, and whispered:

"This is what you've always wanted. Now I know for certain, this is just what you've always wanted. But let me tell you: Maya and I will never leave here. Not for anything. Not ever . . ."

But it wasn't so much her words as her altered face that said everything—in the space of a second it had become suspicious and alien. Her eyebrows seemed to elongate, her lips compressed into a straight line. That drop of Caucasian Mountain blood she had inherited from her father—both proud and wild—surfaced like a sudden sunburn. Alyona lay down on the divan and turned her face to the wall.

From that moment on, she stopped washing, eating, dressing, and talking. She could hardly drag herself to the WC before returning to the divan with tiny, uncertain steps and turning her face again to the wall. Her clinical depression was so obvious, the symptoms so classic, that Mikha had no trouble diagnosing it himself. Even Maya's whimpering entreaties couldn't rouse Alyona from the divan. Mikha floundered in despair and helplessness. For several days he rushed to and fro like a madman, trying to balance work, domestic duties, and taking care of Alyona and the child. Zhenya Tolmacheva came to help. Alyona refused to talk to her as well, but she accepted the help without a murmur of thanks, as though she didn't notice it. Sanya showed up again, and Ilya came after Mikha's phone call.

Ilya looked around, raised his eyes to the heavens, searched for an answer in the invisible expanse of space, and called in a psychiatrist named Arkasha. Arkasha was also one of their own. He was active in dissident circles and had written letters of protest, exposing the judicial-psychiatric establishment. He had lost his job a year before, and was now working as an orderly in a hospital outside of town. He recommended immediate hospitalization, and getting a categorical refusal, he prescribed some strong psychotropic medication.

Maya hovered around Alyona, but she remained indifferent to everything, including her daughter. For a second week in a row, Mikha took his daughter to work with him. He missed his appointment with Safyanov, and he didn't bother to open the mailbox, where—he knew!—he would find another summons.

At the end of a second week lying on the divan, Alyona's mother, Valentina Ivanovna, suddenly arrived from the Ryazan countryside, where Sergei Borisovich had been exiled. Why she had had the sudden urge to come to her daughter was unclear—most likely maternal instinct. She was horrified at what she saw when she arrived. She kept trying to find out what had happened, but Alyona refused to speak to her, either, and turned her face to the wall again.

Valentina Ivanovna recalled some strange episodes from her daughter's childhood, so she didn't insist, but did the only thing that was in her power—she took Maya with her.

Mikha expected Maya to cry and resist, but his mother-in-law behaved very wisely: she whispered to the little girl that in the country she had a real live goat, a white cat, and a speckled hen. Maya, tempted by this domestic zoo, went happily and willingly with her grandmother. Alyona said good-bye to them sleepily and turned back toward the wall.

Mikha finally went to see Safyanov two weeks after their scheduled appointment. He told him that his wife was ill, and Safyanov believed him: Mikha looked completely haggard and miserable. He told him he wouldn't accept the invitation to leave, that his wife didn't want to go, and that he wasn't ready, either.

Safyanov was surprised. He frowned, and began rubbing his marked cheek, thinking hard.

He rang for a deputy, then went out. Forty minutes later he returned, seething with anger. He sent out the deputy, and changed his tack with Mikha. Now his threats were unconcealed and explicit.

"We have a mountain of evidence against you, Melamid. I'm not even talking about the Tatars. Things turned out fairly well for you in the past. This time, you won't get off so easy."

He placed a pile of grayish paper in front of him.

"Casual conversation is over. We had our little talk, off the record. Now comes the interrogation. Under protocol."

"I won't talk. Since you have so much evidence, what need is there for me to say anything?" Mikha said quietly, not looking at Safyanov. He kept his mouth shut for the next two and a half hours.

On the way home, twice he thought he glimpsed the purple mark on the cheek. Could Safyanov really be following him? It was impossible; but his face kept coming into view at the periphery of his vision.

It was late when he got home. He brought Alyona tea, and made a sandwich. She propped herself up on the pillow, and drank the tea. She didn't eat anything, and she didn't want to talk.

Ilya and Sanya arrived before midnight. The three of them sat around talking, just like old times. Mikha said that they had been shadowing him for the last several days, and he was afraid they would arrest him any day now. The telephone was, no doubt, being tapped.

He ran his fingers through his shock of hair, the only thing about him that still had volume. Except for his hair, he resembled a vertical plane, a profile, a cardboard cutout. Since Alyona had taken to her bed, he had stopped shaving.

He scratched his soft red beard with his bony fingers.

"What do you think?"

"What do you think we think! They offered you the chance to emigrate, didn't they? Do it—you'll never survive here." Sanya was convinced that he himself wouldn't survive here, either. But no one would send him, a Russian, an invitation to emigrate.

"Yes. It's the only way," Ilya agreed.

Mikha gestured toward Alyona's back on the divan with his eyes.

"Don't you understand? I can't! I just can't. And Alyona can't, either." His face looked like that of a hunted animal.

"Do you know what I think? Hear me out, now; don't get upset. You should go alone," Ilya said.

"Have you lost your mind? Abandon my family? Do you have any idea what you're saying?"

"Alyona will come to her senses and follow you," Ilya said, as confident as ever.

"We'll get her ready and send her off," Sanya said, with less certainty.

"What the hell? That's rubbish! The situation is completely hopeless. It couldn't possibly get worse."

Sanya embraced him like a child, pressed his cheek to Mikha's stubbly face, and pleaded:

"Mikha, I'm begging you. If you have no pity for yourself, at least think of Alyona and the child. Alyona will regain her health and follow you there. This is your chance! If I had even the remotest possibility to do the same, I'd jump at it in a second! I'd fly away like the wind! Please, go! That's what Nuta would have told you."

It was already after two by the time they left Mikha. Sanya was tipsy, Ilya was sober.

"Listen to what I'm telling you, Sanya. You blamed me once for what happened to Mikha. For his imprisonment, I mean. Well, it's true, I am guilty; only not of what you accused me then."

Sanya stopped in his tracks and shook his head, trying to regain his sobriety. He was not a drinker, and only did it under exceptional circumstances, out of necessity. Ilya went on:

"Everything's more complicated than it seems. But I want you to know that both you and Mikha are like family to me. Even more than that. Do you understand that I would never betray you under any circumstances?"

"Ilya, the thought never occurred to me. What I meant was that you got him mixed up in, you know, the magazine and all that. Lord, how do you guys drink this stuff? It's absolutely vile!"

Sanya stumbled against Ilya, who put his arm around him gently and led him through the Pokrovsky Gates toward home. Everyone felt miserable. Absolutely miserable.

Mikha was wrong about one thing: that things couldn't get any worse. The following day, they did. He went to work, and the personnel director called him in. He said that several parcels had gone missing, and showed him a packet of invoices.

"You see? There's your signature right there! You sent them off, but they never arrived. They were valuable samples; look here."

The director had begun in a quiet, measured tone, but he quickly grew incensed, and three minutes later was cursing up a storm.

Mikha realized immediately what would follow—he would be asked to sign a resignation letter. And that is just what happened: either sign the letter of resignation or be taken to court.

Mikha signed the letter of voluntary resignation and didn't even bother going to the accounting office for his back pay. This was Safyanov's doing, no doubt.

That was Tuesday. On Thursday he was scheduled to see Safyanov again; but on Wednesday something unforeseen happened. And things got even worse. Without warning, Valentina Ivanovna arrived from Ryazan. She came in a car that she drove herself. This was, in itself, surprising. She hadn't known how to drive before. She must have gotten her driver's license. She came with Maya, but not to return her to her parents. She came to fetch Alyona.

It was all very strange. Alyona, who hadn't wanted to see her father at all since the trial, got up and began collecting her belongings submissively. Mikha had never seen this sort of submissiveness in her. She had always been independent to the point of insolence with her parents. Valentina Ivanovna helped her pack, coaxing her softly:

"We've fixed up a room for you, with windows onto the garden. Liza Efimova sent me some mohair, for hats. There's a whole box; twenty hanks. You could make a sweater. Look, I knitted a blue hat for Maya from it."

"Yes, blue," Alyona said, nodding.

Dumbfounded, Mikha watched them pack. The words caught in his throat before he could utter them. Valentina Ivanovna didn't turn her head in his direction, as though he weren't even there.

"You can't imagine what good friends Papa and Maya have become. She never leaves his side."

"Yes, yes," Alyona said in a soft, slow, completely alien voice.

Mikha took the things out and put them in the trunk of the blue Moskvich. Maya waved to him vigorously. Alyona nodded good-bye as though he were just a chance acquaintance. Mikha didn't dare even kiss her.

The next day he would have to go see Safyanov again and listen to all his threats, all that garbage. He realized he was on the edge.

In the morning Mikha got up early, as usual, though he had no need to go to work. The emptiness was so pressing that his ears rang with it. Or perhaps his blood pressure was up? He spent two hours revising his old poems.

Terrible poems. Terrible, Mikha thought, without any particular rancor or disappointment. He wanted to throw some of them away. He made a whole pile of them to get rid of. But he couldn't bring himself to do it.

He arrived at Captain Safyanov's on time. The captain had a formal
air about him, as if it were the eve of a holiday. *Maybe it's some sort of
holiday for them?* Mikha wondered. No, the November holidays were
still two weeks away.

"We've tried to do everything we could for you, Mr. Melamid. We
even offered you something we resort to only in exceptional cases—
letting you go abroad."

Mikha shook his head, and waved his hand dismissively. He didn't
even notice himself doing this.

"Look here," Safyanov said, and showed Mikha a piece a paper
that read, "Arrest Warrant." "It isn't dated. We can sign it today, or
tomorrow. And here is your testimony." He waved several densely
covered pages. "You yourself didn't give us this testimony. No, you
didn't give it. Here, take a look."

Mikha took the standard protocol form. It was a new kind, printed
on large-format paper and folded in half. Written in blunt words, with
grammatical errors, in a woman's handwriting, a secretary's, with a
thick line for the spine of each letter, it was a denunciation of various
people, most of whom he had never laid eyes on.

"This is my final offer. You put your signature here, and I'll rip
up . . ." And he shoved the arrest warrant under Mikha's nose.

It's a risk, but maybe it will buy me another day of freedom? Mikha thought.
*What was it Ilya had said about that hypnotist, what was his name? Yes, Mess-
ing. He could make anyone think or do whatever he wanted them to do. Even
Lavrenty Beria . . . Had he signed something? Or, no; it was what he didn't sign.
He just showed them a blank piece of paper, and they thought they saw a signa-
ture there.*

He picked up the protocol from the table and began to put his signature to it. He was a teacher, and during the years that he had to sign
his pupils' homework assignments and the roll call, he had elaborated
a streamlined signature, like Victor Yulievich—first, "M. Mela . . ."
followed by a long tail that soared upward.

He took the pen, wrote an "N" that resembled an "M," and put a period after it. Then he wrote "Ofuckingway," and sent the tail soaring upward. The likeness was uncanny . . .

"Here you are. But now I have to run home to my wife. She's very ill. Please sign my pass so I can leave," Mikha said in an importunate voice, at the same time tensing the part of his head just under the frontal bone, in the very center.

Safyanov caressed the paper with the surprisingly elegant signature, which looked like it hadn't been written by Mikha's hand at all, and called someone on the phone. A sergeant with a pass entered.

Sign it, sign it, Mikha commanded Safyanov silently.

The captain signed the pass, and Mikha walked backward toward the door, without removing his gaze from the captain. He exited the room with the sergeant. Now he didn't care when they would notice his little joke. He had time!

He walked to Chistoprudny Boulevard at a brisk pace. He went into his house, feeling light, almost weightless, not thinking about anything. He went up to the sixth floor on foot. It was just after four o'clock. The elevator was out of order again.

He sat down at the table. He wanted to reread his poems again, but he suddenly felt that there was no time for that. He pushed the whole pile aside. Childish, childish poems. Soon he would be thirty-four. And still his poems were childish. And they would never be grown-up poems. *Because I never grew up. But now the time has come for me to take my first step as a grown man. To liberate myself from my own absurdity, my lack of substance. To liberate Alyona and Maya from myself, from the utter failure of my existence, from my inability to live like a normal, full-grown man.*

What a simple and certain choice! Why had this way out never before occurred to him? How perfect it was that he had not yet turned thirty-four. Thirty-three was the age when Jesus had committed the deed that proved his absolute maturity: he had willingly given his own life for an idea that didn't inspire any sympathy in Mikha whatsoever—the sins of others.

Being the master of one's own fate—that's what it meant to be an adult. But egotism was an adolescent trait. No, no, he no longer wanted to be an adolescent.

He went to the bathroom and took a shower. He put on a clean shirt. He went over to the window. The window frame was dilapidated, the glass was dirty, but the windowsill was clean. He opened the window— rain, gloom, paltry city light. The streetlights weren't on yet, but there was a gentle shimmer of illumination.

He took off his shoes so they wouldn't leave dirty footprints and jumped up on the windowsill, resting there for a brief moment. He murmured: "Imago, imago!" And flung himself down lightly.

And the wings? Through a fissure in the chitin, the moist, sharp folds of wing rigging burst forth. With a long, fluid movement a wing works itself free, straightens itself out, dries itself in the air, and prepares for its first beat. Gridded like a dragonfly's, or scaled and segmented like a butterfly's, with an intricate map of venation, unable to fold up, if more ancient, or folding up smoothly and easily, when of newer vintage . . . and the winged creature flies away, leaving the empty shell of chitin on the earth, empty grave of the airborne, and new air fills its new lungs, and new music sounds in its new, newly perfected organ of aural perception.

His glasses and a piece of paper with his last poem lay on the table.

> Once amid the bright flash of the day
> The future will shed light upon my credo:
> I am in the people, too, I did not forsake you
> In any way. My friends, for me please pray.

His friends who were believers bid farewell to the nonbelieving poet, each according to his own lights. In Tashkent, the Tatars honored him: they carried out a memorial rite in the Muslim tradition for him. In Jerusalem, Marlen and his friends commissioned a Kaddish, and ten Jews read aloud the ancient, mysterious words in Hebrew to honor his memory. In Moscow, Tamara, Olga's girlfriend, arranged a funeral mass in Preobrazhensky Cathedral, where a freethinking priest was willing to perform a requiem for a suicide.

The face of the deceased was covered. There were many people, and everyone wept. Victor Yulievich, the former teacher, stood with lowered head, tears streaming down his unshaven, unkempt countenance.

"Poor boy! Poor Mikha! I am to blame here, too."

Mishka Kolesnik, the childhood friend of the defrocked teacher, accompanied him. He stood next to him: "Three arms, three legs," as they had called themselves so long ago.

Sanya wept—his tears were never far from the surface. Ilya had his camera, and photographed the memorial. Everyone ended up in the frame: even Safyanov, with the purple growth on his cheek. He had miscalculated, and it had been his downfall. Oh, what a downfall!

Alyona didn't attend the funeral. Her parents decided that it would be better not to inform her of her husband's death when she was in such a frail psychological state. Later they would tell her.

A RUSSIAN STORY

In winter, at the height of the Christmas frosts, Kostya's children came down with measles, and his wife, Lena, suffered a sudden attack of pyelonephritis, a chronic kidney infection. Anna Antonovna, Lena's mother, a retired seamstress who always visited from her village, Opalikha, at the first summons, couldn't make it, due to the frosts. She would have to stoke the oven at her house constantly to prevent the pipes from bursting.

So, until the frosts retreated, Kostya was left to run back and forth from bed to bed with medicine, bedpans, cups, and plates on his own. Lena refused to go to the hospital. She lay on her back and wept quietly, from weakness and from pity for her children and Kostya.

Finally, Anna Antonovna showed up, rolled up her sleeves, and sent Kostya off to work. He set out for his laboratory, where work had come to a standstill without him. Kostya resumed his running back and forth to the lab, now with the aim of salvaging the long-term synthesis process that hadn't succeeded without him. They had failed to guarantee the consistency of temperature, and the results were not what had been predicted. But chemistry is a mysterious science, and mistakes in staging experiments sometime yield interesting discoveries.

In the middle of the day he got a call from home. His agitated mother-in-law informed him that a very strange old woman wearing felt boots had arrived. She said she had something important for Kostya, but she wouldn't leave it. She said she would wait until Kostya returned so that she could give it to him with her own hands. She was sitting in the living room, still in her outer clothes. She refused to eat or drink anything, and she stank horribly. Anna Antonovna told Kostya to hurry home.

Kostya asked what the children's temperatures were, and got a sat isfactory answer: they had fallen. This was after five days of temperatures hovering around 104 degrees. Naturally, this was in part due to Anna Antonovna's beneficent influence and care. For a long time already, Kostya had called his mother-in-law "Mother Valerian," for her pacifying effect on all living beings, from spiteful neighbors to neighborhood dogs, not to mention children and plants. A woman with an open, active heart and soul.

Kostya lingered at the laboratory for another hour, and then went home to deal with the old woman who stank to high heaven.

In fact, the stench in the house was penetrating, but not foul. It was redolent of raw sheepskin, and there was nothing particularly unpleasant about this acrid, rural odor. Evidently, the old woman had agreed to take her outer clothes off and to have some tea, judging by the old sheepskin coat lying on the floor under the coatrack. Kostya wanted to hang it up, but it had no convenient loop under the collar. Next to the coat were thick felt boots, well patched, which smelled of wet fur. The old woman was no longer in the living room. She had moved to the kitchen. She was drinking tea, strong and black.

Her appearance was completely earthy and rural. She was swathed in four different scarves, of which two were on her head—a black cotton one underneath, and a gray woolen one on top of that; a third was wrapped around her waist; and a fourth covered her shoulders.

"Good day, Granny," Kostya greeted her, smiling at the overall strangeness of the situation. His mother-in-law stood behind him and, contributing to the strangeness, said:

"Here is our young master, Konstantine Vladimirovich, Granny."

"Oh, my child, my grandson, you don't look a bit like your grandfather, not a bit," the old woman mumbled, visibly touched, and began to cry, almost as though he did indeed look just like some long-lost unknown grandfather.

Kostya decided not to push things and pester her with questions—he would let the comedy take its own course and play itself out. And things were, indeed, comical. The old granny, herself pinkish, with eyes the color of turquoise beads, nodded her head in its sheath of scarves like a Chinese top, in all directions at once—to the side, to the front, to the side, and back again to the other side. She clapped her little dry red hands together:

"Oh, Kostya, Konstantine, here is the last little branch, here it is, God knows from what a mighty tree sprung forth . . ."

Kostya fell into the folk idiom himself, and said in response:

"And how might you be called, Granny?"

"Call me Mother Pasha. I am Paraskeva. That's what your grandfather called me."

"And how by your patronymic might you be called?" Kostya still kept up the game, but was starting to feel a bit abashed, trying to gauge what his grandfathers—his mother's father, the late General Afanasy Mikhailovich, and, on his father's side, Victor Grigorievich, a fighter pilot who had died during the war—could have in common with this funny old woman . . .

"No one ever called me by a patronymic—Pasha it was, and Pasha alone."

"Which grandfather of mine are you talking about?" Kostya asked her point-blank.

"Oh, what an old fool I am! I'm not talking about your grandfather, but about your great-grandfather Naum Ignatievich. That was his worldly name; but to us he was His Grace Nicodemus." The old woman, seeking something with her eyes and not finding it, crossed herself, looking at the window. "Now our protector and patron in Heaven, to be sure!"

Long, long ago, when his grandmother had died, his grandmother's sister Valentina had come to visit them and had brought some ancient family photographs with her. Olga had ordered the most treasured one restored. It was blown up into a portrait, and Olga had liked it so much that she hung it in the bedroom, where it was still hanging.

"Come with me," Kostya said, nodding to the old woman. "I have something to show you."

And he led her to the bedroom, where Lena was dozing, her kidney infection beginning to subside.

"Shhh," he warned.

Very gingerly, so that it wouldn't squeak, he opened the door and pointed to the portrait on the wall.

The old woman took one look at the picture and fell to her knees. "Father! Oh, Father! And how young he was! And so handsome! There in the flesh, with Mama, and with all of his children! And when you think of everything he would have to endure, it takes your breath away. He endured it all, and he saved himself, and he is praying for us, he will save us, too . . ."

She half-whispered, half-sang the words, and Kostya began to feel uncomfortable, because it was hard for him to empathize with her—the whole story had always been so garbled and obscure, told in snatches, the interstices filled with silence. Yes, it was true, his grandmother had renounced her own father, a priest, and he had died in the camps—that much was certain. Mama had told him a few things, but nothing else was known for sure.

In the meantime, the old woman had fumbled for Kostya's hand, and was covering it with kisses.

Lena woke up, and propped herself up on the pillows. Vera and Misha were whimpering in their room.

"This is nonsense, some kind of mad idiocy," Kostya said, growing irate with himself, and pulling his broad paw out of the clutches of the little red hands.

The old woman crumpled to her knees again, now right at Kostya's feet.

"My boy, please help, you are our only hope. No one will accept our petition. They say only his kinfolk can do it. And we need to rebury him. My house, they're tearing it down, and with it the honest grave, right below the altar, together with the house. They've been talking about tearing it down for many years already. And at the Patriarchate they said he was a heretic, a Catacombian who believed in the Living Church. He was no bishop, they said, but a pretender!"

Lena looked at the scene playing out before her and wondered whether she had succumbed to some sort of feverish delirium.

They went back to the kitchen again, and Anna Antonovna set food out on the table. Mother Pasha sat down to a bowl of borscht, expressed her thanks, then said she was full and didn't need to eat anything else.

After that they drank tea, and their tea-table conversation lasted until two in the morning. Kostya couldn't understand everything Pasha told him. He would ask her for clarification, as if she were speaking a foreign tongue: Mother Pasha, say that again, Mother Pasha, I didn't get that, Mother Pasha, what do you mean? Please explain it to me . . .

And she would elaborate, explain, demonstrate, sing, weep. In the doorway, Anna Antonovna stood listening, her eyes wide with wonder.

Pasha wasn't good with dates. It was impossible to understand from her narrative when his great-grandfather had been imprisoned, and when he had been released. He was first exiled and lived in the Arkhangelsk region. There he became a widower, after which he returned to where he was born, and was arrested.

"And when he ended up in Solovki, they chirotonized him," the old woman said, closing her eyes as a sign of respect.

"Mother, what did they do to him?" Kostya said.

"They made him a bishop. In secret, of course," she said, and smiled at his ignorance of such simple matters.

"Then His Grace was freed, before the war; but he never made it home before they captured him again. During the war he managed to escape, and ran away and hid for many years in the Murom Forest. He lived as a hermit. That was when Mama took me to him for the first time, and after that I served him until the end of his life. Just as my mother had served him, she ordered me to serve him, too. He allowed us to visit him twice a year. People came to see him from all over Russia, religious and worldly people alike.

"One time the enemy came upon him—he kept a cat, and the cat led them right to his door. They destroyed the hut, but he wasn't there. There was another *starets* who lived there, too, about six miles' distance, and His Grace had gone to give him communion, since he was in very poor health. Someone warned His Grace, and he didn't come back. He went still farther into the forest to live. Good people helped me to find him there. That was when my mother died. Sometimes I would stay there by his side and live with him for a time."

"What year was this?" Kostya asked. Suddenly, it seemed to him that the story was set in some centuries-old ancient past.

"I don't rightly remember. He lived there after the war, many years. But in '56—this I remember very well, I was there myself—he became very ill. He had a strangulated hernia that gave him great pain, and he started to die. And we all prayed for him—Mama was still alive then, but she couldn't make it to where he lived. Sister Alevtina was there, and Sister Evdokia, Anna Leonidovna from Nizhny Novgorod, his goddaughter, and me.

"His Grace said farewell to us and prepared to die, but Anna Leonidovna was very commanding, and she said, 'I'm going for the doctor. There's one in Murom.' And she brought a surgeon to him, a believer. He was a good doctor, may he rest in peace. He died young. He was called Ivan, though he was an Armenian. He cried first, and swore that he couldn't do anything unless we got him to a hospital.

"But this was happening in winter, and His Grace's hut was a dugout in the side of a hill. The way in was just a burrow. There were no windows, it was dark night and day. That's how he lived, for years. If it was cold outside, it was cold inside. There was a stove, but it had no pipe to the outside; he was afraid it would be seen.

"How could we get him out of there? No documents, nothing. And it was about twelve miles on foot to the nearest road. Besides, His Grace himself didn't want an operation. He was worn out from pain, and waited for death. The doctor was about to give up and go, when the hernia burst—it poured out blood and pus. The doctor started to clean the wound, and he worked on it for three hours. At the end, we all thought His Grace would give up the ghost at any moment. He was white as a sheet, white as snow, and the doctor kept feeling his pulse, afraid he would die under his hand.

"'Lead me out of here now,' the doctor says, 'and have someone come home with me. I'll give you medicine for him, but you'll have to give it to him with a needle, in the muscle.'

"Sister Alevtina went all the way to Murom with him, and in a day and a half she came back. She brought everything with her: the syringe, needles, penicillin. Ivan had sent her back with a chicken and some flour. He sent bread for us, but told us not to give it to Vladyka. He also said that we should return the syringe and needles to him. Maybe, the doctor said, the cold will save him. It was a wonder! God saved him, not the cold. So Sister Alevtina and I stayed with him, and we sent the others away. Then a funny thing happened: a laugh came out of him. We boiled him half a chicken, but a fox stole the other half right out of the burrow—we looked around, and it was gone! You don't know whether to laugh or cry.

"For three days and nights His Grace's body was barely warm. And then he opened his eyes, and he said, 'I was ready to go, but look! Here I am again with you.' And he got better and better, and finally he got well.

"In April we took him home with us. He settled in, and he brought the Heavenly Kingdom with him, too. He held services every day. The first year, he left the house a few times—in summer, at night, to look at the sky. After that he locked himself in the side room and came out only to hold services. He used a teeny tiny table for it. And he said, 'We don't need an altar cloth with relics of the saints, our entire land is steeped in the blood of the righteous and penitent. Wherever one chooses to pray, it is always on top of the bones of martyrs.'

"He lived and prayed according to the monastic rules and regulations. He often prayed all night, without going to sleep. In the end his legs began to swell. He couldn't stand up, and he had to be led by the arm. But how many people came to see him! And we shook with fear, we thought: now they'll catch him! But he comforted us: 'Pasha, they won't catch me. I'm staying with you here for all eternity.'

"He lived with us for eight years. In '64, His Grace passed on."

Pasha crossed herself. Her face was aglow, as though she were rejoicing.

"How old was he?" Kostya asked.

"Ninety. Maybe ninety-one."

I was already born then. Grandmother was still alive. He could have lived with us, with our family. Kostya imagined a bishop in a dark cassock, with a cross—and next to him his late grandmother Antonina Naumovna. *Fathers and Children. Fathers and Sons . . . no, it would have been impossible.*

Her story had ended. It was after one in the morning; but it was still unclear why Mother Pasha had come.

"Kostya, I wouldn't have come if everyone weren't saying that they're going to demolish our street, tear down our houses. They will give everyone apartments. But what about the grave? It's in our very home! We have to rebury him. And I tell our sisters and brothers— we'll dig up the remains and take them to the Murom Forest, where he hid. And my sisters and brothers say: he has to be buried according to church law, like a bishop, because the times are such that you can get a piece of paper to allow it. So it doesn't say he was in prison any- more. Wait, I wrote down the word here . . ." She dug in the folds of her scarves and took out a fat roll of newsprint, with a piece of paper inside. In an old person's spidery hand, the word *rehabilitation* was written.

Finally, Kostya understood what she expected him to do: request the file of his great-grandfather (evidently from the KGB, he thought) and get a certificate about his rehabilitation. He promised that he would try without fail. He would try to find out and would put in a request for rehabilitation.

Pasha dug around in the newspaper roll again.

"Here is the only document that he left behind. Our people deci- ded it should go to you. Perhaps they'll ask you for it." She pulled out a yellowed, tattered piece of paper: a certificate of graduation from the eparchial college in 1892 for "Derzhavin, Naum Ignatievich."

"Mother, who are these 'sisters and brothers' of yours? Did he have any other relatives?" Kostya thought to ask at the end of the conversation.

"What relatives could there be? One son, a priest, was shot. The others, who renounced him, also died. The little ones died as babies. And his daughters—well, you know yourself . . ."

"Our religious community was a special one. We didn't acknowledge the patriarch; but after the war, His Grace told us to go pray at the common church, because there wouldn't be any other. But he continued to be our spiritual guide, he didn't refuse. And he served until his death. Whoever couldn't live without him, came to him. And there are still several of those people left alive, people who revere him. These are the ones I call sisters and brothers, our people."

The old woman slept on a folding cot, and left early in the morning, leaving behind the smell of sheepskin that Kostya found so surprisingly pleasant.

He was in his final year of graduate school. It seemed he was about to receive not only his Ph.D., but to make a significant discovery as well. His adviser would wrinkle his eyes and nose, and curb Kostya's intentions to hurry with his dissertation, saying:

"Synthesis, synthesis, synthesis! Don't stop! It may happen that you never get this lucky again! You can defend your thesis this year, or next, it makes no difference; I've got a job lined up for you! Come on, come on! Keep going!" his adviser insisted. And Kostya did one experiment after another, and the results were unexpected, and very promising. And, most important, they were able to repeat them with scrupulous precision.

In the midst of all of this, Kostya made inquiries and found out that he didn't need to go to the KGB, but to the prosecutor's office. People who knew about these things said that it was most likely already too late—the era of "rehabilitation" had ended in the late '60s, and the clergy had never been included in the list of victims of political repression, anyway. Only when it was getting on toward spring did Kostya manage to gather and submit all the necessary documents, with a request for rehabilitation of his grandfather. A rotund, pleasant man in the prosecutor's office named Arkady Ivanovich welcomed him. He promised to try to acquire the archive, then call him back. The phone call came two weeks later.

Kostya was asked to come by at an appointed time. Arkady Ivanovich greeted him very cordially. On his desk lay a thin folder.

"Konstantine Vladimirovich! I must say that more than two thousand cases have passed through my hands, and there is not much that surprises me. Your great-grandfather's case is, however, surprising: it turns out that in the beginning of 1945 he escaped from a camp, and he has been on our official wanted list ever since. This is a special case, unprecedented in my experience. I will speak with some experts on the matter, but I think that his escape, coupled with the fact that the priest Derzhavin, Naum Ignatievich, was never found, might present great obstacles to his rehabilitation. Not to mention that for the time being we are not working with this category of individuals. The case is very interesting to me personally, though, and I'll try to find out something through my own connections. Nevertheless, the chances are slim."

Kostya nodded, indicating that he understood fully, and was secretly glad that he hadn't told the man what he knew himself: where his great-grandfather had hidden for those twenty years, right up till the time of his death. He knew, but he kept mum!

When he got home, he found a letter from Mother Pasha waiting for him, as though it had been arranged for it to arrive expressly on that day, at that moment. She asked him to come to her; it was urgent, because the demolition of the house was imminent, and what was she to do about the grave . . . ?

One week passed, then a second, and Kostya still hadn't managed to leave; he was up to his ears in work, and he had to move the family to his mother-in-law's in Opalikha for the summer. Lena was nervous, as always, whenever she had to pack up and move, if only for the briefest stay. She had an inexplicable fear of any sort of journey.

Only at the beginning of June, after he had taken his family to Opalikha, did Kostya find time to visit Mother Pasha. He traveled to Zagorsk, marveled at the cupola of Sergiev Posad, and continued to the address she had named, on the other side of the railroad tracks.

It was a village that had long ago been adjoined to a city. The street was called Podvoiskogo, or Voikovskaya. On one side of the street, future five-story apartment buildings, as yet reaching only to the second floor, rose up out of the excavation pits. On the other side of the street, a steam shovel was hard at work. The little houses were so ramshackle that one sharp blow of the huge bucket was enough to send them crashing down. Number 19 was still standing, awaiting its turn. The steam shovel operator and his partner were busy with number 17, and a dump truck carrying off the demolished remains had just left.

Number 7, which was the return address on Mother Pasha's letter, no longer existed.

Kostya sat on the stump of a recently felled tree, right across from the house. In the new neighborhood, they cut down all the trees, so they wouldn't get in the way of construction.

I'm too late. Yesterday or the day before, this demolition crew dug into the earth with the steam shovel and snatched up the bones of my great-grandfather. They tossed them into the back of a dump truck, and now they're scattered around the municipal garbage heap. It's shameful . . . and that's where they'll be forever. I'll never forgive myself for this. Why did I wait for so long? Before she died, Mama asked me to scatter her ashes on Ilya's grave, and I haven't done that, either. But—where is he, anyway, in Munich? Where is his grave? The love of our fathers' graves . . . My great-grandfather's bones on a garbage heap . . . What a Russian story . . . Yes, that's how we are.

A dog growling somewhere behind him distracted his attention. He casually turned around to look, since his heart was already weary of this unaccustomed sorrow. Two overgrown puppies, nearly full-size, were capering on the young grass. One of them was carrying a massive bone almost too big to fit in its jaws, and the other was tugging at the bone and nudging the shoulder of the first one with its snout.

The bone had long before been picked clean—it was not food, but a toy. He sat on the stump and wept from shame and anger at himself.

When he looked up, he saw two old women standing beside him.

"There, there now. Don't cry. You must be the grandson? Pasha dug up all the bones from under the floor and washed them, then wrapped them in a shroud to take them to Murom. She said, 'I'll find the hut, and I'll bury them there.' Aleksasha Grigoriev went with her, she couldn't have carried them on her own. And we are from that house way over there, on the very edge. Pasha told us to sit here and wait for you. So we did. We were waiting."

ENDE GUT—

At the beginning of the 1960s, a new breed of foreigner, madly in love with Russia, appeared in our midst. There weren't hundreds of them—but they certainly numbered in the dozens. They were well known in Moscow and Leningrad.

The first to come on the scene were the Italian Communists, followed by all manner of Swedes and Americans. They swallowed the hook with the live bait of Dostoevsky and Tolstoy, Malevich and Khlebnikov—depending on their professional interests. All of them were lured by the enigmatic Slavic soul—tender and courageous, irrational and passionate, with a tinge of madness and sacrificial cruelty.

Shaking the bourgeois dust off their impeccable Italian footwear, they fell in love with Russian beauties untainted by the curse of feminism, and married them. Overcoming numerous hurdles, they took them away to Rome and to Stockholm, to Paris and to Brussels; then they returned again to Sivtsev Vrazhek and Polyanka, or else to Konkovo-Derevlevo. These foreigners found Russian friends, grew close to their parents and children, brought them books, medicine, pacifiers, furs, cigarettes . . . In exchange, they received gifts: limited-edition books, with reproductions of Andrei Rublev's icons or the frescoes of Dionysius; black caviar; and rapturous, but not entirely selfless, love.

Since the festival of 1956, Pierre Zand had been sending, either by mail or through another person, all kinds of things: jeans, lace, record albums . . . The records were for Sanya, the Brussels-lace collars for Anna Alexandrovna, and the jeans were for all three friends. In this way he realized vicariously his love for the homeland his ancestors had left long ago.

Pierre occupied a special place among the foreigners who loved Russia: he was Russian, though his roots went back to the Baltic Germans, and his longing for Russia was existential and incurable in nature.

What vexed Pierre the most was that his rare and complex sensibility had long ago been pinned down and preserved for all time by the writer Sirin, thirty years before. As proof of this, he sent his friends books by this author, unknown in Russia, who by this time had replaced his pseudonym with his actual surname: Nabokov.

Like a character in a Sirin novel, Pierre's "feat" was to send the books of a small Brussels publishing house to Russia. They were, for the most part, religious books. This was his form of social activism, akin to Komsomol work. In 1963 Pierre spent five months in Moscow, at Moscow State University, studying Russian as a foreign language. He lived in a dormitory on Volgin Street, rambled around Moscow, explored the dark underside of the city with Ilya, attended remarkable concerts with his friend Sanya, and, once, even visited the deaf-mute boarding school with Mikha. He was researching his beloved Russia.

Five months later someone denounced Pierre—perhaps on account of the books he received through the diplomatic mail pouch for his Moscow friends—and he was deported from the country as a spy. They were very strict about these things at his Institute for Russian as a Foreign Language.

There was a scandal: an article appeared in a major newspaper alleging his involvement in subversive activities and spreading anti-Soviet literature, as well as spying. It was clear that besides the denunciation, they had no evidence against him—only overblown suspicions.

During these five months, Pierre managed to fall in love with a pretty girl named Alla, with light northern eyes and straw-colored hair. But they were not destined to be united, about which Alla grieved until her dotage. She had done a foolish thing. If she hadn't written the denunciation, perhaps she could have gotten him to marry her. They had pressured her, though, threatening to kick her out of the dormitory, to expose her as a prostitute, and to make her life generally miserable. The girl, who was not in the habit of trusting the Soviet authorities, believed them on this count.

Ultimately, being deported was far better than the Nabokovian prospect: "... and presently I'm led to a ravine, / to a ravine led to be killed."

After departing from his beloved spiritual homeland within the three days allotted, Pierre spent the rest of his life yearning desperately to go back to Russia, as so many thousands yearned desperately to leave it. Some they wouldn't allow in, some they wouldn't allow out.

Life, however, led Pierre in the opposite geographical direction. He became a Slavist, and was invited to teach in a California university. Though his ties with his Moscow friends remained strong, communication became more sporadic. Still, this did not prevent him from receiving, in 1970, a book from Russia, soon after it had been published in samizdat. It was the strange novella *Moscow—Petushki*, by an unknown writer named Venedikt Erofeev.

Ilya had done his utmost. He had even written an accompanying letter, in which he explained to Pierre that the novel was the best thing

that had come out of post-Revolutionary Russia. Pierre ardently agreed
with his friend, and began translating it. Within three months, he realized that he couldn't manage. The task was too daunting, the text
too unwieldy. The deeper he delved into the book, the more layers he
uncovered.

Enormous cultural depths rested on the device linking the novel
to the tradition of Sentimentalism. These were the notes of a Russian
traveler. From his roots in Radishchev and Griboyedov, however, the
newfangled author had strayed very far afield—lurching off in the direction of Dostoevsky and Blok, or into the deep recesses of folk idiom, crude and incorruptible. The text was full of citations: spurious
and authentic, twisted, ridiculed. The book contained parody and
mystification, true suffering, and genuine talent.

Pierre wrote a long article about it and sent it to a scholarly journal, where it was rejected. No one knew the author, and the editors
considered the article to be too daring.

Pierre was deeply offended by this, and got very drunk, after which
he started calling his Russian friends. He couldn't get hold of Ilya and
Mikha. Sanya was home, however. Sanya told Pierre about the tragedy: Mikha was dead. He added a few incoherent phrases—along the
lines of life having no meaning, what did it matter when the best
people, and one's dearest, die anyway, or leave you. And even meaning has no meaning.

Pierre sobered up and said that he would think of a way out for
Sanya. They had already talked through his two-week paycheck. He
said that he needed to go back and drink what was left in the bottle.
And that Sanya should be expecting a call from his friend Evgeny.

Sanya immediately forgot about this conversation, as though he
were the one who was drunk, and not Pierre. He had been gripped by
despair, like a fever. He could do nothing but lie there on Nuta's divan, his unseeing, vacant gaze fixed on the tapestry fabric of a tattered
pillow, and a few visual outliers of the dense weave of varicolored
threads—light blue, pale yellow, lilac—which vibrated in front of the

woven image of a flower basket and the bouquet crimped with serpentine ribbon.

When had he left home the last time? For Nuta's funeral? To go to the forty-day memorial service at the church? Yes, Mikha was at the church, too; he stood next to him, and Mikha was crying. Sanya was no longer able to cry. The very capacity of emotional response was already exhausted in him, and he had no feelings except a sense of terrible alienation from everything around him. Yes, first it was Nuta, and then Mikha. The only one left was Mama, whom he kept having to recognize anew, she was so changed. Rather, he guessed it was her. Every day before she went to work, Nadezhda Borisovna, her hair now dyed brunette, would tiptoe up to the sleeping Sanya and, tenderly, warily, leave him some tea with bread and cheese. In the evening she brought him a bowl of soup.

Sometimes Sanya ate his food without even noticing it. A gulp of liquid, a swallow of some chewed-up substance. That was all. He wanted strong, sweet tea with lemon. The kind his grandmother had brought him when he was ill.

Now it seemed that Nuta had died a beautiful death, and the memory of her was beautiful as well. Mikha's death had been horrific, lawless. Sanya was on his way home from the Kirovskaya metro station, and was passing Mikha's house. He turned toward the building as though he were going to stop in, out of habit, as he used to do during Mikha's absence. Sanya was the first of the family and friends to see Mikha there on the ground. He was lying on the stone border of a flower bed that had long since disappeared, his head smashed.

He was wearing an old plaid shirt that Nuta had bought him. Sanya had one just like it . . . For some reason he was wearing no shoes, only socks. A small crowd was already gathering around the body. They needed to hurry and remove it.

They covered the body with a sheet that had been snatched off a clothesline. It had a large patch in the middle.

He already knew that Alyona and Maya had gone to the Ryazan

countryside. Mikha had told him, not even trying to hide his grief and confusion. Now he would have to find Alyona. How would he tell her?

Right after Mikha's funeral, Sanya took to his bed. He would sleep, then wake up, hear Lastochkin's muttering and his belching, or the nauseating grumble of the television—when Nuta was alive they had never had a television! At six in the morning, the anthem assaulted his ears, then there was a surge of coffee-making smells and activity— Mama prepared it in the room, over a spirit lamp, as Nuta had always done. Then everything would go quiet again. Sanya dozed off, woke up, got out of bed when nature called him to the WC, and went to lie down again. Nadezhda Borisovna grew alarmed and tried to ask him questions, which made no sense to him; and again he turned his face toward the wall.

People from the Conservatory stopped in to see him. And some-one else—Ilya? Vasily Innokentievich? Then Kolosov came. He sat down in Nuta's chair. His visit signaled a truce after several conflicts. Sanya had gradually lost the support of his teacher, and had felt more and more distant from him. Now, rather than feeling glad about the visit, he felt indifferent.

It was difficult for Sanya to hold up his end of the conversation.

On the table, Kolosov placed a box of candies that he'd bought at the confectioner's store opposite the Conservatory, as well as an old book, a splendid German edition. As he was leaving, he said that he had arranged for him to take a month's leave. If he was sick, there was nothing like a little *WTC* for cleansing the soul and body, and for healing all one's ills.

"I brought you a very rare thing. You'll appreciate it."

And Sanya did appreciate it. He reached for the volume two days later and discovered it was

The Well-Tempered Clavier,
or
preludes and fugues in all tones and semitones,
in the major as well as the minor modes,
for the benefit and use
of musical youth desirous of knowledge,

as well as those who are already advanced in this study.
For their especial diversion, composed and prepared by
Johann Sebastian Bach,
currently ducal chapelmaster in Anhalt Cöthen
and director of chamber music,
in the year 1722.

Nuta hadn't forced him to learn German for nothing. He was even able to read the ancient title.

Sanya grew more animated when he opened the volume. It was a marvel—the Urtext, the author's original. The fourteenth volume of the first complete works of Bach, published at the end of the nineteenth century. All the publications that he had seen up till then had been redacted and edited. They had inserted accents, tempos, even fingerings. Now he was seeing the "bare" text, and this made an astounding impression on him, as though he had suddenly found himself face-to-face with the genius who composed it. Without intermediaries. Like all theoreticians, he had studied *The Well-Tempered Clavier*, marveling at the transparent simplicity of its construction, in ascending keys from C major, to C minor, to C-sharp major. The third prelude, Sanya recalled, was first written in C major. Then Bach corrected it—he added seven sharps, and it was finished. And so on, with all twenty-four keys. Simplicity itself! A children's exercise. He had written it for his adolescent son, and said: I trained him in the musical alphabet. No author's notations, no directions—play it as you wish, musician! Utter freedom . . .

Modern notation, rectified and regularized by editors, undermined this freedom.

Sanya's curiosity burned: he knew a number of renditions of *The Well-Tempered Clavier*, and now he couldn't wait to listen to them and compare. They had records at home—a wonderful recording by Samuil Feinberg, bought by Nuta ages ago, with all forty-eight preludes and fugues. They also had a recording by Richter, which was marvelous, but the recording was badly scratched and it skipped a lot.

Sanya found the Feinberg and put it on. Kolosov was right—they were purifying, cleansing sounds. He let his entire being pour through the music, or the music pour through him.

For a whole week he either listened, or studied the notes. Feinberg was absolutely magical. Opinions about him differed. Some people extolled Glenn Gould for his *Preludes and Fugues*; but for others, Richter was king. In Feinberg there was such sorrow, delicacy, and refinement. One sensed that life had already passed, and the only thing that remained were these modulations, the breaths of air under a butterfly's wings; not the flesh, but the soul of music.

He wasn't a magnificent man, but an ordinary one with a goatee, who, until recently, had still walked the Conservatory corridors, where people never whispered in his wake: Look, there goes Samuil Feinberg.

Neihaus and Richter were quite another thing. Throughout their lives, wherever they went, people would whisper: Look, there goes . . .

And Sanya listened to Bach over and over again, until, by the end of the second week, he was completely healed.

On the final prelude and fugue in B minor, Bach had written the words: *Ende gut, alles gut.*

"Good," Sanya said. He trusted Bach.

He scrubbed the bathtub, filled it with water, as hot as he could tolerate, and soaked himself for a long time. He trimmed his nails, shaved his stubble (which already qualified as a beard), then put on a new shirt. He had no idea where he was planning to go. He looked at himself in Nuta's mirror. He had become thinner. He had an interesting pallor, and two nicks on his chin. The telephone rang.

"I'm Evgeny, Pierre's friend. Finally, I've managed to reach you! I want to see you. At the usual spot."

Sanya had almost forgotten about the usual spot, where Pierre sent all his couriers—with books, jeans, records . . .

They met next to the beer garden in Gorky Park. Evgeny turned out to be Eugene, an accredited correspondent for an American newspaper in Moscow. Prompted by Pierre, he offered to arrange a fictitious marriage for Sanya. Sanya, who had barely recovered from his depression, was unenthusiastic: Was that even possible? Eugene assured him that they would have to try, and that Pierre was already sifting through the candidates.

"A blonde or a brunette?" And Sanya laughed for the first time since Mikha's death.

The January frosts, which are supposed to arrive either at Christmas or at Epiphany, took hold in the interim, between the two holidays. Eugene Michaels and Sanya Steklov arrived by different routes at the airport: Eugene took the metro to Rechnoi Station, and from there took a taxi. Sanya came on the shuttle van. There weren't many people there to meet the flight from New York, and Sanya and Eugene pretended not to notice each other.

The plane was an hour late. Finally, they announced that it had landed. The people waiting to meet it surged up to the sacred space where the official state border was about to open up and let through a narrow stream of foreign citizens and a few Russian passengers, diplomats and their KGB brothers-in-arms.

The waiting people had gotten into position too soon—it would be another hour before the arriving passengers had gone through customs and picked up their luggage.

The Soviets differed from the Americans primarily in the amount of luggage they carried and the terrified expressions on their faces. The Americans could be distinguished from the Soviets by their height, their air of inquisitive naïveté, and their clothing. If you looked closely, however, the clothes of the Americans and those of the Soviet officials and their wives were the same: tweed overcoats on the men who occupied higher positions, and hooded anoraks or duffel coats on those of a more modest position. All of them wore muted, dark winter tones; but on the Soviets, the clothes wore a different facial expression.

Among this group, sedate and exhausted after the flight, there was one bright spot: a red gnome hat that stuck out above the crowd, boldly and provocatively. Under the pointed cap were lavishly painted eyes, red cheeks, and a mouth covered in a horrendous shade of lipstick. A typical matryoshka nesting doll—but one of foreign make. A detail for the initiated—she wore a luxurious mink fur and hiking boots. In her hands, along with a woman's makeup case, she carried a giant plastic sunflower. This was the signal.

A light-haired young man in a black jacket separated himself from the waiting group. A hat with earflaps was sticking out of his pocket. He moved in the direction of the sunflower, just as sunflowers follow the direction of the sun. He stopped in front of the woman in the red gnome cap and reached out for the sunflower . . .

"Debbie! You are . . . I'm glad . . ."

Debbie, his fiancée, was no beauty, but she had a radiant smile.

"Sah-nee-a! *Ya tebya lublyu!*"

Pierre had managed to find an ideal bride for Sanya. She was a journalist, a feminist, and a hell-raising activist from the American delegation for the International Women's League. A year before, she had been in Moscow for a women's seminar organized by the Committee of Soviet Women. Where she and Sanya had met and started a romance! A watertight legend!

They embraced. From one side, the click of a camera shutter sounded—a photographer from a progressive American newspaper was documenting the meeting of Debbie O'Hara, an activist in the American women's movement, and a young music historian. With her pudgy hands, Debbie grabbed Sanya by the cheeks and kissed him right on the mouth. The soapy taste of lipstick. Sanya put his arm around her weakly. She was half a head taller and seventy pounds heavier than he was.

Another smacking kiss. Another click of the camera. One more kiss, one more click, and Eugene Michaels left: he had accomplished his mission. Two gray suits, who blended into the crowd, crossed from two corners of the hall. They came together in the middle, by the exit, like somnambulists, whispered something to each other, and parted again.

Chirping:

"Your English is wonderful!"

"Yours is too!"

"You're so cute!"

"And you're my life's dream!"

The bride and groom giggled. Sanya was covered in red lipstick. Debbie gently rubbed off the spots of faux blood with a soft handkerchief.

Sanya tried to grab the suitcase, but she pushed him away, protecting it.

"You're a savage, Sah-nee-a! I'm a feminist! I won't allow you to open doors for me, or to carry my suitcase. I'm an independent woman!"

Sanya looked at her, somewhat abashed.

"Well, I just thought it was heavy . . ."

She had already thrown the bristly dark brown fur over her left arm. She bent her right arm at the elbow, saying:

"Look at my muscles! I lift weights!"

Sanya probed her bare arm.

"Debbie, you're simply the dream of my life! When I get tired, you can bring me up in your arms!"

Marvelous, fluent English.

"Oh! You made a mistake! To 'bring up' is what a mother does. You know, nursing your young, and all that. 'Carry me' is what children say!"

Putting down her suitcase, she placed both palms on her heavy breasts to illustrate her point.

Sanya was somewhat alarmed.

Sanya took his bride to the Berlin Hotel. Before Debbie went to sleep—for about twelve hours straight, a logical consequence of jet lag, her revels with friends in New York on the eve of her departure, and a healthy nervous system—they drank vodka downstairs in the bar. They chatted. Then they kissed, and parted until the following morning.

The next day, Sanya had planned to show his bride Moscow, and to take her to the Conservatory in the evening. He hadn't prepared any other surprises for her. There was just one thing on the agenda: submitting papers for registering their marriage at the Palace of Matrimony, the only place that accepted documents from foreign citizens.

Their morning stroll through Moscow began after lunch. Sanya had put together the itinerary. Debbie had seen the Kremlin the last time she was there, and now she wanted to see what she called "real life."

When they left the hotel, the weather was magical: frost and sunshine, a marvelous day, a remarkably blue sky and snow. In the bracing cold and frigid sunshine, the Irish girl from Texas experienced such a corporeal joy and exhilaration that Sanya, who didn't like winter, looked around and was forced to agree: it was great!

Still, winter induced no ecstasy in Sanya, and, unconsciously wishing to deflate his bride's euphoria, took her to the most terrible place of all—to Dzerzhinsky Square, where the bloody knight of the Revolution stood in the middle like a column.

He pointed to the building at his back.

"That's the Lubyanka. Our own Judgment Day."

"I know, 1937!"

He took Debbie's hand.

"Why 1937? That monster is still alive today. And now that I've managed to spoil your good mood, let's walk around some more."

He spoke his textbook English well, and his keen ear immediately picked up on her slightly lisping Texas drawl.

They went to Pushkin Square, stopping at the very beginning of Tverskoy Boulevard. How often the LORLs' excursions had begun here in years gone by! Victor Yulievich would arrange for them to meet at the Pushkin monument, and from there they would take excursions into the past: Ilya with his camera, Mikha with a notebook, and ten other inquisitive lads . . .

Debbie turned out to be an absolute novice, a clean slate, when it came to Russian culture—so much so that it was difficult to know where to begin.

"Have you read Tolstoy?" Sanya asked.

"Oh, yes! I saw the movie *War and Peace.* Two movies! I adore them! Audrey Hepburn, she's just gorgeous! And your Pierre Bezukhov, Bondarchuk, of course. He got an Oscar! I wrote a review!"

"That's a start. I'll show you the house where the family of Count Rostov lived," Sanya said with a sigh.

What a simpleton she is! he thought, and took her to look at the famous mansion.

For four days the bright cold weather held, and for four days they wandered through the city. The bride, despite her naïve simplicity, turned out to be quite capable of sensitivity and sympathy. She was, in fact, a wonderful traveling companion, animated and curious. Her astonishing ignorance about everything concerning Russian culture gave way to a passionate interest in it, which took hold on the empty spot. This interest extended to Sanya.

During the sunny days, they walked through the icy streets, and in the dim, poorly lighted evenings they shivered and stopped into cafés, which were hard to find back then, for a warm-up and a snack. For Debbie, this was the most romantic trip of her life. With the exception of Spain—ten years before, she had spent a month there, and a handsome Spaniard had turned up, shown her Madrid and Barcelona, and then run off with all her money. There hadn't been much of that anyway . . .

After visiting the museum in Khamovniki, where Debbie was so moved she nearly cried ("Sah-nee-a! Your Lev Tolstoy is every bit as great as Voltaire!"), freezing, they had taken shelter in the entryway of an old building. On a third-floor windowsill, they sat down to warm themselves over the radiator. Sanya took a flask out of his pocket—Ilya's example!—and both of them took a gulp right from the bottle.

Debbie chattered almost nonstop. But now she was very quiet, and when they were by the hotel, saying good-bye, she said:

"Sah-nee-a! I can't understand how I have lived without all of this! When I get home I'm going to learn Russian!"

"Debbie, why would you need to do that?"

Debbie blazed up. Her temper was not merely Irish (though that would have been enough), but downright Italian.

"*Ya lublyu! Ya lublyu* the Russian language! You are, of course, very cultured, and I understand! But I am perfectly capable of learning myself! I learn fast! I learned Spanish! I learned Portuguese! I will learn Russian! You'll see!"

Sanya got nervous, and adroitly changed the subject.

"Debbie, do you know who Isadora Duncan was?"

"Of course! Of course I do! I'm a feminist! I know all the extraordinary women! 'The Dance of the Future'! A new style of dance, barefooted and wearing tunics! And her lovers were Gordon Craig and a Russian poet, I forget his name."

"Look, Debbie, they stayed in this hotel in 1922. This is where her love affair with Sergei Esenin began!"

Debbie lifted her hands to the sky in a gesture of prayer.

"My God! It's unbelievable! And I'm staying here, too! And I'm not even having a love affair!" She laughed. "No, I'm having a love affair with Russia!"

The following day, accompanied by Olga and Ilya, for moral support, they went to the Palace of Matrimony on Griboyedov Street, the only place where male foreigners could solemnize their marriage to a Russian woman. This was a rare instance in which a Russian man was marrying an American woman. Debbie's American documents were so well prepared that she even had a few papers too many. Sanya didn't have his birth certificate with him, so he had to take a taxi and go home to find it, not very confident of success. But Anna Alexandrovna didn't let him down now, either. On the shelf with his favorite books, between the French novels, in a folder that was very familiar to him, Sanya found all his documents, arranged in perfect order, beginning with his birth certificate and ending with his Conservatory diploma and certificates of vaccination.

The documents were accepted. The wedding date was set for May.

"Our Fanya always said that you shouldn't marry in May, or you'll rue it the rest of your life," Olga said.

Ilya and Olga fully backed this marriage venture. Olga was eagerly taking part in establishing the matrimonial union: she made borscht and cooked dumplings.

Debbie was over the moon about Moscow, and about borscht, and the Russian people she met. She loved everything about the Soviet country except the position of women. She came to her conclusions after observing how Olga prepared dinner, washed the dishes, and took care of their adolescent son, and Ilya didn't lift a finger to help her. When she tried to express her indignation about this, Olga simply didn't understand.

On her last day in Moscow, Debbie ended up at Sanya's apartment. The visit was unplanned. They had been walking around Kitai-gorod, and she desperately needed to use the bathroom. The closest one, it turned out, was at Sanya's. Neither his mother nor his stepfather were home. Debbie threw her mink coat on Nuta's chair, and proceeded to walk through the communal apartment to the communal WC. After her rest stop, she glanced into the communal kitchen.

The Texas native experienced another shock. She had not been sympathetic to communism before now, and a single WC and kitchen for twenty-eight people did not increase her regard for the social system. The next shock came when she sat down in Anna Alexandrovna's armchair and looked around: an old piano, a voluptuous dressing table on claw feet, painted with flowers and birds, bookshelves containing books in three languages, sheet music, paintings, a valuable chandelier gleaming with crystal . . . She found it hard to reconcile the poverty of the shabby communal apartment with the splendor of Sanya's room.

"Try to warm up. Do you want some tea? I'll put on some music."

"Why don't you play something yourself?"

She took the gnome's cap off her head, and her red Irish hair crackled with dry static.

Sanya sat down on the round piano stool. He thought a bit, and began to play Prelude no. 1 in C Major.

Debbie sat listening, her hands folded over her stomach like a peasant, and analyzed the situation that had unfolded. She was not as stupid as Sanya thought she was. She liked this Russian boy—he was over thirty, and three years younger than she was—very much.

He was younger, better educated, and, besides, he clearly came from a higher class of people than she had ever had anything to do with.

By the time Sanya had finished playing, Debbie had made a decision: since this strange and absurd proposition had already come about somehow or other, let it not be merely for show. She would marry this boy for real.

Sanya had not suspected that things might take such a dangerous turn.

The weather broke on the last evening, as though Moscow had grown sick of trying to make a good impression on Debbie. A damp wind began to blow, it grew warmer, and icy snow started to fall. Sanya wanted to take Debbie to a Richter concert, but it was canceled. They went to Olga and Ilya's on foot.

Olga fed her friends what she called a "prenuptial dinner." By that time, Sanya had grown weary of the endless walks with his bride, and even the idea of the marriage had begun to pall. It hadn't even been his idea in the first place!

Olga served salads and pies. Ilya brought the vodka out of the cupboard built into the kitchen window—the original refrigerator from the time of the building's construction, before the advent of modern fridges.

Debbie ate a lot, and drank a lot as well. She sat next to Sanya and kept trying to tickle him and paw at him; but she did this as though in jest, as if it were all a game. She pushed her smiling face into his, and he noticed, all of a sudden, the glistening pink strip of her gums above her upper row of teeth. It prompted a sharp adolescent memory— Nadia's gums! Potapovsky Lane!

"Sah-nee-a! Why do you resist? If you are so cold toward me, I won't marry you! But if you are a good boy, I'll just put you in my bra and smuggle you out as contraband!"

"Debbie, that wasn't our agreement! When we get married I'll be an ideal husband—you won't even see me at all!"

"No, no, I've reconsidered! I think you might suit me both in the kitchen and in the bedroom."

The next day, Sanya took her by taxi to Sheremetevo Airport. They kissed when they said good-bye. Before she disappeared down the passageway, she waved her hand, clutching the red gnome cap, at him. Sanya went back home by bus. Outside, a snowstorm raged, and snowy porridge stuck to the bus's windows.

———

I won't go home. I don't want to go to Ilya's. I'll go see Mikha, Sanya thought.

And then it hit him again. Mikha was gone. Anna Alexandrovna was gone. His mother was all but gone, too.

What is left is the unhappy Alyona, and Maya, and my mother, who is nothing like me; and the horrible Lastochkin. And a bit of music, that absurd circumstances deprived me of. So Pierre must be right, and his only choice was to flee all of this. Or should he lie down and stare at the tapestry pillow again? Or, like Mikha?

He shuddered. Depression was stalking him.

Debbie arrived in Palo Alto without warning.

The California winter did not resemble the Russian winter in the least: 59 degrees Fahrenheit. While she was trudging up to the third floor, dragging her mink coat behind her, she tried to remember the formula for converting Fahrenheit to Celsius. She remembered precisely that in Moscow it had been minus 25 degrees Celsius.

She pushed on the door to the apartment. It was open. She called out from the doorway.

"Pierre! Russian minus twenty-five Celsius—how much in American degrees?"

Pierre knew the formula.

"Well, about minus thirteen."

From the doorway Debbie flung her fur onto a chair, and it slithered onto the floor.

"Are you crazy? You should have called, I just got home! I might not even have been here," Pierre said angrily.

"I just flew in myself! I don't need your old fur coat! It's totally useless in our climate, anyway! It's insulting, actually!"

"Wait a minute! Have you changed your mind? What's insulting? We agreed about all of this!"

On a small table stood a bottle of whiskey, already opened. Debbie rushed over to it. Pierre grabbed the bottle from her hand, and poured a third of a glass.

Debbie tossed off all of it, then slammed the wet glass down on the glass table with a dangerous, earsplitting crash.

"After all, he could marry me for real, couldn't he? Why not? Why doesn't he want to marry me?"

"Hold on, hold on. We had a formal agreement—the mink coat as an advance, and the money after the marriage takes place. What is the problem?"

Debbie quickly took another tack, and started crying.

"There's no problem. Just explain to me why I'm not good enough! He's the one who's not good enough for me: he's little, and he probably doesn't have a penis at all! And he's useless—and he has some weird profession!"

"Debbie, what does his penis have to do with anything? Or his profession? We had an agreement . . ."

"To hell with the agreement!" Debbie burst out. "What's wrong with me, Pierre? Why doesn't anyone want to marry me? Even your little Sanya? I am an independent, self-respecting woman! I don't give a damn about men! But why don't they want to marry me? Maybe I don't even need to get married! But why? I just want to know. Why?"

Pierre realized the whole endeavor might be in jeopardy. He picked up the fur from the floor and threw it on the couch. He poured two more glasses of whiskey. He sat down next to the large woman and placed a glass in her hands.

"Debbie, I can't answer for all men. You know yourself that you're an extraordinary woman. But everybody's different. I can tell you something about Sanya. Sanya is depressed. I told you he was an extremely talented person. He's special. Have you ever lost anyone who was close to you? In the same month, he lost his grandmother, who raised him, and his best friend, who committed suicide. He himself is . . . on the edge. He's just not up to marriage. And the problem is not with you. He has to save his own life."

"Yes, but he could marry me, and I would save his life. Why doesn't he want to marry me for real? Not a fictitious marriage, but a real one?"

———

Now there was just one last chance.

"Debbie! Did it never occur to you . . . Ilya always had a lot of women. Mikha, his dead friend, was deeply in love with his wife. He never had any other women. But I've never seen Sanya with a woman at all."

Debbie's eyes grew wide with sympathy.

"Oh, do you think he might be gay?"

"I don't know. I didn't say that. I just said that I've never once seen him with a girl or a woman."

Debbie made a new decision: "That changes the picture. Then it doesn't hurt me. If he's not gay, then he's just afraid of women. And maybe he's a virgin?"

"I wouldn't rule it out. But that doesn't affect our agreement."

Debbie calmed down and began to think about the future. She had an intriguing task before her.

"Well, tell me, how was your trip? How's Eugene?"

Debbie pulled a packet of photographs out of her purse.

"Here you go! Photographs! Eugene took them. They're funny. Pierre, the city is amazing! And the people are amazing! I was only there for four days, but it felt like I was there for a whole month. So much happened, and I saw so many new things! Oh, and did I say that the wedding is in four months? So long to wait! You have to wait in line to get married! And then we'll have to file Sanya's application with the U.S. Embassy. For a visa. And he'll have to wait for that, too; they explained it all to me."

Debbie was a little tipsy.

"Listen, Pierre, I want to learn to speak Russian. Will you give me lessons?"

"Why do you want to do that? It will be expensive. You'll have to spend a lot of money on gas, driving back and forth. It's an hour and a half one way. I'll find you a teacher in San Francisco."

"I need a good one!" Debbie pouted.

"Fine, I'll get you a good one."

Pierre realized that his male honor would not be lost if Debbie would get good and drunk, and she was halfway there already.

He poured her another glass.

"I want Sah-nee-a! If I can marry him for real, I won't take the money from you."

"But we made a deal about a fictitious marriage!" Pierre was doing his best to protect Sanya's liberty.

"What do I need the money for, anyway? I have money! I want little Sah-nee-a as my husband!" Debbie wailed, and burst out in hysterical weeping.

Looks like there's only one way out, Pierre thought, and put his arm around her. Instantly she went quiet, and became pliant and limp.

Pierre didn't approve of adultery. He had sown his wild oats before he married, and he took his family commitments very seriously. But his wife and his daughter had been staying with his in-laws in Milan for the last three weeks. Moreover, he attributed his fall solely to his devotion to his Russian friend and the furthering of his friend's interests. Still, the lack of spontaneity of the situation did not detract from its pleasantness.

"If you marry Sanya for real, you'll owe me for both the plane tickets and the hotel!"

"No way! Whatever you spent is already gone. I'll pay you for the Russian lessons." She placed her hands, holding them both in an obscene gesture, over her ample breasts. This was something she'd picked up in Russia.

"All right, if everything works out and we manage to get Sanya out of there, the tickets and the hotel are on me."

They continued kissing gently, rounding out the session.

And now I have the added stimulus of trying to draw him out of his shell, Debbie thought with satisfaction.

The wedding took place in May, as indicated on their application. It was a rainy day, which promised to bring the young couple wealth, according to folk superstition.

Debbie O'Hara was wearing a big white dress. Her hands held a round wedding bouquet of plastic flowers, which she had brought with her from America. She wore white high heels. Sanya wore a black corduroy jacket with a zipper and old blue jeans.

Eugene, wearing a tweed jacket and a tie, looked much more like a groom than Sanya did. Olga, Ilya, and Tamara were all there, dressed in their best attire.

The bride and groom stood side by side, and Eugene took a photograph. Ilya photographed them from the other side.

They entered a hall, the matrimonial holding cell. Several couples were already sitting there: two Africans with blondes, one Arab with a girl with oriental facial features, and several indeterminate Eastern European couples: Czechs or Poles. There was a line.

They sat without speaking. Sanya studied the faces of the couples about to be married. The Africans were most likely from the Patrice Lumumba Institute. One of them, a handsome, dark-lilac-hued fellow, pulled out a deck of cards and asked his bride whether she wanted to play. She declined. He began laying out a game of solitaire. A second young man, small and homely, was holding his bride's hand, admiring the paleness of her skin. He ran his finger across her wrist. The Arab man was older. His profession was unclear, but gold dripped from all his fingers. His bride was also covered in gold, and it was obvious that they were eager for the ceremony to be over. He put his hand now on her waist, now around her shoulders. She luxuriated in it. One Czech (or Pole) was reading a newspaper.

It's in Czech, Sanya observed.

Debbie was visibly nervous. Sanya amused her with conversation. Finally, they were summoned into a long room. A red carpet runner led up the aisle to a table, behind which was sitting a stately woman who looked like the actress Alla Larionova, with a thick red sash over her shoulder—a smaller version of the red runner. The witnesses—Olga, Ilya, and Tamara, and Eugene, with his camera, were admitted through another door. Along the way they got rid of the local photographer. They also got rid of the Mendelssohn.

Then the rigamarole begins. The woman in the sash stands up. She announces:

"Citizen of the United States of America, Deborah O'Hara, and Citizen of the Union of Soviet Socialist Republics, Alexander Steklov, have applied to be married in accordance with the laws of our country . . ."

Debbie wants the wedding. Sanya wants to disappear. Debbie wants a honeymoon. Sanya wants to bury his head in the ground. Debbie wants a wedding night. Sanya wants to fall off the face of the earth.

Olga throws together a wedding party at her place.

Over the past six months, Debbie has learned to speak some Russian. She talks incessantly. Sanya remains silent, in both Russian and English. Toward evening his temperature shoots up, and a headache takes hold.

Ilya takes him to Chernyshevsky Street. Nadezhda Borisovna does everything that Anna Alexandrovna used to do: she presses a hot towel to Sanya's head, gives him sweet tea with lemon, and two Citramon tablets. As always, in such cases, his temperature is near 104 degrees. Nadezhda Borisovna continues to do everything that Anna Alexandrovna did in this situation. She covers his shoulders and chest with vodka, then rubs it in with a woolen rag. No, Anna Alexandrovna did everything much better.

Sanya is sick for the usual three days. Debbie spends these three days in Olga's apartment: the first day she sobs; the second she chats animatedly with Olga. And, on the third day, Ilya takes her to Sheremetevo Airport. Sanya languishes on Nuta's divan with his high temperature.

The farce called a "wedding" is over. The only thing that remains to be done is submit the application for a visa to the American consulate. And then wait, wait, and wait some more.

Eight months later, Alexander Steklov landed in New York. Pierre Zand met him at Kennedy Airport.

By this time, Debbie spoke Russian very well. She met Sanya a year and a half later at the lawyer's, after she had found a real fiancé for herself (also Russian, by the way), and she needed a real divorce to make him her real husband.

Debbie refused the five thousand dollars that she was supposed to receive for the fictitious marriage. She also refused to keep the fur. In the end, she got the fur anyway. Pierre kept the coat in cold storage in Palo Alto for a few years, and gave it to Debbie for her second, real wedding. By this time she had moved to New York, where winters are sometimes cold enough to wear a fur coat.

Sanya lives in New York, too. He teaches the theory of music at a world-famous music school.

Ende gut, alles gut.

EPILOGUE: THE END OF A BEAUTIFUL ERA

They met. They embraced—right cheek to right, then left to left. It was effortless. They were the same height. The woman's face was narrow, her nose aquiline; the man's face was angular, with high cheekbones and a snub nose. The rain suddenly turned white, and it began to snow. The wind blew from all directions at once, whipping itself into a breaker right above the square where they had agreed to meet. Cold moisture blew up from the bay, while, from the other side, from the river, the air seemed to blow stale decay.

"Doesn't it smell like Chistye Prudy, Sanya?"

"Not at all, Liza. Not in the least."

He ran his hand over her hair. It was cold to the touch.

"Let's hurry. Are you cold?"

"I haven't had time to freeze yet. But it's damn cold."

"I made you a tape of Beethoven's Thirty-second, Eschenbach's performance in Madrid in '86. You'll understand what I mean . . ."

He took a cassette tape out of his pocket and put it in her hand.

"Thank you, Sanya. I'm not arguing with you, for the most part. But Eschenbach always has something of the tongue-twister about him. Sviatoslav Richter has a different articulation altogether, much cleaner . . ."

They had parted a year and a half before in Vienna, where Sanya had traveled to hear her perform. Now, on the way to visit a home to which they had been invited, they were picking up the conversation where they had left off in Vienna.

Maria opened the door.

Obligatory air kisses.

"Good evening. Anna is sick. I put her to bed downstairs. Take off your coats, and go upstairs. I'll be right up."

Somewhat distant and disengaged, as always. Of course, her child was sick. It was natural for her to be preoccupied.

Maria's collarbone jutted out of the low-cut collar of her blue dress. Her Venetian glass jewels rolled across it with every movement she made.

"Is the weather awful?"

"Worse than awful. Windy, cold, and damp," Sanya affirmed.

"This weather pursues me everywhere this year. It seems that my performance schedule has coincided with some sort of low-pressure atmospheric system. Wherever I happen to be—Milan, Athens, Stockholm, Rio—there is rain mixed with snow. It started in the middle of November."

The master heard their voices and came out to greet them. The stairs leading to the upper floor were rather narrow, and he stood at the top, smiling.

They went upstairs. Sanya glanced at the table in the room—a Roman anthology was lying open on top of it. It was another coincidence, as so often happened. At home, Sanya was reading Ovid.

"Come in, come in. You see, Liza? We've gotten to see each other again after all."

They kissed.

"I've been hearing that phrase from you for the last twenty years. Do you say it so that I'll value you more when next we meet? That isn't necessary. I value our meetings without being reminded of it!"

"No, I'm just letting you know that we don't have another twenty years," the master quipped.

In his hand he held an unlit cigarette that he lit up and began to smoke after they had kissed.

"You still haven't quit?"

"No, I won't quit smoking. Just wait a while, it will quit me soon enough!"

"But you were going to try!" she said in an old woman's plaintive voice. "You're cutting short your last twenty years!"

The master laughed.

"Liza, I'm cutting into them from the other end, not from this one. Maybe it's not so bad for me. Besides, these years are a gift."

"A gift?"

"If I had stayed in our homeland, I would have died of poverty, frayed nerves, and poor medical care long ago."

Sanya turned away and looked at the heavy curtains, as though he could see out the window.

Yes, even with the best medical care imaginable, my end is not far to seek, Sanya thought.

He must have known that his own illness, already with him for the past eight years, was incurable.

On the table were takeout cartons from a Chinese restaurant. The door opened up just a crack. Maria appeared out of the semidarkness, like a photograph developing.

"Anna won't settle down. She wants to see Sanya before she goes to bed."

"May I?" Sanya stood up.

"Of course," Maria said, nodding.

"I'll go down, too," the master of the house said.

With Maria leading the way, and the rest of them walking in single file behind her, they went downstairs and along a hall, then stopped in front of a door that was slightly ajar. A little girl was sitting on the bed, radiating fever. The light of a lamp that stood behind her next to the bed turned her tousled hair golden. It sparkled like Christmas tree tinsel.

"Papa, you promised . . ."

"What, my kitten?"

My God! This child doesn't speak Russian! Liza thought.

"I don't remember what it was, but you promised," she said, her mouth crumpling. She began to cry.

"Look, here it is," Sanya said, holding something up to her in his closed fist.

The little girl took his hand and tried to pry his fingers apart, but Sanya kept them closed.

"Careful, Anna. This little thing might break."

Then he opened his palm, on which lay a small glass mouse.

"Do you remember what I promised you? That Sanya would come and bring you a glass mouse."

"That's not true! You didn't promise me Sanya's mouse! It's not a promised mouse, it's just a plain mouse. Thank you. No one ever gave me a mouse before."

"Will you go to sleep with the mouse now?" Maria asked.

"Yes," the girl assented. "But don't turn the light off, Mama."

"I'll leave the night-light on."

"The mouse will be scared."

"All right, all right. Tell everyone good night, and close your eyes."

The golden-haired child in the white pajamas embroidered with strawberries, her face flushed with fever, with little swollen lips, settled down in her bed, shifting her arms and legs, and kneading her pillow and blankets to make a little nest for herself. He had a strange sensation that this had all happened before: the golden-haired girl, the glass mouse, tears . . .

Liza waited in the doorway, keeping her distance from the little girl.

How amazing, at this age, when grandchildren should be on the way . . . He's happy . . . No, no, I don't need it, I never did. Not then, not now.

From the love that she had been true to since childhood, children had not been born.

Maria stayed with the child a bit longer, and then joined the guests upstairs. The remains of food from the Chinese restaurant sat on a tray on the floor next to the door. They didn't drink tea after dinner. That Russian custom had faded after a quarter of a century in emigration. They drank Italian wine.

The master ate pastries from a cardboard box. He wiped his mouth unceremoniously with the back of his hand.

"Well? Will you recite something?" She was both sincere and well brought up, but sincerity prevailed in her. She felt somewhat abashed at her own directness, but she need not have. The poet read without any prompting. He himself needed to hear them spoken aloud—the trembling of the air proof of life itself.

"Small towns, where they don't tell you the truth.
And why would you need it? That was already—yesterday . . ."

He read this poem, which was a new one, and then another.

Sanya noticed that Liza was folding her hands in some sort of mudra. Since childhood she had suffered from crippling headaches, and she had tried treating them with pills, with homeopathic remedies, and, lately, through these curious hand configurations. Indian magic. Liza's headaches usually began after performances, sometimes after intercontinental flights. And now, apparently—from poetry. It would seem that contemplating verse was not an easy task.

Liza, her fingers interlaced, pressed her palms against her temples.

The master interrupted his reading. He drank some wine.

He has a headache, too, Sanya thought.

"Is it all right if Sanya puts some music on? Very quietly?" Liza said.

"Do you want a pill?" the master asked her.

"No, but I'll lie down for a bit, if you don't mind." And Liza lay down on the couch.

Sanya put the tape on. It was Beethoven's last sonata, performed by Eschenbach. In fact, Sanya hated mixing music with conversation.

"Here's some Eschenbach for you." Sanya pressed the button.

Liza and Sanya exchanged glances on hearing the first notes.

The poet caught their glances and told his wife:

"They hear what ordinary people can't hear."

She nodded with only her chin. *A flawlessly beautiful face . . . Lippi's Madonna? No. But the same type. Where have I seen it before? Natalia Goncharova. Of course!* Sanya smiled to himself at his belated discovery.

A bit later Maria went down to check on their daughter. She came back, sat with them for another ten minutes, then took leave of the guests for the evening.

They drank another bottle of wine. It was excellent.

Then the master led the guests down to the front door, and crossed the threshold onto the porch with them.

Outside there was no rain, no snow, no wind. Everything was quiet and still. It was warmer. Everything—the asphalt under their feet, the walls of the houses, the branches and trunks of the trees—was covered with a thin layer of ice. It sparkled in the streetlights.

"I'm so glad that we visited him. And glad about . . . everything . . ." Sanya made a vague gesture toward the icy trees gleaming in the soft light.

The door slammed unexpectedly loudly. Liza smiled.

"You're the only person in the world who catches on to my migraines."

"You're the only person in the world who catches on . . . at all."

And, unexpectedly, he asked something he could have asked thirty, or even twenty years ago.

"Liza, why didn't we ever get married? Back then, when we were young?"

"You really don't know?"

"Well, I can guess . . . that fat Boris . . ."

"I never suspected you were so thick! What does Boris have to do with it? Two years afterward he left me for my girlfriend, and that was the end of it. But with you and me—it would be an incestuous relationship. The Egyptians permitted that sort of thing, but in our world, brothers and sisters can't marry. Even cousins! Although we're only second cousins, we're still related. Anna Alexandrovna and my grandfather are cousins."

"No, Liza, no. That wasn't the problem. Grandmother loved her second husband, the actor, who died in the camps. That seems to have been a happy marriage. But I've never seen any other happy marriages. Remember Ilya and Olga? It all ended very badly. Mikha and Alyona . . . even worse. What a beautiful man he was."

"They were all killed by Soviet power. It's horrendous," Liza said, her mouth contorted.

"Not all. Alyona, it seems, is alive and well. She married some sort

of artist, a Latvian or Lithuanian. She's living a peaceful life somewhere in the Baltics. And it wasn't just the Soviet authorities who
were to blame. People die no matter who is in power. That goes without saying. There's more and more of the past, less and less of the
future . . ." he said, smiling. At the past? The future?

Liza smiled, too.

"Oh yes, I wanted to tell you why I don't like Eschenbach. Not
because he has a different tempo, but because the energy is somehow
alien. It's because at the very core of his music is a desire to please the
public. He plays so that they will like it. Yudina never lowered herself
like that."

Liza plucked at Sanya's sleeve, like she used to do when they were
children.

"So what? Rachmaninoff lowered himself in that way—even lower!
He cut parts of his music out altogether when the audience got bored!
And Richter? He's a genius, a true artist! But he's a bit of a clown,
too! He indulges his audience."

"Still, I insist—Maria Veniaminovna didn't depend on her audience in the least bit. She raised the audience to her own level."

"Liza, those times are finished. That's clear. It's clearest of all in
music. Music itself has changed, has become something altogether
different."

"Nevertheless, neither Beethoven nor Bach have been replaced.
Consider the repertoires of young performers. Do you hear them play
Cage very often?"

"Well, often enough. But I'm talking about something else, Liza.
Of course, no one will ever replace Beethoven or Bach. Even if they
wished to, it wouldn't be possible. But that form of culture is over, and
another form of culture has begun. Culture has become a patchwork,
a web of citations. The previous dimension of time is over. All of culture is like a complete sphere. The second avant-garde has entered
culture, entered that part of it that wasn't outmoded. Innovations age
more quickly than anything else. Stravinsky, Shostakovich, even
Schnittke, who betrayed the avant-garde, have become classics. Cycli-
cal time keeps revolving, absorbing everything new into itself; and the

..ew is no longer distinguishable from the old. The idea of the avant-garde outlived its usefulness, because there is no progress in culture, in the sense of a phenomenon that is finite and revealed, once and for all . . ."

"Sanya, I've been wanting to ask you for a long time—'A grand piano floats off the earth in a self-made storm, raising its polished sail . . .'—do you think he doesn't understand?"

"He doesn't understand, apparently, that the storm isn't self-made," Sanya said.

"Don't worry about him. He understands a great deal that we have no clue about."

"Of course. But you know that all the storms here are only reflections, pale shadows, of those he called 'self-made'?"

They stood in the middle of the empty street, having walked a ways from the house, and talking.

"Of course we know that. What did you think of him? How is he?" Sanya asked.

"He seems happy," Liza answered without much conviction.

"Women," Sanya said, and grimaced.

"Did I say something wrong?" Liza said, alarmed.

"No. But I thought he looked tired. And he was unusually quiet tonight." Sanya put his arm around her shoulders.

It was very slippery. Liza held Sanya by the arm, and they walked slowly and cautiously in the direction of the subway.

"Now it has become clear to everyone that he's a genius. In the Russian sense of that word, not the European."

"I don't understand what you mean," Liza said, becoming uneasy. She was used to catching his meanings from the slightest word or gesture.

"Well, he's not simply a person with a divine gift for poetry or music, but a person who, like an icebreaker, moves ahead of time and smashes walls, breaks apart the ice, forges new roads, so that all the little ships and boats can sail behind in his wake. The most sensitive people, the most gifted and capable, follow in the path of the genius, and the crowd surges after them—and what was once a discovery becomes a commonplace. Average people—and here I mean myself, not you—are only able to grasp things through the efforts of genius and the general unfolding of time. The people of genius are harbingers; they precipitate the movement of time."

"Yes, yes, of course. And the Thirty-second Sonata is evidence of that. It transcends all time—Beethoven's own, and ours as well."

"Beethoven was a genius. Unequivocally. He completed classical music, creating a canon and then destroying it himself. The classical structure ended—and only themes and variations remained. He crossed the boundary of boundaries. He composed however he wished—no more rondos, scherzos, all those dance forms—they were just gone." Sanya waved his hand in dismissal. "There are no words for it."

Liza stopped.

"No, I can't agree with you there. The rondo, the scherzo, and all those dance forms were with Beethoven right up to the end. And what do you think 'Arietta' is, in the last sonata? It's the shadow of a minuet! The shadow of some minuet up in heaven, to which angels dance, if no one else. If they exist! It can't be considered a dance—but it's a symbol, a hieroglyph. Already beyond the bounds of life, outside time, in an incorporeal world."

Liza gripped Sanya under the arm. It was terribly slippery, and the ice-clad trees played in the light cast by the streetlamps. She pressed his upper arm through the sleeve of his jacket, as she used to do when they were young, sitting side by side at the Conservatory and exchanging secret signs of understanding.

"Yes, of course. But time has its own complexity . . ." Sanya couldn't stop. "It becomes stratified, and no longer moves from point A to point B. It's more like the layers of an onion bulb, everything happening simultaneously. Closer to the end . . . Hence the tendency toward citation. It seems that what is truly valuable doesn't age. In the world, there is an enormous multitude, as well as a multitude of worlds. The world of Beethoven, the world of Dante, the world of Schnittke, Joseph's world . . . The secret is in that . . ."

"Enough, enough. Stop! I have another quote, do you remember?" Liza interrupted him, and slowed her pace.

"The secret is ta-ta, ta-ta-ta-ta, ta-ta,
and more I have no right to say."

"Yes, of course. He was a rather bad poet. But he did touch upon the secret in his prose. Don't you think so?"

"I don't know, Sanya. It seems that now we've grown up, I know much less than I did when we were younger."

They walked for a while not saying anything, barely able to keep their balance, afraid to fall and bring each other tumbling down—the pavement was like a skating rink under their feet.

"We haven't come across a single taxi! We should have ordered one beforehand." Suddenly, Liza remembered something she had been wanting to say for a long time. "I saw Vera last year in Paris. She was giving a master class. At first I thought, 'How sad, she's not giving concerts anymore.' Then I sat in on one of her classes, and I realized it wasn't unfortunate at all. There are so many performers, and she is creating a school of piano performance. Or continuing one. The Russian School. And you are also part of the Russian School, as Kolosov's student."

"In the conventional sense. You know, until the day he died Yury Andreevich never forgave me for leaving."

"He was a unique person. A patriot in his own way. And we are cosmopolitans. Music is our homeland."

"And the Russian School you were referring to? No, you'll never make a good cosmopolitan. You, with your Tchaikovsky, are also a musician of the Russian School."

"Why do you all hate Tchaikovsky so much?"

"I got over that long ago. Our friend Joseph can't abide him, though, for his unconcealed emotion and pathos."

"Well, there may not be a lot of pathos in the poet's work; but he also belongs to the Russian School."

"No, he belongs to the world."

"I beg to differ, my friend. He writes in Russian."

"Yes, that's so. In Russian."

A cab stopped next to them, almost grazing Liza. A large, drunken man clambered out. Sanya gestured to the driver to wait, stroked Liza's hair, and kissed her. She ran her hand down his face, from his temple to his chin. Anyone seeing them might have thought they were lovers saying good-bye.

"Do you want us to drop you off somewhere?"

"No, I live nearby. I'll be all right."

"See you, then."

"See you."

It was after one in the morning, January 28, 1996. That night, the poet died.

ACKNOWLEDGMENTS

I would like to thank my dear friends, whose love has been a lifesaver.

I am grateful to Elena Kostioukovitch for her daily support of many years—for the wonderful conversations, sharp criticism, meticulous editorial work, and for her priceless friendship.

Alena Smorgunova and Yuri Freilin, for their participation in writing the book.

My friends the Alexanders—Smolyansky, Okun, and Bondarev— for their attentive and creative reading, copious comments, and unwavering interest in the book.

Sanya Daniel, Vitya Dzyadko, Igor Kogan, and Elena Murina, for being fearless and upstanding witnesses of their era—or perhaps, not completely fearless, which makes them even greater in my eyes. I am grateful to them for our long Muscovite conversations about our shared past.

I am endlessly grateful to my dear friends in Israel for their heartfelt, reliable support during the hot summer of 2010: my guardian angel Lika Nutkevich, Sergey Ruzer, Luba and Sandrik Kaminsky, Igor and Tata Guberman, and Lucy Gorkushenko for their warmth, care, and constant concern.

I am grateful to my beloved, courageous friends Lena Keshman,

...afarova, Ira Yasina, and Vera Millionshikova for our corre-
...ndence and conversations, which were so crucial during the
summer of 2010 when the work on the book—and my strength—were
coming to an end.

A special thank-you to my musician friends who led me through
the enchanted forest of music: Vera Gornostayeva, Olesya Dvoskina,
Volodya Klimov, and Olga Schnittke-Meerson.

I would like to apologize to those who I have failed to mention at
this moment, for which I will surely kick myself later. How could
I have forgotten you?

Finally, with gratitude, I would like to remember the dear departed who have served as the inspiration for my characters, the in-
nocents who stumbled into the meat grinder of their time, those who
survived, and those who were maimed; the witnesses, the heroes, the
victims—in their eternal memory.

LUDMILA ULITSKAYA
November 2010

TRANSLATOR'S NOTE

Unless otherwise indicated, all excerpts of poems quoted in this edition are translated by me. In order of appearance, the poems are:

Deaf-mute Demons
by Maximilian Voloshin

Who is blind, but my servant? or deaf, as my messenger whom I sent?
who is blind as he who is perfect, and blind as the Lord's servant?
—Isaiah 42.19

They walk the earth
Blind and deaf and dumb
And draw fiery signs
In the spreading gloom.

Illuminating the abyss,
They see nothing.
They create, not knowing
Their own predestination.

Through the murky underworld
They beam a prophetic ray . . .
Their fates are the face of God
Casting light amid the storm clouds.

29 December 1917

473 *Hamlet*: William Shakespeare.

478 "The Old House": Innokenty Annensky.

509 "Winter's Eve": Boris Pasternak.

518 "When will the pall on my / Ailing heart disperse?": Evgeny Baratynsky.

567 "August": Joseph Brodsky.

570 "Bagatelle (To Elizaveta Lionskaya)": Joseph Brodsky.

572 "The secret is . . ." *from Glory*: Vladimir Nabokov (Wellesley, 1942).